Tapestries
of
Difference

A Novel

by

Roger Riddell

COPYRIGHT

Powerhouse Publications
Suite 124. 94 London Road
Headington, Oxford
OX3 9FN

www.powerhousepublishing.com

Contents

BOOK I
CONNECTIONS

- 1 -

A Chance Encounter

It was 5:45 on a Monday in mid-May. Emma was woken by the early morning sun as it moved across her pillow and warmed her cheek. She opened her eyes and was wide awake at once. Her mind was racing and she was conscious of the quickening beat of her heart.

Emma had never been content merely to live in the world as she found it. From an early age, she had always striven to change it, and she still did. During the spring and summer months she slept with her bedroom curtains wide open, but normally when she woke she kept her eyes tightly shut. She had done this for as long as she could remember, as she so savoured lying in bed suspended in that magical moment between sleeping and waking. Indeed, as a small girl, she drew such comfort from that in-between period bridging sleep and wakefulness that when the sun rose, with eyes still closed, she used to chant made-up spells as she bent and twisted her body into odd shapes under the bedclothes to try to hold onto those precious feelings of warmth and intense security for just a while longer. It was her attempt to influence – to try to alter – the world beyond.

Today, however, was different. Emma was alert and excited as soon as she woke because she was being interviewed for a job which, if offered, she knew would radically change her life and her world. What she didn't know was that a chance encounter that same morning would also set in motion a chain of events that would change her forever, in ways she could not possibly have imagined.

Emma was now in her mid-20s. From around the age of 18, she had known she did not merely want to be a current affairs journalist working on political issues, ideally on television: she wanted to be an extremely successful one.

After leaving school with three good A-levels, she gained an undergraduate and then a post-graduate qualification in journalism, passing both with distinction. With glowing reports from her teachers, she landed exactly the job she had been looking for with her leading local newspaper, where she was still employed today. They worked her hard, and she responded well so that over the course of just a few years she had gained a wealth of experience. Whatever was thrown Emma's way she was well able to cope with; the tougher it was the more she seemed to relish the challenge. She excelled in her work and was well liked by both colleagues and bosses.

Emma was not only growing into a highly competent journalist, but she was also a very amiable young woman whose bubbly personality enabled her to make friends easily. But what set her apart from many of her peers was the way she was always on the lookout to welcome into her circle of friends those people who lacked self-confidence. Indeed, from a very early age, she had tapped into a huge well of inner self-confidence, often going against prevailing social norms to help those who felt excluded: instead of laughing at those too shy to join in and play hopscotch at nursery school, Emma insisted they join in and play as full members of the in-group. Through similar acts of kindness as she grew older, Emma became known as a person willing to challenge conventions which failed to respect people as people; and customs or codes of practice which she felt strongly about and knew to be wrong.

With her professional skills and experience, and equipped with some glowing references, Emma had recently applied for a new job opening for a young journalist at the BBC. Her application had clearly been well received because today she had been asked to come to their London headquarters at Langham Place to be interviewed. She had been told this would be an all-day affair.

The job-title was "trainee political/current affairs journalist" and the successful applicant would join a new unit recently created within the BBC's sprawling news division. This had been set up to provide a fresher, more dynamic and proactive approach to the gathering, analysis and presentation of the news and political affairs in yet another attempt to try to shake up the current division. From friends at the BBC, Emma knew this job was a key position which, all being well, could enable her to transition up the organisation on the path to a permanent and influential position at national level. She also knew the post was one of a number of new "fast-track" positions created as part of an organisation-wide initiative to address the middle-aged male dominance of news and current affairs posts at the BBC.

As a student Emma had excelled in TV work but had been advised to go into local print journalism for a few years before applying for a TV post. Now, she believed she was ready. From early on in her career she had seen herself working one day for a programme like Newsnight or Panorama. However, a job with this new unit looked even more demanding as well as appealing, and the more she thought about the job, with its clear upward career path, the more she felt she was cut out for it. With characteristic determination and self-confidence, Emma had convinced herself this was the job she really, really wanted.

In the past few days she had been told by journalist friends at the BBC (eager up-to-date news-gatherers like herself) that only three people were being interviewed for the position, and by today the panel had already seen the other two candidates. When Emma woke, she felt supremely self-confident. Today, she just knew, was going to turn out well: she *would* be offered the job she so wished to have, and she would then be set firmly on the path to being the influential political journalist she craved to become.

She knew she needed to begin the day with a good breakfast, but, almost as importantly, she knew she had to be totally on top of today's news. This meant she must follow a routine she was familiar with and loved. First, she put on the radio to have the *Today* programme playing in the background. Next, she switched on her TV ready to flick between Al Jazeera, Sky and RT so as to see the way each station was approaching the day's main stories. Then she went online to trawl through *The New York Times, The Guardian, Financial Times, China Daily, The Moscow Times, Pravda* and *Al Ahram* websites, to provide her with the different key perspectives being taken on today's news to place alongside the BBC's views. Knowing the way she often lost track of the time when she absorbed herself in the news, she re-set her alarm for 9 o'clock, then poured some muesli and milk into a bowl, made herself coffee and settled down to soak in the day's main stories. She was soon in another world: the world of news, politics and current affairs, the world she was not only happiest in but the world she wanted to help shape – and change.

Just after nine, Emma grabs her light-weight jacket, puts her charged phone in her bag, steps out of her flat and breathes in the fresh spring air. Though she is understandably apprehensive about what lies ahead, she isn't nervous; her feelings are more those of contented anticipation. She is at ease with herself.

This is East Finchley, where Emma lives, a typical residential district of north London – growing, busy and ever-changing – a mix of people of different ages, incomes and wealth and a melting pot of different races, ethnicities and personal histories. To the bewilderment of many old-time residents, the local council recently tried to recast its identity by erecting "Welcome to East Finchley Village" signs at the approaches to its short and very ordinary high street – suggesting it was quainter, more olde-worlde and homely than it is. But for Emma, East Finchley is far more than the warmth which the word "village" conjures up. This is where she grew up, the place of her earliest memories and where she fell in love with Robbie. East Finchley is the base from which she first ventured out into the wider world and the place she still feels comfortable returning to today. As Bag End was for Bilbo, so East Finchley is for Emma – it means just one thing, and that's home. East Finchley is Emma's piece of England and, warts and all, she not only loves it, she's proud of it too.

Emma is heading for the tube station but instead of going directly from her flat down the High Road, she walks up Church End, turning right when she reaches East End Road on a route which takes her away from the station. This is because she needs to stop at Graham's the butcher to buy a few things her mother, Sarah, has especially asked her to bring with her when the two of them are to have supper at Sarah's flat that evening. Uncertain when the interview will end but aware from bitter experience that

Graham's closes at four on Mondays, Emma has given herself just enough time to pop in before getting to the station. She knows the way well. It will only take ten minutes longer than the direct route, along the narrow privet-hedged passageway to reach the tube that way. Detailed planning and logistics are two of Emma's many skills.

Sarah and Emma are close. Emma has arranged to have supper with her mother both because Sarah will want to be the first to hear how the interview has gone and because Emma will be keen to tell her all about it, too. Since she was very small, Emma has always shared life-changing events with her mother and she still does. It is an integral part of the deep bond between them.

Along East End Road, Emma walks by Nazareth House, the Catholic old people's home where one of her mother's oldest friends, Maggie Joyce, works as a nurse. She feels a twinge of guilt that she has not found time to visit her for years. A little further on she passes the bright yellow sign displayed over the strangely-named Dr Hunger Café and then the black and rather sinister frontage of Sound Gurus, the local in-car audio store. They lie on opposite sides of the junction with Ossulton Way, which she crosses at the lights. Ten paces beyond Sound Gurus, and still feeling in her chest the thudding base-sounds emanating from a new speaker system just fitted to a low-lying BMW 8 Series sports car parked on the street, Emma pushes open the door to Graham's the butchers.

* * *

It is not meat which brings Emma to Graham's but rather the South African groceries they stock and which southern African exiles from miles around converge on Graham's to buy, like bears to a honeypot. Emma is here because her mother was born in Zimbabwe and continually pines for the food she grew up with. Sarah came to England when she was in her early thirties and as the food she had always eaten remained a necessity, Emma also grew up with it and learned to love it too. Perhaps, wonders Emma, the Dr Hunger Café located so close to Graham's is more aptly named than she had thought.

On her shopping list today are five basics: All Gold guava jam; Mrs Ball's Original Peach Chutney, which Sarah always referred to by its Afrikaans name, *Perske Blatjang*; Tiger jumbo oats; milo (chocolate and malt powder used to make a soothing overly-sweet, hot pre-bed drink) and mealie meal (finely ground maize flour). These, together with *boerewors* (spicy sausages) and *biltong* (dried meat) – though these are not on Sarah's list today – are among the main comfort foods any self-respecting southern African exile living in London simply has to have in their kitchen cupboard.

Since Emma's last visit to Graham's the southern African produce which used to be located to the left of the door when you walked in have been moved. Looking round, she sees most of the items she has come in for are now on new shelving on the far right-hand side of the shop. Standing in front of the expanded display Emma picks the jam, oats, milo and chutney she needs off the shelves, but she can't see the mealie meal. As she pivots round to scour the shop in search of the missing item, Emma's right arm brushes against the shelving and the milo, oats and jam tin which were cradled in her right arm crash to the ground and scatter across the slate floor. Fortunately, she is still holding the glass-jarred chutney in her right hand. Emma curses out loud: "Damn it!"

She crouches down and starts to retrieve the missing items, annoyed with herself as she is in a hurry and embarrassed as she moves across the shop floor on her haunches. As she does so, she hears a loud voice right behind saying, "they seem to have moved things around a bit, isn't it?"

"Pardon?" says Emma, turning round to see who is speaking, though she is not entirely sure it was to her. "Are you talking to me?" she adds, even more flustered.

The voice belongs to a lightly-bearded young man, much the same age as her, who is crouching down beside her. As Emma turns towards the man their knees almost touch, their eyes momentarily meet and the man blushes deeply.

"Yes," says the young man as he joins Emma in picking up the dropped items. They reach the last item, the Tiger oats, which he picks up. As they stand up, the young man flushes again as he finds himself – a total stranger – now standing embarrassingly close to Emma, their faces only inches apart. Their eyes meet again and once more they look away from each other.

"Sorry," says the young man as he takes half a step backwards. Words then start to tumble out of his mouth as he tries both to explain what he meant when he first spoke and make amends for having invaded Emma's social space not once, but twice.

"I came in just after you did," he said. "I saw you seemed confused, unable to find what you were looking for. So, like me, I assumed you shopped here regularly but, also like me, I guess, you were perplexed when you saw they've moved everything around.

"If you want the mealie meal – which is the main reason why I popped in today and so it was on my mind and why I am mentioning it – you will find it there." And as he says the word "there," the young man turns to his left and points to the top corner of the new display shelving.

Emma isn't sure quite what to say or do next. She is certainly pleased to know where the mealie meal is, but she is still feeling uncomfortable from their close-body and double-eye encounter. She is also intrigued by how much and how fast he had accurately worked out why she is at Graham's and what she has come to buy. Yet, as she doesn't feel in any way threatened by what has happened, she smiles, albeit a little tentatively, and simply says "yes", quickly followed by "thanks very much."

Encouraged by Emma's response, the young man strides over to the new shelving and extends his right arm upwards almost as far as he is able to reach in order to retrieve two large packets of mealie meal, one for her and one for himself. But after handing the first one back to Emma he realises that, with his left arm still holding tight to Emma's oats and milo, he is scarcely able to touch the second packet of mealie meal as it had been stacked behind the first, further back on the shelf. So he hesitates, smiles, gives back to Emma her oats and milo and then stretches up again – this time on tiptoes – to try to grab hold of it. But he still can't.

Without thinking, Emma puts everything she is holding onto the floor then steps forward and places her two hands gently but firmly against the man's back, either to push him up a little higher or to stop him falling backwards; she isn't quite certain which. After a couple of attempts and a final push from Emma, accompanied by a "you can do it!", he is successful and hands the second package down to Emma.

They both step back again from each other as they start to gather together everything from the floor, laughing as they go through the process of swapping items to ensure each has what they came in for in part to hide the embarrassment they both feel from their close physical contact. They then walk towards the till and stand next to each other as they wait for the only customer in front of them to be served.

"Well, that was different," says the young man, still flustered but trying desperately to regain his composure as he turns towards Emma and smiles. He then holds out his hand for Emma to shake, and, as he does so, half-thought-out words and disjointed sentences tumble out of his mouth. "I'm Simon," he says.

"I live in Muswell Hill.

"I pop in here a couple of times a month on my way back from the gym – the Puregym on East End Road – to buy *boerewors* and mealie meal.

"My family is Zimbabwean, we all love their *boerewors* and since I was small we have always had mealie-meal porridge for breakfast and Graham's is the only place round here where we can buy the genuine stuff."

They both laugh again as they realise at the same time that Emma's arms are too full for her to shake his hand, so she simply smiles, a more relaxed and warmer smile than before, as she ponders what to say. But before she can say anything, the shopkeeper says "Yes please," a little impatiently as she has witnessed the earlier commotion and clearly wants them both out of her shop as she is convinced they have been upsetting other customers.

Although Emma is growing increasingly concerned, she is running really late and nods for Simon to go first, thinking he is only buying the mealie meal. When he asks for 1 kilo of *boerewors*, which needs to be weighed out then wrapped up, Emma curses silently to herself for not taking up his offer of going first. As she turns to walk out of Graham's with her purchases paid for she sees the young man, whom she now knows is called Simon, waiting for her. He politely steps aside and opens the door for her to go out first.

As they leave, they pause a moment outside, not quite sure how to say goodbye. This gives Emma enough time to take a closer look at Simon. He is about the same height as her, slimly-built; his short, trimmed but not particularly well-kept beard is slightly ginger-coloured and he has deep blue eyes. As she rapidly takes all this in, without thinking she smiles again, even more warmly than before, and he reciprocates, unconsciously searching her face to try to uncover further clues about her; he still doesn't even know her name.

Then, realising she hasn't either properly thanked Simon for coming to her aid or responded to his clumsy attempt to introduce himself, she says, "I'm Emma. I am buying all this for my Mum, who I am seeing tonight." And this time with her groceries safely tucked away in her shopping bag, they succeed in shaking hands. "Sorry," she continues, "but I really have to rush as I'm already running late."

Then, aware of how uncharacteristically inarticulate she is being, she realises she needs to say a bit more. "I am off for a big job interview at the BBC," she says. "Thanks so much for coming to my rescue just then. I was so embarrassed, dropping all that stuff and, of course, you *were* right – it *was* the mealie meal I was looking for!"

"Hey, that's fine," replies the ginger-bearded blue-eyed young man, adding, "I hope it goes well – the interview I mean – and you get the job. That is, if you really want it."

"Yes, I really do want it," says Emma, revealing more about herself than her instincts tell her she should but sounding far more relaxed as they part.

She transfers her shopping to her right hand, slings her bag over her left shoulder and strides away down Ossulton Way, raising her left hand above her shoulder as a way of saying a final goodbye.

"It's Simon *Robertson*," he calls out, accentuating the word "Robertson" as he steps off the pavement and heads for the bus stop for Muswell Hill on the opposite side of the road. Emma raises her hand one last time to acknowledge she has heard him but doesn't look back.

Halfway across the road Simon suddenly stops. He feels quite strange: it's as if something deep inside him has forced him to do so. Seeing himself as a rational person with little time for the paranormal and none for the mysterious, his immediate instinct is to reject any such notion. But then even stranger things start to happen. With increasing intensity, Simon realises he must not let this woman Emma simply slip out of his life. He feels his whole being straining to tell him that they have to meet again. He tries to dismiss these thoughts as well, but he can't. Indeed, in an instant, and with crystal-clear clarity, he knows he has to act.

With these thoughts and feelings whirring round inside his head, Simon feels his body pivot and his legs turn as if some involuntary force within him is compelling him to return to Emma. Once on the pavement again, his legs gather pace and his walk turns into a trot and then almost a run. As he hurries towards Emma he becomes aware of his right hand at work in the pocket where he keeps his phone: it is searching for the pen and piece of paper he always carries with him. Simon feels as if his arm is being manipulated from his shoulder blade down to his fingertips by someone – or something – else. It is totally unreal, like a dream, but Simon knows he is not dreaming.

Moments later, Emma feels a hand gently but firmly grasp her right arm at the elbow. Gasping from the shock, she turns and sees Simon right next to her. The sun catches his face in a strange sort of way: it is gleaming brightly as it would if all the spotlights in a theatre were trained on it, and his deep blue eyes sparkle out at her. To Emma, he looks more intense and earnest than he did when they said goodbye just now, but at the same time he seems calm, relaxed and almost serene. She takes in another sharp breath of air, unsure whether this is due to the surprise of seeing him again or his changed appearance.

"Hi again," says Simon. Hurrying on and sounding breathless he asks, "Perhaps we can meet for a coffee sometime?" half-pleading, but with determination in his voice. "Here's my number. Text me if you'd like to. Sorry, I should've given you this when we said goodbye just now but it slipped my mind, but then I knew I had to," he says, the ambiguity in what he said highlighting the confusion still in his mind.

He thrusts a piece of paper into her hand with the numbers 07884 567882 written on it, and with a "Cheers," is gone as suddenly as he had reappeared.

Though she has been quite shaken by their brief exchange, with her mind already refocused on the day ahead, Emma puts the paper into her jacket pocket, momentarily wondering not just why he acted so strangely but what it is about him she really likes. Feeling her phone, she checks the time and quickens her pace, realising she is even later than she had thought. "Terrible planning, Emma Maconie," she says to herself as she returns to rehearsing her answers to the likely questions the interview panel will soon be asking her. By the time she turns left into Brim Hill, Simon Robertson, his face and the piece of paper he has just given her have all been forgotten.

Emma reaches East Finchley tube station a little sweaty as she had been walking fast but pleased with herself as she looks again at her phone to check the time again and relieved she is back on schedule. She taps her debit card on the entry pad and hurries up the stairs to the platform as the next southbound train is drawing into the station. As she knows can take either a Bank or Charing Cross train, she doesn't pause to look up at the display board or the front of the train as it approaches and jumps right in. Since she was young, she has always liked to look out across Cherry Tree Wood and catch a fleeting glimpse of the playground her mother used to take her to as a child. As it is mid-May, the new leaves on the trees overlooking the playground are not yet blocking her view and she smiles to herself as she catches a glance of the bright colours of the swings and slides. Almost at once the comforting sense of darkness engulfs her Northern Line train as it is swallowed up in the tunnel and rattles along on its way first to Highgate and then on into central London.

* * *

The BBC interview had overrun by more than an hour and it was not until after five o'clock that Emma emerged from Broadcasting House. Feeling completely parched, she popped into Boots and bought herself the largest chilled orange juice she could see, which she gulped down in an instant, though it still failed to quench her thirst or raise her sugar levels. Picking up an *Evening Standard* at the entrance to Oxford Circus, she realised just how exhausted she was when she didn't have the energy to skip down the steps. It was only after changing at Camden Town that she found an empty seat and opened her paper, but she wasn't able to absorb what she was reading; her eyes simply travelled over the words. Emma's tired mind automatically returned to the interview, and she struggled to recall the interchanges she had had with different panel members as she attempted to take stock of how it had all gone.

Stepping back from the day's events and reflecting on them was something Emma often did. It was a practice she had learned in her late teenage years, something she found extremely helpful and which continued into adulthood, whether to assess and reflect on important events which had happened or simply to ponder the toll which the daily, humdrum routine of ordinary life was taking on her. She did this because of a discovery she had made. Emma had come to understand that trying to make a difference to the world around her not only required her to continually deepen her understanding of how the world, with all its complexities, worked. She grew to understand that changing the world necessitated changing herself as well. Indeed, she learned that the more deeply she knew herself, and especially the more she understood the flaws, weaknesses and shortcomings of her own personality, the more successful she would be in influencing the world about her. No longer a child living in her make-believe world, Emma had grown out of thinking that changing the world required nothing more than simply curling up in bed and wishing it to happen. However, she was determined as ever to play her part in making it less cruel, more caring and more inclusive.

But now, sitting in the hot tube and trying to take stock of the BBC interview, Emma is unable to focus. As if drugged, she quickly falls into a deep sleep...

Emma is standing outside the lift on the third floor of Broadcasting House to take her down to the exit. As the lift door opens, she sees there is only one other person inside, though she doesn't initially notice who. Suddenly she recognises the woman and immediately feels her stomach tighten: standing at the back is Rosemary Slattery, one of the three people on her interview panel. Wholly absorbed in reading and flipping over the bundles of papers she is holding in her hands, Rosemary doesn't seem to register it is Emma who has just stepped into the lift. Yet by the time the door is about to open, not only is Emma's heart beating ever faster, but she senses Rosemary knows her travelling companion. Indeed, as they step out of the lift, Rosemary's face relaxes and she smiled warmly across at Emma as she gestures her to leave first.

Outside the lift and amidst the bustle of the ground floor, Rosemary turns to her and says, "You did well today, Emma. We were all impressed. I hope to see you again very soon." Then, as they start to walk off in different directions, Rosemary nudges Emma ever so slightly and smiles in a knowing, almost maternal way.

Emma feels a warm glow inside her. She then relives the smiling-nudging interchange at the lift door with Rosemary. The scene repeats itself again – once, twice, three times more. Then as Rosemary nudges her a fourth time and Emma relishes the warm glow one more time, she is woken by the woman seated next to her knocking her elbow against Emma's as she rises from her seat...

At the instant she was jolted back into consciousness, the sounds of the rattling tube suddenly changed and Emma's carriage was engulfed in sunlight as her train emerged from the tunnel, signalling she would soon arrive at East Finchley. As she gathered her things together, checking she had not left behind the bag with her mother's early-morning shopping, a feeling of elation swept through Emma. The reprised exchange with Rosemary while she slept seemed to give her what she was searching for: deep down in her bones, Emma felt the job was hers.

The mix of her dreaming and her sleeping had put energy back into Emma's body. Hardly able to put one foot in front of the other when she descended into Oxford Circus tube station, she skipped down the steps at East Finchley and, with a determined tap of her debit card, strode off towards her mother's. At Emma's pace, it would take her less than 15 minutes. She was now able to play back to herself the key moments of the interview.

She recalled being warmly greeted and fussed over by Janeen, who had initially called to tell her she had been short-listed and with whom she had held further exchanges to fine-tune the details of the day's interview.

When they met, Emma took an instant liking to her. Much the same age as Emma and as self-assured, Janeen was as bubbly in the flesh as she was on the phone, and she immediately put Emma at ease.

At 11 sharp, Janeen ushered Emma into a wood-panelled room where the interview was to take place. It was a recording studio with the furniture rearranged. With a table between them, opposite her were three of the four-person interview panel, one middle-aged man and two middle-aged women. The fourth person, a younger man, was perched above the other three panel-members, peering down at Emma from a TV screen on a video link to the BBC's Media City outpost in Manchester. The middle-aged man, John Ritter, introduced himself as the panel chair and a senior BBC executive. Although she had thought she had done a thorough google before today, Emma did not recognise either his name or his job title and chided herself for her shoddy research. On his right sat Rosemary Slattery, who introduced herself as Head of the new unit, and on his left Polly Turnberry, who said she was a senior editor at BBC News, which Emma already knew from her googling. The man from Manchester, if Emma remembered correctly, was a Current Affairs Coordinator, who had introduced himself as David Hope, adding cheerily that Emma should simply call him Dave. He explained that he had only recently joined the BBC. Being black as well as young, Emma knew Dave was there to complete the two final pieces of the panel's diversity jigsaw.

John Ritter had run quickly through the day. They would start with a formal question-and-answer session and then, after a quick coffee-and-comfort break, return for an in-depth discussion of one or possibly more current news and current affairs issues, depending upon how things went. After a longer break for lunch, John Ritter told Emma she would be asked to role-play a TV interview with a government minister on a topic he would give her later and the day would close with a final wrap-up session.

As the panel members each took it in turn to go through their list of pre-set questions about herself, the job and her expectations for the future, Emma had felt her self-confidence grow as all the questions were ones she had anticipated and prepared for.

"What is it about news, politics and current affairs you find appealing?"

"Why the BBC?"

In recalling now how she had answered these questions, Emma remembered feeling what she had said sounded a bit banal, perhaps verging on trite. She had realised she needed to come across as more engaging and so decided to use an old trick she had been taught by one of teachers: ask a follow-up question herself.

"Should the news be entertaining?" she remembered saying. "Well, it certainly shouldn't be boring," she had immediately replied. "And if it is possible to convey the truth, or paradoxically even the seriousness of a story with humour, or even with a little satire, then all options should be on the table. Sometimes, though, when horrific events occur you need to jolt, even shock, people with the stark reality of what is happening."

"So news is largely focused on reporting the facts, with current affairs programmes providing the broader context?" Polly asked quietly, provocatively challenging Emma to explain to the panel what she really understood the essence of news to be.

Emma had been waiting for this question. She recognised it as soon as Polly had asked it and was quick in her response. "As we all know as journalists," she remembered saying, "news is not only about *who, what, when* and *where;* it is also about the *why* and the *how* of events. And we know that trying to understand why and how things happen can be controversial especially if, as is not uncommon, events elicit competing and widely differing interpretations of what and why they have happened. Indeed, it is even more complicated than this because, as I have repeatedly discovered myself in pursuing stories, it is far from uncommon for the very facts of a story to be contested.

"And it is within this real-world environment that the BBC operates, striving to fulfil its statutory role as an impartial and independent purveyor of the news. As journalists, we will always strive to look for ever different and better ways to try to answer the difficult *why* and *how* questions. We should always be willing to hold up our work to external scrutiny as we attempt to make sense of what is happening first to ourselves and then to our audiences."

Emma then recalled the flourish with which she had rounded off her answers to this first session of the day. "Why do I want to work on news and current affairs issues for the BBC?" she had said, breathing in deeply as she spoke. "Because I believe deeply in the BBC's values of impartiality and independence, because I enjoy working in this important but difficult world of reporting the world's news, and because I really believe I have a contribution to make."

She remembered John Ritter ending the session with almost a smile as he said, "Thank you, Emma, for being so frank."

After the break, Rosemary began the second session by asking Emma how she thought the BBC ought to respond to the new challenge presented by fake news. Emma had also been expecting this topic to be raised given all that had happened following the Brexit vote and Trump's election. However, she was also genuinely interested in how to handle the problem of fake news, and she had read a lot on the subject before she applied for this job. Mulling over now how she had answered the question as she zipped up her jacket to keep out the chill in the evening air, Emma was sure Rosemary had deliberately used the words *"the new challenge"* of fake news to trip her up. Indeed, recalling the smile which Rosemary had given her as she launched into her answer, Emma knew she had successfully negotiated the question's potential trick: it was the only time Rosemary had smiled at her the whole day until they said their final goodbyes outside the lift.

"Of course," Emma had confidently said, "fake news is nothing new. We know that it was deployed as far back as the time of the pharaohs of Ancient Egypt, and even in America, politicians were spreading fake news centuries before Donald Trump and his team began doing so: Benjamin Franklin wrote fake news about murderous scalping Indians working in league with King George III, in an attempt to sway public opinion in favour of the American Revolution."

Emma sensed the rest of the panel had also been impressed she had done her homework. "Today, as in the past," she had continued more earnestly, "the important thing is to ensure people know when fake news is being spread and action is taken not merely to counter it, but to debunk it.

"Indeed, in my view," she added, knowing then that some panel members would probably not agree with what she about to say, such as Polly the senior editor at BBC News, "the BBC and the other main news providers need to be more proactive than they have been in profiling specific examples of fake news far more prominently on the main TV and radio news and, of course, in explaining precisely how and why such news is fake."

And she had been right, as she remembered John Ritter immediately coming back to her with the provocative retort: "Ah, but how does that square with the BBC's principle of impartiality, Emma? Why should the reporting of fake news not be subject to the BBC's requirement to present the news in a balanced way, giving equal air time to differing points of view?"

Emma knew that they had now moved into difficult territory. She was well aware of the debates about fairness and balance which had swirled around the BBC, the wider media and parliament, as well as across the pubs and wine bars of London and among her friends concerning the BBC's approach to reporting on climate change and the Brexit referendum.

"Clearly," she had responded, "the BBC always needs to ensure all its news reporting is balanced and fair in its presentation. But, in my view, there is a crucial difference between two very different things. The first is giving equal air time to differing views on important issues when there is plenty of robust evidence to support both viewpoints or when little research has been done to inform debate. This is where balance is important.

"However, in situations where the overwhelming evidence and almost all of the research points to and supports a particular position – as, in my view, it does in the case of climate change – then giving equal air time to those whose views are supported by the evidence and those whose views are based largely on speculation, or simply sloppy research, violates the principle of balance. In short, providing air time to people just because they have a different view is not what I understand as adhering to the principle of balance. I should add that I am not saying the BBC should not give air time to leading politicians and prominent people propounding views with little firm evidence to back them up or who misuse the evidence, but when it does this, the BBC should always draw the audience's attention to the strength of the available evidence."

Up to this point, Emma had deliberately not mentioned the Brexit referendum and she had been expecting the panel would next ask her views on whether the BBC had got the balance right here. But neither the chair nor any other panel members chose to pursue the issue any further. Emma wondered again why this was and concluded, even more firmly now, that it was because they were themselves divided on the issue – though quite how, she had not been able to judge.

But then, as she thought back again to this particular interchange and knowing that if she got the job she would be working directly for Rosemary, Emma felt certain of one thing: if Rosemary had been one of those panel members who had shared her criticism of the BBC's handling of balance, this could well be a critical factor in determining whether she would be offered the job or not. Rosemary's face, of course, had given nothing away.

Overall, she thought the mock interview session was the lowest point of the day and she suddenly felt deflated. After all, however good she had been at answering their questions, a key part of the job entailed being able to perform well live in front of the camera, and she knew she hadn't. Emma felt herself panicking. Were the good vibes she felt on waking from her tube-journey dreams of that final interchange with Rosemary mere wishful thinking? Perhaps she would not be offered the job after all. Crossing the bridge over the North Circular Road, she felt a shiver rip through her body which she knew wasn't caused by the growing chill of the evening air.

Looking ahead, Emma caught sight of the green grounds of the Finchley Cricket Club. This was where Robbie had begun to teach her the rules of the game soon after they started going out together. Then, all of a sudden, the thought of cricket switched her mind back to the informal lunch she had had with the panel chair. He had invited her to join him in the staff canteen, the News Café, excusing the other panel members from eating with them because of other commitments.

Earlier, Emma had thought little of the lunch. She had enjoyed their salad and coffee, not least as her BBC friends had told her the food was dreadful, and she had admired John for the professional way he had managed to steer the conversation away from anything relevant to the main business of the day. Practically the whole of lunch was taken up discussing cricket and Emma recalled laughing to herself thinking she had never known she had so much to say about the merits of Test Match versus ODIs, T20s and 100-ball cricket.

But the more Emma reflected on their lunch, the more she was beginning to think John's seemingly innocuous question about which forms of cricket appealed to her most had far more to it than she had initially thought. Perhaps this discussion and her lunch had not been *informal* at all? Perhaps it had formed part of the overall assessment of the day? After all, Emma mused, in England cricket is not simply cricket. Current affairs, and even politics, encroach on and are intertwined with this particular sport. After all, it is still *de rigueur* for a British prime minister to be seen at the Lord's test match.

Emma then smiled to herself as she recalled that afternoon a year or so ago when she had popped into the East Finchley library to return a book. She had come in with neither a raincoat nor an umbrella and was a caught in a downpour, so she idled away the time reading through the pages of *Sixty Summers: English Cricket since World War II*. The book had been prominently displayed as it was written by an East Finchley author whose name Emma had now forgotten. Without that rain storm she would never have been able to comment with such authority on the fluctuating fortunes and high points of English test cricket, about which she remembered she had felt some national pride on reading the book. From her ignorance, she had been swayed by the book's view of the pre-eminence of test cricket as the pinnacle of the sport, a view she now sensed John Ritter had firmly shared.

By the time she rang the doorbell to her mother's flat at the end of Moat Crescent, Emma's earlier plunge into darkness and doubt had lifted and she felt once again she would be offered the job after all. She knew this was just the frame of mind she needed to be in for her evening with her mother. Only now did she realise how much she was looking forward to just being with her.

Emma turned the key in the lock and as she opened the door of her mother's front door she called out, "Hi, Ma!"

She heard the cheery reply coming from the kitchen: "Emma, my dear, I want to hear all your news. I'm sure you got the job, isn't it?"

It was only as she opened the front door and smelt Ma's chicken that Emma realised how hungry she was. She put her coat and bag down on the sideboard in the entrance hall and four steps later she was in the kitchen. It was close to 7 pm. Sarah had come in from work a little over an hour earlier and was still wearing the summer dress uniform and black belt with her name badge pinned to the front. On her feet she wore her sturdy workaday sandals.

They hugged and touched cheeks rather than kissed, then momentarily held each other tight as they each patted the other on the back and sighed. They both loved this reassuring ritual as it confirmed their joint sense of belonging, and so each of them savoured the moment. Over time, this physical greeting ritual had become even more important to Emma because, as she had grown into an adult, the intellectual world they shared seemed to be ever shrinking, though their love for each other remained as strong as ever.

Emma placed the things she had bought from Graham's on the kitchen counter and Ma, examining each in turn, thanked her warmly for remembering. Ma liked order and regularity and tried to avoid the unpredictable. In this she was so different from Emma, who relished the new and the unexpected, seeing them as new opportunities from which she could learn.

"Get yourself a drink, my dear, and sit down," said Sarah. "The chicken is almost cooked; I am just finishing the rice and then we can sit down and I will hear it all."

Emma went to the fridge and poured herself some ice-cold water, then walked into the sitting room and sat down as instructed. She was excited and couldn't wait to give Ma a blow-by-blow account of her day, but she also knew Ma was not good at on-the-move interchanges. She loved to listen, and to talk, yet only when she was "settled." So Emma forced herself to hold back until the meal and her mother were ready.

Ma was in her mid-sixties and near retirement. "One day soon," was her constant reply to Emma whenever she had popped the question "When do you plan to retire, Ma?", which she had done an ever-increasing number of times over the last few years. Emma had decided her indecision was probably "for the best," at least for now, because for as long as Emma could remember, Ma's whole world revolved around her work – which she loved – and Emma. And they both knew Ma would be lost without either of these pillars of her life.

Sarah was 30 when Emma was born, much the same age as most of the mothers of those of Emma's school friends whom she knew, and younger than some – an issue of some importance to Emma in her early years as some classmates were teased for having mothers judged by the day's conventional wisdom to be either clearly "too young" or "too old." She was much smaller in height ("half a head," she used to say) than Emma with a smaller body frame and shorter legs and feet (Emma had always assumed her never-known and rarely-talked-about father must have been big). Sarah wore her hair short and her warm rounded face was now dominated by her glasses which for the past ten years she had worn all day, currently large, round, brown tortoise-shell ones. Emma didn't much like them and thought they would soon be out of fashion and look silly, but at least they matched the shape of her face.

Sarah was a warm, outgoing and caring person which is probably why she had originally decided to become a nurse. For as long as Emma could remember, Ma had worked at the North London Hospice, a short walk and easy bus-ride from her Moat Crescent flat, a slightly shorter journey though not as straightforward as the one she used to make from The Grange, Emma's first home in East Finchley. Since opening in the 1980s, the Hospice had steadily expanded in size and reputation to become a much sought after home-from-home for the terminally ill of which North Londoners had grown to be proud. Though it now received considerable state funding, it remained financially dependent on private donations, most still coming from a generous group of loyal North Londoners.

As well as giving Sarah professional fulfilment and some very close friends, the hospice crucially provided their small family with a sure and steady income. Ma and Emma were poor, but they "managed," in large because Sarah spent so little on herself and was a savvy shopper. An early memory of Ma was her singing the lines from Porgy and Bess, "I've got plenty of nothing and nothing's plenty for me!"

This evening, however, was not about Sarah, it was about Emma, her interview and her future. Before Emma had finished her iced-water, Ma walked into the sitting room carrying napkins, mats, knives and forks, which she placed on the low-lying glass-topped table in front of the two-person settee. Emma jumped up to follow another familiar ritual – first, laying out the supper things neatly on the table, then going back with Ma to the kitchen to bring in the chicken and rice, the dinner plates, a water glass for Sarah, the water jug and, finally, the small glass jar of piri-piri sauce – an earlier purchase from Graham's.

As Emma knew, Ma's chicken was reserved for special occasions. Emma had never tasted anything quite like it outside her home, even though Ma insisted this was the way everyone cooked it back home; and on those rare occasions when relatives or friends from Zimbabwe visited, they concurred. The chicken was first cut into smaller pieces than is common in England; these were then fried fast in (far-too-much) hot oil to brown all over, covered and placed in a hot oven to roast. Next, the sauce was prepared by frying chopped onions and tomatoes in (also far too much) oil and salt until soft and browning, to which were added very finely chopped up green cabbage or kale stalks. When the chicken pieces were thoroughly cooked and tender they were mixed with the sauce for the final frying, to which even more oil and a few drops of piri-piri sauce were added. The meal was served by first placing plain boiled rice on a plate, over which the chicken pieces and gravy were poured, topped off by dripping the excess oil from the surface of the unserved gravy from the chicken pot over any of the remaining and still-dry rice.

There was a time in her late teens when Emma became alarmed at the quantities of grease she was consuming when enjoying Ma's chicken. However, she managed both to cope with her guilt and to continue enjoying the chicken by telling herself that, as Ma only made the dish on special occasions and these were rare, no long-term harm would be done. Emma loved not only the taste and texture of Ma's chicken but also crunching the chicken bones with her back teeth and sucking out the succulent marrow juices. This was a way of eating chicken her mother had never explicitly taught her, but as Ma had always chewed and sucked her chicken bones Emma had always imitated her once her grown-up teeth had come in. Though bone-crunching usually led to odd looks from unsuspecting visitors, the practice had spread to a number of East Finchley households.

"Well," said Emma, drawing in breath after swallowing a couple of mouthfuls in silence to savour and enjoy the taste, "let me tell you what happened." She then alternated between eating and talking, sometimes speaking slowly to emphasise a point of particular importance, sometimes hurriedly in order to include all the complex details. It was part of her nature to be thorough. Knowing her mother's keenness to get to the point, Emma began with a short summary of her assessment of the day's events.

"I won't hear for two or three days, but I am pretty certain I got the job. Yes, Ma, I really do think I will soon be working for the BBC and you will be seeing my face on the TV."

On hearing this, Ma sighed, sensing any remaining tension of her workday gently ebb away and feeling good both from what Emma had just told her and the evident pleasure the chicken and rice had started to give her: comfort news and comfort food.

"But tell me all that happened, dear Emma," said Sarah, who was perhaps at her happiest at moments like this: sitting close to Emma on her settee and eating food she had lovingly prepared for her. Sarah felt the lonely gaps between such periods of closeness had grown wider as the months since Emma moved away had turned into years.

Emma then recounted the bits of the day she thought Ma would be most interested in but, as she suspected, Sarah wasn't really interested in the details, so she quickly fast-forwarded to the end of the day and her encounter in the lift with Rosemary.

Holding her mother's hand, Emma said, "And on leaving the lift, Rosemary turned to me and said, 'you did well today, Emma, we are all impressed. I hope to see you again very soon.' And as we parted, she nudged me ever so slightly with her elbow and smiled in a knowing, almost maternal way."

As Sarah turned towards Emma and gave her a hug, Emma said "So that, Ma, was my day." Then suddenly, feeling a twinge of guilt she quickly added, "and what about yours – was it a good one too?"

Ma smiled again as she patted Emma on the knees with both her hands and said, with deep feeling, "My day was good, Emma, because it ended with you".

Emma came back rapidly with "No, Ma! I really do want to hear what happened with you, at work."

"Well," said Ma slowly, "there was bad news, actually sad news, and good news. The sad news is that old Mrs Patel, who seemed to have been getting stronger during the weekend, took a turn for the worse and died in the late afternoon. Frail old Mr Patel came in as usual at lunchtime and we walked together to her room. As it was clearly near the end, I told him so as gently as I could, and, ever so sweetly, he asked me to stay with them both. So I sat there until eventually she passed away just after 4 pm."

Ma paused and they shared a moment of silence, as if to honour the parting of Mrs Patel. Emma knew how good Ma was at supporting loved ones and close family as her patients neared the end of their lives. Indeed, she was so well known for this role and was so often recommended to assist that she was constantly in demand. Emma was immensely proud of her mother.

When Ma spoke again, her mood had changed. "And the good news, my dear," she said, and Emma could sense the excitement in her voice as she spoke, "is I received word about my annual pay rise. It will go ahead this year after all. The increase will appear on my pay slip as from next month."

Emma leaned over and gave her mother another hug. She knew Sarah ought to be paid far more money than her annual pay rise would give her, but at least this was some sort of recognition of the contribution she continued to make to the care of the dying.

It was now after 9 pm and both Emma and Sarah were tired after their very different, but emotionally draining, days. Ma took away the dishes and boiled the kettle to make them each a mug of milo from the newly-opened tin Emma had bought from Graham's. This they drank together when they were both back on the settee. They talked a little more, just small-talk, then they both yawned and knew it was time for their goodbye ritual.

Emma went to the hallway, put on her coat, picked up her bag and returned to Ma, who was still sitting on the settee. Emma thought she looked washed out and the thought suddenly flashed across her mind that her mother might be ill as well as tired. But she immediately dismissed the idea, though she did wonder how her mother – and she – would cope when Sarah did become really ill. She prayed it wouldn't be soon as she sat down again close to her mother for their final, lingering hug.

Emma then walked to the front door, calling out, "see you at the weekend – call me."

"Bye," said Ma, "and go well, my dear. I am so proud of you – and don't forget to call Robbie."

As Emma stepped outside, it was far colder than when she had arrived, and dark too. She was glad of her jacket and the street lights were on. She took her phone from her bag and checked her emails. As her eye ran down the list of six or seven people whose names appeared, she quickly formed the view no one e-mailing her was sufficiently important to merit her having to deal with it tonight. She was pleased as she felt far too tired to shift her mind to anything new.

She had one text message. It was from Robbie, of course! It read: "Thinking of you today. Hope it all went well. Talk soon. Love Rob-bow xxx."

Emma smiled to herself. She was glad he had texted, though she would have been shocked if he hadn't. Though they usually spent the weekends together, she realised how much she was looking forward to their time together this coming weekend. Hopefully it would come after she had heard whether she had been offered the job, giving them the opportunity to discuss the future together. She then recalled how helpful Robbie had been when she was thinking of applying for the BBC job and how reassuring and supportive he had been when she had some, albeit minor, self-doubts.

Emma had fallen in love with Robbie at school and she loved him now even more deeply. They had known each other the whole of their adult lives, and Emma's understanding of who she was, her views of the world and her growing self-knowledge had been shaped, formed and developed with Robbie. She knew how well he had filled the intellectual space which had widened between her mother and herself. She loved them both in totally different but – she thought – very complementary ways. Nothing, she felt, could ever come in the way of the completeness she felt in her love for both of them.

Emma was daydreaming. She suddenly realised she was nearly home. She knew it was already too late to call Robbie, so she quickly composed a text in reply to his. "Great day, my dear," she wrote. "I think I got the job. Thanks for everything. Really looking forward to the weekend together. Lots to talk about then. Love you loads. Em-and-Em xxx."

Emma picked up her post from the doormat as she walked into her flat: one utility bill, otherwise junk mail and a bunch of glossy fliers for all sorts of takeaways, home-delivered and 2-for-1s. She tossed her keys onto her dressing table, plugged in her phone and was quickly in bed. She would shower in the morning.

As she sank beneath her duvet, Emma momentarily lay on her back, resting her head in her cupped hands folded together on the pillow behind her and consciously breathed in and out deeply four or five times. She was far too tired to take stock of it all, she thought; it had been a very good day.

Then, as she turned over onto her side and put her left arm under her pillow as she drew up her knees and curled up – the way she had always fallen asleep since she was tiny – the encounter she had at Graham's the butcher early on in the day suddenly came back to her. She was shocked that she had completely forgotten about it until just then.

There was something about him – about Simon – she had really liked, even been attracted to, but she couldn't quite put her finger on it, and she was far too exhausted to think what it was or might be. Though it would be completely out of character for her, she thought she might contact him – but where had she put the piece of paper he gave her? She couldn't remember and then decided she wouldn't call him after all. Why should she? Their meeting was simply a chance encounter, and she had had plenty of those in her life. Why would this one be any different? Then, as she began to fall into the deepest of sleeps, unnervingly warm and positive feelings seemed to well up from the pit of her stomach, causing an ever-so-small twinge of excitement, and begin to latch themselves on to her unconscious.

deliberately as she replied. However, she wasn't really able to disguise the joy welling up inside her.

Emma had rehearsed what she would say if offered the job dozens of times over the last few days – far more often than the short sentence she had memorised if she had not been offered the job – but she forgot it all in her excitement and simply said, "Thanks so much, Janeen! I am so delighted the panel had the confidence to offer me the job and I can tell you now I *will* take it: it means *so* much to me.

"I am also keen to start as soon as I can and I am sure I can sort everything out here to begin in four weeks or less," she continued. "But I will need to discuss my leaving the *Times* with my line manager, and I won't be able to do this until after the weekend. So if it's okay with you, can I call you back to confirm the start date on Monday?"

"Yes, Emma, that's absolutely fine," said Janeen, who sounded less official now. "You will also need to pop in to see HR to sign a couple of preliminary documents, mostly about BBC confidentiality rules and regulations, as well as go over the nitty-gritty of your draft contract. We would hope you could come in and do all this next week."

"Yes, that sounds fine, Janeen," said Emma, without stopping to check her diary for next week.

"Great," said Janeen. "Talk to you Monday, then. Bye!"

Emma held the phone loosely in her hand as she kept telling herself that what had just happened was not simply a repeat of her recurring daydream. It was a dull and unusually chilly day for May and, as she was replaying the conversation with Janeen in her mind, she realised how cold she was standing outside, having left her sweater hanging over the back of her office chair. She needed to get back into the warm and to act as if nothing had happened. When she had sat down again at her desk, she allowed herself a sigh of relief as she said ever so quietly to herself, "Emma, well done, my girl."

The rest of her working day was a blur. Emma texted Robbie and called her mother, who wasn't picking up so she left her a message. She remembered receiving a note from the day's sub-editor saying he had liked her piece on the flower sellers and telling her it had now been published online, with only one minor edit, under the provocative and not entirely accurate headline of "Revolt over Cemetery Flower-Seller Restriction Edict." Besides that, although she had kept herself busy (she always did), Emma couldn't remember what calls she made or received in preparing for next week's stories, or with whom she spoke until the office fell silent for the weekend. She was one of the last to leave and headed for the lift with her last few remaining colleagues. As she stepped out of the building with them, exchanging mutual good-byes and wishing each other a good weekend, all of a sudden Emma realised she would miss them all. It had been – she was ready to acknowledge to herself – a very happy four years.

Just after 8 pm that same evening, Robbie rang the bell at Emma's flat. As she opened the door, Robbie's face broke into a warm smile and Emma stepped forward to embrace him. He wrapped his arms around her and momentarily cradled his cheeks against hers saying, "I'm proud of you, Em. You did it, as I knew you would." Emma felt a warm glow of satisfaction inside her as they linked hands and walked into the flat.

* * *

Like Emma, Robbie was in his mid-20s, though a few months older. When friends asked how long they had known each other, neither quite knew how to respond as they had been vaguely aware of each other since they were young. This was because they had gone to the same church, St. Mary's East Finchley. As shy children they used to exchange a few embarrassed words standing next to each other as their mothers briefly chatted after Mass, but for years that was about it. Their mothers had not become friends and their relationship had never extended beyond exchanging pleasantries after church on Sundays. The two families didn't live close to each other; Robbie and Emma had attended different primary schools and they had grown up with different circles of friends.

It was in 2010 – halfway into the school year – that all that changed. The previous September Robbie had transferred to St. Michael's Catholic Grammar School in North Finchley to start his A-levels. Until then, St Michael's had been a single sex school for girls. It was where Emma had been since leaving her primary school some six years earlier.

Though it had become increasingly common for former single sex secondary schools to open their sixth forms to pupils of the other sex, when it happened it invariably caused quite a stir, and St. Michael's was no different. It was an event Emma and her friends had been eagerly awaiting, the subject of endless discussion and, inevitably, embarrassed and excited giggles. The girls were not disappointed in the boys, and the boys were delighted with the attention they received, not least because the ratio of girls to boys in the sixth form still lay heavily in favour of the girls for the first few years.

Robbie found himself a particular focus of attention because he stood out from most of the other male newcomers as tall, slim and athletic as well as articulate, astute and academically bright. Also, as the girls were quick to notice, he came across as kind and considerate –indeed, he was both those things. However, it took until the following spring, soon after Emma had turned 18, before Robbie had the courage to ask Emma to go out with him.

In the grand order of things, what happened to them was unremarkable. Though the details were unique to them, in essence the story of how they got together was repeated dozens of times across the country's secondary schools every year.

It began quite slowly. As Robbie and Emma were taking different A-levels, they were only thrown together in class twice a week for their RE classes. Sometime after the Christmas break, Robbie found himself chatting to Emma more frequently after class and she responded warmly. Then, increasingly trying to find reasons to be with her, he would search her out at lunch, in the playground and eventually in the after-school walk to their different bus stops. It didn't take long for Robbie to realise he had become captivated by Emma. He daydreamed about her longingly and she visited him encouragingly in his dreams at night. He gazed at her when he thought she wasn't watching and felt down when they couldn't be together. He joined the school's Amnesty International support group, one of Emma's initiatives, which met twice weekly to write letters to political prisoners, just to be with her. However, he didn't know what to do next.

Then, one day, knowing she was a keen runner and almost without realising what he had done, Robbie asked Emma if she would mind their going out jogging together, and she agreed. Just before they entered the school gates at the end of their run, Emma tripped on a loose paving stone and Robbie caught hold of her arm. It was the first time they had touched each other and both sensed the significance of what had just happened. When school closed for the day, Robbie waited for Emma. He caught her eye and they walked out of school together. Without saying anything, they awkwardly made their way down unfamiliar streets to be on their own and, when they were sure they were alone, they kissed, briefly and rather clumsily.

After three or four such after-school meetings, Robbie managed to blurt out, "I love you Emma," feeling relieved as well as excited as his recurring dreams of the past weeks had now become reality.

"I love you, too," said Emma, tingling with teenage glee as well as deep satisfaction.

The following weekend Robbie invited Emma to meet him at the Finchley Cricket Club where he regularly played for the youth team; he was a talented fast bowler. By then he knew the ground was near to where Emma lived and she readily agreed. By the Monday Emma eagerly told her girlfriends at school she and Robbie were now together, but they said they already knew.

What was far more remarkable than their getting together was that Emma and Robbie remained a couple. Instead of growing apart when they moved into adulthood – they were the only ones in their year to be together five years after leaving school – their relationship grew ever more solid as they discovered new areas of common ground between them.

Understandably, as they were at a church-based school, Robbie and Emma already shared a belief in the dignity of *all* human beings, black and white, male and female, straight and gay. They were also well aware of the divisions in the world between the rich and the poor, between the haves and the have-nots. Embarking on their new lives as young students, their horizons broadened further when they met and were influenced by a new group of teachers, developed new friendships and read more widely. As a result, their beliefs in the value and worth of all people grew ever stronger and their awareness of the deep divisions in society was sharpened.

But what affected them most on their path towards greater social awareness was discovering what had happened to a growing number of their less fortunate school friends, especially those from their primary schools who had failed to transfer to one of Finchley's better secondary schools. Many had wanted to pursue further studies and all of them eventually wanted a fulfilling job, just like they did. But, again and again, Emma and Robbie learned either directly from their friends themselves or indirectly from others that many were not offered a place in university or college and were unable to find almost any sort of work. Rather, they found insurmountable barriers to further education or a proper job laid in their path. This drip-fed into them a growing sense of hopelessness, eroding their self-esteem. Eventually it shattered their dreams and destroyed all the expectations they had had for their futures.

Over time the list of names and the personal stories of those whose hopes and ambitions were thwarted grew longer; some were deeply disturbing. For Robbie, there was Joanna, Nurun, Hamish and Jo. For Emma, there was Michele, Mohammed, Bobbie and Jen; and for both of them there were Kojo, Ayana, Janek and Mateusz. Losing all hope, two friends killed themselves: Nurun when she was 22 and Mateusz just a week after his nineteenth birthday.

For the most part it was not ambition which their friends lacked. The primary cause of their problems lay in their being poor and the fact that neither they nor their immediate family members knew the right people or had the right connections to help them. Their paths were repeatedly blocked repeatedly by lack of money, by prejudice or by overt discrimination. Whatever the specific cause – and each case differed in the details – the outcome was almost always terrifyingly familiar. With comparative ease, as one friend after another began to lose hope, they started to drift. Many couldn't cope with the stress and easily slipped into a vicious cycle of life of drugs and debt, but thankfully only two were sucked into the underworlds of crime and hard drugs from which they found it impossible to escape. To make matters worse, these two were disowned by their families, tipping them into mental breakdowns for which they obtained only derisory support from the medical profession on the few occasions when they had the strength to try to seek help.

Emma's rollcall of the distressed included one of her oldest and closest friends, Jennifer, or Jen, which she found particularly hard to cope with because all her repeated efforts to help her had failed. By her early twenties, Jen had joined the aimless drifters, living a stressed and unpredictable life. Quite soon she hardly noticed the difference between day and night and no longer seemed able to distinguish between right and wrong; she became listless and uninterested when Emma and other old friends sought her out to try to support her, though she seemed grateful when Emma came to visit her in prison. Emma found herself joining the Saturday afternoon queue of family and friends assembled outside Holloway prison, waiting for it to be opened to visitors of inmates: women and young offenders. Though she didn't share this with the friends she came to see, it did thrill Emma to know a number of suffragettes had been imprisoned in Holloway. One of these, Charlotte Despard, a particular hero of hers, was sent to Holloway twice. She devoted most of the rest of her life to trying to make life a little better for the poor people of Battersea. Emma not only knew about the pub named after her but had once taken Robbie to the *Charlotte Despard* at the end of Despard Road in Archway to have a drink in her honour.

Robbie and Emma used to talk about all these upsetting events with growing dismay; they grew to love talking deep into the night. And their discussions led them both to feel a growing desire to map out career paths for themselves which would contribute to helping root out the causes of these tragic problems. Young and fired up with enthusiasm, they became convinced that the cogs which turned their world – their country, London and their part of it, their neighbourhood – needed to be adjusted and realigned. And they convinced themselves and each other that if this change was to come about, they had to be part of the process to make it happen, however small their contribution might be. Indeed, they increasingly felt their lives would only have meaning if they chose jobs which, directly or indirectly, would help to change their world; to shift those cogs. Their growing and shared desire to contribute to making a difference to the world became fundamental to Emma and Robbie's relationship: it strengthened the ties which bound them together and nourished their love for each other.

As Emma and Robbie began to articulate their emerging view of the world and what they wanted to do with their lives, their parents and some of their friends responded by telling them they were idealists, even dreamers. At times they admitted they were, but this didn't cause them to waver in their beliefs. If anything, it had quite the opposite effect. What's more, although their circle of old school friends certainly shrank, their relationship with those they continued to see regularly deepened and they also gained plenty of new friends who shared their outlook on life. But important though all this became to their lives, neither Robbie nor Emma lost the zest for living which initially attracted them to one other: none of their closest friends or work colleagues would ever accuse them of not being fun people.

Emma knew the source of her desire to change her world: it was rooted in her self-confidence. Even as a toddler, grown-ups not only noticed but remarked upon her exceptionally strong inner strength as they listened to her repeatedly saying she wanted to help make the sad children she played with as happy as she was. She grew into a girl self-evidently at ease with herself. Indeed, her zest for living could not be contained: she had such *joie de vivre*, it seemed forever to be bursting out from her for others to try to capture for themselves. As a teenager and into adulthood, her bubbly and caring personality provided a welcome, warm and reassuring shoulder for others to cry on. Quite soon after they got together, Emma told Robbie she was sure the seeds of her self-confidence could be traced directly back to the love showered on her by her mother.

Sarah was a single mother and Emma an only child; she never knew her father. Not surprisingly, Emma and Sarah were extremely close and Ma's life revolved around Emma, to whom she was totally devoted. Sarah had acquired the skills to be both father and mother to Emma though she could also, with apparent ease, slide into the chummy or playful role of sister or the wise and forgiving role of grandmother as the occasion or need arose. Consequently, Emma felt at ease confiding in Sarah.

Emma's first home was a small second-floor flat on the Grange estate, just off the High Road towards North Finchley. Although it had undoubtedly earned its reputation as a rough and at times dangerous area, as hard drugs were exchanged and gangs operated there, Sarah had some solid friends on the estate. Many of her first playmates came from troubled families, but Emma's memories of those early years of her childhood were predominantly happy ones.

From the age of three, she went first to Martin's Infants and then on to Martin's Primary School on the East Finchley High Road next door. The schools were less than ten minutes' walk from their home, even when she was small and only had little legs.

At Martin's, it was common (as it was in other schools) for one or two pupils to be the centre of attention: the ones whom others wanted as their best friend. It took a while for Emma to realise *she* was the one whom others in her class (and even some in the class above) wanted to be best friends with. *She* was the one who would make the decision of what games to play or what songs to sing in the playground. If *she* said something happening in the classroom or playground was wrong, nearly everyone else soon thought the same. Then, as Emma and her friends grew older, if *she* said a particular boy was attractive, all the other girls readily agreed.

In later life, Emma began to wonder why and how she had achieved such status among her peers. She came to the view that her self-confidence had been significantly boosted by a single event which occurred when she was quite young, around six or seven. Whatever the precise year, she remembered the incident well.

It happened on the opening morning of the new school year. Her class teacher, Mrs Murray, starting her first job after college, stood before the whole year and in a strong Glaswegian accent announced loudly to all, "I am delighted to announce to you all that in my class this year we have three Scots lassies: Laura McCabe, Jennifer Macrae and Emma Maconie. Please come forward the three of you and stand up here next to me."

Emma didn't feel Scottish, largely because aged about six and having lived all her conscious life in London she wasn't sure what being Scottish was – or being a lassie. However, she was keen to lay claim to both as they were clearly the attributes one needed to have. What she did clearly understand, though, as she stood in front of the whole class was she was one of three quite "special" people – indeed, so special, everyone needed to know. Prompted by Mrs Murray, the other children even clapped to express their approval.

This incident was also the catalyst for Laura and Jen to become Emma's earliest and closest friends, and, as they were both far more reserved than her, it was Emma who was always the most dominant of the three. Had it not been for the young Mrs Murray's misguidedly anointing her that morning, Emma might not have so easily slipped into a range of different leadership roles later in life. But, looking back, Emma was certain that from then on, she became a more self-assured person, comfortable in herself, happy simply being Emma; Emma Maconie.

An important way Emma's growing self-assurance manifested itself was in the strong sense she had of *belonging*; of identifying herself with and being identified as an integral part of the mix of children from very different backgrounds who attended Martin's school. Typical of contemporary London, it was made up of a diverse group of ethnicities, customs and beliefs. Besides "white English" and Protestant, Martin's pupils were made up of Greek Cypriots (mostly Orthodox), Indians (mostly Moslem and Hindu), Bangladeshis (Moslem), Irish (mostly Catholic) and those from the Caribbean (different Christian denominations). There were children from eastern and southern Africa (mostly Jewish from South Africa and Ugandan Asians – Hindu, and some Christian) and a number of mostly second generation Jewish children whose families had predominantly come from mainland Europe and Russia around the time of World War II. Most, like Emma, came from poorer homes, though a minority came from richer ones as well, and she happily made friends with fellow pupils from most of these different groups and backgrounds.

As they grew up together, their different backgrounds produced a widely-shared outlook on life which was rooted in the values they brought from home and those they absorbed in the classroom. These were mixed together, initially in the playground, to create – quite unconsciously – the modern English identity which Emma absorbed and became a part of. It was an identity she shared with the overwhelming majority of her peers, built on the core values of tolerance and respect for all, a penchant for the truth and, of course, an obsession with orderly queuing. But it included three inter-linked attitudes to others which were fundamental to the way Emma and her friends related to each other at school and which, later in life, they would all live by: the welcoming of others, a respect for otherness and the championing of difference.

As a young and growing girl Emma's popularity, as well as her self-esteem, were enhanced by her physique (she was tall for her age), her intellectual abilities and her prowess at sports, starting with her playground hopscotch skills and culminating in becoming a good middle-distance runner and a skilled mid-field football player. She not only had an inquisitive mind but was quick-witted to boot. She was one of the first in her year to learn to read and this was probably a key factor in developing her interest in books. She became a voracious reader of English novels and still read for pleasure. Most schoolwork came easily to her and she sailed successfully through primary school.

After Martin's, aged 11 and comfortably equipped with both the exam qualifications and a nod of support from the local parish priest, Father Underhill, which she needed, Emma easily made the transition to the Catholic grammar school, St. Michael's, in North Finchley. It was a big school, but she continued to do well academically and to shine socially. Aged 16, she sat her GCSE exams and easily obtained the grades needed to move to the sixth form. It was during this time, parallel to her interest in boys, that her love affair with journalism and the media began to develop, shaping her choice of A-level subjects: English, Sociology and Politics and Media Studies.

Just before Emma's sixteenth birthday, she and her mother had left the Grange and moved into a modern flat in Moat Crescent, a dozen or so streets to the west. Not only was it bigger and brighter, but the area had a more open feel to it: the surroundings were dominated more by grass than concrete, and there were no dark corners permanently filled with leftover takeaway wrappings and smelling of urine. Its main drawback was that it lay right next to the ever-busy North Circular Road, and the flat had seemed really noisy when they first visited. This probably explained why the rent was far lower than if the same flat had been located in a quieter area, and why they could afford to move. However, as Moat Crescent was on high ground above the rebuilt sunken highway and their windows were double-glazed, in no time at all they hardly noticed the 24/7 traffic noise. Indeed, it was only after they moved that Emma realised quite how noisy the Grange had been, from the raucous noise of drunkenness to the screams of domestic violence and the heart-wrenching whimpering of abused women.

Their new flat was also warmer and far better insulated than the Grange, so it cost them far less to heat in the winter. Soon after they left the Grange, a man was murdered there in a gang shooting. Sarah said this confirmed to her that their decision to move had been the right one.

In the summer of 2007, aged 16, Emma was fortunate to land a holiday job with the *Hendon and Finchley Times* with the assistance of David Gould, one of the paper's sub-editors, whose son, Joe, had been a classmate and later good friend at Martin's School. She often met David at his home when she went to play with Joe; their house was one of the smaller ones on Brim Hill on the posh villagey side of East Finchley. Though the job was fairly menial (she seemed to spend more time making tea than writing), she followed a number of local news stories, including one about London Greek Radio, located down the road from Martin's, where the eldest sister of another of her school friends was working as a part-time DJ.

The six weeks in Hendon nurtured Emma's growing conviction she wanted to be a journalist, which was reinforced the following year when she applied and was accepted for a three-week holiday job at the BBC World Service at Bush House. Here, she shadowed and worked alongside a World Service newsreader. The work involved long hours, sometimes at night. Though Emma never got near to reading the news, she experienced the buzz of the newsroom and loved it. She was given background research assignments and wrote short, summary pieces on current news stories, which she found absorbing and exciting. The high point of her placement was on the second to last day, when three sentences Emma had written on the war in Georgia and South Ossetia were read out word-for-word on the World Service news. She was thrilled!

These experiences and her emerging career ambitions developed in Emma a new sense of who she was – a modern North Londoner – and who she wanted to be: a modern North London journalist. That same summer she had had another experience which, though fleeting, reinforced her identity as well as bringing a smile to her face whenever she recalled it. St. Michael's had arranged a short sixth form trip by coach to Paris and funds had been arranged to enable those who, like Emma, could not afford to pay to go on the trip. When the bus reached the Calais Euro-tunnel terminal on its return journey, everyone had to pile out of the coach to have their passports inspected by the English immigration officials. Emma's passport was taken by a dour-looking, slightly overweight, round-faced, bearded man with chubby hands and short fingers. He looked first at Emma, then at her passport and back to Emma again and as he did so, she grew increasingly nervous. This was her first trip abroad and this was her very first passport, obtained specifically for this trip to France.

The official said to her inquiringly, but firmly, "Emma Maconie?"

"Yes," said Emma strongly and confidently, in part to hide her nervousness.

"Mac-con-ie," he said, enunciating each syllable of her surname in turn and imitating (poorly) a Scottish accent.

"You're Scottish, are you?" he asked, flicking through the pages of her passport, which were all blank. "And you don't seem to have been anywhere? I thought the Scots were great travellers?"

Not quite knowing which question to answer, Emma said, "No, I am not Scottish," then mumbled something about being British. Why was he hassling her? she thought to herself.

"I know you're British, Miss Maconie, or you wouldn't have a British passport, would you?" he retorted.

"Yes," said Emma quickly followed by "No!" She was even more nervous now, but then bravely said first in an upper-class accent, "Actually, I am English, proper English and posh," before switching to broad cockney, "from Norf Lundun."

This seemed to clear the air. The previously dour official looked at her passport for the final time, closed it and handed it back to her. Then as a smile broke out over his face, he said, "Well then, young lady, welcome back home – to England, Emma's England."

The other girls giggled, as did Emma when she was out of earshot, but in her case more out of relief. Though brief, she had found this short exchange quite an ordeal. But it was over now and when she sank back into her seat on the bus she breathed deeply to herself, thinking that if she ever met her old teacher, Mrs. Murray, again, she would confidently tell her she was now sure she definitely wasn't Scottish.

Emma stopped growing before she left school. At a little over 1.7 metres (or "just under six foot", as Robbie's mother put it when they first met) Emma was tall and, though she was not thin, her height gave her the air of being slim. When growing up, she was told she could have been a basketball player or a high jumper but she had no interest in either. She kept in shape these days largely by jogging regularly from her home, once or twice a week, something she and Robbie often used to do in their early days together.

Her skin was smooth and slightly oily. She had a fair complexion and browny-black hair which, following a short-lived "funky stage" in her mid-teen years, she had subsequently worn straight. It was now shoulder-length hair, long enough to be tied at the back when she wanted to, with a short central parting; she always ensured both her forehead and her eyes were clear of hair so you could see her whole face. Though her cheekbones did not stand out particularly, they were sufficiently distinct to accentuate the length of her face, which was neither long nor round. Her brown eyes were slightly smaller than average, but exceptionally bright; they lit up when she smiled, which she often did, exposing her white and well-shaped teeth. If there was one feature of her face which had troubled Emma when growing up it was her lips. She would have liked them thinner and could never

plenty of other people: close friends of her mother and their children and schoolfriends and their parents or carers. Emma never felt friendless: she hardly thought about, still less worried about having no siblings or cousins to play with; being an only child and living just with her mother never bothered her.

When she was 21, and had a steady income as a young journalist, she had moved out of the family flat at Moat Crescent and into her own (far smaller) one, the bottom half of an already-small post-war and poorly-built terraced house which stood in a row with others on a short street between the High Road and East End Road. Though Emma had felt guilty about moving out and leaving Sarah on her own, it was her mother who first suggested it was time for her to do so; she knew Emma was keen to spend more time on her own with Robbie and she understood and accepted that. Emma knew Sarah was right that she would only be a small walk away so felt less guilty about it. Emma's flat certainly had its problems – thin walls, poor plumbing, leaky roof and a lousy landlord – but it was her own home, her very first, and she loved it. It was to this flat that Robbie came as often as he could, as a male homing pigeon regularly returns to the comfort of his nest.

* * *

Robbie Hall, like Emma, was a North Londoner, but from North rather than East Finchley. At 1.9 metres and with a strong physique, he was a good deal taller than Emma. Though not fat and far from obese, he was heavily-built, in large part because he had progressively been taking less exercise since his late teenage years when he had been, and had looked, athletic. His runs with Emma had become less frequent as his workload had become more and more demanding. He knew (because Emma told him) he had to watch his weight and also (because she told him that, too) that he needed to exercise more than he did. He wore his hair short and was clean shaven; he had a long face, thinner than might be expected given the size of the rest of his body. Like Emma he had brown eyes and a warm smile.

What Emma had at first failed to register about Robbie was his hands. She had known almost from the day she set eyes on him that Robbie had wide wrists and large hands which matched his body size. But it was only after they first started going out together that she noticed his fingers, which were exceptionally long and thin. She played with his hands: when he straightened them with his fingers outstretched, you could see the light shining through the large gaps between each and every one of his finger joints. There were 12 gaps in all: Emma knew, she had counted them. It was this which created the illusion his hands were thin. Emma had told him they were "knobbly in a nice way." She loved lying lengthwise along her settee with her head resting on his lap as he sat at one end and placing her hands inside Robbie's as he, in turn, gently cupped his hands around hers, enclosing them as if they were being swallowed up.

Robbie had always felt himself fortunate not so much to have fallen in love with Emma but for her having fallen in love with him. This was less because he found Emma exceptionally attractive – which he definitely did – but more because his self-image was of an ordinary if not boring person.

What Robbie initially failed sufficiently to notice about Emma related less to her body and more to her character. He knew she was ambitious and strong-willed; this was in part why he found her so attractive. But what he hadn't realised at first was quite how determined she could be. Over time he learned how single-minded Emma could be in pursuing tasks she considered urgent or important. Objectively they could be quite trivial, such as trying out different recipes for fennel which she suddenly discovered and had never cooked before until she found one which worked; or they could be far bigger and even controversial issues, such as when *The Times* told her not to run a story on a local businessman she discovered was charging excessively high rents on shoddy accommodation because he was such a generous supporter of local charities. Whenever her vigorous determination kicked in, she became almost obsessive about the issue she had decided needed to be resolved. What was more worrying was that when this happened she would sometimes become so wrapped in what was absorbing her attention she couldn't hear when people were advising her to be more cautious and less hasty. Deep down, Robbie worried that her single-mindedness could get her into serious trouble, especially if it affected her judgement. But as such actions had never caused any real damage and had often led to the change Emma was pursuing, he had been happy to let things be. He didn't know how concerned he should have been until it was too late.

It was not surprising Robbie liked cricket as his parents were from the Caribbean and an equally tall and famous uncle had played cricket for the West Indies but well before Robbie was born. Robbie's father, Trevor, had been born in Barbados: in Holetown, on the west coast of the island, north of the capital, Bridgetown. His family were strong Methodists. Soon after leaving school, in the 1950s, Trevor had the same journey as a number of his friends and came over to London, where he found employment with London Transport, eventually becoming a Northern Line tube driver based in North Finchley. It was here that he met and socialised with other London Transport workers drawn from the different islands of the Caribbean: it was only in London that he began to feel West Indian rather than simply Barbadian, or Bajan.

It was through one of these new London Transport friends, Frank George, that Trevor was first introduced to Robbie's mother-to-be, Cynthia Thompson, who, like Frank, also came from Tobago. Cynthia was born into a strong Catholic family in the capital, Scarborough, and grew up round St

Joseph's Church, attending the linked Catholic primary and secondary schools where, she used to tell her children, she was given a "proper English education." After school, she studied nursing. Soon after qualifying at the Scarborough General Hospital she came to England, and shortly after arriving, met Trevor. Soon after that they were married. Leaving Tobago, she moved directly to North Finchley as a nursing job at Barnet General Hospital seemed ready and waiting for her – as Robbie recalled her telling him. They met in North Finchley and were married at the Catholic Church of Philip the Apostle in Finchley Church End, where Cynthia had regularly gone to church ever since she had arrived in England.

Being a good Methodist, it was with some reluctance that Trevor allowed Cynthia to bring up Robbie and his two brothers as Catholics. Robbie was also a family name, chosen because, coincidentally, Trevor and Cynthia discovered they both had grandfathers named Robert. A few years after their marriage, when Robbie was in primary school, Cynthia made the difficult decision to move their place of worship to St Mary's East Finchley because of what she judged to be the racist attitudes of some of the parishioners at St Phillips directed at her three young boys. It was then that Robbie and Emma started going to the same church and when they must have first sort of met each other on one of those Sunday mornings after Mass.

Unsurprisingly, they had already started going out together before she told Ma. Emma, who shared everything with her mother, didn't quite know when and how to break the news. Some six weeks or so after it had become well known at school that Robbie and Emma were "an item," Robbie urged Emma to tell her mother about him. By this time Emma had already, quite formally, met Robbie's mother, Cynthia, at her house. Cynthia immediately took a liking to "my Emma," as she soon began to call her. Though they had not spoken about the matter between themselves, Cynthia followed up on Robbie's initial comments by taking Emma aside the second time she had come to the house and told her, in a supportive but firm manner, she had to let her mother know. This was in part because that was simply what was done back in Tobago but also because, as she told Emma, "As the mother of an only child and daughter, she'll already know something is going on, and she will be worrying what it is, so you simply have to tell her."

That same evening, when Emma had finished her homework and they were sipping their milo together on the couch before going to bed, Emma turned to Sarah and said with deliberation, "Ma, I have something important to tell you."

Pausing a little before replying, Ma said, "I know, Emma – it's a boy, isn't it?"

"How do you know?" exclaimed Emma, clearly surprised.

"I am a woman, my dear Emma, and also a mother," answered Sarah, deploying, whenever she became emotional, those expressions which sounded quaint to Emma's friends, but which she found so comforting.

Then, smiling as she did so, Sarah told Emma how she knew. "Though you may not have realised it, the positive way you have been talking about the world, the excitement you have expressed about the future, the even more careful way you have been dressing and ironing even your school uniform, the longer hours you have spent at school on those extra, unexpected and oh-so time-consuming work assignments – all these things, my dear, and more, can really only add up to one thing! Tell me, about him. First, what is his name?"

The easy part was the name; the difficult part was to tell her his family came from, and his roots were in, the Caribbean. To her knowledge, no one in their family had ever married any sort of outsider, never mind someone from the Caribbean. What would she think? Surely she would not approve? Should I not say anything about his origins and his ethnicity, Emma had wondered, and just bring him home and let her see him? No, that would be too cruel. "He is a Catholic, and you know his Mum as she goes to our church" – maybe I should start with that?

Emma decided the direct approach was the one she should take as Ma would respect her for that, even if she would likely have problems with the answer. So, taking a deep breath and with her forehead slightly wrinkled, Emma said slowly, "Ma, Robbie's dad is from Barbados and his Mum from Tobago: his roots are in the Caribbean. But," she added quickly, "he is English, born here in Finchley, and he speaks like me too. You'll really like him: he is kind and caring as well as bright and clever. And…"

Ma stopped her there, raised her hand and said, "Slow down, dear Emma, slow down," in a voice which Emma couldn't tell was signalling approval, concern or, God forbid, hostility.

Sarah put her mug of half-drunk milo down on the coffee table in front of her, looked down to the floor and paused as she carefully thought how to put what she was going to say next. She spoke slowly and in short sentences.

"You are right," she began "people from the Caribbean are not the same as us. Their culture is quite different from ours. From the little I know of them they have a more happy-go-lucky way of looking at things. I don't know many people from the Caribbean, but people at the Hospice tell me many of their men leave their wives and divorce rates are high among Caribbean people.

"But I am sure you know this, and you will have thought long and hard about what you are doing." Then her mother started to speak more quietly, as if she was talking as much to herself as to her daughter. "But the heart moves in all sorts of unexpected ways; it has an understanding of its own. The man I married was different as well. He was kind and caring and bright and clever, but, oh, was he also determined! He went when we were still so young. We had such little time together. I love him now, though he is long gone, just as much as I loved him when I last saw him, last touched him, last smelt him. I told him then I would never forget him. There is no other man that I have loved, and I never will."

Emma was startled at what she was hearing for rarely had Ma talked about her husband – Emma's father – and certainly never in this way. Clearly Sarah had not only experienced deep pain and suffering in the past for the man she had loved but she still did. Though he was long-dead, her love for Emma's father was still both strong and alive in her heart. Emma felt now a little ashamed to be here asking Ma to approve of her love and to support her when it had never crossed her mind that her mother might have needed *her* love and support to help her live with the perpetual grief of having lost the man she so clearly continued to deeply love.

Fortunately, Ma rose out of her melancholy as rapidly as she had sunk into it. She turned to her daughter and said, "Emma, my dear, if this is the man you want to be with, then you have my blessing. Love him, and as you do so learn more about him and in doing that learn more about yourself. Test your feelings to ensure your understanding of yourself and the deepening knowledge you have of each other reinforces the initial promptings of your heart. If it doesn't, then pull back, and do so as soon as you sense discord or dissonance or else the later pain you will feel will be deeper, more intense and even more difficult to bear. If it does, then thank God for the blessings he has given you."

Then, as suddenly as it had come, this unique and deeply tender interchange between mother and daughter was over. Ma rose and gave Emma an intense and lingering hug which Emma returned in kind, Ma then confirming the mood-change by saying cheerily, "And when will I be lucky enough to meet this man of yours, this Robbie? If he is free on Sunday, invite him for lunch. I would like that."

Still affected by what Sarah had said about her own father and, rarely for her, lost for words, Emma mumbled, "Yes, that would be nice – I will ask him; and I am sure he would love to meet you properly now. Sunday lunch would be good." Although she was delighted with her mother's initial approval of her relationship with Robbie she was now desperate to know more about her father and her past. She wouldn't have to wait long. Within a few months she would discover far more than she could have possibly imagined.

As it turned out, when at last they met, Ma took an instant liking to Robbie, and he to her. She could clearly understand what Emma saw in Robbie as, above all else and though still young, he struck her not only as a good and honest, but as a gentle and caring, person. In some ways Robbie reminded her of her lost love. A while later, she admitted to Emma her earlier views had been based more on prejudice and "what people had said" rather than on first-hand knowledge of people she knew and apologised for what she had initially said. Indeed, she told Emma how fortunate Robbie was to have been brought up in a stable family environment with a father as well as a mother, which was more than she had been able to give Emma. Within a few weeks, Sarah had accepted Robbie almost as part of their family and was soon calling him laughingly "the son I never had," in the same way Robbie's mother Cynthia had begun to call Emma "my own daughter."

However, though they continued to see each other after church and now had something more to talk about, Cynthia and Ma never became close friends. Cynthia could not have been more welcoming to Sarah, inviting her over for a meal on a number of occasions. But Sarah found the socialising difficult, admitting to Emma that the fault was hers and not Cynthia's. The truth was they didn't really get on. Neither their common calling as nurses nor their shared Catholic faith was able to bridge the many things which separated them. Their different cultural worlds certainly divided them, but so too did their very different personalities – Cynthia bubbly and outgoing, Ma quieter and more introverted. All this prevented them from becoming close as both Robbie and Emma had hoped – perhaps naively – they would.

After leaving St. Michael's with excellent A-levels, Robbie went to Heythrop College, part of London University, to study theology and philosophy, where he gained a respectable 2:1 three years later. He was initially attracted to Heythrop as it claimed to offer its students "an education marked by intelligence, scholarship and generosity of spirit," and in that he was not disappointed. He also chose Heythrop because he could live at home for the duration of his degree, though he never got used to Kensington's affluence. When the Grenfell Tower tragedy happened, Robbie felt really bad that he had been so unaware of the deprived pockets of London's richest borough.

At first sight, Robbie's decision to study theology looked odd: he was the only one at St Michaels to do so and many of his friends told him it was a strange choice. He certainly didn't choose theology because of any desire to become a priest. Far from it. As a young child Robbie had enjoyed going to church; by the time he had reached the age of 16 or 17 he was finding church services pretty meaningless. Like so many people of his age, he found them formulaic, ritualistic and dull. However, Robbie had a more substantial complaint. His church and the Christianity it presented seemed incapable of providing him with answers to the questions he was now beginning to ask himself about the meaning and purpose of his own life as he was about to launch himself into the adult world. Worse still, the questions which were so pressing and urgent to Robbie seemed to be wholly irrelevant to the church-world he encountered: Robbie was interested in the here-and-now, while the church seemed to be only interested in the hereafter, deploying words and concepts such as saviour, salvation, kingdom and redemption. As Robbie didn't feel any need to be saved or to be redeemed, he had no interest in a saviour or redeemer. It was this world and this planet which interested him. For Robbie, talk of kings and kingdoms obscured present-day reality and conjured up images of obscure medieval chivalry and the make-believe world of fairy-tales.

So why did Robbie want to engage theologically rather than to simply disengage? The beginnings of the answer lay deep within his Caribbean roots. For Robbie's and for almost all other Caribbean families, religion had for generations been a core component of everyday, family life, as it still is today. There was, and still is, something akin to a golden thread linking the world of the family and the world of the church, such that the flourishing of the family unit is seen to be both rooted in and catalysed by the world of worship and church. What this means is if someone chooses to stop going to church, there is a strong sense that the bonds which bind family life will be affected as well: certainly damaged and at worst irreparably ruptured.

As family was really important to Robbie he did not want to sever the umbilical link his family had to worship and to Christianity which had been so central to his family for generations. This prompted him to start to channel the discomfort he felt for his church into a growing interest into the historical origins of Christianity. He knew there was a sharp disjuncture between modern life and the life and language of the church today, but as he read he became increasingly aware that Christianity had huge appeal to those who first heard its message, and it excited him. Why was this? He wanted to know what the core – the very essence – was of Christianity: what did people find so alluring in the Christian message when Jesus first proclaimed it, as this was clearly why it caught on and spread so rapidly? And if it did grip his hearers so completely, why did the Christian Gospels – which he knew meant *good news* – seem so uninspiring today? What had happened to switch the good news if not into something bad, then into something irrelevant to most people's lives? Had the message been altered by the church or had people and the context changed? It was the search for clearer answers to these questions which led Robbie to choose to study for a degree in theology and philosophy, and the more he asked them the keener he was to try to find answers: he felt this was what he really wanted to do.

As it turned out Robbie was not disappointed. His time at Heythrop provided him with many of the answers he had sought about the essence of Christianity. But there was more. To his surprise, Robbie found the Christianity he discovered hugely appealing, so much so that he realised he now had a far clearer idea about what he should do with his life. His formal degree courses certainly helped, but Robbie knew his radically new outlook on life was due predominantly not to something else, but to someone else.

His world was turned around largely by a man Robbie met, almost by chance, at Heythrop, and who was to become a close friend first to himself and then to Emma as well. He was a middle-aged Jesuit priest from Peru, Father Pedro Paulo González.

Don Paulo, as he was widely known – or simply Paulo, as Robbie and Emma soon called him – had worked in the slums of Lima for the past 15 years. He had been destined to be a theology lecturer and studied for his doctorate at the Sorbonne in Paris. But before embarking on his teaching career he became increasingly keen to have some hands-on experience working as an ordinary priest. So he asked his superiors if he could first spend a year or two in a parish, requesting specifically to work among the poor. With some reluctance they agreed, and Paulo soon found himself not so much as working for but living alongside some of the thousands of rural migrants who make their way down from the Andean villages in what has become a permanent migration. These poor peasant farmers leave their homes in search of a better life, initially struggling to make ends meet in the ever-expanding slums of Lima. And it was in in the Lima district of Flora Tristan that Don Paulo first encountered some of them, listened to their stories and realised that if he had any role at all in their lives, it was to help them. His initial two years were extended to four, which then became six, grew to ten and had now passed 15. Though fit and strong when he began this work as a young man, the work had exhausted him; he had recently become ill and his superiors ordered him to have a spell away from Peru. Don Paulo had reluctantly agreed.

One of Paulo's closest friends from his student days was Father Bill McKnight. They had remained in touch, so Paulo knew Bill had recently been appointed the Principal of Heythrop College and Bill knew Paulo needed a place to rest and recuperate. Paulo emailed Bill to see if he could spend some of his year off in London, as he was keen both to pick up with his old friend again and to spend time working in Heythrop's world-famous theology library, and Bill readily agreed, coming back to him with a proposal. In exchange for his board and lodging, Bill asked Paulo if he would be willing to give a few lectures to any students at the college who were particularly interested in knowing about the challenges of bringing the Christian Gospel to the very poor – people so caught up in the struggle for the day's necessities that they wouldn't have much time for church and religion. Paulo agreed and ended up facilitating more than eight sessions in all, and in the second year of his degree course Robbie was one of the first to sign up. He was surprised to discover he was one of only a handful of students to do so, almost certainly because the lectures turned out to be more like informal talks which didn't count towards their London University degrees.

From his first greeting, Robbie sensed the warmth and charm of Don Paulo and he never forgot their first session. Don Paulo was seated as the students walked into the room, informally arranged with easy chairs to make a small circle around a small low table. He was a tall thin man. Though young, the skin on his face had been darkened by many years' exposure to the tropical sun, which had created premature old-age furrows spreading out dramatically from the edges of both eyes as if he had just emerged from a theatre's make-up room. His forehead was marked by lines as deep as one would normally expect to see on a man twice Don Paulo's age: they were as straight as tramlines, unlike the higgledy-piggledy lines of older men. His cheek bones protruded from his thin face, suggesting to Robbie some sort of illness. Not knowing a lot about potentially life-threatening diseases more prevalent in poor countries, Robbie thought it was TB. He learned later it had been typhoid, from which Don Paulo had only recently begun to recover.

The warm smile of initial greeting, Don Paulo's firm handshake of personal welcome and his gentle but strong voice spoke of an inner strength. Robbie quickly sensed he was in the presence of a quite special human being and was soon captivated. Exuding an air of peace and calm, Don Paulo appeared to be as interested in Robbie as a person as he was in conveying to him the substance of the material he had prepared for them. And so it proved to be: as his talks progressed, Robbie increasingly felt Don Paulo wasn't so much lecturing *to him* as much as reflecting *with him* what it meant to be a Christian in today's world.

"What makes you dismayed – even angry – about the church today?" Don Paulo asked as he looked searchingly at each of the students in turn. His question was provocative, but it was also clear he knew today's young people and genuinely wanted to hear what they really felt about the church. It was the first time Robbie had been asked his personal views about his beliefs since arriving at the college, but he didn't feel uncomfortable answering: already coming under the spell of Don Paulo's warm personality, Robbie felt himself wanting to genuinely share with him his deepest thoughts, and especially his doubts.

After Robbie had expressed his views about the irrelevancy of the Christianity he had been taught, Don Paulo began to talk of his experiences living among Lima's poorest people, and so began an exchange between Robbie and Don Paulo which drew them ever closer together. Like the people who first heard Jesus' message, the Gospel was indeed good news to them. Why? Because it gave them not just some distant hope their lives could get better but tangible proof it would. Don Paulo helped wave after wave of rural immigrants – many frightened and most disoriented – to make new lives for themselves. He did this first by bringing them together as a group, then by accompanying them as they struggled to make their collective voice heard, as they lobbied, campaigned and at times openly protested at the inhumane treatment they were receiving. Though they often experienced setbacks, the outcome was largely positive, reaping real and tangible benefits. Most new arrivals soon had a roof over their head, followed by access to clean water and basic medical care, then places for their children in makeshift schools.

Over time most were able to find steady jobs with almost-decent wages, and, in the interim, Don Paulo was able to mobilise some support for those in need of immediate assistance using funds he elicited from priests working in Lima's richest parishes, though there was never enough. Especially during rough periods, Don Paulo sowed a message of hope, saying things *would* get better, not hereafter but here-and-now, as he encouraged the new city dwellers to believe in themselves, for then they would succeed. It was a message he passionately believed in himself.

The essence of what Don Paulo told Robbie and his fellow students was this: Christianity is not about going to church and saying your prayers to a distant God in order to accrue credits in order to get to heaven. And it is definitely not about distancing yourself from the world in order to purify your soul.

"What Christianity is *really* about," said Don Paulo slowly and with deep conviction in his voice, "is *this world*. It is about becoming involved with and engaging with it. To be a Christian is really quite simple. First you need to celebrate the fact that the world was made by God for the good of the whole of humanity. Next you need to look at the world carefully, with fresh eyes, so you can begin to understand how it looks from the underside; from the viewpoint of the marginalised and the discarded. Then, thirdly, inspired to participate in the work of God, you need to work out how best to help especially the most deprived, those who are suffering the most, as they struggle to live more fulfilling lives.

"When the Christian message was first proclaimed, it was directed to the poor and they were captivated by what they heard. Why? Because it gave them hope that change really was possible; that the drudgery, toil and hardship of their daily lives could be lightened. They were not told to wait patiently for a better life in a world to come after they died. The good news then was that this life can be better, and it remains good news today.

"And that," said Don Paulo, "has been my experience working in Peru. My job was supposedly to bring the good news and sprinkle it liberally onto the poor in the hills of Flora Tristan, but I quickly discovered it was these same poor people who were inspiring and teaching me. Through their struggles, by working together and praying, they have taught me the meaning of the Gospel. The Christianity I believe in sees *all people* as having worth simply because they are human, made in the image of God and in my work, I have discovered the captivating power of this truth."

Listening to Don Paulo speak, Robbie warmed to this view of the Gospel and his faith in Christianity revived. Although he had become increasingly attracted towards postgraduate work after completing his undergraduate degree, over the course of the year after he met Don Paulo,

It set her mind racing. Ever the planner, she re-thought their time together: evening in tonight, probably take-away pizza; get up late Saturday; a run for her after a late-breakfast while he works, followed by the evening out. She would suggest this started at the Phoenix, as she knew the film *Calvary* was playing and Robbie had already said he wanted to see it. Then they would treat themselves to dinner out at *the Quality Tandoori* on the High Street. They would get up late, have a lazy Sunday morning and Robbie would then decide (he rarely decided in advance) if it was to be home to North Finchley directly or later after lunch with Ma.

What she said was, "*Calvary* is on at the Phoenix; would you like to go?"

"That would be nice," said Robbie, removing his tie and sinking into Emma's comfortable second-hand leather settee, which filled one side of her small main room which doubled as both a sitting and dining room. He beamed across at her and said, "Emma, I'm so proud of you, though I expected nothing less!" She smiled, knowing Robbie *was* proud of her.

"Beer?" she asked enquiringly. "There's still one left in the fridge."

Emma knew what the answer would be so didn't wait to hear it. She was dying to discuss both the interview and now the realities of what the job meant with Robbie. While out, she made a mental note of needing to buy the cinema tickets ahead of time, knowing from bitter experience that the chances were slim of there being any left if they tried to buy them just before the Saturday night show started.

Emma returned, carrying Robbie's opened beer bottle plus an empty glass in one hand, and a glass of ice-cold water for herself in the other, then sat down next to him. Robbie smiled on seeing it was his (and his late father's) favourite, Banks Caribbean Lager, brewed in Barbados. He liked Emma's predictability.

As he poured his beer and took a deep satisfying gulp, Robbie turned towards her and said "Now Em-and-Em, I want to hear it all – in every detail!"

Needing no prompting from Robbie, Emma launched into the account of her day at the BBC, describing each session in turn and her reaction to it, with Robbie only occasionally halting her flow to ask a question. Robbie received the long version, not the short one she had given her mother. When she had finished Emma turned to him, smiled and said, "And that's about it, except to say that in spite of the worries which had initially haunted me earlier that evening, overall I felt I had presented myself well." She then ran through the morning's exchange with Janeen, expressing her delight not only that she had clinched the job but also that her instincts about being offered it had been spot on.

As Robbie listened, he could feel the power of Emma's self-confidence rubbing off on him, and he suspected it had probably had the same effect on the panel members. He thought they must have felt that in Emma they were appointing someone competent, reliable and predictable.

What he said was, "An impressive performance, Em," then repeated what he had said earlier: "I am proud of you, though I would have expected nothing less.

"I suspect resigning from *The Times* in time to start with the Beeb in mid-June will be pretty straightforward, but what about your new contract? You will need to go through the nitty-gritty of that."

"Well," she said, "I will clearly have to read the draft carefully but as the basics were set out in the job particulars and they looked fine to us both then, I am not expecting to find anything which could throw a major spanner into the works. But I really do need to ensure I can get a week off at the end of August and link this to the Bank Holiday so we can have that break in Ireland we promised ourselves before the start of the next school year. It might be tricky as I will likely only have accrued three or four days by then."

"Ah," said Robbie. "I had been meaning to talk to you about our plans for August because..." Emma turned and looked at him directly. "Because," continued Robbie "because things may not work out as we had initially thought they would."

He went on to explain. "You remember my telling you that one day I would like to continue my theology studies? Well, I have been doing a little investigating and discovered I can register to do a part-time postgraduate degree, starting with a Masters and perhaps transferring to a PhD at Durham, Birmingham or Sheffield. Well, August is the time when they have residential "taster" periods of between one and three weeks when one can read and discuss with possible tutors a potential programme of future work."

"That all sounds really exciting," said Emma in a voice that sounded rather flat. Though she didn't blame Robbie for it, she felt quite deflated both by the way the conversation had suddenly switched from her future to his and because their planned holiday she had been so looking forward to would now not happen, at least in August. "Lots to discuss there, but we have the whole weekend ahead of us and I'm getting hungry. Pizza?"

"Yes," said Robbie who also realised he was getting hungry and only then remembered he had bought a bottle of white wine with him, which he took out of the ruck-sack. "I'll put this in the fridge and then let's go out and get the takeaways."

Friday nights had something of a ritual air about them. Robbie and Emma would leave the flat together, grab the pile of glossy pizza fliers which had dropped through her letter box during the week and scour them in turn as they walked down to the East Finchley High Road to see which of the alluring offers could be used on a Friday night. As ever, they found most could not.

Robbie bought the pizzas while Emma bought the cinema tickets. As they started to walk back to Emma's flat Emma – the planner – said, "How about a curry tomorrow night?"

"Sounds good to me," replied Robbie, who knew they were coming up to the *Quality Tandoori*, owned by the father of one of Emma's old primary school friends, Rashid, from Martin's. Like almost all other restaurants run by Bangladeshis (and most of those were run by families from the Sylhet region), when the *Quality* first opened it called itself an "Indian" restaurant. Then, a few years ago when it was refurbished, it was adorned with a new bright yellow sign with the words *Bangladeshi* boldly displayed on it; a sign, thought Emma and confirmed by Rashid, of the growing self-confidence of the London Bangladeshi community. Today's even newer orange sign read even more self-assuredly: *Contemporary Bangladeshi Cuisine.*

Emma opened the restaurant door and Robbie followed as Rashid's elder brother, Syed, on seeing Emma, greeted her with a "Hi, Em!"

"Hi, Syed. Two for tomorrow?" she asked inquiringly.

"Sure, Emma," he replied, "what sort of time?

"After the 7:45 show at the Phoenix," said Emma. "Best guess around 10."

"Should be okay," said Sayed as he scribbled in the well-worn diary which doubled as a booking chart on the counter in front of him. "I'll tell Rashid you'll be in. It might encourage him to come tomorrow and do his stint," he added, laughing but clearly only half in jest.

As they left the restaurant they felt the evening was getting chilly and as neither was wearing warm enough tops they quickened their pace for the short walk back to Emma's flat. Emma put the pizzas in the oven to keep warm just after Robbie said he would take a shower and change into clean clothes, as he always did.

It was almost 10 o'clock when they sat down to eat. Emma brought in the chilled white wine and two glasses, and they had a glass sitting next to each other on the settee before Emma brought in the pizzas which, through much practice, they skilfully ate on their laps. They could both feel the tension of the week leaving their bodies as they relaxed and, as ever, Emma began to experience the effects of the wine before her glass was half empty. Robbie ate a little over half of the pizza – a *Pizza Legend* (30% off), thick-crust with four toppings: pepperoni, olives, mushrooms and extra cheese – and drank two thirds of the wine. They chatted light-heartedly, recalling and recounting different events of the week they had banked to share with each other, especially the odd and amusing moments. Robbie still got a thrill hearing Emma laugh out loud: he loved her spontaneity. Once the pizza had gone and there seemed no need for more talk, they turned on the

TV and began to watch an old Eddie Murphy movie, the original *Beverly Hills Cop*. They both knew it well and so it didn't matter it was already halfway through.

Try as they might to keep awake, they soon gave up and made their way to Emma's bedroom. She had put clean sheets on that morning after getting up, as she always did. They kissed warmly and, already half asleep, made love gently. They dozed for a while, their bodies tight together and then, as they separated, Robbie fell into a deep sleep almost at once. Emma turned over and lay on her back for a moment or two, still with her eyes closed. She sucked in that feeling of complete contentment she missed when she slept alone as her satisfied body sank down further into her welcoming mattress, emptying itself of any remaining tensions from her momentous week. Sleepily, Emma reflected on how good life was to her at that moment with the excitement of the new job and the safety and security she felt in her relationship with Robbie. But, all too soon, tiredness enveloped her too and curling her body up next to Robbie's, her knees tucked in behind his, she stretched her free arm out and over his torso, rested her hand softly on his breast, pushed the hairs of his chest slowly between her fingers and fell into a deep, contented sleep.

Emma was the first to wake. Though the room was light, as the sky was grey and overcast, it was later than she had expected, which explained why she had not woken earlier. She checked the time and then smiled to herself as she rolled over to Robbie's side of the bed. Slipping easily back into the comfort and secure zone between waking and sleeping, Emma touched Robbie. Though barely awake, he needed little encouragement and they made love again, more slowly and deliberately than the night before. Then, their bodies still entwined, they fell back into a deep sleep, breathing as one, with Emma savouring the smell of his body, or was it her soap? It didn't matter – and she didn't care.

It was past 11 o'clock when they got up. As it felt cold and she was naked, Emma dressed quickly, putting on first her tightly-fitting sports bra and pants, followed by her white running shorts over which she slipped on her loosely-fitting grey trackie bums, and finishing with her dark blue ill-shaped T-shirt which she knew was not flattering but which she loved to wear as it had once been Robbie's. Across the front, it read *Stop the War in Iraq*, written in fading black letters. Aged 13, Robbie had been given it when he had gone on his first London demonstration and to this day he remained both proud of having gone on that historical anti-war march and of this precious but now fading souvenir of when he had first really felt like a grown-up. It was the first piece of Robbie's clothing Emma had asked if she could wear and keep, and she knew his sense of loss was eased a little when he saw it on her, so it was special to her, too.

Emma first went to the kitchen to fill the coffee machine with water and coffee and to warm the ready-made pancakes and plates in the oven; she arranged a tray on which she had assembled what they needed: the knives and the forks, a carton of milk, sugar, mugs and the most essential item for today's breakfast, *Aunt Jemima's Original Syrup* – the cheaper and sugar-based substitute for maple syrup – and took it into the sitting-dining room. When Robbie had dressed – in a reprise of the jeans and matching blue denim shirt he had worn after showering the night before – he walked in and sat down just as Emma placed the now-warmed pancakes on the table in front of him. "Thanks so much, Em-and-Em," he said, clearly delighted. "The perfect breakfast!"

They didn't hurry their food but when they had finished, they both changed gear. Emma took away the dishes and then slipped off her trackie bums and put on her (well-worn) grey running shoes, which she tied tightly over her new white socks. She then began her pre-jog stretching exercises in the sitting room at the same time as Robbie began to remove the dozens of exercise books from his briefcase, assembling them in neat piles on the breakfast table which had now morphed into his work-desk.

"Bye Rob-bow," said Emma cheerily as she left the room. "Hope it goes well."

"Bye Emma," replied Robbie half-distractedly as he had already begun to read the first book on the pile, but he then extracted himself from his books and looked back at Emma. As he did so, he suddenly took in the beauty of her body and felt his own urging him to return with her to the bedroom. Instead, he said to her, "Take care of the T-shirt. I hope the rain keeps off. Enjoy and have fun. See you soon, lovie."

By the time he had finished speaking, she had already waved, swept up the front door key she used when out jogging, placing it in the small pocket of her running shorts and left the flat. He turned back to the books and, in an instant, was totally absorbed again in the marking.

Emma had never joined a gym. Once she found out how much it cost she realised she could get as much exercise she needed for free simply by bending and stretching at home and running around the local streets. The more she ran the more she liked it, plotting different routes, learning about different neighbourhoods and observing what went on. Her goal was to jog twice a week: once at the weekend and then on a weekday evening after work, though more often than she wished, the working week finished without the mid-week jog materialising. Initially when this happened she told herself she needed to do three runs the following week to make up, but this now rarely happened and over time she quietly shelved her self-made rule. However, she remained fit and enjoyed her running.

* * *

Today, as on other days, within a couple of hundred yards of starting off, Emma is breathing rhythmically and her stride lengthens as she sets herself a strong and steady pace. She has chosen a fairly hilly route along leafy side streets, to avoid the diesel fumes of the busier roads whose health dangers she had read about during the week. She reckons it will be about a five-mile run, her route taking her through the posh west side of East Finchley up to the edge of Hampstead Heath, then on to Highgate and back home to her flat. She knows it well; it is one of her favourites.

She runs along Church Lane, past the former church hall, now a Hindu temple, and the small brightly painted terraced houses and turns left at the junction with East End Road. Passing the Five Bells pub, she cuts through the narrow hedge-lined footpath leading on to Brim Hill. Soon she passes David Gould's house, a small white-stuccoed brick terraced house which still retains the old single-glazed windows, as required by the ever-vigilant Hampstead Garden Suburb Trust. She glances in through the windows but the little of the rooms she can see conveys a sense of absence. David and Esther, Joe's mother, had divorced when Joe was in his early teens, and David had never married again. Since then the house has become more a base from which David and his two sons, Joe and his elder brother Nathan, launch their different activities rather than a home where they spend lots of quality time together. They are all activists. Thus the house is often empty, and it looks empty now.

She runs down to the busy A1, which she crosses at the pedestrian lights. Already she has passed three builders' skips on the road. On her right is the synagogue where the Goulds are members. Like other North London synagogues, it is now heavily protected and burly uniformed men are nearly always visible outside especially on a Saturday morning. Following another attack on Jewish graves in the week, they have been joined today by an armed policeman. Emma shivers as she passes.

Although Emma's schoolfriend and David's son Joe had their Bar Mitzvahs here, they now only attend services on the High Holy Days and by no means all of them. Emma had not been invited to Joe's Bar Mitzvah because David judged (correctly in her view) that Emma would not feel happy having to sit far away from Joe and himself in the segregated upstairs section of the synagogue reserved for women, none of whom she would have known.

His parents' separation and eventual divorce affected the young Joe deeply. In the end it revolved around the issue of Israel: Joe's mother was staunchly pro, with his father a strong advocate of Palestinian rights. Emma knew how deeply troubled Joe had been because the family break-up happened the year they started to sit next to each other in class, her last year at primary school. She not only saw his grief and heartache but what Joe went through taught Emma something which stayed with her for the rest of her life. Though she was hardly 12 at the time, she understood that when someone tries to do good they can cause pain even if they don't mean to. She later learned posher words for this: exposing injustice and working to right the wrongs it has caused will usually result in new pain and distress, but this is often a price worth paying.

Past the synagogue, Emma soon starts the long and steady mile climb up to Hampstead Lane. Now she is running past even bigger properties, owned by those she calls the mega-rich. Most are detached, lying behind high, electrified and locked wrought iron gates on substantial plots. First up on the left are two adjacent houses which are widely believed to be owned by the Sultan of Brunei. To be more precise: there is one house and one house-front as the second house, so everyone says, was knocked down to construct a sports complex including a squash court which lies concealed behind the false-fronted façade. Both properties lie empty for most of the year; rarely has Emma ever seen anyone going in or out of either, and seldom are cars parked outside.

She climbs more steeply now. Up the hill and on either side, she passes some grand residences which today house, or in the recent past have housed, the ambassadors or high commissioners of Pakistan, Kenya, Botswana and Malawi, among others. Some have recently been renovated. She likes the feeling of being close to such important people. However, the dominant feeling Emma has when she nears the top end of Winnington Road is not one of grandeur but grand squalor. What she sees is a disordered array of white vans, builders' trucks and rusting, chipped and dented old cars belonging to the men who work here. They line both sides of the road and are not parked neatly but randomly, some half on the pavement and some half on the grass verges.

Week by week, she sees all shapes and sizes of lorries and delivery vans passing through the clumsily-erected high wood-panel or metal fencing temporarily put in place to hide the massive construction sites which lie behind them. Here, colossal new mansions in various stages of erection are being put up and some of the most charming older houses in various stages of destruction are being pulled down, discarded to make way for the new. All is overseen by tall cranes which eerily watch overhead and pollute the skyline of both this road and its parallel twin, The Bishops Avenue.

Emma's first reaction to the wealth she passes is more pity than either jealousy or envy. Poor people, she thinks to herself: you have so much money you are not even aware of how much you are wasting. But then today, as has happened many times before, Emma feels an anger welling up inside her as she thinks about the unfair and unjust way the world we have created works. Alongside the rich, our world has forced billions of other people to live in squalor in tiny hovels without clean water and sanitation. She thinks about the poor in Lima's slums which Don Paulo had spoken about, as well as the hardship and suffering of young friends from school and those she has written about over the last few years – what she found most difficult to accept was that so many would die young. She quietly says to herself, "It doesn't have to be like this."

Emma reaches the top of Winnington Road and takes a left onto Hampstead Lane, giving out a small satisfied sigh as she turns, having ended her long uphill climb. The road now begins to descend gently for a few hundred yards till she reaches and crosses The Bishops Avenue before continuing on, almost flat for well over a mile, when it gently climbs again to reach Highgate Village.

Soon she crosses Courtney Road, which, like all the other neighbouring roads, was built as a public thoroughfare and for many centuries stayed that way. Now, however, this road, and Compton Road ahead, are blocked off by electrically-operated gates which bar entry to all but those able to convince one of the gates' guardians to let them pass. Here at Courtney Road Emma sees two dour-faced men sit in their newly-built glass-fronted cabin whose roof and walls bulge with security cameras, spotlights and other state-of-the-art surveillance equipment, ready 24/7 to open the gates to those they deem worth of entry.

Jogging on, she crosses Sheldon Avenue and has to swerve to miss a young Filipino woman who is making heavy weather of controlling a brown and boisterous Labradoodle. It is clearly not hers and she is clearly not used to dog-walking: another instance, says Emma to herself, of the maid being sent out to walk the dog. As Joe had told her, most houses in this area employ house-workers, many live-in and mostly Filipino women. Indeed, as Joe told Emma, so common are they that for the men, women and children of the families who employ them the word Filipino and maid has become interchangeable: "I need to get a new Filipino" means "I need to get a new maid." Even when their children chat to each other they talk about what "our Filipino" did or what "our Filipino" said. Do these people not have names?

The road turns to the right as she passes the historic but run-down Athlone House, now owned by a Ukrainian billionaire. Passing the playing fields of Highgate School on her left, she sees that young boys have already begun their afternoon cricket matches, though the sky is beginning to darken and play could soon be interrupted, she thinks. The road narrows and it becomes even darker as, briefly, overhanging trees line this part of her route and almost touch, after which the road widens again and, with fewer trees, it becomes lighter again as Hampstead Lane starts its final, gentle climb to Highgate Village. As it does so, the houses also change. Emma begins to pass a succession of three- and four-storey square Victorian houses, some cream-coloured, all now converted into apartments; between them a number of more modern-looking flats of different shapes and sizes have been built, creating an architectural mishmash.

She takes special pleasure in passing these old Victorian buildings, not for any particular love of their design, but because she knows the Scottish comedian, Stanley Baxter, lived in one of them and still does as far as she knows. In her intensive television-watching days as a young girl, Emma was fascinated by his mischievous Mr. Majeika character. When she feels in a particularly boisterous mood, as she does today, she looks to see if anyone is around and to make sure no one is in earshot, then shouts out loud: "Hi there, Mr. Majeika, I love you!"

Reaching the island at the end of Hampstead Lane, Emma turns to the left, her route taking her along North Road. In front of her stand the gleaming new gates and behind them the grand red brick buildings of Highgate School. Highgate was originally established as a free grammar school by royal charter in Elizabethan England. It is now an independent fee-paying school which in recent years has become co-educational. Among its many illustrious former pupils, the one Emma knows best is the English poet Gerard Manley Hopkins, a pupil at Highgate way back in the 1850s and early 1860s – coincidentally her favourite English poet. Her arrival at the gates of the school usually prompts her to start reciting to herself as she jogs along some of the opening lines of Hopkins' poetry which she especially likes. Though first made aware of his poetry in the sixth form at school, she became particularly enamoured of Hopkins after Robbie gave her a book of his poems a few Christmases ago.

Emma had never thought it odd to jog and recite poetry at the same time; she loved doing that. But it suddenly came to her one day while running along and reciting one of his poems that of all the poets Hopkins is *the one* for joggers. After all he was the inventor of "sprung rhythm" and the key to good running lies in developing a good springing action between heel and toe. Wondering if anyone else had ever thought of this, she had checked out Google but found no clear answer. Today, with the gates of Highgate School in front of her and with a fresh spring in her step, Emma begins to recite the opening words of *Pied Beauty*.

> *Glory be to God for dappled things –*
> *For skies of couple-colour as a brinded cow;*
> *For rose-moles all in stipple upon trout that swim;*
> *Fresh-firecoal chestnut-falls; finches' wings;*
> *Landscape plotted and pieced – fold, fallow, and plough;*
> *And all trades, their gear and tackle and trim.*

As she finishes, the sky begins to darken and she feels gusts of cooler – even cold – wind on her face. She passes St Michael's School and Church on her left and has just said to herself the words of the final line *He fathers-forth whose beauty is past change* when she starts the steep downward descent to the A1. Feeling drops of water on her face, she prays the rain will hold off for ten more minutes. She passes the house where Charles Dickens once lived and, to counter the gloom which had set in around her, begins to recite the opening words of Hopkins' *Spring*.

Nothing is so beautiful as Spring –
When weeds, in wheels, shoot long and lovely and lush;
Thrush's eggs look little low heavens, and thrush
Through the echoing timber does so rinse and wring
The ear, it strikes like lightnings to hear him sing...

She begins the first line of the second verse, *What is all this juice and all this joy?* but then stops, calling an abrupt halt to the poetry as she no longer feels in any way joyful. The drops have turned into real rain and Emma is now focused entirely on her running, quickening her pace to try to keep warm.

Soon it is raining really hard, her T-shirt is soaked through and sticking unpleasantly to her back and her wet running shorts are rubbing against the sides of her legs. Though she is running faster, she is becoming colder and focuses on getting home as quickly as she can. Nearing the flat, her numb, wet fingers struggle to get inside the pocket of her shorts to retrieve her front door key, and she curses as she is forced to wait on the mat until she is finally able to recover the key and turn it in the latch. Inside, she half-hops in the hallway as she forces off first one then her other running shoe, managing a quick "Hi, I'm home!" to Robbie as she hurries past the sitting room door on her way to the bathroom.

When Emma steps into the shower, the water is already steaming and in no time, she has warmed up. As she knew it would, her post-run after-glow feels immensely more satisfying when she comes back from her run cold. As she dries herself, she feels her spirits rising again and sings "I've got plenty of nothing" to herself as her thoughts turn to her mother. Though Emma's body has now stopped running, as ever her mind is still racing, and by the time she has dressed she has already planned the route she will jog next weekend.

* * *

The rest of the weekend turned out much as Emma had expected. As Robbie had not finished his book-marking when she joined him after her run, he continued working while she sat on the settee, computer on her lap and iced-water at her side, and read the papers online. For the evening, she had decided to wear the new pink blouse she had bought the previous weekend for her interview and he had not yet seen on her. It took until they were about to leave the flat for Robbie to notice it, but he redeemed himself by saying how much he liked it and she was pleased enough with that. By four

She then heard a woman's voice saying clearly and distinctly, "I'm sure you got the job, isn't it?"

She recognised the voice at once. First, she felt comforted then she felt puzzled: it was clearly Ma, but why was she saying this? She then realised her mother had spoken these exact words to Emma – but when and why? *Why was Ma saying this to me and why am I dreaming it now?*

As she was searching for the answer, she heard the voice of a man, as clearly and as distinctly as she had heard the first voice, the voice which had turned out to be her mother.

The man said, "They seem to have moved things around a bit, isn't it?"

What on earth did this mean, thought Emma? Out loud she said, "Who was this man? Who was he talking to – was it me?"

The same two words came back to her again: "Isn't It?" But this time they didn't sound strange; they were familiar and real. Emma said to herself, *I know that voice and I remember distinctly those words being said to me, but who was speaking, and when did it happen?*

The answer then came to her, appearing initially as a still frame of a video sequence, frozen in time. In the centre of the still picture Emma saw herself. She was crouching down on the floor but completely still, as if frozen in time. Next to her, she saw the young man who had helped her pick up the fallen groceries at Graham's that Tuesday morning, the day of her interview. Simon Robertson. Yes, that was his name. That was him.

At the same moment as his name came to her, she heard herself repeating it out loud, slowly and deliberately, and she paused between the two words: Simon…and Robertson…. As she spoke, she was aware more of hearing the words of his name than of speaking them, as if the voice talking was not hers, as if someone else was speaking.

Then the words "Simon Robertson" started to whizz around and echo in her head, growing ever louder. Then they suddenly stopped, and the frozen frame still in front of her started rolling. Simon Robertson started to come to life but in a strange way, as if she was controlling the process, her mind urging the scene on from the pause to the play button. But it was not only he who came to life, but she did as well; the two of them, crouching down next to each other, began to move, though everything was happening in slow motion.

He smiled at her and sitting in bed she was conscious of him; his face and his blue eyes were present to her as clearly as if he were here next to her. The encounter which had taken place some days before at Graham's seemed to be happening not as a rerun of the past but for real, right now in her darkened bedroom. As he smiled, she reached out to try to touch him then and there in her bed. He *was* there, it *was* real; she wanted to touch him, she needed to touch him. Then, as she stretched out her hand and she could see it almost reach his face, everything disappeared. In an instant, everything was gone. The vision, if that's what it was, had passed. Neither Simon nor her mother was there any longer. She was totally alone.

Emma tried to take stock of herself and of what had happened. Alone in bed and in the dark, she felt herself moving out of what she was now realising had been an extremely vivid dream and into the real world of the night, her bedroom and her bed. She felt cold as all this while she had been sitting upright in bed, so she hurriedly pulled up the bedclothes and, as her back sank into the mattress, tried to work out what it all meant.

As she attempted to piece everything together in her mind, she not only began to understand what the dream meant but knew – with crystal-clear certainty – that it carried a message for her. It was not merely a signal or a cue for her to act; it *required* her to act.

Though completely fluent, English was Ma's second language and on occasions Sarah used expressions a native English person wouldn't. The first thing Sarah had said to Emma the night of the interview, when she opened the front door of the Moat Crescent flat, was, "I'm sure you got the job, isn't it?" A native English speaker would have said, "I'm sure you got the job, didn't you?"

The first thing Simon said to Emma that morning at Graham's was, "They seem to have moved things around a bit, isn't it?" A native English speaker would have said, "They seem to have moved things around a bit, haven't they?"

This way of talking, this way of answering questions – by using the phrase "isn't it?" – was the way Zimbabweans and people from other parts of southern Africa spoke. It was something they all shared; a sort of invisible sign or signal which bound people from southern Africa together. It symbolised their shared roots; it was a sort of blood-bond creating a solemn pact among southern Africans, thought Emma, whose imagination was now beginning to take her back into the world of fantasy. Emma had used the same expression herself until about the age of 12, when she had said "isn't it?" incorrectly when answering a question in an English class. After the lesson, her teacher took her aside and carefully explained her mistake to her and she never made the same mistake again. But the incident had made her especially aware of when people used the words "isn't it?" incorrectly to answer a question.

Simon had told Emma his family was from Zimbabwe. What Emma had failed to tell Simon, she now realised, was that she and Ma were originally from Zimbabwe too, though she couldn't now recall why she hadn't told him. Whatever it was, she knew she needed to see Simon again so she could tell him of their shared roots. Emma felt she really had to do this: this was what her dream was about. It was telling her she had made a grave mistake.

Simon had said his *family* was from Zimbabwe, but she was pretty sure he had not said whether or not he had *been born* in Zimbabwe. Had he? Did he learn the "isn't it?" mistake just from his family as he grew up in London or had he been born in Zimbabwe too, just like her? As she pondered all these things in her mind, she realised even more clearly that she had to have answers. Emma had been born in Zimbabwe; if Simon had too, then perhaps there was an even closer bond between them. She should have told him explicitly she was also from Zimbabwe. Her dream was clearly telling her of her omission and the need to make amends.

Simon had scribbled his phone number on a scrap of paper. At the time she thought nothing of it, but now she remembered not only his giving it to her but also where she had put it. It was in her jacket pocket, in the pocket of the jacket she realised she hadn't worn since Tuesday because the weather had turned warmer.

Emma threw back the bed clothes, jumped out of bed and half ran across the floor to the far side of her bedroom where the jacket had hung those four days on the back of her chair. She couldn't recall which pocket she had put it in. As if possessed, she plunged her right hand into each of the pockets in turn, extending her fingers outwards ready to grab hold of the paper when she felt its touch. In her mind's eye she saw the cranes which hovered over cuddly toys in cheap slot machines at bank holiday funfairs, enticing you to give them your spare coins to make their arms twist and turn but almost always failing to clasp the alluring toy. But now they were working fast, in double or triple time. Emma felt she was watching one of those old Charlie Chaplin films where everything has been sped up.

One, two, three pockets – nothing! Her heart beat faster as she failed to locate that precious piece of crumpled paper she was so desperate to find, and she cursed out loud. It was only when she reached the fifth of the six pockets that her fingers touched and at once recognised the feel of paper. She pulled it out, jumped back into bed, turned on the bedside light, opened it carefully and read what was written on it: the numbers 07884 567882.

She turned the paper over three or four times and, as she did so, turned over in her mind what she should do.

He cannot contact me as he doesn't have my number, but I can contact him... Only I have the ability – the power – to enable us to meet again... If I don't make contact with him, I will have let the opportunity go... I will have let slip the invisible link between us... My dream was telling me I must not let this happen... Should I? Isn't it?

Emma felt her head starting to spin, so she returned to her bed, sat down and initially felt a little calmer, though her heart continued to beat fast. Then her mind revved itself up once again.

Plenty of other people, lots of men, have given me their numbers; in some cases, I have given them mine, though rarely. Why should I do so now? There are thousands of people from southern Africa in London. I have met many, including Zimbabwean men, and even quite liked some. What is so important about this meeting, this person, this man? It was just a chance encounter, why should I take the initiative and get in touch? Should I?

It was Emma's next thought which clinched it: *what have I got to lose?* Then her mind started to race again as she convinced herself this was what she had to do, and why.

He seemed nice and didn't in any way try to force himself on to me. Indeed, he seemed rather reserved, even a little shy.

He was clearly reluctant to give me his number as he only did so after we had parted, and I clearly wasn't much bothered either as I failed to reciprocate.

I will text him and ask him to call so we can arrange a time to meet – just for a coffee after work. It can't do any harm.

Does he work?

God, I don't know, I don't know much about him at all!

He said he lived in Muswell Hill, that's pretty near.

Perhaps we can meet for a coffee there on evening when I get back after work?

I'll text him and suggest he calls me. When he does so I will merely suggest a quick coffee.

What's the problem with that?

It's a good idea.

It's less forward than phoning and if he has already forgotten me he won't respond – and that's okay, too.

As Emma became clearer that her considered decision was to text him, she realised how even more excited she had become. Not only was her heart beating faster but she felt the paper had become damp from the sweat on her hands. Something deep inside her wanted her to meet him. Her head – she had now worked out – had told her that that would be okay. She had decided. She *would* do it.

Once she had made her decision, Emma impulsively wanted to text him at once, straight away. But looking at her clock, she saw it read 2:15, and her more rational self told her she needed to wait until the morning. She couldn't text him now – that would be crazy! Yes, she would wait until then. She wouldn't text at 7 when the alarm went off, either, as that would be too early. She would wait till 8:30, just before she left for work.

But what should she write? She decided to start by telling him she had got the job – after all, his final words to her were to say he hoped she would get it, if it was what she wanted. She would next thank him again for coming to her aid at Graham's, apologising she had been in a bit of a state. She was happy to say that because it was absolutely true! She would end by saying that, if he wanted to, they might meet for a coffee early one evening. Should she write "one evening soon," or "just one evening"? Not sure. She would end by suggesting he call rather than text her – and she would say at the end he should text her very soon – so they could agree then and there when and where to meet.

But then Emma realised this was more an essay than a text message and decided to wait till the morning to decide what she would write. With that settled, she switched off her bedside light, turned over and closed her eyes, but she couldn't sleep immediately. Instead she went over in her mind the scene with Simon at Graham's and outside, trying to recreate it all in the vivid way it had come to her just now in her dream. She wanted it to be real again, as it had been just now. After four attempts and four failures to re-enter her dream, she fell back asleep. As she did so, the blue of his eyes seemed to expand outwards in her mind and envelop her. Though she wasn't really aware of what was happening, her body started to relax in just the way it always did when she fell asleep after making love to Robbie.

Just before she left for work the next morning, Emma pressed the send button on her phone, but in the cold light of day decided not to end her text with the word "soon."

- 3 -

Simon

The bus to Muswell Hill took forever to arrive. After waiting for almost 15 minutes Emma gave out a sigh of frustration, knowing she would be late. She was on her way to *Jenny's* restaurant in Muswell Hill and was now sure she wouldn't make it for 6:30 pm, the time she had arranged to get there. Since waking that morning, Emma's emotions had been running high, lurching between excitement and nervousness; now a growing sense of irritation was added to the mix. It was Wednesday and so much had happened since the calm of the weekend.

As soon as she arrived for work on Monday, Emma phoned Peter Smith, her line manager, to ask if she could pop in for a moment. She was at his desk within two minutes and back at her desk ten minutes later.

Peter was clearly busy but he greeted Emma warmly when she walked in. He had always liked her. Now he respected her as the best of the current wave of young journalists under his watch. Emma told him about the BBC job she had been offered and that they wanted her to start as soon as possible. Unemotionally she mouthed the words she had rehearsed about how much she had enjoyed working at the *Times*, how much she learned, about the good friends she had made and how she would miss them all, but she felt it was now time to move on.

As Peter had had plenty of similar conversations with young and smart reporters who had used the *Times* as a career stepping-stone over the years, Emma's news was anything but headline-grabbing. However, his response was not quite as formulaic as Emma's announcement she was leaving. He smiled and thanked her for the contribution she had made and he genuinely meant it. Knowing full well he was overstepping the mark, he told Emma she was a person of exceptional talent as well as charm. Their brief exchange ended with his telling Emma he would call HR to tell them he fully supported her request to terminate her employment as soon as possible, foreshortening her final days in the office by using her accumulated leave days. Within half an hour of her returning to her desk, HR had called Emma to ask her to pop in before lunch to sign the forms for her release. That, too, took only a moment. By the time she went out to lunch with a few close colleagues with all the formalities completed, Emma felt able to share with them – confidentially – the news she was leaving, and she told them a little about the new job. She was touched by what she sensed was real sadness at her imminent departure.

She stayed outside the building after her lunch so she could call Janeen to tell her she could now formally accept the BBC job and confirm she could start by mid-June. A little more business-like than the day before, Janeen asked Emma to hold on a moment while she checked the diary then asked her if she could come down to Broadcasting House late on Thursday or Friday to read through the draft contract and sign the initial confidentiality documents she had mentioned earlier. Emma said 5 pm on the Thursday would be good for her.

"That's fine," said Janeen. Emma had become used to the reassuring way Janeen spoke to her on the phone. As Janeen said, "bye, see you on Thursday then," Emma wondered how the ever-cheery Janeen sounded when she was the bearer of bad news.

That evening, on her way back from work, Emma phoned Robbie but he wasn't picking up, so she texted him to say all had gone as expected but with the BBC meeting scheduled for Thursday she would be completely tied up with work till Friday. He was still at school when her text arrived, preparing for a lower sixth parents' meeting, but he texted back almost immediately repeating his weekend congratulations on her new job and telling her that now everything was sorted they would have another excuse to celebrate at the weekend: he said he was now sure he would be able to get to her place on the Friday evening.

Less than ten minutes later Emma was surprised to see another text from Robbie. It was an apology: he had completely forgotten he was not going to be able to see her at all as his mother had just called to remind him this weekend was a family "maroon-line" event. It had slipped his mind, just as it had Emma's.

For the Halls, the term "maroon-line" was used for a family gathering deemed to be so important it superseded all other commitments and everyone was required to attend. As Robbie had explained to Emma, maroon is the colour of the West Indies cricket team, and when they are playing in the Caribbean, the cricket trumps everything else. For those unable to acquire tickets, all eyes and ears are glued to either the TV or radio for the duration of key international matches and normal life is suspended. This coming weekend was the sixtieth birthday party of his mother's sister, his Aunt Betty, who lived in Walthamstow with his uncle and five first cousins. Robbie and his two brothers were required not only to attend the Sunday party to be held at his Mum's house. She needed him to be there early on the Saturday as well to help her prepare the full spread of Caribbean dishes her mother always provided for such occasions. Robbie was also the one always tasked with putting together the music, largely a mix of old and new reggae, Motown and a little rap.

Emma was just about to call Ma when Robbie's text came in. After reading it and taking it in, she chatted briefly to her mother, who also congratulated Emma once again on the job and reminded her she was away on Sunday. When she put the phone down, it dawned on Emma she would have the weekend all to herself. This was such a rare event she couldn't remember when it last happened.

There was, however, far more going on in Emma's mind than the complexities of changing jobs, remaining in close touch with Robbie and Ma, keeping abreast of their changing schedules and wondering what she might do at the weekend. Emma's thoughts were dominated by Simon Robertson.

Before sending her text to him as she left for work that Monday morning, instead of reading the days' papers online, Emma googled his name, searching for clues of who he was. Her search threw up plenty of Simon Robertsons, many dead, but the list was dominated by a famous New York surgeon and academic, and almost all the images appeared to be either of the surgeon or an American college football player from Ohio State University. The only Simon Robertson she felt certain was British had been a student at the University of Kent, but she wasn't able to find out when he was there or what he had studied and no images she found looked anything like him.

After sending Simon her text message, Emma became increasingly focused on her phone. As he hadn't called by the time she reached work, she placed it on her desk next to her computer just as she had done the previous week waiting for news of the BBC job, keeping a watchful eye on the screen. She had memorised the last three digits of Simon's number, 8-8-2, to herself. Though she sometimes willed the phone to vibrate, he didn't call the whole of Monday.

Emma did a further Google search that evening before she went to bed, adding references to Zimbabwe and Southern Africa, but she still wasn't able to find anything else she thought at all significant. There were plenty of South African references to Robertsons, including a number of rugby players from Gauteng, a family of pineapple growers in Port Elizabeth and what looked like two or three generations of Robertsons who had studied accountancy at Cape Town University. Initially she was annoyed she had dug up so little as she prided herself on her investigative research skills, but her annoyance soon mellowed into a growing curiosity. Who was this mysterious man Simon Robertson, and why hadn't he replied to her text message? By the time Emma was seated at her desk at work on the Tuesday, looking at her phone, waiting for it to ring and then checking each caller's ID had almost become an obsession.

Then, suddenly, late on Tuesday, just before the end of her working day, Emma felt her phone vibrating. It was still in her hand. She was about to put it back into her bag after finishing a confidential work call she had gone outside to take. Initially she thought it was her last caller redialling to tell her something he had forgotten but then as she checked the number, she felt her heart jump: 8-8-2. Her wait was over. Relieved she was still outside so she could talk freely, Emma pressed the green "answer" button firmly.

Before the phone touched her ear, she had swept her free hand across it to ensure there was no hair in the way.

"Hi!" came the voice at the other end. "Is that Emma? Simon here, Simon Robertson. I was so glad to hear from you."

Simon hurried on before Emma had worked how to respond. "Sorry not to have called earlier but I was tied up all yesterday and guessed you were at work, too, and I thought I should wait until I thought you would be likely to be free before I called. So glad to hear about the job. When are you starting? Yep, it would be great to meet up properly this time and have a chance to chat. Coffee after work sounds great. It would be good to meet soon."

He sounded as nervous as he did the first time he spoke to Emma that morning in Graham's.

"Oh, hi, Simon," said Emma failing to sound matter-of-fact. She picked up the nervousness in his voice and sensed he had spent some time rehearsing his opening remarks. Whatever he said – and she wasn't too bothered with the detail – the message was clear: they were going to meet up, and soon.

She hurried on. "Thanks for calling back, Simon. I thought it would be simpler and easier to try to fix something up on the phone than to endlessly text each other."

Her cautious journalistic instincts had told her not to sound too eager, though she certainly didn't want to wait until the weekend. What she said was: "I am free tomorrow evening after work, busy on Thursday, having to go down to the BBC to sign papers, and Friday looks difficult."

There was a pause. Simon had expected her to suggest the weekend, so was a little surprised she had proposed they meet earlier. However, he was delighted.

"Well, Emma, I am doing work all this week in Crouch End: I'm deep in an audit. This means having to work over there until at least six, but tomorrow after work should work." He knew how flustered he sounded.

Emma smiled to herself, recalling that Simon Robertson's slightly disorganised manner was one of the things she had found attractive about him. She was also pleased he replied with the word "Emma," an indication, she thought, he had been thinking about her, or at least mulling over her name. She now knew he was some sort of accountant, though probably too young to be qualified? Then her mind set to work: if he is working in Crouch End, then the suggestion in her text they meet in Muswell Hill had been a good one.

With only a slight pause, Emma said, "I finish work at 5.30 so why don't I come over to Muswell Hill and we can meet around 6:30 – I mean tomorrow, Wednesday, the day after today?"

Oh dear, she said to *herself, his nervousness seems to be catching. Calm down, Maconie!*

"That sounds great," said Simon. "I am sure I can make it by then and if I am running late, which is pretty unlikely, I can always text you now I have your number."

He added, "Are you sure it's okay for you to come to Muswell Hill? If we were to meet a little later I could come over to East Finchley." Then, rather contradicting himself, he continued, "How about meeting at *Jenny's*? *Jenny's* restaurant? Do you know it? It's on Muswell Hill Broadway next to Oxfam; I mean the old Oxfam shop on the opposite side to where Woolworths was before it closed, not the newer Oxfam bookshop opposite the older Oxfam."

"Yep, *Jenny's* sounds great. We'll meet for a coffee then," said Emma, as calmly as she could. She definitely didn't want to risk their first real encounter extending to supper. Though now excited at the prospect of their meeting, she was also sufficiently streetwise to acknowledge to herself that if she took a dislike to him, she didn't need to spend the whole evening with a creep. "I am sure I'll find it okay. So, 6:30 it is, at *Jenny's*. See you then," she said.

Then, thinking she had sounded a little too unfriendly, she added, "It will be really good to have the chance to talk this time."

"Fantastic," said Simon, "'til tomorrow, Wednesday, then? Cheers, Emma!" As she put her phone away in her bag, she thought he no longer sounded nervous and said to herself, *he really does like my name.*

Ending the call with Simon seemed to be the catalyst for Emma's whole being to step up a gear. For the rest of that day and until they met the following evening, she felt excited in a way she couldn't recall feeling for ages. Again and again, she replayed in her mind every detail of their original encounter at Graham's to search for more clues as to why she had found it so significant and, of even greater importance, what it was about him which had convinced her she needed to see him again. She tried to reassess the way her subconscious had processed it all in her Sunday night dream, driving her to make contact with Simon – all in the hope a little more might be revealed.

The closer it got to their Wednesday evening coffee the more she started to think how their conversation might go, what she would say to him and what he might ask her. Why was she so nervous, preoccupied and even edgy about it all? It was so unlike her – the matter-of-fact, business-as-usual, all-under-control, self-assured Emma?

She reached home just after five on the Wednesday evening and already knew what she would do and what she would wear: she had rehearsed this part of the day as well. They were meeting up after work so decided her outfit should say "smart work clothes." After a quick shower, she looked in the mirror, touched up her mascara but decided that was it. She put on a clean pair of comfortable blue jeans and a predominantly pink long-sleeved check cotton shirt which she had bought a year or so ago, a designer brand but massively reduced at TK Maxx and still in fashion. She had ironed them both the previous evening. She wore black slip-on shoes which looked a little too old but had the merit of being extremely comfortable to walk in – she did not need the distraction of painful feet. Around her neck she wore a thin gold-looking tattoo choker.

* * *

It is just after 6:30 pm when Emma jumps off the No 102 bus. Turning the corner into Muswell Hill Broadway she immediately sees the Oxfam Bookshop ahead of her so knows she is on the right part of the road. The red sign for *Jenny's* Restaurant soon comes into view on the opposite side of the street. She walks in and quickly looks around to make sure she has arrived first: it's more than half empty and he's not there.

Notwithstanding its name, *Jenny's* is less a restaurant than a café. It is laid out with groups of brightly-coloured melamine-type rectangular tables, garish pink, bright scarlet, dark blue, light and dark green, each with four matching chairs. On the walls Emma sees a TV screen which is on but with the volume turned down and a random display of pictures, photographs and posters: one looks like the Grand Canal in Venice, another reads "Make Tea not War", but most she doesn't recognise. *Jenny's* has the feel of a 1950s American diner, though Emma is uncertain whether this is by accident or choice. She avoids the pink and scarlet table and chairs and decides to sit at the dark blue set in the far-right corner from the entrance, choosing a chair which faces the door. Sitting down, she places her bag on the table, slings her jacket over the back of the chair next to her, takes her Orwell out of her bag and opens it on the table in front of her. She has no intention of really reading it: she brought it merely as a prop. Her attention is focused on the entrance door to the café in front of her. She can feel, and almost hear, her heart beating in anticipation.

This is clearly not a busy time for *Jenny's*; more people are leaving than coming in, and as it empties she worries they might be the only customers there when he arrives. Fortunately, first one, then another and finally a third group of what look like East European construction workers arrive, all male. Emma has recently interviewed a group of local Polish migrant construction workers in a piece about whether they plan to go home permanently given all the uncertainties surrounding Brexit, but she doesn't recognise any of them. They are talking intently in what she thinks at first is Polish but, on second thoughts, could be Czech or Slovak. They choose the bright-pink and scarlet tables, which add cheer to their plain and soiled work-clothes and their tired faces. They are all thin and clearly extremely hungry.

She does not have to wait much longer. A sudden noise announces Simon's arrival: he almost falls into the café as he pushes open the door.

He sees Emma at almost the instant she sees him and they raise their hands in the air almost in unison as he confidently makes his way across to where she is seated. By the time he reaches the table Emma is already on her feet, but she deliberately stays on her side of the table. He smiles and she smiles back. Sensing a handshake would seem silly, he pulls out the chair opposite hers and they both say "Hi," and sit down at the same time without making physical contact, though neither senses any awkwardness.

Simon is wearing a dark grey work suit, white shirt and half-undone tie which makes him look a little scruffy. He speaks first, by which time Emma has registered his dishevelled appearance has probably less to do with its being the end of the working day and more with having run at least part-way to *Jenny's* as she can see beads of sweat forming on his brow.

"Sorry to be late," he begins as he takes off his jacket and tie and places them on the back of the chair next to his. "But," he breathes out, saying enthusiastically, "it's great to see you."

"Yes," says Emma. "I haven't been here long. I had to wait ages for a bus and have really only just sat down myself."

Not quite certain how to continue, Simon blurts out a little awkwardly: "Shall we order?" He reaches out to take the only menu which is on their table; it is propped up against the wall and gives it to Emma. He then leans back to the table behind him to pick up another. They each look at the menu and glance at each other but their eyes don't meet. Emma takes the plunge by saying she will have a small mint tea; he chooses a large latte.

Simon then says, "I missed lunch and am dying of hunger. Do you mind if I get a toasted sandwich? Their egg and mushroom *panini* are great."

"That's fine," says Emma as she takes a look at the food choices, none of which she finds appealing. She had not intended to eat and isn't hungry but says she will have a chocolate brownie. Simon gets up and goes to the back of the café to place their orders. Emma smiles to herself while he is gone as the one thing she had forgotten about Simon in all her post-dream re-runs of their first meeting are his small, somewhat sunken but penetratingly deep blue eyes.

When he sits down again he says, "they'll bring it to the table when it's ready".

The ordering ritual has succeeded in dispelling their initial nervousness and they know it is now time to start the real conversation.

Emma looks directly across at Simon and says, "So you're an accountant, are you?"

"Yes, sort of," says Simon, somewhat taken aback. "But how do you know?"

"Well, when we spoke on Monday you did say you were doing an audit all this week, and unless I am mistaken accountants do audits, isn't it?" said Emma, smiling to herself as she deliberately uses the words "isn't it?"

As Emma had expected, Simon didn't pick up on the phrase but suddenly became more serious as he realised Emma had given him the opening to say a little about himself, and he was happy to make full use of it.

"Yep, accountants do audits, but so do trainee accountants and I am still one of those. I work for Falkland, Fairbridge and Hayes – you may have heard of them?" Emma purses her lips and raises her shoulders to convey a no which Simon notices, but he hurries on while she banks the information for potential future Google searches.

"They're a local Muswell Hill accountancy firm. I have been with them now for – what? – some five years; ever since I left uni. I am about to sit more exams probably this autumn or winter and will then be all set to take my finals. So, assuming I am successful, *then* I will be an accountant!" He turns to her and smiles.

"So you like numbers?" says Emma, trying to get Simon to open up a little more.

"Well," says Simon, happy with the ease with which the conversation is already flowing, as he had not resolved in his own mind how he would begin talking to Emma and was delighted she was making the running, "do you want the long answer or the short one?"

Emma smiles back. "For now, how about a short-ish one?" She is taken by Simon's sincerity and has already decided he isn't a creep. She also likes the lilt in his voice, the slightly clipped way Zimbabweans speak with the voice rising at the end not quite hidden underneath his dominant North London accent – or was she imagining it? Emma even knows people born in England to Zimbabwean parents who speak like that, though there is no trace of a foreign accent in the way she speaks.

The waitress arrives with the drinks and food, and Emma points towards Simon as she hesitates with the *panini* plate, telling her the latte is for him as well. She places the bill next to Simon which prompts Emma to say, "We'll split this, won't we?" but he says, "No, we won't. This is definitely on me." Simon's insistence is not something Emma has noticed about him. She banks this away too. There is far more about Simon Emma is about to learn.

"Yes," says Simon, distractedly, as he is keen to answer Emma's earlier question and so repeats what she has just said – "Do I really like numbers?" – before replying. "Well… yes and no.

"I sort of fell into accountancy as I grew up with it. It was in the blood: an accountant is what I was expected to be. You see my father is an accountant; actually, he is a partner at Falkland, Fairbridge, which is why I have ended up there. And my grandfather, my father's father, was an accountant too, as was his father before him. Long ago, the family used to live in South Africa and the men all studied accountancy at university in Cape Town. My grandfather moved north and became a founding partner in one of the big Harare firms in Zimbabwe, where my father also worked till we all moved here, to England, in 1992. I was three years old at the time. So that's why I 'do' numbers, though I realise it doesn't really tell you whether I like to do them."

As Simon talks, he takes a bite of his *panini* and a sip of coffee then stops talking so he can concentrate fully on his panini, which he quickly finishes, together with his latte. Emma senses he could easily eat two more and says, "And do you like them? I mean the numbers. I can see you like paninis!" Her face lights up as she laughs out loud.

Hit by the intensity and warmth of Emma's smile and the engaging warm brown eyes which fill her entire face, Simon loses the thread of what he is saying. He now notices the choker around Emma's neck, takes in her neatly-ironed shirt and is suddenly aware of Emma as the woman she is.

But there is more. Although she hasn't yet begun to talk about herself, Simon – ever awkward when talking with women one-to-one – is conscious of how deeply reassuring he finds simply being in her presence. It is as if Emma has the power to remove his inhibitions, giving him the freedom to speak to her freely and frankly about himself – something he would normally shy away from – though he doesn't quite know why. He not only feels comfortable telling Emma more about himself but he senses she is keen for him to do so. Indeed, he feels the urge to go further – even to start talking to her about his feelings, something he knows one normally never does on meeting someone for the first time. Just as he ran back to give Emma his phone number without quite knowing why, so now something inside him seems to be urging him to start to share with her some of his innermost secrets. Then, all of a sudden, he relives the huge relief he felt the moment Emma's text message came into his phone. Simon sees this as an omen to reassure him that opening himself up to Emma will not merely be okay. He feels he has the green light to do so.

"Well, I certainly seem to be good at numbers," he continues, having recovered some of his composure. "And to date the exams have not proved too much of a problem. And I also get a bit of a buzz out of pursuing expenditure trails and trying to unpick complex problems in audits. You would be amazed how much scope there is for massaging facts.

"But…" he begins to speak more slowly now, "I have always felt there is far more to life than numbers and increasingly over these four years since I left uni and the closer I have become to qualifying as an accountant, the more I have felt I actually want to do something else with my life. What I am really interested in is not numbers, but people and the problems of our wider society. I am increasingly interested in how people live, in understanding what 'drives' them, what 'values' they have and live by, how they 'fit in' and especially what happens to them when they don't. I think what I would really like to do is to spend more of my life helping people who don't count much count more, rather than counting even more numbers.

"I have always wanted to understand better how and why society seems to favour some people over others. But my real interest lies less in trying to work out how to resolve the big political and economic issues of the day and more in working with individuals, especially in assisting people who face immediate personal problems, to help them get back on track."

Simon hesitates and glances across at Emma, looking for some signal to tell him she would like him to say more. There is something about Simon Emma really likes but she can't pin down precisely what it is. Perhaps it is his honesty, concealed in part by his rather embarrassed, almost bumbling manner which she finds endearing. Whatever it is, she knows she does want to hear more, so she encourages him to continue, saying, "tell me more, Simon. Go on. Yes please, *do* go on!"

"Well," says Simon, regaining his confidence, "I know these ideas have been bubbling deep within me for a number of years and that's why when I went to uni I deliberately chose to do courses on the anthropology and sociology of health and medicine as well as to study accountancy. It was because Kent allows you to include these sorts of modules in their accountancy degree that I chose to go to uni there."

Emma smiles to herself on hearing the word "Kent".

"So, I was in my second year at uni when I had an experience which really affected me –indeed, it probably changed me for ever. I discovered the guy in the room next to me in our Hall of Residence was beginning to spend more and more time alone in his room. Once in the fourth week of term, he stayed in his room for three whole days without coming out: he didn't go to lectures; he didn't even eat. On the fourth day, I gently knocked on his door and very reluctantly he let me in. He looked simply dreadful. As I later discovered, he was suffering from acute depression. He simply couldn't cope: he was totally distraught both physically and mentally, right at the end of his tether, as you might put it.

"Over the course of the next few weeks I went in to see him loads. To begin with we just sat there and we said very little; then, slowly, things began to change. Sometimes he would speak, just saying a few words, and sometimes I would. He was really suffering. In time, I persuaded him to get some professional help, which he did. Then it all happened so quickly: before the end of term he had left university (he was a first-year student) and I have never seen or heard of him since. His name was Martin Speke and he was studying psychology. Strangely, I have never felt the need to contact him again, but that encounter with Martin really changed me and my whole outlook on life. Seeing someone suffering like that made me think quite deeply about life, about my own life and what I really wanted to do with it. I know it was that experience, those hours and days sitting with Martin, really feeling his suffering and seeing how desperately he needed help, which started me thinking I wanted to do something more with my life than simply become a rich accountant.

"And, as I said, Emma, these feelings seem to have grown stronger inside me ever since. In the last few months becoming some sort of therapist, psychiatrist, psychologist, social worker, or even becoming a doctor *en route* if that would help, has increasingly appealed to me. I guess, perversely, that the closer I have come to qualifying as an accountant the more I have felt this is not what I want to become. The question is: will I have the courage to do what I feel ever more strongly I want to do? The problem, Emma, is that our family is so wedded to the profession that I am sure my Dad would never understand my wanting to abandon accountancy – even if he knew this is what I really wanted to do."

Emma listens intently, sipping her mint tea, her fingers cupped around her cooling mug as Simon talks, sharing his very private thoughts about his life and his future. And as she listens, she wonders what it is that has prompted him to reveal so much, and why to her, someone he hardly knows? She doesn't have anything like a complete answer but she thinks it is partly because he sees in her someone he feels immediately able to trust. Emma feels duly flattered, but she is also aware of something else stirring within her. As a journalist, she has listened to dozens of personal stories just like Simon's, many far more heart-wrenching than his, but she feels Simon's story is different – or, rather, she feels it differently. What Simon is telling her is having an effect on her: it seems to be drawing him closer to her as if what he chooses to do with his life is important not just to him but to her as well. This not only creates a warm feeling inside her, it also makes Emma feel the need to reciprocate, to tell him about herself, to begin opening herself up to him. This makes her nervous: she feels she wants to, but she isn't yet ready.

"More coffee?" says Emma to lighten the conversation. "I'm ready for another mint tea."

"Yes," says Simon, "that would be great."

They get up at the same time, but as Emma is seated closer to the counter at the back of the café, she beats him to it and gestures to him to sit down again while she goes off to place their orders.

As if he had had some inkling of what Emma had been thinking, when she returns Simon says, "You know, Emma, I am a pretty shy and reserved person, though I often try to hide this by acting as a bit of an extrovert. What I said to you just now about wanting to work with needy people and to step away from accountancy is not the sort of thing I normally say to *anyone*. In fact, I *have* never said it to anyone until now.

"But when we met so totally by chance and out of the blue at Graham's last week I just felt there was something between us. Since our all too brief encounter last week – and I am being totally honest with you now – I had desperately been hoping you would get in touch, but as the days went by and you didn't, I then began to convince myself I was mistaken – that our meeting was nothing more than a chance encounter and I would never see you again. But when I got your text, all this changed. I felt quite elated. I know it sounds utterly daft, but it was if our meeting up was something which *had* to happen."

Simon suddenly stops, realising he has embarrassed himself even more by telling Emma so openly and frankly what has been swirling round in his head even though he hasn't really been able to make sense of it. He looks at Emma, then looks down at the table. He is suddenly gripped by fear that he has made a fool of himself and she is seeing him as odd, a strange and an unbalanced person, or worse. Overcome with remorse, he glances over at his jacket and tie on the chair beside him, thinking perhaps it might be best if he simply apologises to Emma for embarrassing her as well as himself, gets up, quickly leaves the café and walks out of her life for good.

Just then the waitress returns and places a second *panini* in front of Simon. He looks surprised and smiles at Emma, who beams back at him. It immediately breaks the tension.

He blurts out: "Oh my God, you knew how hungry I really was. Thanks so much, Emma. You really do seem to be able to read my mind. But enough about me. I have talked far too much."

Simon's black cloud has lifted as quickly as it engulfed him. Enormously relieved and realising she *is* keen to engage, he is now even more desperate for her to do the talking. What he really wants her to do is to simply talk about herself: who exactly is this woman who is having such an unnerving effect on me, he asks himself. As Simon is far too shy to ask her to talk about herself directly, he rather lamely says, "tell me more about this job you have landed, it sounds amazing."

Emma peers into her new mug of mint tea and takes a couple of sips as she tries to gather her thoughts. Though she doesn't know precisely what she will say, she is finding what is happening between them alluringly exciting. Her instincts had been right: they did have to meet. Her dream was a portent for what *was* meant to be! Though Emma sees herself as a rational and sensible person, she had seen enough as a journalist to know how odd life can be, even mysterious at times. She is keen to engage, to join the conversation which up to now had been pretty much a one-sided monologue from Simon. But what should she say? When and how should she say it? She is aware that at this moment she doesn't know the answers to any of these questions.

For a little while longer there is silence, but not an uncomfortable one. Emma doesn't feel the need to hurry, to talk until she is ready. When she does, she looks across at Simon quite intently.

"Well, Simon," she says, "you know next to nothing about me and you have told me loads about yourself and I hugely respect you for that. So let me try to 'balance the books' a bit. First, you don't even know my full name! You know I'm Emma but I have still to tell you my surname. Its Maconie: I'm Emma Maconie, the girl from East Finchley!" As she says this, she raises up her shoulders as she opens the palms of her hands outwards and smiles across at Simon.

"Sounds Scottish to me," he says, smiling back.

"You are not the first to say so," responds Emma. "But in spite of my name – and I will tell you more about that some other time – I have still never set foot in Scotland: I am English, I feel English and I speak good 'Norf Lund'un' to boot, just like you." They both laugh and Simon feels even more at ease, reassured once again he did not embarrass himself after all by telling Emma so much about himself.

Spurred on by hearing the confident sound of her own voice, Emma continues in a more measured tone. "You, Simon, are an accountant – correction, *trainee* accountant. Telling you about my new job is as good a place to begin to tell you about myself because I am not only a journalist, as you know, I am a *passionate* journalist and I really want to explain why."

Emma starts by telling Simon how, rather than why, she became a journalist. She explains why she never went to uni, even though she had good enough grades, tells him about the journalism courses she took and how they led to her getting her current job at the *Hendon and Finchley Times*, embellishing this with some of the more interesting and successful assignments she has undertaken for the paper. She stresses the importance of this job as a stepping stone to something bigger and her ambition to become a prominent current affairs journalist at the national level. She then starts to talk about the BBC job, but says little about what it entails, focusing more on the selection process and how she was called for the interview as she is keen to explain to Simon how she came to be in Graham's that morning. However, she says little more than that she was buying things her mother needed for the supper they would have that evening so Emma could tell her all about the interview.

"I hadn't planned on dropping all those things on the floor at Graham's," says Emma, as if she had been reading his mind, and laughs. "But I guess I was nervous I was going to be late for the interview. Well, I don't need to go into all the details, but the interview went really well and, as I told you in my text message, on Friday I got the call I had been on tenterhooks for, to say they were offering me the job."

Simon finishes his second *panini* while Emma is talking, then pushes the plate to one side and leans towards her, putting his elbows on the table as an encouragement for her to say more. He is both sharp and perceptive; he wants to know what Emma means when she says she wants to make a difference. "Go on, Emma, I'm all ears," he says eagerly. "Tell me a little more about your passion for journalism." He is already feeling Emma's enthusiasm as well as her self-confidence rubbing off onto him.

Emma glances across at Simon again, choosing her next words carefully, and catches his eye. He smiles back, the earnest look on his face urging her on.

"You spoke just now, Simon, of helping those who have suffered as a result of personal problems," says Emma. "Well, like you, my interest in journalism and especially in current affairs is also driven by a really strong desire to help people, though in a rather different way from you. As a journalist I am keen to present the world as it is, to uncover the reality with no spin, no distortion. And this means exposing the truth about the injustices which haunt our world. Most especially, I want to lay bare the reasons why some people, not just individuals but whole groups of people, suffer and are forced to live on life's margins. I want to explain how and why our world – the real world – enables some people to grow hugely rich while others are forced to live in poverty with an underlying sense of hopelessness."

As Emma feels herself firing up she sees Don Paulo's face in her mind's eye; the person who, with his stories of the slums of Peru, has helped to bring home to her more than anyone else the harsh and living realities of poverty and the knowledge that things really can change.

"I am not starry-eyed, Simon," continues Emma. "To be a success in the world of current affairs at the highest level is my goal, but I know it won't be easy. I know I need to become a hardened journalist, strong enough to confront those who benefit from the world's injustices, to challenge those striving to preserve the status quo. At times, I am likely to be intimidated, threatened and bullied and, as a woman, I know it is going to even more difficult to stand up to these pressures. It is not an easy life I have chosen, but I know I want to do it."

Emma stops; then says, "I know I haven't expressed all this as well as I might. But, Simon, I hope what I have said at least starts to explain why I have such a passion for journalism. It's actually very, very personal.

"*Why* do I want to do this?" she asks, emphasising the word *why*. "Because I believe getting to the truth of how and why things are the way they are is one of the best ways of bringing about change. Simon, you want to help individuals who are suffering mentally and psychologically and you are willing to abandon a secure job and a prosperous life to do this. I admire you immensely. I am also keen to help individuals and I have already done this in a small way in our part of North London by shaming the authorities into action as a result of some of the stories I have written. But the reason I am so interested in current affairs is because I know so much more can be done if I am able to help pinpoint the underlying causes of people's problems. This will sometimes mean challenging the prevailing narrative, uncovering the truth and exposing the lies. At the extreme, I need to be tough enough to stand up to those who will use their power to try – at all costs – to preserve the status quo."

Emma pauses and looks down into her now empty mug as she knows she hasn't yet shared with Simon half of what she wants to say to him. Having talked about becoming the hardened journalist she knows she needs to be to make a professional success of her life, she now feels ready to begin to expose her softer and more vulnerable side to an expectant Simon. It is now her turn to begin to tell him what she has been feeling deep inside her about their chance encounter and how it has affected her.

"Simon, you were incredibly honest with me just now when you opened up about how you reacted both during and after our chance encounter last week," she says. "Now it is time for me to try to be just as honest with you.

"Just as you said you felt sort of compelled to give me your phone number and doing this was out of character for you, so I knew I had to get in touch with you: I knew we had to meet again, but properly this time. What you also need to know was that texting you as I did was totally out of character for me too: it went against all my instincts as a supposedly *hardened* journalist.

"I am not a shy person – indeed, my friends would say I am precisely the opposite of shy: outgoing, bold, and even boisterous, someone who is not afraid to speak her mind. That said, I don't really 'do' spontaneity either. I like to plan and as far as possible to be in control. But three nights after our encounter at Graham's I had this amazingly vivid dream. It was all about you and also about Ma – Ma, that's my mother – and what seemed to be some sort of link between us, something which bound us together. It was so vivid and powerful, upsetting in a way, but its message was absolutely clear: I needed to get in touch with you. It was after having that dream that I texted you, I felt I just had to! Like you, I wasn't sure you would want to meet up again; in fact, I thought you wouldn't. So I was so pleased, actually relieved, if I am being honest, when you agreed to do so."

Emma then says, half to herself and half to the man seated opposite her, that she increasingly feels in a muddled sort of way she needs to get know even better. "Simon, I don't really know why I am telling you all this. Before coming here this evening it never crossed my mind I would mention my dream to you, and even as I speak to you now I am still puzzling to try to understand why I have."

Just then the lights in *Jenny's* are suddenly turned off, then on again, then off and on again a second time. A voice from the back calls out, "Finish up, please – we are about to close."

"Oh my God," says Simon looking at his watch, "it's almost nine already. I've completely lost track of the time."

They realise they are the only ones left in the café; all the other customers have long departed, and neither of them had noticed.

They stand up as one and quickly gather their things, trying to make sense of what has just happened. Their thoughts are pretty much identical. On the one hand they are both a little embarrassed at the intensity and frankness of their exchange and what they have said to each other about their feelings. On the other hand, they both feel deflated as their intense conversation has been prematurely brought to an end. Likewise, they each sense their frankness cannot be recreated tonight.

Aware of the changed atmosphere as they rise, Simon says, "Emma, I meant to say how much I like your shirt and your necklace; they really suit you, you look great."

"Thanks, Simon," said Emma, adding with a Jesuitical gloss on the truth, "I'm really only in my work clothes but I'm glad you like them." Emma's voice, like Simon's, is sounding a little nervous again.

After paying, they move towards the door which Simon opens, standing to the side to let Emma pass through first, reprising what he had done when they left Graham's, and they laugh as they both recall the event. They step outside and face each other on the pavement, the loud noise of a passing bus allowing them both a moment to think of how they should re-engage.

"What's short for Emma?" asks Simon.

"My close friends call me Em," she replies cheerfully, "or Em-and-Em" she is about to say but checks herself. Even before she has started mouthing the words, Robbie sweeps into Emma's consciousness, unexpectedly, powerfully, and unsettlingly: Em-and-Em is the nickname Robbie uniquely uses for Emma.

Another noisy bus moves towards them and until it passes conversation again becomes impossible. Then, as Emma says nothing, Simon says cheerily, "Well, Em, we have hardly started talking and the evening is almost over. There is so much more to say and so many things I want to ask you. We need more time. How about dinner? You said you are busy tomorrow and Friday: would you be free on Saturday? I would really like us to get together again so we can pick up where we left off."

"I would, too," says Emma, who has only half-heard what Simon was saying.

She is still trying to process Robbie into what has been happening to her here in Muswell Hill with Simon. His mention of Saturday jolts her memory and brings at least some temporary calm to Emma; it certainly dramatically reduces the sense of disorientation and panic she is feeling. She remembers Robbie is going to be away the whole weekend. As he will be away, Emma reasons to herself, she can't tell him what has been going on not only tonight but earlier, in her powerful and disturbing dreams. In any case, she says to herself, as she isn't at all certain what exactly *is* happening, she wouldn't know quite what to tell him anyway. For all she knows her relationship with Simon could be leading nowhere. By the end of the dinner Simon is proposing they have together on Saturday, they might have exhausted what they have to say to each other. They may well then decide to go their separate ways, possibly saying goodbye for good. Best, she thought, to talk it all through with Robbie when they are next together, when everything is bound to be clearer. What's more, Emma reasons to herself, it would be impossible to explain it all to Robbie on the phone, still less by text. So until they next see each other, Emma convinces herself she doesn't need to involve Robbie with Simon but promises herself she will at that point.

This seems to satisfy Emma, and she quickly regains her composure, though it takes a while longer for Robbie to leave Emma's consciousness entirely and she remains quite shaken.

"And, yes, I am free on Saturday," says Emma, trying to rebuild her self-confidence. "You are right, there is plenty more I want to tell you about myself, Simon, and far more I would like to know about you.

"First up," she continues as she turns right towards the roundabout, "is I haven't yet told you where I am now living. The reason I am walking this way is I need to catch the bus back to East Finchley. I have a small rented flat in East Finchley off the High Road, which I moved into a couple of years ago. It's old and objectively a bit grotty, but it's mine and I love it." She then adds, fully aware of what she is saying, "and I live there on my own."

"I'll walk with you to the bus stop, then, Miss Maconie," says Simon.

"Oh, you don't have to, Simon," says Emma.

"Yes, I know I don't have to, but I would like to!" says Simon, smiling. They cross the roundabout and continue along the Broadway. It is already quite dark and only a few people are still out, mostly young couples like themselves.

"Well, as you know, I live here in Muswell Hill," continues Simon "but in the opposite direction to where we are walking now, on Wellfield Avenue. I am sure you don't know it, it's a typical middle-class Muswell Hill street of terraced houses, but at least it is quiet and has a garage. Unlike you, I still live with my Mum and Dad but have never really felt the need to move out, though, of course, I did when at Kent."

As they reach the next roundabout, overshadowed by the fading edifice of the old cinema, Simon says, "Sad they sold the old Odeon cinema, I loved the retro-seats and the musty smells."

"Yes," says Emma. "I wrote a piece about the new Everyman to replace it for the *Times,*" and they both laugh.

"Impressive," says Simon, "there doesn't seem to be much round here you don't know about!"

"I told you I was passionate about news and current affairs. Try me on Brexit, Grenfell, Trump or even the Arab Spring," says Emma as she tosses back her head and laughs.

"The Arab Spring," repeats Simon. "Way out of my depth there, but there's always more to unpick about Trump. My God, I don't think one dinner is going to give us nearly enough time for everything we need to talk about."

They both laugh again. When they near the bus stop, they see two other people standing there waiting, so they stop some yards short so they can keep chatting more freely, without being overheard.

Emma becomes more serious as she turns to Simon and says, "You know Simon, the real reason we met that day at Graham's was because southern African food drew us both there. You remember you told me your family was from Zimbabwe? Well, I never told you about either myself or my family though you guessed – correctly – I came to Graham's because of the southern African groceries they sold.

"This evening you told me you were born in Zimbabwe. Well, what I was about to tell you when they switched off the lights at *Jenny's* is I was born in Zimbabwe too. You said you came to England in 1992 when you were three. Well, I came over to England in 1993, a year after you, when I was just two. So how about that for a coincidence. It's amazing – isn't it?"

Just then they both turn their heads as they hear the sound of a bus rounding the corner to their right. Emma checks: it is the 102. Thinking ahead as she always does, she asks Simon with some urgency in her voice where they are going to meet, and at what time.

He raises his arm and points across the road opposite the green sign which reads "*Feast On The Hill*", saying, "Either there or further down at *FASTA* the home-made pasta bar – you will see the yellow awning if you look out of the right side of the bus when you go past just now. As the Feast closes a little earlier and we seem to need plenty of talking time, let's go for *FASTA*. Anyway, let's meet here outside the bookshop say at 7:30, Saturday, and we can decide then. How does that sound?"

As Simon is speaking, they both turn and hurry to join the queue of waiting passengers. As the bus draws up to the curb and the doors open, just before stepping on to the bus, Emma turns to Simon and hurriedly offers him her cheek which he obligingly touches, a fleeting peck, before she is gone. She pulls her debit card out of her bag ready to pay and shouts back to Simon as the doors close behind her. "Let's go for *FASTA*. You are right, we will definitely need more time."

"Bye Em," says Simon as he waves to the departing bus. "See you Saturday." But Emma has already crossed to the other side of the bus and is peering out of the window just in time to see the yellow awning of the *FASTA* pasta restaurant before the bus lurches to the left to turn onto Fortis Green and accelerate on its way to East Finchley.

As Emma sits alone on the bus and Simon walks home alone, they each begin gathering their thoughts to try to sift through and make sense of what has happened. They both have much to ponder: about the coincidence of their first meeting at Grahams; about discovering their joint roots in Zimbabwe and their growing up in North London so close to each other; about their surprisingly similar and keenly-felt outlook on helping the needy; about how well they got on; about how much they shared so quickly about themselves; about how honest they each were in revealing their thoughts about that first meeting at Graham's and why they were both, seemingly independently, so keen to see each other again; about how much they still needed to know and learn about each other; and, finally, about how eager they both are to meet again on Saturday and continue where they had left off.

* * *

Simon was the first to reach Fortis Green Road on Saturday night: it was a few minutes before half past seven. He knew he needed to be early. He popped into *FASTA* to confirm the booking he had made late on the Wednesday night. To kill time, he wandered back down the street and gazed through the window at the new books displayed at the Muswell Hill Bookshop and then, because she still hadn't arrived, he crossed the road and did the same at the Children's Bookshop opposite.

Since saying goodbye to Emma on Wednesday night, Simon had endured a busy three days at work, which was not unusual. He had been pleased the audit had been completed by Friday night and so he knew he would not have to work on Saturday morning and could put in a few hours of study towards his next accountancy exams. However, he was not surprised that by midday on Saturday he was no longer in the mood to study so he decided to abandon his books because, as he had suspected, he was not able to concentrate: he could not get Emma out of his head. This didn't distress him; far from it.

As he had walked back home after their Wednesday meeting, he had admitted to himself not only that he had liked her even more than he ever thought he would, and his expectations had been pretty high, but he was certain she liked him too. This pleased him hugely but also quite terrified him. Could Emma be the one? He knew asking such a question was to tempt fate.

Simon saw himself as down-to-earth and practical, a person whose views on life were grounded in facts and evidence; he would run a mile from anything remotely close to the world of superstition. Yet he did find it at least a little odd not only that *he* had found their quite coincidental meeting so meaningful and significant, but that *she* had as well. What exactly was it he had found so appealing and attractive in Emma as she clearly had found in him – and why? Try as he might, he could find no rational explanation. He had certainly hoped their coffee evening at *Jenny's* would confirm his strong feelings for her and they did, but he had not expected such reciprocally intense feelings from her. What exactly did she mean by there being a sort of link or bond between them, and what precisely had she dreamt which seemed to compel her to get in touch when he had almost given up on their ever meeting again?

Simon was aware of challenges he faced in getting close to and feeling at ease with women of a similar age. Of course, there was Meg at Kent. After a hesitant and embarrassing start, he had certainly enjoyed both the physical side of their relationship and being in her company, both on their own and with other friends. But after not quite two years together she had ended it because, as she told him, she thought it was going nowhere and he, Simon, seemed to be less interested in her as a person than the thought of having her as his girlfriend. Their relationship, said Meg, had become too "lop-sided." When it was over, he had admitted to himself a growing awkwardness in being with her for more than a day or night and he certainly found it difficult confiding in her.

Why was it he felt so completely different with Emma? How was it he could be so honest and frank with her? How had he felt able to share with her some of his innermost feelings about himself, things he had never said to anyone else before, and do so even before she had scarcely opened her mouth? Was this infatuation; was this love as he had never experienced it before? Or was it something else? Had he been initially attracted to her more as an idea, or an image created in his mind after their first momentary meeting? Lots of questions and too few clear answers.

Then, to cap it all, there was the Zimbabwe link. That was an amazing coincidence. He had always viewed Zimbabwe as remote; a place which clearly meant something really important to his parents but little to him. He had rarely met anyone locally with direct links to Zimbabwe but here was Emma, also a North Londoner, who, like him, had been born in Zimbabwe. Now that was weird!

So Simon spent Saturday afternoon mulling over and trying to make sense of these thoughts and questions. One more hour to kill. He googled "Emma Maconie" yet again, scrolled down and re-read the random selection of articles she had written for the *Times*. He then clicked "images" to see the three pictures which had come up before, only one of which he thought was any good. She was clever and she was pretty, no doubt about it; but precisely why he found her so attractive was far more difficult to say. That was puzzling too.

Like Simon, Emma's time between their parting on Wednesday and their meeting again on Saturday had been busy, though, like Simon, that was not unusual either. She arrived early for work on Thursday so she could finish everything in time to leave for the BBC for her five o'clock appointment. Her first meeting was with her future line manager. To her surprise, this turned out to be Rosemary Slattery, the older of the two women from the interview panel.

Whereas at the interview and afterwards in the lift, Rosemary had showed her charming side, today Emma became more aware she also had a tough side to her. As Rosemary made clear to Emma, much would be expected of her. Though Emma had been selected because she had the core skills necessary to start, Rosemary explained there was a huge amount she still had to learn. She would be expected to use her spare time to keep abreast of and read around those aspects of the news she was working on. Especially during her first six months, Rosemary said Emma would be given feedback on how she was doing to review progress and address any potential shortcomings.

Rosemary was a no-nonsense person, oozing professionalism. Nevertheless, Emma thought she would grow to like her. Following her meeting with Rosemary, Emma went to HR to sign the BBC confidentiality papers and to read through and discuss her draft contract, confirming her start date for mid-June. Though her starting salary was only marginally higher than the finishing salary at the *Times*, there would be a huge jump at Christmas on completion of her initial six-month probationary period. Reading through the small print of the draft contract on the tube back home, she was pleased to see she would be able to take leave days in anticipation of future days worked providing these days were agreed with her line manager.

As always, work was busy, but Emma's mind repeatedly wandered back to Simon, both when she was at work and back home. Before Wednesday, she had been preoccupied with wondering, and worrying, about what would happen when they first really met, what she would say to him, and he to her, and, of course, whether she would like him, and he her. Now she spent very little time going over in her mind what they had said to each other. Her thoughts were dominated by her wish simply to spend more time with him and pick up where they had left off in their journey of mutual discovery. As Saturday night drew nearer, she was aware of how excited she was becoming. The only other thing she kept mulling over in her mind was whether Simon had a current girlfriend: she was already clear he wasn't gay. He had said he had had a girlfriend at uni and seemed to suggest the relationship was over. But did he see her occasionally? Had there been others since? Was there anyone now? Deep down, she felt she needed to know.

Emma woke on Saturday morning excited about the evening ahead. She had dreamed that night of Robbie and then remembered this had happened on both Wednesday and Thursday nights as well. In many ways, Emma found this reassuring. She knew how much she loved Robbie and she saw her dreams as confirmation of this. For Robbie's sake as well as her own, Emma knew she needed to sort out what was happening with

Simon and the sooner she did this, the better. But until things *were* clearer Emma knew she wouldn't really be able to tell Robbie what was going on.

Emma liked routine. As usual, she went for her weekly run, choosing one of her longest routes right across Hampstead Heath to Parliament Hill and back. She then food-shopped and returned to do her weekly laundry and house cleaning, which she finished by six o'clock. As she planned to reach Muswell Hill a little later than their agreed 7:30 rendezvous time, she turned on the TV and started flicking to kill time. Soon she came to the dying moments of a *Harry Potter* film which, as she watched distractedly, she vaguely remembered having seen when it had come out. Her mind wandered: it was the *Harry Potter* books, not the films, which she had really enjoyed growing up. Saving up to buy them and queuing for the next hardback was still such a strong memory for her. She recalled now waiting outside the Muswell Hill bookshop early on a warm July morning to buy the sixth book, *Harry Potter and the Order of the Phoenix*, when she was 14. It is there that she was soon to meet Simon for their second evening together.

It was time to leave. As her bus made its way towards Muswell Hill, in her mind's eye Emma instinctively started to plan the evening, but she quickly stopped. It was, she said to herself, going to be one of those rare occasions when she didn't need to make a plan. She knew what she really wanted was simply to enjoy being with Simon and to let their time together simply run its course.

* * *

Simon's phone vibrated, then rang just before 7:45. He checked to confirm it was Emma and, looking around him as he began to answer it, saw her waving to him from outside Muswell Hill Bookshop. He motioned for her to stay on that side of the road as he crossed and they met up just outside *FASTA* pasta.

Simon opened the restaurant door, standing aside to let her pass, and as he did so she leant towards him and gave him a fleeting but firm kiss on his right cheek, placing her hand on his shoulder as she did so. Simon motioned to the waiter he had spoken to earlier, who recognised him and pointed to a table with a "reserved" sign on it to their left. The tables came with benches not chairs, and they both slid to the end of their black plastic-covered seats, ending up opposite each other next to the wall. As the evening had started chilly for early summer, they had both worn jackets, which they now took off and placed on the bench beside them.

Half in jest, Simon announced they had three hours before the restaurant closed. This was the catalyst they needed to re-engage, sharing first the recent days' events before moving on to recount to each other stories about their pasts, nibbling initially on olives accompanied by a large bottle of cold sparkling water, and at once the conversation flowed effortlessly. From the start, they were at ease with each other. Only when both the olives and water were finished did they turn to the menu.

Simon asked Emma if she would like wine, which prompted a discussion of their attitude towards alcohol. Emma said she really only drank at weekends and then she only liked the odd glass. Simon said he could drink three glasses without feeling any substantial after-effects and rarely drank more. He added that he never drank when he was driving, which Emma filed away; she didn't drive.

They both said they ought to cycle more, but neither did, and Emma added she did not know how to and had never owned a bicycle. This led to them sharing their views on exercise. Emma started by saying she ran at least once a week and had done a seven miler this morning across Hampstead Heath. Simon was clearly impressed. He said cricket was his major sporting love and he had been good enough to play for the first team at uni. He said in the winter he jogged to keep fit but admitted if he did so once a month, he was doing well.

Emma said he looked pretty fit and in shape and then went on to ask him if he liked test match cricket better than the shorter forms of the game. Simon was quite taken aback by the question and asked her if she played. She said she didn't, and then told him about the incident at the library when she had been caught in the rain and had been forced to read a book on test match cricket, explaining how this might have influenced the interview and the chairman's decision to give her the job at the BBC. They both laughed as Simon went on to say his preference was for ODIs followed by T20s, adding that his father, who had played club cricket when young and still supported Zimbabwe, only ever watched test matches. They both chuckled.

When the wine arrived, Simon launched into the story of a memorable trip he had made to Sicily one August when a second-year student at uni with a group of his male Kent friends. The main reason for their going was to climb Mount Etna and peer inside Europe's biggest active volcano.

"For four nights," began Simon, "we stayed in a rather run-down boarding house halfway up the mountain on the outskirts of the village of Fornazzo, overlooking the sea. We chose it because it was on a bus route and seemed incredibly cheap. It was owned and managed by a charming if eccentric woman, Signora Occhipinti. As she was half deaf, she always shouted *at* you rather than speaking *to* you.

"Anyway," he continued, warming to his story, "the accommodation was cramped. All four of us slept in one room, two sharing a large double-bed. We had known this when we had booked but what we didn't know then was that the beds were old and the mattresses and pillows were rock-hard. Neither did we know their room had no air conditioning or ceiling fan. This was something we had completely overlooked when booking and clearly the reason why Signora Occhipinti's rates were much lower than any other place we had researched. Remember, Emma, this was before the days of TripAdvisor.

"Well, while it was hot during the day, at night the heat was unbearable. But it wasn't only the heat and the beds which made sleep almost impossible. Even worse were the mosquitoes. Lying hidden in the dusty wooden rafters during the day, they swooped down on us as soon as we switched off the lights and the room became a hellhole. The heat was so unbearable we were forced to ditch any pretence of modesty and sleep naked, but this created an even larger target for the hungry attackers. Their noise grew louder as they buzzed around our naked bodies as they pondered where and when to bite. We tossed and turned to try to keep them off us and this added even more noise to the mix: the continuous squeaking and creaking of the old beds. At first, we tried to fend off the mosquitos with our hands; then we tried hiding beneath the bedcovers, but this merely raised our body temperature from the almost to the totally unbearable so that we had to throw the covers off again. The extra heat our bodies generated sweating under the covers sent the temperature soaring even higher. Of course, we had earlier opened the windows, but as this prompted in a new wave of hungry mosquitoes we hurriedly closed them again. Sleep was impossible until just before dawn when the temperature at last started to fall. As we emerged from the room in the morning, we all felt more exhausted than we had when we had turned in the previous night."

Simon glanced across at Emma. She was smiling but he hardly noticed.

"Signora Occhipinti insisted on our rising early if we wanted breakfast," said Simon, "and we were always among the first in the dining room as getting out of that hot room was a relief. As each of us walked in each morning, Signora Occhipinti was at the door to welcome us. She gave us each a warm lingering embrace, holding her face unsociably close to ours. Though she was very short-sighted as well as deaf, it was if she was trying to count the bites on our arms and faces from the night's battle with the mosquitoes.

"Surprisingly, the food she served was excellent. There was an infinite supply of bread for breakfast, plus often the odd cake, but the dinners were the best: huge quantities of home-made pasta with lashings of exotic toppings and fresh parmesan cheese. Most nights this was served by her 18-year-old daughter, inevitably called Maria, dark-skinned with sparkling dark brown eyes. You can imagine the effect she had on us, four testosterone-charged young males egging each other on."

Then, remembering who he was recounting his Sicilian story to, Simon said there was a choice of only one wine at supper, *Arpeggio Bianco*. He told Emma it was exactly the same wine he had chosen for them tonight, which was why he was telling her about his fateful holiday.

"Even to us as poor students, that wine seemed incredibly cheap," he said. "On our first night, before we knew what the night had in store for us, we drank three bottles between us. But by the fourth night, they were up to nine, believing, with some evidence to prove it, that the more we drank the greater the chance of us falling asleep and the longer and deeper our sleep would be.

"To cap it all, we never did manage to peer inside Europe's live volcano. When we reached the top of Mount Etna after a strenuous six-hour hike, we found it was "zoned off" to visitors, another key fact we had failed to pick up from our clearly too rapid trawl of the guide books. On our descent from the summit, we did put a few pieces of cold lava into our rucksacks to bring back home as souvenirs, but within a week of our getting home, we had tossed them away.

"But I do still have one souvenir of that disastrous holiday." He beamed across at Emma. "Although the huge amounts of wine we ended up drinking certainly enabled us to get at least some sleep, we suffered even worse mosquito attacks. Our bodies were covered in even more bites which, after a few days, became so itchy none of us was able to resist scratching them. Inevitably, the bites became sores which took weeks to heal. And to this day, I still have the scars on my back to remind me of that unforgettable Sicilian adventure."

Emma laughed loudly as Simon finished. The evening was going as well as she had hoped it would, if not better, and she had learned one more thing about the strikingly handsome blue-eyed man sitting opposite her: when not feeling shy, he was a great story-teller.

For the rest of the meal, they continued to chat away, flipping from one subject to another, often sharing other amusing stories or anecdotes and always keeping the conversation light. The more they shared, the more they realised how much they were really growing to like each other: the chemistry was working. They each sensed this was a relationship which could easily flourish and deepen, though Emma resisted thinking through how this might occur. For now, she was simply content her plan for the evening – to let things happen – was working so well.

They finished their main course and their bottle of wine at much the same time: Simon had drunk a little over half the bottle, Emma a little under but slightly more than she normally drank. She congratulated Simon for his choice of restaurant. He didn't tell her he had chosen FASTA because Paul, the Senior Partner who led this week's audit, had recommended it to him, and he had never set foot in the place before.

To round off the meal Simon said he would like a chocolate gateau. Emma declined but then, prompted by Simon, asked the waiter for an extra fork and they shared the one dessert when it came, taking it in turns to dig into what began as a mountain of cake between them.

It was just past nine when the waitress cleared their table and asked if they wanted anything else. Simon said "no thanks," just as Emma said "we're fine," and they leaned back, stretched and looked at each other as if to say it was time to switch gear and move their conversation to a different level. They both felt ready to open up to each other once again.

* * *

Emma took the initiative. She leaned forward, folded her arms, laid her elbows on the table in front of her and, looking intently at the slim-faced, light-bearded man opposite, said "I think it's time to pick up where we left off on Wednesday, Simon." He responded by sitting up and replicating Emma's folding of the arms. It gave her the reassurance she needed.

"You remember I was starting to tell you a little more about myself after you had spoken your doubts about accountancy and shared with me so touchingly your possible different future career ideas?" she began. "Well, Simon, I promised to tell you more about my surname – Maconie – so why don't I start from there?"

"Fine by me, Em," he said. "Fire away!"

"I'll go back as far as I can. I already told you I came to England in 1992, so that was when I was just two. Ma and I were what you would now call refugees but I never really thought of myself as one. We arrived here at a time when it was easier for Zimbabweans both to get into the UK and to be allowed to stay. As I later realised, this was just another period when waves of Zimbabweans felt they had to leave the country of their birth – like you, I guess?"

She looked at Simon, who nodded and motioned to her to continue; he did not want to interpret the flow of what she was saying.

"Of course," continued Emma, looking down at her hands now, "I have no memories of the move and, try as I might, I can't recall anything at all about my life in the village of my birth and my first two years of life. Ma told me my father died in Zimbabwe either before I was born or when I was very young, I can't clearly remember which now. It's funny, Simon, but I never really asked. I suppose it was because my father was never any part of my life and Ma never spoke much about him, though I am pretty certain she once told me he had died of AIDS. I think she told me his first name was Kenneth, but I don't recall Ma ever telling me his surname. She was always vague about him; it was as if they had had quite an odd sort of relationship – it seemed sort of private, and I felt I shouldn't pry. As I said, Ma never really spoke much about her Zimbabwean past as I grew up, and as it meant nothing to me, I wasn't too bothered then to ask as it all seemed so remote and irrelevant. My world wasn't Africa but England; actually, not really England but this part of north London around East Finchley where I first went to school and have lived all my life. You know, Simon, though I am embarrassed to say it and have never told Ma, I don't feel African at all – I never have. I have always felt English because that's what I am!

"Anyway, back to my story. Ma never married again and I have no brothers or sisters; there is just Ma and me. We are and always have been very, very close, a really happy family unit, even if it is the tiniest you could imagine." Emma looked across at Simon and smiled. "Ma's family came from near Mutoko in Zimbabwe, a town about 90 miles east of Harare. Have you heard of it?"

"No," said Simon, "but then my Zimbabwean geography is pretty lousy."

Emma hurried on. "Now here's a funny thing. Ma's name is Sarah Makoni – spelt M-A-K-O-N-I. There is a place called Makoni near to Mutoko – if you google it you will see it – and this is where the family, on my mother's side, originally came from. Ma said her father, so my grandfather, moved away from Makoni to a village closer to Mutoko after he was married and that's where both she and I were born.

"Anyway, I arrived here in England with, as Ma tells it, only the most basic of documents Ma needed for us to get into the country. These she had somehow managed to get from the British High Commission in Harare. Anyway, the point of the story is to tell you that when I arrived here my surname was also Makoni – that is, Makoni with a "k." It was only when I began nursery school a year or two later long after the papers which enabled me to get into England had expired that the school authorities asked for my birth certificate. Well, Ma had never had one, though she did have my baptismal certificate. It was handwritten by the priest in charge of the huge Catholic complex called All Souls which was close to our village and where I was baptised. We are Catholics, you know. When she was young, Ma was a pupil at the big secondary school at All Souls Mission and after leaving school she went on to train to be a nurse at the hospital there. Once qualified, she worked as a nurse also at All Souls until she moved to the UK. Sorry. I am wandering again. It was my name I was talking about."

"That's fine," said Simon. "It's nice to know a bit about your Mum as well."

Emma then told Simon how the school secretary had misread her name on her baptismal certificate and had written it down as Emma Maconie with a "c" rather than with a "k" – M-A-C-O-N-I-E.

"This was probably," said Emma, "because she had never come across the name Makoni. Anyway, from then on my new name stuck."

She then told Simon the story of Mrs Murray, her Scottish teacher, telling her to stand out in front of the whole class to announce to everyone she was delighted she had three people in the class who *were* Scottish: Emma Maconie and two others.

"So," she said looking across the table and chuckling, "the muddle of the spelling of my name has led many people – not only you, Simon – to enquire about my Scottish ancestry. I have sort of got used to it by now!

"At about the age of six, the school and our parish priest at St Mary's Church in East Finchley, where Ma and I went to church, helped Ma gather together all the bits of paper needed to enable me to become officially what I already felt I was – namely, a British citizen. That document also has me down as Emma Maconie – that's Maconie with a "c" – as does my British passport, which I got as a teenager before my first school trip abroad, to Paris. Paris, Simon, I so loved it – but that's for another time, too! Anyway," she finished, looking across at Simon and smiling, "that explains how and why I am Emma Maconie."

He stretched out his hand and momentarily clasped hold of Emma's folded arms as he said, "That's quite a story, Em. In time I would like to hear more about your mother; she must be quite a woman both to have succeeded in getting you over here and then to bring you up all alone."

Emma was pleased with Simon's response and reassured by his touching her. She would have been glad to talk more about her mother, but she was keener to tell him more about herself. She explained how she was accepted at St Michael's Catholic Grammar in North Finchley, and Simon nodded to indicate he had heard of St. Michael's – he had not heard of St Martin's, her infant and primary schools.

"When I was about 15, Ma and I moved out of the flat I had always known as home – we lived on the rough Grange Estate in East Finchley – to a much nicer flat on Moat Crescent – near to that gym of yours. Then about three years ago I moved into the rented flat I spoke to you about and now call home, which I really feel it is."

She looked across at Simon again as she mentioned her two homes: from his reaction, he clearly knew nothing about the infamous Grange Estate.

As Emma seemed to have finished, Simon shuffled a little on his bench as if to indicate he was preparing to start telling Emma a little more about himself. But before he could begin, Emma suddenly remembered there was one more thing she was really keen to share with him.

"I have never gone back to Zimbabwe, Simon," she began. "When growing up on the rare occasions when I mentioned that one day I would like to visit the home of my birth, Ma was not only unenthusiastic but she was dead against the idea. However, as a teenager many of my first-generation British friends told exciting tales of their visits back to the countries where their parents came from and I grew desperate to be able to tell everyone *my story*. So I began to ask Ma again, more seriously this time, sort of badgering her about when we could go back and visit our family in Zimbabwe. Well, you know, Simon, she became quite agitated, almost angry. It was really odd, quite unlike her, so I reluctantly backed away even though I felt quite bitter about it at the time. It is the only time I ever felt any sort of rift or barrier between Ma and myself.

"Then, all of a sudden, it was certainly less than a year ago, sometime after I had moved into my own flat and had settled in to my life as a journalist, Ma's attitude to my visiting Zimbabwe dramatically changed. Instead of discouraging me from even talking about going out there, she not only began speaking to me more about what she still always calls 'home,' but she told me that as I am now an adult and earning my own money, I need to think seriously about making a trip to Zimbabwe. She told me I need to go out to our village near Mutoko, to stay with the family and meet all my relatives. In fact, even in the past few weeks she has been urging me again to go out as soon as I can arrange to have time off work.

"It's really funny," she continued, reflecting out loud what she had been mulling over in her mind. "When I was growing up, Ma seemed to be sheltering me, almost trying to protect me from our past and from Zimbabwe. Whenever the subject came up in conversation she quickly steered the talk to something else. Now she wants me to go out and learn about the very past which, for all the time I was growing up, she seemed so desperate for me *not* to know about.

"You know, Simon," she turned to look at him, this time straight in the eye, "I really do want to go, and go soon. I really do! When I was finishing secondary school, I wanted to go to Zim so I could come back with exotic stories to impress my friends. Now I want to go because I think if I know more about my past it will help me understand better exactly who I am. Perhaps it is the journalist in me trying to find the 'story'? Only last week, I even googled "flights to Harare" and got even more interested. I am really, really keen to go."

Simon had not only been happy to sit and simply listen to Emma talking about herself and when she was growing up. He had felt a sort of warm glow of contentment come over him as she was speaking. When she started talking about her growing desire to go back and visit Zimbabwe he sat up straight, as he could feel something stirring inside him. When she described how her mother had suddenly switched from deterring her from going out to positively encouraging, even pleading with her, to go, he knocked over his empty wine glass in disbelief. As it rolled across the table, crashed to the ground and broke, Emma looked up and was startled by what she saw. Simon was clearly upset. He was flustered and looked confused, even disoriented. It clearly wasn't from breaking the glass or the effects of the wine. Emma tried to catch his eye but he didn't seem to see her; he was staring through her almost as if he was in a trance.

"Simon, are you alright?" said Emma, her voice raised, though not too loudly as she didn't want to attract attention. She grabbed his hand in hers and shook it. Slowly, Simon returned to his old self and Emma waited for him to speak.

"What you have just said beggars belief," he said, searching for the right words. "Indeed, I find it all quite strange, disturbing actually. If I was the superstitious type I might call it eerie or even frightening."

"What do you mean?" said Emma, who was racking her brain to try to recall what she had said which could have so upset him.

"It's the coincidence of it all," said Simon. "I can't make sense of it at all."

"What do you mean?" said Emma, even more eager to discover what it was she had said to trigger such a reaction. "Simon, please tell me what it is and let me apologise if there is anything I have said which has so distressed you."

"No, it's not you," said Simon, "it's me, or I should say it's neither you nor me. It's us."

"You're talking in riddles now," said Emma, even more perplexed but ever more curious to know what it now seemed was happening not just to Simon but to both of them. "Simon, take a deep breath and then tell me what on earth is going on in that head of yours!"

"Well," said Simon picking up Emma's hand and holding it loosely in his. "You won't believe this but until a few months ago my parents were dead against my going back to Zimbabwe. Just like your mother, Emma, they simply didn't want me to go, and whenever I suggested it they ignored me or, if I was persistent, they became quite confrontational. It was unpleasant not least because this was really the only issue between us I can recall where they were so defensive. Then, all of a sudden, totally out of the blue a few months ago, all this changed. My Mum and Dad, but mostly my Dad, started to tell me I needed to go to Zim, to return to the place where I was born. He said I needed to see where he and my mother grew up and got married, experience Harare and visit my relatives who still live there. One time, he also said I needed to understand, but when I asked him what he meant he immediately retreated and seemed embarrassed by what he had said. It was really weird.

"At first Dad raised the subject in rather a matter of fact way, but in recent weeks, especially, he has grown more persistent. Sometimes his persistence has veered towards the obsessive, and I have to tell you, Emma, when this happened it quite startled me. You see, Em, what he so wants me to do now is precisely the opposite of what he was so keen for me not to do all the time I was growing up.

"Now," said Simon gripping Emma's hand more tightly, "here *you* are telling *me* this is pretty much exactly what has been happening to you. I can understand coincidence, but this seems to be something a whole lot bigger than that. You remember on Wednesday how I told you the day we bumped into each other at Graham's I had felt the urge, I felt almost compelled, to run back and give you that piece of paper with my phone number on it? Then you told me your dream and its telling you that you had to text me and we had to meet? Well, what we have just shared about your mother and my parents almost at the same time totally switching from not wanting us to go back to Zimbabwe to now positively encouraging us to do so is another huge sign to me – to us – telling me – telling us – that our coming together may not have been the chance encounter we both initially thought – assumed – it was. Emma, we both need to go to Zimbabwe; unless we do, this mystery, if that is what you can call it, will remain unsolved.

"As you know," Simon was speaking fast now, a little breathless, "we both left Zimbabwe when we were tiny: you were two, I was just three. Except for a very vague sort of memory I still have of sitting on my grannie's lap, I have no real memories of Zim and certainly no particular feelings about it. Yet when you started speaking about the country just now, I began to feel inside me a growing urge to go. Indeed, by the time you had finished I felt I needed to go, that I really ought to go.

"Perhaps, Em," Simon laughed as he said the words half-jokingly to try to lighten the conversation, "we should go out together so each of us can see where we were born and then share our thoughts and reflections. We have nothing to lose and they say the more you know about your past the better you will know yourself, who you really are and what makes you tick!"

"Yes," said Emma, cautiously but at the same time feeling herself warming to Simon's suggestion. "Perhaps our going out to Zim is the final part of the jigsaw of all these different, though perhaps linked, coincidences. Perhaps it will shed some clearer light on this mystery, if mystery is what you can call what seems to be happening between us?"

Simon said nothing in reply, but it then occurred to both of them independently that going out to Zim together might not be such a crazy an idea after all. The seeds of travelling together to Africa, to their past, seemed to have been sown in each of them.

There was a short silence while they both tried to make sense of what they were each thinking: not so much travelling to Zimbabwe – which each of them clearly wanted to do – but of going out together. But it was too sudden and novel an idea for them to digest and play through all its implications. They both felt they needed more time on their own to process this new twist to the coincidence of their coming together and being drawn to each other. As if by mutual agreement, nothing more was said about this and neither of them raised the issue again for the rest of that evening.

Even keener now to get to know each other better and for the mood of the evening to revert to what it had been as they were eating, Emma leaned back and said, "Simon, please tell me a bit more about yourself and your family. Go on!"

As Simon had earlier been waiting to do just that, he was delighted with her suggestion, and as he began talking, they both felt relieved the atmosphere between them returned to the growing warmness which had characterised their earlier exchanges. He started with a self-derogatory comment, which Emma was soon to learn was a technique he often used when trying to conceal the embarrassment he always felt when starting to talk about himself.

"Mine is a far less exciting story than yours, I'm afraid," he began. "I was born Simon Robertson. I came to England as Simon Robertson and here I am today, still Simon Robertson. No name changes for me.

"My dad is Peter Robertson and his family was among the first white settlers to the country," he continued. "He was an only child, I think, because Gran was ill when he was born and they were advised to have no more children. He went to Prince Edward School in Harare" – it was Emma's turn to look blank – "and, as I told you, he studied to become an accountant. He joined my grandfather at the family firm of Robertson and Lewis. Besides accountancy, his other great love was sport and especially cricket, which he played competitively until the family left Zim. Like others of his generation he was caught up in the pre-Independence war and had to go into the army for the first two years after he left school, delaying for a couple of years his entry to Cape Town where he did his accountancy exams."

Simon was feeling his old self once again and, as he glanced across at her, he was pleased to see he had Emma's full attention.

"Ma was also from Harare," continued Simon. "She was born Cathy Stander and she and Dad met, apparently at a dance in Harare in 1984; they were married in the Anglican Cathedral three years later in 1987 by Bishop Hatendi – a grand affair, I am told – and their wedding pictures confirm this. Ma's dad, John Stander, had come to Zim, or Southern Rhodesia as the country was then called, after the Second World War. He had met and fought alongside Rhodesians against Rommel in the western desert and liked them, and as he didn't know what to do after the war, he decided, like a good many others, to emigrate from Britain. He became a tobacco farmer and lived in the Mazoe area just outside Harare. You must have heard of Mazoe? It's where they grow all the oranges."

Emma nodded, as Ma often spoke of Mazoe orange juice, but she didn't want to interrupt him.

"Ma and Dad loved the country, they really loved it. They told me many if not most of their friends left after the country became independent in 1980, but they chose to stay on. While they certainly wanted to continue living in the country they had always loved, they were also keen to make a contribution to what they knew was in many ways going to be a new country after all the killings and horrors of Zimbabwe's pre-Independence war. However, when the 1980s turned into the 1990s, as Dad tells it, they felt there was no future, not so much for them but for me and any other children they might have. What they saw deeply upset them – nepotism, greed and corruption – the country was being torn apart and the prospects for peaceful political change and steady economic growth seemed more and more remote.

"You know, it's funny, Em, when you think about it, both your mum and my parents seem to have left Zim more to give *us* the opportunity of having a better life than *them*, though neither you nor I seem to know very much about what precisely it was they gave up for us. I am curious about the past – our pasts and our parents' pasts – as you seem to be.

"Ma's father died of cancer when she was 12 and the family then continued to live in Mazoe for a few years, but apparently it never really worked. So, some years later, they sold the farm just before the compulsory purchases of white farms became widespread, and my Gran, my Mum and her younger sister and my auntie Sheila moved to a small flat in town. However, that didn't work either: Gran and Sheila didn't get on – apparently, they never had done – and when Ma and Dad were married and Ma moved in with Dad, Gran moved in with them. She never really settled after John, my granddad, died, and she gradually retreated into herself. Soon after moving in with Mum and Dad, Gran's memory began to deteriorate and she had to move to Nazareth House, a home for old people run by nuns on the outskirts of Harare. This happened when she was 60. Quite soon after the move, she developed Alzheimer's and died two years later. Her death was really the catalyst for Ma and Dad leaving Zim as with Gran dead Ma no longer felt she had any need to stay.

"Ma's sister, Sheila, still lives in Harare. She is married to the person who without a doubt was Dad's closest friend, James or Jim Reddy. Uncle Jim and Dad were not only in the same class at Prince Edward but they went into the army together straight after school. Mum and Aunt Sheila are close; Mum has been over to Zim to see them a couple of times and Aunt Sheila and my cousins, Arthur, Janet and John, have all been over here to stay with us. Arthur and Janet went to live in South Africa after leaving school but John is still around as far as I know; apparently, he lives in a sort of squat in Harare.

"Strangely, it has only been in the last couple of years that Mum has begun to start to pass the odd comment about Dad's and Uncle Jim's time in the army, but Dad will still never speak about the war and I was never sufficiently interested to ask him much about those days. It seemed to be pretty much a taboo subject when we were growing up. As children we had a sort of sixth sense that that wasn't something we should talk about.

"Uncle Jim is in the hotel business," he continued. "For many years he worked for the big Delta Corporation, but now he is an independent consultant, and Aunt Sheila is a physiotherapist who works for the church. I think they switched and became Pentecostals or Mormons – something like that – I was never quite sure which. But whatever denomination it is, Ma says they have become very keen churchgoers. Actually, it seems it is their church life which motivates them to stay on in Zim. Aunt Sheila has always been keen for me to come out and stay with them but I never have really felt I wanted to, that is until now.

"So," Simon sped up as he felt he had given Emma more details about his family than she could possibly want to hear, "Mum and Dad and I came over to England in 1992, as I told you. Dad managed to move straight into a job with Falkland, Fairbridge and Hayes here in Muswell Hill because one of the partners of the firm had been at Balliol in Oxford with my Uncle George. Uncle George – or Professor George Stander – is Mum's first cousin, the brother of Mum's dad. He is not only quite a character but he is known as the family 'fixer.' He is a consultant at St. Thomas Hospital, but also inherited the family house in Kent where he and my Aunt Margaret still live today, with their children Harry, Amelia and Lydia – all second cousins of mine.

"Anyway," he took a deep breath, "I am sure I have told you more than enough about my family – it must sound pretty boring, just lists and names of people who mean nothing at all to you, why should they? Sorry I got carried away."

Though Emma would not have been able to repeat the names of all the people Simon had mentioned and their relationship to him, she was far from bored. She was grateful to get a feel of Simon's large extended family and she was also enjoying simply listening to him talk. Indeed, it made her realise how keen she was to go out to where she was born so she could at last meet, especially, her Uncle Prosper and Aunt Emerentiana, whom she knew her mother was closest to, as well as her numerous cousins whose names she always had difficulty remembering. But what she really wanted was for Simon to tell her even more about himself.

"No, I am finding all the details of your family really interesting, Simon," said Emma, "I really am. However, what I would really like you to do now is to tell me a little more about you."

"Well," he continued, "when we arrived in London, as you know, I was just three. We first moved to a flat on Woodberry Crescent, just a couple of roads away from where we are now, where my sister Jane was born in 1994. I am five years older than Jane: I think Mum and Dad delayed having another child in Zim because of all the uncertainties – worrying about whether to stay or not and Gran's deteriorating health. Soon after Jane was born we moved to our current house on Wellfield Road. Jane and I both went to Muswell Hill Infant School and then on to Fortismere, if you have heard of it?"

"Of course," said Emma smiling. "They call Fortismere 'the big school for the smart kids!'"

"Jane and I get on fine now, far better than when we were younger, though I wouldn't say we are all that close. Our family seems to divide along sex lines: Dad and me, the sporty ones on one side, and Mum and Jane on the other.

"So, Em, we didn't get to England as refugees but because of our family ties to Britain. We all came over with Zim passports but it was pretty easy first for Mum and then me to get British passports. Jane was okay as she was born here. Finally, and again I think with a little help from Uncle George who knew someone in the Home Office, Dad was able to get a British passport, too."

As Simon talks, Emma observes him closely and starts to daydream. She hasn't interacted so rapidly, intensely or so frankly with anyone quite like him before. She is well aware of how much she likes him. He is sincere and honest, which she likes, but he is also dreamy and a little awkward as well as often earnest, and she likes that too. What else? She knows she finds him handsome and if pressed she would probably have to admit to finding him attractive. She is certainly enjoying being in his company. As a journalist, when she delves into and begins to immerse herself in a new story, Emma has been trained always to continue searching to discover if there is anything more to root out which she could initially have missed. Is there anything more about Simon, about her and Simon, she hasn't yet considered? Possibly, but she can't put her finger on it or, rather, she is not yet ready to begin to acknowledge what it is. For now, she is happy just to enjoy being in Simon's company, to listen to him as he opens up more to her about himself, his views of the world and his future. What she does know is that the longer she spends in his company the more she knows she is growing to like him, just as she knows he is growing to like her too.

Just then, one of the waiters comes up to their table to tell them the restaurant is about to close. Simon looks at his watch; it is after 11:30, well beyond closing time.

"Just like Wednesday at *Jenny's*," says Emma. "We're running out of time again before we have finished."

Simon feels a little deflated as he has so much more he wants to tell Emma, so he speeds up to try to finish off what he had wanted to say – he rehearsed this bit during his walk earlier that afternoon.

"You said you feel English, Em, well, so do I. As I said, I have a vague memory of sitting on Gran's lap before she died, but I wonder whether this is a real memory, or just something I know about from seeing old pictures of me on her knee and the photos sort of coming alive in my mind's eye. Anyway, besides that memory, or non-memory of Zim, my other distant memories of my early childhood are all of England. Ma and Dad still speak with recognisable Zim accents, though these have mellowed in the more than 20-odd years they have lived here, and though they miss Zim, I sense it is more the past they miss than the present. From what I can tell, they have adjusted pretty well to living in north London and seem pretty content. They neither live in the past, nor do they deliberately mix with an inward-looking circle of southern African expatriates. None of the hard white racists I have bumped into have had any links with Ma and Dad. It is more the old Zim, its food and beer, they pine for today, not the outdated views of bitter ex-Rhodesian Zim emigrants. They seem to have really adjusted well."

"Wow, Simon," says Emma, as they stand up ready to leave the restaurant, "we have covered so much ground in so short a time, and I feel I know you so much better now. I have really loved our evening."

"Me, too," says Simon.

In summing up their evening, neither of them makes any further mention of any potential visit to Zimbabwe. It is clearly a far too difficult a subject to return to tonight; they both need more time to digest it.

On leaving the restaurant, they turn to their right to walk the 20 or so yards to the crossroads with Fortis Green. Neither speaks. They are each too busy pondering what should happen next.

For now, Emma's immediate feeling is one of needing time just on her own, but, like Simon, she is also eager for them to see each other again soon. When they reach the lights at the crossroads, Emma tells Simon she wants to walk back home and turns down his suggestion of going back part-way with her. Knowing Emma always spends Sundays with her Mum, and desperate to see her again soon, he asks her if it would it be okay if he calls her tomorrow evening to fix something up for next week. She not only says yes but that she would really look forward to it.

Simon takes this to be the signal to say goodbye. He turns to Emma and kisses her affectionately on both cheeks. She gives him the warmest of smiles as she loosely grabs his hand in hers before quickly letting go, and they part, walking away from each other in opposite directions. Simon senses Emma was distracted when he had kissed her and her hesitation when she took his hand. He is now worried he might have been too forward and forthright. Or perhaps it was what he had said earlier? Whatever it was, he feels quite desolate. He panics, thinking everything might rapidly unwind.

They haven't walked more than ten yards away from each other when a hand gently but firmly grasps the right arm at the elbow, replaying what had happened the first time they said goodbye outside Graham's, when Simon ran back and took hold of Emma's right elbow. But this time the roles are reversed: now it is Emma who has run back and taken tight hold of Simon's arm. Simon turns back as he feels her hand on his arm and as he does so, Emma's lips close in on his. He does not resist: he is spellbound. Emma's kiss is a kiss of certainty. Simon is immediately struck by both the passion of her kiss and the smell of her perfume. He knows he has to respond but as he ponders how, Emma's demonstrative kiss rapidly turns into one of uncertainty, hesitancy and doubt and she hurriedly disengages.

Then, a little breathless and with her confidence restored, Emma steps away and, looking deep into his eyes, she asks Simon whether he was doing anything important tomorrow as she tells him she will be free because she won't be having lunch with her mother as she always does, as she will be away on a church outing.

"So," says Emma, "wouldn't it be really nice if we could spend the day together and continue where we left off tonight?"

Still recovering from Emma's unexpected kiss, Simon first mumbles something about cricket but then, back-pedalling fast, tries to swallow his words by saying, with far more conviction, that meeting up again tomorrow is what he really, really wants, too. He says he could easily re-arrange what he had vaguely planned to do – it wasn't so important anyway – and how lovely it would be to do that.

Relieved, and with growing excitement in her voice, Emma says that quite exceptionally the forecast for tomorrow predicts a balmy summer's day, still with no wind and with temperatures expected to be close to the 29-degree record level for May last reached in 2010. So why don't they have a picnic on Hampstead Heath?

Emma's excitement is contagious. "That sounds a great idea, Em," says Simon, smiling broadly now. Emma's spur-of-the-moment idea fast develops into a plan. She suggests they meet at the ungated entrance to the Heath on Hampstead Lane, the one she calls the "ice-cream" one, next to the nursery and herb garden. She is delighted when Simon says he knows it. But just to make sure, Emma says it is the entrance between Compton and Sheldon Avenues, right opposite the sign for Park House. Simon smiles to himself as he is becoming used to Emma's ways and reconfirms he really does know the place.

She asks what time they should meet and he suggests one o' clock (it is almost midnight by now), adding that he will buy some stuff to eat and bring it along. They both smile and kiss again, a longer kiss this time before they go their separate ways, each with a spring in their step.

Emma reaches her flat some 20 minutes later and, rarely for her, draws the curtains before getting into bed, as if she wants to keep out the world and preserve within her the feelings of excitement for tomorrow bubbling up inside her. As she quickly falls asleep, the warm feelings in the pit of her stomach which had visited her when she fell asleep on the night after their initial encounter at Graham's return. Now, though, they are warmer and they linger, and this time Emma is conscious of what she is feeling. It is as if she is on the cusp of a wave.

Simon had arrived back at the family home in Wellfield Road a little earlier. As he turns the key in the lock, he hears his mother call him from the sitting room where she and Simon's dad are watching the end of a late-night movie on TV. When he opens the sitting room door both to greet them and say goodnight, his mother tells Simon she has ironed his cricket kit and left it for him on his bed. He thanks her but then quickly goes on to say something has come up and he will not be playing cricket tomorrow after all. He says he had just texted Bill (Bill Southerton, the cricket secretary-cum-captain) to let him know and Bill replied saying that would be okay.

Quick as a flash but in what successfully came out as a rather detached and matter-of-fact question, Simon's mother enquires whether what has just come up for tomorrow was the same as the thing which had come up tonight and whether this, in turn, had anything to do with the thing which had come up on Wednesday evening.

"Yes," says Simon, who knows his mother well. "Exactly the same thing! And as you are clearly so interested, her name is Emma, Emma Maconie to be precise, and we have arranged to have a picnic on Hampstead Heath tomorrow, so cricket's clearly not going to happen.

"And Dad," he continues, looking across at his father, who has begun to wake from his slumbers as Simon was speaking, realising something important was being said, "I am sure you will be interested to know Emma is originally from Zimbabwe. Like me, she was born there and like me, she came over here when she was young. She's a journalist and is about to start a big job for the BBC. You will really like her."

And with those words, Simon lets out a chuckle, wishes them both goodnight then closes the door to walk up the stairs to his room and to bed, a spring in his step. As he climbs the stairs, he can hear the sounds of their voices; they clearly turned off the TV as soon as he left the room. He can't make out what they are saying but it doesn't bother him in the least as he sleepily continues to relive the evening he has just spent with Emma.

Above all else, he ponders all the different things her kiss meant then and what it might mean for the future. However, by the time he has got into bed and turned off the light he has reached no firm conclusions other than knowing he wants to reciprocate. Weary but happy, he falls asleep knowing the opportunity of another kiss will arise tomorrow though he has no idea exactly how or precisely when. It just has to.

- 4 -

Hampstead Heath

Sunday dawned without a cloud in the sky but as Emma had her curtains drawn, she slept until just after nine. Before showering, she had asked her phone for Hampstead's weather. The reply came back in an instant: clear blue skies and highs of 28 expected by mid-afternoon. Though it was still only May, it was going to be one of those rare balmy early-summer days and she knew at once what she would wear: grey running shorts; her trim, if ageing, loose-fitting light-blue T-shirt and recently bought coral canvas shoes.

With the weather and her clothes taken care of, Emma settles down to breakfast and her thoughts immediately turn to Simon. If anything, she is even hungrier for his closeness than when she had impulsively kissed him only a few hours earlier. However, as she begins to munch on her cereal in the cool light of day, she knows she needs to come to grips with the jumble of different emotions which has been building inside her. Indeed, she is now ready to admit she has deliberately welcomed and engaged with the thoughts and feelings she has found warm, comforting and reassuring, and tried to ignore or fend off the confusing, troubling and upsetting ones. It is these – the uncomfortable ones – she knows she needs to confront. But as she starts what she had feared would be the difficult and unsettling process of trying to take stock of what has been happening to her, Emma feels quite calm and in control. Perhaps, she now thinks to herself, her problems will be far simpler to resolve than she had thought they would be? Emma starts by trying to unpack precisely why she feels the way she does about Simon and she finds this easy too.

Although she is not prepared to admit to herself that she has fallen in love with Simon, she is ready to acknowledge that he is already exerting an increasingly powerful hold on her. Of course, there is the physical side. She knows she finds him hugely attractive: he is strikingly good looking, tall, with those alluring deep blue eyes, and she finds his sometimes slightly embarrassed and awkward mannerisms increasingly captivating. She also knows him to be a sensitive, upright and honest man, with a commitment to justice which seems to closely match hers. Another big box was ticked when Simon told her of his decision to ditch a secure career in accountancy to respond to the growing desire within him to help those less fortunate than himself, as this resonated strongly with Emma's own passion to make life better for the disadvantaged.

Then there is the whole business of the weird set of coincidences between them which began when they bumped into each other at Graham's. Quite independently, they both felt almost compelled to see each other again. On its own this would have been odd, but there was so much more. When they did meet up properly, they warmed to each other at once and then – defying normal convention – each of them felt comfortable opening up and sharing innermost thoughts about themselves. That was strange too. On top of that there was the remarkable coincidence of their discovering they had both been born in Zimbabwe and moved to England at pretty much the same age. But strangest of all was the discovery that the turnaround in Sarah's attitude to Emma's going out to Zimbabwe – from being dead against the idea to now urging, even pleading, for her to go, and go soon – was mirrored almost exactly in what had happened between Simon and his parents.

As she weaves all these strands together in her mind, Emma can't bring herself to believe that her meeting Simon was simply some chance encounter. Indeed, she ponders, couldn't her meeting Simon in some inexplicable way be something which was *meant to be*? Couldn't the series of events which unfolded be seen almost as providential? And if this was the case, then aren't the strong and growing feelings she clearly has for Simon *meant to be* too? These musings prompt the return of the comforting warm glow Emma felt on waking and steer her mind to the day ahead. She knows this is likely to draw them even closer together: after all, this was what lay behind last night's impulsive kiss and Emma's wish for them to spend the day together. So if all this is also *meant to be*, then she should surely feel comfortable simply going with the flow of the day ahead?

But then all of a sudden Emma's stomach tightens. She puts down her cereal spoon, sensing the need to take a step back and think all this through more clearly, but immediately she is distracted. She sees herself tottering precariously on the steaming edge of a volcano and a sense of panic envelops her as she feels herself being sucked in over the side, falling headlong into the molten lava below.

Emma lurches back to reality and knows why she is starting to panic. She may be on the brink of falling in love with Simon, but it's all happening too quickly. It's not only all too new, but there are far too many unknowns. How does she *know* all this is *meant to be*? How does she *know* this is the correct path for her to take? How does she *know* she should go with the flow of her emotions? Emma forces herself to re-engage with her critical self. She knows that she needs to be wary; to be suspicious of the facts as they appear. She has been taught to challenge the seemingly self-evident and to question people's feelings, and she knows what a good student all her teachers told her she was. Then, as she starts to revisit what has happened to her through the lens of the professional journalist she is, Emma finds herself raising a very different set of questions.

Could the strong feelings she has for Simon simply be infatuation dressed up as something which appears to be more substantial? Would she wake up and find herself lying in bed securely next to Robbie, realising these past days had all been a dream? No, this was real. But then could the string of strange and still unexplained coincidences be a trap? And if it is a trap, has it been set solely for Emma, or could it be a trap which both she and Simon are being tempted, or worse, being lured, to fall into?

Emma breathes in deeply and then sighs loudly as she exhales, pushing her half-eaten bowl of cereal into the centre of the table. Her rational self tells her that her fast-developing relationship with Simon isn't that simple after all: even if she adds her troubling thoughts about Simon to the mix, they still make up less than half the story. Simon has exploded into Emma's life, but Robbie hasn't left it.

As Emma brings Robbie into the frame – something she has resisted doing until now, fearful this would both confuse as well as distress her – she is surprised by what happens. Instead of Robbie distressing Emma, feelings of warmth and reassurance start to flow, and Emma welcomes them in. Why? She doesn't need time to reflect; Emma already has the answer. She knows deep within her bones that the bonds which bind her to Robbie are not merely still intact but remain extremely strong. Over the course of many years, Robbie has helped to shape and mould Emma into the person she now is; so much so that Robbie has almost become a part of Emma, in the same way as she has become a part of him: their lives are enmeshed. Together. A snake may shed its dead skin and forget it, but Emma knows she is incapable of simply discarding Robbie and walking away, just as she knows Robbie would find it immensely difficult casting her aside. So, as keen as a part of Emma is for Simon and her to be drawn more closely together today, another part of her knows she is as much in love with Robbie this weekend as she was last weekend. This was why last night, when one part of Emma drove her to run back and kiss Simon, another part of her wrenched her away from him.

But with Robbie joining Simon at her breakfast musings, Emma senses she is now ready to confront the dilemma she has tried so strenuously to avoid. She has to choose between Simon and Robbie: she cannot have an exclusive loving relationship with both men, the one she still loves deeply and the one she is within a whisker of falling in love with. Working as a journalist, Emma has met a number of two-timers, but for her there is a fundamental contradiction in believing it's possible to share her life completely with more than one other person. She knows it would be totally dishonest to both Simon and Robbie if she ever tried, but more importantly, she knows she cannot deceive herself.

She also knows she has to choose soon because the longer she delays, the more dishonest she feels she is being – to Simon, to Robbie and to herself. And because Emma is the sort of person she is – always keen to get to the point and to have things clear in her mind – she tells herself she needs to make her decision today as she starts to go over the different arguments she has used to attempt to justify to herself not having yet told Simon about Robbie, or Robbie about Simon.

In Simon's case it is comparatively simple: she hasn't felt the need to tell Simon about Robbie because their relationship is still so new. Not only has it scarcely begun: it might well soon end. If it doesn't end, she will certainly tell Simon about Robbie.

In Robbie's case, things are more complicated. Emma knows she will need to open up completely to Robbie about Simon whether her relationship with him continues, and blossoms further, or whether it peters out. In either case, she knows she will need to tell him face-to-face what has happened and to honestly answers the questions he is bound to ask. She knows she needs to do this soon but she also knows that when they do meet and she lays bare her soul to Robbie, she needs to be absolutely clear precisely what it is she will be telling him. And that's her problem: she doesn't know the fate of her relationship with Simon. This only fuels her determination to resolve the dilemma she faces as soon as possible. She knows she owes Robbie this clarity even more than she owes it to Simon and to herself.

Emma senses she is going round in circles again. She doesn't believe she has acted dishonestly – except, perhaps, last night's kiss, though it was impetuous, unplanned and not premeditated. But she is aware of a growing sense of guilt about what is happening – or rather about what is not happening. Her feelings of guilt not only bother her, they are now upsetting her, which is another reason why she has to make her choice today and stop prevaricating.

Thinking about it now, Emma knows there are many ways she could have kept both Simon and Robbie in the picture of what was going on. For instance, she could have begun her very first conversation with Simon by telling him up front about Robbie, but she didn't. She tells herself she didn't because she had no idea then how her feelings for Simon would develop; but was it dishonest of her to think like this? Likewise, she could have told Robbie about her chance encounter with Simon right after it happened, and she could have called him to tell him about her vivid dream of Simon just after she had had it, before it drove her to text Simon. She knew it would have been too difficult to have tried to explain everything to Robbie in a text or phone call, but instead of doing nothing, she could have told Robbie they needed to meet urgently. But she didn't. Emma's growing guilt is making her feel ever more uncomfortable with herself and it only adds to her conviction that she needs to resolve everything today.

But how can she decide? How can she choose, and choose quickly? As she carries the breakfast things to the kitchen Emma feels despairingly lost; she still seems to be going around in circles. Then, as she turns on the kitchen tap and idly watches the soapy water bounce off her cereal bowl into the sink, the beginnings of an answer start to form in her mind. Soon she thinks it's actually quite simple and chides herself for not having had the courage to see the solution before.

Emma knows there is one outstanding matter she still hasn't broached with Simon. She hasn't asked him about his faith, his underlying beliefs; what drives, what is the basis, the essence, of everything he does. She already knows quite a bit about the values he lives by and knows how closely these resonate with her own value system. But what informs and shapes Simon's values? In short, what does Simon believe? Knowing what Simon believes deep down will provide Emma with the final piece of the jigsaw to enable her to choose between Simon and Robbie, but the freedom it will give her terrifies her. If she discovers that he shares her faith, then she knows there will be no barrier left to prevent her responding to her instincts and falling in love with Simon. She will be free to be with Simon and free to leave Robbie, even though she also knows that this freedom will come at the cost of a long period of pain and deep distress for both of them.

Emma knows why she hasn't discussed her own faith with Simon and in turn asked him about his faith. It is because she is deeply afraid of what will transpire. If the account Simon gives her of his faith and his innermost belief strikes no chord with her, if there is no clear resonance, no common ground between his beliefs and hers, Emma will know – and know for certain – that their relationship can have no future. This is because Emma's Christian faith and her relationship to Robbie have become so intertwined she could not conceive of ever being in a relationship with anyone unless her partner shared her faith – it's as simple as that. But Emma also knows that if it comes to that, turning her back on Simon will not be easy for her either, given what has already happened between them. When a car is already traveling at great speed, it's not possible to bring it to a sudden stop without risking the lives of those inside.

Then, in part to try to prepare herself for the day ahead, and in part to try to calm herself down, Emma plays over in her mind all that Simon told her about his family and his past to search for clues about his beliefs. As she strains to recall what he said, the more encouraged she feels. It seems pretty certain his roots are Christian, as Emma remembers him using the word "switched" in explaining that his uncle and aunt had now become evangelical Christians. This surely meant they were Anglican, Methodists or something else? It's a long shot, but he could even be Catholic, she thought. Now that would be a coincidence! But he could be: hadn't he said his grandmother died in a Catholic old people's home? Yes, said Emma to herself, I am absolutely sure he said that. And if he had been brought up as a rather traditional Catholic, so had she. So even if he had stopped going to church, as most people she knew had, then just as she had recast her Catholic faith into a very different form, so too could Simon.

These more comforting thoughts linger and stay with Emma as she dries her hands. She then checks the time again and gathers her things together; she knows she mustn't be late. In the brief time left to her before setting off for the Heath, she feels her self-confidence returning. By the time Emma opens her front door to join Simon for their day together, she is wearing a smile on her face and has a distinct spring in her step.

Simon's early morning had a far more mundane, matter-of-fact air to it. Emma was very much in his thoughts, but so too were the more practical and immediate issues of what to wear and what he should buy for lunch. Emma had said it would be warm – no, she had said it would be hot – and his light khaki trousers caught his eye as soon as he opened his top drawer. Rummaging down, he found his short-sleeved, khaki shirt which he thought sort of matched. When he had put them on, he feared Emma would be more critical of his choice of clothes not so much because they didn't match, but because they were so crumpled, notwithstanding his best efforts at trying to iron them by pressing his hands on the creases. Such a pity, he thought, that his mother had spent all that time ironing his cricket kit which he would not be wearing today after all.

Although he knew he was running a little late, as he reached the kitchen he saw Ma had put some bread out for him on kitchen table, as well as – still the thoughtful mother – some suntan cream. Where food and sunburn were concerned, she still treated him like a dreamy teenager and, on this occasion at least, he was grateful to her. After making himself two pieces of toast, each of which he covered with thick layers of butter – comfort food – he grabbed the car keys his father had left for him on the table and headed for the family car, which was soon weaving its way to the car park behind the M&S store in Muswell Hill. As Simon couldn't decide what to buy for their lunch, he opted for a medley of different types of food for them to munch on through the day. For drinks, he bought a large bottle of ice-cold fizzy water, two smoothies and two smaller bottles of still water, currently frozen, which he hoped would help to keep the rest of the food chilled. As he left M&S, he worried that Emma might criticise him for buying too much food but thought she would be pleased to be given plenty of choice. It was apparent that Simon, too, was also both excited and nervous about the day ahead.

Given the forecast, he knew the Heath would be crowded, but fortunately he would have no problem parking. One of the partners from Falkland, Fairbridge and Hayes, John Fairbridge, his father's closest friend at work, lived close by, in Sheldon Avenue. Simon hadn't thought to call John to ask if he could leave the car in their driveway. He assumed it would be fine as his father and mother always parked there on their regular walks on the Heath. After carefully manoeuvring their now ageing blue VW Passat into the corner of the Fairbridges' sweeping driveway, Simon grabbed his M&S bag of goodies and the rug which always lived on the back seat of the car, turned the key in the lock, carefully placing it in the

zip pocket of his trousers having mislaid it in the past, and then strode off
to meet Emma only a couple of minutes' walk away. Like her he had a
spring in his step, and he now felt able to focus on their day together.

His first hope was that the day would "flow" naturally and they would
enjoy each other's company as much as – no, even more than – they had
done last night. He also hoped they would build on last night's kiss but he
wasn't sure how or when that would happen, or the extent to which he
needed to be forward in such matters. This led his mind to wander back to
one thing which had been troubling him and which he really hoped would
be clarified today: Emma's love life.

He didn't think she had a current boyfriend, though she hadn't
specifically said so. She had said she lived on her own, which was good,
but it was only a start. She must have had one, or more likely a number of
boyfriends in the past given her good looks, her bubbly nature and her
magnetic personality. But what had happened? Simon thought the odds
were loaded in favour of her currently having a boyfriend of sorts, but he
told himself it was very unlikely she was currently in any sort of long-term
relationship, or why would she have texted him and been so keen for them
to meet? If she had had a succession of different boyfriends, would he end
up simply being the next one to be added to the long list of names of those
she had ditched? As Simon had a rather self-deprecating image of himself,
he thought the odds of his joining that roll call were pretty high.

As he turns the corner onto Hampstead Way and sees the entrance to
the Heath where they had arranged to meet. Simon tells himself not to fret
too much about all this because he trusts Emma. He tells himself she will
tell him what he needs to know about her other relationships, former or
current, when she thinks the time is right, and the more he thinks about it
the more he convinces himself that will be today. So everything will be
okay. But after only a few more paces, Simon feels a churning in his
stomach which his thinking self has clearly not been able to suppress.
Everything is not okay. There is a dissonance between his head and his
heart.

Emma reaches the Heath a little after Simon. Keen to reserve them a place,
as he sees so many other picnickers pouring in, he decides to walk ahead a
short distance to a grassy area looking down on London. Torn between
standing up so Emma can see him and squatting down to spread his rug to
mark their "territory", he bobs up and down on the grass, shopping bag
tightly held in one hand, rug shaking in the other, his eyes trained on the
entrance where they had agreed to meet. He had never been any good at
multi-tasking. Fortunately, Simon's dilemma is quickly resolved. Almost
at once, Emma sees Simon and waves, feeling her heart skip a beat as she
does so. He waves back and she quickens her pace. As the distance between
them narrows, their eyes meet and they smile; when together they give each

other a tender but brief kiss. Simon follows this up with a tight and longer hug which Emma warmly reciprocates, giving him the sort of hug and affectionate pat on the back she normally reserves for her mother.

As they part, they step back to take each other in. Without a thought Simon blurts out, "Em, you look lovely." It is an instantaneous explosion of delight at seeing her, not a considered comment on her wardrobe. Though she is modestly dressed in her shorts and sleeveless top, this is the first time Simon has seen so much of Emma. As his eyes rest on her, he is aware of the effect her body is having on him, the tall, strong but gentle female form momentarily still and so close. He has said no more than that she looks lovely, but his face and bearing must have conveyed the warm and wholesome feelings welling up inside him because she senses his pleasure at seeing her and feels pleased. Then, as suddenly as it had been cast, the spell is broken.

As he had feared, Emma laughingly asks him if he likes ironing, though seeing him for the first time in bright sunlight she is keener for him to answer her next question, which is how often he shaves. He says since wearing a stubble beard he usually "neatened himself up" once a week, on a Sunday night before the working week. Standing before Emma in the sunshine, Simon suddenly feels exposed, scruffy and unshaven, sensing she would have liked him to have neatened himself up for her, for today. Emma quickly dismisses her own criticisms as unimportant as she sees through all this to the man behind. Her anticipated excitement at simply being with Simon again is overwhelmingly confirmed by the warm feelings she has simply being close to him again.

Realising she has embarrassed him, which had not been her intention, Emma cheerily says, "Shall I help you with the rug?" as she points to a different patch of grass a few yards ahead of where Simon thought they should sit, adding "I think this place would be better". It was on a small ridge slightly further away from the other picnickers who have already settled down to enjoy a day of uninterrupted sun, the younger ones hurrying in with their throw-away bags of fast food, the older ones with their carefully packed cool-boxes, already sitting on their folding camping chairs.

"Yes, that's perfect!" says Simon. "If it gets too crowded, we can always move further in. I know loads of quiet, out of the way places where we can be more 'alone.'" He then quickly adds, a little embarrassed for fear Emma might have misinterpreted what he had said, "that's if we feel we need to."

They lay the rug out together and sit down, legs outstretched, their bodies almost touching. In front of them is the breathtaking view of London, its iconic buildings, old and new, rising from the side of the Thames, all clearly visible against the backdrop of clear blue sky in spite of a slight heat haze. With his bag between them, Simon goes through what he has bought for the day, as if to seek Emma's approval. As he had hoped, Emma seems pleased with his selection and praises him for his choice of both food and drink, though it does cross her mind he has bought a massive quantity of food. However, she doesn't say anything as she fleetingly recalls that whenever she and Robbie go off on a day-long picnic there is never any food left over, however much she has brought. But Robbie vanishes from Emma's consciousness as suddenly as he had unexpectedly (and unwelcomingly) appeared, as she makes a roll-call in her mind of all the men she has picnicked with. Whenever any of them opened up honestly about themselves – as Emma wants Simon to do today – the more they had needed to eat.

When they are settled they begin to chat freely, reprising the same relaxed way their dinner had started the previous evening, and they both delight in the ease they feel being in each other's company once again. Emma tells Simon how captivated she was by the smells of the early English summer, the lilacs and magnolias, as she walked to meet him, and Simon tells Emma about the brief exchange he had with his parents on getting home the previous night.

"And what did they say?" she asks, somewhat taken aback that Simon had already mentioned her to his parents, but surprising herself more as she realised how eager she was to know their reaction.

"They were clearly very interested," says Simon, "especially when I told them they would really like you!" Emma smiles. "With her sixth sense Ma told me if she had counted correctly, today would be the third time we will have seen each other in four days, even though," he adds hurriedly, "I never told them where I had gone on either Wednesday evening or last night.

"I then turned to Dad and told him you worked for the BBC and were Zimbabwean. He seemed to be pleased you had what he called a 'proper job' but he became *really* interested in you being Zimbabwean which was really unlike him – quite odd and out of character. What I mean is although he was initially excited when I mentioned your Zimbabwean roots, he suddenly became quite distracted, as if his mind was far away, focused on something else though he didn't say anything at all. Mum picked this up too and I could see she looked a little worried. Anyway, I then said my goodnights, left them to talk and went up to bed."

With these warm-up introductions completed, their day proper together begins. It is filled with a succession of relaxed and light-hearted moments. As anticipated, they relive and deepen their joy of simply being together, laughing and joking as they chat, eat and drink. However, these are interspersed with a series of engaging, and some intense, conversations, most introduced by Emma. As the Heath fills up they decide to move after having eaten most of their lunch, and they end their day lying out on the grass above Highgate Ponds. Between times, they travel to the Heath's highest points, cross its open ground in the full sun, marvel at its budding spring foliage and flowers and meander along its wooded shaded footpaths.

By the end of the day they are both exhausted. This is hardly surprising as they have spent a long day in the hot sun and have walked – and sometimes run – up and down some of the steepest hills on the Heath. Yet it is not only their bodies which are weary. They have also travelled deep into the recesses of each other's minds and their heads are tired too. To the end, Simon remains a willing participant, even during their most delicate and tricky interchanges. At times, he even surprises himself at how passionately he speaks about beliefs he hadn't really realised he held so strongly.

When they eventually leave the Heath, Emma has the answer to the question she had nervously posed to herself earlier that morning. As the shadows lengthen and the evening starts to draw in, she knows for certain the future of their relationship – whether it is destined to end abruptly, wither and quickly die; or whether, with the brakes be released, it will be propelled forward unimpaired. And an hour or so later, when they say their final goodbyes after darkness has fallen, Simon knows the answer too.

As they start to nibble on nuts and crisps and sip their fizzy water, Emma uses their view of London in front of them to launch into their first substantial discussion of the day.

* * *

"Isn't this an amazing sight? You get such a panoramic view of our city," she begins as she sits up alert, knees bent in front of her. "In many ways it tells a story in microcosm not only of the development of London but of our changing attitude to life.

"Can you see St Paul's straight ahead of you down there? With all the new buildings around it, it's difficult to make it out these days, "isn't it?", partly answering her own question, and pointing out into the distance. Simon nods.

"Now try to picture the scene when St Pauls was completed over three hundred years ago," she continues. "Then it was a colossal building which towered over the rest of London and the countryside beyond, symbolising both the power of the church and the importance of religion and Christian belief to the life and rhythm of the city and its inhabitants, indeed to the whole of England."

Simon glances across at Emma and he sits up himself, right next to her so their knees almost touch. It has now dawned on him that Emma is warming to something and he knows he needs to listen even more carefully to what she is saying.

"Look across to your right," says Emma. "In contrast to the elegance of St Pauls, you can see the really ugly BT Post Office Tower. For a couple of decades this utilitarian pole replaced St Pauls as the tallest building in London." Simon nods again. "To your far left," continues Emma with growing excitement in her voice, "over the hill there – look – you can just see the tops of some of the tallest buildings of the Canary Wharf complex, London's very first modern-day skyscrapers. It's odd to think they only started building them in the early 1990s, when we were born, but they were only the first wave of even taller buildings which soon changed so dramatically not merely the London skyline but London itself."

Again, Emma points, and again Simon nods. He knows there will be no stopping Emma now and he can feel her excitement being transferred to himself and goose-bumps down his back. He is loving this!

"It's significant, isn't it," Emma goes on, "that these first skyscrapers were built some distance away from the buzz of the West End, theatreland, Whitehall and Westminster. But fast forward 20 years and you see the current skyline taking shape, with its even taller skyscrapers going up here as if they had been advancing westwards like Tolkien's Ents in Middle Earth tearing apart whatever is in their path to occupy and take over the heart of traditional London."

Simon is now keen to join in and make this more than a monologue. "Yes," he says as he points and names some he knows. "In front of us, there, is the NatWest Tower. There is the Heron Tower and over there a bunch with those funny names that have stuck: the cheese-grater; the Gherkin; the Walkie-Talkie, and – now dwarfing all these – the Shard."

"Yes," continues Emma, "and even more are still going up. Already these new buildings have almost hidden St Pauls and even more are planned. Soon that once massive edifice which for centuries dominated the London skyline will have completely disappeared from view.

"And," she adds, "it's not only the physical structure of St Pauls which is disappearing. The worldview St Pauls symbolised is also vanishing. Indeed, it has practically gone already. For most people today, the caring world and respect for all human beings which Christianity boldly proclaimed have been almost completely eclipsed by the 'me-world' and the religion of the market with its lie that the more we consume the happier we will be. London's new make-believe world is symbolised by the grandeur, opulence and masculine power of these buildings."

"You are right and there is more," says Simon, warming more to Emma's new theme. "These icons of London's modernity conceal another reality of modern-day London, and England more generally: widening inequalities and a growing number of people who feel alienated by the society we are creating.

"In fact, it's even worse than this. In many ways, the wealth which has built these skyscrapers has *created* the new wave of poverty and deprivation we are witnessing." He can feel himself being carried away by what he is saying and ends with a flourish, even surprising himself as he says, "Indeed, as the skyscrapers have grown ever taller and the gap between the rich and poor have widened, you could even say the one has been caused by the other."

Emma turns to Simon with a surprised look on her face. She hadn't expected him to make such an acute observation and is clearly delighted to concur. "I really do agree with you, Simon. It worries me, and at times makes me feel angry. The skyscrapers grow in number and reach up higher and higher to encroach upon *our* lives, to push us out, and all this becomes what some journalists call the 'new normal' in *our* world."

"In many ways I agree," says Simon. "But if I'm honest I would have to admit I also find modern London exciting. I wouldn't want to live anywhere else."

"I agree," says Emma. "Even though I do get angry, at times even feel bitter, don't get me wrong, I really love London too. And if I'm honest I also get a sort of buzz looking out across at it all from here. I really like the quirkiness of the new buildings and once inside, the views from the roof tops of many of them are truly breathtaking; I've been to a couple myself. It is a great city and I consider myself fortunate to live here. I guess what I really am is sad.

"Sometimes – actually only very occasionally – I go down to the South Bank on a summer evening and have drinks outside with friends looking out over the river. I really get a kick out of mingling with so many lively people: even though I don't know them, I feel a sort of bond with them. But then I am hit by the reality of it for people like me. Even spending a couple of hours down there, going out in 'our' city burns a hole in my pocket. However much I feel I would like to be a part of 'cool' London, I realise I am not. It needs more money than I could possibly earn."

"So, you're jealous then, as well as sad, Em?" asks Simon enquiringly, and slightly provocatively.

"Like a typical modern Londoner," Emma responds, "I dream of eventually buying my own place, but even on my new BBC salary, a mortgage – just for a simple two bedroomed house in my little old East Finchley – seems like an ever-distant dream. Dynamic London is now driven by the profits of the big companies who pay these high salaries to those who can afford the flats and houses that are beyond our reach and is less and less responsive to the needs of people like me – the ordinary Londoners who grew up and live here."

There is a short silence as Emma takes stock of her first exchange of the day with Simon. She puts her hand down on top of Simon's and squeezes it. She likes what she has heard. Her instincts confirm she had been right in her initial assessment: underneath this slightly shy young man sitting beside her is someone with quite a fire inside him, a man with a very strong sense of what is right and what is wrong. This, she says to herself, is a good omen for the rest of the day.

Emma *is* passionate, and knows she has strong views about London, but her purpose in sharing her thoughts on the capital's skyline was to prepare the ground for what she really wants to discuss with Simon: not just their shared values and outlook on life but the beliefs each of them has which underpin them.

"Why don't we have some more to eat?" Emma asks Simon as she brings their first conversation to an end. She is happy with the way it has gone. From the speed with which he finished off the nuts while they were talking, she can see Simon is now pretty hungry.

"Good idea," he says, pulling his bag towards him. "Let's start with the first course proper!" Emma helps Simon take the lids off an array of dips then tears off a small portion of pita bread and scoops out some hummus, gesturing to Simon to join her. He needs little encouragement and is away. Emma picks rather than eats. Then, unnoticed by Simon, she disengages from their small talk and goes quiet as she gathers her thoughts together to launch into their second proper conversation of the day.

"Simon," she says, "we were talking just now about buildings. What interests me far more than architecture and buildings is the meaning which lies behind them. We are all builders of ourselves – we construct our own lives; we create who we are. And I want to tell you what has shaped my life. Not wanting to sound too corny, I want to talk a little about my core beliefs, what it is that drives me in what I do."

With his immediate hunger pangs subsiding and feeling far more relaxed, Simon is happy to hear more from Emma. "Go on, Em," he says. "I really want to hear what you have to say. If this doesn't sound too corny either, I am keen for you to tell me!" They both laugh.

"If you want to understand me, Simon," said Emma, "you need to know more about Ma and me. As I told you, Ma and I have always been very close – not surprisingly as we are a mini-family, there's just the two of us after all!" She lets out a short chuckle and Simon smiles.

"Ma was raised as a Catholic," continues Emma, "and her faith and religion are really important to her. They were among the very few things she could bring with her from Africa: they didn't need to fit into her tiny suitcase and they were a constant reminder to her of the home she loved and left behind."

Emma then tells Simon about how Sarah took her to Mass regularly each Sunday, how she prayed daily and often read her bible at home, explaining that as her mother's faith and religion were precious to her, Sarah had wanted to pass these on to her. Emma explained that from her early teenage years she became increasingly aware that her mother's strengths – her warm personality, her positive attitude to life, the caring way she looked out for others and the skills she had in working with the dying and their families – all flowed directly from her Christian beliefs;

they were part and parcel of her faith. The two, said Emma, were inextricably bound together.

"Why am I telling you all this about my mother, Simon?" Emma asks rhetorically. "Because I also saw faith and religion, trying to lead a good life and helping people as all being inter-linked, sort of intertwined. Like Ma, I, believed my faith really helped me to be a better person."

Emma glances over again at Simon to make sure he is still listening to her. He is, and she is pleased.

"Inevitably, I guess, as I grew older," says Emma breathing in deeply, "I came to realise all was not well with me and my religion, my Catholicism." She pulls up a long strand of grass from the ground and rolls it between her fingers as she gathers her thoughts together for what she is about to say next. "When I was young, church and the Catholic faith were a really positive experience for me. But then, as a growing and questioning teenager, I found church and the ritual of the Sunday service increasingly meaningless. I felt a growing gap between the world of religion and what I wanted to do with my life, and it was *my world* which excited me."

Emma looks at Simon, who nods affirmatively as if to say that he agrees with her and possibly to confirm that this was his experience too.

"As we all know," she continues, "these sorts of feelings about church are commonplace these days: most people in Britain today give up their religion and stop going to church when they grow up. Indeed, you could say not going to church has become a sort of cultural rite of passage for most young people today. Go to any Catholic or Anglican Church for a Sunday service these days and the benches will be filled with the old and very old. The only other people seem to be married couples with their young children; the vast majority attend either because their children already go to the local church school or they want them to in the future."

Emma looks across again at Simon. This time he is keen to chip in and says, "Yes, Em. I know. That's me exactly – join the crowd!" Then, to his astonishment, Emma responds to his quip quite differently from the way he had been expecting.

"Well," says Emma, sitting up, her body rising with the importance to her of what she is about to say. "That's just where I was different and I now want to tell you why."

Quite taken aback, Simon puts down the bread he is holding and sits up. She waits until he is still again before continuing.

"I said just now Ma's faith was very important to her, that she and I are very close and that part of the bond we have between us had its roots in Ma's faith and those beliefs. Because of this, I knew if I had turned my back on the church completely and abandoned the faith Mum nurtured within me, then I am certain this would not merely have saddened Ma deeply and created a huge gulf between us. It would have ruptured our relationship and torn us apart. And you know, Simon, I not only *couldn't* do this, I *didn't want to* do it!

"So there I was, unhappy to keep going to my church, but also unwilling to simply abandon the Catholic Church and the Christian faith because I knew the devastating effect that would have on my relationship with Ma. As I said, I felt such a move would both be cruel to Ma, and would tear us apart.

"So what did I do?" she asks rhetorically. "I began to reflect upon and try to unravel precisely what it was about my church, its ritual and the way the Christian faith is presented which put people off – put *me* off.

"Undoubtedly prompted by my desire to maintain my bond with Ma, I wanted to know what it was about Christianity which across the centuries had made it so enticing, so captivating then to those who heard it, and so boring and irrelevant to me today?

"Well, do you know what Simon? I have found, if not the complete answer – not sure you ever can do that – then at least a strong and clear enough answer to satisfy me. But before I tell you any more, I think we should tuck into more of your delicious food."

Simon digs into his bag again and brings out what he calls 'the main course'.

"It's mostly more salad-y things," he says, perplexed by her last remarks but relieved to be back again with the Emma he knows and is now ready to admit to himself he has fallen in love with. "But appropriate I thought to the heat and this amazing weather."

Emma smiles as she watches Simon place a collection of plastic covered containers in the middle of the picnic rug between them. There is a large artichoke and olive oil salad and two more substantial ones: a filling pasta, bean, celery, feta and herb, and a couscous, lentil and goat's cheese salad. Next, he produces the two smoothies: one deep green in colour, the other red, and ends by triumphantly producing from his bag paper plates, plastic forks and, with a final flourish, a pile of paper napkins.

"My God," says Emma, "this really is a feast!"

"Sunday lunch, Em," says Simon. "You told me you and your Mum always have Sunday lunch. I may not be your Mum but I am certainly up to the challenge of producing a good spread."

Together they peel off the plastic covers and laugh as Emma tells Simon to go first, but he insists she does, telling her she clearly needs more sustenance after all the talking. With her blood-sugar levels rising again, she is not only re-energised but now feels incredibly hungry. She digs in, piling a mixture of different salads onto her plate. Simon can see she is pleased with his food choices and he is delighted. Feeling relieved and the pleasure of their being together, he digs in too.

Quite soon their plates are empty and, at Emma's promptings, Simon takes more and easily finishes off all the salads. The combination of food and sun has made them both feel sleepy and Emma knows there is no way she can immediately launch back into a deep conversation – nor could Simon keep awake to listen to her, so she suggests they have a short nap.

Just as she is saying this and as Simon is putting all the dirty things back into to his bag, his hand comes into contact with the suntan cream his mother left out for them. He pulls it out and announces they need to put it on before they do anything else; as he tells Emma, his mother would kill him if he came back home burnt. Then they have fun coating themselves and each other in sunblock before they lie down on their backs side by side and hand in hand, their arms and legs nestled next to each other. In no time at all they both sink into a deep sleep.

Emma is the first to wake. She sits up and looks around. Seeing others with ice creams, she impulsively decides to buy some. Not wanting to disturb Simon, she gets up quietly and heads off to the Heath entrance where she knows the ice cream van is always parked and waits in the queue to buy each of them an ice lolly. When she returns, Simon is still fast asleep. She kneels down beside him and wakes him by touching his cheek with the ice-cold lolly. He jumps up with a scream, which Emma reciprocates.

After they finish their ices Simon says, "It's getting really crowded here, let's move to somewhere quieter." Emma replies by grabbing his hand, pulling him up and racing him down the hill to the Goodison Fountain at the bottom of Cohen's Fields. Here they pause, a little breathless, and take a long drink of the cool flowing spring water, flicking water at each other from the running tap before walking on.

They cross the tarmacked road to the next field ahead of them. Soon, behind the trees to their left, they hear noises of women bathers and laughing children enjoying themselves in the still quaintly named Kenwood Ladies Bathing Pond. The unseen swimmers and sunbathers remain hidden today, as successive generations have done before them, behind a curtain of white hawthorn blossom, early-flowering sweet-smelling orange honeysuckle and the new leaves of the trees planted round the Pond to free them from prying eyes. Simon and Emma pause to breathe in the perfumed air before walking on. As they cross the bridge by the Bird Sanctuary Pond the loud squawking of green parakeets above makes them look up and they see half a dozen of them diving and swooping around the tops of the tallest trees in the distance to their right.

Ahead of them is a gravel path which they decide to join, turning to their right as it hugs the north side of South Meadow on its way up to the top of the hill. As they climb, Emma becomes quiet and, sensing the mood change, Simon smiles across at her as if to give her the all clear: he knows she is keen to launch back into the conversation she had earlier suspended. With Emma leading again, they take to the path in front of them and, as they enter the shade of the oak trees, they feel the coolness of the air around them and their energy levels rise.

"Before we had lunch, Simon," she begins, "I was just about to tell you how I resolved the problem I had about not wanting to turn my back on and abandon the Catholic Church in spite of the growing problems I had been having about its irrelevance to my life. Well, I became a time-traveller. I tried to try understand what Christianity meant to those who first heard it and why so many people found it so appealing.

"What I discovered was that the fundamental Christian message I had unearthed resonated so strongly with me. This not only amazed me but it came as a huge relief."

Then, turning to look across at Simon, Emma says, "Like you, Simon I suspect, I had been taught that Christianity is predominantly about going to church and saying your prayers to a distant God in order to get to heaven."

Emma can see Simon nodding as she speaks, though he continues to look straight ahead and doesn't make eye contact.

"But Christianity is not about that at all," says Emma. "As I discovered, what it is *really* about, Simon, is *this* world – becoming involved and engaged in it, getting your hands dirty in it. It is about trying to make *this* world better.

"You remember, Simon, I told you how passionate I am and always have been about changing the world? Well, the Christianity I discovered is focused above all on doing just that. The acid test of whether you actually are a Christian is whether you are willing to engage with the world and its injustices and strive to help especially those who are forced to live on the margins of life."

Simon can hear the enthusiasm in Emma's voice. He warms to her excitement but the ache he had started to feel in the pit of his stomach before they had lunch returns as she says, "In short, Simon, I did not need to turn my back on Christianity after all. It was the distortions of the religion taught to me which I needed to reject. My new faith in *this* Christianity is the key driving force in my life today."

As she speaks, Emma is conscious she has made mention of neither Don Paulo nor Robbie, but she has already convinced herself this is not necessary. After all, she is telling Simon about her faith, not anyone else's, and for a good purpose: in order to encourage him to open up and talk about his beliefs. Clearly, she tells herself, to bring in anyone else at this point of their discussion would only be a distraction.

"Goodness me, Em," says Simon. "I certainly hadn't realised quite how important your faith is to you."

"There is far more I could add but I would really like to know whether what I have said resonates with you. Can you do that for me, Simon?" she asks quietly, even a little hesitantly.

"I am not sure, Em," says Simon, "how good I am going to be at articulating my own thoughts on where I am on all these deeper issues. To be frank, though I have read and reflected a lot, I don't think I have thought through everything in such a careful and considered way as you evidently have, and I certainly haven't shared my deepest thoughts with anyone else. But let me try now to respond as best I can with a few thoughts to help you to understand where I am coming from."

"You'll be fine, Simon," said Emma tapping him on his back to encourage him, "you know I'm not looking for a long treatise." Then she adds, smiling, "What are *your* thoughts, that's what I'd really like to know?"

But Simon is deeply worried and he knows full well why; it can be summed up in just four words: he is an atheist. Until Emma started to speak about her faith, he had never thought this could possibly be an issue between them; an impediment to their getting together. But now he knows that her Christian faith and belief in God are not merely important to Emma, but that they are pivotal to her. Even more troubling is that Emma seems to be hinting that sharing her faith would appear to be crucial for embarking on a serious relationship, a *sine qua non* for everything else. Indeed, from what she has just said, he senses that his telling her about his atheism could rapidly bring to an end everything which had been developing between them.

But will Emma see things simply in stark black and white terms? Will the knowledge that Simon does not believe in God, has no real interest in her Christian faith and no affinity with her Catholicism mean their relationship now has no future? Knowing Emma's need for clarity, will everything come crashing down as soon as today? The raw aching feeling he had had when they parted last night returns to churn inside Simon even though Emma is right next to him, still within touching distance.

They reach the edge of the Vale of Health Pond and, to aid Simon along, even though they have not been walking for very long, Emma suggests they pause for a while. She points to an empty bench overlooking the Pond and motions for them to sit down. Simon willingly agrees. For a moment they say nothing. They watch a group of newly-hatched ducklings swimming with their ever-vigilant mother, around the island in the middle of the Pond, far from the commotion of two Labradors jumping into the water to cool off, to the delight of a set of twins safely strapped in their double buggy. The dogs splash the twins, and they scream first in surprise, then in delight.

Simon knows he has to talk and, feeling some additional reassurance from sitting close to Emma, he now starts to tell her what she has been waiting to hear. She is about to clasp his hand to help him along, but decides not to, saying to herself he needs to do this totally on his own.

"We share so much, Emma, in terms of our views of the world and how it needs changing," he says, repeating what he has already said to try to give himself the courage to say what he knows must come next, addressing her more formally with her full name rather than the 'Em' he now always uses. She immediately notices and glances across at him.

"How-ev-er," he says, enunciating each syllable in order to try to boost his self-confidence, "there is a difference in how we arrived at this shared position, an important difference in terms of your fundamental beliefs and mine. You have eloquently described the crucial link for yourself between your worldview and your Christian faith and I must say, Emma, I have rarely, if ever, heard anyone explaining the relevance of Christianity to life in such a powerful and compelling way."

Simon then gets frightened and launches into something of a diversion from what he had been about to say, recounting a particular incident when his mother had once spoken to him about God and heaven soon after her mother, his grandmother, had died. He remembers it all so well even today, he tells her, because it was so exceptional and out of the ordinary.

"I think she spoke to me about God as part of the grieving process. I am pretty certain she prayed then, but whether for her mother or for herself I can't tell. She must have found it a comfort, a help in getting through the pain of Gran's parting.

"She never prayed with me, and neither Dad nor Ma ever suggested I should ever pray outside church," he continues. "I never felt I needed to do much more than mouth the words of the prayers I read when in church: it was all so far removed from real life – just as you seem to have said as a teenager it had become for you.

"I am telling you all this, Em, to give you the context for what I am about to say next. And it is this. From around the age of 16, certainly by the time I left school, I had come to the pretty firm view I simply did not believe in God. You see, Emma – and I am conscious of the importance of what I am saying so know I mustn't mince my words – I am an atheist."

Simon feels his mouth dry up. He swallows and continues. "I'm not just any old atheist but a strong, you might almost say, a card-carrying, atheist. I simply don't believe there is a God either out there or intervening down here to add anything to my life which I don't already have."

He has said it; it's now out in the open. Having plucked up the courage to tell Emma he is an atheist, Simon surprisingly relaxes and feels confident enough to say more. Her reaction could not have been more different. As Simon mouthed the words *I am an atheist*, Emma felt her body tense up and her tummy muscles tighten. She forces herself to carry on listening to what Simon is saying but she feels sick to her stomach and is fearful of what is now happening. She is glad she didn't clasp his hand in hers.

"While I would be among the first to acknowledge there is still a huge amount we don't know about human beings and the way we function and communicate," continues Simon, "I have never felt I needed, and still don't believe I need, God as an explanation to fill these gaps in our knowledge. The key difference between us, Emma, is pretty clear. You have found a new way of understanding Christianity and your faith clearly re-energises you. But I have continued to be a non-believer. I have remained as much an atheist today as I was when I was 16."

As Simon speaks, Emma is as still as a statue. There are no visible signs of distress – she is neither moaning nor shaking, but she is in severe shock. She can feel her world collapsing inside her and around her; she can sense her relationship with Simon is fast slipping away her from her grasp, and she is unable to retrieve it. Her body aches, telling Emma it will now never be united with Simon's. He doesn't seem to notice as he is so focused on continuing to explain his atheism to her.

Simon talks a little more and when he feels he has said enough, he turns towards Emma and moves in a little closer to her. He takes her hand and she turns instinctively towards him, and their eyes meet. He sees hers are filled with tears and they have started to flow down her puffed checks and it is only now that he realises how upset she is. He tightens his grip on her hand and senses not even the faintest of responses from her. She is clearly in pain.

It is Simon's turn to panic. He knows he has to continue talking because his declaration of atheism is by no means the end of his story: it is merely the prelude to his explaining what he really wants to tell her about his beliefs. He knows that announcing to Emma he is an atheist has really told her nothing – it was merely a statement of what he *doesn't* believe. He knows he urgently needs to tell her what he *does* believe. Though Simon has registered Emma's pain, he is now thinking about himself. He knows that if there is to be any chance of saving their relationship, he has to keep talking and she has to carry on listening.

"And this, Em," says Simon, "brings me to the faith I certainly *do* have, to the things which motivate me to have the views I do have about humanity, to what drives me to want to change my career to help those for whom life is unfulfilling or meaningless."

He looks across at Emma and waits for some response – almost any response so he knows she is listening. After a moment or two as she shifts a little in her seat and he feels her hand moving in his. "How do I," he says, "without God, get to much the same place on all this that you have arrived at, but in your case with God? Well, Emma, I think a good part of the answer lies in our actually drawing our inspiration from the very same roots."

Emma senses Simon is starting to say something of huge significance and she forces herself to listen even more carefully to what he is saying. Though she knows there is an unbridgeable gap between her faith and his atheism, she draws some comfort from Simon's assuring and confident voice.

"Before I explain to you what I mean by this," he says, "let's continue walking."

As Simon starts to get up, Emma impulsively leans over and slides her fingers through his hair, ruffling it in the reassuring way a mother does to comfort her young son as he lies on his pillow before he sleeps, though it is Emma who is grasping for grains of comfort. The instant her fingers touch his head she senses his body quivering, then feels it start to relax as her fingers busy themselves, returning his ginger head to its former order. He had hoped she would follow this clear demonstration of affection with, if not a tender kiss, then at least by sliding the back of her hand gently across his cheek, but she doesn't. Emma's ruffling of Simon's hair is a reflex response to the distress she is feeling, brute animal instinct driving her to touch him, to make contact, not unlike the kiss she found herself impulsively giving him last night. Touching him soothes her pain a little.

Feeling slightly deflated, Simon gets up and, as he does so, Emma says, "yes, let's do that." Her voice sounds strange, as if it's coming to him from a distance, almost as if it's another woman from the other side of the Pond answering his question.

They exchange a few brief words, agreeing to head back to South Meadow. Simon gestures for her to lead the way. Emma chooses the path which will take them to the Viaduct Pond, one of the less frequented parts of the Heath. When out running, she often stops at the bridge; it is a favourite spot of hers. In desperation she makes a wish.

"Please God," she groans to herself, half in hope and half in prayer. "Please help me! Please show us how to bridge the unbridgeable gap between us, between my faith and his atheism."

"The first thing I need to tell you, Em," says Simon, picking up where he had left off, "is that I recognise the huge importance religion and religious thinkers have played in helping us not only to know right from wrong but to deepen our understanding of what it is to be human. But at least since the Renaissance, or the Enlightenment as I prefer to call it, we have learned the importance of science and reason to help us answer many of life's key questions.

"I had my own 'enlightenment' as a teenager, Em, when it dawned on me one evening as I sat in my room that I didn't need a God to tell me the difference between right and wrong. Then, as I began to read more, it struck me as remarkable that religious thinkers and believers were in the vanguard of the Enlightenment. Why? Because the Enlightenment sowed the seeds of the secularist view of the world we hold today, a view which over time concluded you didn't need God to explain either how things worked, how to be good, and how to lead upright lives as human beings.

"Like many other people, I have been influenced by the lives and writing of the towering figures of our own age – people like Gandhi and Mandela. But I have also been inspired by the lives of number of Christians, such as Martin Luther King and Dietrich Bonhoeffer, as well as plenty of Catholics, many of whom seem to share your views on the importance of engaging with the world."

The word "Catholic" induces a Pavlovian response in Emma, and she pricks up her ears.

"People," says Simon, "like Helder Camara and Oscar Romero, who have been leading champions of justice. What's more, especially when he talks about the poor, the marginalised and the environment, I even find your current pope, Francis, says quite inspiring things at times.

"So, Emma," becoming a little more formal as he rounds off what he had wanted to say, "even though I no longer believe in God (I'm not sure I ever did, actually), I don't find it in the least surprising that the views you have, which are rooted in what you call a different Christianity, resonate so strongly with me."

He goes on to explain to Emma that his views have also been profoundly influenced by his experiences of knowing people on a very personal level whom society has discarded. He mentions his after-school visits to pensioners in the depths of winter without the money to heat their homes and two friends from primary school he is still in contact with who are still unemployed, one of whom took hard drugs and feels totally alienated from the world which their school told them they could expect to inhabit. It is all this, Simon tells Emma, which has led him to understand the importance of trying to live a morally good life. As he speaks, Emma can't help thinking how similar all this is to her own experiences.

"The point I am making, Em," he says, "is that my beliefs are drawn from both religious and non-religious people and thinkers. It is the mixing of their ideas with my own experiences which has given me the faith I have. While my own faith does not have any place for God, it is rooted in my strong belief in the worth and value of humanity, all human beings, and from this comes my own drive to contribute to making the world a better place. And this, dearest Emma, is the same destination you arrived at, propelled, in your case, by your faith and belief in God. So, while I am certainly an atheist, I would prefer to describe myself as a believer, indeed a pretty strong believer, not in a God, but in humanity."

As Simon rounds off what he had wanted to say about his beliefs, they reach the Viaduct Bridge and, once they are on it, Emma gestures to Simon to stop. She leans on the metal railings and, bending over, looks down at the water below them. There they see a family of coots swimming: the two adults are coaxing their six young chicks to venture out from the protection of the pond's undergrowth to the unknown world beyond. Two courageously set off but soon scurry back to the safety they know.

Emma glances across at Simon as if to coax him on to say more, but he doesn't. He just peers down and watches the coots swimming below them. As she is soon to discover, the reason Simon has stopped talking is that he is desperate to know what Emma thinks about his declaration of atheism, but even more about the way he has articulated his beliefs.

Simon turns to face her and says, "And that, Emma, brings me to the question I need to ask you and it is this. Can you explain to me why you *need* God? What 'value added' do you get from believing in God? Twisting around what Alistair Campbell once said to Tony Blair: how and why do you 'do' God?"

Emma is taken aback by the directness of his question: she had wanted Simon to continue to talk about his beliefs, not for her to be challenged by him. But she then remembers that talking about *their* deeply-held beliefs, not just *his*, was precisely the plan she had had for today. She realises she needs to explain what difference God really makes to her. But it is her turn to feel uneasy as she has never before had to try to explain all this to someone who is neither Catholic nor shares her Christian faith.

"Perhaps the easiest way in to understanding how I 'do' God," begins Emma, a little nervously, "revolves around what or who I understand God to be. As this isn't easy, let me start by saying a little about what I believe God *not* to be. That's far simpler!"

Emma explains to Simon how she has come to reject many of the images of God presented in the Bible. She says talking of God necessarily as being a "He" is simply wrong, adding that she doesn't see God as a "She" either. She says representing God as a king is for her not just off-putting but distasteful. Kings, she says, are associated with elitism and privilege on the one hand and subservience and submissiveness on the other. She says she has no interest in being part of any movement led by a king whose central mission is to try to build a kingdom – any sort of kingdom. Simon says he agrees and, warming to the theme, chips in to comment on what he was taught as a child about the world being divided up into two parts, the natural and the supernatural. He says even as a young teenager he had had a problem with there being a supposedly supernatural world with spirits – good ones, like angels, and bad ones, evil spirits – hovering around us. But immediately he regrets he may have voiced an opinion which Emma disagrees with and starts to backtrack, saying he hopes he hasn't offended her in what he has just said.

"Not at all," says Emma. "I agree with you entirely. I believe there is only one world we inhabit, not two; indeed, I would go even further. I was taught we are made up of two different bits, bodies and souls. I could never understand this split – indeed, I never wanted to. How could 'I' exist and function without my body? My body is an essential part of who I am. I am not a mix of half-bits!"

Emma stops, worried she has lost Simon, or worse that he is finding her "God-talk" vacuous and irrelevant, even if it was Simon who had asked her to talk about how she understood God. But as if he is reading her mind, Simon urges her to continue. "Go on, Em, please do!" he says. "I am finding what you are saying really fascinating."

"Okay, Simon, I will," she replies, "but only as long as you promise to stop me when you have heard enough".

"I will," says Simon. "Rest assured I will!"

They have now reached South Meadow and start looking for a place to settle overlooking Highgate Ponds. They move off the gravel path to a piece of flat ground where they intend to spend the remainder of their day together. Simon lays out the rug and they sit down close to one another.

Simon plunges his hand deep inside his bag and produces further sustenance to aid their discussions: this time two nectarines, two egg custards and the remaining water. The bottles are no longer frozen but, as Emma confirms when she takes the one Simon hands her, they are still cold. She declines the food but is eager to drink: the walking and talking have made her incredibly thirsty again. In sharp contrast, they have revived Simon's hunger and, after being given the affirming nod by Emma, he devours one of the egg custards and a nectarine. He could easily have eaten both.

"So far, Simon," says Emma as they resume their discussions, "I have told you what I think God is not. Let me now move and try to explain how I understand what or who God is. It's not easy; it's rather like trying to catch your shadow, but as you have asked, let me try – so here goes!

"Many believers say they get some sense of God by stepping back from and sensitively engaging with the world about them," says Emma. "For some this can happen when they are taken away by the beauty of a breathtaking landscape, for others when they peer through a microscope and wonder at the intricate detail of the world's tiniest creatures. It can happen when we realise how tiny we are compared with the immensity of the universe as so many of us have done when first seeing those awe-inspiring pictures of our planet taken from outer space. Likewise, people can be moved to tears – transported out of themselves – when they listen to exquisite music, stand silent in front of stupendous works of art in museums, masterpieces in art galleries, or when they read or listen to poetry. In all these instances, it is the sense you have of being uplifted out of your everyday self and your everyday world to what is beyond which believers say confirms or reconfirms that there is someone or something out there which they call God or helps them experience God.

"All this certainly resonates with me. But this is just a beginning to the way I understand God. To search for God only when you feel uplifted by a beautiful landscape or an exquisite painting is, for me, far too limiting and restrictive. The God I believe in is also to be encountered right here in the everyday and the mundane, in people and deep within each one of us. When we experience the unbounded love of another human being, when we are bowled over by the beauty of the human form, and when we feel within us the goodness, honesty, truthfulness of other people, in some ways we are also, so to speak, brushing up against God. I have not found anyone express this better than the Quakers, who say there is 'that of God' in all of us.

"Quite how to describe either how I encounter or experience God either in the world about us or deep within us is difficult, Simon, and you can see I am struggling," says Emma, knowing she is delving deep into the worlds of philosophy and theology which she would be the first to admit she knows so little about. "For me, God is not static and unmovable, but needs to be seen in a far more dynamic way. I view God as the ultimate cause and the first mover of everything. What I mean by this is captured really well by my favourite poet, Gerald Manley Hopkins, in his poem *God's Grandeur*. It starts with the line *'The world is charged with the grandeur of God,'* and that word 'charged' is for me such an evocative word, Simon: you can almost feel the dynamic movement of God at work!

"But how exactly is God at work within humanity?" Immediately, she tries to answer herself. "Well, I think the Quakers have got it absolutely right. They don't say God is in us secretly determining what we do, how we think or how we behave. No, when they say *that of* God is in us, I see this as meaning we have within us – within our grasp so to speak – those attributes of God which resonate with what it is to be human.

"Let me try to explain this a bit better, Simon." Emma gives out a nervous laugh, trying to hide the difficulties she is having expressing clearly what she believes so passionately. "We all know people whose honesty and integrity and sense of what is right sort of shine out from them in such a powerful way that their goodness seems almost as if it will rub off on us. Likewise, we use the word 'inspirational' to describe the impact that the lives of great people like Nelson Mandela have had on so many people. As Hopkins might put it, these people are participating in charging the world with God's attributes, thereby extending and deepening our sense of God's presence in the world. And in our small way, to the extent that we respond to 'that of God' within us and try to do good, and act justly ourselves, then we add to the total sum of goodness in our world.

"But there is one final element to my overall understanding of God, and in many ways, it is the more important to me," says Emma, casting a glance in Simon's direction, encouraged by seeing he is still listening. "And this concerns the difference my Christian faith makes to my understanding of God. For me, Simon, it is not sufficient to respond to 'that of God' – to join God in 'charging' the world – when I've got nothing better to do! My Christian faith demands of me far more than adding a dose of goodness to our world only when I feel like it, as you would when choosing whether to add topping on your ice-cream cone or not. I know this sounds very preachy, but my faith requires me to help make the world more human for more people. And the more this happens, the greater is the overall gain for humanity as a whole. And the greater the overall gain, the more God-like will humanity become."

Emma's voice strains and rises with emotion as she struggles to get out these last words, as they mean so much to her. She knows the difficulty she has trying to explain her faith to Simon and how poorly she thinks she has done, and she knows why: she has never had to try to make sense of her faith to an atheist, a radical non-believer. She also knows that much of what she has been saying has been echoes of what Don Paulo told her on the many occasions when she pressed him to explain to her what difference his Christian faith made to him. Emma knows her faith is deeply rooted, but she also knows much of the language she has used in explaining it to Simon has been Don Paulo's, and not hers.

She apologises. "I'm sorry, Simon, I know I haven't put this as well as I might, but then I am not a theologian. Someone trained in theology who shares my view of Christianity would explain all this far better than me."

She looks across at Simon but for a fleeting moment in her mind's eye, she sees the face of Don Paulo.

Simon has not heard anyone speak like this about God; nor has he really thought about God in this multi-dimensional way before. He knows what Emma has said doesn't alter his own views about God, but it does make him wonder. He takes another sip of his water. Emma is clearly an even more exceptional person than he has given her credit for, and the bar was already set at a pretty high level.

Emma is parched from all her talking, and she takes another gulp of her fast-disappearing water. She knows there is one final question Simon asked her which she needs to answer: how does she *do* God? As they settle again, Simon asks if she would mind his taking the last egg custard. She urges him to take the last nectarine, too, which he also rapidly devours, and Emma waits for him to finish.

"So far, Simon," says Emma picking up from where she had left off, "what I have said to you about my understanding of God has been pretty much all positives. Human beings are hard-wired to love, and most strive to be honest, kind and generous and tell the truth at least to their nearest and dearest.

"But," she says a little more gravely, "we also have within us a tendency to be selfish and dishonest, even to do harm not just to each other and to the planet, but even to ourselves. We are all capable of self-deception, concealing evil as good, even convincing ourselves we are acting altruistically when we are doing precisely the reverse.

"What's more, just as good can be catching, evil can be toxic as well, corrupting the young, infecting families, poisoning communities and blinding whole countries. Most of us have met people who have made us feel really uncomfortable and know of others who have done terrible things to their fellow human beings. My work as a journalist has forced me to at least skim through reports of horrific atrocities brought before the International Criminal Court in The Hague. Sadly, these are not exceptions, they are part of the new normal."

Emma pauses to take another drink of water, but seeing her bottle is now empty, Simon passes her his and nods in agreement, though he is a little unsure where all this is leading and what it has to do with 'doing' God. Emma seems to be taking the conversation in quite another direction.

"You may be wondering, Simon, why I am talking about all these negative and destructive forces?" Emma asks, as if she is reading his mind. "Well, the reason is that I recognise a number of them in me."

She hurries on to explain what she means. "You see, Simon, however much I would like things to be different, my thoughts and actions are not always driven by my better self. Indeed, I know myself well enough to admit I can easily deviate from the path my better self and my faith urge me to travel along, and when this happens I need to try to put myself back on track again. But even more importantly, I need to understand what makes me do and say things which, after the event, I regret having done or said. If I do understand, then in the future I will be better equipped to stop myself veering away and deviating from my chosen path.

"And the way I do this, Simon, is that every so often I take a step back from the busyness of my life to pause and take a hard, honest look inwards at myself. Sometimes I do this on the bus on the way back from work, sometimes at home before going to bed, or when I am walking to Ma's for Sunday lunch – really any time when I have a moment to be quiet."

Emma then goes on to tell Simon what she does when she takes stock of what has happened in her life. She explains that it seems to be a rather ordinary and routine exercise, as she simply goes through the events of the day, recalling whether there was anything in her behaviour she was particularly pleased about or saddened by.

"The reason I step back and look inwards," says Emma, "is not to sprinkle myself with feelings of guilt and remorse. Far from it: I don't see life as a trial. No, the purpose is to know myself better: if things have gone well, to try to understand why, and if they have not gone well, to try to think through why they have gone wrong so I am less likely to make the same mistakes again. It sounds simple, Simon, but I can tell you it's not, because it requires me to be completely and scrupulously honest with myself. And I never find that easy.

"I view my life more as a project than as a trial, a project to strive to make myself a better person, one who is more God-like. So, looking inwards at myself, Simon, is one very practical way of getting closer to my inner core to help me to become more God-like."

Emma looks across at Simon and a nervous smile sweeps across her face. She knows she has exposed a chink of vulnerability which normally lies safely hidden away behind her bubbly self-confidence.

She has finished. Emma leans back and takes a long drink from Simon's bottle. As the cool water travels down deep inside her, she is aware of a change occurring between herself and Simon: she feels she is reconnecting with him again. Whereas just then she felt she had been laying out her thoughts about God to a sceptical stranger, she now senses she has been sharing deeply personal and intimate details of herself not just to a close friend, but with her partner in an enterprise they are participating in together. In short, she is shocked to discover she no longer feels she has lost Simon or that their relationship has been irretrievably torn apart. To her surprise, she senses it has not merely survived, but is very much intact. Yet Emma is puzzled. How, she asks herself, can her struggling to explain how she 'does' God draw her more closely to Simon when he so clearly doesn't believe in either God or 'doing' God? She doesn't have to wait long for an answer.

* * *

Simon leans over, takes back his bottle then looks directly across at her and says, "My dear Emma, I have heard lots of people talk about their faith and what they understand by God, but this has to be the most moving and powerful way of putting it I have ever heard. What's more, I don't think anyone has ever explained to me what 'doing God' means to them as clearly as you have. So that is the first thing I want to say."

Simon takes hold of Emma's hand and squeezes it firmly, but she responds with an uncertain smile. She is confused inside herself: should she focus her mind on what he is about to say or go with what she is starting to feel for the man sitting next to her? She strains, aware that she needs to listen closely to every word Simon is about to utter.

"You know, Em," says Simon, eager to pick up from where she left off, "when you were recounting what God means for you – and I am sure this will surprise you coming from an atheist – so much resonated with me.

"I, too, am enraptured by the beauty of our planet and often deeply moved when listening to music or reading poetry. You mentioned Hopkins and his alluring metaphor of the world being charged by the grandeur of God, but you could have mentioned another Jesuit, the French palaeontologist Pierre Teilhard de Chardin, whose theories about the universe and the human mind growing in complexity I came across at university and found pretty convincing."

Emma looks blank, and Simon says, "that American bishop, Bishop Curry, mentioned him at Harry and Meghan's wedding."

Emma smiles to herself at the way Simon's mind is able to jump from the serious to the almost flippant with such ease. She feels goose-bumps at the back of her neck: she knows how much she loves him.

"You talk of prayer and meditation, Em," says Simon. "Well, you may be surprised to know I participated in a course on transcendental meditation when at uni and recently I've been practising mindfulness. Every so often I like to spend time alone and still in my room and I find such periods of quiet not merely satisfying but sometimes strangely fulfilling.

"I also understand exactly what you say about the weaknesses of our human nature, Em. I also sometimes feel bad about what I have done or more often about what I haven't done, and occasionally I resolve to act or think differently in future. I may have rid myself of God but I haven't shaken off feelings of guilt for my misdemeanours; indeed, I am pretty certain I never will, they are built-in parts of the human psyche. Yet there was something totally new to me in the way you described the quite structured and disciplined way you look inwards at yourself to help you understand why you do things you feel bad about afterwards. This really struck a chord with me: I thought this was something I might try doing myself. And when I do, I will certainly let you know how I get on."

Simon laughs. He senses Emma is hungry for more, though she hasn't moved a muscle. He obliges, unaware of how uncharacteristically articulate he is being and feeling ever more confident as he speaks.

"Indeed, Em," says Simon, summing up, "what repeatedly occurred to me as you were speaking was that the main difference between you and me seems to lie more in the words and the language we use to describe what we believe and what we feel rather than in there being any fundamental difference between us.

"You open yourself to the beyond, which you label God, and you reflect, pray and meditate in the presence of God, Em. I practise mindfulness and meditate, but I don't feel any need to do this in the company of anyone or anything. For me, Em, there is no one 'there' beside, beyond or inside me, but this doesn't undervalue what I am experiencing. Perhaps, then, it is more a matter of language than of substance? You use God-talk to describe what you are doing but I don't. As I see it, the main difference between us is I don't need a God to make sense of it all, to describe what I am doing or to explain what I am striving to become."

Then, turning directly to Emma, Simon says, more slowly now, "So this leaves me with a final question to you, Em, and it is this. Does it really matter that you call yourself Christian or a Catholic and I call myself some sort of atheist? Having heard you speak, I am far less certain than I was that it really matters how we label ourselves and what the precise language is we use."

As Simon says all this, Emma can feel herself warming once again not just to Simon's words, but to him. At breakfast, she had drawn her red line, telling herself she and Simon could not be together if there was no clear resonance, no common ground between their beliefs. An hour or so ago, she had come to the firm view that there was no common ground between them; their relationship had definitively hit the buffers. But now, notwithstanding Simon's unwavering declaration as an atheist, Emma is convinced there is sufficient resonance for them to have a future together. Emma, the believer, could be in a relationship with Simon, the atheist. The unbridgeable gap between them and their beliefs could, it seems, be bridged after all. Stepping back from the roller-coaster ride she has been on, Emma is surprised how easy it has been for her to arrive at this destination.

"Oh, Simon," she says, "I love to listen to you as your mind races, and it certainly seems to be working in top gear now! What you say about language and labels contains some important truths. However, being a Christian and believing in God are really important parts of who I am, of my identity, so for me talking to you today, it does make a difference. But you are right, there is plenty still to talk about, and labels and language are certainly a central part of that discussion. I am also excited to learn more about your experiences with mindfulness and meditation. I never realised you had done that, indeed, that you are still doing it – though why should I given how recently we have met?"

"Well, all in good time," says Simon, "but not today, as it is already getting quite late. But before we finish I need to dip into my bag one final time."

He brings out two large chocolate brownies, reminding Emma that she has told him she loves chocolate though she feels guilty about this and so severely rations her intake.

"I know you ate chocolate last night, Em, but today is the start of a new week. So, unless you had chocolate for breakfast, you don't have to feel guilty."

Emma can't resist, and as Simon holds a brownie up in front of her she momentarily touches his hand before taking it and nibbling her way through it. As they both finish, she gestures to Simon to speak, seeing he is keen to tell Emma one more thing about himself.

"Although I *am* an atheist, Em," he says, "I don't really like to *call* myself an atheist. This is because the atheism label has been hijacked by Richard Dawkins and I part company with him in what he says about faith and religions. He seems unwilling to accept there are *any* people who can hold religious views and believe in God and who can also have a genuine and passionate interest in this world and strive to make it a better place, like you, Em."

"I can see your problem, Simon," retorts Emma, "as I have similar difficulties when I try to come up with a word to accurately describe who I am." She laughs her old carefree laugh, no longer feeling she has to carefully weigh every word before she speaks. Emma has almost become her old self again.

"In many ways," she continues, "I would like to continue to call myself a Catholic because there is nothing in what I believe which has not been laid out by Catholic writers, even though they are not considered mainstream. So, fear not, dear Simon, I am not the unique person you may have thought me to be!

"My trouble is that mainstream Catholicism perceives itself as still monolithic: you are either a Catholic who toes the party line or you are not a Catholic; you are either in or you are out. If you can't accept the whole package then they will label you either a lapsed Catholic, or worse, a heretic.

"So, what would I call myself?" Emma is half asking herself and half Simon. "Frankly, Simon, I don't know! Ma sees me as a Catholic and so, in many ways, do I, so I am happy to call myself Catholic. As you say, it's all very much a question of labels really, isn't it?"

She smiles across to Simon, leans over and touches him briefly on the nose with the tip of her finger then pulls away as she says, "The problem – as it often is with belief and religion – does not lie with us, Simon. It resides in other people."

They both chuckle, though it is a weary laugh as neither of them has fully recovered from the intensity of their day of emotionally draining exchanges. They know it's time to intellectually disengage. Then, at almost the same time, they both feel the first waft of cooler air slicing through the exceptional heat of the late spring day. Emma glances at her phone and is shocked.

"My God," she says, looking about her, "I have lost all sense of time; it's already gone past 7:30."

She points to shadows starting to appear around them on the grass. They both know it's time to leave.

"Today has been quite a day for both of us, hasn't it Simon?" says Emma as they both start to stand up. "It has certainly had its difficult and troubling moments, but it's also had its tender moments. But above all, Simon, today had to happen. It has been so important to me, but now we need to get going before the evening chill sets in properly. Shall we start heading back?"

"Yes, Em," says Simon dreamily, still trying to make sense of it all. "It has been a remarkable day. I will never forget it."

They gather up their things then start to wend their way back towards the entrance where they had met up at the start of their day. It seems such a long time ago. As they set off they are aware of how empty and quiet the

Heath has become. Soon, they begin to notice – and Emma comments on – the Heath's newly-arrived invaders: dogs of all shapes and sizes, looking fresh as they run across the fields in spite of the day's heat, followed by their minders, poo-bags at the ready.

Simon suggests she walk backs with him to his car, offering to drop her back at her flat. Without thinking twice, she readily agrees, prompted more by the thought of not having to make the long trudge home than by the prospect of spending a little more time with Simon. She is so tired even her usually over-active planning genes seem to have shut down.

Almost immediately, they loosely link hands, every so often swinging them back and forth as if to urge their heavy legs on. They walk in almost total silence, each keen to try to make sense of what has happened over the course of the day and what it will mean for the future. They are aided by the musty smells which are beginning to rise up from the dampening ground of the Heath in twilight and which the dogs' more sensitive noses have already caught.

* * *

Before it had begun, Simon had few expectations for the day ahead other than his yearning to be with Emma. Two days ago, he knew she was already captivating him. Now he was even more certain he was deeply in love with her. But if he was honest with himself – and Emma had taught him something about that today – he would have to admit to being a bundle of mixed emotions.

One thing which surprised Simon about the day was the pleasure their conversations had turned out to have given him. He had known Emma had wanted to 'dig deep' and he had feared having to answer her challenging questions about himself. In any event, their more intense discussions had gone far more smoothly than he expected. He reckoned he had handled her questions about his beliefs pretty well and had not felt nearly as uncomfortable as he thought he would when talking about his own faith. He hadn't known how pivotal her Christian faith was to her and was surprised how troubled she had been when he told her he was an atheist. But it was only when he had seen her tears that he had realised how deeply upset she had been and he now chided himself for what was clearly such a cold and inadequate response to her extreme distress. In the end, however, he felt she had not merely accepted where he was coming from but, in a way he didn't fully understand, he thought the outcome of their interchange was to have brought them closer together.

For his part, Simon's assessment was that their beliefs were not all that different. Indeed, it struck him that they could quite easily practise mindfulness together with neither of them thinking they were in any way compromising their own beliefs. He thought it might be an idea to suggest they try this soon. He wondered what made him suddenly think that the differences between what they believed were more to do with language and labels than anything fundamental; but, looking back on it now, he believed that really was true.

So as Simon walked on, he felt even more at one with Emma and tightened his grip on her hand as if to seal his positive thoughts, but she didn't seem to notice as he sensed no response. Perhaps it was this which prompted him to start having doubts again about the future of their relationship. Although she had appeared to be accepting of his atheism, she had also made it clear that she remained strictly wedded to her belief in God and her Christian faith. He then realised it was he who had said the difference between them lay more in the labels they gave to their beliefs than to anything more substantial. He had thought she had agreed with him, but had she? He tried to recall precisely how that bit of their conversation had gone, but he couldn't. It struck him that she had never made her position clear. If so, could this have been deliberate?

Simon broke into a cold sweat. He was terrified he was going to lose Emma and this only made him more distressed. While she had certainly been affectionate towards him during their day, she had never made any mention of love; nor, come to think of it, had she last night when she had kissed him. What did she really feel about him? He realised he didn't know. But then he hadn't actually told her what his feelings for her were, had he? Were these warm thoughts of his mere fantasies and desperate hopes? Why hadn't he been totally honest with Emma?

Simon now saw their time together as some sort of test, a test which had been set up and conducted by Emma. Initially this didn't trouble him as he told himself how much he had really enjoyed their day together on the Heath. But then he thought that if today had been some sort of test, what was the outcome? Had he passed? If he had, how would he know, and would there be more tests to come? His head and his heart were both aching.

Emma's musings travelled along quite different pathways. Before today and deep down, she knew she was falling in love with him. Today not only confirmed this but it brought it all far closer to the surface. But her growing love for Simon – with his tall thin body, his deep blue eyes and his dreamy air – had not been the main focus of the day. Today was all about resolving the more pressing question of whether Simon could be her soulmate. The answer seemed to change as the day proceeded, as Emma's determination to have a clear-cut response veered from one extreme to another.

Their initial discussion of the London skyline had excited Emma far more than she thought it would. It led her to believe far more clearly than she could have hoped that they really did share a passion for trying to make the world a better, more humane place. But when he announced he was a card-carrying atheist, she knew they were poles apart on the thing which mattered most to her. She shuddered as she recalled that part of the day.

But as they had talked more, she had begun to realise how wrong her initial reaction had been: her emotional distress had clouded her judgement. As she had struggled to try to explain how she understood God and he told her how much of what she said resonated with him, it began to dawn on her that there might be common ground between them after all. Then, when he went on to tell her that his beliefs were shaped in part by Christian writers and thinkers, that he was inspired by some of the same Catholic priests and activists as she was and that he practised mindfulness, she knew she was crossing her Rubicon.

But what had really struck a chord with her were Simon's final comments about their seemingly diametrically opposed views on God and atheism being due less to any disagreement about the fundamentals, which they discovered they so evidently shared, but more to do with the language used to describe their respective beliefs. Though Emma told herself she would need to reflect far more about the language and labels we use to describe what we mean by God, belief and atheism, for now she thought he might be right. She felt excited at the prospect of their embarking on such a search together.

So where did all this leave Emma? Had the day answered the questions which, sitting at breakfast, she had been so desperate to have answered? Though she had not expected the day to end with such certainty, and she found her assessment a little surprising, her feeling now, as they walked together, hand in hand, across the Heath was that Simon pretty much did tick all her boxes. At least enough boxes had been ticked to enable her to banish from her mind the terrifying thought she had had halfway through the day: that their relationship had no future and they would have to go their separate ways. Indeed, it was more than ticking boxes. Emma felt quite attracted by a number of Simon's ideas about faith and belief. Yes, she said to herself, not only could this work, I really think it *will* work, and work extremely well.

But this firm, even if still preliminary, answer only added to the underlying turmoil which she had tried to keep well below the surface over the course of the day. Deep down, one part of Emma had rather hoped the day would turn out differently. In some ways, it would have been far simpler if she had been able to end the day firm in the view that she and Simon could never be soulmates. Then her future would be clearer. She would wrench herself away from Simon and return to Robbie, initially upset and hurt but not wounded and scarred, comforted in the knowledge she could continue living with him, the man who before this week she believed would never – could never – be replaced. But this was not at all the way she felt now.

So today had made Emma's life even more difficult than it had been when she had woken up. Then she had one love and one soulmate. Now she seemed to have two. It certainly looked as though Simon was here to stay, but she knew she now faced a massive problem as Robbie had not departed, either from her feelings or from her life. But she told herself she would postpone embarking on that journey, traumatic and necessary though she knew it would be. Today was Simon's day, and she wanted simply to wallow in the pleasure of the decision she knew in her bones she had just made. At least one part of her felt as if she had been set free.

As they reached the car, Simon and Emma extracted themselves from their inner worlds and re-engaged. From the time they had left the grass overlooking Highgate Ponds to the time they drew up outside Emma's flat, they simply talked light-heartedly and inconsequentially. They both felt they had had their fill of deeper conversation. Neither of them said a serious word about the day, their relationship or what they were now feeling about each other.

It was close to 10 pm when they finally decided to part. They were both extremely tired and, as each knew they needed to sleep to be ready for the working week ahead, they were keen to keep their parting brief. Before their final goodbyes, they had readily agreed to see each other again in the week ahead.

"Soon," said Emma.

"On Wednesday or before," said Simon, and they agreed, laughing.

Their parting told them what they had not had words to express. Emma opened the car door, then leaned over and kissed Simon firmly on his lips as her left hand found, clasped and held on to his right hand. Then, putting her right hand round the back of Simon's head, she drew closer and kissed him more intensely. Simon responded in kind as he, in turn, gently stroked her hair. For some moments, they remained locked together, feeling the stresses and strains, the rejections and the comings together, the doubts and the certainties of the day draining out from them. They didn't need language or labels to tell them what they both knew.

When they separated, Emma gently rubbed the stubble on Simon's cheeks with the back of her right hand, looked deep into his eyes and smiled, and then gave him a brief final kiss before she stepped out of the car.

As Emma left, Simon could feel a sense of calm and reassurance flooding deep into his veins. This was not merely the relief of being kissed by the woman he loved. Their kiss confirmed to him their relationship was destined to continue. If today's discussions had been a test, in kissing Simon lovingly the way she had, Emma was telling him he had passed. If there were more tests to come, he knew he would be up to them, though he sensed there wouldn't be.

Reaching her front door, Emma turned back and waved. Simon had watched her every move and waved back, waiting till she had closed the door of her flat before he restarted the engine and drove off. Well on his way back to Muswell Hill, he cursed himself for not looking more carefully at the outside of Emma's flat which he had told himself earlier he wanted to examine more closely. He had been too absorbed in watching her disappear. As he had predicted, he felt an aching pain enter his tired body as Emma left him which grew more intense as he started his engine and drove away. By the time he parked the family car, though he felt lonely he also had an incredible feeling of freedom.

They knew this week and this day had been pivotal to their future. Their individual reflections walking back to the car, their final words before they parted and their goodbye embrace had laid the ground for the future. This they each hoped and both now felt would bring not only themselves but also their families closer together – though this, too, remained a matter they had still to discuss. What neither of them then knew was how close their families had already been drawn together. There was so much more they were to discover over the coming months – and a lot of it would turn out to be deeply, deeply upsetting.

The Journey Out and The Summer's Couplings and Uncouplings

Simon shook Emma's shoulder a little more vigorously this time. He had tried to wake her a few moments earlier but she had remained in a deep sleep, her mouth half-open, her head lying across him and her chest rising and falling as she breathed deeply, in…out, in…out, in…out. This time she stirred, though it took her a while to wake and a good deal longer to realise where she was. As she opened her eyes, she peered out of the window beyond Simon. All she could see was blue sky, a more vivid blue than she ever remembered having seen before.

"Africa," she said, smiling with delight.

"Yes," said Simon "we should reach Lusaka in just under an hour. They have already switched on the fasten seatbelt signs and told us to raise the window blinds in preparation for landing. I saved a glass of water for you, Em, they just brought it round. Here, take a drink, it's ice-cold. How are you feeling?"

"Thanks, Simon," said Emma as she pulled away from him, lowered the arm rest between them and began to straighten up her clothes just as the cabin attendant asked her to pull back her blanket to show him her seatbelt was fastened for landing. She drank all the water in one gulp; it was cool and refreshing, as he had said.

It was just after 2 pm on a Monday in mid-September. Simon and Emma had left London the previous evening and were heading for Zimbabwe – together, just the two of them. After this brief stopover in Zambia, Zimbabwe's northern neighbour, they would soon reach their ultimate destination, Harare. They were due to land in the late afternoon after 18 hours in the air.

They had decided to travel to Zimbabwe on Emirates as it was the cheapest flight they could find, but it meant having to change planes in the middle of the night, London time. A few hours after leaving Gatwick, they landed to a clear Dubai dawn which they scarcely noticed as they were ushered bleary-eyed into the airport's newest terminal. This only added to the surreal feeling they had on entering this vast space-age building, pristinely clean to almost hospital-like standards, with its dustless marble floors, its sweeping walkways, its complex web of escalators and the see-through lifts housed below its massive arched glass roof.

Still half asleep, Simon and Emma and their fellow travellers were shuttled efficiently through state-of-the-art security machines by teams of well-trained and impeccably-dressed staff, all migrant workers, and then ushered on by another team towards and into an eerily silent automated people-mover which whisked them on to another terminal. There they found themselves in what looked more like a high-end shopping mall than an airport concourse, the aisles filled with designer-label shops overflowing with the latest luxury goods and technological gadgets, smart restaurants, food shops and branded fast-food outlets. In spite of its being so early in the morning, the place was alive with shoppers alert and hungry to spend.

Dehydrated from the combined effects of their first flight and the free wine served with their dinner, Simon and Emma were on the lookout for only one thing: a cheap cool drink. But they couldn't find even a small bottle of water or a simple tea or coffee priced at less than $5, so they set off in search of a drinking-water fountain. They eventually tracked one down hidden away off the main thoroughfares, and both drank deeply from the trickling tap.

With the risen sun now bright in the Dubai sky, they boarded the plane which would take them to Harare. As it was still only two o'clock in the morning London time, they were both fast asleep before it took off, and slept through breakfast. A few hours later, they were woken by the smell of lunch, which they ate ravenously as the captain announced they were passing over the Kenya-Tanzania border. They gazed down eagerly from their window, keen to have their first sight of Africa, but at 40,000 feet and with thick clouds, they were disappointed not to be able to see the land below them.

"I was really hungry for that lunch they gave us an hour or so ago," said Emma. "Since then, I have been in and out of a succession of really deep sleeps. When I woke just now, I had no idea where I was."

Simon said he had dozed and flicked through the different music channels until he discovered the Paul Simon and Ladysmith Black Mambazo's tape of *Graceland*, which he listened to in his earphones at top volume from start to finish, telling Emma how well it had got him into an African mood.

As she put her phone away, Emma pulled Simon's arm towards her to look at his watch and said, "It looks like we will land in Lusaka on time at two thirty."

She was fully awake now and slid easily back into planning mode. "With luck we should only have to sit on the tarmac here for an hour or so before taking off again so should land in Harare just after five. Can you believe it, Simon, we will be in Zimbabwe in a couple of hours? It's so close now.

"How am I feeling?" she then asked, remembering Simon's earlier question. "*Really* excited. I have to pinch myself to make sure I'm not dreaming!" She laughed and leant over to give Simon a peck on his cheek. "I can't believe we are sitting on this plane together on our way to Zim," she added. "It's going to be such an amazing experience, a huge adventure,

I just know it is. I don't think I have felt as excited as this since I was in primary school!"

Simon returned one of his earphones to his left ear and put the other one into Emma's right ear as he started playing the *Graceland* tape again. They listened hand in hand as the plane circled before straightening up to land at Kenneth Kaunda International Airport. Emma started to tap her toes gently on Simon's shoeless feet in time to the music as the tape played *She's got diamonds on the soles of her shoes.* Ta-na na-na-na, ta-na na-na-na, ta-na na-na-na, ta-na na-na-na ... ... Bump! They had landed on African soil.

* * *

So much had happened that summer. The chance encounter which led to that intense, emotionally-charged and at times almost surreal week in late May set Emma and Simon firmly on their path together. Once Emma's compulsive, desperate and almost manic need to know whether she could commit herself to Simon had been resolved – in a relationship which had been as unexpected as it has been unforeseen – life began to settle down to a more normal and familiar pattern. As May turned to June and June to July, they saw each other regularly, spending many evenings and, when they were able, the occasional day together. As they both had hoped – and as Emma had almost willed it to happen – their feelings for each other grew, their relationship blossomed and they both became more certain their futures lay with each other. Not only did they become more physically close, but they became more intimate intellectually as they continued to chew over their deepest beliefs, repeatedly surprising themselves as they discovered new areas of common ground between Simon's approach to atheism and Emma's brand of Christianity. If Emma had had any lingering doubts about Simon as a soulmate after their day together on Hampstead Heath, by mid-summer she seemed to have tossed her concerns and worries deep into the long grass.

However, things did not go as smoothly as either of them had hoped they would. Their attempts to spend time together were continually aborted by their ever-growing work commitments which, as the weeks went by, repeatedly encroached into their private space. At times, work prevented them from firming up the next time they would see each other or meant they had to cancel plans they had already made. While this frustrated them both, it did have one very positive outcome: it massively increased their desire to simply get away so they could be together undisturbed. This in turn spurred them to act on an idea whose seed was sown during that first tumultuous week –to visit Zimbabwe together. As they talked about it, they grew ever keener to revisit the country where they had each been born and to learn more about their pasts which, until very recently, neither of them had had much interest in doing, convincing themselves this would deepen their understanding of each other.

By the end of June, they had taken the decision to travel out to Zimbabwe and by the end of July, they had both arranged time off work and booked their September flights to Harare. And by the end of August, they had discovered one more thing they had in common: they were both closet romantics. As they started to plan the details of their trip, they began to see it as their first real opportunity to weave themselves back inside that magical first week which had brought them together, a time and place they both yearned to re-enter and explore further.

Of course, there was one matter which – one person who – hovered ominously over Emma's decision to embark on a relationship with Simon, and that was Robbie. As she acknowledged to herself both on the morning before and the morning after the day's events on Hampstead Heath, uncoupling from Robbie was going to be a momentously difficult, long and painful process. And so it had proved to be. In spite of her growing love for Simon, Emma could not find within herself the strength or the courage to simply walk away from Robbie. In her head, she knew her relationship with Robbie had to come to an end, but, try as she might, she found it well-nigh impossible to disengage herself from him.

As a result, her efforts to resolve the conflicts in her love life were messy. It had taken her far longer to bring up the subject of Simon with Robbie than it should have, and when she eventually did, she knew she had handled it badly. When, a while later, they spoke about their own relationship, it was Robbie rather than Emma who ended up proposing the course of action they should take. And, in many ways, this only made matters worse as Robbie's evident courage in being able to work through his own pain and anger and propose a workable way forward for them only endeared him to Emma all the more. By the time she and Simon left for Zimbabwe, although Robbie was fully aware of Simon and Simon knew a lot about Robbie, there was plenty about her past relationship with Robbie and her ever-deepening relationship with Simon which Emma knew she had to, but still hadn't, revealed.

Emma had had far greater success in her wider efforts at coupling. Soon after the whirlwind of the first week of their relationship, Simon met Sarah then Emma met Simon's parents and they all got to know each other more as the weeks went by. However, before they left for Zimbabwe, Emma had still not arranged for Sarah to meet Simon's parents.

In mid-June, Emma slid comfortably into her job at the BBC. Her new colleagues could not have been more welcoming and, as always happened with Emma, she was well-liked almost from day one. Her new boss, Rosemary, had set up a structured and rigorous induction programme, then an equally taxing training schedule. Emma was sent on elocution and TV presentation courses, which she found professionally beneficial as well as enjoyable. When not away on courses, of which there were many, Emma began shadowing three of the older hands on the current affairs team. Initially she watched and absorbed, then she began working alongside them and every so often she started to step into their shoes completely. Her initial reviews and performance assessments were uniformly positive.

Though life was always hectic and often chaotic, Emma loved the work even if she increasingly recognised how difficult it is to navigate one's way through the fog of spin, misinformation and outright deception and retain one's integrity as a current affairs journalist. Though it required a mix of courage and tenacity to combat bullying and sometimes intimidation, she was not deterred by any of this. Indeed, she relished the challenge and fought with a mixture of charm and dogged determination, to the growing admiration of many of the senior members of the unit.

In a comparatively short time, Rosemary had almost become a friend, though she was always scrupulously careful not to let her positive feelings for Emma influence the management of the young woman whom she believed, with the right guidance, would become a huge asset to the team and to the BBC. Her first big break occurred in mid-July. After some delicate discussions, London's mayor had agreed to give a live interview to BBC London TV news on the difficulties he was facing in extending the all-night tube service across the capital. As the two senior presenters were on annual leave, Rosemary asked Emma to do the interview. Her performance was scrutinised carefully by the team and she received overwhelmingly positive feedback when she got back to the office. Even the Mayor of London had wanted to know more about this new interviewer the BBC had recruited.

It was just after this interview that Emma approached Rosemary to ask if she could have two weeks off in September to make a trip to Zimbabwe. Rosemary was fascinated to hear about Emma's Zimbabwean origins and gently prodded to see if Emma might be interested in doing some media work while she was there, saying she could easily ask the BBC's reporters and main stringers to make contact with her when she was out there. But Emma immediately felt uneasy: she wanted the visit to remain what she had increasingly dreamed it would be, very special but private. What she told Rosemary was she would love to have the e-mail addresses and phone numbers of her contacts but would prefer to make contact herself as her schedule was already over-full, but she would get in touch if she could. Emma was pretty sure Rosemary had understood what had been left unsaid.

A few days later, in early August and scarcely six weeks after she started at the BBC, Rosemary called Emma in to share some preliminary thoughts she and senior colleagues had been having about a series of TV programmes about British values in modern-day, multi-cultural Britain.

Rosemary rarely showed her feelings, but her voice was unable to disguise her excitement.

"Quite by chance," she began, "I saw David Attenborough in the staff canteen and he invited me to join him for a quick, informal lunch, just the two of us. He asked me about our new unit and when I explained its brief was in part to do more challenging things using different approaches, he told me how in the late 1960s, as the new controller of BBC2, he came to commission Kenneth Clarke to present that pioneering 13 part series called *Civilisation.*"

Glancing across at Emma and seeing neither the words 'Kenneth Clarke' nor '*Civilisation*' triggered any visible response from her, Rosemary explained that the programmes provided a sweeping history of the best of western art, architecture and philosophy.

"Commissioning that series was an extremely controversial decision at the time," continued Rosemary, "but it proved to be the right one as *Civilisation* was hugely influential not only in Britain but abroad too; it was bought by more than 50 TV companies. Anyway, the idea emerged over our lunch of developing a TV series which would provide a sweeping view not of art through the ages but of contemporary Britain which would profile and discuss the essence of what being British is today and the things which make the country great in our age. Given the growing polarisation of views on these issues, it would be a hugely controversial decision for the BBC to work on and eventually commission such a series, and, like Attenborough's *Civilisation*, its success would likely turn not only on the preparatory research undertaken but, crucially, on who is chosen to present it."

Rosemary ended with a flourish. "Although it's all very sketchy at the moment," she said, "the more I think about it, the more excited I'm becoming about the whole idea."

As Rosemary had rightly surmised, Emma didn't know much about the original series, though she had seen mention, and watched odd snippets, of the more recent and far less ambitious programmes called *Civilisations*. So Rosemary pulled from her top drawer the box set of the original series and gave it to Emma, encouraging her to think through how a series on British values, possibly with a similar sort of format, might work for today's television and audiences. Emma was duly flattered to have been asked for her input, and it crossed her mind then how closely the proposed series resonated with her passion to make Britain a more caring, inclusive and united country. After all, this was, in many ways, why she had decided to become a journalist.

Emma dutifully made her way through the box-set, but it didn't make much of an impact on her. Indeed, though she learned a lot about art, churches and cathedrals, Emma found Clarke's supercilious manner not merely distasteful but off-putting: in the way he spoke, he seemed to be projecting values she disdained rather than wished to emulate. It wasn't until after she came back from Zimbabwe that the idea of working on a series of programmes on contemporary British values took hold of Emma and well into the New Year before Rosemary's initiative came to take over her life.

Even without the time she needed to spend on Rosemary's new programming ideas, trying to keep up to speed in her new job was already taking a heavy toll on Emma's personal life. She knew almost as soon as she started that she would need to spend even more hours than in the past trawling the internet to ensure she kept abreast of all the day's main news stories. But it then began to dawn on her that many seemingly parochial domestic news stories could not really be understood without reference to events happening in the wider world. This meant her having to set aside huge chunks of additional time doing in-depth research of what lay behind major news stories in Britain's increasingly complex and interconnected world.

At one level, Emma fully accepted her personal life would have to bear the cost of her growing workload. But this meant she was forced to spend far less "quality" time with Simon than she yearned to and to devote far less time than she knew she needed in trying to sort out her relationship with Robbie. If she was honest, her failure to confront what she was feeling and thinking about Robbie made her feel far guiltier than the lack of time she was able to spend with Simon.

The time Simon had to devote to work also increased substantially over the summer. This was driven partly by the growing volume of work Falkland, Fairbridge and Hayes was succeeding in attracting. They initially tried to manage this by increasing the workload of all but the most senior staff, which meant Simon was forced to work longer hours. It was not until well into August that the partners agreed to increase staff numbers, but the recruitment process was slow and none had joined before Simon left for Zimbabwe.

There was, however, another reason why Simon worked even longer hours before they left for Zimbabwe. Telling Emma he had been toying with the idea of making a major career change acted as the catalyst he needed to push him into doing something about it: in the week after they met, Simon told Emma he had made the decision to abandon his career as an accountant.

Perversely, however, the exit path he chose required him to work even harder. At the start of the summer, Simon was two exams and two years away from being a certified accountant. But, in large part because of the impact he knew his decision would have on his father, he decided to leave the world of accountancy only after he was fully qualified. So, he decided to write his exams within a single year and, as he knew it would, this meant he had to spend far more time at his books over the summer months: in the early morning before work, in the evenings after work and over the course of many weekends.

As a result of these twin workload pressures, and for the first time in his life, Simon played no cricket in June, July or August. He spent far less time with Emma than he hungered to, though, as he was so absorbed in his work and they were soon to go off on holiday together, he found this easier to manage than he had thought it would be.

Deciding he wanted to leave accountancy and enter one of the caring professions was the easy part. Deciding precisely what new career path to follow proved a far greater challenge. Unlike Emma, Simon wasn't a natural planner so he benefited greatly from chewing over possible options with her whenever he could. By the time they boarded their plane to Harare he had decided becoming a medical doctor was the best first step towards pursuing a more specialised career in mental health. It had two advantages. The first was he could postpone applying for a place in medical school for the following year's intake until they returned from Zimbabwe. The second was that he could therefore delay telling his father he would be abandoning the world of accountancy – the first in the family to do so for at least four generations.

When Simon set his mind on something, he invariably achieved it. And so it was this time. At the end of August, he heard he had passed his advanced level exams: as he had hoped, his summer of intense study had paid off. As he busied himself with the practicalities of their upcoming holiday, he could now focus all his energies on Emma. As he did so, he started to regret how much of the summer he had wasted; how often he had forcibly suppressed the promptings of his aching heart.

One Saturday in early June, Emma had arranged to pop in for a quick lunch with her mother the day before she usually came for her regular weekly visit. She had phoned a few days earlier to say she was free and asked if it would be okay if she brought over a Zimbabwean friend she had bumped into quite by chance a week or so ago. Her mother said little except that that would be great and she was looking forward to it. Emma said she would bring the lunch as she knew that otherwise Ma would panic and she needed her to focus on Simon and not on the meal and its preparation.

When Emma opened the door and saw Simon standing there, to the surprise of both of them, Sarah immediately welcomed him into the flat with such warmth it seemed as if she had always known him. Almost before they had stepped into the hallway and at a cracking pace she started to fire a succession of questions at Simon, about himself, his family, his Zimbabwean links and how he and Emma had met. Emma had expected Ma's face to express some astonishment on first seeing Simon – she hadn't even said her Zimbabwean friend was a man. As Ma didn't show any surprise, Emma was led to conclude her sixth sense had already been at work.

Well before today's first meeting with Simon, Sarah must already have picked up something significant was happening in Emma's life – just as she had known plenty about her relationship with Robbie well before Emma had first told her about it. Blissfully unaware of all this, Simon responded in kind to Sarah's immediate and positive welcome, not least as Emma had told Simon to be ready for Ma to show surprise, possibly even some shock, on first seeing him. She had told Simon that Sarah would probably be initially a bit lost for words, but he needed to see beyond these embarrassing, possibly tense, first few moments to the warm-hearted person she was. Emma could not have been more wrong.

As the questions started to fly, it struck Simon that Sarah's directness was so like Emma, just as over lunch as the conversation grew he relaxed as he began to see Emma in Sarah's warm and engaging personality. He liked what he saw, sensing not merely that developing a solid relationship with Sarah was going to be far less difficult than he had feared, but their relationship could – indeed would – become genuinely warm. As Emma became aware of the dynamic between them she was delighted, though she was also a little puzzled just how well it was all going. Too good to be true?

Of all the questions Sarah asked Simon, she seemed most interested in the coincidence of their bumping into each other on that Monday morning at Graham's. She kept coming back to that initial encounter and must have asked Simon to tell her all about almost half a dozen times. As Sarah did so, Emma grew ever more conscious she had never mentioned this first meeting to her mother, even though she had had many opportunities to do so.

She now felt she had been wrong to have said absolutely nothing to Sarah of the incident the very first evening when Emma had come round to recount what had happened that day. After all, Sarah was the reason Emma had gone to Graham's in the first place. Equally, Emma knew why she had deliberately not mentioned Simon in the days and weeks which followed. If she had, she knew not only that she would have had to explain how and why she and Simon had subsequently met up but that she would not have been able to avoid starting to tell Ma about her strong and growing feelings for Simon. This she had not then been ready to do.

After lunch, Emma was in for one more surprise. When Simon had finished answering her question about their first meeting for the umpteenth time, Ma turned to her daughter and spoke to her as forcefully as Emma had ever heard her speak.

"Emma, my dear," said Sarah, "this is a sign. It is a sign you really do need to go out to Zimbabwe. It's funny, isn't it, that only in the last few months I have been telling you that you needed to go back to where you were born, to return to the village where your life began and meet up with all your close relatives – my brother and sister, their children and all the rest of our extended family."

"Yes," chipped in Simon, "Emma mentioned that to me as well."

"Well, my dears," continued Sarah, "what I have heard today makes me even more certain the time *has* come for you to go."

Then, turning to Simon, Sarah said to him directly and earnestly, "And you *will* go soon, isn't it? It will be good for you to go together too: you can relearn about the country of your birth together."

As she spoke, Simon was immediately struck by the intensity of Sarah's demanding question; it was not unlike the way Emma had almost interrogated Simon about his beliefs on Hampstead Heath. It clearly overrode any worries a mother might have about her daughter going off alone with someone she had only just met. But it was Emma who interjected.

"Well, Ma," she said, "we have actually spoken about it a bit and we are both pretty keen to go, but I am not sure when it is going to be possible to find the time, what with my new job and Simon's need to study for his big exams."

Simon interjected, "But you are right, Sarah, we are both eager to go as soon as we can, and, as you say, it would be great to go together," adding, "my uncle and aunt are pillars of their local church in Harare and I am sure they would host our visit and keep a watchful eye over us."

"Yes," said Sarah, "I'm sure they would." Then, returning to what she said earlier, "but you do need to get yourselves organised so you can go out soon."

With that, Sarah seemed to be satisfied and for the rest of their first lunch together the conversation switched back to the more chatty and informal. They parted with Simon and Sarah both saying they were looking forward to seeing each other again soon, and each of them meant it.

After introducing Simon to her mother that Saturday, Emma began to open up to Ma about her feelings for Simon, starting the very next day, when Emma came over for their regular Sunday lunch. Emma felt Ma was supportive and was grateful she scarcely made mention of Robbie when they spoke: her sixth sense was at work again.

Simon came to see Sarah a couple more times before they flew out to Zimbabwe, for two Sunday lunches when both he and Emma felt his relationship with Ma deepening, though nothing was said. During these visits, they rarely talked about the past. Emma thought this could have been linked to her beginning to tell her mother a little of what she had begun to pick up about Simon's and his family's history. She seemed far keener to talk about the future.

Sarah was particularly supportive of Simon's pending career-switching decision and she happily shared some of her own experiences of helping people with mental health problems at the Hospice. She told him that in her experience mental health issues were far more common than most people, even health professionals, were ready to acknowledge. She also stressed to Simon how important it was for him to complete his accountancy studies. Like all Zimbabweans of her age, Sarah was obsessed with qualifications.

However, each time Simon came over, Sarah raised again the subject of Emma going to Zimbabwe, always emphasising the need for this to happen soon. Indeed, as Emma and Simon were soon to remark, the whole Zimbabwe trip seemed to have become an obsession with Sarah. When Emma and Simon told Ma their flights were booked and they would be going out in mid-September, Emma immediately saw a change in Sarah. She became less tense and anxious, the furrows on her forehead less deep when the subject was next raised. On the day they showed Sarah their ticket confirmation emails, she gave both of them one of the warmest hugs Emma ever remembered her giving. It was only matched by the one she gave them on the day they flew to Harare.

Emma first met Simon's parents, Peter and Cathy, in mid-June, the Saturday following Simon's initial lunch with Sarah. Simon knew his mother in particular was dying to meet Emma and when Simon first broached the subject, she insisted Emma come for supper. Simon had brought his uni girlfriend Meg home on a couple of occasions, but she and Cathy had never got on. When Simon told Ma their relationship had ended, she was quick to express her approval, though it was only then that Cathy told Simon that Meg was both pushy and more interested in herself than him. At the time he had resisted his mother's harsh assessment but, on reflection, thought she may have been right. That was some five years ago and, in the intervening period, Cathy had become more concerned there was no one new even remotely on the horizon. Seeing how clearly happy and far more engaged – with everyone – Simon had become since he had met Emma made Cathy even keener to meet her.

The night before Emma's first visit, both his parents asked Simon if any subjects were taboo or likely to be sensitive. Simon confirmed there were none, saying that if Emma disagreed with what they said, they would soon know and adding she could hold her own with anyone. It was Emma who was a little nervous as she pressed the doorbell on Wellfield Avenue just before 8 pm that Saturday evening. Simon answered the door and welcomed Emma with a warm but brief kiss. This failed to relax her; indeed, seeing he had shaved and was wearing a freshly-ironed shirt for the occasion only increased her nervousness. He ushered her into the sitting room where the introductions took place just as Simon said they would. Peter and Cathy stood up together; Peter shook hands warmly while Cathy gave Emma a kiss on the cheek and they all sat down. Simon motioned to

Emma to sit on the beige leather settee, and, as she sat down taking in her surroundings, he slid in next to her.

Although she had never set foot in the house before and Simon had not said anything about its interior, as she stood in the hallway Emma was immediately struck with how familiar it all seemed, a feeling which grew on her as she entered the Robertsons' sitting room. To earn a little extra money while doing her journalism courses, Emma had taken a succession of temporary jobs at different stores at Brent Cross, and during this time, though she had never worked at John Lewis, she had walked through the store hundreds of times, rarely stopping there herself, except to buy the odd light bulb. As she looked around, Emma saw a sitting room she knew: a John Lewis suite and side tables, John Lewis light fittings and curtains. A little later she sat in their dining room with its John Lewis dining table and chair, decked out with its John Lewis tablecloth, cutlery and candlesticks. The Robertsons were typical middle-class North Londoners. Their house was fashionable without being overdone; it felt "just right" without looking opulent. Emma knew the John Lewis strapline of "never knowingly undersold," and she smiled to herself, thinking Cathy had done an excellent job in ensuring their home was neither knowingly under- nor over-decorated.

Emma was seated close to Peter. He was tall, looked fit and wore clothes which could easily have come off the men's rack at John Lewis. However, she was more interested in his eyes, which she was quick to notice were not just blue, but almost midnight blue, just like Simon's.

Cathy was considerably smaller than both Peter and Simon and slimly built, her makeup half concealing deep wrinkles round her eyes brought on by years of living under the African sun.

The evening started well and when they moved into the dining room, everyone enjoyed the food. Cathy and Emma drank a little wine, Simon more, and Peter more still. It was apparent almost from the start that Cathy liked Emma and the two of them dominated the conversation around the dinner table. Emma answered Cathy's questions – about her life in Britain, her love of journalism, her passion for current affairs and her new job at the BBC – but Emma never sensed Cathy was interrogating her or going through a checklist of pre-prepared questions.

They seemed genuinely to like each other and as the evening progressed it became clear to both Simon and Peter that Cathy was delighted with Simon's choice. Simon knew she would; Emma came across as a sharp, amusing and quick-witted young woman with strong views and a sensitive social conscience. As the evening progressed, Cathy confirmed and deepened her initial assessment of Emma. Over drinks, she had been assessing whether Emma was good enough for Simon. When dinner was over and they were returning to the sitting room, Emma lightly and affectionately rested her hand on Cathy's upper arm to signal the warmth she was feeling towards Simon's mother. She really did like her. As she sat down after she and Emma had jointly served the coffee, Cathy had come to the view that Simon was not only lucky to have found in Emma a woman who was so clearly in love with him but was fortunate to have found someone who was probably even smarter than him – her boy!

Peter and Simon chipped in to the conversation when given a chance. As the evening progressed, Peter, who was also becoming increasingly charmed by Emma, felt he wanted to prod her gently with a question about her family in Zimbabwe. Emma replied, saying she really knew very little about them or her Zimbabwean past except her family had come from the Mutoko area some 80 miles east of Harare, where she herself had been born. Without thinking, Peter said he had been there a couple of times but he didn't know it well.

Though Emma and Simon had earlier decided the evening should be about themselves and not Zimbabwe, she could not resist a follow-up question. She liked Peter and was keen to bring him more into the conversation. What's more, she was genuinely surprised to meet someone who had not only heard of Mutoko but had actually been there, so she couldn't resist asking him more, wondering why Simon had never mentioned this. Perhaps he had never told Simon? This made her even more curious.

"What was Mutoko like?" enquired Emma, with some eagerness in her voice.

"Well, I guess Mutoko is pretty typical of that part of the Mashonaland East Province," replied Peter confidently, clearly pleased they were now talking. "When I was there, which must have been some 30 years ago, it was pretty underdeveloped and I gather it remains much the same today: villages surrounded by fields growing maize and groundnuts and a bit of tobacco and plenty of bush where cattle and goats graze. The bush used to be teeming with trees, but now it seems to be covered more by tree-stumps as the people have hacked down the trees in their continual search for firewood which they need for cooking. Most of the roads are still gravel or sand as they were when I was last there; they become pretty impassable in the rains. The town itself is still tiny, with only a handful of stores, a police station, a post office and little else. When I was there, the liveliest places seemed to be the sprawling old mission stations, established decades ago by Catholic, Anglican and Methodist missionaries, competing with each other to draw in people to their schools, clinics, hospitals and churches.

"However," he continued, apparently lost in memories, "the most distinctive thing about the Mutoko area are the granite outcrops, the growing numbers of massive rounded hilltops of bare rock you begin to see as you near the town. Oh, and beyond, to the east of the town as the road starts to descend to the *low-veld*, you start seeing baobabs appearing as if from nowhere with their huge trunks and amazing shapes. When you first see these trees, it looks as if some giant has turned upside down, their bare branches looking more like their roots. The people are mostly poor, but the place is lively. Above all, though, it is beautiful; stunningly beautiful."

Emma warmed to what Peter was saying and couldn't resist asking one last question. "What took you there?" she asked, wondering why Peter had travelled to what seemed like a pretty remote, out of the way spot.

"It was the war," said Peter, launching into a topic he had wished to avoid. But having started, and because Emma had explicitly asked him, he felt he had to say something about Zimbabwe's pre-Independence war. He knew this was tricky ground and he was moving into potentially dangerous territory.

"Like all young white males at that time," he began, not quite certain how much he would end up saying, "and we are talking about the mid- to late-1970s, the years leading up to Independence in 1980, after I left school, I was required to do my stint of two years in the army. Following our initial training, we were sent out to the rural areas on army patrols to track the insurgents. I was sent east, mostly to patrol quite close to Harare, or Salisbury, as it was then called. But I was then told I had to go further east, and the unit I was attached to started patrolling in and round the Mutoko area so I got to know it pretty well. A couple of times I ventured even further afield down the escarpment and on the road through Mudzi right up to the Nyamapanda border with Mozambique."

Emma looked blank; these names meant nothing to her.

"Everyone was affected," said Peter. "As it was a guerrilla, rather than a conventional, war, both sides tried to win over the hearts and minds of the civilian population, those caught in the middle. There were many killings and many dreadful atrocities – committed by both sides, as l came to realise more fully later. Over 25,000 people were killed in all and there was a huge amount of suffering, especially among rural people who were in the frontline. As the fighting was particularly intense around the Mutoko area, the people there suffered probably even greater hardship than others."

Then, turning and looking directly at Emma, Peter said, "I don't know if any of your relatives fought in the war, Emma, but when it ended and Zimbabwe became independent I gradually came to view those years in a different light. At the time, I genuinely thought what I was doing was right: I was fighting for the preservation of civilisation against terrorism and the spread of communism. I felt I had a part to play and I played it as best I could."

Peter paused and took a deep breath. As he didn't want to say any more about his time in the army, he turned the conversation on to the post-war period.

"After the hostilities ended and the war became more a memory than the immediate day-to-day reality of my world – when I met men and women, some deeply impressive human beings, who had fought on the other side – I began to see the killings and suffering people went through, indeed the whole war, in a different light. In retrospect it was so unnecessary, so utterly pointless.

"Part of me was angry, especially with the politicians on both sides for the deaths and suffering their stubbornness caused; but mostly I was sad, especially for the friends who had died or been wounded and for the way the country was torn apart. As you know, many white people left the country after independence, but we remained. I met so many wonderful young Zimbabweans, men and women, too young to know about the war. We stayed on for 14 years after independence, trying to help build the new Zimbabwe, and the first few years were incredibly happy: we felt we were making a real contribution. In those early years, life almost returned to what I remembered when growing up: we played cricket and even Mugabe used to come and watch, especially when international teams came to play.

"Then the politics of greed and power set in and corruption began to spread like a cancer; farms were taken over and occupied by the political elite who had no knowledge of modern farming. The economy imploded, workers were laid off and the early post-Independence improvements evaporated – they were blown away. Years ago, even in times of drought we grew enough to be able to send grain to South Africa to help them feed their people when the rains failed; now we often have to import food from South Africa and other countries beyond even in the years of plentiful rain."

Emma had never heard anyone speak like this about Zimbabwe and she listened with growing fascination, as did Simon, who had rarely heard his father talk with such feeling. She was struck by his use of the words "we often have to import food"; though he had lived in England for more than 20 years, deep inside it was clear he still felt himself to be Zimbabwean.

Peter was no longer looking at Emma but was now speaking into the middle distance. He was clearly very sad; Emma could almost feel it emanating from him. Cathy was watching Peter closely. If Emma or Simon had turned and looked at her, they would have seen she was nervous.

"We watched what was happening and increasingly came to the view there was little hope of a future, not merely for ourselves but for our young family," said Peter. "So, with heavy hearts, we decided we had to leave, just as I guess your family felt they had to leave as well, Emma – together with hundreds of thousands of young educated Zimbabweans. The cream of the country and the hope of its future voted with their feet and simply walked away to pastures new. What a waste! It's all so tragic and it could have been so different. I loved that country and its people. I still do. Zimbabwe and Harare were my home, just as Rhodesia and Salisbury had been: different names but in essence the same place: home."

Emma had not been expecting Peter to open up quite like this; she had clearly touched a raw nerve, maybe many raw nerves. Simon had told Emma his father didn't often talk about Zimbabwe and never spoke about the war or shared his deeper feelings about the country, past or present, even within the family, never mind with outsiders.

As Peter spoke, Emma felt she needed to respond but knew she needed to tread very carefully herself. As an English woman with English instincts, the last thing she wanted to do was ruin her first evening with Simon's parents.

"Peter," said Emma, "I know so very little about the war or even much about post-war Zimbabwe except from what I read and from the media. You are right; my mother left because things had got so bad in Zim. As Simon may have told you, I was two at the time so can only tell you what she has told me, and that's not very much.

"Ma was a trained nurse and, as she tells it, the high hopes everyone had at independence fast disappeared. By the early 1990s, the health service had deteriorated so much she could no longer be sure of her monthly pay cheque arriving; sometimes it didn't. In the year she left, the harvest failed and the family farm had run out of maize and was unable to feed everyone; the local stores were starting to run out of even the basic essentials. The local politicians were growing rich from corruption and kept in power by intimidating and threatening the people. Everyone was frightened. As Ma put it, "fear stalked the land." With a heavy heart, she decided to join the ever-growing exodus of Zimbabweans and, with the help of the family, she managed to scrape together enough money to come to England. In many ways she did it for me: she believed I would have a better future here."

Emma knew she hadn't wanted to talk about all the bad stuff but felt she just had to. Just as Peter had cleared the air by talking so frankly, so she felt she needed to say more than she had intended.

"As for the war," continued Emma more solemnly, "Ma has told me very little and I never really asked. But I do know the family suffered greatly, especially during the last few years of the war and, as Ma worked as a nurse, I guess she was in the front line helping those affected. Ma never spoke to me about who she helped and how. Like many others, our family was forced to move into camps behind barbed-wire fences. It is difficult to believe this really happened. There were beatings, awful atrocities, even deaths."

"Yes," said Peter, who felt the need to butt in, "in what were called Protected Villages."

Emma glanced across at Peter, who was now sitting up alert, engaging fully with what Emma was saying.

"I don't know for sure whether any of our relatives fought in the war," continued Emma, "and whether they joined the liberation struggle as guerrillas, comrades, freedom-fighters or what you will. But, from the little I know and have read, I guess a number of them must have done."

Emma was aware old wounds were reopening so, having said what she thought was sufficient in response to Peter's musings, she tried, as he had done, to shift the conversation away from the past to the future.

"You know, Peter, I am quite keen to go back to Mutoko and see my family and where I grew up, and when I do I guess I will learn more about the past as well as present day Zimbabwe. I really want to see it all for myself and talk to my relatives, both those too young to know the war years and the old who I am sure still do. Actually, Simon and I have already talked about going out to Zim one day to learn more about our roots."

"Yes," said Peter, "Simon mentioned this to me and I have recently been urging him to go myself. The time has now come when he needs to see Zim for himself. As he may have told you, his Aunt Sheila, Cathy's sister, still lives there and both she and Simon's Uncle Jim, one of my oldest and closest friends, have for years been urging him and Jane to go out and stay. As Simon probably told you, Sheila has been over here a couple of times since we moved to the UK but Jim hasn't and I really want Simon to get to know them both, to see the country and get a real feel for Africa.

"It's winter just now and I have told Simon one of the best times to go to Zim is September, when it starts to get warmer but before it gets too hot, in October, and before the rains come in November. There is so much to see. In September the jacarandas will be out in Harare, and in the game parks the animals will be coming down to the water holes to drink as the long dry season draws to a close.

"You must also see at least some of Zim's great tourist spots – the Vic Falls of course, but also Kariba, Nyanga, Chimanimani, the Matopos Hills, Mana Pools and Great Zimbabwe – all different but all well worth a visit."

There seemed to be no stopping him now.

"But more than all this, you need to walk in and really experience the African bush – to feel the heat of the midday sun and the chill of the breaking African dawn, to see Africa's changing colours and the tricks the light can play. You need to hear its noises – to be deafened by the chirping crickets and to grow angry at the never-ending deep-throated calls of mating frogs at night preventing you from sleeping. You need to be captivated by its silences and you need to catch the unforgettable smell of the first rains in your nostrils. It is truly awesome and I still miss it so."

The room falls silent for a moment. Peter breathes in deeply and suddenly tenses up as other memories of the bush, other sights and sounds, return to visit him, experiences he would want no one to share. He momentarily shudders. Cathy knows the signs well and glances across to Peter, ready to rush to his aid if she must. Fortunately, she can see him relaxing and the danger passes. Peter then says, as if to no one in particular, "sorry, I got carried away."

After a brief pause, he turns to Emma and says, "Simon really needs to go out to Zim, Emma, and now you have both met and given your own history I really would urge you both to go. Why don't you go together, and soon! I am serious, really serious, hey! You really should go!"

"Yes, Dad," said Simon, "I think you've made your point". It was his turn to laugh. "When we spoke to Sarah, Emma's Mum, last week she also urged us to go. We have decided to go haven't we, Em?"

"Yes," said Emma a little hesitantly. "We have, we will, and it will be sometime soon. Your description of Zim, Peter, makes it sound even more enticing. Who knows, September might just be possible and if not this year then definitely next."

At this point Cathy joined the conversation, eager to turn it away from Zimbabwe and the sensitive issue of the war and back to England. She began by amusing both Simon and Emma with anecdotes about the oddities of the English when she arrived.

She told them the story of when she first popped into Martin's, the olde-worlde grocery shop in Muswell Hill, to pick up a packet of tea-bags. When Cathy said she would like to buy some tea, the elderly shop assistant asked where she lived. Thinking her hard of hearing, Cathy repeated her request for tea and again she was asked where she lived. Exasperated, Cathy demanded to know why the woman was being so nosy in asking her such a personal question when all she wanted was tea. The shop assistant then explained that because the water to the north and west of the village of Muswell Hill was different from the water to the south and down the hill, Martin's would always recommend a different blend of tea to customers determined by where they lived.

They all laughed even though Simon had heard the story before, and the relaxed atmosphere of the early evening returned. When she realised it was close to midnight, Emma said she should leave and Peter jumped up, left the room and called for a mini-cab, insisting it was far too late for her to walk back on her own and adding that he and Simon had drunk far too much to drive her back themselves. The taxi came quickly and they said their goodbyes.

As she travelled back to East Finchley, Emma thought back on the evening. Overall, she rated it a success. She was pleased she had got on so well with Cathy and had certainly enjoyed listening to Peter as he began to open up about Zim. She thought Peter definitely liked her but sensed there was far more to his time in the army than he had been willing to share; matters he seemed to be struggling to suppress. What was it like being a young soldier in the African bush? Simon had told Emma his father never talked about that part of his past. Why? Did he have things to hide? Perhaps Simon's Uncle Jim would tell them more? Yet another reason, thought Emma, for both of them to go out to Zim and find out. She felt her investigative journalist instincts rise within her, but this time it was Emma's turn to try to suppress them. This had never happened before, but she knew why. She didn't want her professional life ever to encroach upon her personal life.

She then started to recall the interchange they had had about Simon and herself visiting Zimbabwe. At the time, she had been struck by how sharply his insistence mirrored Sarah's that they should go out soon and go together. Now she saw how consistent this all was with all the other coincidences that had happened since their first meeting up at Graham's not so very long ago. It really *was* all very strange.

But before Emma finished mulling all this over in her mind, the taxi had reached her flat and she was jolted back into the present. As she pulled her wallet out of her bag, she discovered Peter had pre-paid her fare. This confirmed the view she was forming of him: that behind his somewhat nervous, shy exterior lay not only a deeply sensitive but an incredibly kind man. As she turned the lock on her front door, Emma felt sure Simon had inherited his shyness from his father. What attributes and character traits – positive and negative – she wondered had been passed on to her by her own father, that rarely talked about man she had never known?

Emma popped into the Robertsons' a number of times over the following weeks but mostly before going out with Simon, so her visits were brief. She did go over to dinner once more before they left for Zimbabwe, where she met Simon's sister Jane for the first time. However, Cathy had set up the evening primarily to help them prepare for their impending trip and they spent almost all of the time poring over tourist books and old photos she had assembled, being careful beforehand to remove any pictures of Peter or Jim in their army days. She dispensed tips and made countless recommendations of how they should fill their time – much of it while on their knees in the sitting room with a large map of Zimbabwe laid out in front of them. This was partly why Emma and Jane had little time to talk. When she had left, Emma thought Jane had inherited even more of her father's shyness than Simon had, or was it that she hadn't liked Emma? She wasn't sure.

Simon had forewarned Emma that Cathy would lecture them about the dangers of the African sun, and so she did. Peter told them never to swim in the lakes and rivers, not because of the crocodiles, though he said he had seen one once, but to prevent them catching bilharzia, which was far more common as well as life-threatening. He also insisted they take their malaria tablets, especially when they went to the Lowveld. He said he didn't think Emma would need them in Mutoko as it was the dry season, but she needed to check in Harare, just to make sure.

Emma and Simon arranged their time off work in September without much difficulty but they could only manage two weeks away. They didn't see this as a problem; it was Sarah and Simon's parents who had wanted them to go out for far longer. Emma had never taken a break of more than a few days, nor had Simon since his student days, and his Sicilian holiday had only lasted eight days even if at times it had seemed longer. While they were both keen to spend times with their respective relatives, what was uppermost in both their minds was spending time not just together but alone. To make sure this happened, they made it clear to their parents they would be spending the last four or five days at the Victoria Falls, just the two of them. Indeed, as the time for their departure drew ever nearer it was the prospect of their having a holiday-within-a-holiday which was exciting them the most.

With the dates agreed with work, Emma went into top gear to book their flights. After a little online research, she easily persuaded Simon they would fly Emirates as it was the cheapest, even if it meant a middle-of-the-night plane change and slightly longer in the air than the second-best alternative, Ethiopian Airlines. To fix visits to their respective families, phone calls were made and e-mails and text messages criss-crossed as Emma developed and finalised her masterplan.

To arrange Emma's visit to Mutoko was the greatest challenge. Sarah told Emma the key person they needed to make contact with was her eldest brother, Prosper, who Emma knew was in his early sixties and had just retired from a lifetime of teaching. Prosper was the patriarch of the Makoni family, whom Sarah called her *sekuru*, the Shona name for both elder brother and uncle. He did more than simply live in the family homestead near the town of Mutoko where Sarah and her siblings grew up, where Sarah's youngest sister, Emerentiana, still lived and where Emma herself had lived for the first two and bit years of her life; he presided over it. However, most of those currently living there were his children and grandchildren. On hearing the news that Emma was planning to come out and visit them, the family went wild with excitement, telling Sarah that Emma had to stay for at least two months, and certainly for no less than a month if it was to be just a quick visit. Emma had plenty to still learn about Shona hospitality.

Communicating with the family in Mutoko proved a constant problem. Although the Makonis had a couple of mobile phones between them, their home had no electricity and an uncertain signal and Emma soon realised relying on the phone wouldn't work. After a week of trying, Sarah did manage to talk to Prosper, who told her the best way to communicate was through his eldest son Francis, who also lived in the family compound. Francis was employed by the only hotel and guest house in the area, Nyamakwere Lodges, travelling there each weekday by motorbike. He worked in the Lodges' office, which had an internet address and a connection which sometimes worked, though there were many days when it didn't.

Communication with Simon's aunt and uncle, Sheila and Jim, was far easier as they lived in Harare. They had a landline, reliable mobile phones and good internet access, except when they had power cuts, which were becoming more frequent again. As with the Makonis, the Reddys wanted Simon to stay longer, insisting he could not possibly visit the country properly in less than three weeks. Whereas for the Makonis it was the never-ending numbers of relatives Emma had to see which required her to stay for so long, for the Reddys it was the large number of must-see tourist spots Simon needed to visit.

Besides their time alone at the Victoria Falls, they also decided it was going to be far easier if Emma visited her family on her own, so Simon would not travel to Mutoko with her. With those parameters settled, this was the itinerary which everyone eventually came round to agreeing. Arriving early evening on the Monday, they would spend the first two nights staying with the Reddys in Harare. On the Wednesday morning, Emma would take the bus to Mutoko where she would be met by either Uncle (*Sekuru*) Prosper or Cousin Francis. Meanwhile, Aunt Sheila and Uncle Jim would drive Simon down to Lake Kariba, where friends had a houseboat. They would both return to Harare from their separate trips at the weekend, when they would book their flights to the Falls, arrange their accommodation and buy their tickets. Sheila and Jim advised them to delay doing this till the last minute because if Air Zimbabwe flights were grounded (an all-too-common occurrence) they might have to hitch a ride with a charter company and there were more and cheaper last-minute options than making an advanced booking.

Sarah explained to Emma the bare bones of how the bus system worked and warned Emma about the potential dangers she might encounter en route. But she spoke at far greater length about the clothes Emma could and could not wear. Where women's clothes were concerned, rural Zimbabwe, she insisted, would be as conservative today as it was when she left some 20 years ago, when dresses below the knee were the norm, jeans could be worn providing they were not tight, but definitely and absolutely Emma must not wear shorts. Together they went off to buy Emma an "appropriate" dress which Emma thought made her look like a hospital matron. When Emma checked, Cathy said that in town, and at Sheila's and Jim's, shorts and shorter skirts would be fine. Simon already knew about footwear – flip-flops and *takkies* – and the need for a sun hat. The Reddys had a pool, so to take swimsuits, though whether it would be warm enough then to swim remained somewhat in doubt. Warm sweaters would be needed as the evenings could still be cool, as well as *DEET* to keep the mosquitos away, especially at the Victoria Falls. Peter also told Emma not to forget to pack a small torch for Mutoko.

Neither Simon nor Emma had realised what a problem health was going to be for them; not so much in relation to their general wellbeing but both logistically and financially before they even began their journey. Indeed, if Rosemary had not mentioned travel vaccinations to Emma, followed closely by Peter insisting Simon needed to make an early visit to the travel clinic to discuss their travel plans, they would have set off without most of the vaccinations and pills they were soon to discover they needed.

A day or two before they left, Simon and Emma suddenly realised they would have to take presents out with them; fortunately, Cathy and Sarah knew what they needed. For Sheila and Jim, Cathy said they should stick predominantly to food and drink: Cadbury's milk chocolates; Stilton cheese; shortbread; smoked salmon and whiskey. For the family in Mutoko, Sarah said the thing they would most welcome would simply be cash in American dollars, the most welcome of the currencies now regularly in use in Zimbabwe. Although she had very few savings of her own, almost since Emma could remember Sarah had regularly sent out money to her family in Zim. Initially it paid for school fees and medicines, but a year or so ago Sarah told Emma she had send out money to help to pay for water, which at the time Emma didn't really understand. Before she left, Sarah gave Emma $500 in crisp new dollar bills, which she told her to immediately give to Prosper when she arrived, and a further $100 for her sister Emerentiana. Emma felt sure the $500 was in part to pay for her keep as Sarah said they were bound to buy food they never normally bought, and could ill afford, in honour of her visit. Besides the money, Sarah and Emma also bought a mass of cheap loose sweets for all her younger relatives, which Sarah said she should give out to those who seemed most deserving, adding they would not last long.

Then, on the day they left, just before their last goodbyes at her Moat Crescent flat, Sarah sprang a final surprise. She went to her bedroom and returned with a small, clear, plastic container about ten centimetres high, its lid tightly wrapped and sealed with sellotape. It contained what looked to Emma like sand. She handed the container to Emma which she said was quite precious, instructing her to give it to Prosper on her arrival.

When Emma asked her what it was, Sarah said, "Prosper will understand; he will know what it is. Thank you, Emma. This means a lot to me."

Emma carefully placed the plastic container in her bag, puzzled by her mother's behaviour, saying, "I'll be sure to keep it safe until I see him, Ma".

With that they embraced, and her mother wished her a good journey with the words "Go well, my dear, I will miss you."

She then added, her voice quivering as she spoke, "you will come back, my dear Emma, isn't it?"

Surprised by the question and taken aback by the quivering nervousness of her mother's voice Emma replied, "Of course I'll come back, Ma," adding in her usual cheery way, "Miss you too!"

* * *

Emma's seemingly buoyant mood and the endearing way she interacted with new work colleagues, with Simon's parents and even with Simon himself over the summer months was deceptive, for all her new relationships were overshadowed by one old one: her relationship with Robbie. From the moment she and Simon parted outside her flat late in the evening after their pivotal day on Hampstead Heath, Emma was not merely conscious of Robbie, but her relationship with him continually gnawed away at her and all too frequently churned up her insides.

Emma knew her decision to be with Simon required her to talk to Robbie both urgently and face to face. But, for a series of practical reasons, they saw far less of each other over the summer than either had intended. In part this was due to Emma's new job. Not only did she need to keep on top of her growing workload but Robbie completely understood this and went out of his way to discourage Emma from having him around to give her the additional time and space she needed. However, it was the changes taking place in Robbie's professional life, not Emma's, which prevented them far more often from meeting up.

At the end of May, Robbie learned the usual taster weekend for potential PhD theology students had been brought forward this year from August to June. Eager to go, this not only meant Robbie would be in Durham the first weekend pf June, and away in Sheffield two weeks later, but, being the conscientious teacher he was, his time away meant he would need to work even longer hours on weekdays and weekends, catching up with his marking and preparing lessons. To add to all that, in the early spring Robbie had been approached by the Catholic development agency CAFOD to ask if they could put his name forward to join their Board of Trustees. As a black British Catholic theology graduate with a known interest in third world issues (he had started a CAFOD group at school), he ticked almost all the right boxes. Though flattered and attracted by the idea, he initially declined as he knew he didn't have the time, but they leant on him hard and he eventually wavered and then agreed. Unsurprisingly, his appointment was approved at the May board meeting. Almost at once he was asked if he would be available to make a trip to Haiti in early August to see the work the agency had been supporting following the latest emergency. As it was the school holidays, he found it difficult to say no, but, in the event, he was pleased he had gone as the visit had a profound effect not only upon him, but indirectly on his relationship with Emma.

The upshot of all this was that both Emma and Robbie met far less regularly during the week and repeatedly had to cancel even hurriedly-arranged evenings together. What's more, the more precious weekends they used to spend at Emma's flat became a far less common occurrence. Indeed, Robbie only managed to come over for two weekends between Emma's decision day on Simon and their departure for Zimbabwe.

However, the practical barriers to Emma's and Robbie's meeting up were a very minor part of the complete story. Her biggest problem lay less in finding the best moment for *when* to tell him about Simon, but in working out precisely *what* to tell him. This was the main reason why the first agonising week passed and, although she did see Robbie briefly, she failed to raise the subject of Simon. It was why she didn't do so either the following week or the week after that. And the longer things continued to drift, the worse Emma felt. Indeed, as things turned out, it was only in early July – after Simon had met Sarah and she had had her first dinner with Cathy and Peter – that Emma plucked up enough courage to broach the subject of Simon with Robbie for the very first time. By then she was feeling totally wretched inside.

Unsurprisingly, Robbie had picked up that something serious was troubling Emma well before then. From almost the moment they were together after her whirlwind first week with Simon, Robbie sensed that a change had come over Emma, which was confirmed on every subsequent occasion they met. It manifested itself physically. Although Emma was always pleased to see Robbie and to be with him, the way she touched him was different: her kisses were warm, but they were hesitant, and when she caressed him, he knew she was holding back. But there was far more. Robbie became aware of a growing distance between them when they spoke which he found even more upsetting. He could see Emma was distracted but she wouldn't say why and he chose deliberately not to pry. What's more, although Emma had always been the more proactive of the two of them, Robbie became aware of her texting him less often. However, the first thing which really hurt him was when he realised she had stopped asking him to join her for Sunday lunch at her mother's. Even then, Robbie continued to hold back and didn't ask Emma directly what was so evidently distracting her.

It didn't take long before it had crossed Robbie's mind that Emma could have met someone else. By the third or fourth time they met, brief though each encounter had been, he was almost certain this was the root cause of the change he noticed in her. He knew the signs because this was not the first time Emma had been drawn to other men. There were two other occasions which he knew about. The first was on her postgraduate journalist course, when she had become very attracted to one of her tutors; the second was when she had been smitten by someone she went to interview when working for the *Hendon and Finchley Times*. The first was far more serious than the second, which was quickly over. However, on both occasions Emma had not only confided in Robbie about her feelings almost as soon as she realised what was happening to her, but she had asked him to help her to "work it through" with her.

Many people might have viewed the way Emma had been attracted to these other men as a warning sign about their own relationship, but this was never the case with Robbie. Emma's honesty in sharing with him what she was feeling and the support Robbie gave her seemed to strengthen rather than weaken their relationship. Perhaps perversely, Emma's evident willingness to expose her vulnerability to Robbie increased his love for her, at least to the extent that it made him realise how deeply upset he would be if she ever left him. Though he knew many men were different from him, from a very early age Robbie had always been a very forgiving person. Even at primary school, if his classmates were brewing for a fight, he was always the one who would step forward to try to reconcile them before things became violent. Then, as an adult, partly under the influence of Don Paulo, Robbie grew to understand more about the power and importance of forgiveness in human relationships, and he committed himself to strive to become an even more forgiving person, though he also understood how difficult that was. As a result, he had always told himself he would stand ready to forgive Emma if she ever strayed or was about to stray, provided she had the strength and honesty to tell him what was happening and the courage to say she was sorry if she had wronged him. Emma knew this too, as forgiveness had been one of those subjects they had discussed long into the night. It was yet another thing which attracted Emma so much to Robbie.

However, if his instincts were right and the cause of the changes he could now clearly see in Emma was another man, the fact she still hadn't told him about it signalled that something quite different was happening now. Though Robbie didn't yet feel he was losing Emma, he realised he was becoming increasingly worried when, totally out of character, he started to snap at some of the kids in his class. Quite soon, it was his turn to start to feel his stomach churning, and the longer Emma said nothing the more wretched he felt inside.

To add to the complexity of what appeared to be going on and was still not being talked about, Emma knew she was incapable of hiding anything from Robbie, not least the turmoil she was feeling within herself and the guilt which accompanied it. So, she could assume Robbie would know there was something troubling her without her ever mentioning it. What's more, she knew Robbie would know she knew. Indeed, she even guessed Robbie would suspect it involved another man without her telling him that either. Confusingly, therefore, Emma thought that as she was already communicating quite a lot about what was going on without having to spell it out in words, she wasn't being totally dishonest either with herself or with Robbie – or at least not as dishonest as an ill-informed bystander might think.

Emma's problem was that her feelings for Robbie seemed to block her whenever she tried to broach the subject. On almost every occasion she set her eyes on him, she could feel Robbie still working his old magic on her. Their embraces only confirmed how strong her feelings for him still were

– Robbie's tall body up against hers, his tender arms wrapped around her and the touch of his lips on hers. Though Robbie may have sensed a certain doubt and hesitancy in Emma, she continued to feel she was embracing Robbie not merely with deep affection, but with love. The prospect of losing Robbie as he stood before her now was simply too dreadful to contemplate. But *were* they going to part for good and for ever? Would this *be* the reality? Emma's problem was that as she became more enmeshed with the second love of her life, she still wasn't able to let go of her first.

When Emma was with Simon, she could usually blot Robbie out of her mind, but when she was with Robbie, she was continually aware of Simon. When she was alone and wasn't absorbed in her work and when she was with her mother, she was conscious of thinking of both of them. If she had ever done a tally, which she never did, she would have realised that most of the times when she was alone it was Robbie who was dominating her thoughts.

Then, one evening when she was alone, her work finished and trying yet again to make sense of what she should say to Robbie, all of a sudden Emma remembered the problem she had had as a very young girl when learning to swim. Whereas academically and on the sports-field Emma was always at or very near the top of the class, when it came to swimming, Emma was at the very bottom. Long after everyone else in her class could successfully swim unaided in the water, Emma was still unable to swim. She recalled her teacher leaning over her at the pool edge and repeatedly telling her to "let go," to force her foot off the bottom of the pool and have the courage to launch herself off and just swim.

"Thrust yourself forward, Emma," said Miss Raynaud in a heavy French accent. "Let go! Trust yourself, Emma, and you will swim!"

Emma remembered telling Miss Raynaud again and again she *had* lifted foot off the bottom of the pool when her toe hadn't left the ground. It was as if she had been trying to convince herself she could keep one toe touching the bottom of the pool and swim at one and the same time. With the security of her long relationship with Robbie in jeopardy, for the second time in her life Emma found herself unable to let go.

Emma finally told Robbie about Simon on a sultry Sunday afternoon, sitting on a park bench in Cherry Tree Woods, East Finchley. Though Emma had been nervous and she could feel her heart beating faster as she started by saying a little about her chance encounter with Simon, their whole interchange turned out to be less upsetting than she had expected. Robbie confirmed he had known something was going on and thanked Emma for telling him; Emma apologised for not having done so sooner. They then talked around the subject rather than about it: Robbie didn't ask Emma anything about Simon and they didn't talk at all about what all this might mean for them and their own relationship. Robbie concluded Emma had already fallen in love but he didn't say anything about this to Emma either. By the end, she even thought the clamminess of her hands and the dampness under her arms were due more to the humidity than to the emotional energy she had expended.

When Emma confirmed to Robbie what he had already suspected, his initial feelings were of relief, as things were now out in the open, and, partly because this first interchange between them was so brief, it was only after they parted that Robbie realised how distraught he was. As Emma left, saying she didn't want to say more for now as she knew it would upset her, she kissed Robbie possibly as warmly as she had ever done in the past. But then, as they parted with Emma turning back to smile and wave to Robbie as they strode off in opposite directions, he started to feel he was going to be sick and had to steady himself as he walked along. Then, as he stood waiting for his bus, he felt tears start to stream down his cheeks and instinctively turned away so the three or four other people at the bus-stop wouldn't see him. This upset him further as he had never cried in public before. As he stepped onto the bus he felt a hollowness inside which remained with him the rest of the evening; it affected him so much he couldn't sleep. All these emotions were very new to Robbie.

Emma's telling Robbie about Simon didn't give her a hollow feeling because she didn't really feel she was losing him, though the act of telling him did make her feel less guilty. And as if to confirm that in her view Robbie remained very much a part of her life, Emma had insisted they meet again the following day, which she confirmed with two text messages, one sent that evening and the other early the following morning. She and Robbie met, briefly again, at the Five Bells pub the following evening, and then spoke again on four or five other occasions before she and Simon flew to Africa.

A little earlier, just before Emma told Robbie about Simon, they did spend the weekend together at Emma's flat. She had intended then to tell him about Simon but found she couldn't. They both slept together in Emma's bed on the Saturday night, as they always did, but they didn't make love. Although this had happened a few times before and so it wasn't totally without precedent, in their different ways they both sensed this was a watershed moment. It was only in late August, just after Robbie returned from Haiti, when they agreed, at Emma's insistence, to spend their second weekend together at Emma's flat that they spoke about Simon; indeed, they talked about little else.

In the interim, though, Robbie and Emma continued to meet up and they spoke little about Simon. However, his presence was never far from either of their minds, though its effect on each of them differed sharply. What was happening was far more complex than if they had been going through the motions of a simple break-up.

For Emma, these meetings did not seem to signal a major rift developing between herself and Robbie. With her head, she said to herself her telling Robbie about Simon would lead to her and Robbie inevitably moving apart, and even if some sort of break-up did occur, it would happen gently and amicably. But Emma's heart told her their relationship would survive and Robbie would remain her best friend. They would still see each other and continue to confide in each other, though she had no idea in what precise form. Emma was clearly in denial. She could not think – or feel – straight. The only thing she knew for certain was she couldn't let go: her toe was still touching the bottom of the swimming pool.

Although she didn't realise it at the time, part of the reason Emma seemed incapable of letting go of Robbie was that she couldn't shake off the series of coincidences which thrust Simon and her together. Although her day-to-day self didn't doubt or question her growing love for Simon, below the surface her inner self – or was it her journalistic instincts? – gnawed away at her, keeping open the possibility – or was it the probability? – of potential dangers ahead. The building-blocks of the life she was planning to construct with Simon still lacked the certainty of the mortar it needed to hold it all together. Until things were far clearer, Emma's subconscious continued to tell her not to let go of what she already had: her precious relationship with Robbie.

For Robbie, things were very different. As soon as he realised what was happening, he first felt deeply sad but quite quickly his sadness was swamped by feelings of emptiness, and then terrifying loneliness. The more often Robbie was with Emma, the more he dreaded losing her. When he looked into her face, touched her hand and stroked her cheek as they parted, the more distraught he felt. When they were apart, what he missed most was her bubbly personality, her zest for life, her enthusiasm for the world and, above all, the long evenings they used to spend committing themselves to putting the world to rights. He knew how much he would miss the physical side of their relationship – his body had already told him that. But he increasingly recognised what he would miss most was Emma his companion and soulmate. He started to dread the future as he knew he would become even more distraught. Never before had Robbie thought much about grieving, but now he knew what mourning felt like.

Then, all of sudden one evening, when he sat up from the pile of books he was bent over marking to stretch his aching back, Robbie was hit by a totally different emotion. He began to feel a wave of anger sweep through him the like of which he had never experienced before. He could feel it rising up his back and tensing all his muscles. His fingers gripped tightly then viciously snapped in half the marking pen he was holding. Then his hand picked up the empty coffee mug on his table and threw it across the room: as it hit the wall opposite and shattered, Robbie's voice bellowed out long and loud the single word... NO! As he sat trembling, unable to move, a stream of questions poured up from deep inside him, all of which revolved around Emma. Why was she leaving him? What made her turn her back on him for another man after all they had going for them? What did this person Simon whatever-his-name-was have which he didn't have? Robbie felt he was about to be sick. Then, just as the bitter taste of bile rising from his stomach touched the taste buds in his mouth, he realised what was making him most angry: Emma was so wrapped up in *her* world that she hadn't for one moment thought of *his*. It was as if she didn't care about his feelings. This was what was hurting him and making him feel so bitter. Up till now Robbie had repeatedly told himself he loved Emma, but had that love now suddenly turned into hate? Had she really ever loved him? Could she possibly have just been using him until someone else came along?

The intensity of his anger stayed with Robbie the rest of the evening. He looked for relief in alcohol but cursed as he found only three beers in his flat he downed them quickly, but they didn't have any effect. When he eventually went to bed, he tossed and turned, slept little and woke up feeling drained. For some time afterwards, though these feelings of anger and bitterness stayed with Robbie, their intensity diminished and they became a persistent sore and a nagging backdrop to his life as he tried to get on with it. Then, in the two weeks between his initial anger attack and his departure for Haiti, Robbie did something he had never done before. He turned down Emma's repeated attempts for them to meet up. He didn't tell her the reason even when he realised how upset this made her.

It was when he was in Haiti that a profound change came over Robbie. It happened when he was visiting a rebuilding project in Cité Soleil, one of Port-Au-Prince's roughest neighbourhoods, and was introduced to a group six young mothers, all earthquake survivors. As they talked and the women relived what had happened, two of them told him they had each suffered the death of a child killed by falling masonry when the earthquake struck. Robbie was shaken by what he had heard, but a moment later he was even more shocked when all six of them told him they had been robbed at gunpoint of practically everything they owned by gangs of looters who swept through their neighbourhood in the chaotic days which followed. Even more remarkable were the stories each of them took it in turns to tell Robbie about how they had begun to rebuild their lives, practically from scratch. Quite soon, Robbie picked up a thread common to their accounts of what happened. They had all successfully journeyed through the horrors of the earthquake and its aftermath, parked the bitterness and anger they all felt, picked themselves up and were now moving on. Touched by their dignity and calmness, Robbie urged them to tell him more, and he was even more astounded by what they said next. To a woman, they told him they forgave God for allowing them to be caught up in the horrors of the earthquake, but – more surprising still – that they had forgiven the looters, too, for what they had done. Robbie couldn't understand how they had it within them to forgive but he could see their forgiveness was genuine. Then, without his asking, the oldest of them said quietly to him in broken English, "When my sons grow up they may also be forced to become robbers. If they rob people like me, I will need to ask these mothers to forgive my sons. But I will only be able to do this if I have forgiven these sons of other mothers for what they have done to me."

It didn't take Robbie long to start placing what he had heard from these remarkable women alongside his feelings about Emma. He knew he needed to draw a line under the anger and bitterness he still felt towards her and find within himself the strength and courage to forgive her. Given the lead part Emma had been playing in the ending of their relationship, Robbie knew how difficult that was going to be, but he also knew that continuing to be angry and bitter was destructive. The women had showed him the creative power of forgiveness and he knew that forgiveness between himself and Emma was necessary to give the freedom they would need to rebuild their lives anew. But he also knew the mountain he had to climb to put the theory into practice.

Robbie's biggest problem was that however hard he tried, he felt he wouldn't really be able to forgive Emma unless and until she showed at least some remorse. If she could acknowledge to herself, and tell Robbie she was sorry for, what had happened and the part she had played in creating the hurt inside him, only then did he feel it would be possible to start the process of forgiving her. Without that, he didn't believe he genuinely could: for Robbie, sorrow was the necessary flip side to forgiveness. On the plane back home, he not only prayed that one day soon Emma would understand the pain she had inflicted and ask him for forgiveness but racked his brains trying to work out precisely how he might help her do this. But he couldn't. He knew he was moving on from his anger and he almost felt ready to start forgiving Emma for what had happened, but he also knew he was not yet there.

A few days after his return from Haiti, Robbie came over to Emma's flat and they spent their final weekend together. It turned out to be shorter than either of them had anticipated: Robbie arrived after eight on the Friday evening and was gone by lunchtime on the Saturday. They didn't go out; Emma had planned that. As she knew they would both be running late, she had bought chilled ready meals which were waiting to be put into her ageing microwave. After their meal, which Robbie accompanied with the couple of beers Emma had thoughtfully provided, they sat together on the couch and started to talk, both of them aware how different the atmosphere between them was from the comfortable intimacy of old. At times they loosely held hands, at times they didn't and their fumbling reminded Robbie of when they had first started going out together.

However, it provided Emma with the setting she needed to give her the confidence to start telling Robbie far more about Simon than she had had the courage to do up till then. She said a little more about the coincidence of where and how they first met and their both being born in Zimbabwe as a prelude to telling Robbie more about Simon as a person: where he lived, the work he did and his intention of switching careers. However, she said nothing about the stage her relationship with Simon had reached or how often they now met. Emma still couldn't tell Robbie what her growing love for Simon meant, either to her or her own relationship with him, though she did admit to being both deeply confused as well as feeling guilty – indeed, she kept returning to her confusion and guilt, to the point where even she realised she was becoming repetitive. Robbie took it all in, but he didn't say much. He didn't feel he needed the detail of either the past or the present; he was focused on trying to work out what all this meant for the future.

Emma then threw a bombshell into a conversation which began by her telling Robbie more about Simon's Zimbabwean links. When she explained Simon had never returned to the country of his birth but his parents had recently been encouraging him to go, Robbie chipped in to say how well he remembered Sarah having been dead against her doing the same. No sooner had Robbie said this, than – to his total surprise – Emma told him she had recently changed her mind. Indeed, she said, her mother had become quite obsessed with the idea of going to Zimbabwe and had been urging her to go out there as soon as she possibly could. Once she had said this, she told Robbie she and Simon had not just been discussing the possibility of their going out to Zimbabwe together, but they had bought their tickets and were leaving in a couple of weeks' time.

Robbie went numb, as he took in the magnitude of what Emma had just said. However, he didn't become angry as he had already worked through most of his anger and bitterness. Instead, his mind set to work as he tried to work out how best to manage this new twist to what was already a complex saga. By saying she and Simon were about to go off alone to the other side of the world without making any reference to their own relationship, which she had been trying to keep alive, was Emma implying that even now she was expecting it could remain intact in some form? Robbie knew this was not merely nonsense; it was delusional. So, quite out of character, he decided that from here on in he would take over the running of their conversation. This he did until they went to bed and for most of the following morning.

Robbie could see the positive side of what was happening: Emma's going to Zimbabwe with Simon could provide her with a unique opportunity to decide, once and for all, whether her future would lie with Simon. However, Robbie also knew Emma would only be able to make this decision if she was no longer tied to him. Only then would she have the clarity and freedom to make the decision he knew she needed to make. The trouble was that as Emma was clearly incapable of letting go of her relationship with him, Robbie had to do that for her. He had to tell Emma their relationship had finally come to an end, and he had to do so now. But just as he was on the point of telling her it was all over between the two of them, Robbie hesitated; he wasn't able to enunciate the words. In spite of all the hurt that had accumulated inside him and the release he knew he would feel if Emma said she was sorry as the prelude for him to start the forgiving process, he knew a part of him was still clinging to the hope Emma would return to him. At that moment, he realised he still loved her and he knew that, just like Emma, he couldn't bring himself to tell her, in effect, to draw a line in the sand and forget about him. It was as simple and as complex as that.

But then, all of a sudden, Robbie saw the answer; a clear way out of his dilemma. He would tell Emma not that their relationship was over, but that they should suspend it, at least for the duration of her and Simon's trip to Zimbabwe. Why hadn't he thought of it before? It was his turn to lob a bombshell into their midst.

Robbie turned to Emma and told her he had decided it would be best (for all three of them) for their relationship – his relationship with Emma – to be put on hold, kept in abeyance, temporarily shelved – call it what you will, it came to the same thing. He quickly explained why. He said suspending their relationship would give Emma the freedom to enable her to make the decision she had to make about Simon and herself. Repeating himself, he said he wasn't asking her now to choose between himself and Simon. Instead he told her that – for now – she was not to think of the two of them as being together because – for now – he and Emma no longer *were* together. And as they weren't together, when she and Simon were in Zimbabwe, she would have the freedom she needed to decide whether or not she wanted her future to be with Simon.

It took a while for Emma to grasp precisely what Robbie had said about the difference between their ending and suspending their relationship. As he feared, when Emma began to understand what he had meant and seemed close to accepting it, her response was driven by her feelings. She told Robbie how much she loved him for what he was doing for her and, drawing near to him, she leaned over and kissed him fondly as they were sitting next to each other on her sofa. A little later, instinctively, and as her dormant feelings for Robbie increasingly awoke, Emma began to signal to him in ways he knew only too well, and without her saying a word, that they should move off together to her bedroom and to her bed. Robbie wondered if this was her subconscious confusingly wanting to seal their suspended relationship.

To prevent what was already complex from becoming even more complicated, and suppressing his own feelings, Robbie persuaded Emma it would be best for them both if he slept alone on the sofa. This he did, though he hungered not just for Emma's body but for the whole of Emma the entire night. Though Robbie knew what he had proposed was the right thing to do, he also knew the coming weeks were going to be especially painful for him; they already were.

In the morning, Robbie was woken by Emma snuggling in close to him on the sofa. She was affectionate but didn't try to overstep the boundaries he had established. There was both huge warmth as well as an underlying sadness to their non-lovemaking. She asked him about his trip to Haiti. He told her he had found it both an enlightening as well as a depressing experience: enlightening because he had not realised the extent of anti-Haitian racism across the black Caribbean and depressing because, in spite of some good post-disaster work undertaken, Haiti's underlying poverty and its vulnerability to the next disaster remained largely untouched. He added that he was relieved his team came across no evidence or even hint of any sexual abuse by the employees of the local aid agencies with whom CAFOD worked, and they were satisfied that effective safeguarding measures were in place to ensure nothing like that could happen undetected in the future. However, he didn't tell Emma about his meeting with the young mothers caught up in the earthquake and what he had learned from them about anger and forgiveness. He was still hoping against hope Emma would return to him and he would not need to forgive her for the hurt she had caused him, which, as they lay close to each other, he started to feel was becoming just a little more bearable.

Robbie left shortly after breakfast. Emma made them pancakes and coffee; at least those bits seemed like normal. They did not see each other again before Emma flew to Zimbabwe, but she texted him regularly right up to the time their plane took off.

Emma also talked to Simon about Robbie before they left for Africa but she didn't go into much detail. The more she said, the more Simon wanted to know, especially about how Emma now felt about Robbie, but he knew this was a subject Emma found particularly difficult to share, even with him. Just like Robbie, Simon didn't want to pry and he continued to tell himself Emma would tell him all he needed to know when she felt the time was right.

Emma had first broached the subject of Robbie in a distant, almost matter of fact, way. It happened a week or so after their day on Hampstead Heath, as they began to volunteer more about their respective lives. Emma recounted the story of her first love, how she and Robbie had met and got together. She went into some detail about the importance of Christianity to their relationship and explained how her current views of her faith had evolved in part from the long discussions she had had with Robbie. However, it took a while before Simon realised their relationship did not appear to have entirely ended: Emma said they still saw a lot of each other without explaining what "seeing" exactly meant. At the time, Simon wasn't unduly concerned as he knew his relationship with Emma was bedding down well and establishing ever deeper roots.

So it came as quite a shock when Emma told Simon less than two weeks before they were to travel out to Zimbabwe, just after their final weekend together at her flat, that she and Robbie had now formally suspended their relationship. However, he chose, yet again, not to pursue the matter any further as it immediately became clear Emma did not want to discuss it any further. But when she saw the look on his face, she added in a rather off-hand way that she and Robbie hadn't slept together since she had first met Simon.

As Emma was speaking, Simon could see she was struggling even to tell him this much and he suspected part of her still had strong feelings for Robbie. Strangely, his thoughts then turned to Robbie. He wondered what Robbie felt and thought he must be feeling pretty wretched; then he began to feel for him in a way Emma had clearly still not managed to do.

But trumping all this, Simon felt an enormous sense of relief knowing there were no more skeletons in Emma's cupboard. These same feelings returned to Simon when their plane took off with Emma sitting next to him, her hand in his, her head resting on his shoulder, the now familiar smell of her perfume on her skin and in her hair, and her body warming his whole being. He knew they were on their own, just the two of them and he felt he needed to pinch himself to reconfirm all this was really happening.

BOOK II
REVELATIONS

- 6 -

First Impressions

The sun was low in the cloudless sky when their plane neared Harare and the captain announced they would soon be landing. Emma pressed her body next to Simon's who, in turn, leaned against the window, his cheek touching its cold surface. They both peered down, eager to catch the first glimpse of the country of their birth. Yet, like a film in fast-motion, too much was happening too quickly for them to take it all in.

As the plane turned steeply to line itself up for its final approach to the still distant runway, clusters of traditional grass-roofed huts swooped into view, nestled close together against the backdrop of a parched and barren, almost desert-like, land beyond. Then, as a rumbling sound below signalled the wheels of the aircraft were being lowered, the panorama of rural tranquillity abruptly gave way to a very different urban scene: hundreds upon hundreds of houses, row upon row. Most were tiny, matchbox-sized, many half-built, almost all with corrugated iron roofs. They were so densely packed together that from above they looked like tins of sardines. Any gaps between the houses seemed to be filled with sand, gravel or mud. Largely absent were paved or tarmacked roads and footpaths to give them that more familiar neighbourhood or suburban look.

"They have a bleakness to them," said Emma, "and look to me more like institutional dormitories than homes."

"Mmm." Simon mumbled his agreement.

Then, as suddenly as they had appeared at their aircraft window, the houses disappeared. The plane had reached the airport and was now so near the ground it looked as if it would clip the top of the security fence as it steadied itself to land: the closer it came to the ground, the faster it seemed to be travelling. Looking out of the window to their left, they could clearly make out the shapes of tall buildings in the middle distance, silhouetted in front of the setting sun behind.

Emma pointed and said to Simon, "Look over there. That must be the centre of Harare. It has far taller buildings and is a lot bigger than I had expected."

"Yes," said Simon, "and it looks quite modern too. Exciting, isn't it?"

Emma didn't say anything but answered his question by squeezing Simon's hand, feeling the excitement grow inside her.

Just before touch-down, the wings suddenly wobbled as the incoming plane met an unexpected blast of air rising from the hot tarmac. Then bump... rattle... The plane landed, and almost at once clapping and the release of nervous laughter broke out from a group of Chinese tourists sitting in the middle of the aircraft. When the plane stopped a moment or two later outside the terminal building, the clicking of released seatbelts resounded before everyone rose and gathered their things, ready to disembark.

As they stepped out of the plane, Simon and Emma felt the warm dry air on their faces and they paused to breathe in deeply before going down the steps and taking in their surroundings. There were very few other planes on the tarmac. The airport was quiet; it seemed underused, even ghost-like, against the lengthening shadows cast by the setting sun behind them.

Being British passport holders, they joined the longer line for "Visitors" rather than the shorter queue for "Returning Residents and SADC Citizens", even though, as Emma said to Simon "we *are* (former) residents who *are* returning." There was no special line for people like them, Zimbabwean-born returning, with foreign passports, to the land of their birth.

They didn't have to wait long to reach the immigration desk, where they handed over their passports, their landing cards, their immigration forms and what they thought were extortionately high pay-on-arrival visa fees: $55 each. The neatly dressed official behind the desk took their money, stamped their passports and asked them how long they were staying; they told her just short of two weeks.

She then asked, "Are you together?"

Simon said "yes," just as Emma said "no," then almost before their words were out of their mouths, Emma said "yes" at precisely the moment Simon said "no."

The official looked up and, eyeing them across the desk, said, "Well, I hope by the end of your stay you will have worked out whether you are or whether you are not together." They both laughed.

She then gave them back their passports and, having seen from their passports they were both Zimbabwean-born, said, smiling, *"Titambirai,"* meaning "welcome". "Welcome back to Zimbabwe!"

Their bulging rucksacks were soon on the luggage carousel. Picking them up, they walked purposefully past the customs officials to the world beyond without being asked to stop. By then, Emma had been greeted by a succession of officials enquiring if they were okay or needed anything. Most greeted her in the Shona language and she felt chuffed at the ease with which she was able to understand them and to reply. After Emma's third such exchange, Simon said, "I'm impressed, Em." She was surprised by the sheer number of officials milling around them, impressed by the courtesy and politeness shown to both of them and inwardly pleased she seemed to be seen as a local. Not a white face among them. Emma breathed in deeply once again. She felt good. She really was in Africa.

When the doors opened to the arrivals waiting area they were shocked to discover it was already dark, and initially felt quite disorientated: in the short time they had been inside the terminal building, the day had turned into night without any noticeable period of dusk. As they were trying to adjust to the darkness, they heard their names being called out and, looking round, saw two people waving at them and smiling. Simon immediately recognised Sheila and they both assumed (correctly) it was Jim who was standing next to her.

"Welcome to Zimbabwe, the two of you," said Sheila, giving Simon a hug as Jim shook hands warmly, if rather formally, first with Emma and then Simon, adding, "you must be tired after such a long flight."

"Thanks so much for meeting us," said Simon. "Yes, tired, but more excited than anything else, so it's difficult to tell quite how we're feeling."

"Yes," said Emma, unusually lost for words, adding, "We're both really excited to be here at last."

"Yes, it is still a great country, hey! And we are so pleased you are staying with us first," said Jim. "Come on, though, we need to get going."

He took Emma's rucksack from her and told them to stick close by as he strode out of the airport building and they followed. As they struggled their way through a group of taxi-touts congregated at the exit, they took it in turns to firmly decline the repeated offers of rides to town at bargain prices. They soon reached Jim's car, parked close by, piled in with Emma and Simon in the back and drove away.

Harare's Robert Mugabe Airport lies some 10 miles south of the city centre. The drive to Sheila and Jim's house in the eastern suburb of Mandara took them a little over half an hour. Given the darkness, and with few street lights on the main airport road, they could see very little at first, but once they had turned off and come to a more lively built-up area, they passed a few shops, petrol stations, and lots of houses, most hidden behind the walls which surrounded them. Sheila announced "We're nearly there," just as Jim slowed down. He then reached forward and pressed hard on the electronic remote housed in its cradle on the car's dashboard.

They heard a creaking sound and saw in the car headlights what must have been a seven- to eight-foot-high metal gate ahead of them which creaked as it slowly moved sideways. When the gate was almost open and the driveway beyond was visible, Emma and Simon could just make out the shape of a tall man in a heavy coat and balaclava-type hat standing in the shadows. He waved at the car as it entered the property. It didn't stop, but Sheila raised her hands in greeting at the same time as Jim rolled down his window and said, as he passed the dark figure next to him, "you can bolt it now for the night, Matthew, we won't be going out again," in what was clearly a familiar ritual for all three of them.

Jim pressed the remote again and there was a reprise of the same creaking sound as the gate rumbled along its unoiled runners and shut behind them. A succession of rattling sounds, metal on metal, followed as, they subsequently learned, the coated figure double-locked the gate, securing it with a large metal padlock and chain, barricading them in behind the seven-foot-high walls topped with broken glass and razor-wire which surrounded the Reddys' property. As they heard the noises behind them, Simon nudged Emma and she knew just what he was thinking – it was as if they were entering a prison, and Emma felt a nervous chill run down her back. But her thoughts took her to a different place: for an instant she imagined herself back in Hampstead Garden Suburb, being whisked inside one of the gated and guarded mansions on Winnington Road she had only ever either run or walked past, adding a dose of embarrassment to her nervous chill.

Jim took Emma's rucksack again as they climbed from the car and then welcomed them to the house and started to show them round while Sheila disappeared into the kitchen. The Reddys lived in a large red-tiled solid brick-built bungalow. From the hallway, Jim took them left along a long corridor and pointed to the doors at the end which he said were an en suite master bedroom and office. Nearer to them were six doors, behind which were four smaller bedrooms and two bathrooms on either side. Jim opened the door to the first room on the left, indicating this was to be Emma's room, dropping her rucksack down on the bed. He then opened the door opposite, which was to be Simon's. He said they would be sharing the first bathroom: the one nearest to their rooms. He then invited them to retrace their steps to the hallway through the open double doors into the large sitting room which dominated the right-hand side of the house. From there he pointed to two doors, the first to the kitchen, the second to the dining room, inviting them to unpack and unwind, shower if they wanted to and, when they were ready, come back into the sitting room for drinks prior to supper.

As Emma and Simon were to discover, the Reddys lived quite formal, structured and tidy lives which were in part reflected in the design of the house. The living room and bedrooms were all identical, off-white plastered and un-wallpapered, with white ceilings and a single central light; the bathrooms all contained the same simply-designed white enamel basins and baths and surrounding wall-tiles which stopped at chest-height. Emma's and Simon's rooms were mirror images of each other, with a bedside light placed on a wooden table next to a single bed, a small built-in cupboard with rough wooden shelves and simple mirror on the door, almost empty bookshelves next to a simple matching unpainted wooden desk and chair set.

Some fifteen minutes after Jim had left them, Simon knocked on Emma's door; she had showered and he had not. She said she was almost ready, and Simon waited so they could go into the sitting room together. As they walked in, they saw Sheila was already there with a drink in her hand. Jim politely rose and walked to the bar in the corner where he offered them the choice of a soft drink or a beer, either a Castle or a Lion, a brandy and ginger ale or a rock shandy which he told them, though Simon knew, was a mixture of bitters, lemonade and ginger ale with ice. They both opted for beer. Emma chose a Lion, after Jim had said it was the sweeter of the two; Simon chose a Castle, which they both drank while Simon dipped his hands repeatedly into a large bowl of salted peanuts placed too near to him to resist. He hadn't realised how hungry he was.

It was now almost 7:30 pm and in a matter of fact way Jim said they usually ate far earlier, at six, and went to bed usually before nine as they rose at five. Soon afterwards Sheila rose to invite them into the dining room where she served ample portions of macaroni cheese followed by ice cream and a plentiful supply of fruit and cheese. Simon and Jim both had another beer but Emma asked to try a rock shandy, which she loved.

The evening was relaxed and they chatted freely, with Sheila – just like her sister Cathy – doing most of the talking, and Jim – like Peter – mostly listening. They continued the conversation they had started in the car with Sheila wanting Simon to give them an update on all the family news, though she seemed rather more interested in giving Simon and Emma an overview of present-day Zimbabwe. Early on, Sheila asked Emma to say a little about herself and why her family had moved to England, but she didn't pry. It was a relaxed conversation, with Emma sensing Cathy had filled Sheila in on her background. After supper they moved back to the sitting room for coffee and chatted a little more about their plans for their stay in the country. Very soon it was clear they were all too tired to talk more that evening and both Emma and Simon were relieved when Sheila suggested they finalise their plans for the coming days in the morning.

"I'm really keen to show you round Harare tomorrow," she told them. "It's the only thing I have scheduled for the day so we can take our time. But you need to rest now and remember that, as we are at 5,000 feet, it will probably take you a day or two to acclimatise yourself to the altitude."

They all helped carry the dishes into the kitchen, but when Emma offered to wash, Sheila said Matthew's wife, Jessica, would do it in the morning, adding that she came in to work in the house a little after six. As they bade each other good night, Sheila told them to sleep in as long as they wished but that she would be up and about early and would have breakfast with Jim before he left for the office around 6:45. She then led Emma to her room and gave her a warm kiss on the cheek as they parted saying, "I'm so glad to have met you at last, Emma. Sheila has told me so much about you. Simon is a most fortunate man."

Just before she said goodnight to Sheila Emma remembered she hadn't asked how to connect to the internet. Yet, uncharacteristically, she did not ask Sheila for their password. She was simply too exhausted and everything – both her emails and even catching up on the latest news – could wait until the morning.

Simon stayed in the sitting room and leafed through a few glossy books on Zimbabwe he had not previously seen before he turned in – not ten minutes later – unable to keep his eyes open.

Emma fell asleep immediately but was woken well before dawn by a very loud and unfamiliar noise. When she had worked out what it was – the dull, rhythmic croaking of African bull-frogs – she turned over and smiled to herself as she pulled up the bedclothes to keep warm, surprised at how cold her room was. She hadn't thought of Africa as cold but she could have done with another blanket. As she lay listening, she decided the sound of bull-frogs was not, as Peter had told her, one which made one angry. On the contrary she thought it was rather pleasant and mesmerising as she sank back into another deep sleep.

Just after 8:00 am – 7:00 in the UK – Sheila knocked on Emma's door to let her know what time it was and then did the same for Simon, inviting them to come through and have breakfast when they were ready. As the sun had been up for two hours already and sensing Sheila thought they had overslept, they dressed quickly. Emma left her room a moment or two before Simon; he took longer to emerge as he knew Emma would like him clean-shaven for breakfast.

Emma walked through the sitting room on her way to the dining room, where she assumed they would have breakfast. As she did so, she was greeted by an elderly woman, slightly-built with a thin but kindly face, almost a foot smaller than Emma. On hearing Emma's footsteps in the corridor, she had hurriedly left the kitchen and now stood respectfully in front of her in a welcoming manner. The woman was dressed in a perfectly-ironed white uniform, her head covered by a brightly coloured headscarf. She smiled, curtsied slightly and spoke confidently if quietly to Emma.

"Good morning!" she said, clearly comfortable conversing in English. "Welcome! My name is Jessica. I hope you travelled well and had a good night's sleep." She then added, "And I hope everyone is well back home."

Jessica then gestured to Emma to continue onto the terrace outside, beyond the sitting room French doors, which she hadn't seen the previous evening as the curtains had been drawn, to where breakfast had been laid out for the two of them.

Surprised at seeing the woman and somewhat confused about how she should respond to Jessica's deferential manner, Emma thrust out her hand, wished her a good morning and then proceeded in quick succession to say how delighted she was to be in Zimbabwe, apologise for sleeping for so long, tell Jessica her name was Emma Maconie and enquire of Jessica's other name.

"Jessica Mashayamombe," came the reply, as she held out her hand to clasp Emma's, which she shook gently, curtsying again as she did so. She then walked over to and opened the French doors for Emma to go out onto the terrace, with Emma feeling even more at a loss about how best to interact with this kind but clearly subservient woman.

Just as Emma was sitting down, Simon's door slammed closed as he left it with a plastic bag in his hand, tracing the route Emma had just taken down the bedroom corridor across the hallway and into the sitting room. Hearing his footsteps, Jessica promptly abandoned Emma, turned and walked back into the sitting room to greet him. Seeing the uniformed woman hurrying towards him and being better prepared to interact with servants than Emma clearly had been, Simon thrust out his right arm to shake Jessica's hand and spoke before Jessica had had a chance to greet him.

"Simon Robertson," he said, confidently introducing himself. "And who do I have the pleasure of meeting?"

"I'm Jessica," she replied, then glancing back at Emma she added with a little embarrassment, "Jessica Mashayamombe," curtsying in the same formal way she had done when greeting Emma moments earlier. Hardly noticing, Simon took hold of her hand and shook it firmly.

"Good to meet you. Jessica's a fine name. As for Mash-eye-whatever," said Simon stumbling over her surname, "well, that sounds like a bit of a tongue-twister to me. Does it mean anything in particular?"

Then, seeing Emma out on the terrace, he quickened his pace to join her and Jessica stepped aside as he passed her. Simon and Emma gave each other a quick hug and a smile as they sat down next to each other. Stunned by the brightness, they were both keen to take in and focus on their first morning together in Africa. Breakfast could wait.

"In English, Ma-shaya-mombe means you lacked cattle," said Jessica, enunciating each Shona syllable slowly in the hope Simon might remember it. She had followed him out and was now standing next to him. "We are descended from a famous chief," she started to say but was cut off mid-sentence.

"Oh," said Simon who, on seeing Emma had stopped listening and already forgotten the question he had just asked Jessica and which she had been patiently been trying to answer.

Realising he had made Jessica feel uncomfortable, Simon turned to Jessica and said, "I think I shall stick to Jessica if that's okay, as Mash-a-mom-bay sounds far too difficult for me," this time almost pronouncing her name correctly.

As Jessica said nothing and he was struggling to sound friendly, Simon changed the subject. Cheerily he said, "So what's for breakfast then?"

Emma had heard Simon's initial interchange with Jessica and knew he had embarrassed her again. What she had not sufficiently picked up, however, was Jessica was troubled not so much by Simon's rapid repartee but because he had moved on to practical, day-to-day questions – talking about breakfast – before they had finished greeting each other properly. This was the underlying reason Jessica had been so flustered.

As Simon was soon to learn, when greeting someone, and especially a stranger, Shona etiquette requires one first to "focus in" on the person you are talking to and ask about themselves and their well-being, before moving onto practicalities. In fast-moving Britain, it would seem odd not to say all in one breath "hi, how are you, what's on the agenda for today, are you free for lunch?" but in Zimbabwe, and across much of Africa, getting started is both merely a far gentler and slower process than it is in London and other big European and American cities. You begin by saying "Hello so-and-so," "Good morning my friend," or something of the like, and then wait for the person you are addressing to reply with a "Hello" and a "Good morning to you too," or something similar. You then move on to enquire about the well-being of the person you are talking to, asking, for instance, if you first meet them in the morning, "Did you sleep well?" or in the evening, "How did the day go?" If they have just come from afar you might ask, "And how was your journey?" or, as Jessica had said to Emma, "Tell me, are the family well?" The gentler response will commence with the immediate answer "I slept well", "The day was good" or "The family are well", but it will not end there. The person replying will then add something like "And how about *you*?" or "And how is *your* family? Well, too, I trust?" Only when this series of greetings has been completed should you launch into the pressing matters of the day, however urgent they might appear to you to be.

To the busy, modern-day urbanite, such a ritual smacks of the formulaic; it all seems quaintly naïve. Yet by the time Simon was preparing to take his leave of Africa, he would be ready to admit to himself that the greeting ritual did convey something of underlying importance. Behind all the word-play, what you are saying in essence is you are a human being like me. Let's pause to acknowledge and recognise this. Let us show the respect which all human beings deserve simply because they are human beings before we become absorbed with, and are totally lost in, the busy-ness of life; the matter-of-factness of the everyday.

Likewise, although Emma was well aware of the importance given to greetings in Zimbabwean culture because Sarah had spoken to her about it in England, this was the first time she had encountered it in so dramatic a way. In first greeting them, it was not Jessica's reserve and deference which Simon and Emma later recalled. Rather, it was her lesson on human dignity she had treated them to which remained with them for long afterwards, a lesson Emma now realised, sitting at the breakfast table, she had singularly failed to reciprocate.

In this brief interchange Emma already felt she had learned a huge amount not only about traditional Zimbabwean culture but also about herself, the young self-confident go-getting English woman. What other things of importance were there, she wondered, which contemporary Britain had forgotten how to value? This was the first of many instances when Emma would ponder what was really important to her as she began her journey back to her roots.

Jessica points to the lidded marmalade and jam pots on the table and lifts the covers off the milk, the sugar bowl and the butter dish, all there to keep off the flies. She asks Emma and Simon if they would like tea or coffee, says she will bring them porridge and enquires whether she should cook them an egg – scrambled, boiled or an omelette. They both express their delight at being offered what they know will be mealie-meal porridge as it will remind them of their childhood and say they would like coffee. As the offer of an egg is too much for Simon to resist, he asks Jessica for an omelette.

With that taken care of and happy to be on his own with Emma for the first time since they landed, Simon takes hold of her hand and they look about them. From where they are sitting on the terrace to the garden below and to the hills beyond they take in their surroundings: it is a scene of exquisite, almost magical beauty.

Emma and Simon are seated above an arbour overflowing with red, purple and white bougainvillea, dense enough to shade them from the glare of the sun rising in the sky in front of them but which they can feel already warming their faces. Climbing up the latticed trellises on either side are thinner and more delicate vines which carry today's display of morning glories, delicate light-blue and white petals each newly opened but by sunset doomed to wither and die. On either side of their table are low beds of flowering sweet peas – a jungle of pinks, whites, reds and purples – their fragrant aromas wafting up to them. All around, they can hear the humming of bees already busily at work. But what they both find most captivating is the intoxicating early morning September air – crystal-clear and fresh in a way they never remember having experienced before as they deeply breathe in.

In front of them, the terracotta tiles of the terrace floor give onto a manicured lawn, lush, green and now damp after the morning sprinkling of water pumped up from the Reddys' own borehole. The lawn drops down steeply after a couple of yards, disappearing from view to reappear at the bottom of the slope, where it levels off to stop at a low freshly-painted white fence. Behind the fence lies the expanse of swimming pool, large enough to swim laps in, surrounded by white tiles on which loungers, plastic chairs and closed umbrellas have been higgledy-piggledy placed. The sides of the pool are painted blue and the water glistens in the morning sun, though when set against the shadows of the tall trees behind, its brightness is easily trumped by the even deeper hue of the cloudless sky above.

Two formal flowerbeds are set on either side of the pool fence, the left one dominated by the red, pink and yellow flowers of mature hibiscus shrubs and white and pink flowering frangipani trees. The right-hand bed is filled with mature standard roses planted in concentric circles and a mass of colour: whites in the centre, then yellows and oranges, with red, purple and crimson petals dominating the outer edges. Beyond the pool and formal flower-beds they can see an irrigated vegetable plot and Emma calls out the names of plants she recognises: the reds and greens of ripe and ripening tomatoes, the purple fruits of the more robust aubergine plants and the yellowing tops of ready-to-eat onions.

Directly behind the vegetable garden and grown to hide the property's ugly perimeter wall is a dense line of tall evergreen trees. Simon points to two tall trees and a cluster of smaller ones which he tells Emma are avocado and mangos and she says she can see fruit on both of them. But what impresses her most is when Simon says, "and I'm pretty sure that huge tree in the centre with its giant deep-green ribbed leaves and bulbous hanging fruits is a breadfruit tree." Surprised, Emma asks how Simon could possibly have known that, and he then tells her that during the week before they flew, and with his exams over, he had started to study in some detail a book on Zimbabwe's fauna and flora which had sat on their sitting-room table for as long as he could remember but which he had hardly ever flicked through the pages of before. Simon was immensely satisfied when Jim confirmed later it was indeed an *atocarpus altilis* – a breadfruit tree.

Their eyes then move further to their right to the garden gate they both recognise from the previous night, Beyond the driveway, Emma points to half a dozen citrus trees, their shiny green leaves half-hiding their ripening crop. They strain their eyes to try to guess what fruits are on them, coming up with grapefruits, lemons, oranges, possibly limes and what they say are tangerines but which Sheila later tells them in Zimbabwe and the rest of southern Africa are called *naartjies*.

Almost touching the citrus trees further to their right stand a number of rather dishevelled-looking banana trees, behind which they can see a number of tall and elegant-looking pawpaw trees, growing in deep red soil next to a small compact and low grey *brise-soleil* brick structure with a tin roof. This, they later learn, houses the Reddys' diesel-engine borehole, lying idle now until dusk, following its early morning watering session. Largely hidden behind the bananas and the paw-paws, they can just make out a rather old white brick building with a narrow and rickety green front door, with two square poorly-fitting windows on either side and a sloping roof that, they learn from Sheila later in the day as they drive past and ask, is made of asbestos. They rightly guess this is where Jessica and Matthew live. In front of the house, a large black dog lies asleep in the sun; behind it a washing line hangs between two trees, already filled with today's almost-dry clothes.

The main road runs alongside the Reddys' property in front of them but they can't see it as it is hidden by the boundary wall. Beyond the road, the land falls sharply, rising again to the hill beyond, over some quarter of a mile away they reckon, on the top of which Simon is pretty sure is a line of tall grey-barked eucalyptus or gumtrees. Scattered across the hill are a number of sizeable residential properties, each of which is surrounded either by walls or tall fences, and half-hidden by trees. Simon wonders whether, like the Reddys' wall, these too are topped with broken glass and razor wire, but they are too far away to tell.

As it is now well after 8:00 am, the rush-hour and school-run traffic has long passed, and the world immediately beyond the Reddys' land lies quiet except for the sound of the occasional vehicle passing along, the shouts of passing pedestrians greeting each other and the gentle rustling of the wind in the trees.

"It's so good to be here," says Emma. "No one told us how beautiful it would be. But I'm getting really hungry."

"Me, too," says Simon.

As if on cue, Jessica returned with a tray carrying their breakfast. Catching the enticing smells, they both thanked her warmly as she placed everything in front of them and quickly put a few lumps of butter on their steaming porridge and whisked it round as it melted. When they had both finished their porridge, and Simon his eggs, and had started on their coffee, Sheila swept onto the terrace, also as if on cue, and sat down to join them. She apologised for not coming earlier but said she always spent an hour or so at her desk after breakfast to attend to her pressing paperwork, adding she was sure Jessica had taken good care of them. Then, looking at Simon, she said she had already called Cathy to let her know of their safe arrival, and all was well in Muswell Hill.

Almost before Sheila had finished talking, Simon stood up and, apologising, proceeded to take the presents out of the plastic bag he had brought with him to breakfast and which he had forgotten about until this morning as he had been rummaging around the bottom of his rucksack to find something suitable to wear for the day. As each gift appeared, Sheila's excitement grew, until Simon produced the Stilton, followed by the smoked salmon, when she jumped up in horror and rushed to the kitchen to put them immediately in the fridge, fearing they might already have spoiled. While she was gone, Emma hurried back to her room to pick up the Cadbury's Milk Tray chocolates she had also forgotten about and which still lay buried deep inside her own rucksack.

As Emma opened her bedroom door she let out a loud gasp and jumped in surprise on seeing there was someone in her room. Her shock quickly turned into embarrassment when she realised it was Jessica; she was busy laying out the clothes from her rucksack neatly on the cupboard shelves, having already piled her cosmetics, books and the chocolates on her desk, made her bed and arranged her shoes in a line under it. Never before had Emma experienced life with servants; no one but her mother had ever looked after her, and Sarah had stopped doing that by the time she was five. Though she was grateful for Jessica's kindness, first for making them breakfast and now for tidying up her room, she felt hugely uncomfortable, just as she had the previous night when witnessing the gate-scene with the shadowy man. While it was now evident that servants were part of normal everyday life for the well-to-do in modern-day Zimbabwe, this was not something Emma had been expecting to encounter on her return trip to Africa. What she knew for certain was that being waited on and formed no part of her African roots.

Sheila was already back at the breakfast table with Simon when Emma returned. Cathy had been right: Sheila was delighted with the chocolates, explaining British chocolates were far tastier than Zimbabwean ones, which included additives to stop the chocolate from melting in the heat but which, she said, ruined the taste. Back again in good spirits following the Stilton and salmon incident, Sheila said they should now discuss the day ahead.

As it turned out, there wasn't much discussion; the rest of the day happened much as Sheila had decided it should. She began by announcing it would be best if the two of them had the morning to themselves to further acclimatise themselves to the altitude, saying they would then be ready to start their tour of the city following a quick lunch. As she rose to leave, she produced a piece of paper with their internet code, saying Jessica would have mid-morning tea ready for them on the terrace at 10:00 am and she would re-join them then. Although they did log in on Simon's iPad and felt they needed to catch up on their emails, they were far keener to get going – not just to see, but to get a taste of, Harare. Emma was thus not surprised when Simon told her he felt a little as if he was being held captive.

Although she felt the same, she was determined to make the most of their morning and so, before they sucked themselves into the internet world, Emma said enthusiastically, "Let's at least explore the garden," as she took hold of Simon's hand, pulled him to his feet and ran onto the lawn, running down to the pool below. They were both reminded of that day on Hampstead Heath when they had raced each other down to the Goodison Fountain and splashed each other with water. By the time they reached the Reddys' swimming pool, their melancholy had vanished. Emma dipped her fingers into the pool; after a chilly night and before the sun had warmed the water, it was far too cold to contemplate a swim.

For the next half hour or so, they meandered round the garden, inspecting the flowers, touching the trees and hopping between sun and shade, absorbing so many new sights and smells and simply enjoying being alone with each other. Their wanderings began with Simon plucking a bright red hibiscus flower from its stem and placing it behind Emma's ear.

Near the borehole, Emma shouted in amazement when she saw the vivid yellow markings of a bird darting across her path. Following it, she screamed in delight when she saw three intricately-woven nests hanging precariously from the branches of the tree ahead of them and exclaimed without thinking "weaverbirds!" She then told Simon that as a class project in primary school, Mrs Murray had shown them pictures of weaverbirds and had even brought in a nest for them to hand round and touch, one she had smuggled back in her suitcase on a trip to India. Emma remembered at the time wishing she could go to exotic India to do the same, and here she was now in Africa not just seeing the bird of her dreams but able just to stretch up and touch its nest. As she did so, she relived a little of the excitement she had felt as a young child.

As they walked to the mango trees, Emma reached to touch the green fruit; it was hard and uninviting. As she pulled her hand away, she suddenly froze, for next to it she saw a chameleon, cleverly disguised, its back speckled green like the mango, its front grey-brown matching the branch it was standing on motionless. Emma grabbed Simon's hand and they watched in silence as it began to walk almost regally away, each hand in turn clasping the branch as it climbed, its bulbous eyes individually swivelling back and forth as it surveyed its surroundings to make doubly sure it was safe to proceed.

They each picked up an orange which had fallen from the tree they'd been growing on; these they decided to keep for later. When they reached the bananas and saw a yellowing bunch they could reach, Simon picked two and handed one to Emma. They were far smaller than the ones you buy in England and they were eager to know whether they tasted different. They did; these ones were far sweeter.

A moment later, and with their eyes now scouring the vegetation more carefully, Simon cleverly spotted a six-inch-long stick insect which had caught his eye. Seeing what he thought at first was a stick rhythmically swaying back and forth though there was no wind, he prodded it gently and as it flinched he saw its elongated legs tense up before it froze. He told Emma he thought its movement could be a mating dance, though he admitted that was just a guess on his part and, search though they did, they couldn't see another. "It's just like the ones I used to see at London Zoo," said Simon. Emma had never stepped inside the zoo, though she said when visiting Regent's Park she had longingly gazed in from the grassy fields outside.

Their walk completed, they returned to the sitting room where they sat busily in front of Simon's iPad until, promptly at ten, Jessica emerged from the kitchen with the tea, and, at almost the same instant, Sheila swept in from her office and ushered them out to the terrace to drink it. On their way there, Simon almost stepped on a giant millipede, black with orangey-brown legs, walking across the tiled floor. Sheila told him it was called a *chongololo* and was harmless, so Simon gave it a prod and immediately it rolled up into a ball. Emma smiled. Before today, she hadn't really noticed Simon's boyish side, but first with the stick insect and now with the millipede she could see him as a wide-eyed child, delighting in each new discovery. She could sense how carefree and relaxed he felt; she liked what she saw, realising this was precisely what she was feeling too.

After tea, Sheila offered Emma her phone so she could text Sarah to let her know they had arrived safely, apologising for not having thought of it earlier. Emma said she had wanted to double check her relatives would be meeting her bus so had earlier emailed Francis to say she would definitely be on the 9:30 bus and to ask him to reconfirm that he, or one of the family, would be there to meet her at Mutoko. As he hadn't replied, Emma then asked Sheila if she could use her phone again to text her uncle Prosper's mobile to repeat the message she had emailed to Francis. Sheila said she was happy to do so but added that she was doubtful it would reach him, though she did admit she had never tried calling or texting anyone in the Mutoko area. When she handed the phone back to her, Sheila said she confirmed she would drive Emma down to the big bus station in Rezende Street tomorrow in plenty of time for her to catch the 9:30 bus, though she couldn't resist adding it was almost bound to leave late. It only emerged later she had never taken anyone to that bus station before either.

At midday all three of them had an early lunch which Jessica had prepared and served outside on the terrace – a leafy salad with hard-boiled egg and home-grown tomatoes and American-type cucumbers which Emma had never eaten before but had seen growing in the garden and had wondered what they were. It was all washed down with iced-water and hunks of freshly-baked and still warm bread which, Sheila explained, Matthew had gone out on his bicycle to buy for them. Sheila herself had a slice of the newly-arrived smoked salmon which Emma and Simon politely declined, as they did her offer of a Coke or Fanta: Cathy had warned them they put far more sugar in these drinks in Africa than they did in the UK. After lunch, they set off on Sheila's tour of Harare, which she had drawn up without consulting either of them. Emma had already concluded Sheila was not a strong believer in participatory planning.

* * *

It took them little time to reach the city centre and, as they drove, Emma and Simon's first trip in daylight, they were struck by how wide the streets were, how old the cars seemed, how many pedestrians they saw walking and, overall, how clean everything looked. They were surprised Sheila could leave her car in a multi-storey carpark but later learned that Harare boasted a number of them. Their first stop was the Eastgate Shopping Centre, where Simon and Emma bought local SIM cards for their phones.

They connected easily to the NetOne phone network which, the shop assistant told them with little conviction, usually had coverage as far afield as Mutoko. As they were close by, they walked across a couple of streets – learning traffic lights are called "robots" here – to the Anglican cathedral where Cathy and Peter were married. Simon recognised the grey sandstone entrance and tower, granite-pillared interior and the main stained-glass windows from his parents' wedding photos. Emma thought its thoroughly English look was completely out of character overlooking Africa Unity Square, ablaze with the colours of the tropical flower market. It was, she felt, a cathedral in the wrong place; a cathedral of otherness.

Returning to the car via First Street, which Sheila said was the city centre's most upmarket shopping district, they drove west along Harare's widest thoroughfare, Samora Machel Avenue. Sheila pointed out Pearl Assurance House, once the city's tallest building. It was here that Simon's family's accountancy firm, Robertson and Lewis, set up offices in the optimistic days of the Federation of Rhodesia and Nyasaland, before Northern Rhodesia broke away to become Zambia and Nyasaland to become Malawi, and before the family business was eventually absorbed into one of Zimbabwe's big-four accountancy firms and its name passed into history. Turning left into Rotten Row, on their right they passed the opulent gold façade of the Sheraton Hotel and the cock-adorned headquarters of the ruling party, ZANU (PF) on their way to the city's only hill, unimaginatively called "the *Kopje*" – Afrikaans for "hill" – where Sheila told them they have a good view of the city. Sheila said in the old days she would have parked the car on the roadside and walked up to the top with them, but nowadays it wasn't safe to leave vehicles unattended in most parts of town, especially round the *Kopje*. So she sat and waited while Emma and Simon walked the few yards to the top to take in the panorama: they had an almost 360-degree view of the city.

Aided by two young entrepreneurs eager to tell them what they were looking at and give them some of its history for what they said would be a little loose change, they looked about them. To the northeast they could see the current city centre with its odd mix of buildings and architectural styles, from the Federal boom to the more recent additions, many glass-fronted as in London, vaguely recognising the skyline they had first seen at a distance from their plane when they came into land. To the east and southeast, their newly-appointed and supremely confident guides told them lay the older centre, now a mess of busy, noisy and dirty roads, the oldest tin-roofed houses and shops huddled together in a mishmash of what looked like confusion between the railway lines, marked by long unused and rusting goods wagons and some mostly old factories and warehouses stretching out as far as the eye could see. Simon said it looked like a town planner's nightmare.

In the distance beyond, to the southeast and to the southwest, their eager tour guides pointed to the older high density suburbs half hidden in the dry dust and beyond, in the haze, the old Pioneer cemetery. Closer in, they gazed down onto the decaying Mbare hostels which their budding local historians told them had been built to house tens of thousands of single migrant workers in dormitory-type accommodation where they were packed in like caged-chickens and froze in the cold nights of winter. Emma shuddered; they did look grim.

Back in the car and light of two $1 notes they had handed over for their briefing, which Sheila said was far too much, they drove back along Rotten Row to pass Prince Edward School where both Peter and Jim had been pupils. In those days Simon knew it had predominantly been a school for white boys; today as they saw the children – still only boys – spilling out onto the pavements on foot and on bicycles, smartly-dressed in their school uniforms, there was not a white face to be seen.

The final destination of their tour was Nazareth House, slightly out of town to the northeast of the city in the Highlands suburb of Harare. Simon reminded Emma this was where Sheila and Cathy's mother, his grandmother, had lived for her final years and died when Simon was just two. Sheila's route took them passed the manicured fairways and greens of the Royal Harare Golf Club, where neatly-dressed men in hats, and a number in shorts and long socks, were swinging their clubs or walking, their bag-carrying and sweating caddies hurrying along besides them. Beyond the golf course, they passed through some of Harare's most affluent northern suburbs, with their wide tree-lined roads and their walled or high-fenced properties, many surrounded by red, orange and yellow-flowering cannas, their walls spilling over with dazzling bougainvillea. In front of some of the large plots they saw national flags flying; these were either embassies or ambassadorial residences. Between them Emma and Simon named the flags of Greece, Algeria, Norway, Iran, Ethiopia and Switzerland before they turned and left this affluent residential area. Sheila only named Switzerland, admitting laughingly even that had been a guess, but adding how impressed she was with the numbers of different flags they recognised. These magnificent houses with their strong gates, high walls and smartly-attired security guards and the general air of opulence they gave off provided Emma with her second reminder in as many days of London's Winnington Road.

When they reached Nazareth House and Simon saw the white brick buildings and bright red-tiled roofs in front of them, it all seemed strangely familiar to him. This wasn't so surprising because as a baby he had been a frequent visitor when Cathy had brought him on visits to see her dying mother. However, he quickly dismissed this as an explanation, believing he owed his strong sense of *déjà vu* more to the many photographs of Nazareth House and of his sitting on his grandmother's knee he had thumbed through as a child in London than his actually remembering these visits. After all, he was only two years old when Gran died.

Sheila told Simon how comforted she had been in those difficult final days by the Nazareth House sisters and insisted they pay a visit to the chapel where she knelt down, eyes closed in silent prayer. Simon stood at the back feeling extremely uncomfortable amongst the statues, crucifixes and holy water fonts, the waxy smell of burning candles and the lingering odours of Sunday's incense. Just like when she had seen Harare's Anglican out-of-place cathedral an hour or so ago, Emma was struck by how un-African the chapel looked, the statues and paintings of Jesus, Mary and the early apostles depicted as Caucasians, with not an African or even Jewish or Arab feature in sight. Yet she smiled to herself, thinking how happy Sarah would have been in such a traditional Catholic setting. In some mysterious way Emma could never grasp, these religious symbols gave Sarah great comfort.

Nazareth House was hardly a five-minute drive back to the Reddys' house in Mandara. This time when they reached the house and the gates opened, Emma asked Sheila to stop the car so she could greet properly the man who last night had been half-hidden in the darkness. Though Sheila found the request a little odd, she brought the car to a halt just as Emma jumped out and walked towards the now hoodless gatekeeper, and Simon followed.

Emma held out her hand and, trying hard not to sound like a brash foreigner, said "Mr Mashayamombe."

He began with a deferential "Madam," but beamed as they took the time to greet each other properly and then chatted briefly in far more halting English than Jessica spoke. He was clearly as delighted with the exchange as Emma.

As they stepped back into the car, Emma thought she had made up in some small way for their insensitivity in the manner they had greeted Jessica earlier in the morning. Emma readily acknowledged to herself their actions were little more than gestures. They had hardly done more than stop and take a little time to say hello, but she felt good about it all the same.

Jim was already home when they got back. On hearing the sound of the car he came outside, greeted them warmly and ushered them through the house and out onto the terrace for a pre-dinner drink: it was now past 5:30, so well within the comfort zone of sundowner time. Sheila excused herself, saying she needed to freshen up, and told them she would join them as soon as she could. Jim and Simon had a beer, but Emma said she would like another rock shandy. As she drank deeply after her dusty afternoon in the city and the sugars began to do their work, it felt good, and she told Jim his drink really did hit the spot. By the time Sheila joined them, they were all well into their second drinks.

Jim was keen to know what they made of Harare. Simon began by sharing some of the factual details of their day out: the sim-card purchase, their visits to the *Kopje*, the Anglican cathedral and Nazareth House, and their drive past the Pearl Assurance Building and Prince Edward School. Emma was far more interested in feeding back to Jim her first impressions of the city: the near-perfect weather; the wide and quite empty streets; the sheer numbers of people on the move; the vibrant colours; the paucity of pushchairs and the ever-present sight of mothers with babies tied to their backs, some with packages balanced precariously on their heads.

She said the main thing which struck her about Harare was the sharp contrasts in what she saw. Jim asked her to tell him more, which nicely warmed her up to launch into an explanation of what she meant while Jim and Simon drank their beer, finished the peanuts and listened.

"On the one hand," said Emma, "there is the wealth and orderliness of that part of the city centre clustered around the modern high-rise buildings and the affluence of the extensive northern suburbs. On the other hand, there is the dust of the industrial sites and the dirt and grime of the more tightly-packed housing of the older southern suburbs we saw at a distance from the top of the *Kopje.*"

Emma did not add what she was also thinking – that Sheila had not included the rougher and poorer parts of the city on today's tour.

She continued in the same vein. "On the one hand, the city is bristling with stores stocked with the latest gadgets, shop windows displaying clothes as fashionable as you might find in Oxford Street and coffee shops alive with the young-with-money willing, even eager, to part with their dollars. On the other hand, these upmarket shops all seemed pretty empty, especially of customers willing to part with the sort of money needed to buy the goods enticingly displayed in their shop windows.

"For most people, this sort of shopping is not so much a distant dream, more an irrelevance. Most of the people we saw walking, the majority of people on the move, were not only far away from the commercial centre of the city, but they were clearly walking because they had to walk, many obviously having to cover quite long distances. Most were dressed in drab-to-shabby work-a-day clothes; some were even walking barefoot. We encountered small groups of women and a few individuals trying to sell us what they were carrying, and what a variety, from lace tablecloths to, in one case, live chickens. When the car stopped at the lights, we were met by jay-walkers encouraging us to buy matches and kitchen cloths, and one enterprising man was egging us on to buy an Arab version of Monopoly.

"I couldn't help laughing," she said. "But, more seriously, Harare seems to be full of budding entrepreneurs. But then there were also the beggars. A few people approached us directly with outstretched hands, most of whom by looked in a quite a bad way; some were clearly hungry.

"A number stuck with us, I have never experienced such persistence." Emma, even as a journalist, had been upset by her interaction with the beggars. "In London I am well used to beggars, but there they park themselves in strategic locations on the city's most-frequented streets. Here it was quite different: I was challenged by beggars on the move, something I have never met before, and a number ran along beside us."

As she was speaking, Jim realised that in the short time she had been in Harare Emma had noticed things he had scarcely been aware of his whole life. He looked across at her in a new way: she was an impressive woman – that was for sure!

"You have a sharp eye, young Emma," said Jim, trying to sound exactly the opposite of condescending. "I guess it's your journalistic training, hey? But I can tell you the begging problem was far worse in the past. The police and local authorities have at least recently had some success both in moving such people along and in stopping them coming into the centre of the city, which is starting to get to the root of the problem."

Emma felt she should respond, but she held back. There was one final observation from their tour of Harare she was eager to share and, as no one else spoke, she said, "Finally, there were the children. On the one hand, we saw plenty of clean, neatly-dressed and laughing book-carrying children leaving what looked like pretty affluent schools on foot or on their bicycles, or watching vigilantly for the cars and mini-vans to pick them up and take them home. On the other hand, we saw plenty of un-uniformed, simply dressed, rucksack-less children, a number without shoes, many walking along on their own quite aimlessly on pavements far from the entrances to any school and probably far from home. The contrast could not have been greater.

"In short, what my first day taught me is that Harare is a city of huge differences between the haves and the have-nots."

Jim and Sheila, who had come in on the tail of Emma's reflections, nodded but Simon and Emma couldn't pick up what their nodding conveyed. They were disappointed. Keen as they had been to share their impressions of the city Simon and Emma were even keener to hear what Sheila and Jim's views were about the country as they saw it today. Having followed Zimbabwean news over many years, more recently as a journalist, Emma had developed strong views about the erosion of democracy, corruption and the abuse of power so she wanted to hear what Jim and Sheila had to say about party politics and human rights in contemporary Zimbabwe. Understandably, she also wanted to know more about the freedom of the press and how the rise of social media had influenced people's access to news and political debate. Simon wanted to know why they had chosen to stay on in Harare, when his own parents had decided to leave. It was quite an agenda, but at least they hoped they could make a start.

With their sundowner drinks over and as the four of them sat down to dinner, which Jessica had prepared just before she left at six, Emma and Simon encouraged Jim and Sheila to share their own views about at least some of these issues. Repeatedly, however, they could not be drawn into saying much of substance when first Simon then Emma tried to move the conversation on to party politics and human rights issues, and then to differing living standards and the huge gulf between rich and poor. Indeed, the more they prodded the more they realised they were getting nowhere.

It didn't take them long to realise why their questioning never seemed to lead anywhere. It wasn't because Jim or Sheila were deliberately trying to be evasive. Dinner was a very happy affair, free from any tension. Indeed, as they parted for the night, Emma felt the tenderness and clearly heartfelt embrace both Jim and Sheila gave her summed up the growing and genuine warmth which had developed between them in the short period – scarcely 24 hours – since they had first met.

No, the reason for their reticence lay in the way the Reddys looked at the world. For Jim and Sheila, life, all of life, was to be understood – *could only* be understood – through the prism of their Christian beliefs. This is what really mattered to them. It was the one topic of conversation they were keenest to engage in and certainly the one which interested them the most. So whenever either Emma or Simon raised any new topic about present-day Zimbabwe, the discussion always came back to their Christian faith. Why? Not because they were trying to be evasive, but rather because it was this which provided them with the fundamental answer to everything.

* * *

Simon had known from his mother that, quite soon after they had married, Jim and Sheila had become evangelical Christians and were active members of their local Pentecostal Church. What he had not sufficiently understood until this evening was quite how pivotal their faith, their evangelical Christianity, was to them both. It was the bedrock to their life. It not only informed and shaped their view of their own world and the wider world beyond. It also influenced their relationships and determined who were likely to be their closest friends and explained why they continued to live in Zimbabwe when so many of their friends had left, and why they would go on living here.

Sheila began by saying they had both been brought up as Christians, she a Methodist and Jim an Anglican. But then she explained they only really became true, believing Christians after having a joint conversion experience soon after they were married.

"It overwhelmed us at the time," said Sheila and Jim nodded in agreement. "And it changed everything afterwards."

Jim then took over, explaining that it happened because they were open to the grace of God, which was poured out onto them and flooded into their souls.

"Our new faith led us to understand, fully and completely, the meaning of life. It opened our eyes to the fact that God had sent Jesus onto the earth to save us and our purpose in life is to participate in his life-giving mission. The way we do this is to scrupulously follow God's law as revealed by Jesus and preserved forever in the Bible.

"And what a gift that is," he couldn't help adding.

Sheila then picked up the story. "The Bible," she said, "is the Word of God. It is true, no ifs, buts or maybes, because God told us it is true. You need to read it, we all need to read it and do what it unambiguously instructs us to do. It is not merely a guide to life; it is the surest guide there is. As we read the Bible and understand how Jesus lived and loved, we draw inspiration to follow in his footsteps, to love others as Jesus loved us and taught us to do."

Emma was very familiar with the views of evangelical Christians, but what struck her about Sheila and Jim was the matter-of-fact way they described their beliefs. There was no sense of any embarrassment. However, what did surprise her was that neither Sheila nor Jim seemed to want to try to convert others – Simon and Emma in this instance – to their point of view, as had many of the evangelical Christians Emma had known in London. They were evangelical in their beliefs but not in terms of wanting to proselytise. Indeed, even Simon, who did not share with them the fact he was an atheist, was struck by how, over the course of the whole evening, neither of them asked either Emma or Simon what they believed.

At one point, Emma did say she was a Christian but, as she told them, a rather different, free-thinking one. However, neither Sheila nor Jim seemed eager to dig and discover how and why her Christianity might differ from theirs. It didn't seem to interest them. What Emma and Simon saw in Sheila and Jim were kind, caring – yes, decent – human beings, so secure in their faith they felt neither challenged by anyone who thought any differently from the way they did nor the need to discuss their different beliefs. It was as if their faith encouraged them to cocoon themselves in their own world, a world of order, of regularity and – dare they say it – of comfort?

"Our lives revolve around our church and the community life and fellowship which flows from our church membership," said Sheila. "I work for the church, both as a physiotherapist as well as helping to run the administrative side of the church."

"All our closest friends are members of our church," added Jim. "A few are white, but the vast majority are black Zimbabweans."

They explained that since their conversion they have gone out of their way to welcome all their close church friends into their home, and when they holidayed inside the country, they did so with far more black than white Zimbabweans. And as they spoke, neither Simon nor Emma detected any hint of racism from either of them. Jim then went on to explain how his job, his work and his faith all fitted together.

"God," said Jim, "gave me the attributes, talents and opportunities I have to enable me to obtain a good job with a steady income, first with the Delta Corporation and now as an independent consultant. Each day I thank the Lord for his God-given gifts, the economic security he has given me and the rich life with which Sheila and I have been blessed."

It was their God-given faith, their God-given economic security and their God-given friends which explained why neither Jim nor Sheila had felt any need or desire to leave the country. All they wished for and needed, they had here.

As Sheila succinctly put it, "Life is satisfying, life is predictable and life is meaningful.

"Two of our three children have gone to live in South Africa. That was their choice and we are happy for them. However, we are additionally blessed as Mary-Louise, our youngest, chose to stay and she remains a pillar of our church.

"If we were allowed to be proud," she added with a smile, "we would be proud of her. She is soon to be married and if it is God's will, we will be blessed with grandchildren."

Jim went on to tell them the Mashayamombes, Jessica and Matthew, were also evangelical Christians, though not members of their own worshipping community, and this was why they employed them.

"My God-given wealth enables me to pay them a good salary," continued Jim. "I am able to pay them far more than the going minimum wage. I am also able to contribute to their pension fund so they will be comfortable in their old age, just as we will be. It's all part of what we understand as Christian justice."

Emma was also pretty sure they gave a significant proportion of their income to charity, almost certainly church charities, as Sheila had mentioned during the course of the evening the Gospel's insistence on feeding the hungry and helping those in need.

Although they didn't talk about it directly, their evangelical faith and outlook also shed some light on Jim and Sheila's approach to Zimbabwean politics. While they clearly recognised and were ready to acknowledge the problems of present-day Zimbabwe, with its beggars and its vast number of unemployed, they viewed all failings, all weaknesses and all evil as rooted in and caused by individual weakness and human selfishness. As a result, in their view the solution to these problems lay principally and most fundamentally in personal conversion.

As Jim put it, "The abuse of power, the corruption, the disappearances and even torture, all of this can be traced back to the evil in people's hearts. People need to acknowledge the evil in themselves and open themselves up to God's grace so as to have the strength to turn away from evil and lead better, more Christian lives. Social evils, economic evils and political evils are clearly terrible but they need to be seen mostly as cumulative and as extreme cases of the evil and potential evil in all of us."

"Yes," said Sheila, "and that's why we always pray for our leaders to ask God to open their hearts to His goodness, to turn away from evil. For us this is far more important, providing a far more potentially powerful force for change than if we were ever to get involved in politics ourselves and join any particular political party."

Seeing neither Emma nor Simon looked convinced, Jim added that, like everyone else but even more so as Christians, they had a responsibility to vote when elections came round. But he said they believed real change came less from what politicians promised and more from people being true to the Christian Gospel and leading lives of personal honesty and integrity. However, he went on to say he knew well a number of evangelical Christians who were heavily involved in national politics, and he admired them hugely for their courage in speaking out against human rights and other abuses. But, he said, he and Sheila had decided to take a different approach.

"I would be the first to say the social, political or economic order in this country needs to change, to improve," said Jim. "But as I have said already – though perhaps I need to spell out even more clearly – Sheila and I believe the best way for this to happen is for us to engage with, talk to and work *with* all people, including politicians, not to simply to *oppose*."

Dinner had begun with a pause for silent prayer and it ended with Sheila thanking God for bringing Emma and Simon into their lives. As it was already late, Emma knew it was time to bring their evening to a close. She briefly thanked them both for supper and for everything else they had done for them since their arrival, saying she was sure they were both tired now and they should all turn in for the night. Sheila and Jim were hugely relieved because even though it was not yet 8:30, they were both struggling to keep awake. In less than half an hour, they had taken leave of their guests, and were asleep after holding hands together to thank God for his innumerable blessings – as they had done without fail every night since the day of their joint conversion.

When Sheila and Jim had retired for the night, Simon and Emma went back to the sitting room. Although they were also tired – Simon admitted Sheila had been right about the effects of being new to living at 5,000 feet – in part wanting to recapture the mood of their morning walk, they both felt the need simply to be in each other's company.

As they talked, they both said how pleasantly surprised they had been at how well they had got on with both Jim and Sheila in spite of the frustration both of them felt with their conversation about present-day Zimbabwe not getting anywhere. Simon commented on the fact that neither

Jim nor Sheila saw themselves as particularly affluent when to both him and Emma they so clearly were, with their large and stunningly beautiful garden, their pristine swimming pool, their servants and their economic security. Emma laughed as Simon said Sheila was even more of a control freak than his mother.

They then shared a few thoughts on the Christian faith discussions, with Simon agreeing with Emma when she said, "You simply can't engage with them about their views on Christianity. Just like their London co-evangelicals, theirs is a self-contained system, logical and internally consistent, and impossible to penetrate to anyone who doesn't share their fundamentalist beliefs."

"So unlike you, Em," said Simon.

"Yes," said Emma. "You know, I was holding back because you told me before supper you didn't want me to upset the applecart. But it seemed so pointless anyway as I knew it would get us nowhere, though I do wonder how they would have responded if I had said what I really believe."

"And I know pretty much what you would have said," chimed in Simon. "Let me see how right I am!

"You would have said the essence of Christianity is to look afresh at the world, with eyes that see. You would have gone on to say that for you, Christian belief requires you to see the world from the viewpoint of the poor and to seek to change it so they can participate and fulfil themselves as the rich can. If you had been really courageous you would have told them the Jesus of the Gospel challenges us to continually look at our own lives because routine breeds complacency, and complacency, ever so subtly, perpetuates the *status quo*. And you would probably have finished with a flourish, telling them that, in your view, charitable giving is only Christian if it is accompanied working for a more just world."

Emma smiled, leant over and kissed Simon, saying "you know, I do believe you now know my take on the Christian faith almost as well as I do myself. The pity, my dear, is you don't share it, and I fear you never will."

"You're right," said Simon. "But because I don't believe in God doesn't mean I can't empathise with you. The conclusions you draw from your Christianity about how life should be led make total sense to me. It's simply that I don't believe in God or think belief in God is necessary to do that."

"Actually," said Emma laughing, impressed by Simon's first-ever encapsulation of her Christian faith, "I would have added two more things. Firstly, I would have said Christianity which looks at the world solely through the lives and motivations of individuals is a cop-out. And then I would have added that, in my view, believing God blesses you in your wealth is the polar opposite of what I understand the essence of Christianity to be. Indeed, it's what Jesus criticised the Pharisees for and was the prime reason they had him killed." Emma knew she was repeating Don Paulo's words almost verbatim.

"But enough of this," she went on, knowing it was the days ahead of them they were both keener to focus on.

Now they had had their first "taster" of the country, Emma told Simon how excited she was to see her family and learn more about what she was sure was the very different world of rural Zimbabwe. It was a world, she said, that she had come from but which she realised she knew even less about than she thought she did 24 hours ago. She was even keener now to go and visit her family than she had been before they left London. As they sat next to each other, chatting about what they might discover over the next few days, she could feel the excitement rising inside her. Simon said how novel, even thrilling, it felt being in Africa today for what to him seemed like the very first time, though he added that he hadn't yet had time to process it all in his head. He went on to say how much he, too, was also really looking forward to what was to come.

"Dad was dead right," he said. "I did need to come here. I'm now so pleased he was so persistent and pushed me.

"I'm particularly pleased to have begun to get to know Jim," he went on, more reflectively. "For all our differences, he strikes me as a really honest and sincere person. Already I am beginning to understand how he and Dad had become friends and I'm really looking forward to our time together at Kariba where I can get to know him even better."

Simon knew his relationship with his father had never been as good as either of them would have wished it to be, and he was hoping Jim would provide him with a new way in to his father. Besides that, he was even keener now to know more about the life his parents had led before they left the country and why they had decided to abandon it all – things he had always found so difficult to discuss at home, especially when it came to his Dad. Simon's main worry now was there wouldn't be enough time for everything he wanted to talk about and to do.

They were too tired to talk further, so they reluctantly agreed to part. As they rose to go to their rooms, they hugged, their bodies aching for each other even more than they ached for sleep. As they walked the dozen or so paces to their bedroom doors on opposite sides of the corridor, fearful of waking Jim and Sheila, they bade each other goodnight as quietly as they could – their arms coiled around each other like an African cobra as they drew their bodies tightly together. Then they kissed tenderly and lingered for a final moment outside their rooms with hands outstretched and fingers just touching before separating for the night.

Though they were both greatly looking forward to their next few days, they also knew they would miss each other terribly. As they fell asleep they both dreamt of the few days they would be spending together at the Victoria Falls for the last few days of their trip. They both knew this holiday-within-a-holiday, their time alone, just the two of them, following their respective visits to Mutoko and Kariba, was going to be the high point of their entire time in Zimbabwe.

So powerful and comforting was the thought of her time together with Simon at the Victoria Falls that, for probably the first time since they had been together, Emma fell asleep without either a conscious or subconscious visit from Robbie.

Mutoko

Mutoko lies some 90 miles east of Harare. Confusingly, if you google "Mutoko" on TripAdvisor you are shown a picture of the Victoria Falls – as far from Mutoko as Geneva is from London. It is rarely visited by outsiders unless they are travelling all the way to the international border with Mozambique through Nyamapanda and need a break. It boasts no hotel and its commercial centre looks more like a temporary settlement than a longstanding urban centre. The town itself is difficult for even alert passers-by to notice: most of its scattered low-rise buildings are hidden from view by the rocky granite hillocks and outcrops which, as Peter had told Emma, are a dominant feature of this part of Mashonaland East. No wonder the outside world knows so little about it.

The Makoni family homestead, where Emma is headed, is about 20 miles to the east of Mutoko, a brisk half-hour walk from All Souls, the Catholic mission staked out from the bush by early missionaries well over 70 years ago. In contrast with Mutoko town, All Souls is thriving, with its primary and secondary school, its extensive hospital and its nationally-recognised nurses' training centre abuzz with activity. All this now eclipses the decaying church with its once magnificent but now cracking dome-topped tower, which still attracts thousands who flock there for Mass each Sunday. Fortunately for Emma, her bus goes on to All Souls after stopping briefly in Mutoko town, and this is where the family have arranged to meet her.

This morning's journey began on time, leaving the Rezende Street bus station exactly at 9:30, arriving at All Souls at about 1 pm, a little later than scheduled. Emma handed over her US $6 single fare to the driver, reckoning this was less than she would need to pay to go two stops on the London underground, a journey of at most a couple of hundred yards.

Arriving early, with a small backpack filled with gifts she had brought from England and the clothes and toiletries she had packed for her five nights away, the money Sarah had entrusted her with safely tucked away on her person, Emma found an empty row of seats half-way down the bus, sat next to the window and settled down to read. Ever the planner, she had brought out with her the local author Charles Mungoshi's *Coming of the Dry Season*. When she had first come across his books as a young teenager she had found his descriptions of rural Zimbabwe so evocative she had decided to read them again on the bus to aid her transition from urban to rural Zimbabwe and prepare herself to meet her family as she watched the changing countryside unfold before her. She wanted to recreate the intoxicating feeling of Africa she had felt so intensely as a teenager so far away in London and which she was on the point of experiencing first-hand.

Old Musoni raised his dusty eyes from his hoe and the unchanging stony earth he had been tilling and peered into the sky. He looked to the west. Soon the sun would go down. He looked over the sun-blasted land and saw the shadows creeping east, blearier and taller with every moment that the sun sheds each of its rays. Unconsciously wishing for rain and relief, he bent down again to his work and did not see his son, Nhamo approaching....

Emma is not disappointed by what she sees from her window as the bus journeys east. Once they have left Harare behind and everyone has finished greeting each other, the journey is mostly quiet save for the chug-chug-chugging of the bus's ageing diesel engine. The tarmac surface shimmers in the heat, every now and then creating the illusion of pools of water suddenly appearing then disappearing before often reappearing again further down the road.

Occasionally the quiet and emptiness of the road are interrupted by the noise of passing vehicles – mini-vans, cars, trucks, motorbikes and a rare bus – and the commotion caused by the blaring of horns as impatient drivers wave their arms in frustration before vanishing as quickly as they have come. Every driver is aware lethal potholes lie in wait along the road – some wide, some deep, some both but all potential death-traps. But, as Emma can see though she is not a driver herself, many are driving far too fast, and she knows a common reason why: they are the worse for drink.

They pass the 35-kilometre peg which marks the place where 26 people died in a horrific head-on bus crash earlier in the year; closer to Mutoko they pass the spot where 13 others died six months earlier, drink being a likely cause of both. Emma knows about these horrific accidents because on her regular trawls of the internet she has seen the coverage given to them by the local press. She also knows these accidents and deaths were deemed too remote and unimportant to BBC news editors to merit any mention in the British domestic media, reinforcing her view that foreign black lives don't matter.

She sees rickety old three-sided, open-backed, two-wheeled trailers – scotch-carts – pulled reluctantly along by unwilling donkeys or oxen goaded on by barefoot, scantily-clad boys in shorts running alongside, their crudely-made but skilfully wielded, long-roped sticks at the ready. She watches a few wizened old men and a number of carefree teenage boys riding rickety bicycles and sees some being pushed off the tarmac into the dust by irate drivers, incensed they should have trespassed onto their road. She observes sweating women walking alone or in lines of two or three, one behind the other. All are weighed down by heavy burdens and some have babies on their backs as well. Many are also carrying packages on their heads which balance precariously on rolled-up cloths placed between their loads and their scarf-covered heads: heavy packs of mealie-meal, metal containers of cooking oil, unknown parcels wrapped in brown paper, and, in one case, an empty glass Coca-Cola bottle. Their progress is slowed not only by the heat of the day and the bundles they are carrying but also by their long skirts which are wrapped tightly round their waists. Emma remembers as a five-year-old trying to balance a book on her head and walk across the sitting room after her mother had shown how, but she could never do it. She marvels at what she now sees.

The bus makes a brief stop at Murewa town, about a third of the way to Mutoko. Afterwards massive outcrops of bare granite rock, increasing in size and number, begin to come into view. Some are tall, almost elongated, some long and flat. One massive rock stands out, arched and majestic like the long back of a lion poised, alert and ready for the chase. Thin wisps of smoke start to appear, rising vertically in the distance, blown this way and that by unpredictable gusts of heat-driven wind. From reading Mungoshi, Emma knows the smoke is likely to have come from bushfires, increasingly common here in the late spring, some lit deliberately, some caused by human error, others started for no clear reason. But whatever the reason, the outcome is the same. When the fire subsides the earth will have turned black and a lingering smell of burnt and smouldering wood remains. Then, suddenly, the scorched soil will witness the birth of new shoots with green leaves, new life rising from the scarred and seemingly-dead soil which, every farmer hopes, heralds the coming of this year's rains. Emma is keen to be out there to smell for herself the burnt bush she has read and dreamed about.

Birds of prey circle, keen-eyed, high above, catching the thermals, flying alone or groups of two or at most three, ever watchful. They look like eagles, or perhaps they are vultures? They are too high to tell.

Then, standing out from other trees in the distant hills, Emma catches her first sighting of the deep oranges and wine-reds of the *msasa* trees, their leaves as vivid and distinctive as a New England fall. Here, though, their bold colours, so distinctive against the backdrop of the other forest trees which are still brown and leafless, is not a sign of autumn but of spring. The *msasas'* new leaves announce that the raw winter nights will soon be over. Soon the biting and bitter cold of this part of Africa will be but a distant dream.

However, Emma's plans to read are thwarted almost as soon as she has opened her book. When she turns the second page of the chapter she opens at random, a bright-eyed, fresh-faced young woman about her age tumbles into the seat next to her. She is breathless from running to catch the bus and from the burden of carrying three or four heavy bags which she lets fall around her as she sits down. Apologising for nearly hitting Emma with one of them, the woman smiles and they greet each other. In an instant, following a quick glance at Emma, the woman knows they will be conversing in English, which is fine for her because, like almost all young urban Zimbabweans, she is fluent. A moment or two later it becomes clear to Emma she is not going to get any reading done because, as she is soon to discover, Farisai (she never volunteers her other name and Emma never asks) is a serial talker.

As Farisai talks about herself and her world, what she has to say more than compensates for Emma's aborted plan to read. Chatting away almost non-stop, Farisai opens up new and totally different windows on the realities of present-day Zimbabwe, different either from what Emma has already observed or from what she is about to experience with her family. It dawns on Emma that her book is redundant.

The conversation, however, starts off with Emma. As soon as she opens her mouth, Farisai knows she is different. But it isn't just the way Emma speaks: the clothes she is wearing and the way she does her hair are all different too. Emma's bearing speaks of a confidence and self-assurance which fascinates Farisai to such an extent that her inquisitiveness overcomes her cultural reserve. She wants to know more about this woman sitting next to her, who she is and why she is here, sitting on what is after all a pretty ordinary and old inter-city bus travelling to such an out-of-the-way destination.

So, after a few pleasantries, Farisai turns directly to Emma and says, "So let's start with you. Tell me your name, my dear, and how you come to be my travelling companion today."

Emma tells Farisai her name, that she was born in Zimbabwe and her family come from the Mutoko area, but she grew up in England with her mother and has not been back to the country since she was two years old. She is now heading off to meet her extended family. It is clear they will get on so Emma explains why she is called Maconie with a *c*, then an *on* and then an *i-e*, and not Makoni with a *k*, then an *on*, and then a single *i*. When she has finished Farisai bursts out laughing and Emma knows they will get on. She is just about to add that she sees herself as English and not Zimbabwean, but she holds back.

Almost from the moment she stepped foot in the country, certainly from the time she started chatting to the different officials she encountered at the airport, Emma had felt a sort of bond or link between herself and those she met and greeted. It was difficult to put her finger on it, but she felt sort of at one with the Zimbabweans she spoke to, or rather black Zimbabweans. She certainly felt it with Jessica, perhaps a little with Jim but certainly not with Sheila, and she was having that same feeling now as she sat and talked with Farisai. Though she knew she was English, she felt English and until now had been more than happy to say she was English, in some strange way she couldn't really explain, Emma now felt part of her belonged here. At the airport, she had had the beginnings of the feeling of a homecoming, and those feelings were even stronger now. Emma sensed she wasn't simply or just English.

Farisai is aware of Emma's hesitation but she doesn't enquire or probe further. She is a very straightforward person. She *knows* Emma is different and that is enough for her. It is sufficient for Farisai to convince herself she is on safe ground to begin to open up to Emma about herself, and once she has started there is no stopping her. And the more Farisai tells Emma about herself, the more Emma is at first fascinated, then increasingly aghast, by what she is hearing. As a journalist Emma knows the power and importance of what she is hearing, and as she does so she recalls Rosemary's suggestion about doing some interviews about contemporary Zimbabwe while she was here and making contact with BBC colleagues or stringers. But as a journalist she also knows the ethics of her profession. Farisai is about to tell her life story not to a professional journalist but to Emma – the person who quite by chance has been thrown next to her on the bus and in whom she feels comfortable confiding. Unless when they part Emma is to ask Farisai if she could retell her life story to the wider world – which she has no intention of doing – Emma knows the price of listening to Farisai is that she will have to keep pretty much all of what she hears to herself.

Farisai is a qualified nurse who works at the large government hospital in Harare, the Parirayanetwa. She lives with her husband in Highfield, one of Harare's most pleasant high-density suburbs, old enough to have been designed with tarred roads and trees. Farisai is travelling to Mutoko today to visit her mother but, more importantly, to be with her five-year-old daughter, Rudo. Rudo lives with Farisai's mother and not with her in town. Yesterday Emma had classified Zimbabweans into two groups: the poor and unemployed she saw walking the streets of Harare and the rich Zimbabweans, far fewer in number, she saw in the up-market shops and cafes. Here was someone in between; someone from a poorer background but in work with a permanent job, married, living in a house with running water and electricity, clearly cheerful and with a caring mother ready to step in and help with child-minding – it all sounded very positive to Emma. But then, as Farisai begins to flesh out the details, a very different sort of reality emerges.

"I am a nurse," repeats Farisai, "and I know that means having to work extremely long hours."

"But you're paid well," says Emma enquiringly.

"No, I'm not," says Farisai bluntly. "I get $15 a day and when I do nights they give me only 50 cents more each night I'm on. It costs me more than almost $2 a day for transport."

My God, says Emma to herself, after paying to get to work that's less than £10 a month with a measly 30 pence for a night shift.

Farisai explains it is her lack of money which necessitates her having her daughter Rudo live with her mother, a widow, 100-odd miles away in Mutoko because she can't afford even a few dollars a month to pay for a childminder when she is at work.

"Rudo has lived with Ma almost since the day she was born, well before she was weaned," says Farisai. "It takes me three or four months to save the round-trip fare to come and visit them for just a few days, and I have to use up my annual leave to do so.

"And today, as usual, my bags are filled with what I have managed to scrape together since my last visit to help feed and clothe my beautiful Rudo." She opens her bags to show Emma a mishmash of second-hand clothes and plastic toys, a random bag of onions, a few sweets and the heaviest, containing a big sack of mealie meal.

As they talk, Farisai reveals the complexity of her marital arrangements, the details of which would appal even a hardened journalist. Her husband is a doctor at the hospital where she works. He is still married to his first wife and is about to marry a third: Farisai is the one in between. Some ten years into his first marriage and having already fathered five children, her husband began seeing Farisai and brought her home to live with him. After a while, and at her prompting, he started the process of exchanging gifts with Farisai's family in order to formalise the process of her becoming his second wife. However, the arrangements were never completed and now are never likely to be because, soon after Rudo was born, he began seeing someone new, a woman still in her teens.

The familiar pattern was repeated: soon she became pregnant and then she moved into the house in Highfields to join his two wives and five of the doctor's six children. When the newest bride arrived, Farisai was instructed to leave his bedroom and move into the room his first wife was now occupying, joining as many of her children as were able to sleep there; the house had only two bedrooms. The arrival of the third wife coincided with the doctor's starting to assault Farisai physically.

"Recently," said Farisai, "the beatings have become more frequent," and she lowered the nape of her dress to show Emma the bruising round her neck and arms to prove the point. Emma gasped in horror and grabbed Farisai's hand. Farisai turned to her and attempted a smile; Emma had tears in her eyes.

"My husband, the doctor, was not the first man to abuse me," said Farisai, whose confidence in telling Emma even more upsetting things about her life had been boosted on seeing her tears.

"No, the first time happened when I was just 14 and I was forced to sleep with one of my teachers. It was terrible: he kept demanding me and there was nothing I could do to stop him. What's more, it happened to other girls in my class as well. And if you don't know, it still happens all the time here. Everyone knows but no one seems to care enough for it to be stopped. If you want to pass your exams you have no choice."

Fortunately for Farisai, her teacher was young – a first-time abuser – and she did not contract HIV, unlike a number of her friends who had been forced to sleep with some of the older teachers. Many had been unable to access the anti-retroviral drugs they needed and, to Farisai's knowledge, three had died. Fortunately, she said, reverting to her account of the present day, her doctor-husband had always been careful.

"As a nurse," said Farisai, "I am able to carry out my own test at the hospital and I did this again last month. Fortunately, the results came back negative once again. I am one of the lucky ones."

Emma was struck by Farisai's use of the word "fortunate". *It's I who am the fortunate one* she said to herself. She had not had to grow up where schoolgirl rape and violence in marriage seemed to be so prevalent and where a steady job was no passport out of poverty and hardship, rather the opposite. She began to feel sick to her stomach, though it could have been from the swaying of the bus as it lurched from side to side to avoid the potholes in the road.

Farisai had more to say and pressed on. She told Emma that as jobs had become scarce in Zimbabwe two of her cousins had managed to leave the country and now lived in Glasgow. She said she was not in regular touch with them though she had written twice to see if they could help her to find a job in the UK. She was keen to follow and give Rudo a better life but nothing had come of her enquiries. Occasionally they sent money back, though this had gone to Farisai's mother and her sisters and not to her. Still, Farisai was glad of the help all the same as even a few dollars were always shared out and this meant she could keep back a little more of her own money for herself. A few months ago, she told Emma, her Glasgow-based relatives had sent across $50 and this helped her to buy herself the dress she was wearing today. It was second-hand not new, she told Emma, but then, she said, she hadn't worn new home clothes since the day she stepped out of her last school uniform, explaining that when at school she wore her uniform not only there but at home as well.

As Farisai shared more of the increasingly grim story of her life, Emma marvelled even more at her cheerfulness. For all she had gone through in the past and for all her current problems, she had not given up. Indeed, what shone through was her toughness, her resilience in the face of such hardships – and on top of all that a cheery, even bubbly, disposition. Farisai expressed little bitterness; in fact, she seemed to exude a stoic optimism which Emma found remarkable.

As they draw nearer to Mutoko, where Farisai is getting off, Emma, knowing they're never likely to meet again, is pleased to have been there for Farisai, simply to listen. She feels Farisai's unburdening herself of her problems has been cathartic; a means of releasing some of the tensions she constantly has in life. Emma hopes Farisai's act of telling her about herself and her troubles may also have helped strengthen her inside, nurturing and feeding the sheer determination to soldier on.

When Farisai begins to gather up her things, Emma's mind begins to race. Should she give Farisai her contacts; should she give her some money? Above all else, Emma knows what she really wants to do is simply to give Farisai a huge hug, to wish her well and thank her for sharing so much with her, the stranger on the bus. But Emma knows these instincts come from a different way of interacting; they are driven by different cultural norms. A moment ago, Emma had felt so close to Farisai; now she feels so distant from her. She wants to wrap her arms around her in the warmest of embraces but she knows she can't. Instead, as Farisai is about to rise to say goodbye Emma holds out her hand. Farisai takes it and, before gathering up her things, pauses, smiles and says nothing except to wish Emma well for the rest of her visit. It is her eyes which speak what Farisai feels deep inside: gratitude. For Emma, that look in Farisai's eyes considerably eases the pain she feels in her chest for not having been able to give her the hug she had so wanted to impart.

Then, as she prepares to leave, Emma thrusts two $10 notes into Farisai's hand.

On feeling the dollar bills but not knowing their value, Farisai says, "No, you keep that for yourself, I'm fine, really. It's been good just to talk."

"Please," says Emma as she presses both her hands over Farisai's, "You really must take it, I insist. Here, let me help you hide it."

Farisai folds the money up then tucks it inside the front of her dress before saying she has to rush as she sweeps up her parcels and runs down the bus.

"Thank you, again, Emma," she says again, straining to raise up her heavy bags as if she is trying to wave, saying respectfully – this time in Shona – "Stay well (*Chisarai*)."

"Go well," replies Emma in Shona (*U-fambe zvakanaka*), but Farisai has already jumped off and is gone – from the bus, and from Emma's life.

As a journalist, Emma had listened to many stories of human hardship, but Farisai's touched her more than almost the all others she had heard. She had wanted to help not only because she could, but because she felt guilty listening to Farisai, as if she were somehow to blame for what had happened to her. She knew giving Farisai money would at least ease her pain for a moment, but she also knew it wouldn't solve any of her problems. That was far tougher. Then she thought back to last night's conversation and Simon's telling her that her Christian faith told her giving to charity without working for justice was a cop-out. She then realised why she was feeling so guilty.

With Farisai and Mutoko behind her, Emma's thoughts turn unexpectedly towards her mother. Farisai's story makes her think about

Sarah in a new and different way. Emma knows, like Farisai, that her mother is resilient; she, too, is strong-minded; she, too, has huge determination. What she wonders now is whether, like Farisai, Sarah's strong-mindedness hid things she hadn't shared with Emma. Sarah had told Emma so little about her life in Zimbabwe, her early life. Farisai had a dreadful marriage; Sarah had told Emma almost nothing about her husband except to say Emma's father had died when she was very young. Had Sarah suffered at his hands? Had Sarah, like Farisai, hidden former suffering, had she concealed dreadful former hardships? Was Sarah ever raped? Emma is soon to find out.

Some 20 minutes later, the bus turns off the tarmac and onto the 10 miles of dirt road which the signpost tells her leads to All Souls. Within a few hundred yards, the bus starts to shake, then the whole chassis begins to rattle violently. Emma grips her seat, petrified something dreadful is about to happen, though she doesn't know what as it doesn't look as if they are about to hit anything. She can see that no one else seems particularly upset so she tells herself to calm down: this is clearly normal.

As her Uncle Prosper later told her when she recounted the incident to him, the bus was merely speeding up in order to ride over the corrugations which form on the surface of ungraded gravel roads in the dry season. Counterintuitively, as all drivers know, the faster you go over them the smoother the ride, providing you and your vehicle can endure the shaking and rattling as you race to reach the optimum speed.

After the corrugations, Emma's bus faces another challenge: deep gullies in the road formed in the last rainy season by the continual churning of tyres into the soft road surface, which rendered the road impassable but which had never been properly repaired. Undeterred, her driver brakes heavily, lurches the wheel to the left and takes to the bush, negotiating his way along the tracks which successive vehicles have created to form a makeshift route around the blockage. Again, no one else on the bus seems concerned, so Emma decides not to worry either. Back on the proper road again, the bus rattles and shakes as it picks up speed to try to ride over the next wave of corrugations.

Emma then sees in amazement coming up to her left the most enormous baobab tree, its trunk as wide as two London buses. Its branches are bare, having not yet begun to send out their early summer leaves, but she sees a few grey-green bulbous fruit pods dangling down, still unpicked from the end of the harvesting season. She has never seen a baobab before but she quickly recognises it from pictures she saw as a small child. Seeing the baobab with its wide, elongated, horizontal and bare branches, she had imagined some enormous giant had picked up the whole tree and thrust it back into the ground. Looking at her very first baobab now, Emma thought it did indeed look like just like an upside-down tree.

Soon after Emma loses lost sight of the baobab, the arched entrance with the words *All Souls Mission* painted across it announces their imminent arrival. It is now Emma's turn to gather up her things ready to leave. As the bus draws into the mission, she is welcomed by a blaze of purple from the blooming jacaranda trees and a sea of eager faces ready to greet other dust-covered passengers like herself.

* * *

"Emma? Emma Makoni?"

"Yes, hi! That's me. I'm Emma, Emma Maconie."

As she stepped down from the bus, she was greeted by a blast of hot air, a smiling face, a hand to shake and a warm greeting: "I'm Francis. You are most welcome, Emma."

"Ah, Francis," said Emma smiling and relieved they had met up without any problem. It was clear Francis was happy to converse in English.

She looked about her and was pleased to see some of the white-uniformed student nurses had straightened hair like herself, so it couldn't have been her hair which had marked her out as different. She then thought it must have been her clothes as hardly any other female bus passengers were wearing jeans. Or could it have been her dark green rucksack, the old *Fjällräven Kånken* backpack she had picked up cheaply at an Oxfam shop before that teenage trip to Paris?

It turned out to be none of these as Francis next said, "You look just like Emerentiana, Sarah's sister, I recognised you immediately from your face. You will see her shortly, she's really lovely," adding laughingly, "as are the rest of us!"

The bus was late, and as Francis knew everyone at home was waiting for Emma, he was keen to get going. He pointed to a well-used but still shiny blue Chinese-made motor-bike standing under the shade of a tree some yards ahead of them. To disguise her nervousness, Emma said laughingly she had never ridden on a motorbike before, but Francis assured her she would be fine as long as she hung on to his waist, did what he said and always took her legs off the foot-rest as soon as she felt the bike skidding to stop it toppling over into the sand. He smiled and said she would soon get the hang of it, but the mention of skidding only increased Emma's worries. She was glad she was wearing jeans and had brought her backpack, which she slung over her shoulders. She put her arms round Francis' waist after she got on as instructed and pressed her body close to his. There was more room on the seat than Emma had thought. She felt snug and they were away. As Francis had predicted, the bike started first time.

Their ride to the Makoni homestead took them about a quarter of an hour. The first couple of hundred yards were to prove the fastest, ridden on firm gravel with few corrugations. This gave Emma the confidence she needed, which Francis added to by tilting his head backwards and shouting to make himself heard above the engine noise in order to tell her how good she was at keeping her balance. They both laughed and she loosened her grip around his waist, only to tighten it again when they took a sharp left turn and the bike hit the softer sandy road. A small skid, feet off the footrest, but Francis kept the bike upright and on they went.

At times, the road narrowed to what seemed to be more like a footpath, and occasionally even the footpaths disappeared. When this happened, Francis had to skilfully navigate the bike through virgin bush, weaving his way around bare tree stumps, their branches and bark torn off by modern-day hunter-gatherers – firewood collectors. At other times, Francis took to the wide-open plains, known by their Afrikaans name, *vleis*, joining scotch-carts and bicycles travelling along the same unmarked but clearly well-known routes. Francis knew every twist and turn of the way, unsurprisingly, as this was the route of his daily commute. He deliberately rode more slowly than he normally did, even when carrying passengers, because today's pillion-rider was someone very special: their relative from far-away England.

As they rode on, Emma began to focus less on the bike and more on her surroundings. Her mood shifted first from calm to contentment, then to sheer delight as a sense of carefree joy began to bubble up inside her. With every new experience – eyeing Africa from afar from the plane, touring Harare yesterday and seeing rural Zimbabwe race by on this morning's bus ride – Emma had felt she was getting ever closer *to* the Africa she had had in her mind's eye. Now she felt she was really *in* that Africa: she could not only see it, but could touch it and smell it.

They passed ant-hills – termite mounds – some massive red-soil edifices constructed over decades, rising three, four, eight and even ten feet from the ground. Next to one as they slowed in the sand and almost came to stop, Emma witnessed ants hurrying along in lines and understood how apt the term "soldier ants" was. She spied a dung beetle dining on fresh cow-droppings; she saw lizards, some lying lethargically on a passing rock, others disturbed by the bike's vibrations, scurrying away to avoid being crushed under the bike's wheels. She had her second sighting of weaverbirds and, just once, caught sight of the brilliant reds and crimsons of a group of carmine bee-eaters. She smiled on seeing – and smelling – goats in search of food, some carefully pulling low-growing leaves from shrubs to avoid their protruding barbs, others standing erect on their hind legs, balancing momentarily in the air, tempted by the juicier leaves on the higher branches. Francis steered his way along the bush carefully so as not to pass too close to the thorny shrubs which lined their path, and at times Emma had to lean in quickly to avoid being pierced by their long, menacing spikey needles.

Emma waved to a nearby group of smiling barefooted boys in oversized torn khaki shorts, skilfully turning the long steering wheels of the cars they had created by twisting and wrapping bits of old wire together, their wheels covered in rubber from old car tyres. In the distance she returned the wave of two giggling green-uniformed young girls hitching rides on a scotch-cart packed with firewood, their bare feet dangling down from its open-ended back. They passed two teenage boys, clearly close friends, walking triumphantly hand in hand, their unlinked hands each carrying a small dead bird brought to an early death by stones skilfully propelled by the home-made catapults now triumphantly slung over their shoulders.

They rode past a small and rickety two-doored tin-roofed building with a short veranda in front and a billboard displaying the faded words "Coca-Cola" at one end and "Family Butchery" at the other. A small group of old men were standing chatting in the shade of the veranda. As their bike drew near, one lifted a bent stick in greeting, another raised an arm and a third lifted his hat to wave as they passed and, riding more confidently now, Emma raised a hand to wave back. Then, noticing the whiteness of their hair, she suddenly realised neither she nor Francis was wearing a helmet. But this discovery prompted neither fear nor panic in Emma, such was the sense of security and oneness she was feeling in amongst her newly-found African surroundings.

Nearing the end of their ride, Francis chose a shortcut which took them close to an outcrop of granite rising to a height thirty or so feet above them to their left. As they neared the *kopje*, the bike's engine scared three or four monkeys hunting for early-season fruit in the thick branches of what Francis told Emma was a *muhacha* tree, its roots clasped onto and seemingly growing right out from the rocky boulders at the base of the *kopje*. Startled by the noise, the monkeys scattered, one appearing on the bare rock above them. It paused for a moment, inquisitively trying to see what had disturbed them – just long enough for Emma to see a baby tightly clutching its underbelly, its tiny head just visible between her mother's front legs. Francis and Emma both laughed. As the bike emerged from behind the *kopje*, Francis pointed to a group of buildings, some with thatched roofs, a hundred or so yards ahead of them surrounded by a rather makeshift-looking fence. As he did so, he shouted back to Emma to tell her they had arrived.

As they rode into the family homestead, Francis pressed repeatedly on the motorbike's horn. He needn't have done so as the sound of the motor had already forewarned the Makoni clan they were here, and the welcoming party had already gathered. Emma could feel the excitement welling up inside her as the bike slowed to a halt. It did so in an open area of hard-packed earth around which the family's main buildings stood. It was, she thought, a cross between a yard and a courtyard. The absence of any fallen leaves and the presence of brush marks were clear signs of its having recently been swept.

To one side, standing alone, was an elderly man with greying hair, tall and thin though with a protruding (though not huge) stomach, his frame bent slightly to the right as he stood waiting. Francis gestured for Emma to move forward and stand next to him. He was wearing an open-necked white shirt, a badly-fitting suit, old black leather shoes with no socks and a welcoming smile. Emma saw Sarah in the shape of his face and the sparkle of his eyes and immediately knew it was Prosper, her mother's eldest brother, the acknowledged head of the Makoni family. Francis stood on the other side of Emma.

This was not the moment to greet Prosper properly because as Emma and Francis walked over to join him, on the other side of the courtyard the women, all grouped together, had already broken out in loud song and jubilant dance. Barefoot in their long dresses and head scarves, their bodies swayed to and fro and their hips rocked from side to side as each woman first raised one foot in the air, then the other. Then, shuffling their feet from side to side, they raised the dust from the dry ground as they stamped their feet on the hardened mud beneath them, their feet and twisting torsos responding rhythmically to their changing songs of greeting. As they danced, they raised their cupped hands to their mouths and ululated loudly, sometimes together, sometimes individually, producing protracted high-pitched trills emanating from their trembling tongues and half-open mouths which resounded loudly round the family homestead. Next, they raised their arms upwards and waved their hands in the air, then lowered them, their swaying hips responding to the changing tempo of their home-grown music. They danced in line, they danced in circles and they pivoted, at times performing full 360-degree turns. One dancer advanced towards Emma, shook her whole body, ululated then retreated, followed by a second and a third. More ululating, more singing, more twisting and turning of feet on the ground, creating yet more dust. They laughed as they sang and soon they were all sweating. And so it continued.

Grouped together on the edge of the yard stood the children and young teenagers, both boys and girls. They were all neatly dressed, the girls in school uniforms, the boys in shorts and short-sleeved shirts. Although most were bare-footed, a couple stood in flips-flops, known locally as *pata-pata*, their name made famous by Miriam Makeba's popular song of the same name. As the women danced and sang, the young onlookers clapped. They all smiled and waved their hands in the air. Some giggled coyly, the younger ones chuckling the most.

Prosper nodded to Emma, motioning to her to join in. A little self-consciously at first, she started to clap and then to tap her feet. By the time the welcoming ritual was drawing to its close, she was stamping her feet, waving her arms and moving her hips around with the women, her initial slightly embarrassed smile having turned into loud laughter. Before they finished, Emma had danced with each of the women in turn and the more she moved her body the more they laughed. She couldn't remember the last time she had enjoyed herself so much. By the end, to screams of laughter from everyone, even Prosper and Francis had joined in the dancing as well and the joyous expressions on their faces as they raised their arms and wiggled their hips on their faces were more than a match for Emma's.

When the singing and dancing, laughing and ululating finally died down, everyone came forward in turn to greet Emma. So much happened so quickly she was not able to take it all in or absorb everything which was said to her.

Prosper was the first to formally greet Emma. He turned to her – she was standing next to him once again by now – and started to shake her by the hand and tell her who he was. But almost before he had begun, she spontaneously threw her arms around him and gave him the hugest of hugs, the sort she normally reserved for Sarah.

As she did so, she said "*Sekuru* Prosper, Uncle Prosper." She then took a pace back, sized him up and stepped back for a second warm hug, repeating, "*Sekuru* Prosper, Uncle Prosper."

Recovering quickly from the shock of the hug – as men and women don't demonstrate their affection for each other in such a way in public – Prosper smiled and simply said in an attempt to regain his briefly-lost status, "Emma. My dear Emma. You are most welcome!"

Next, the now-breathless women half walked and half ran towards Emma to greet her. When they were in touching distance, they grasped Emma's two hands with theirs, some ululating again. As each one stepped forward, Francis and Prosper introduced them. First up was Prosper's wife, Tendai, who was well-built. Next to greet Emma was Francis's wife, the far younger and thinner Fadzai. Emma responded to both in turn with vigorous, yet more appropriate, handshakes rather than hugs. Then came Emerentiana, who looked so like Sarah in build and facial features she could have been her twin.

Even before Francis had had a chance to say who she was, Emma blurted out: "Emerentiana – *'mainini* (my little mother)."

Emma used the word *'mainini* both because in Shona there is no one word which corresponds to the English word "aunt," and because the words "little mother" capture so well the closeness and special relationship you and your mother have with your mother's sister.

Speaking now in English, Prosper said, "No, Emma. Emerentiana is not your *'mainini*, she is your *ambuya*, your great aunt in English. She is one generation higher up."

"No," said Emma, who was only half listening and didn't stop to take in fully what Prosper had just said as she was so focused on greeting each relative in turn and trying desperately to remember what name went with what face. Emma was so enjoying herself and could hear herself laughing as she repeated each name as it was called out either by the person greeting her or by Francis.

"No," she repeated, pausing to reply to Prosper. She turned to him and then said, "What I know is Emerentiana is my mother Sarah's sister, but I do get a bit muddled with the way you address different relatives in Shona. I never really understood why the word you just used – *ambuya* – means both grandmother and aunt, and if you pronounce it differently with the accent on the first syllable– **am**-*buya* instead of *am-bu-ya* – it means something even more different, your mother-in-law, or is it the other way round, I can never remember!

"For now," she laughed, "I will just stick to people's actual names: I find names a lot simpler than working out relationships. You, Prosper, and Francis here are both called *sekuru*, but in English that can mean either great uncle, or uncle or even cousin – one name but three possible generations. You see, it is confusing." And Emma laughed again; she was clearly enjoying herself.

"Anyway," she said, turning back again to Emerentiana, who was still standing opposite her and reverting to Shona again, "Emerentiana, you and I have so much to talk about!"

"Yes," said Emerentiana, who was as struck as Francis had been at how like Sarah Emma looked, "it is true, it is true. We certainly do. What a wonder!"

While Emma was speaking, Prosper caught Francis' eye. They exchanged glances and Francis, in turn, nodded back knowingly to his father. It was just as they had suspected; Sarah had not told Emma. He knew he had a lot of talking to do in the coming days but he now knew there was even more to do than he had suspected. But he had already decided not to even start *that* conversation until tomorrow. Today was a day for rejoicing, not one for confronting and exposing the hidden pains of the past.

Unaware of this exchange between Prosper and Francis, Emma laughed again as she next turned to the children, motioning for them to come up and introduce themselves. Far too embarrassed to approach Emma individually, they moved forward together and clustered round her in a group, each in turn eager to make physical contact with Emma; to touch and feel her. As they remained close to each other, Emma asked them each their names and they replied in turn, some laughing, most giggling. The two youngest remained next to Emma after greeting her. The girl, Zuva, aged seven, snuggled up to Emma and rested her head against Emma's arm, and Emma put her arm around her – that was allowed!

Emma later discovered Zuva was Francis' youngest daughter. Indeed, it turned out most were Francis' children. Besides Zuva were Clemence, aged 11, Tafara, 13, and Chipo, 15. Two other girls, Spiwe and Stella, both aged 8, were children of Prosper's two married daughters, Madiwa and Mary, neither of whom was present today. As was the custom, both had moved away to their husband's homes when they were married but Spiwe and Stella lived here during term time as they attended the local primary school, the one where, until recently, Prosper had been the head teacher.

With the greetings over, Prosper invited Emma to accompany him as he walked, limping slightly, towards one of two identical brick-built buildings which stood on either side of the central yard. Its double-doored French windows were latched open to reveal a welcoming, formally laid out front room with two easy chairs either side of a central sofa, in front of which was a low wooden coffee table covered with a plastic tablecloth and adorned, for Emma's benefit, with flowers, even though they were faded and plastic. Prosper and Francis sat down on the settee and motioned to Emma and Tendai to sit on the chairs on either side of them. Everyone else sat down on the floor, most spilling out onto the yard.

Prosper made a short formal speech of welcome. Emma then replied, saying she brought greetings to all from Sarah, and produced her phone to share a couple of recent pictures she had taken. The older women ululated again. Then Emma began to remove the gifts she had brought from her rucksack. She handed one envelope of money to Prosper and another to Emerentiana, explaining these were gifts from Sarah. They were shocked to feel how much the envelopes contained, but both were delighted. The women ululated once more. Emma then opened her bag of loose sweets, which she began to distribute to the eager hands of the women and children. Though she thought she had brought plenty, within seconds she had had to dip into her reserves and soon they were all gone as well. While the sweets were being gobbled up, Emma handed Prosper the small plastic bottle filled with sand which her mother had given to her on leaving for the airport. Emma recalled Sarah telling her Prosper would know what to do with it – he clearly did, and without comment he simply nodded and placed the bottle carefully inside his jacket pocket. Francis was the only other person to notice the exchange.

Prosper then signalled to two of the older girls, who jumped up, crossed the central yard and went into the large hut opposite. It was an imposing building of typical *rondavel* design, dominated by a conically-shaped thatched roof. Its rounded wall was well-built, with cement and bricks to a height of about seven feet, on the top of which were long wooden poles firmly fixed in place to come together at the centre and on which long roof-grass was tied in tightly bound clumps. Emma knew this was the most important building of all. It was always referred to as the kitchen as the food was cooked there but, as she knew, it was really the centre of the homestead, the place where everyone gathered to eat as well as talk.

The girls emerged from the *rondavel* with their hands full of seeds taken from a dry maize cob. These they proceeded to scatter on the ground in front of them, making clucking sounds. Almost at once five or six hens hurried into the yard and began eagerly to peck at the seed. Immediately one of the girls skilfully grabbed hold of a leg of one of the hens and triumphantly walked back with it into the kitchen hut, to emerge a moment later carrying it upside down by its now tightly-bound legs. She gave it to Prosper, who in turn handed it to Emma. This was her gift and she thanked him for it.

As Emma looked a little perplexed about precisely what she should do next, Francis stood up and took the leg-bound hen from Emma. However, she knew why she had been given it: the hen would be taken out and killed (Emma wondered precisely how the execution would be carried out) to reappear as the centrepiece of their celebratory supper later that evening.

Prosper, who was now clearly enjoying himself, announced it was time for tea. It was now the turn of Tendai and Fadzai to disappear into the kitchen. They soon re-emerged, carrying two trays, one with a huge enamel teapot and lots of empty mugs, the other piled high with thick slices of white bread dripping with homemade peanut butter. As the guest of honour, Emma took hers first. She was hungry and tucked in. The sandwiches were delicious. But she almost gagged on taking her first sip of the milky tea: because it was so thick with sugar, she was unable to drink it. Though they all thought it extremely odd to drink unsweetened tea, Tendai made Emma a fresh mug, this time without sugar, and everyone made a mental note for the future of Emma's strange tastes.

When tea was over, Prosper took his leave and Tendai showed Emma where she was to sleep. Two rooms led off from the rear of the front room where they were sitting; the one to the right was Prosper and Tendai's and the other was to be Emma's. It contained a single bed with a thin lumpy mattress, made up with sheets, a blanket and a thin and equally lumpy pillow. The only other furniture was a small bedside table and, in the corner, next to a four-paned window, its frame unpainted, stood a narrow wooden cupboard. Next to the cupboard were packages wrapped up in plastic which Emma thought probably contained the normal contents of the cupboard which had been removed for her visit. The floor, uneven in places, was made of highly polished cement; there was not a speck of dust in sight. Her room had no ceiling, just the bare corrugated iron strips of the roof. Emma hurriedly dropped her things onto her bed and walked back through the French windows to the central courtyard.

As Prosper had explained before retiring, most of the rest of the day was to be taken up with Emma being shown round the family homestead. It was the children who were going to conduct the tour and they were standing waiting for her expectantly as she emerged from her room. Walking, she soon realised, was going to be something of a challenge as the four youngest clasped Emma's hands as they set off and were clearly reluctant ever to let go. As they set off, Emma felt a little like the Pied Piper.

They started by crossing to the kitchen *rondavel* which it was clear the children wished Emma to go inside to inspect and which she duly did, her four limpets in tow. It was far larger and darker than she had expected and, until her eyes had adjusted from the brightness outside, she couldn't see much. Then, as her pupils began to widen, her eyes travelled first to the central fireplace, a few red cinders still visible on the ground, evidence of earlier activity and giving off a welcoming homely aroma. Opposite the doorway and behind the fireplace on the far wall stood an assembly of cooking pots stacked up by size from the bottom, from very large to small, most dark from years of service over countless open fires, as black as the grass and roof rafters above. On either side of the pots and pans, a large can of cooking oil and a number of closed sacks were neatly assembled. Emma was invited to inspect them: some contained mealie-meal flour, others whole peanuts ready to be ground; some housed vegetables and gourds, a small one salt. Next to them four or five black metal trunks were piled on top of each other which the children told Emma contained their blankets: the kitchen doubled as a family dormitory at night.

Still inside the kitchen, stretching out from either side of the doorway to the left and right, a low-level brick seating bench swept round along the hut wall, finished off, like the floor, with a thin layer of dark polished cement, adding to the overall sense of darkness of the hut. It provided enough space for a dozen or so people to sit on, six a side. Outside and against the kitchen wall, firewood was piled up, sheltered from any rain by the overhanging grass roof. Also sheltered by the roof was a large wooden mortar and pestle.

When Emma stepped out of the kitchen, the children pointed to the tin-roofed building which stood opposite the one where they had all gathered earlier for the welcoming speeches. This, they told Emma, was Francis and Fadzai's house, built to an identical design as Prosper's and Tendai's.

The troupe left the central yard and stopped a few yards away at the washing-up area. The children pointed to a newly-installed tap above a waist-high slab of concrete and told Emma to turn it on. As the cold water flowed out they all cheered: it was still clearly a novelty. The mud floor below was damp from recent use and upturned mugs, pots, plates and cooking utensils were drying in the sun on raised wooden slats. A few hens were pecking the ground in search of food. Emma suspected they all knew they were one less in number now and were also well aware of the fate which had befallen Emma's gift.

A few yards beyond the washing area, they came to the grass-roofed grain and fresh-food store hut, a small square, wooden construction with a padlocked door, built on stilts to keep animals, ants and rats away.

Underneath, two thin nondescript dogs were sleeping and the children started to shoo them away but they were reluctant to move off. The children encouraged them to leave, shouting "S*va, sva, sva. Ibva, ibva*", and the boys picked up pebbles which they threw at the dogs to hurry them on their way. One suffered a direct hit and yelped as it ran off with its tail between its legs. The children all laughed but the incident upset Emma though she didn't say anything.

Beyond the grain store, they came to a collection of trees which provided partial shade to two round roughly-built animal pens, *kraals*, the larger one for cattle, the smaller one for goats. Both were constructed from ill-shaped pieces of wood gathered from the branches of local trees, thrown together in what looked a rather haphazard way between vertical wooden posts, the entranceway made of two straight moveable poles loosely bound together by barbed wire and frayed strips of sisal rope. The floors of the *kraals* were covered in trampled stalks of last year's mealies, intermingled with freshly-dropped dung to create a strong rich sweet odour which, to her surprise, Emma found alluringly pleasant. The *kraals* lay empty now as the animals were loose in the fields, but by nightfall, the children told her, they would all be secure inside.

Beyond the animal *kraals* three or four of Emma's guides broke into a run, encouraging her to follow them, which she did. They were heading for the family's two arable fields, each about half a football pitch in size and bordered by a crudely-constructed fence made of irregular tree poles and barbed wire. They pointed in turn to the family's twelve head of cattle, some grazing among the dry mealie stalks, some resting in the sandy soil under the shade of the trees.

Emma saw a boy waving at them from under a tree in the middle distance. The children explained he was their herd-boy. They told her he was from a neighbouring village and Emma thought he looked about 16. They said he minded their cattle for them as he didn't go to school anymore. He looked happy enough; Emma wondered what he was paid though she didn't ask.

Chipo went on to tell Emma that serious herding didn't need to be done in the dry season as there was little of value left in the fields once the harvest had been gathered. She said soon the men would come with the oxen to plough the fields for the new season and when the crops reach knee-high they would all be in the fields for an hour's weeding each day before they went to school, returning for another hour before sunset.

Walking back from the fields, they picked up a path which led to the vegetable garden. It was quite large – the size of a couple of classrooms – and was surrounded by a far more secure-looking wooden and barbed-wire fence than the one around the crop fields. They went inside and the children in turn pointed to the ripe tomatoes, the onions, a few chilli peppers and, on one side, a mass of dark green vegetable leaves, laughing when Emma correctly named them: *muriwo*. At the far end of the garden was an old well, protected by a low brick wall across which was attached a round piece of wood with a metal handle screwed into one end. At its centre was a wound-up rope attached to an old-looking yellow plastic bucket. A low grass roof covered the crude pulley mechanism. As Emma peered in she could see the well was deep; one of the children threw a stone in and she waited, but there was no splash. They told Emma the well had recently run dry, explaining it always did at this time of year.

At the near end of the garden, closest to the central yard, stood a far newer hand pump rising up from a round cement slab. Two of the children started to work the pump and in a few moments water started flowing. Initially it was browny-coloured but soon what came out looked to Emma like reasonably clear water. It was cool to the touch. Chipo again stepped in to explain the pump covered a far deeper well, recently dug, which meant they no longer needed to walk the mile to the nearest river-water source to fetch their water in the dry season.

Just outside the garden fence stood two small tin-roofed brick buildings with an entranceway which twisted round as you walked in. Each had a chimney running up the side. These were the family toilets which Emma was required to go in to inspect. As it was a tight squeeze to get in, she went in alone while the younger children giggled outside. It was dark inside, the building designed deliberately like this to keep away the flies and mosquitoes. However, Emma could see two pit latrines, each covered with a small concrete slab with foot-holes marked on either side of the holes where you squatted down. Two jugs and a small empty container lay on the floor of each latrine next to a basket containing a few dry bare mealie husks and some sheets of torn newspaper; one jug was half-filled with water, and the other was dry. Emma was surprised at the absence of any putrid smells and how clean it all looked.

She was next shown a large covered open-fronted shed of locally-made *brise-soleil* bricks. Inside she could see three or four old black bicycles, some old batteries and a few fertilizer bags. Outside stood an old cattle-drawn plough lying alongside a well-used scotch-cart, its wheels touching the brick wall, its drawbar or diesel-boom leaning over and against the wall above.

Their tour nearly completed, they came to a small open yard area surrounded on three sides by three mango trees, under which were four wooden chairs. From the yard Emma could see back to the route along which she and Francis had travelled to All Souls with views across the plain to the *kopje* where she had seen the monkeys and to rising hills in the middle distance. Immediately ahead of them and far closer was a smaller hillock with a cross on it, which the children told Emma was the family burial ground though there were no visible signs of any tombstones. As none of the children seemed particularly interested in telling Emma who exactly was buried there, she made a mental note to ask Prosper or some other older relatives later on.

Finally, the children proudly showed Emma the homestead's newest building: the recently-completed shower. Though locally-made of roughly-hewn bricks, it was clearly professionally-constructed, well grouted using high-quality cement, with an unpainted rust-coloured metal door which swung effortlessly when being opened and closed. It was covered by a well-fitted shiny tin roof, above which Emma could see a single sheet of solar panelling and a small water tank. Encouraged to go inside, children in tow again, Emma could see the walls were made of grey rough plaster and openings at the top let in the light. The floor was a smooth cement base which sloped down towards the back wall to an open channel which took the water away under the wall to drain out on the ground outside. She was asked to turn on the single tap attached to the side wall. As Emma turned the tap, water flowed from the shower head above to the applause of the watching children; it was hot to the touch but not scalding. Chipo explained it had only been completed last year. Emma subsequently learned from Francis it had been paid for with the larger amounts of money Sarah had been sending out once Emma had started earning and moved into her own flat. The newly-installed solar panels and plumbing work were a technological leap forward for the Makonis.

The tour completed, Emma went to her room and lay down to rest. She must have fallen asleep as the next thing she knew was being woken by a gentle tap at her door and a voice beyond: "*Go-go-goi!*" ("Knock, knock, knock!"). It was her aunt, Emerentiana, checking she was fine and telling her they would come over and call her shortly for supper.

When she left, Emma decided to unpack what little she had brought with her and hung up her clothes in the still empty cupboard. As she knew the women would feel more comfortable if she changed into a dress for the evening, she slipped on the one she and Sarah had bought together, a just-below-the-knee tied-at-the-waist green and red striped non-iron dress with a folded down collar. She felt a little like a hospital matron but, having seen what the women were wearing, acknowledged to herself her mother's wisdom in advising her to buy that dress. There was no mirror in the room so she simply felt her hair and rearranged it as best she could. It was getting dark now and Emma suddenly panicked she might have forgotten to throw her torch into her rucksack and was relieved when she felt it at the bottom. She flicked it on and shone it round the room, only realising quite how much darker it was when she switched it off again. She lay down once more and gazed upwards but the roof had already disappeared from view. She felt so good to be here as she relived the warmth of the welcome she had been given.

It was completely dark when the knock on the door came again, accompanied by the repeated words "*Go-go-goi.*" It was Emerentiana, who began by apologising for forgetting to bring Emma a paraffin lamp and who was therefore relieved when she saw Emma's torch. She was holding a lamp herself which she used to motion to Emma to follow her and join the family for their evening meal. Emma slipped on her flip-flops and followed her aunt out.

As Emma and her aunt stepped into the kitchen hut, they were immediately met by applause and cheering. As Emerentiana held up her paraffin lamp, Emma saw pairs of eyes peering across at her from the floor where almost all the children were seated around the fire. The room was warm and she could feel the fire's heat on her face. She recognised Prosper's voice as he invited Emma to sit down on the brick bench to the left of the door where he and Francis were already seated. Emerentiana moved in next to Emma. Another welcome speech from Prosper – this time brief – was followed by his raising his right hand, at which everyone fell silent. When all heads were bowed, he said a prayer of welcome and then turned to Francis to say grace. After grace, Prosper began to recite the Lord's Prayer and everyone joined in: *Baba wedu muri kudenga…* ("Our Father who art in heaven…")

It was during prayers that Emma caught an all-familiar smell, her mother's chicken, and knew she was in for a real treat. However, before supper could begin, one of the younger girls came up to Emma and knelt down in front of her. On her lap was a bowl of water and over her arm a folded towel. Emma dipped her hands into the bowl of water, rubbed them together then wiped them dry with the towel. This ritual was then repeated in front of Prosper, Francis and Emerentiana. The preliminaries completed, it was now time to eat. A narrow wooden table was put in front of them, followed by four plastic mugs filled with water.

Another of the younger girls now brought two bowls to their table. The larger one was piled high with *sadza*, the basic staple carbohydrate made from mealie-meal and eaten daily. As she had expected, the smaller bowl was a bone-laden stew of vegetables and chicken, the same chicken she had been given earlier, alive; cooked in the same way her mother always cooked it. It looked and smelt good and, as she was about to verify, it tasted good too, just like Sarah's: tender, thick in rich gravy, far too oily but, oh – so tasty! Other bowls of *sadza* and chicken stew were placed in front of the rest of the family, grouped together round the fireplace. There was an air of expectancy: all eyes were focused on Emma. She knew what to do. She cupped her hands, fingers close together and brought them together one on top of each other, once, twice, three times. As her cupped right hand came down on her cupper left hand below, the captured air created a hollow-sounding clapping noise as her hands met and everyone laughed in delight. Then she said the word "*Pamosoroi*" ("Excuse me") and leaned forward to begin eating. There were no knives, forks or spoons.

Emma peeled off a small amount of *sadza* with her right hand which she moulded dextrously and speedily (the *sadza* was piping hot) into a small ball with the tips of the fingers of her right hand. She then dipped the *sadza* into the stew, skilfully picking up a piece of chicken then some oil-drenched gravy and a few bits of tomato and onion relish, all with her right hand. Popping this delicious mixture into her mouth was the signal for everyone else to begin. Eating was a serious business and meat a rare treat. As much as Emma would have liked to chat while they all ate, most of the meal took place in almost complete silence. She listened out expectantly for the noise she was sure was about to come and then smiled when it did: the unmistakeable sound of teeth crunching right through the chicken bones and mouths sucking the juices out from the insides could be heard right across the kitchen.

As Emma sat eating in the warm dark hut amidst the largest gathering of close relatives she had ever been with, she suddenly felt herself overcome with emotion, but a very different and new sort of emotion. Inside the warmth of the Makoni kitchen, sharing familiar food with so many blood relatives who had until now been simply names, mere shadows in her mind, Emma knew what her family really meant to her. She felt complete; at one with the others gathered around the kitchen's central fireplace, a real part of this – of *her* – extended family. Though she was well aware of how different she was, she felt accepted simply as herself, as Emma: no superficiality, no show and no pretence. She felt one of them. Emma breathed deeply: it was good to be here, so *very* good to be here. Sarah had told her she should come and she was now so grateful Sarah had nagged her and she had eventually stopped resisting. Her only regret was not being able to share the feelings she was now having with her mother, with Sarah, though in a strange way she couldn't explain she also felt Sarah was very close not just to her, but to all of them.

Amidst her closest relatives, Emma suddenly thought how wonderful it would be to have children of her own, to bring new life into the world and for them to be able to experience that sense of oneness and family she was now feeling. And this made her think of Simon. She missed him and she wanted to share these feelings with him too. *Wow,* she thought to herself, feeling an even warmer glow in her cheeks, *I am drunk with happiness!*

But she was suddenly snapped out of her dream as she felt something moving on her leg. Initially she wasn't sure what it was and instinctively brushed her leg with her hand. Then it returned and she suddenly realised it was alive and moving and she gave out a sudden scream. One of the girls had noticed what had been happening and came over to Emma. She brushed her hand down both Emma's leg and then stamped on her feet and said, smiling, "*bete, mapete.*" Emma smiled back and racked her brains to try to remember what the Shona word *bete* meant in English, but she couldn't.

The evening was drawing to a close. There was no stew left, but bowls of uneaten *sadza* were removed, and tossed outside to the waiting dogs and chickens. In due course everyone was served with a hot mug of milo. It was a perfect end to a perfect meal, though Emma was still being bothered now and again by something light and feathery tickling her legs: she knew it wasn't mosquitos, they weren't biting, but what was it? What did the word *bete* mean? Mugs were emptied then, with the youngest already asleep round the fire, Prosper stood up, announcing the time had come to retire. He wished everyone a good night and left, motioning for Emma to follow him as he had noticed she had started to nod off herself. Then, becoming a little more formal, he repeated once more how pleased he and everyone else was Emma had come and said she should sleep as there was a lot they needed to discuss in the morning. Unaware of what was to come, Emma said how much she was looking forward to that.

As she stepped outside, everything seemed so different in the darkness but Emma remembered enough of the route to the toilet to get there, aided by her torch. When she emerged, her eyes had grown more accustomed to the night, and looking up to the sky she was blown away by the magnitude and beauty of what she saw. Though there was no moon, she thought it was almost bright enough to be able to read by the light of the stars. Above her, the night sky seemed vast – twice or even three times the size it was in London. The Milky Way formed a huge arc of brightness over her head; it was made of far more stars than she had ever seen before, sparkling brightly against the jet black of the night beyond, the Southern Cross shining out almost like a beacon. How to describe the vastness of it all? Perhaps, she thought, it was like seeing a movie for the first time in an IMAX cinema…

Emma then realised how tired she was. She soon returned to her room and slipped into bed. In the distance, she could clearly make out the sounds of drums beating and the muffled accompaniment of people singing in a distant village, interrupting the stillness of the African night. She wondered whether they were mourning a death or celebrating at a mid-week beer drink; she didn't know enough to tell whether she was hearing drums of merriment or drums of grief. Whatever their cause, they comforted her.

As Emma turned over to go to sleep, the word she had been searching for suddenly came to her. *Bete* was the Shona for cockroach. It was *mapete* – cockroaches – which had been crawling up her legs while she ate. Ugh! She shuddered at the thought. But the horror of what had been walking across her skin quickly faded and, in spite of her lumpy mattress and even lumpier pillow, she was soon fast asleep.

* * *

"Go-go-goi." Emma was woken by the quietest of voices and the gentlest of taps on her door.

She opened the door to find seven-year-old Zuva weighed down with a jug of warm water held in both hands. She stood there with an empty bowl balancing on her head, a towel over her shoulder and a bar of soap in the pocket of her dress. Emma hadn't had time yesterday to look carefully at each of her many cousins but now here was the youngest, standing silent and alone in front of her, and she could begin to take her in. She was a thin-legged, barefoot girl, as delicate as a twig, dressed in a threadbare hand-me-down dark green school uniform frock which hung loosely over her frail shoulders, her hair knotted tightly together in braids – but she was wearing the warmest of smiles.

Emma thanked her, the first of many times she was to do so over the coming days as Zuva – the only young cousin not in school – had been given the task of attending to Emma's domestic needs for the duration of her stay. Later Emma discovered Zuva making her bed, which she did each day Emma was there. Then she found her dusting and sweeping out her room, which she did every morning and evening. Zuva also took away Emma's dirty clothes each morning and returned them washed and ironed before nightfall. When Emma had embarrassingly bumped into Jessica making her bed at Sheila and Jim's, she had told herself being waited on was not part of her African roots. She was now beginning to realise how wrong she had been: not only had she had someone look after her wherever she stayed, but this time her new servant was a mere child. Emma had not only benefited from domestic labour; she was now a direct recipient of child labour. As she washed in Zuva's warm water, it was her turn to feel very small.

The sun was high and the air already warm when Emma stepped outside. She breathed in deeply as she took in her surroundings, the crisp freshness of the air only adding to the happiness already welling up from within her. She felt relaxed and ready for the day ahead. The Makoni homestead was already beginning to feel like home.

But almost at once the day started to unravel in unexpected ways. On crossing the smaller yard on her way to the toilet she caught sight of the outline of a man silhouetted against the morning sun, walking slowly and deliberately on the mound which, on their homestead tour yesterday, the children had told her was the family burial site. She knew who it was at once: it was Prosper. She also recognised the upturned plastic container he was shaking in his raised right hand, scattering the final grains of sand on the ground around him.

He saw Emma, waved and hurried down to meet her. They greeted each other warmly: he enquired, and she replied, saying she had indeed slept well. He didn't say then what he had been doing but satisfied her curiosity by telling her he had important things he wanted to speak to her about, and they needed to have a long talk. He told Emma to first go and have breakfast and when she had finished to come back here to the small yard where she would find him.

When Emma entered the kitchen, it was deserted except for Emerentiana, who was sitting next to the fireplace, barefooted, legs crossed and outstretched in front of her. The older children had all eaten and already left for school, and none of the other adults was anywhere to be seen. On seeing Emma come in, Emerentiana greeted her and immediately began to poke the cinders and the unburnt wood lying in the fireplace. The flames quickly returned and she re-heated the mealie meal porridge she had made earlier and re-boiled the kettle to make Emma's tea, remembering to make it without sugar.

They chatted a little about nothing in particular while Emma ate, but the atmosphere had changed from yesterday. Emerentiana was far quieter, even subdued, and Emma sensed she was also a little nervous. When Emma said she was going out to chat to Prosper when she had finished breakfast, Emerentiana said, "I know. I am coming as well."

They left the kitchen together and made their way to the smaller yard overlooking the family burial ground, Emma carrying her mug of half-drunk tea. She was by now a little nervous, too.

Prosper stood up when he saw Emma and Emerentiana approaching and pointed to the two chairs he had placed close to his, all three positioned so they were well in the shade of the largest mango tree; it was thick with leaves and already laden with hard unripe green fruit. When they were settled, Prosper spoke.

"My dear Emma," he began, speaking slowly, "there are things I need to talk to you about, delicate things, things which are difficult to put into words. It is not easy for me to say the things I am going to tell you and I do so with a heavy heart so please forgive me for that. But I am telling you them because you need to hear them and because I know Sarah wants me to do so. I have asked Emerentiana to sit here with us and she already knows much of what I will be telling you. We will speak mostly in English even though Emerentiana may not fully take it all in, as it's far more important for you to fully understand everything that I say."

At Prosper's words, Emma tensed up and felt her insides tighten. She had no idea what was to come but she just knew it was going to be dreadful.

"Yesterday, Emma," began Prosper, "you may recall when you greeted Emerentiana you referred to her as your 'mainini, and I said to you she is your *ambuya*, your grandmother's sister, one generation higher up."

"Yes," said Emma who only vaguely remembered what Prosper had said and couldn't now recall precisely what words she had used in reply.

"Well," said Prosper, "Emerentiana *is* your grandmother's younger sister."

"No," Emma immediately interjected as Prosper had clearly made a mistake. "Emerentiana is Sarah's sister," she insisted, "so she can't be my grandmother's sister. She is my mother's sister. Sarah and Emerentiana are sisters – *that* I know for sure!"

"Yes," said Prosper, "what you say is partially true. They are indeed sisters, but – and this is going to come as a huge shock to you – Sarah, my dear Emma, is not your mother. Sarah is your grandmother."

Emerentiana nodded when Prosper said these words, and slowly said the words: "It is true."

Emma couldn't believe what she was hearing. Her immediate reaction was to dismiss what Prosper had just told her as complete nonsense. She felt annoyed with Prosper and said, quite combatively, "so if Sarah is my grandmother, as you say she is, then who is my mother?"

"Your mother," said Prosper turning his eyes away from Emma as he spoke, "is dead."

Emma said nothing. It was all too unbelievable for her to begin to comprehend what she was hearing.

After a pause, Prosper continued. "Alice, your mother and Sarah's only daughter, died in England less than a year after she had brought the two of you to London. You came over together, some months after Sarah had arrived in East Finchley. Sarah arranged it all. Alice – your real mother – was already suffering from full blown AIDS. She died in the hospice where Sarah worked; she was nursed by Sarah and was buried quietly in London; none of us could go and Sarah would not have wanted it."

Prosper looked down at his upturned hands, which were resting on his lap, and went on. He was too nervous to look directly at Emma.

"You were just two years old then, Emma. Sarah brought you up. She cared for you, looked after you and loved you as a mother – so much so that, in effect, she became your mother. Indeed, as nothing was said to the contrary, you grew up believing Sarah was your mother and loved her as a mother as, clearly, you still do today."

Prosper glanced across at Emma, who was listening intently to what he was saying but, as far as he could tell, unemotionally.

"When you were a young child starting school," he said, "it seemed to Sarah at first difficult and then unnecessary to tell you – or anyone else – she was your grandmother, not your mother. After all, as she told me in letters at the time, when she met mothers at the school gate, she was pretty much the same age as most of them so they all assumed she was your mother as well.

"Alice was the only fruit, the sole surviving blossoming, of the love Sarah had for Alice's father. As I will explain shortly – for there is so much I have to tell you – Sarah's husband, your grandfather, passed away long ago, even before Alice was born. Sarah loved Alice not only with the love a mother has for an only child, but also with all the pent-up love she had within her for the husband she had lost. When Alice died, all this love was then transferred to you. You, dear Emma, became the daughter Sarah had lost. The plastic bottle of sand Sarah gave you and which you carried out here was taken by Sarah from Alice's grave in London. Sarah gave it to you because, as is our custom, she wanted it to be scattered here on the family burial ground, and that was what you saw me doing earlier this morning.

"Sarah wanted Alice to come home, to return to the Makoni homestead where she had grown up as a child, to the ground where she had played, the place where she had been her happiest. And as the eldest of the Makoni family, in scattering the sand of her grave right here, I have enabled Alice to complete her journey home. It is our custom I should do this. You and I will walk across to the spot later where we will pray together, just as it should be."

"It is good this has happened," added Emerentiana, speaking solemnly and with a heavy heart.

"Dear Emma," continued Prosper, "I know this all sounds totally unbelievable, and your first reaction is probably to dismiss what I have told you as completely untrue. But you have not been listening to an old man telling you a fable: none of it has been made up; all of it is true. I am sure it will take a while for it all to sink in and there is still more I need to tell you. For now, though, what I want to say is none of this changes anything – you are and will always be a member of the Makoni family. We love you as one of us and always will because you are one of us."

Prosper now leant over and gently took hold of Emma's hand. Then he said, "And of even greater importance, Emma, Sarah loves you. Indeed, it is the love Sarah has for you which caused her to keep the truth of who she is and who you are hidden from you for so long. But she now wants you to know the truth, the whole truth, because you are an adult and because she believes you to be sufficiently strong to understand why she has waited until now to let you know what really happened all those years ago."

Prosper gripped Emma's hand a little more tightly. "Emma, Sarah is my young sister. I grew up with her, as did Emerentiana here. We know her through and through. We know she is a truthful person, a woman of great integrity, not one who deceives, and I suspect you know that as well as we do, even possibly more so. What Sarah did and what she failed to do in not telling you about Alice, your blood mother, was done out of love for you. She was convinced you would grow up into a better, a stronger, person, if you had a mother. In fact, because you had no father, she felt even more keenly what you needed above all else was a mother."

Emerentiana added quietly, speaking in Shona: "It is true (*i-chokwadi*)."

As Prosper started to reveal Alice's existence and her true relationship to Sarah, Emma began to feel she was being hit violently and repeatedly in the stomach; the air had been taken out of her. The usually confident, bubbly and self-assured Emma felt no urge to speak, to say anything in response. She simply sat there, stunned. By the time Prosper had finished speaking, Emma had closed her eyes, cupped both hands around her tea-mug and sat motionless, as still as a stone. She was numb.

She sat there silent for five minutes, maybe longer, unable to take in the magnitude of what Prosper had said. Then she began to stir. She dropped her mug of half-drunk now-tepid tea onto the ground, wetting her feet as it fell to create a pool of dampness in the dry earth below. She hardly noticed. She felt quite alone. Why was she here, why had she come? Were all those warm feelings she had had last night a trick, a con?

Then the tightening Emma had started to feel in the pit of her stomach seemed to spread outwards to her whole body, down her legs, across the back of her neck and up into her head. She felt terribly afraid, but almost immediately her fear changed to panic. Part of her wanted to run, to get away fast; everything here now seemed so utterly alien to her. But she didn't move. She couldn't move. It was as if she were frozen to the spot. Emma wanted Sarah; she missed Sarah desperately. She needed to hold Sarah. She wanted Sarah to tell her what she was hearing wasn't true; they had got it all wrong. She was becoming muddled; her mind was racing. She felt tears rolling down her cheeks; they were tears more of confusion and self-pity than tears of sadness. Emerentiana moved her chair closer to Emma and put her arm around her, clasping her own hands – hard and calloused, a farmer's hands – tightly around Emma's. This made Emma think of Robbie and the security she used to feel when his hands were wrapped around hers. Where was Robbie? Where was Simon? No one who knew her was here, no one who could really help her was here. She felt so alone.

"God," she thought to herself, "what a mess I'm in! I don't know what to do; I don't know what to feel; I don't know who I am. Who on earth *am I*?"

Prosper and Emerentiana waited. They could now sense the pain and turmoil inside her and glanced across to each other. Emerentiana moved in still closer. Emma's thoughts turned again, but kept on returning to Sarah. She forced herself to go back in time to as far as she could remember, to try to tease out from deep inside her the very first thoughts she had ever had of Sarah. She remembered and was comforted. Then she tried to go even further back in time and force out of her subconscious hidden memories of Alice. But, try as she might, there was nothing: just a blank, a total blank. Alice was nowhere to be found in the deepest recesses of her mind. What's more, now she came to think of it, there had been no photographs of Alice at home which she could recall ever having seen. Sarah had always been her mother. There had been no other. Sarah *was* her mother, she was Sarah's daughter. She knew that – everyone knew that!

With all these thoughts whirring round in her head, the silence was eventually broken by Emma. She opened her eyes and released her hands from Emerentiana's. Everything was blurred. She looked out into the middle distance and, speaking to no one in particular, said very quietly, hardly recognising her own voice as she spoke, "Tell me about Alice then. Tell me more about Alice, my mother."

Prosper took a little time to respond; he wanted to be sure Emma was capable of understanding what he was saying to her. When Emerentiana gestured to him, Prosper said, "Your mother, Alice was such a lovely, bubbly, outgoing child who grew into a confident and self-assured woman, single-minded, strong-willed, though at times a little stubborn. Sarah was so proud of her – we were all proud of her and loved her, and you have every reason to be proud of her, too.

"Because of the war, Alice was born at the hospital at All Souls in October 1976. I can't forget the year Alice was born as it was the same year as Francis, my firstborn, came into the world. They grew up together like brother and sister. If she had lived, like Francis she would have been almost 40 now."

Recalling the happier days after the war, Prosper said, "Alice grew up here with us all. She played in the family courtyard; she ate and slept in the kitchen where you have eaten; she worked in the vegetable garden you walked in yesterday; she swept the yard; she weeded our fields as the mealies were ripening; she played with her cousins and went to school with them. She played and she laughed, and such a laugh she had! I can hear her laugh now as if it was only yesterday. We loved Alice, we all loved her; she was Sarah's child, but she was ours too.

"Alice and Emerentiana, here, were especially close." Prosper motioned to his sister. "Emerentiana was ten when Alice was born and, though she was her 'mainini, her little mother, Emerentiana was really Alice's big sister. Indeed, Emma, they were so close that when Alice knew she was pregnant with you, she chose to name you Emerentiana. It was only later, in England, that Sarah shortened your name to Emma.

"But this doesn't really explain why Alice was so special to Sarah. To really know about Alice, you need to know about and understand the love between Sarah and Alice's father and what was happening here in Zimbabwe at that time."

Emma's ears pricked up when she realised Prosper was about to reveal to her things about Sarah.

"Sarah was just 16 when Alice was born. The story of her birth can only really be understood in relation to the final years of Zimbabwe's struggle for Independence. By the mid-1970s the guerrilla war here was beginning to hot up. In ever larger numbers, young men and women were starting to cross into Mozambique to join the liberation struggle, to train in the camps and then return to the country as fighters."

"Yes," said Emma a little impatiently, "I know about the war, but what has all this got to do with me, with Sarah and with Alice?"

"Be patient, my dear Emma," said Prosper. "My sister Sarah had met and fallen in love with Joshua Makonde. They were at school together. He was a fine man, handsome, good looking, but above all a man of integrity, a strong character. He was as much in love with Sarah as she was with him. When Sarah brought him home – brought him here – we all took a liking to him. We knew how lucky she was to have found such an upright and honest man, bright-eyed, alive, with an alluring smile."

Prosper was struggling as he tried to tell Emma about Sarah's relationship with Joshua as he knew how difficult it was for him to explain to her just how much Sarah loved Joshua and how much he loved her. He said that though they were still young when they met, they were totally devoted to each other and almost from the outset had wanted to get married. "Joshua," said Prosper, "started the process and a few head of cattle passed between his family – he lived nearby – and ours to start to cement the relationship. Both families were delighted."

He then went on to explain to Emma their falling in love happened in the growing climate of first growing political unrest and then war. So, he said, no one was surprised when, one day in June 1975, Joshua told Sarah he had decided he had to leave; he had to join the liberation struggle.

"He told Sarah he felt he had an obligation to join the guerrillas," continued Prosper, "to play his part in freeing our country from decades of white settler rule. Sarah, of course, was devastated by the news, but as they kept no secrets from each other, she knew it was coming. She supported his decision fully even though she knew he might never return, and she might never see him again. Those weeks before he set out one evening after dark to walk through the night the 70 or so miles to the Mozambique border were, as she told us at the time, heart-tearing, as we would put in Shona, or heart-wrenching as you would say in English.

"After Joshua left," he went on, vividly recalling these events, almost reliving them again, "he and Sarah saw each other one more time, though it was only a brief encounter. It happened the following year, in February 1976. Joshua came back in the dead of night when everyone was asleep. He woke me, and I woke Sarah.

"I remember it as if it was yesterday." Prosper turned to look at Emma. She was now hanging on his every word, totally absorbed in his narrative.

"He was dressed, as all guerrilla fighters were, in their uniform, boots, a T-shirt and khaki trousers," said Prosper. "He had been toughened by his training, though beneath his hardened exterior I could still see the same Joshua. He was not here for more than a few hours and was gone well before the sun rose, to rejoin his comrades in the bush. I told no one Joshua had come and Sarah never told anyone, not even me, what passed between them.

"As I said just now, their daughter Alice, your dear mother, was born in the October of that year," said Prosper. "It was nine months after this first, and what proved to be his only, his final visit back to Sarah after he became a soldier.

"What Sarah didn't then know was Joshua had almost certainly been killed before she gave birth to Alice, probably the month before. Indeed, Sarah lived for years at first fully and then at least half-believing he was still alive, waiting expectantly in hope, day after endless day, for his return. It was only when the war finally ended, once independence was achieved in April 1980, some four years after Alice was born, and when there was no sign of him after all the guerrillas went back to their villages and Joshua was not among them, that Sarah was ready even to start thinking Joshua might never come back. And this was only after following up on hearsay and rumours about Joshua all which led nowhere.

"Accepting he was dead was not easy for Sarah because no body was ever found.

"I will tell you more about Joshua and his life as a guerrilla fighter in a moment but what you need to know is your grandfather was a man of whom you can be justly proud. Though sadly not remembered by our politicians, he was a true hero.

"But first I must finish telling you about Alice and Sarah." Prosper was aware he seemed to be flitting between one bit of the story and another and was worried he was not making himself as clear as he had tried to be. Emma would never know the time he had spent rehearsing what he was now recounting to her.

"Sarah was completely devoted to Alice," said Prosper. "With no Joshua and no news of him, Sarah became Alice's father as well as her mother. While Alice grew up here as part of our wider family, as I have told you, she remained precious and special to Sarah. Alice was a warm, loving and outgoing child with something of a magnetic character. Indeed, dear Emma, it is quite eerie how like her you are not only in your looks but in the way you laugh and in so many of the different mannerisms you share. We older ones have seen this repeatedly since you arrived yesterday and we have been astonished by the similarities!"

Prosper then told Emma that after independence Sarah trained and worked as a nurse at All Souls and saved what little money she was able to provide as best she could for Alice. Sarah, he explained, was an exceptional nurse and was well known not only within the hospital but across the local villages, especially for the way she cared for the dying – and growing numbers of people were then starting to die of AIDS. Sarah, said Prosper, seemed to have a special understanding not only of HIV/AIDS but of the way it leads to death and especially the effect it has on the dying as it increasingly takes hold of the body. She often took Alice to the hospital at

All Souls where she worked and became well known not only to the other nurses but to the Italian doctors and missionaries who ran the hospital, to the priests who ran the mission and to the nuns who lived and worked there.

Prosper told Emma the nuns had a special love for Alice, explaining, as Emma clearly did not know, that Emerentiana had gone away to become a nun herself when she was 17 and Alice seven.

"When she left here," continued Prosper, motioning once more at his sister with the open palm of his hand, "Alice had just started school. During her training in Harare. Emerentiana got to know some of the nuns who were then sent to All Souls. Emerentiana herself was sent to the convent in Makumbi to the north east of Harare and it was while she was there she learned Alice had become pregnant. As soon as she heard the news she decided she had to leave the convent and abandon her idea of becoming a nun in order to return to help Sarah, and, most of all, to help Alice."

"It is true," said Emerentiana in Shona, before switching to English. "I was the one who had to come home to help my sister. I needed to look after her and the newborn baby – you, dear Emma." As she turned to look at Emma and smiled, Emma could see Sarah so clearly in her face. Emma was beginning to understand why Sarah had always told her how important Emerentiana had been to her.

"First, I helped so Sarah could carry on working," continued Emerentiana. "Times were very hard then; people were losing their jobs and sometimes neither teachers nor nurses were paid at the end of the month. For six months before you were born, not even my brother here, Prosper, a headmaster, was paid. Then there was the terrible thing about the money people did have: if you had money it was soon worthless. Whenever you went to the shops you were asked for more. Eventually they wouldn't take money; you could only buy things by exchanging what you had for what you needed. Life became mad. We didn't know what was happening from one day to the next.

"It was so... crazy," she added, looking across at Emma unsure whether she had used the right English word.

Prosper nodded, and then took up the story. He told Emma that Alice was a bright child; she did well at primary school and easily won a place to go to secondary at All Souls. However, said Prosper, she was also headstrong and self-willed and fell in with a rough group of older pupils, among them Kenneth Banda, who was two years older than her. Kenneth's family, explained Prosper, were farm workers from Malawi. His grandfather had come here in the 1940s and worked on a tobacco farm in the Mazoe area, just north of Harare, where Kenneth had been born.

"But when he met your mother Alice," said Prosper, turning to Emma, "he was staying with his father's sister in a village near to All Souls so he could attend secondary school.

"Just before her 15th birthday, Alice became pregnant and Kenneth was the father but, totally unlike what had happened between Sarah and Joshua, there was never any intention of their getting married and Kenneth never set foot inside our family home here. Indeed, soon after Alice became pregnant Kenneth and his family were forced to join the stream of Zimbabwean-born farmworkers whose fathers and grandfathers had come from Malawi and were being forced to return there, deemed by the powers that be to no longer be Zimbabwean citizens. As a result, Alice had lost touch with Kenneth even before you were born, Emma. But we understand he died of AIDS in Malawi soon after he returned there. His family apparently came from Chikwaka near to the Zimbabwe border. I'm sorry, Emma, that's really all we know of your father, Kenneth Banda."

Prosper looked across again at Emma. She was listening carefully to what he was saying but he didn't detect any emotional change in her when he told her of her father's death, just as had happened a little earlier when he had told Emma of her mother Alice's death. Emma couldn't stir up any emotional feelings for the deaths of the people she was hearing about for the very first time. It was as if she listening to a story being read to her about the deaths of people she had never known.

Prosper then switched back to talking about Alice. "You were born, dear Emma, when Alice was still young. She was just 15 when she had you. Like your mother, you were born at the hospital at All Souls. Before she gave birth, Alice knew she was already HIV positive but in spite of that, she had a good pregnancy. As about half of women who were HIV positive at that time passed the disease on to their babies, we were all so worried you would be born HIV positive as well. But as soon as you were born, they tested you and, miraculously, you were born free of the disease.

"But that was about all that was miraculous. The future looked bleak."

Alice had no qualifications and no job at a time when the prospects of finding work in Zimbabwe were almost non-existent, especially as she was so young, HIV positive and had just given birth to a fatherless baby. Sarah's own job, said Prosper, was also looking far from secure and she knew she could not depend upon the extended family to help make ends meet.

"Francis had children in school and we needed to pay for their school fees, and there was no certainty he would be paid at the end of the month.

"Sarah was beside herself when she learned Alice was HIV positive. At the time it was almost impossible to get hold of the medicines Alice had to have; the only way to get hold of the drugs, if they could be tracked down, which was not easy, was to pay for them and the money needed was way beyond Sarah's means or dreams. It was all this which led Sarah to decide to try to leave the country and go to England. She knew Zimbabwean nurses could get jobs there and, when settled in England, her plan was to arrange for Alice and you to follow so Alice could get hold of these anti-retroviral drugs she desperately needed."

Prosper then told Emma how Sarah set about trying to get to the UK herself and, once there, how she fixed up for Alice and her young baby to follow her. Sarah could not have succeeded, continued Prosper, without the help of the priests and missionaries at All Souls.

"They worked hard on her behalf, using their contacts to persuade the British High Commission in Harare to include Sarah among the few thousand Zimbabweans who Britain, at that time, was willing to accept into the UK as refugees. She was fortunate to be helped by Archbishop Chakaipa, the head of the Catholic Church in Zimbabwe, who knew our family from when he had been the priest in charge at All Souls in the early 1970s.

"Sarah worked with and became a close friend of his niece, Elizabeth Tarira, at the hospital at All Souls. Elizabeth later joined the Italian missionaries who ran the hospital; she qualified as a doctor in Italy and returned to work here in Zimbabwe. Tragically she died of breast cancer a few years ago, so young.

"What a loss." Prosper sighed as another painful memory returned. He had known Elizabeth from when she was a little girl, and he paused as he fought to keep back his tears and waited to regain his composure before completing what he needed to tell Emma about Alice.

"Within a year of Sarah's arrival in London, and with the help of both the priests at All Souls as well as her new friends in England, Sarah managed to get together the papers needed to enable Alice and you to follow her to the UK. We never quite knew how she managed it, but I guess it was a mixture of dogged determination as well as a bit of luck.

"You were just two years old at the time we said goodbye to you." Prosper turned back to face Emma again. "However, within six months of your arrival, Alice's health began to deteriorate rapidly; she had developed full-blown AIDS which had advanced so far it was too late to save her. She died on 18th September 1994, a few months before your third birthday. I remember it well because it was a Sunday and I had been at All Souls for Mass and got a message to come back in the evening to take the phone call from Sarah. I don't know how she got through but she did. And when she broke the news, she broke down: it was so terrible."

Emma thought she saw Prosper wipe a tear from his eye. Emerentiana had started to sob to herself quietly.

"As a teenager Alice was healthy and strong," said Prosper, taking a deep breath, "but, as Sarah told us in her letters, she weakened as she got close to death and eventually had no resistance left to fight the disease and quietly died with Sarah at her bedside in the hospice."

Prosper paused for a moment before he continued speaking. He had spent a lot of time preparing this speech to Emma, but as he spoke, he was overcome with emotion as he relived the tensions, worries and uncertainties of those troubling times.

"The rest, dear Emma," he said, "you know. Sarah brought you up as the child she lost, the only remaining link with her beloved husband Joshua. With Alice's passing, you became Sarah and Joshua's child. The story of how she cared for you, dear Emma, is yours. You know it far better than we do.

"But what I can say, is Sarah has produced a fine young woman, one we can all be proud of, immensely proud. Alice would be proud of you, too, Emma, as would your grandfather, Joshua Makonde.

"You asked about your mother, Emma, and I have told you the events of her short life of most importance to you, as best as I could. But as I said earlier, I also need to tell you more about your grandfather, Joshua Makonde, and this is what I must do now."

Prosper, Emerentiana and Emma had been sitting together in the small yard for much of the morning and they were by now all quite drained and in need of sustenance. So, before Prosper started to tell Emma more about Joshua, Emerentiana asked him to take a break while she went to the kitchen to make tea for the three of them. He readily agreed. Presently she returned carrying a tray with mugs of tea and chunks of bread covered in peanut butter. While she was away Prosper started to tell Emma about some of the people who lay buried in the family burial mound.

On Emerentiana's return, Prosper said they should move their chairs back into the shade as they were now almost sitting in the full sun. As they did so, two lizards who had been sunning themselves on a rock in the sand scuttled away.

When Prosper resumed his recounting of those past events, Emma was fully alert. She was eager to hear more from Prosper about Joshua, Sarah's husband. Although until today she knew next to nothing about him, she already sensed she had a far stronger emotional connection with him than with Alice or Kenneth, her real mother and father. New though he was to her, it was as if she was learning about her close and just-discovered father rather than her distant deceased grandfather.

"Joshua," began Prosper, "played an important part in the process of Zimbabwe becoming the independent nation it is today and you should be proud of him. After crossing to Mozambique, he underwent training as a guerrilla fighter and became a member of the Zimbabwe National Liberation Army, or ZANLA.

"We are told he was one of the finest recruits they ever had. Like many others, he was physically fit, mentally alert, and soon became a proficient soldier, well able to cover 40 to 50 kilometres across rough terrain at nights, even without the aid of the moon. He was also an excellent shot with an AK47, ably handled even the heavy rocket-launchers and quickly became a skilled and speedy layer and concealer of deadly landmines. He was also able to survive on his own in the bush for days on end. This was because as a child he had been good at catching birds and trapping animals and his grandfather had taught him which berries and leaves he could eat and which were poisonous.

"But perhaps most critically, through his grandfather he had learned how to detect where to find water, both through using his nose to smell it out and by carefully watching wild animals as they searched for the bush's most precious commodity. Sarah thought he had once told her he had acquired these skills because he had bushman blood running though his veins, though she wasn't sure it was true."

"Anyway, after five weeks' training, Joshua was considered ready to return to the country where he soon engaged the Rhodesian Security Forces in three or four encounters on his first tour of duty. But where he differed most crucially from so many of his fellow fighters was in his leadership skills.

"Very early on in his training, Sarah's Joshua was recognised not only as a great tactician and a man of cunning, but as someone with a wealth of person-skills, a man who had the potential to be a leader. As a result, and as everyone had expected, within a few months he was leading sorties himself. What was even more surprising was that all his early missions were highly successful with hardly any deaths of those under his command. This was quite exceptional."

As he spoke, Prosper grew increasingly aware of how intensely Emma was now listening and he began to feel the whole process of telling Emma about the past, which he had been dreading, was having a very positive effect on her. He sensed Emma was not only sifting through in her mind everything he was saying about Joshua, but she was continually linking what she was hearing back to Sarah.

"Joshua was not merely well liked, he was trusted," Prosper went on, "rapidly earning a reputation as a successful commander and strategist. Young guerrillas were keen to be part of his unit and as a result he was able to attract the better junior fighters to join him. This not only enhanced the fighting capabilities of the units he commanded, but further successes only fuelled his growing reputation. He rarely drank and never took drugs while on his missions, and he expected all under his command to follow his orders meticulously. Soon he was commanding groups of up to 20 fighters on successful missions and after that his reputation had spread beyond his own troops to the enemy. By the end, so daring and so successful were the surprise encounters with the security forces he set up that he was viewed by some as having almost mystical powers. He was said to be invincible."

Did she know all guerrilla fighters were given or chose new names when they joined up, Prosper asked Emma. These were referred to as their *Chimurenga* names, or names-in-the-struggle. Emma shook her head to indicate she didn't.

"Well," he continued, "almost from the first week he joined up, and seeing his potential, his first commander gave him his *Chimurenga*, which was *Rupango*. This means "Lightning". And from then on, Joshua Makonde was known as Comrade Lightning, and very few people knew his real name.

"Perhaps it was inevitable, given his prominent role on the front line," mused Prosper, "that Joshua's life as a guerrilla was destined to be short. As far as we have been able to discover, he lost his life at a massive fire-fight in an engagement he led in a farming area just north of the Mhondoro Communal Area, some 70 kilometres off the main Harare-Masvingo road."

Prosper lifted his arm and pointed in a westerly direction, telling Emma Mhondoro was about 50 or 60 miles from here as the crow flies.

"It was a daring attempt to either kill or kidnap a top Rhodesian Front politician-cum-farmer, a friend of Prime Minister Ian Smith and the Rhodesian Front founder, Boss Lilford," he said, resuming his account of the likely end of Joshua's short life. "We certainly know such an incident took place and most if not all the guerrillas involved in that fire-fight were killed, and we are pretty sure Joshua – or should I say Comrade *Rupango* or Lightning – was involved. Why? Because that was the last bit of news we ever had of his wartime activities. No subsequent stories about Comrade Lightning have ever come to light."

Prosper then took up his own part in the story, explaining to Emma the role he had played in trying to piece together what happened to Joshua.

"It was back in 1982," said Prosper, "two years after independence and seven years after this incident took place when I became directly involved. After the family had heard a number of different stories about the farmhouse attack, and urged on by Sarah, I decided to travel to Mhondoro to see if I could gather any new information about Joshua and his likely death there. I stayed three or four days trying to find out anything more concrete about what had happened, trying especially to gather any details about who precisely was killed and when and where they might have been buried.

"I did manage to track down three former *mujibas,* the name given to the young villagers who used to support the guerrilla fighters. I spoke to three people, two boys and a girl at the time, who had been active in the area. Although they were reluctant to speak to a stranger like me, they were able to confirm the incident had taken place. They told me a number of bodies had been buried, but as none of them had been directly involved in this particular incident, they said they didn't know any more. I wasn't sure whether they knew anything else and were still afraid to say anything more or whether that was all they knew; it was very frustrating.

"However, two other people gave me the name of a teacher who they said still taught at the school near to the big Catholic mission in Mhondoro, St Michaels, a Mr Svosve. They both said independently they had been told he knew about the incident. Though a little obscure, it did seem to be an important lead. But in the end, it led nowhere: though I spoke to dozens more people, I wasn't able to track down or even find anyone else who knew of this elusive Mr Svosve.

"After I returned home, I wrote to the priest in charge at St Michael's, asking him for Mr Svosve's contact details, but he never replied so I have no idea even whether such a man existed and if so, whether he is still alive. And if he is alive, I don't know whether he could shed any more light on the incident where Joshua probably died than I had managed to find already.

"Then, partly because I was keen for Sarah's sake to try to solve the continuing mystery of Joshua's death and partly because after my initial visit I had grown more interested myself in discovering what had happened, a few years later I tried to arrange a second trip to Mhondoro. This is because I had heard there had been a change in the priest in charge and the new man, I was told, was keen to help in the search for people missing from the war days. Over the course of a year, we corresponded but, in spite of his best efforts, I failed to find any more firm information about either Joshua or the mysterious Mr Svosve than I had before.

"I told the priest I would like to come back to Mhondoro for a follow-up visit but he strongly advised me not to come. He said it was no longer safe for someone from outside the area to come and ask questions because political intimidation had grown so much worse and no one would talk to strangers about such matters anymore. He even told me two people who had come to the area and had started to ask questions had disappeared. I told Sarah and she forbade me from making the journey.

"And that just about sums up all we know – or I should say all we don't know – about Joshua's death," said Prosper. "No firm evidence of his death, nothing about where a body might be buried, but pretty strong circumstantial evidence he probably died and was hurriedly buried somewhere in and around Mhondoro."

Prosper was nearing the end of what he had promised Sarah he would recount to Emma, and he was now visibly tired. But he had one more thing he felt he needed to say to her.

"Sarah has never acknowledged to either Emerentiana or myself she was ready to admit Joshua is dead, though deep down, she must know it," said Prosper. "In the recesses of her soul, Sarah knows Joshua is dead, but somewhere else inside her she retains the spark of hope he didn't die and he will come back to her. Without the firm evidence and with an initial swirl of rumours after the war ended which included third- or probably fourth-hand reports Joshua had been sighted, it is so hard for Sarah to have closure.

"Sadly, Emma, there are literally hundreds of people who are in the same situation as Sarah – their loved ones never returning home and no hard news of what ever happened to them. It's all so sad; so very, very sad. These are the people who gave their lives for our independence, our young, our flesh and blood. Without them we would not have been free. Yet too many of them have been forgotten by both our politicians and even by those who purport to represent former guerrilla fighters. In many ways they have become non-people. They have been erased from the nation's memory except by their nearest and dearest, like Sarah, who will never forget."

At the mention of Sarah's name, Emma suddenly recalled the first and only time Sarah had opened up to Emma about the man she loved. It was when Emma first told Sarah about her love for Robbie. As she did so, what Sarah had said then came vividly back to her.

> *The man I married was kind and caring, bright and clever, but, oh, was he also determined too! He went when we were so young. We had such little time together. I love him now, though he is long gone, just as much as I loved him when I last saw him, last touched him, last smelt him. I told him then I would never forget him and I never will. There is no other man I have loved, and I never will.*

Emma had never before thought about the man Sarah had loved: up until now, she had only ever focused on Sarah. But thanks to Prosper, Emma now knew something about him. She knew his name: it was Joshua Makonde. As she repeated his name to herself and as Sarah's words came back to her, the feeling grew in Emma at first in a small way but soon very powerfully that she, Sarah's "daughter" needed to find out what really happened to Joshua Makonde – Comrade Lightning – her "father." It was as if in some way, through Prosper, Sarah was asking for the help of Emma, her daughter, the journalist, in finally finding the truth about Joshua's disappearance.

Prosper was right: Sarah still hadn't had closure. If she had, she would surely not have said "he went when we were so young". She would have said, "He died when we were so young". Deep down, did Sarah think Emma could help? Was this, thought Emma, either the conscious, or the underlying reason why Sarah had been so keen for Emma to come back to Zimbabwe?

It was late that Thursday afternoon when Prosper, Emerentiana and Emma left the lengthening shadows of the mango tree, their intense conversation over, and three more days before Emma left the Makoni family home to return to Harare. In the intervening period, she revisited in her mind, again and again, what Prosper had said and, on the occasions when they were together, sometimes asked him further questions. Sometimes he added the odd detail he regretted he had earlier forgotten. They only talked extensively again one more time; it was on the following evening as they stood together watching the sun go down after Prosper had taken Emma to the family burial ground and started to pray for Alice, and Emma said they should pray for Joshua as well. Yet, as far as Emma could remember at the time, it was only small, insignificant details which he mentioned. When she left Mutoko, Emma was not aware of anything substantial Prosper had added to his basic narrative.

What surprised Emma was how calm she felt in the days immediately after learning who she really was – news which had caused her initially to feel at first tearful then upset and disoriented and, for a time, totally distraught. She seemed to be adjusting to the new "her."

This was, in part, because the more she thought about it, the more she realised she didn't really feel any different. Deep down inside, she was still the same Emma. She felt as safe and secure as the woman she always had been, and what she now knew about herself would not alter in any way her plans for her future life on the path she had started to tread as a journalist.

Emma also thought that, if anything, knowing what she now knew would draw Sarah and herself closer together. This was because Sarah would now be able to open up and talk freely about the things she had been compelled to keep hidden for all these years. And, as she did so, Emma would support her and this sharing would, in turn, only deepen their already close relationship. Nonetheless, Emma was also realistic enough to know it could well be hard at first to re-establish their relationship as she knew Sarah would be terrified that Emma would think ill of her for hiding her true identity for so long. This was why a part of her wanted her time in Zimbabwe to quickly come to its natural end so she and Sarah could be together again and start the process of rebuilding their precious relationship. It crossed her mind she should text Sarah to tell her she now knew everything, but she dismissed this almost as soon as the idea had occurred to her. She knew they had to sit down and go through everything together. When she broached the subject with Prosper in a roundabout sort of way after they had prayed together and were watching the sun set, it was clear he thought the same.

But more immediately Emma needed to get back to Simon. He was the person she now shared everything with – and him her – and she was desperate to do so. *He* had to know the truth about who she was: *he* had to know about her mother, Alice, and how Sarah really was related to her, and *she* had to tell *him* all about Joshua. But she also needed to tell him how she felt when Prosper began to tell her the real story of her life and how disoriented she felt. Sunday afternoon, when she would see him again – that seemed like an eternity away. She missed him terribly.

Emma did try to text Simon a couple of times but gave up; not because she wasn't able to get a signal but more because she knew she couldn't even begin to tell him what she needed to say even in a long text message. She knew they needed time: she needed a reprise of their long day on Hampstead Heath, simply to talk it all through and be together, just the two of them.

moving towards each other, then falling back, hips moving, hands raised, hands clapping, elbows in, elbows out. They laughed and laughed until exhausted they gave up and collapsed on the ground one by one, calling for water to quench their thirst.

The days, however, were not all spent in merriment. One time Emma asked Prosper why he walked with a slight limp. This provided an opening for him to talk a little more about the pre-independence-war days and how the war had affected them directly. Emma was horrified by what she heard.

The year Sarah gave birth to Alice, 1976, was the year the war really impacted on their lives. To try to place a wedge between the guerrilla fighters and the villagers upon whom they depended for food and intelligence, the government created what were euphemistically called Protected Villages. These were enclosures surrounded by barbed-wire and landmines, guarded by armed soldiers and overlooked by raised platforms which looked uncannily like control towers in Nazi concentration camps. At dusk, everyone in a specified area – men, women, children, the old, the crippled, and the disabled – had to make their way to the Protected Village where they were required to sleep until daybreak, when the gates were opened and they were let out. It was, said Prosper, just like the way they kept their animals in at night, except, unlike with the animals, if people were discovered outside the village fence at night, they were not coaxed back in, they were shot.

Prosper said All Souls Mission was converted into a Protected Village in the year 1976, and for four years families living up to 20 kilometres away, including the whole Makoni family, had to walk each evening from their home to All Souls for the night and stay there locked up, often for 14 hours, till they were let out in the morning. Neither food nor shelter was provided, nor toilets. During this time, it was impossible to farm as the fences around their fields and the animal kraals fell into disrepair. If they did manage to plant their fields and weed their crops, most were eaten by ay by wandering goats or cows and at night by hordes of marauding baboons. The family lost all their cattle, goats and chickens and most of their vegetables were either eaten by animals or stolen.

But, said Prosper, they were luckier than many. Some villages were burnt by the security forces and dozens of villagers from the Mutoko area were maimed or killed by landmines. A few were killed by sniper bullets, whether deliberately or "caught in the crossfire," but practically none of these killings were ever investigated.

"But most terrifying of all were the beatings – and worse," said Prosper. "Cooped up in Protected Villages and with their livelihoods undermined or in some cases destroyed entirely, people talked. Some gave accurate accounts of the movements of guerrilla troops because they were so desperate for money they were willing to be bribed for information.

Some made up stories because they bore a grudge against someone else. Whatever the truth of the allegations, the stories had consequences."

Prosper then explained to Emma that on several occasions he was interrogated, but, as he provided his interrogators with no real information (he knew very little) he was whipped on his back and on his legs. "I was beaten hard," said Prosper, shuddering as he recalled what he had tried to forget.

At one particular beating, Prosper said he was hit so hard his left leg was severed and torn, and it became infected. The hospital managed to save the leg but that was why he now walked with a permanent limp. Emma said how sorry she was, but he told her he was one of the lucky ones.

"Some were tortured," said Prosper. "Their heads were immersed into water to simulate drowning; some were beaten so hard they caused permanent brain damage; electrodes were placed on different parts of the body, including their genitals, and sharp electric shocks were repeatedly administered which left people trembling and shaking. But probably the worst of all were the psychological effects the war had on so many people. Not hundreds but many thousands of people were scarred and deeply traumatised by the war years so that five, ten or 20 years afterwards many were still in need of psychological counselling.

"Of course, it was not only the security forces who were guilty of inhumane treatment and the killing of civilians. Sometimes villagers reported the presence of guerrillas in their area to the police and security forces, and some of these were tortured, maimed or killed if they were found out. Likewise, some innocent people were undoubtedly killed and tortured by both guerrilla fighters and their supporters in and across the villages. Some people supported the guerrillas because they believed they were fighting for justice; many others were simply too frightened not to do so.

"It was not only villagers who were caught up in the war," Prosper went on. "The Italian missionary after whom the hospital at All Souls is now named, Dr Luisa Guidotti, was shot by the security forces after leaving a road block while returning to All Souls in her ambulance after attending to a patient in mid-1979, only months before the war ended. She bled to death. Whether she was killed by accident or deliberately was officially disputed; some even claimed she had been killed by the guerrillas. But we all knew this was nonsense. Doctor Luisa was so well liked right across the region and known as the dedicated medical doctor she was. She was unafraid to assist anyone in need, including guerrilla fighters. Indeed, she was the first white woman in the entire country to be imprisoned and charged for not reporting the presence of guerrillas. As the security forces admitted after the war, they had planted bombs outside churches to make it look as if they had been set up by those they referred to as the terrorists. Claims and counterclaims of who killed who were all too common. It was not only a military war which was being waged, Emma, it was also a propaganda war.

"Two months after Dr Luisa was killed, her close friend and fellow missionary, John Bradburne, was abducted," added Prosper. "He was killed, shot in the back, his almost naked body found by our local priest, *Baba* ("Father") Gibbs, in a ditch on the main road early one September morning. He was also extremely well-known locally, the bearded Englishman who for the previous ten years had run the old settlement for lepers at Mutemwa, on the outskirts of the town of Mutoko. He had lived with the people and devoted himself to building a community among his leper friends. He was a poet and not in the least political; you used to her him singing loudly as he walked along; some called him a dreamer.

"Why was the singing, bearded poet John who looked after the lepers killed?" asked Prosper, almost as if he was talking to himself.

"People believe what they want to believe, but, in reality, we still don't know for sure, even if we have our suspicions. But if you really want to know who was ultimately responsible for the deaths of tens of thousands of us who were killed in the war which should never have been allowed to happen, that is a far easier question to answer."

On the Friday of her stay, Emma herself made the journey on foot from the Makoni homestead to All Souls and back again. She went with Francis' wife, Fadzai, who had worked on and off as an administrative assistant both at the hospital and in the parish office at the mission. The reason for their trip was that the only official piece of paper which documented Emma's birth was the certificate of her baptism, which took place a few weeks after her birth at All Souls. Emma was keen to see the parish ledger for the year in which her baptism took place, which Fadzai said would have her date of birth recorded, and, if possible, have another copy made with her date of birth added.

Having worked in the parish offices, Fadzai said she knew where all the old church record books were kept, and she easily found the right one in its correct place on the shelves of the dusty old archives. Fortunately, the 1991 ledger was made of good quality paper, not the more modern newsprint, so it had not been eaten by termites as had some of the more recent ones. Before they set out, Prosper had reminded them of the date of her baptism, 26th December 1991.

Fadzai pulled the dusty book from the shelves and opened it on the page for the correct date and between them Emma and Fadzai's fingers went down the line of names to find entries for those born on 10th December. Suddenly, everything became quite surreal. Next to the name of the only infant born on 10th December 1991 were inscribed the names of her mother, Alice Makoni, and her father, Kenneth Banda. Not only had Emma never known until this week the mother or father recorded here had any connection to her but the name of their daughter, written boldly next to theirs, was not hers. The girl born on that day was *Emerentiana Makoni*. The young woman looking down at the page of the baptismal register and touching the name of the Zimbabwean Emerentiana Makoni was a young English woman named Emma Maconie.

What a strange world, thought Emma to herself as she thanked Fadzai for bringing her to see the book and said, aloud, "The only official written record of my entry into the world turns out not to be me at all." But she did take a photo of the page with her phone.

The walk to and from All Souls was the first time Emma and Fadzai had spent time together, just the two of them, and on their way back, Emma asked Fadzai about her dead mother. It was mostly a reprise of what Prosper had told her. But as they chatted, Fadzai told Emma about other young members of the Makoni family who had died young or unexpectedly. She explained why there was a gap between Zuva, now aged 7, and Clemence, now aged 11. Francis and Fadzai's fifth child, Mary, was born in 2006 but passed away five years later. She would have been nine now but she had died of malaria and been buried in the family burial ground. Emma learned she was not the only one to die young. In 1997, when Emma was six, Sarah's older sister Angelica died, aged only 30. She had had tuberculosis and had been sent to the sanatorium at Makumbi, where she died of pneumonia. Emma vaguely recalled Sarah telling her about this when she was a child, but only now did it come alive and make sense to her. Sadly, two of Francis' nieces, children of his sisters Madiwa and Clemencia, had also died. Spiwe's younger brother, John, had died of measles when he was less than two, and Stella's oldest sister, Shamiso, died as a baby of six months from diarrhoea and dehydration.

Fadzai explained it was partly because of the deaths of these young ones that the decision had been made for Spiwe and Stella to move away from their own homes in more remote villages and come to live with them. All these deaths, thought Emma, as Fadzai was speaking, were deaths which need not have happened, and, if they had been born in England, would almost certainly not have happened. Deaths from poverty, deaths from avoidable diseases. *What a tragic waste*, she thought.

There was great sadness when Sunday came and Emma had to depart and return to Harare. Given the spate of horrific accidents on the Harare Mutoko road, Prosper and Francis were not keen for Emma to take the bus back. Fortunately, an Italian couple who had been staying at the Nyamakwere Lodges where Francis worked were returning to Harare by car and were happy for Emma to hitch a ride with them.

Amidst many tears and after endless hugs, Emma left the Makoni family homestead the way she had come – on Francis' motor bike. The last person she said goodbye to was Prosper. He stepped forward and, for a moment, they stood in front of each other a yard or so apart, without moving or saying a word. Then Prosper stretched out his arms and Emma couldn't help herself: she moved forward and, after hugging him, gave him a kiss on both cheeks. She knew she had overstepped the mark, but the tectonic plates had moved and she felt herself somehow exempt from normal custom and able to violate tradition. Seeing how grateful Emma clearly was for all he had done for her, Prosper immediately forgave her – or was it forgiveness? As she sat on the back of Francis' motor bike and grasped tightly hold of him when the bike slipped on the sand, this time with warm affection, and thought about it, Emma wasn't all sure the word forgiveness sufficiently captured what had passed between them. It was far more complicated than that.

The young Italians, Francesco and Sofia Benini from Modena, were waiting for them when they reached the motel, and they greeted Emma warmly. They had been staying there for a week, travelling between the Luisa Guidotti hospital and the leper settlement at Mutemwa as they had been keen both to help and to learn more about John Bradburne and Luisa and the work they had done in the area. They had come more as tourists but were now hoping to return one day soon as volunteers.

When Emma first saw her hosts sitting in the car, she got the fright of her life. She had not been with a white person for days and when she saw these two pale faces smiling at her they looked very strange to her. Their faces looked so pasty, they looked ill. Indeed, to Emma their features appeared so plain and dull she wasn't initially able to distinguish them apart: they looked almost identical. But once in the car and when they had begun chatting, these early impressions and feelings of Emma's quickly faded and within a few moments her white companions no longer seemed so odd, so different. *That was funny*, Emma thought to herself, as she adjusted to their all being together; *I have never experienced anything like that before.*

As they passed the massive granite outcrops around Mutemwa, Francesco pointed out to Emma the two summits of *Chigona* and *Chisosera* and told her they had climbed to the top of both hills, following the track which led upwards from the leper settlement. This was the route, they said, which John Bradburne had often taken to watch the eagles, to run round what looked like a crude running track at the top of *Chigona* and to seek inspiration and sometimes sit down and write his poetry. As they passed it, Francesco pointed out to Emma the sign on the tree-lined side road which, he told her, led down to the settlement where the lepers lived.

Sofia said that, as a young Englishwoman born here in Mutoko, Emma must be particularly proud of John. As Emma seemed perplexed, Sofia explained John had written over 6,000 poems and was said to be the most prolific poet of the English language. Until Prosper had first mentioned his name a few days' earlier, Emma had never heard of either John or his poetry, but she typed out a note to herself on her phone to find out more about him, his life and his poetry when she got back home.

Late that afternoon, after a hot but otherwise uneventful ride, the Beninis dropped Emma at the gate outside the Reddys' house, refusing all offers she made to contribute to the costs of their petrol and declining her invitation to come in. She had enjoyed her time with them and wished them well. But it was Simon who was already the focus of her attention. As she walked up the driveway to the house, she prayed he had got back before her as there was so much she was really desperate to tell him.

The Feedback

Simon was sitting by the pool, the late afternoon sun warming his back, a book lying open on his lap. It was Abraham Varghese's *Cutting for Stone*, about an American doctor born in Ethiopia who only as an adult learns who his father was and how he had met and fallen in love with his mother. Simon had brought it out with him to read on holiday and was gripped by the storyline as well as by the beautiful descriptions of everyday life in Africa, though it was set in Addis Ababa rather than Harare. However, he was too troubled to read; he was restless waiting for Emma. As well as having missed simply being with her, there was so much he needed to tell her. He felt no urge to distract himself by taking a swim even though, after almost a week of hotter weather in Harare, the water was now just about warm enough for a quick dip.

Emma arrived an hour or so after Jim and Simon had returned from Kariba. As she opened the front door, which was never locked, she was met by Jessica, who told her Simon was by the pool and Jim had joined Sheila in their room, where they were both resting. Without diverting to drop her rucksack in her room, Emma hurried on through the house to the terrace; she quickened her pace as she stepped out from the French doors, calling out to Simon as she ran down the slope to the pool to join him. On hearing her voice, Simon jumped to his feet to open the narrow gate of the fence which bordered the pool just in time for her to squeeze through. They embraced, then held each other tight in a gesture which was now so familiar it had almost become routine. As they parted, they picked up two of the white plastic chairs which lay by the poolside, placed them side by side and sat down. They were both as keen to start talking as they were to be physically close to each other.

There was so much Emma was desperate to tell Simon, but immediately sensing how eager he seemed to be to talk, she motioned to him to go first. She wasn't upset. She thought it best for Simon to tell her first about his lazy days of fishing, swimming, game-viewing and lakeside barbecues before she took the time she knew she would need to relate to him the shocking and deeply upsetting things she had discovered about herself since they parted.

However, as she was about to discover, it wasn't his adventures at Kariba which Simon wanted to relive with Emma. What he was bursting to tell Emma about were the unbelievable things he had learned about his father and his father's past, which, it was now clear to him, his parents had deliberately kept hidden from him and his sister Jane when they were growing up. Simon could hardly believe the most horrific events Jim had described to him but he knew they had happened because Jim had been there either as a witness to or participant in them as they had unfolded.

"Okay," said Emma, unprepared for what was to come. "You start, Simon, and when you're finished, I'll tell you what I need to – so fire away!" She smiled nervously, knowing how much she would need Simon's comfort and support when the time came for her to tell him what she now knew about Sarah and her past and who she really was.

"It's about Dad," began Simon hesitantly, not quite knowing how to start.

"Dad was always reluctant to tell us much about what he did here in Zim during the war years. I have seen the few odd pictures of him in uniform in family albums but he told us next to nothing about those initial post-school years before he went down to Cape Town to study accountancy.

"Well, as I knew Jim and Dad were the closest of friends and they had been in the army together, when we were alone on the boat at Kariba I asked Jim if he would tell me a bit about those days. He was clearly delighted as he told me he had wanted the opportunity to do just this, saying something vague about how he and Dad felt now was the right time for me to know. So over the course of the four days we were away, he told me what I am now going to share with you, Em. Jim seemed to feel a sense of relief as he unburdened himself of the story of Dad, hinting towards the end that Dad had specifically asked him to do so. It was as if his telling me what happened was fulfilling a really important obligation to his closest friend. What he told me was simply dreadful, it completely blew my mind, Em, and that is why I have been so desperate to share it all with you. But be patient as I do so as I became quite upset and tearful when Jim told me, and I'm afraid this may well happen again just now."

Emma was both shocked and worried, but at least she was ready. Of course, she had no idea what Simon was about to tell her, and already she was starting to feel nervous. What's more, as she knew she would have to wait even longer to give Simon her account of what had happened to her, she was also feeling quite disoriented. She said quietly, "Go on, Simon, tell me everything, in your own time and at your own pace."

"According to Jim," continued Simon, who hardly noticed Emma had spoken, "Dad was a hero. Indeed, this wasn't just Jim's view, and he wasn't just an ordinary hero. Towards the end of his time in the army, Dad received one of the highest military decorations given out during those pre-independence war years. He was one of the very first of only about thirty people to be awarded the Silver Cross of Rhodesia. Jim said those who fought alongside Dad, including him, were convinced he should have been given the country's highest military medal, the Grand Cross of Valour."

Though Emma knew nothing about Rhodesian war medals, she knew enough about Zimbabwe's pre-independence history to understand that what Simon was telling her meant his father had played both an extremely active and prominent role in the bush war. This didn't really come as a surprise to her because from what he had told her – and held back from telling her more – about his time around Mutoko, Emma had already suspected he had been a member of the Rhodesian Security Forces.

"The story of how all this came about," said Simon, "starts with Dad's joining the Rhodesian Light Infantry, or the 'RLI' as it was always known, pretty much as soon as he left school. This was not unusual because all white male school-leavers were required to go into either the police or army: it was compulsory. By this time there was conscription."

However, as Simon explained to Emma, unlike many who joined with them, his dad and Jim didn't begrudge having to go into the army. They were not among those, and apparently there were many, who would do anything to get out of it.

"Jim said those thinking of 'gapping it' (leaving the country) and joining the 'chicken-run' (going south to live in South Africa) were accused of being sell-outs or worse, traitors to the cause.

"As Jim put it, both he and Dad were *very* keen to make a contribution. They both felt they needed to play their part in helping to defend the country from the threat of communism which the government had worked hard to try to convince people would destroy their country unless everyone played their part in stopping such a terrible thing happening."

Simon added that from what Jim had said it was easy to understand why they all thought they were playing a crucial role in defending western civilisation from the communist onslaught, as such beliefs were both deeply held and widely shared by those closest to them. Jim said their families, their friends and those they looked up to and respected, their teachers and sports coaches and even those who preached to them when they went to church, indeed practically everyone they came across, including the nannies who had brought them up and whom they still saw and loved, shared this view of the world.

Simon said that when they were fishing Jim had spoken at length about precisely what he and Simon's dad were committed to and what they thought they were fighting against. It was, Simon said, as if he felt he had not merely to explain but to justify what they had done.

"Strangely," said Simon, "they didn't view what they were doing as a sort of last ditch stand for white supremacy. On the contrary, they saw the war as the only way of ensuring a secure and prosperous future with equal opportunities for all, a future which, as they saw it with crystal-clear clarity, was now under attack from the guerrillas and their political leaders. Jim told me that as teenagers he and Dad had known many black Zimbabweans who were vehemently opposed to communism. Some had been called in to give talks to the sixth form at their school to explain their views. Jim said the armed forces and the police had more black than white members, and they were never short of black recruits as the war heated up.

"Even at that time, neither of them had been against majority rule, they had simply wanted to ensure the future Zimbabwe would be a democratic country where the rights of all people would be respected. Jim repeatedly emphasised how much he and Dad loved the country they grew up in and wanted it to remain essentially the way they remembered it, a country where all future Zimbabweans, black and white, would live happily together. Indeed, Jim said they both felt really uncomfortable listening to the few white extremists they knew talking about racial superiority: neither he nor Dad were supporters of South Africa's system of apartheid which, in their view, was simply wrong. Rhodesia, they believed, was very different, a country where black and white had lived alongside each other, mostly happily, in the past, and where they would in the future, too."

As Simon spoke, Emma began to feel a little less uneasy. Perhaps Peter's role in the army had not been quite as bad as she had feared? After all, it seemed to have been based on some principles, hazy and muddled though they appeared to Emma and not ones she even remotely shared. But again, Simon was so focused on what he wanted to tell Emma about his father that he scarcely noticed how she was reacting to what he was saying.

"Until 1973," continued Simon, returning to the story of his father's life in the army, "the RLI was made up entirely of professional soldiers. But then it began to take conscripted national servicemen and Dad and Jim were among this group of new recruits.

"Their army life began and was initially centred on Cranborne Barracks in Harare, the home of the RLI. They both threw themselves into their training and in these early months started to learn the way the war was being waged. After a few months of life in barracks, much of it tough as they had expected, they had their initial hands-on experience, joining ten older recruits in a week-long patrol in the bush. It was challenging but when it was finished both Dad and Jim knew this was where and how they wanted to do their soldiering – on the ground, in the front line. Sitting in an office doing intelligence work, learning to fly planes or helicopters or sitting in command centres waiting to be parachuted in for quick assaults, none of this was the type of soldiering they felt cut out to do. They wanted to be the foot soldiers slogging it out deep in the bush, doing the grinding work of locating and then engaging the enemy.

"As a result, two things happened," Simon went on. "First, they opted not to join most of their friends on the accelerated training route to become officers. Second, they spent many long weeks understanding more about the craft of guerrilla warfare and the skills of counter-insurgency. Jim said they read and re-read a book called *The Law of the Flea*, a classic on guerrilla warfare, until they practically knew it off by heart. They learned first-hand how to survive in the bush, both physically and mentally. They understood how to track, locate and, once found, how best to engage the enemy. Jim said they quickly came to understand the pivotal importance of teamwork, the need to get to know the other members of your patrol, and how different people reacted to and functioned under extreme stress."

All this, Simon told Emma, provided the backdrop to what Jim told him about his father's leadership skills.

"Jim said it soon became clear to everyone that Peter – Dad – was not only fast becoming a superb bush soldier but he had quite exceptional leadership qualities with all the attributes needed to become a crack patrol commander. Just short of a year in the army, he was made a Lance-Corporal, and a few months later was promoted to the rank of first acting then full Corporal, giving him command over a ten- to twelve-person patrol. In short, before he had reached the age of 20, Dad fulfilled his early ambitions of playing a key role in the front line of the war. His youthfulness, said Jim, proved no impediment. He knew how to play to each person's strengths to get the best out of each member of his patrol to achieve their common goal, and the men under his command developed enormous respect for him and totally trusted his judgement. Jim said that whenever they succeeded in locating and drawing near to an enemy unit, the initial tension which the rest of the patrol always felt seemed to trigger an aura of calmness in Dad which, in turn, spread back to the rest of the patrol, boosting the confidence of them all."

Simon hurried on. "Jim said Dad quickly understood the crucial importance of local intelligence in guerrilla warfare and that longer term benefits often lay not in killing but in capturing enemy soldiers, hoping they might be persuaded to switch sides and join the security forces – and many did – transferring their skills and knowledge as well as their loyalty to their new commanders. Many captured guerrillas gave them vital intelligence about current or planned operations and Dad fed this back to HQ, resulting in many lives being saved. Jim said they were all aware of horrific things done to force informants to divulge information in violation of all the Geneva Conventions, but he told me Dad strongly disapproved of all of this. To him and Dad and to most of the younger recruits from school, torture was completely contrary to their core values, even, as Jim admitted, very few people raised their voices to protest when they saw it practised.

"According to Jim, however, what most marked Dad out from all the other commanders was his keenness to obtain as much personal information as he possibly could about any guerrilla commanders who had started to inflict a disproportionately large amount of damage in the areas where they were patrolling – whether it was killing farmers and farm workers on isolated farms, laying mines, murdering villagers whom they learned had informed on them and were thus judged to be sell-outs, destroying government buildings or, more daringly, attacking army posts and protected villages.

"As information about and especially as the names of particularly successful guerrilla commanders reached Dad," said Simon, "he saw it as an obligation – a sort of personal mission – to seek them out and to hunt them down. Indeed, Jim told me that the names of influential guerrilla commanders grew into something of an obsession with Dad. It was as if by knowing the names of the best commanders he was up against, and marrying the name with what he learned of their activities, Dad could form an image of them in his mind. This, in turn, enabled him to focus on them as people, which helped him to understand them better, almost as if he was trying to get inside their heads, or under their skin, in order to know the way they thought. This, Dad believed, would give him an edge on them, helping him to see their strengths and to uncover their weaknesses so he could anticipate where they would strike next and the tactics they would use.

"Jim said Dad was unique in never referring to these commanders as terrorists, or '*terrs.*' He would always refer to them by their title – calling them Comrade 'this' or Comrade 'that.' This was because he respected them as fellow fighters; in some ways it seems Dad saw his enemy counterparts as co-strategists and leaders like him who just happened to be on the opposite side in this war. Jim said it was as if Dad was playing cat and mouse in his mind with these commanders and, for Dad, knowing their names was an important part of the cat's weaponry."

Up to this point, while Emma had been listening to what Simon had been saying, she was not half as interested in the detail as Simon clearly was. Indeed, she was hoping Simon would soon finish what he was clearly so keen to tell her about his father's war exploits so she could tell him the far more troubling news she needed to share with him. If the truth be known, she was getting rather bored.

It was then that Simon said something which shook Emma to the core. "By the middle of the year – the year was 1976 – Jim told me that the names of three guerrilla commanders in particular kept coming up. These were Comrade *Pfumo* (or Spear), Comrade *Museve* (or Arrow) and Comrade *Rupango* (or Lightning)."

As Simon said the words "Comrade *Rupango*, (or Lightning)," Emma felt her body tighten. She froze and sat bolt upright, then turned to Simon and asked him in a penetrating sort of way, the strength of her voice forcefully indicating she was demanding an unequivocal answer: "Did you say Comrade Lightning, Simon?"

"Yes," said Simon who had picked up neither the shock in Emma's voice nor her evident intense interest in the names of one of the commanders. "Yes, I am pretty sure that was the name of one of the three commanders Jim mentioned Dad had become almost obsessed with hunting down."

Simon was about to reach the climax of the story of his father's life in the army and he didn't want to stop the flow of what he was saying. So, after quickly confirming that one of the three guerrilla commanders he had been hunting was Comrade Lightning, he hurried on. He didn't turn to look at Emma and so wasn't aware of her contorted look and fear which visibly spread across her face.

"They were easy names to remember," said Simon. "Comrades Spear, Arrow and Lightning.

"In the middle of that year, Dad led the patrols which ended in the deaths of two of these commanders in what Jim said were absolutely horrific engagements. The first lasted a couple of hours and Dad's patrol was successful, without needing to call for any external help: it involved a pre-dawn assault on a guerrilla unit which had been attacking a succession of government buildings in the rural areas. Dad tracked them down to a makeshift camp they had set up in dense bush and surprised them under cover of darkness in an engagement which involved close-quarter fighting. It was, said Jim, pandemonium, but Dad kept his head and maintained control of the patrol in the chaos of the fight. Two of the ten guerrillas were captured, the rest died and none escaped.

"The second engagement involved an attack at dusk on a unit which had been causing havoc by planting a succession of landmines on arterial farm roads, severely disrupting the shifting of that year's tobacco crop. After a week or so of observing the unit unnoticed from a distance, Dad's patrol located their position on a hillock of rocks and trees, and Dad decided they should launch an immediate attack. This began with Dad's leading the assault party which had to cross open ground; Uncle Jim was with a small group giving them cover from the side. Just before the attack, they radioed for assistance and the group was flushed out with a final assault led by Dad, aided by a *Fireforce* helicopter gunship. Five guerrillas died, three were captured but six or seven escaped into the darkness.

"In each of these incidents the names of the commanders Dad was pursuing were confirmed by the guerrillas whom they captured: the first was 'Comrade Spear' and the second was 'Comrade Arrow.' So it was two down and one to go.

"However, what happened to the third of these three commanders was never satisfactorily resolved," Simon continued. "Though the outcome was successful, what happened to the commander remains in doubt to this day: in rather mysterious circumstances he seemed to have vanished."

If Simon had turned to look at Emma, which he didn't, he would have seen a statuesque figure, eyes open wide but with head and body frozen as if in time, waiting to hear and process what Simon was about to say. But he hurried on, unaware of what was happening to Emma.

Simon then recounted Jim's story of what had happened, which, he said, they had pieced together in part from what his father remembered of the incident, in part from the information which Jim and other members of the patrol provided in their initial debriefing and afterwards as they each recalled additional snippets of what happened, and in part from the post-operational ballistics analysis.

For two months after the killing of these first two guerrilla commanders Jim said Peter had been totally focused on trying to locate and hunt down the last of these three commanders. He scoured intelligence reports and spoke to dozens of villagers, government workers, teachers and nurses, which convinced him he had located the area where this last commander was operating.

When he caught up with the guerrilla unit, it had recently attacked a local government office and then a remote cattle farm. Both resulted in three or four civilian deaths but no guerrillas were either killed or captured, so Peter was never certain these really were incidents led by the last of the three commanders he was pursuing. There then followed a long month of silence: for some four weeks they received no new local intelligence of any event which could be traced conclusively to the unit led by this commander. With his own mind focused on the mind of the commander he was hunting Jim said he was sure the group had gone back to Mozambique, most probably to rest, regroup and obtain new supplies.

Then word began coming in of a crack unit moving speedily in from the east, led, it was said, by Comrade Lightning. If it proved to be true, this was the surviving and elusive third commander Peter had been trying to find. Jim said his father had been so determined to find him himself that he persuaded his commanding officers to send out a patrol under his command to try to locate him.

After a week or so, and following a few minor attacks, Jim said Dad was able to piece together their movements, enabling him to locate the general whereabouts of the unit and soon after to begin to track them, though initially from a distance. Peter tried to work out where they were heading and what sort of target they might be aiming for. Jim said Dad had felt sure it would be something big, and he was right.

Late one afternoon, the guerrilla unit launched a hugely ambitious assault on the heavily-guarded farm of a well-known farmer-cum-politician, a senior member of Prime Minister Ian Smith's cabinet. If it had been successful and the farmer killed, given his standing the whole venture would have made world headlines. However, the farm was extremely well fortified: surrounding it were two security fences, erected about five metres apart, with landmines randomly though strategically placed between them. The property had round-the-clock surveillance, guarded by a small team of highly trained army personnel so that at any one time at least two men were always on duty. As the guerrillas would have known all this from their own intelligence-gathering, everyone assumed the farm was safe as practically all guerrilla attacks up to then had been either "soft" unguarded targets or lightly guarded ones.

How wrong they were. When news began to come in of an attack either near to or at this location, Peter immediately realised what was happening. This was so big and so ambitious, said Jim, Peter was sure it had been masterminded and was now being led by the third commander he had been hunting – his final nemesis.

As Peter was later to discover – as it took him a while to reach the spot – the assault began with the blowing up of the farm's *Leopard*, one of its two anti-landmine vehicles, which had left late in the afternoon to pick up supplies from the nearby town, aiming to be back by nightfall. Peter's patrol was probably a mile, possibly a little further, away when they heard the first noise. It was a huge bang, the all-too-familiar sound of a landmine exploding. Jim said that once Peter assessed what was happening – he knew the Cabinet Minister lived on a farm close by and his map showed him precisely where – he rushed his patrol to the farm, radioing to the *Fireforce* response team for support as he did so. Jim said that from his earlier research, Peter was already familiar with the farm layout, most crucially where the safe room was located – toward the back of the house and only accessible by way of a corridor which led off the hallway from the front door. He knew that as soon as an attack was launched, the farmer would immediately run to the safe room and bolt the door to wait until help came. Peter confirmed all this during a hurried inspection of the security plans of the farmhouse which he had had the foresight to have with him and was able to quickly review as they headed for the farm.

Simon was totally absorbed in his account of the raid on the farmhouse, as was Emma, now.

"Given the two fences with the landmines between them and the guards," said Simon, continuing his narrative, "Dad assumed the firefight would take place outside the farmhouse around the perimeter fence, and that the farmer would be safe until they arrived. However, when Dad's patrol reached the farm they thought they were too late and the farmer had already been killed as the electric fence had been neutralised, the inner and outer barbed wire fences cut, the generator blown up, the phone lines were down and two armed guards lay dead outside the front door of the farmhouse, which lay open in front of them. As he saw what had happened, Dad was now certain the farmhouse attack had been planned and led by Comrade Lightning.

"With Jim and two others covering for him," said Simon, speaking faster now as if he was trying to match the pace of the narrative, "Dad ran through the open farmhouse door, across the hallway and down the long narrow internal corridor which led to the farm's safe room. There, at the far end of the corridor, with his hand on the still locked door to the safe room where the politician-cum-farmer was hiding stood a man Dad assumed was the guerrilla commander: he was screaming and shouting as he kicked the door, trying to break it down.

"Then, suddenly sensing danger, the attacker stopped screaming and kicking and realised someone was behind him. He momentarily turned round and saw Dad, but before he had time to lift his *AK47* and shoot, Dad had shot him in the chest and he fell to the ground. Dad, however, had no time to run up to him to see whether he was dead because just before he had squeezed the trigger, he heard automatic gun fire behind him and the sound of someone, or possibly two people, running in through the farmhouse door. Based on the pre-operation assault plan he had devised and knew his patrol would be rigorously following, Dad knew these had to be the enemy and not his own men. In an instant, Dad sprang forward down the corridor towards the body lying bleeding and slumped against the locked door behind, immediately jumping to his right as he landed. He pressed his body tight against the corridor wall to conceal enough of himself behind the side of a bookcase which stood halfway down the corridor, holding his automatic rifle aloft and also hidden against the wall. It was, said Jim, the *Norwood R-76* Dad always used. As he tried to pin himself ever closer to the wall, two guerrillas came running into the corridor tracing the route Dad had taken moments earlier. Dad judged correctly that when their eyes fell on the body of their commander lying ahead of them in a pool of blood they would be distracted and come to an abrupt stop, their attention momentarily focused on their dead or dying commander.

"In that instant," said Simon, breathless now from the emotion of describing the climax of the firefight to Emma, "Dad jumped out from behind the bookshelf and lowered his rifle in a single movement. Then, standing face to face in front of the two surprised guerrillas, Dad shot them both dead in a hail of bullets. As they fell to the ground, he jumped over them and ran out of the farmhouse the way he had come in as fast as he could, firing shots in the air as he left."

As he paused for breath, Simon was suddenly aware of a quiet whimpering sound coming from Emma. Thinking she was upset about what was happening to Peter in his narrative and not noticing she was crying, Simon hurried on.

"As Dad emerged from the front door," continued Simon, "he heard Uncle Jim shouting to him to run, run, run. Dad turned to his left and, crouching low, he ran along the side of the farmhouse building to where he knew Jim and two others were covering for him. On the opposite side of the front door, two or three more guerrillas lay hidden behind an outhouse building about ten yards away. But it took them a moment to realise the figure running out of the door was Dad and not one of their two comrades who, moments earlier, had gone in. Once they did, they started firing, but it was too late. The side wall of the farmhouse Dad was running along, the cover Jim's group gave him and the growing darkness were sufficient protection to enable Dad to reach them in safety. By this time realising their comrades inside the farmhouse were probably dead, the guerrillas covering the front door had abandoned their position and were running away from the farm as quickly as they could."

"However," said Simon, taking in a fresh gulp of air, "the battle was not over. Instead of scattering into the bush as most guerrilla units did when their attacks resulted in failure, failing to hit their targets, these men were different. Disciplined, well trained and knowing what they needed to do, even without their commander, they ran purposefully towards the nearby hill which overlooked the farm to re-join the main group of their comrades, who were dug in and ready equipped, as Dad was later to discover, with at least one rocket-launcher and a machine gun. Checking no other guerrillas were left within the perimeter of the farmhouse fence, Dad knew his immediate priority was to follow them and to neutralise what he was soon to discover was the far larger group.

"Jim said Dad couldn't understand then why neither the additional ground forces nor the helicopter support he had radioed for had still not arrived," continued Simon. "Only later did he learn the ground troops had been despatched but they had been held up by landmines, smoke bombs and booby traps which the guerrillas had carefully laid at the place where they had blown up the *Leopard* truck to delay their arrival at the farm. To compound this problem, the lead helicopter pilot misread his map and initially went to the wrong farm, some 10 miles further north.

"Dad took stock of what was happening and, guessing rightly that there were more guerrillas on the hill, he ordered his patrol to surround it as best they could. For 20 minutes they managed to prevent the guerrilla group from escaping, but given the guerrillas' superior firepower, they could not risk attacking them without the additional support they desperately needed but which had still not arrived. Then, after what seemed an age, they heard the deep thudding sound of the blades of the helicopter gunships in the distance. A flare was sent up and within seconds two helicopters were overhead, their searchlights scouring the hill and the surrounding ground for movement. It was only at this point and seemingly without waiting for any order, that each of the guerrillas unilaterally decided it was all over: they abandoned their position and ran willy-nilly into the bush under the protection of the moonless night. Twelve were killed, none was captured. The rest – no one ever knew how many, perhaps there were none? – escaped into the bush.

"Dad and two others then rushed back to the farmhouse and to the cabinet minister," said Simon, whose voice then slowed to its normal pace now the fire-fight was over. "They were relieved to find him alive and unhurt, but he had been traumatised by the attack and was in shock. As Dad returned to the corridor where the first shooting had taken place, accompanied by my Uncle Jim, all they saw at the far end was a pool of blood on the floor where the body had lain. There was no sign of the guerrilla leader. On closer examination, they could see blobs of blood on the corridor floor. Dad and Uncle Jim followed the route of the drips which led back along the corridor to the front door and over the bodies of the two fallen guerrillas across still lying at the end closest to the hallway and the front door. But then, just outside the front door, though difficult to make out clearly in the dust and the darkness, the drops of blood simply disappeared. Although they scoured the ground beyond with their torches, they weren't able to see any more blood on the ground. The body from which the blood had been dripping had simply vanished."

Simon couldn't conceal the excitement he was feeling as he relayed the most mysterious part of the whole affair as he said – his voice raised almost an octave – "If the guerrilla commander was still alive, he was badly wounded so he must have been helped to get away, but who had come to his aid and how did he make his escape? If Dad had killed him, the dead body had been removed. But whatever happened, why was there no sign of footprints or boot marks? It was all very strange then, and it's remained a complete mystery ever since.

"The next morning," Simon's voice was returning to near normal, "further searches were made both inside the perimeter fences and along all the different farm tracks but nothing was found. All Dad and Jim knew was that from that day on no word was ever heard again of Comrade Lightning, the last of the three guerrilla commanders Dad had pledged to find. To this day, no one knows for certain what happened to the third commander Dad had committed himself to hunt down, except that if he had died that night it would have been at Dad's hand."

Simon was not quite finished. "It was the planning, execution and hunting down of these three commanders," he said, "his command and leadership of what had become one of the country's most crack patrols and, most notably, his skill and incredible bravery in stopping the third leader just before he would have killed the Cabinet Minister which led to Dad receiving his decoration, for gallantry and valour.

"Tragically, though, these three episodes, but particularly the final one, took their toll on Dad, as Jim told me in quite some detail.

"Soon after the third and most frightening engagement, Dad started to have nightmares. He would wake up at night sweating profusely to find himself reliving particularly that final shoot-out in the narrow corridor of the farmhouse. At times, he would dream he was the one killed and he could see his own face looking up vacantly as he lay in a pool of his own blood on the floor. At times he would be the one who pulled the trigger but as he did, the scene would always freeze with him looking at the face of the guerrilla commander and the commander staring back at him, eye to eye, no one moving.

"Jim said that once when Dad was reliving the same episode, the body of the guerrilla fell to the ground, but as it did it transformed itself into the dog Dad grew up with as a child, a Maltese terrier, the white tips of its paws reddening as it jumped up and down on the bloodied floor. On another occasion, as the shot body fell, it started to shrink, transforming itself into a huge scorpion, almost as large as his pet dog. It began to advance towards him, slowly at first but then it sped up, its tail quivering over its head ready to strike; as quick as lightning it struck Dad on his thigh and he felt a pain shooting through him and up his leg like an electric shock when he suddenly woke in a pool of sweat.

"Dad then started to be affected during the day," said Simon. "He would find himself beginning to shake all over uncontrollably as he sat at his desk or in his chair, feeling first incredibly hot, then icy cold.

"Jim said no one really knew what triggered Dad's post-traumatic stress, but it could have been his realisation that he should have left someone back at the farmhouse to ensure the Cabinet Minister was indeed still alive and safe rather than to order his whole patrol to surround the guerrillas around the *kopje*. Dad, said Jim, certainly told him that this was a major error, a fundamental misjudgement – *his* error and *his* misjudgement – which might well have resulted in disaster.

"Whatever the cause, Dad never led another patrol, and, except for the debriefing sessions following his return to barracks, he never spoke again about his life in the bush as a frontline soldier or made mention of his having been singled out as one of the best patrol leaders the RLI had ever had, except for the one or two brief discussions he had with Uncle Jim. Mum, of course, got to know what had happened very soon after they started going out together, and she was a continual help to Dad. She supported him when he had further terror and shaking attacks which fortunately grew less common – at least, that is what Jim said. Mum always protected him when socialising with friends by steering the conversation away from any discussions of those war years and what Dad had done in the army.

"Jim said that though he seemed to recover and outwardly appeared to be the same old Peter Robertson he had known from school days, deep down he was a changed man," continued Simon. "When he went to Cape Town, he had to have regular counselling sessions for the first year of his degree course and, he told Jim, without these weekly meetings with his therapist he would not have been able to finish his course at uni. Even when he began work at the family firm in Harare, he still went for the odd counselling session.

"Oh, Emma." Simon leant over and tightly gripped her left hand, which he was now holding. "Poor, poor Dad. I now know what he went through and why he wanted to keep it all hidden from Jane and me. He went through so much and he suffered greatly, and I never ever knew.

"I also now understand why he and Mum were so keen for me to come out to Zim, not merely to see the beauty of the place he still loves but so Uncle Jim could tell me what they both now wanted me to know – about Dad's past – but which, up to the day we left, he still felt unable to share with me."

Simon had finished telling Emma what he had been dying to share with her, and he now wanted Emma to speak. He knew she wanted to tell him about her family and the time she spent in Mutoko and he did want to hear all about it. But he really hoped she would comment first on the deeply upsetting things he had learned about his father and which he had just shared with her. Though he knew this would not be easy, given Emma's very different views about Zimbabwe's liberation war, he really felt he needed her support.

Without turning to look at her, Simon took his hand away from Emma and waited for her to speak.

Before Simon had spoken, Emma had wanted to tell him the momentous things she had learned since they were last together – about herself and her true identity; about Alice, her real mother and her dying of AIDS; and about how Sarah, really her grandmother, had brought her up as if she was her daughter. But most of all she had wanted to share with Simon what she felt as she reacted to Prosper's each new revelation about her past. She had also wanted Simon to know that although she now knew Alice was her mother, try as she might she couldn't bring herself to feel any sense of loss for a person who had only just entered her life, someone she had no memory of either knowing or losing. But, in sharp contrast, she wanted to tell Simon how much she did feel a loss for someone else she had discovered but hadn't known: Sarah's husband, Joshua Makonde. He didn't seem to her anything like a distant grandfather who had died years before she was born with whom she had developed no close emotional bonds. On the contrary, he felt to her more like her father who, even now, she hungered to know more about in spite of not having been aware of his existence until a few days ago.

But after Simon first mentioned the name of Comrade *Rupango*, Comrade Lightning, and as the stories of Peter Robertson's life in the army and his tracking of guerrilla leaders unfolded, the whole thrust of what Emma had planned to talk to Simon about was thrown awry as she began to grasp the enormity of the things he was saying – none more so than when he started to recount, with all its gruesome details, what took place in the corridor of that farmhouse on that fateful afternoon.

Oh my God, Emma had said to herself as the full meaning of what she had been told started to dawn on her – *Simon's Dad killed... Sarah's husband...* Then it hit her right between the eyes: Simon's Dad, the father of the man she was in love with, had both plotted and planned in minute detail and then tried with all the strength and skill he could muster to kill the man she had begun to feel was like a father to her. "Oh my God," she heard herself calling out into the ether, the hollowness of her voice sounding as if she was in a vast cave. But instead of her words disappearing, they boomed back at her with the intensity of the speakers at a rock concert, growing louder and louder as they echoed round her head and pounded her chest – "*Oh My God. Oh My God. Oh My God. Oh My...*"

But in reality, there was total silence round the pool; Simon heard and felt nothing. Then, as he waited for Emma to speak and she still said nothing, he turned to look at her and was shocked by what he saw. Her face was haggard and drawn: in some thirty seconds, it looked as if she had aged thirty years. She was not simply upset; her darting eyes had the look of a frightened woman. Emma was far more upset than Simon would ever have expected her to be, though he had suspected she would find what he had told her about his Dad pretty upsetting.

He took hold of Emma's hand once again then, holding both her hands tightly together, he looked straight at her and said, "Em, what is it? You look as if you have seen a ghost. What on earth can have caused you to react in such a way to what I was saying? I know what I told you came completely out of the blue. It was disturbing, horrific in many ways, but..."

Emma didn't seem to either see him or hear what he was saying.

Simon halted mid-sentence and, as he placed the warm palm of his right hand tenderly on Emma's left cheek, he tried again, saying, "but, dear Em... Dad is fine. He's alive; he didn't die and time has all but healed the pain he suffered. I am sure, too, that once I tell him all that Jim has told me about his past, the groundwork will have been laid for us to get even closer together than we have ever been before.

"I even think..." Simon leaned forward once again and at last managed to make at least the beginnings of eye contact, "I even think that if I approach the issue with the necessary sensitivity, Dad may even come round to supporting, even encouraging me in my decision to switch careers and work in the area of mental health, given what I now know of the psychological distress he has been through."

There was another pause. Simon could see Emma was now struggling to speak. He sensed she had a huge amount bottled up inside her which she needed to get out, but he could also see she was having enormous difficulty. Was it not knowing where to start or not being able to articulate what she was feeling? He couldn't tell.

He also knew what he had just said had pretty much misfired. He could see from her face she was in as much mental anguish now as she had been before his clearly failed attempt to cheer her up with his ill-judged, almost flippant remarks about changing careers. He thought he knew Emma pretty well, but this time he knew he had totally misread her: there really was something deeply, deeply wrong. He had to know what it was. He felt her pain. He waited. She would speak; she had to speak. He just had to know what it was.

As Emma gradually emerged from her almost hypnotic state, she began to speak. She started quietly, almost in a whisper, stammering as she tried to articulate what she was struggling to make sense of and say.

"I think, Simon..." she said, then stopped.

She then tried again, repeating herself, "I think, Simon..." and stopped again, unable to continue. She felt limper than she did after even the longest of runs in the roughest of weathers.

Then, at her third attempt, she said, blurting out the words quickly in staccato style, still not wanting to believe what she knew to be true, "I think Simon, your father killed, might have killed, possibly killed, did kill – oh I don't know..."

She stopped again in mid-sentence and twisted her fingers together as if this would help to force the words out then, speaking quickly, said, "Simon, I think your father killed Sarah's dear, dear husband."

Having said this, Emma found it far easier to continue. Taking a deep breath, she said, "I have learned so many earth shattering things about myself and my past in the last few days. Among these are that soon after Ma – Sarah – married, with their child starting to grow inside her, her husband, Joshua Makonde, left Mutoko and joined the Zimbabwe National Liberation Army, ZANLA. Like your father, he too became a soldier, but he joined the other side; he became a guerrilla fighter. No, he didn't merely become a guerrilla fighter, he became one of ZANLA's finest commanders and strategists." Emma could feel a sense of pride welling up inside her as she spoke. Her voice became stronger and she began to sound a bit more like her old self.

"As you know, Simon, all guerrilla fighters took war names, *Chimurenga* names as they called them. Well Joshua's *Chimurenga* name was *Rupango*. He, Ma's, Sarah's, husband – *he* was Comrade Lightning. The Comrade Lightning your father was hunting for was my own... my very own flesh and blood.

"What you have told me, Simon, means the closest of your family, your flesh and blood, tried to kill – and probably did kill – the closest of my family, my flesh and blood. Simon, our families were at war with each other!

"There, I have said it," she said with relief, adding, more tenderly now, "Dear, dear Simon, this is so terrible, just dreadful, awful, unbelievable."

And with that Emma burst into tears.

It took only a moment for Simon to take in the magnitude of what Emma had just told him, and as he did so, he turned white and felt cold, then his stomach began to churn. No wonder, he said to himself, Emma had looked as if she had seen a ghost.

It was his turn to say – out loud this time – "Oh my God." Then he repeated the words two or three times more to himself as he tried to work out what all this meant not merely for their two families but most especially and more immediately for the two of them.

Then, ever the practical one, as he began to think through carefully the sequencing of what Emma had just told him, Simon suddenly exclaimed, "Hang on, Em, there's something wrong here.

"If Comrade Lightning was Sarah's husband, then he would have to be your father. But if he died way back then, in 1976, the baby Sarah was carrying would have been born in 1977 at the latest, which would make their child almost forty now. As you are nowhere near forty and you were born in 1991, some fifteen years after Comrade Lightning was killed, whoever this person was who Dad shot in that farmhouse corridor, he simply couldn't have been your father and the woman he was married to couldn't have been your mother, Sarah, either. So whoever Dad killed, if indeed he did kill him, it couldn't have been Comrade Lightning, or at least he wasn't *your* Comrade Lightning. You see the logic in what I am saying, Em, don't you? It's simply not possible."

"Oh, Simon," said Emma half-groaning, "you don't understand," adding, "but how could you? Let me try to explain.

"Among the many things I learned in Mutoko is that Sarah, the person I had grown up thinking was my mother, is not actually my mother after all. She is my *grandmother*. Sarah and Joshua's daughter – or, if you will, Sarah's and Comrade Lightning's daughter – *was* born in 1976. Sarah named her Alice. Fifteen years later, in 1991 and at the age of 15, Alice got pregnant and had a daughter and that daughter was me! A year after Sarah arrived in England, Alice followed with me in tow as a two-year-old toddler. A year later, my mother Alice had succumbed to AIDS; she died in my mother's (that is, Sarah's) hospice in North Finchley, and from then on Sarah looked after me. She not only cared for me as a mother, in effect she became my mother. So the dates absolutely *do* work, Simon. There *was* only one Comrade Lightning and he *was* my father, or, strictly speaking, he was my grandfather, though just as I still feel Sarah to be my mother and I always will, I feel he was my father, and probably always will too.

"What is more," continued Emma, "my Uncle Prosper told me that my grandfather Joshua Makonde – or Comrade Lightning – was probably killed while leading the attack on the farm of a bigwig politician south of the town of Beatrice on the main road from Harare to Masvingo, a few miles north of the Catholic mission of St Michael's in Mhondoro. That was the last firm evidence the family had of his whereabouts."

Then, turning to Simon, she said, "where exactly did Jim say your father's farmhouse killing happened?"

"I don't remember," said Simon. "He probably did tell me the place but I am pretty rubbish at Zimbabwean geography so even if he did, it didn't mean anything to me. At the time it didn't seem to be of much importance."

"There's something else Prosper told me which I need to tell you," said Emma, pausing for a moment. She was trying to remember what Prosper had told her about Mr Svosve and it suddenly came to her that among the odd things he had told her after their first discussion there was something which now seemed of huge importance, and she wove this into what she said next.

"You told me, Simon," said Emma, speaking more slowly now, "your father never knew for certain exactly what happened to Comrade Lightning. You said Jim told you his body seemed to vanish and was never found. Well, when the war was over, because her dear Joshua never returned home, Ma – Sarah – was convinced he was still alive. Even after everyone else had given up hope of his returning, Sarah never stopped believing he would come back to her. So Prosper decided to go St Michael's to make enquiries to see if he could get any more news about the incident, the last time anyone had any firm news of Joshua. For Sarah's sake and so they could have closure and she could mourn properly, he wanted to find out if it really was Joshua who had been killed at that farm shoot-out and if so, what had happened to his body. Well Prosper went and made enquiries but he couldn't find the hard evidence he needed to confirm exactly what had happened.

"He told me," continued Emma with some urgency now in her voice, "that he did manage to locate a number of people who confirmed there had been a horrific shootout at the farmhouse and the name of Comrade Lightning was mentioned unprompted by at least half a dozen of those whom he met. But he couldn't find anyone who knew for sure what had happened to the body of the guerrilla leader who most people assumed did die during the fire-fight, only general and pretty vague comments like 'He must have been buried nearby'. However, Prosper did tell me later of rumours which had circulated that not all the guerrillas had been killed, though no one was able to verify that to him either."

As Emma was speaking, Simon's mind started racing again. The full force of the fact his father may well have killed Emma's father/grandfather had hit him earlier; now he knew how vital it was to focus in on the details of what had happened on that fateful day. Emma was right: clearly the most crucial thing was whether the shootout at the farm which Jim had recounted to him was the same incident which Prosper had spoken to Emma about. But there was so much more. And if it was the same farmhouse incident, was the person Dad shot really Comrade Lightning, and if so, did he die? If not, what did happen to the body? No one seemed to understand quite how it could have disappeared, but it clearly had. When that happened was he still alive, and if so, did he die soon afterwards or might he have recovered?

If so, perhaps he was so traumatised that he couldn't ever remember what happened? Perhaps that's why he never returned home?

Simon knew some of what he was thinking seemed pretty farfetched, but he was well aware of why he had become so caught up in all these questions: his relationship with Emma was dependent upon the answers. He knew his future with Emma hung in the balance: if his father *had* killed her grandfather, he wouldn't need to ask any more questions, because once they told their parents, as he knew they'd have to do, their relationship would effectively be over.

"We need to know exactly what happened," said Simon almost pleadingly, "don't we, Em?"

Emma had not only been mulling over these same thoughts in her own mind but, ever the planner, she had begun working out how best to answer them. The process of doing this was therapeutic: focusing on what to do now eased her pain and helped her to pull herself out of the disturbed state she had been in.

First, she needed Jim to confirm the precise location of the farm where the killing of Comrade Lightning had taken place. Assuming it had been on a farm somewhere reasonably close to St Michael's Mission, she knew that she and Simon needed to go to the mission. They would talk to people there and to the local people in villages closer to the farm. Perhaps they could even go to the farm itself? Emma sensed the key to their investigations would hang on whether they would be able to locate and talk to Mr Svosve. It was Mr Svosve, she felt, who held the key to the mystery of the missing body. She was convinced they must find him. Then she realised she was getting ahead of herself. She hadn't yet mentioned the elusive Mr Svosve to Simon.

"What I haven't yet told you," said Emma, "is a couple of people Prosper spoke to in the villages close to St Michael's Mission made mention of a Mr Svosve who, they said, had stories to tell about the incident. When he got back to St Michael's to make further enquiries, thinking it would be easy to meet Mr Svosve and speak to him directly, he discovered no one had heard of him. When Prosper first told me about Mr Svosve he said he hadn't been able to track him down on his first visit to St Michael's but had planned to return to try again to find him. But he never went back. He was advised by the new parish priest that people had become even more afraid of talking to strangers, especially about the war years, and so he was unlikely to discover anything new. The priest kindly said he would ask around if anyone knew of this Mr Svosve but, as before, no one he asked seemed to know who he was, still less where he might be found.

"But then, when we spoke again," continued Emma, "Prosper slightly changed the account he had first given me of his trying to find Mr Svosve. He said he now remembered having gone back to the villages to try to speak again to the two people who had given him the name of Mr Svosve and had told him he knew a lot, and probably more than most about the incident. Although he told me he had failed to meet the first of his informants again, he did manage to speak to the second one. This time, however, Prosper told me he was even less forthcoming. All he would tell Prosper now was that Mr Svosve kept very much to himself and although immediately after the war ended he did talk a little about the incident, he would no longer speak to anyone about either what happened at the farmhouse or how he knew about it. Prosper asked him directly where Mr Svosve lived, but he wouldn't tell him. He told me he wasn't sure whether someone had got at him and told him to keep quiet or whether he never knew where Mr Svosve lived, though he said he did find the whole thing very strange.

"Although Prosper told me how frustrated he was that he learned nothing knew," said Emma, "on reflection I think he actually did. The first is that we have further confirmation the elusive Mr Svosve actually existed. The second is that he may well be the only person who will enable us to get to the bottom of the mystery of what actually happened that day."

Please God, he hasn't died, Emma finished to herself. *And please God, we are able to find him.*

* * *

They were interrupted by Jim, who had walked down to the pool to invite them both up to the terrace for a pre-supper sundowner. As Jim approached them, smiling, Emma greeted him civilly, though not warmly. Before she could ask the question uppermost in her mind, Jim had launched into the speech he had prepared but which he had thought he would be giving on the terrace over drinks. But, having concluded from what he took to be Emma's frosty greeting that Simon must already have spoken to her about Peter, he decided he couldn't wait till then.

"I am sure Simon has spoken to you about what I told him while we were away at Kariba," began Jim. "Those were terrible days, Emma, not ones I like to think about now, though I do believe we need to be honest and truthful about what happened."

Emma nodded, as did Simon; it was Jim's signal to continue.

"We were all so young and naïve back then," he said, "headstrong and sometimes foolhardy. Peter was a real hero, incredibly brave and deeply committed to what he was doing. I was more the follower but – don't get me wrong – at the time I sincerely believed what I was doing was right. Peter, like many real heroes, suffered terribly afterwards. After that final incident at the farmhouse, the horror of what he had been doing hit Peter when it suddenly dawned on him he had been on a mission to kill human beings and he recoiled as he now saw what he had been doing not as something brave and noble but as something repulsive, almost animal-like. It has a name now, post-traumatic stress disorder or PTSD, and we had certainly read about similar things happening to returning Vietnam War vets in the United States. Over the years, the psychological terrors, the nightmares, the flashbacks and the pain – and, boy, did he suffer and feel pain – have eased. But Peter is a far quieter, more reflective person now than he was when we were young. Cathy has been such a brick. Without her care, support and love, he would be in a far darker place today. The fact that Simon told me he never knew anything of the horrors of his Dad's past is surely a credit to both of them, hey?"

It soon became clear, however, that Jim was far keener to tell Emma about himself rather than Peter. "I don't like to talk about the war these days, we have enough problems today to grapple with without having to remind ourselves of, and relive, past horrors," he said.

"But what I didn't tell Simon was that soon after independence and the war was over, our church was one of the first to lay on healing sessions and services of reconciliation to try to mend the wounds of those days and I must say I found them really, really helpful. You see, Emma, and I'm telling you this as you said you were a Christian, I believe God is a forgiving God and His words of forgiveness have made a profound impact on me, helping me to change my views on many things. Most of all, they have helped me to see everyone – black and white, male and female – as precious. Thank God, I never went through what Peter had to go through, but no longer would I ever want to kill another human soul. That's what my faith and God's grace have taught me, Emma."

But there was more Jim felt he needed to say. "During these sessions," he said earnestly, "I came to realise we are all sinners in the sight of God. We make mistakes, even horrific mistakes, but God is a forgiving God. He forgives us even our worst transgressions."

Jim was repeating himself and both Emma and Simon were afraid they were going to have to listen to more of his home-spun theological musings when they had already heard quite enough the other evening. But fortunately they were spared. All this had been the prelude to what Jim had been building up to – what he had really wanted to say to Emma – and he said it quickly.

"I now know God has forgiven me, just as I have forgiven those who killed, tortured and maimed. God, the forgiving God, has set us, set me, free and for that I am and will forever be eternally grateful."

Emma wasn't really listening to what Jim was saying. What she wanted from him were not his reflections about the war years and why everything was now all pretty much okay for him. She needed concrete information about the location of where the last attack had been carried out. Where exactly was that farm?

So, with her journalistic determination and ignoring what Jim had just been saying, Emma asked him directly.

"You know that final assault at the farm of that politician where Peter shot whom he thought was Comrade Lightning, Jim? Well, Simon couldn't recall the name of the place where you said it happened. Where precisely was that farm? Was it south of Harare near Mhondoro, not far from St Michael's Mission, if you know the place?" Emma was aware she was struggling a bit with places which were merely names to her which she would have difficulty herself trying to pinpoint on a map.

"I'm not sure precisely where St Michael's is," replied Jim, a little taken aback Emma had said nothing about how his faith had made sense of the horrors of the war, "but I certainly know Mhondoro, and the farm where this last firefight took place was a little way north of Featherstone, south of and closer to Beatrice, just in from the main road from Harare to Masvingo, the old Fort Victoria road. So, yes, it must have been pretty close to the northern tip of Mhondoro."

Emma was even more confused now, as was Simon, but they were relieved when Jim said he had a map in his office and would check, inviting them to meet him back on the terrace for drinks when he had taken a look.

It didn't take him long. Simon and Emma had scarcely sat down on the terrace before Jessica arrived with a tray of cold drinks. As they started to discuss whether they should start or wait, Jim strode out from the sitting room to join them. He looked pleased with himself and said to Emma, "Yes, you are right, St Michael's Mission is almost at the north-east tip of Mhondoro, so pretty close to the farm. Come to think of it, I seem to recall our passing through a big mission station after that last engagement. If it is the same place, it has a huge church with a corrugated iron roof which I remember to this day as it was painted bright green. But what really struck me about the church was the inside: it only had a couple of benches at the rear; I guess everyone who worshipped there simply sat on the ground. With such a huge empty floor area between the altar at the front and the few benches at the back, I thought it really looked more like a mosque than a church."

Once again, Emma wasn't really taking in what Jim was saying. He had confirmed what she had needed to know: the shootout at the farm which Simon had described to Emma *was* the same incident which Prosper had described to Emma. The Comrade Lightnings each had described were the same person. She had the answer to their first question; now they needed to find the answers to their other ones. She was determined she would succeed. Emma had the bit between her investigative journalist's teeth.

As supper began that Sunday night, Emma gave Sheila and Jim just enough information from what Prosper had told her about herself, Alice and, of course, Joshua. They were both duly shocked to learn Comrade Lightning was so close a relative of Emma's – though Emma didn't explain just how close – and they fully supported Emma and Simon's decision to go out to St Michael's to try get to the truth of what had really happened.

The rest of the conversation at dinner and afterwards was subdued. Neither Jim nor Sheila wanted to pick over what Emma had shared with them or reflect aloud about what it might mean for them. Simon provided a little light relief by recounting to Emma and to Sheila, who had not gone, what he and Jim had done at Kariba, passing round his phone to share some amazing photographs of elephants coming down to the water's edge to drink. Though she was distracted, Emma focused enough to learn how the combined impact of low water levels and poor maintenance was leading to an impending crisis at Kariba dam, which could cause even more severe electricity generation problems for both Zimbabwe and Zambia. She had never felt less interested in news and current affairs.

Regular as clockwork, Jim and Sheila excused themselves at nine, but Emma and Simon stayed up late into the night. They talked and they planned. Emma filled in more from what she had learned from Prosper and Emerentiana about herself and Sarah and her family – the things she had planned to tell Simon earlier. She told him the amusing things which happened to her and how much she had felt at home among her relatives. She even told him that at times she had felt a bit like a rich male arriving from an alien planet. At times they laughed and it seemed like old times, but the atmosphere of the final part of evening when they got down to discussing what they should do now was heavy and at times quite subdued. They both understood – but kept to themselves – that what they could discover over the next few days could have profound effects on their relationship.

It wasn't only the future of Emma's relationship with Simon which was troubling her. Both that night and over the following 24 hours, Emma felt increasingly uncomfortable being at the Reddys. Though she was certainly grateful for the generous way they had offered to help and for the amazing work Sheila did the next day in arranging their trip to St Michael's, Emma knew she needed to leave the house as soon as possible. It wasn't just that Jim had been a member of the patrol which may well have killed her father/grandfather – though she did return again and again to the thought of Sarah and the suffering she had gone through. It was the thought that she should be accepting their hospitality and carrying on talking to them normally as if nothing had happened.

Emma was particularly upset by the way Jim seemed so easily to explain everything away in what he had said at the pool, delivered as a speech, or even a sermon. He said he was sorry for what had happened, that he had forgiven those whom he had participated in killing and maiming during the war and he believed God had forgiven him. But where was the remorse? Where was the understanding of the permanent harm and damage which war does to people, destroying relationships, ripping families apart?

And where was the sorrow? What difference did their forgiveness mean? In Emma's view what Jim had said about a 'forgiving God' was at best incomplete and at worst a cop-out.

In her late teens, Emma had given up going to confession, not only because she found it ritualistic and formulaic but it struck her as profoundly dishonest. All she had to do was to confess to the priest she had done wrong and say she was sorry – indeed, even to believe she *was* sorry – and, hey presto, God would forgive her, the slate would be wiped clean and she would feel good. When she was younger she even felt a warm glow after the priest blessed her and mouthed the words of absolution. It seemed like magic; indeed, in many ways it was magic. What did she have to *do* to be absolved, to demonstrate she genuinely was sorry? She simply had to mouth a few prayers.

Emma had thought then this was all wrong, and these thoughts returned to her now as she recalled what Jim had said to her. If Jim really was sorry, shouldn't he at least have tried to find those who he had abused and the families of those he had killed to ask *them* for forgiveness? Unless forgiveness is rooted in trying to address the ills in the society where harm was done, she said to herself, then it has no content; it is meaningless – just words. What did Jim – and all the others – *do* to show they really *were* sorry?

The reason Emma felt she could no longer stay with Jim and Sheila was that she felt Jim's forgiveness was hollow; it had no content. It was an escape. Emma felt it would be disrespectful to Joshua and to Sarah for her to continue staying with them, living off their generosity and benefitting from their hospitality. It would, she thought, be a lie to them and their lives. She didn't tell Simon what she was thinking, in part because there was no time, but in part, too, because she knew it would be but a small step to apply these same thoughts and feelings to Peter and Cathy: how could she be civil to them knowing now what she knew about what Peter had done with Jim at his side? She knew she was far from being ready herself to forgive. What she did say was this.

"You know we are trying to get to St Michael's, hopefully as early as tomorrow to discover the truth. Well, if we finished what we need to do at Mhondoro by Friday night and return to Harare the night before we fly back to London, I can't come back here, to this house. We will have to move into a hotel or guesthouse or something. I'm sorry, Simon, but I have to do this, not so much for my own sake as for Sarah's sake."

Simon was gracious in his response. "I know how you feel, Em," he said, "and I also understand why you feel the way you do. If I were in your place, I would want to do the same. That's fine, we'll find somewhere else to stay. But I'm not at all sure we will be able to unearth what we need to, even before it's time to fly back to London: we have a mammoth task ahead of us."

Simon and Emma spent the rest of that evening and the whole of the next day immersed in discussing their trip to St Michael's Mission and how exactly they should use their time when they were there. Planning their trip wasn't easy and they couldn't have done it without Sheila and Jim's considerable help. Though they had optimistically hoped to be able to travel down to Mhondoro the next day, Monday, it was not until the Tuesday morning that everything had been fixed and they were ready to go.

Before they went to bed, they had both marked "cancelled" over the trip to the Victoria Falls they had planned, and had been so desperate to make. Though it was meant to be the highpoint of their holiday, they both knew it was now just a distant dream, trumped by the far more urgent and pressing matters at hand.

Early on the Monday morning, Jim announced he had decided not to go to the office but would stay back and help with the arrangements, and after breakfast Emma and Simon pored over Jim's map as he worked out how to get to St Michael's. He estimated it would take a good two hours to drive there given the likely state of the 25 or so miles of dirt road. He generously offered them his 4x4, which they gladly accepted. Simon thanked Jim for lending them his car while Emma mentally ticked that off her to-do list.

While this was going on, Sheila began to deploy her considerable networking skills. She quickly found the phone numbers of the mission through one of her Catholic friends, a woman who lived down the road from them. Contacting the mission to invite themselves to stay and arrange accommodation, however, proved to be a challenge. All the phone lines, unreliable at the best of times, were down and no one was answering the mobile phone numbers Sheila had been given. By midday they had got precisely nowhere.

Not to be deterred, Sheila tried a series of different, more indirect, approaches. She called up the pastor of her church and through him obtained a list of Catholic diocesan organisations in Harare. After seven or eight calls, she discovered that the parish priest of St Michael's, the Reverend Ambrose Ngoni, had come to town that morning and was out shopping, but his mobile phone wasn't working so couldn't be contacted, which she already knew. Crucially, however, she learned he was scheduled to meet the Archbishop in the middle of the afternoon and she managed to talk to his secretary who, with some relief, Sheila quickly sensed was genuinely keen to help. She agreed to ask Fr Ngoni to stay back after his meeting with the Archbishop in order for Sheila to have a brief word with him.

The timing was tight. Sheila jumped into her car and set off for Archbishop's House arriving just in time to catch Fr Ambrose before he left to drive back to the mission. He was in a hurry to get back before nightfall, but Sheila was able to convey enough about the need for and urgency of the

had dismissed his former prejudices – hurriedly formed by having to make polite conversation with a habit-wearing nun who was a member of a religious order with a simply terrible name – and he and Immaculata were merrily chatting away.

As Immaculata explained, she had developed a special affection for children with both physical and learning difficulties and, over the years, had tried out a succession of different ways to help them. It was apparent from the stories she told that children with disabilities were fully integrated into the mainstream of school life, largely because she had succeeded in getting both teachers and the other pupils not merely to accept but to welcome and help their less able classmates and to see this as simply a normal part of daily life. As they chatted and he found out more of her background, Simon was amazed how here, deep in the African bush, was a woman with little schooling, no degree and no access to university courses, books or professional journals, implementing cutting-edge approaches to early childhood development based solely on her own insights drawn from years of hands-on experience and immersion in the real world – the university of life.

Immaculata moved effortlessly on from her work to her health, recounting how she had been rushed into hospital in Harare two days ago. Showing no visible self-consciousness, she explained how over the past weeks she had lost her appetite and suffered periods of extreme tiredness, which, in turn, led to dizzy spells and to her fainting. In hospital – as she quaintly put it – they "took away my blood," and when the tests came back earlier that morning she had been given a "Jackson" – her word for an injection – which needed to be repeated in three months' time. She wasn't able to explain exactly what the problem was; nor did she know the results of the blood test. She wasn't too bothered with the details, she said, because she was now back to her old self again and her appetite had returned. The main thing, she said, was that she was feeling well and happy to be returning home to her teaching job, or her "family", as she put it.

Immaculata's most immediate job, however, was to be Simon and Emma's sat-nav on the journey to St Michael's. To start with, all went well. On leaving Sheila and Jim's, Emma and Simon between them remembered the route to town and down Samora Machel Avenue to Rotten Row, where they had viewed the city from the *kopje*. When they reached Rotten Row, they were in a part of town which Immaculata seemed to know well. She confidently told them to turn left off Cripps Road and go under the flyover to Simon Mazorodze Road. This put them onto the Beatrice Road heading south. It was one of the county's few arterial roads, carrying goods and people to Masvingo, lying 200 miles south of Harare, and beyond down to the South African border. They were soon out of the city and made steady progress southwards. When they had passed the signs to Beatrice they knew they were getting close to the 90-kilometre marker sign which they had been told to look out for; here they would take a right to continue the rest of their journey to St. Michael's on dirt roads. This they did.

The first few miles on the dirt went well. Jim had been right – and as Emma already knew – if you drive faster over the corrugations in the road, the ride becomes less rather than more bumpy, and Simon began to feel rather proud of his skills as a bush-road driver. Then things started to go awry.

They came to a fork in the road with no signpost. Simon asked Immaculata if they should go left, and she said yes. Soon afterwards, they came to a three-way junction, again with no signpost. Simon thought the main road was either the one to the left or the one straight ahead. He asked Immaculata if he should go straight on, and again she said yes. Within a few hundred yards the road Immaculata had told Simon was the one they should go on came to an abrupt halt at a local bottle store. On turning the car round to make their way back to the three-way junction, Simon looked across at Immaculata with a questioning look on his face, but she simply smiled back at him. He enquired of Immaculata whether they should have turned left at the last junction rather than going straight on. She beamed back at him and cheerfully said yes, that was right, and Simon then took the second road Immaculata indicated was the correct one. A little further on, they came to another fork in the road. The road they were on looked as if it was narrowing to become little more than a track, whereas the road to the left seemed to be the more major road. Simon was confused.

"Should I take the road to the right?" Simon asked Immaculata, trying to sound confident, though by now he was growing suspicious they were lost.

"Yes," came Immaculata's equally confident reply. "You should take the road to the right."

By now, Simon realised what was happening: Immaculata's way of giving directions was always to agree the road he suggested they should take. If Simon asked if they should go left, Immaculata said yes; if he enquired whether they should take the right turn, she would agree with him and confirm they should go right, just as if asked if they should go straight on, again she would agree with his suggestion. Simon knew Immaculata had lived at St Michael's for 20-odd years and had, presumably, travelled these roads scores of times before. But he now knew she didn't have a clue about the route to the mission. Whenever they came to a junction she had no idea which road to take but being polite – trying to please the person one is talking to by always agreeing with what they said – was an instinct which lay deep within her bones; she would always agree with Simon's suggestion. Immaculata knew this was the correct way to answer a question: it would be far too rude either to disagree or even to say "I don't know."

To test out his theory, when they came to the next junction, it was a three-way junction; instead of asking Immaculata the way in the form of a question which required a yes or no answer, Simon asked her which way they should go by deliberately asking an open-ended question.

"Which road should we take here?" he enquired.

There was a total silence from Immaculata. Then, instead of coming to her aid and enquiring "should we go left," or "should we go right," Simon asked another open-ended question. Though he knew he was being cruel, he asked: "which of these two roads is the one to St Michael's, Immaculata?"

No answer.

Simon then turned to Immaculata, who he could see was now feeling uncomfortable with his probing questions, smiled across at her and said, "Immaculata, you don't know which road we should take, do you?"

"Yes," she said quietly. "I am sorry, but I don't know."

Simon then said, "Immaculata, you don't drive, do you?"

"Yes," she said, "I don't drive."

"And you never ever learned the roads to take from the tar to St Michael's, did you?"

"Yes," said Immaculata, "I didn't."

"So," said Simon, tossing back his head and laughing, "perhaps when we next see someone, especially if they are traveling in a truck or car, we should stop and ask them if they can help us with directions?"

Just as Emma had learned when first greeting Jessica at the Reddys', so now it was Simon's turn to be given a lesson about Zimbabwean politeness and Shona customs.

"Yes, that's a very good idea," said Immaculata, who was relieved Simon had not taken offence at her replies.

Up to this point, Emma's mind had been so preoccupied with thinking through and trying to devise a plan for what they exactly they would do when they reached St Michael's she hadn't noticed Simon was having trouble working out which road to take, but as she started to listen to this exchange between Simon and Immaculata she suddenly realised they were lost. She began to panic as she thought through what this could mean. She grabbed her phone, hoping to pinpoint where they were on Google maps but, as she had feared, she wasn't able to get a signal.

Then, putting her hand on his shoulder and sounding a little on edge, Emma said, "It's almost five and the sun will be setting in an hour. Simon, we *have* to get there before it gets dark or we'll be even more lost and then I don't know what we'll do."

Oh my God, when we set off, Emma said to herself, I felt in such a positive mood, even elated that we really were going to find the answer to the mystery of Joshua's last hours. Now I feel our getting lost is an omen of bigger problems to come. Even if we do get there, perhaps no one we talk to will know what really happened. Maybe we won't be able to track down Mr Svosve, and if we do, maybe he won't know either, or worse still, he will refuse point blank to answer our questions. Why would he want to talk to strangers from abroad about events which took place so long ago when he had been unwilling to share with fellow Zimbabweans soon after they had happened? Emma, what are you doing here? Are you the shrewd and careful planner you think you are, or are you mad? Was coming here the good idea you believed it to be, or is it all crazy?

Keep calm, Emma, keep calm. She felt her heart racing.

Catching the concern in her voice, Immaculata turned back to Emma and said, "Don't worry, my dear. We may be deep in the African bush but remember this is our home. We are not among aliens to be frightened of, or strangers unwilling to come to our aid. The people living here are *our* people, willing to help those in need. If you get lost in big cities like Harare or London, you may have reason to be afraid, but getting lost here is nothing to worry about; it's like getting lost among friends."

Then, turning round to the back seat where Emma was sitting, Immaculata reassuringly leant over and took hold of Emma's hand and, giving it a squeeze, said, "Anyway, I am sure we are not lost. You'll see."

Immaculata was proved right. As things turned out, they reached St Michael's before nightfall – just. This was in large part due to Immaculata who, in the end, turned out to be the asset Sheila had expected her to be, even if not quite in the way she had envisaged.

Over the course of the next hour, they came across three other motorists, two young men on motorbikes, three cyclists and two elderly people walking by the side of the road. Each time Simon slowed the car to ask the way what immediately caught the eye of those they spoke to was a smiling Immaculata, resplendent in her white habit. This was Christian country and the LCBLs, as Immaculata called them, were well-known and deeply respected, even by those they first spoke to, who were Methodists, and even more so when those they flagged down turned out to be Catholics, as most were the closer they came to St Michael's. Everyone was keen to help.

As Simon had already discovered and was to have repeatedly confirmed, asking directions here was an art, not an application of geographical science. Whenever he stopped the car to ask directions, Immaculata would spend some time greeting those they met and indulging in what seemed like idle, time-wasting and general chit-chat. Yet, as Simon soon realised, what Immaculata was doing – besides being polite – was sizing up the person. She did this in order to determine, when she decided the moment had been reached, whether to ask them if they knew the road to St Michael's. Immaculata knew everyone, without exception, *would* give them directions whether they knew the way or whether they didn't. The

the room was a thin simply-made cupboard and small table and chair on which a second candle-and-matches set stood. From the middle of the ceiling hung a bare electric light bulb which dangled lopsidedly from an old piece of wire. In the corner opposite the bed was an old kneeler made of hard wood. Ambrose was delighted Simon knew what it was also called, a *prie-dieu*; it was just like the ones he had often seen in the old Anglican churches he had enjoyed visiting around Canterbury when at uni. As he gazed at this one, their dampness and musty smells now came rushing back to him.

Seeing Simon pause to examine the kneeler, Ambrose mistakenly assumed Simon would be making use of it later and enquired whether he was Catholic. He said Emma was but explained that, as he put it, he was brought up an Anglican, emphasising the words to convey the added meaning he was no longer a believing Anglican. However, Simon realised Ambrose had not picked up the subtlety of his reply as he immediately went on to invite Simon to join him at the early 6:00 am Mass the next morning, assuming Emma would join them too.

He was pleased he had not been more explicit and told Ambrose outright he was an atheist. Before they left Harare, Emma had cautioned Simon if they were to have any chance of achieving their purpose in coming to St Michael's, he had to be on his best behaviour. *Little did I think when planning my trip to Zimbabwe*, thought Simon to himself, *that in the space of 24 hours I would have sat for hours next to and really enjoyed chatting to a nun decked out in her full regalia, spent the night at a Christian mission, attended morning Mass and, to top it all, been mistaken for a Catholic priest.* What other surprises, he wondered, were in store for him and Emma in the next 48 hours?

It was now after six, the sun had just set and darkness was already descending upon the mission. Ambrose picked up the torch and towel which were lying on Simon's bed and said if they were quick, there would just be enough light to show him the ablution block some 20 yards away. This turned out to be another tired-looking single-storey brick building which had seen better days. Inside, the walls were made of rough plaster which hadn't seen a coat of paint in 40 years or more and the floor was polished cement with deep cracks running through it. The building was equipped simply with two old toilets, two old showers, two old basins and two old pieces of soap. As they entered, Ambrose explained that although the mission had its own electricity generator, which would soon come on, it was temperamental and even if it worked it would switch itself off around 9 pm. However, he added, even when it was on, there were very few lights between the different buildings so Simon should never be without his torch after dark. With that, Ambrose left Simon to freshen up, saying he would come by his room in about ten minutes to take him to supper.

After a quick wash (the cold water was warm), Simon returned to his room. As he did so, he heard the thud-thud-thudding sound of the diesel engine generator starting up. He was delighted when he flicked the switch by the door to see the old bulb in the centre of the room hesitate but then light up and stay on. However, it threw out so little light as he hurriedly rummaged deep inside his ruck-sack to try to find something less casual to wear for dinner that he needed his torch to see his clothes. It had never occurred to him they would have a formal dinner, but then he hadn't given the matter much thought. The best he could manage was a long-sleeved blue shirt which didn't look too crumpled and a pair of khaki trousers to replace the jeans he had been wearing. He knew his mother would not have been impressed. He also rediscovered Jim's whiskey bottle which Emma had passed on to him to give to Ambrose. On his return, Simon handed it to Ambrose. As Jim had predicted, Ambrose was delighted, but he asked Simon to leave it in his room until later as they were going off to eat. This was because there would be women in the dining room and, as Simon was later to discover, in these more traditional rural parts of Zimbabwe whiskey was both rare and exclusively a man's drink.

While Ambrose was showing Simon to his room, Immaculata took Emma to the LCBL convent. The sisters lived in a complex of single-storey buildings on the opposite side of the mission from where they had come in, which opened up behind a single door of a windowless brick wall.

As Emma stepped inside the convent, she was transported back in time – not so much to when the buildings were erected, some 60 years ago, she thought, but to an even earlier era. The whole place had the feel of a convent built almost anywhere in Catholic Europe in the mid to late 19th century. The plain walls were adorned with crucifixes and faded pictures, many of which were very familiar to Emma: saintly figures (mostly male) with that "faraway look" in their eyes, and halos above their heads: St Francis of Assisi among the birds; the wizened face of the Italian priest, Padre Pio; St Teresa of Avila in her austere Discalced-Carmelite habit and others who faces were familiar, but whom she couldn't name.

In most corridors and in both the dining and recreational rooms were statues of the same genre – the Virgin Mary here, St Joseph there and a number of saints which even Emma with her Catholic upbringing wasn't able to recognise. She searched in vain for anything even vaguely African. The best she could find was an old photo of Cardinal Montini on his visit to colonial Rhodesia before he became Pope Paul VI (which was in 1963), on the tarmac of the old Salisbury airport surrounded by an assembly of almost entirely white clerics and dignitaries. She noticed two pictures of Pope John Paul II, who she remembered had visited Zimbabwe more recently, but these were devotional pictures, with the Pope's hands joined and eyes closed in prayer, clearly taken in Rome not Africa.

Immaculata showed Emma to her room, explaining this was the one reserved for important guests and adding that although the convent had been built for more than 30 sisters, the current community comprised just 10, all of whom still slept in dormitories. What struck her most about her room was not so much its simplicity – it contained only a bed, a bedside table, desk, chair and small cupboard as she had expected – but how neat and clean it was: the sheets and blankets would have passed the most rigorous of military inspections and there was not a speck of dust to be seen on either the floor or tables. In the middle of one wall was a crucifix and opposite it one of those traditional, iconic and, Emma had always thought, rather effeminate-looking pictures of the Sacred Heart, with Jesus not looking remotely like the Middle Eastern Jew he was but depicted as a long-haired and bearded European white male.

"I'm sorry Sister Superior is not able to greet you," said Immaculata as they left Emma's room and made their way to the washing area, "but everyone is now in in the chapel for evening prayer." As if to confirm this, in the middle distance Emma could hear the sound of voices singing. She smiled and felt far more uplifted as the rhythm was definitely African.

At the end of the corridor, they came to an open area with lines of toilets, showers and basins, each adorned with a small square bar of soap and a long row of newly-ironed and neatly folded towels. The smell of newly-applied disinfectant hung over the place.

In the hallway as Immaculata had showed Emma to her room and now here along the corridors of the convent, young girls were scurrying around, clearly hard at work. Emma thought they couldn't have been more than about 15 years of age and they could well have been far younger. They were bare-footed and all dressed in the same uniform: a simple short-sleeved light-coloured dress and a small light blue veil pinned into their hair, resting lightly on their heads and tied behind at the back. A simple silver-looking metal crucifix and chain hung down from their necks as they bent down to dust, brush, polish, scrub and mop. They all had beads of sweat on their brows. Emma greeted the girls in turn as she almost bumped into them, but instead of responding they lowered their eyes to the ground, stepped back a pace, turned away and said nothing. After the third girl had done this, Emma realised this is what they had been trained to do.

Inquisitive, surprised and somewhat dismayed, she turned to Immaculata and said, "Who exactly are these young girls and why are they acting so strangely?"

"These, my dear Emma," said Immaculata with some pride, "are our postulants and pre-postulants."

As she could see Emma was unfamiliar with the terms, she explained. "They are our young ones, girls who have applied to join the LCBLs and who are having their vocations tested by living in our communities."

As Immaculata was speaking, Emma thought back to Jessica, the first person to look after her, then to her seven-year old niece, Zuva, who made her even more uncomfortable. But she felt even sorrier for these young girls, far from home, working unpaid and probably for long hours, and drilled, it seemed to her, into subservience. Emma had not come to Zimbabwe to be looked after by servants, but this was now the third time it had happened. Although she found each experience distasteful, this was by far the most medieval of the three types of servitude she had encountered, and she marvelled even more at how well Immaculata had survived her training.

Seeing Emma was upset, Immaculata said, "Perhaps we do have to change our ways, Emma. But some of the older sisters would say this is the way we were brought up and it worked for us. If the young of today are to stay the course, they need to have their vocations tested."

Emma wasn't convinced, and Immaculata was shrewd enough to pick this up but she said nothing more. Emma wasn't here to upset the sisters, especially Immaculata, whom she had grown to like a great deal. She knew she needed to keep herself focussed on why they had come to St Michael's and, at least for now, resist pursuing her inquisitive journalistic instincts. It was Emma's turn to be meek and remain silent; to practise a different sort of servitude.

Immaculata said, "Emma, my dear, have a wash and get yourself ready for supper." Then, looking long and hard at her jeans so she would be sure to understand, Immaculata added with a smile, "I am sure you will want to change before you go over to join the others for supper."

From the moment she stepped inside the convent, Emma knew she should have put on her dress that morning, or a long skirt, and not her jeans, even if they weren't her skinny ones. Back home Sarah had warned her about wearing the right clothes when visiting the family in Mutoko, but she had felt far more out of place wearing jeans here than she ever had in Mutoko and, as she hurriedly changed, she prayed her poor judgement about what to wear would not adversely affect their relationship with Father Ambrose and the help and support she knew he needed to give them. She chose her long skirt, the one which went all the way down to her ankles, and as she buttoned it up, she became conscious of slipping into yet another form of servitude. She then heard the rumble of an engine and, after flickering for a few moments, the electric light bulb in the centre of the ceiling came on.

Immaculata knocked at Emma's door almost as soon as she had finished dressing to ask if she was ready, reminding her to take her torch with her, and as she led Emma out of the convent to cross to the dining room, she smiled and told Emma how pretty she looked. At the doorway to the dining room, Immaculata motioned to Emma to go in and join Simon and Ambrose, who were already there. She then turned round and retraced her steps to the convent, bidding Emma a hurried goodnight as she parted. Emma knew what was going on. Though their food was all cooked in the one kitchen in the convent, the sisters still ate separately and apart from the priests and any male religious who lived and worked at the mission or had come to stay. But as Father Ambrose's guest, an exception was being made for Emma. Once again, she was being treated as an honorary male.

* * *

Without rising, Ambrose Ngoni welcomed Emma with a smile and motioned to her to sit opposite him, next to Simon. When she was settled, Father Ambrose bowed, crossed himself and said grace, then invited them to join him in their simple three course meal, adding that he wasn't one for formalities and would be happy for them to refer to him as plain Ambrose when it was just the three of them together.

They began with a tasty, if salty, thin soup of indeterminate vegetables which Ambrose served them from a faded yellow enamelware pot. This was followed by a large bowl of steaming mealie-meal *sadza* which he placed in the centre of the table next to a smaller bowl of finely-chopped green vegetables and tomatoes swimming in an oily sauce, inviting them to help themselves. In contrast to the way Emma had shared *sadza* with her family at Mutoko, they served their own food onto their individual plates, eating it with a knife and fork and helped by a spoon. To drink, Ambrose offered them water and Mazoe orange juice. Though they all ate plenty, more than half was left when they had finished. Emma and Simon helped carry the dishes back to the hatch in the wall between the dining room and the convent kitchen, where it was swept away from the other side by a waiting nun. In return, she handed them a chipped ceramic bowl heaped high with fresh fruit: oranges, *naartjies* and the same small bananas Simon and Emma had first had at the Reddys'. Finally, Ambrose boiled the kettle which lived on the sideboard and offered them all a hot cup of milo. Emma eagerly accepted, but watched with growing alarm as Ambrose poured first one, then a second and finally a third heaped spoonful of sugar into his cup of what Emma knew was sweet enough already.

Observing him course by course, Simon could see Ambrose took a very functional approach to eating: he picked at his food and ate because he had to rather than because of the taste or any pleasure it might give him. Eating was simply something which had to be done, one more item to be ticked off the list of life's daily chores. Perhaps it was because he was served up pretty much the same food every day, or because he usually ate alone? Whatever it was, food did not seem to provide Ambrose with much joy and his thin body confirmed this.

What he was really hungry for on this particular evening were the details of precisely why Emma and Simon had asked to come to the mission and what they hoped to achieve. As soon as he had served the soup, Ambrose asked them, as he put it, to "enlighten him" on their mission. Emma was as keen to do this as Ambrose was to listen but, as she and Simon had agreed, she would only share a part of the whole story.

Emma gave him a quick rundown of herself, focusing in particular on her relationship with Sarah, whom she referred to as her grandmother. She told Ambrose Sarah had urged her to come out to visit her family in Mutoko and learn more about her past.

"It has only been since being here," she said, "that I discovered my grandfather was a renowned guerrilla commander who never returned home after the war ended. Apparently he died leading an attack on a white farm a little to the north of here in, if not strange, then at least unexplained circumstances."

She went on to say it had only been while she had been here that she began to fully grasp what pain her grandmother had suffered and still suffered today not knowing if her grandfather had been killed and, if he had, where he had been laid to rest, and she felt the onus was now on her to try to get to the bottom of what still remained a mystery. Eyeing the cross on the collar of Ambrose's shirt, Emma said, "I really feel I have a moral responsibility to do this; it is the least I can do for her after everything she has done for me." Ambrose caught her eye as she looked across at him.

Next, she told him about Prosper's initial visit to St Michael's and its generally disappointing outcome, and how he had wanted to come back again but had been warned not to because the local people were even more reluctant to talk to strangers than they had been before. She explained how Prosper had been told by a few people here the person most likely to provide him with the answers to what really happened at the farmhouse shoot-out was a Mr Svosve. Mr Svosve, he was told, apparently lived somewhere in the vicinity of St Michael's but Prosper hadn't had time to travel much beyond the mission to track him down. Emma said she was therefore particularly keen to try to find him and talk to him, reemphasising the point that as she and Simon were returning to London at the weekend, she was not merely intent, but quite desperate, to get to the truth before they left.

Emma rounded everything off by telling Ambrose a little about her relationship with Simon and Simon chipped in to add a few details, with them both hoping this would be sufficient to satisfy his curiosity and deter him from asking more. Just as Emma had made no mention to Ambrose of Alice and her believing Sarah to have been her mother, so Simon deliberately said nothing about the part his father played in the war.

Father Ambrose listened carefully to everything Emma had said, but when she had finished he didn't immediately say anything. Instead, he picked up the clean knife he hadn't used to eat his *sadza* and proceeded to play with it, his eyes staring out ahead of him as his fingers set to work. He was lost in thought. He stood the knife upright with his right hand, holding

Then, realising himself he needed to get back to the point, Ambrose said a little less earnestly, "I had cousins, two of them, who joined the ZANLA army and who never came back. We made numerous enquiries but they all drew a blank; we still don't know what happened to them. We assume they were killed but try as we might, we have never had any firm news of what befell them. They sacrificed their lives for us and ended up as two more names to be added to the thousands our country inexplicably forgot.

"So," Ambrose drew a deep breath, "I am all too well aware of what your grandmother must have felt during all those years and long lonely nights of waiting and not knowing, and I am happy to help you as best I can. Even firm evidence of death is far, far better than having to live through even one more night of uncertainty."

Even keener now for Ambrose to explain how he could help them and quite frustrated by his detour into why he had become a priest, to chivvy him along Emma said, addressing him quite formally, "But what do you really think we should do, Father Ambrose? Do you have any ideas, any concrete suggestions?"

Slightly taken aback, Ambrose shuffled again on his chair as he asked rhetorically, "What can I do to help you?" hardly pausing before answering his own question to share at last what he had been thinking.

"Well, almost as soon I arrived here to be the Superior at St Michael's, some five or six years ago, and I got to know more of my parishioners as well as meeting non-Catholics," he said, only to add to Emma's suspicion he was still not getting to the point, "I became increasingly aware of the sheer numbers of people who are still deeply troubled by what happened during the war years, even though it was so long ago. And just like the continuing suffering of the families whose loved ones never returned – like yours and mine, Emma – the pain continues and can be just as deep for so many of those who survived, though all too often their troubles lie unseen where they can so easily fester.

"Well, as no one had done this here before, I decided to set up counselling sessions for those in need of psychological support, and the response was astounding. Over the years, literally hundreds of people have gone through the basic group talking sessions I started running, sharing with each other, under my guidance, their fears and talking about what was troubling them. As they talked it became clear so many of them were still deeply distressed by the traumas they had suffered. If I had had more money, I could have done far more." Ambrose momentarily sighed.

"Anyway," he continued, "because I am that sort of person, I have kept detailed notes on everyone who came and, as you were speaking, Emma, it occurred to me that a number of people who had benefited from these sessions might have information which may be relevant to your enquiries, and, most importantly, might well be willing to help you, provided I explain to them a little about who you are and why you are here. I will go over my notes when I get back to my room to try to jog my memory and get back to you in the morning, hopefully with a list of names and how we can contact them.

"Helping people such as these has been important in nurturing and sustaining my vocation as a priest," Ambrose went on, unable to shake himself free from his reflective musings. "There are so many whom society has forgotten and let fall between the cracks. In recent years, as jobs have become scarcer, wages eroded by inflation and the cancer of corruption spread rapidly across the country, I have become weary of politics. I have grown increasingly angry at the growing affluence of our politicians and the continuing grinding poverty of the mass of the people. People's lives need to improve now; they need a better future not next year, not when they next vote, but today. Making a tangible difference to the lives of people right now is, for me, the very heart of Christianity, the reason why the Gospel really is good news."

Ambrose looked across the table to Emma. As their eyes met she realised she had been wrong a moment ago. What he was saying *was* relevant to what they had come for: it *was* part of the point! Just as Jim had told Simon his father had understood the need for him to try to enter the minds of the people he was fighting against, so Emma was beginning to grasp the importance of the emotional pressures which guerrilla warfare forced not only upon the fighters but the civilian population, those caught in the middle. If she was to succeed in drawing out from the people she was hoping to talk to the truth of what they knew about the circumstances surrounding Joshua's probable death, she realised she would have to do more than simply ask them to tell her what they knew. She would need, above all, to treat them with the respect they deserved.

But there was more. Emma realised how relevant to herself was what Ambrose had said about why he had become and continued to be a priest. His view of Christianity seemed to be almost identical to hers: Ambrose was Christian, and a priest, because he wanted to make a difference to people here and now – just like she did.

This caused Emma to ask herself what had prompted Ambrose to talk so frankly and honestly about himself, and, as she did so, the conversation she had had on the bus with Farisai came flooding back to her. As a journalist she had learned the skills to encourage people to talk but in the case of both Farisai and Father Ambrose, she hadn't prodded in the least; they had told her about themselves completely voluntarily. Why had this happened now on two separate occasions? Emma knew she came across as a self-confident and independent-minded person but this sort of thing had never happened to her back home. She then began to wonder whether her bearing and demeanour as a confident young woman made her appear different to people in Zimbabwe, or was she just imagining it? Was it this which triggered, first in Farisai and now it seemed in Father Ambrose, if not the impulse then at least a strong desire to open up and share intimate details of their lives with her?

Emma was ready to dismiss such thoughts as soon as they came into her head as she was sure Zimbabwe had plenty of strong and self-assured young women; it was simply that she hadn't yet met them – although she was doubtful Ambrose Ngoni ever mixed in the sorts of circles where they were to be found. But if there was something about her which stimulated, or prompted, at least some people in Zimbabwe to open up and talk to her about difficult things, she hoped this "something" would come into play again in the next couple of days – for Emma knew she had scarcely two days to find out the truth about her grandfather. And if she was lucky enough to find people who knew what happened, she needed to deploy every weapon in her armoury to encourage them to tell her what they knew.

But Emma's wave of optimism was quickly dashed by what Ambrose said next.

"I should warn you both," he said, "that getting people to talk is one thing, uncovering the truth of what happened quite another. For a start, I should tell you I have never heard of this Mr Svosve of yours. But I know the power of rumours so I need to warn you he may never have existed, and if he did, whether he is still alive. There's so much you – or I should say 'we' as I have said I am keen to help – need to find out and there are so many unknowns and so little time. You have scarcely three days with us. It may not prove to be enough time: things tend to work slowly round here. We may be lucky but be prepared for us to draw a blank. If I'm totally honest with you, I think this may well be the most probable outcome."

Then, rising from the table and gesturing for Emma and Simon to follow him, Ambrose said, "But that's quite enough of such talk for tonight. It's getting late, I have spoken too much – I have certainly said too much about myself. I should never have inflicted that upon people as young as yourselves. We all need to sleep. Let's rest and pray the morning will give us at least some answers to the questions you have come all this way to find. I will do my very best to try to help remove some of the pain your grandmother still feels. It's the very least I can do."

As they parted outside in the dark, their torches now on, Ambrose turned back to Emma and said more cheerfully, "I have already told Simon I am saying an early Mass at six and you are both welcome to join me. Otherwise I shall see you here again for breakfast, which is at 7:15. *Kusvikira mangwana* ("until the arrival of tomorrow"!)"

* * *

Neither Emma nor Simon had woken early enough for Ambrose's Mass so they reconvened in the dining room. Breakfast at St Michael's was simple but satisfying: steaming mealie-meal porridge with melted butter, fresh milk, a hot mug of *Tanganda* tea and a reprise of last night's fruit. Father Ambrose again revealed his weakness for sugar, shovelling it liberally onto his porridge and into his two mugs of tea, expressing genuine surprise at their steadfast refusal to join him in his first sugar fix of the day. Emma wondered whether his teeth survived the daily onslaught, but she couldn't see.

Ambrose was in a buoyant mood when he started discussing his plan for the day ahead. He said he had been through his files and had drawn up a list of about ten people from his counselling sessions who lived relatively close to the mission whom he thought looked extremely promising. He said he would ask his office assistant, Manos, to try to get in touch with them, adding that he felt confident he would be able to find a number of them.

He then talked through a number of parallel initiatives he proposed they jointly pursue. He said he would go over to the convent and talk to the two or three nuns who had been at the mission for 20 or more years to seek their help in locating those they knew from pre-Independence days. He suggested Emma join that meeting and work on any immediate leads, which she readily agreed to do. Next, he said he would use his early morning meeting with the catechists which was taking place at the mission today to seek their help in gathering additional names of people who might have heard about Comrade Lightning or the farmhouse attack, or who might have heard of Mr Svosve. He suggested Simon should stand ready with his car to drive out to any village where any catechist believed there was a potentially helpful key informant. Father Ambrose said he would also contact the former head of the Parish Council, Peter Claver Ngara, an elderly man in his mid-60s who lived close by, asking him to come up to the mission to discuss other possible leads.

Initially, as they all set off after breakfast, things looked quite promising. Emma spoke to the three elderly sisters at the convent and by lunchtime, through them, had met with two women and two men who still vividly remembered the war years. Following the catechists' meeting, which had ended by 9:30, Simon set off with two of them who knew of people they thought could help. They lived in villages to the north of St Michael's which, they told Simon, were not far from the farm where the attack – which most people seemed to know about – had taken place. They returned to the mission via the home of the local traditional leader, Chief Chivero, a staunch Catholic and friend of the mission, whose knowledge of the war years was said to be second to none. Meanwhile Mr Ngara joined Ambrose and Emma for an early lunch and shared what he knew about the war years, and after lunch the first of Manos' list of people had started to assemble outside Ambrose's office.

Yet when they reconvened in the middle of the afternoon in the dining room, as agreed, to compare notes over a welcome cup of tea, it quickly became apparent they had made little headway. On the plus side, between them they had tracked down almost ten people who knew about the shootout at the farm, half of whom had attended Ambrose's counselling sessions. They also thought they had made a major breakthrough early in the afternoon when Mr Ngara brought to the mission an elderly woman who had been a young *mujiba* during the war and who seemed willing to talk. They were further encouraged when she confirmed that Comrade Lightning had been active in the area and said she was certain he had been the mastermind behind and led the assault on the farm. However, on further questioning it became clear that her own involvement with the guerrillas had only begun a couple of years after the farmhouse attack and, when pressed, she admitted what she knew about Comrade Lightning was based almost entirely on hearsay rather than on hard personal evidence. It then emerged that most of the people they began to interview had not been even indirectly involved in the farmhouse incident themselves and could not give the name of anyone they knew who was still alive who had. And, to Ambrose's surprise and dismay, the two or three people he was convinced had some knowledge of the attack were clearly unwilling to talk.

In short, they had gathered far less information than Prosper had obtained during his visit all that time ago and no one had been able to help enlighten them about the whereabouts of Mr Svosve. They knew they needed more time, but they also knew it was never going to be easy to discover anything new about an event which had taken place almost 40 years ago. But what was most depressing was Ambrose's reflections on their morning's work.

"Although for a while people have felt able to talk about what happened within the security of the group counselling sessions, they are clearly still unwilling to talk about these events in the open," he said. "People are still afraid to talk, it's as simple as that. Life today is difficult enough without uncovering old wounds and revisiting the pain of the war years. I know there is an atmosphere of fear about, but I must say I hadn't fully realised how pervasive and deep it still is. I continue to be shocked at the power of political intimidation and the hold it has had over so many people here for so many years and still has today."

Although no one had the courage to say so openly, they all knew they needed to radically rethink their whole approach. The problem was no one could think of what they could do which was likely to work, especially given the little time they had left. Even Ambrose's early morning optimism seemed to have suffered a mortal blow.

Just then there was a knock on the dining room door. Ambrose crossed the room and opened it, and there on the step stood his very good friend Vincent Vambe. Mr Vincent Vambe was the district's most senior education officer, a very old friend of St Michael's and a Catholic whose loyalty to the church ran deep in his veins. They greeted each other warmly, first by shaking hands and then by giving each other a brief pat on the back before stepping back, smiling and shaking hands once more and chuckling in what was clearly delight. Respect and trust had cemented their relationship, one built between a priest known for his care of those dealt a rough hand by the war and its aftermath and an education inspector known for his passion for schools which taught the old-time values of hard work, honesty and respect. Ambrose then introduced Mr Vambe to Simon and Emma.

Vincent Vambe had held the prestigious post of Education Inspector for almost 30 years and was now close to retirement, the prospect of which filled him with dread as he loved his job and his work was his life. Notwithstanding his age, *Va*-Vambe, as he was respectfully addressed by the young teachers, still had an encyclopaedic mind. Not only could he name all the schools within his jurisdiction, but he prided himself in being able to tell you the numbers of pupils enrolled in each of them each year as well as the names of every teacher in the more than hundred primary schools for which he was responsible.

Although the schools Mr Vambe was in charge of no longer had any formal link to the Catholic Church – they had all long ago been taken over by the government – he personally kept an eye on them, not just to ensure the standard of teaching remained high, but also to ensure they continued to teach and pass on the Catholic faith to each new generation of children. What's more, even though it was no longer part of his job description, Mr Vambe still considered it his duty to provide the Superior of St Michael's with a regular assessment of the state of religious education in what he still considered were his Catholic schools, though he did so more informally than in the past. Whenever he was near, he would drop into St Michael's to give his report orally to the Priest-in-Charge. Very soon after Father Ambrose took over the reins at St Michael's, it was clear the two men, who were much the same age, would get on, and, over time, they grew close and became very good friends.

When they were all seated, with Mr Vambe now holding a steaming cup of richly-sugared tea and at Ambrose's prompting, Emma briefly explained the purpose of their visit to St Michael's and told him – her frankness informed by her frustration – what little progress they had made after almost a day of trying. He listened carefully to what she said about the farm attack, politely interrupting her to ask for more details of where and when it took place, and nodded in an understanding way when she spoke of her grandmother's distress at not knowing what had happened to her grandfather.

"Yes," said Mr Vambe, "I know from so many people I have met since the war ended how important closure is."

"I had hoped," said Emma, "that we would have found someone who might at least have heard of a Mr Svosve, even if he is dead by now, because he seems to hold the key to the information we so desperately need. But we have drawn a complete blank."

"Why exactly do you need to find this Mr Svosve?" enquired Mr Vambe, who had become noticeably more alert on hearing Emma mention the name.

"Well," said Emma, who had not noticed the change in Mr Vambe, "when my uncle visited St Michael's many years ago to try to find out what became of my grandfather, he was told by a number of people the person he really needed to talk to was Mr Svosve, and at least one person he met told him he had heard Mr Svosve had had had some direct involvement in the incident where my grandfather could well have been killed."

Pausing to inform the Schools Inspector that her uncle had been a headmaster at a school near All Souls Mutoko for very many years in the hope of his having known him or heard of him, but he hadn't, Emma continued. "But my uncle wasn't able to track him down and, although the priest then in charge at St Michael's said he would make further enquiries after my uncle had to return home, that was the last the family ever heard of Mr Svovse."

As Emma was speaking, Vincent Vambe stiffened. When she had finished, he put down his tea cup, glanced at Ambrose and then looked directly at Emma. Simon knew he was about to say something important, and he was right.

Speaking slowly, he said to Emma, "I know a Mr Svosve, indeed the Mr Svosve I know could well be the one you are looking for. He is a teacher at my school in Gavaza. It's not a common name."

Emma couldn't believe what she was hearing. She could feel the sap of expectation rise inside her and was desperate to hear more. She looked across at Simon, who was also now fully aware of what was happening.

"It is highly unlikely anyone round here you would have spoken to would have known or even heard of Mr Svosve," continued Mr Vambe. "Gavaza is too far away. It's about 15 kms north of us and, as Fr Ambrose knows, priests from St Michael's rarely visit these days so the old links have largely been severed. They used to say Mass there regularly but with the shortage of priests, they no longer do.

"Old Svosve is getting on now, rather like me," added Mr Vambe as he began to dig into his mind to retrieve the information stored there about this particular teacher.

"He is probably in his early to mid-60s by now, so he would have been a teenager when that attack at the farm you spoke about took place. He is a local man, he grew up in and around Gavaza," he said, still trying to remember more details and waiting for his memory to come to his aid. A moment later it all came flooding back to him and, with a nod from his friend Ambrose assuring him it was alright to share at least some of the personal things he knew about him, Mr Vambe began to tell them a lot more about the Mr Svosve he knew.

"He's an incredibly knowledgeable man," he said, "and extremely keen to impart that knowledge to his pupils. From having talked to him quite often in the past I know he is a voracious reader and particularly interested in politics. He can talk with authority about distant places and knows more about obscure political movements across the globe than anyone else I have ever met. Most importantly, as a teacher I would rate him very highly especially when compared to many of today's younger teachers: he is conscientious, he always prepares his lessons and never misses a class unless he is ill, which is rare. And though he doesn't come across as religious in any traditional sense, he remains a regular church-goer.

"That said," Mr Vambe continued, as if he was reading from a teacher's assessment report, "he has always been considered a bit odd – quite strange, in fact. For instance, he is known for his fastidiousness; he always keeps his classroom impeccably clean.

"Oh, he's pleasant enough when you talk to him and the children seem to like him, which is perhaps the acid test, but he is a very private person. Actually he keeps to himself to such an extent that the other teachers will tell you he is something of a recluse. He is single, has few if any close friends, never married and likes his own company, preferring to stay in his room than to be with other people. You will never see him down at the beer hall, and if he does go out it is to go right away – no one quite knows where he travels to – rather than to socialise with the other teachers.

"The oddest thing of all about old Svosve," Mr Vambe was recalling stories about him he thought he had quite forgotten, "is he'll never let anyone come into his room. He lives in a single accommodation block with three other teachers; they each have their own room. Mr Svosve keeps his door securely locked at all times, and, as far as I know, not one of the seven headmasters Gavaza has had since I have been inspecting the school has ever set foot inside his room. It has always been his own private domain. I remember the previous headmaster at Gavaza telling me it was his Holy of Holies."

As Mr Vambe shared more of what he knew about Mr Svosve, Emma realised the huge importance of what he was saying. She thought his apparent oddities could well be linked to his having been through some traumatic experience quite early in his life as he seemed to have been acting strangely for quite some while. It could, she felt, all fit in. She caught Simon's eye; he was nodding knowingly, as if the same sort of thing had crossed his mind too.

After Mr Vambe had stopped speaking, things happened very quickly. They all agreed Emma and Simon should travel to Gavaza early the next day. Sensing Ambrose was keen for him to help, Mr Vambe kindly said he would reorganise his schedule for the rest of the week, drive up to the school, introduce Emma and Simon to the headmaster and, using his weight as Schools Inspector, lean on him to request they talk to Mr Svosve. Ambrose then invited Mr Vambe to stay for supper, which he agreed to do: this was not unusual. Whenever he arrived at the mission in the afternoon – which he always did – Ambrose invited him to dine with him and stay over for the night – which he always did.

The meal was a relatively quiet and uneventful affair. The food was an exact replica of the previous evening but Emma and Simon weren't in the least bothered, and Ambrose and Vincent didn't seem to notice. The two older men were happy chatting away quietly; they clearly enjoyed each other's company and relished their time together. Emma and Simon were delighted as there was so much they needed to think through and talk about as they tried to work out what they would say to Mr Svosve. They spent some time devising follow-up questions, depending on how Mr Svosve might react to what they would first ask him, though Emma, in particular, realised it was a rather pointless exercise. As a journalist she trusted her instincts, reassuring herself she would be able to manage her discussion with Mr Svosve by letting it evolve as it happened.

After they had finished supper, they all reconnected and chatted briefly to reconfirm arrangements for the morning before both Ambrose and Vincent shared kind parting words of goodnight to Emma about Sarah, Prosper and her wider family as they all left the dining room. It was the signal to Emma that her presence was no longer required. Then the three men adjourned to the priests' recreation room where they consumed two-thirds of Simon's whiskey.

Though she tried hard, initially Emma was too apprehensive to sleep. Tomorrow was going to be a defining day. She knew the stakes were high and although her body usually responded when she told herself to be calm, this time it wouldn't. It looked as though her plan to track down Mr Svosve had worked, but what lay ahead? If he was able confirm to their satisfaction that Joshua had been killed, what would that mean for herself and Simon? Although in normal times she prided herself on her planning skills, by the time she did eventually fall asleep Emma hadn't even started to focus seriously on that crucial question, still less to begin to try to work out what the answer would be.

- 10 -

Mr Svosve

Mr Gumbo Netseka, the head of Gavaza's primary school, heard the sound of two vehicles approaching, and as he looked out of his window he was shocked to see the District Education Inspector's car. By the time he had stepped out of his office to greet his unexpected visitors he had become extremely nervous as he knew only too well unplanned visits meant surprise inspections and these only happened when schools had problems. He grew even more agitated when he saw two people emerge from a second car, one white and one black, for their clothes and general demeanour suggested they were not local but foreign visitors. He was now confused as well as on edge: this was no ordinary school inspection.

Mr Vambe greeted Mr Netseka warmly and then introduced him to Simon and Emma very formally as Mr Simon Robertson and Ms Emma Makoni, and he, in his turn, welcomed them all to the school. As they walked to the headmaster's office they exchanged pleasantries. In conformity with Shona etiquette, Mr Vambe held back in telling Mr Netseka the purpose of their visit while Mr Netseka successfully disguised his shock at seeing the Schools Inspector, saying how delighted he always was to have Mr Vambe drop by and how honoured he and the school were to receive him and his visitors.

Although you would not have guessed it from his bearing, Mr Vambe was itching to get away. He had been genuinely pleased to accompany Simon and Emma to Gavaza but he was a busy man. Even though they had left St Michael's early and it was now only just past 8:30, the diversion to Gavaza had already made him a couple of hours late for his first meeting of the morning and he was keen to leave as quickly as politeness would permit. Simon told Mr Netseka this was his first visit to an African school and said how pleased he was to be here. In truth, he was appalled at how rundown it looked from the outside. Emma was struck by how similar it looked to her uncle Prosper's old school and the two schools she had passed when walking to All Souls with Francis's wife Fadzai.

When they were seated, Mr Vambe reassured Mr Netseka he had not come for an inspection. He said the purpose of his visit was for his two new friends, who had travelled all the way from England, to meet with Mr Svosve. Disguising at the same time both his relief this was not a surprise inspection and his curiosity that people in England should even know of the existence of Mr Svosve, Mr Netseka confirmed that Mr Svosve was in school and teaching today – it was a normal Thursday school day – and said he was happy to arrange for them to meet him. Mr Vambe went on to explain – it was a point he made with great emphasis – that, as they might need to talk to Mr Svosve for quite a while, he was sure Mr Netseka would be able to juggle today's teaching roster to cover for Mr Svosve if he had to be out of the classroom for any length of time.

Mr Vambe knew both that Gavaza School, like most others under his care, did not have its full complement of teachers and that Mr Netseka was not one to want to alter his daily routine, so he went on to say if no one else could be found to teach Mr Svosve's lessons for him he was sure Mr Netseka would be only too delighted to step in and take over himself. He added he would expect the changes to be written into the school's daily logbook, counter-signed by his Deputy Head, Ms Munetsi. Mr Netseka knew Mr Vambe would ask to see the logbook on his next visit to ensure the changes had been duly recorded and signed. In reply, Mr Netseka said this was just what he had decided he would do, forcing a smile as he spoke, knowing there was no escape: Mr Vambe was meticulous and had a reputation for never forgetting anything.

With everything arranged, Mr Vambe announced he had to be on his way. He told Mr Netseka not to trouble seeing him off the school property as he did not want to delay his making the necessary arrangements for Mr Svosve to meet the guests. Instead, he invited Emma to accompany him back to his car.

As they walked away from the school buildings, he apologised for having to leave so soon but said he was sure he had done enough to ensure they met with Mr Svosve, adding that he hoped good would come out of their discussions. Emma, who had been overwhelmed by his kindness, uncharacteristically fumbled for words to express her appreciation for all he had done for them. Keen to express her appreciation while being sensitive to custom and to Mr Vambe's age and status, Emma clasped both his hands in hers and while she shook them vigorously surprised herself by making the smallest of curtsies. If back in England and before her trip you had told Emma she would perform such a non-pc gesture, she would have laughed out loud. How her instincts had changed over the space of a little more than a few days.

As he stepped into his car, Mr Vambe confided to Emma that his elder brother had also gone missing during the liberation war. This was, he said, something he kept to himself, but, like her, his family had never had final closure on his disappearance. So, as he told Emma, he knew well what she and her family had been going through and felt.

"So I was happy to help you, Emma," he said as he prepared to close the car door. "If I can take a couple of hours out of my life to help ease your family's suffering, this is the least I can do."

Emma waved as he drove off and, as the dust swirled up from the wheels of his car, she felt a tear running down her cheek. Mr Vambe was now the third person who had voluntarily shared deeply personal things with her and, yet again, she wondered why. She had wiped her face dry before she reached Mr Netseka's office as she gathered herself together in preparation for her encounter with Mr Svosve.

A few minutes later, Mr Netseka returned to his office accompanied by a man Simon and Emma assumed was Mr Svosve. He had forgotten Simon's name and introduced them as Mr Robinson and Ms Makoni from England. They shook hands, Simon and Emma firmly, Mr Svosve rather limply. He said his name was Shungu Svosve as he eyed Simon and Emma closely. Though he said he was pleased to meet them, it was apparent he was a little on edge and certainly not at ease. They sensed he was suspicious of them, even slightly hostile.

They judged Mr Svosve to be in his early to mid-60s, as Mr Vambe had quite accurately told them. He was a small man and looked even shorter than he was standing next to them: a good head lower than Simon and a few inches less than Emma. He was small all over: small torso, arms, hands and fingers, and small legs and feet. His back and shoulders were slightly arched and though he didn't have a hunchback, it looked as if he soon might. His greying hair, balding at the temples, was trimmed short; his face was round and his eyes, slightly sunken into his skull, never seemed to stay still. He was dressed in a plain white shirt and a thin dark, almost funereal, tie, grey trousers and a pair of black sandals. Although he looked neat, his clothes were old, almost threadbare. His shirt had turned grey from years of washing out the sweat which had accumulated, especially round the neck and under the armpits, resulting in clearly visible and now permanent stains. His dark trousers were baggy and unpressed and covered in a fine sprinkling of white chalk-dust, as were his hands.

"How can I help you?" were his first words.

Given his diminutive stature, his rather scruffy appearance and the limpness of his handshake, Emma was surprised by the confidence of his voice: strong but without being aggressive. There was a sense of purpose lying behind his question. The way he had spoken his first words seemed to be conveying a mix between what-do-you-want-with-me and I've-got-nothing-to-hide.

Emma replied, still trying to process what she had seen and the little she had heard from Mr Svosve. She was nervous but her voice was also strong. She started by saying how pleased she was they had this opportunity to meet, apologising for their arriving so unexpectedly. She then thanked him for leaving his class and said their coming here had nothing to do with the school or his teaching so neither he nor the headmaster need have any worries on that score. Her half-joking introductory remark fell rather flat. Neither Mr Svosve nor Mr Netseka said anything; they were waiting for Emma to say something more substantial.

"Our reasons for coming here," continued Emma, "are both personal and rather confidential, so I think it would be better for us all if we found somewhere quiet where we could talk, somewhere more private."

Keen to ensure any feedback to Mr Vambe was positive, Mr Netseka said, "Mr Svosve, why don't you take our guests over to the teachers' house away from the classrooms where you won't be disturbed?" As he spoke he stood up to indicate his question was really a command.

Mr Svosve responded by saying, slightly grudgingly, "Come, follow me." He then led them away from the noise of the classrooms, across the football pitch with its broken and bent goalposts towards a brick building with a green corrugated iron roof and a built-in veranda some distance away, separated from the school by an untidy hedge. The place had the air of a bachelor's pad to it: the yard area in front of the ageing building had not been swept for days; there were no dogs about and a few lumps of uneaten *sadza* had been tossed under the thorn bushes, where a few birds were hungrily pecking at them. When they reached the yard, Mr Svosve told Simon and Emma to wait while he went inside. He soon returned with a simple wooden, roughly-made, straight-back chair which he placed on the veranda and then he went back inside to pick up the next. When he had brought out the third chair, he beckoned to Simon to help him carry them down to the yard, gesturing to a shady spot where they all sat down.

When they were seated, Mr Svosve repeated the question he had first asked: "How can I help you?" He spoke more gently this time, but he was still wary: his eyes darted nervously from Emma to Simon and back again.

Looking directly at Mr Svosve, Emma said, "I have come to talk about the war." Immediately she sensed a change come over Mr Svosve; it was small but discernible. "My grandfather was Comrade Lightning, a key ZANLA guerrilla commander who operated in this area of the country."

She was observing Mr Svosve closely as she spoke. On hearing the words "Comrade Lightning", she was sure his ears sharpened. He became noticeably more alert. It was enough. It was the signal Emma needed to come explicitly to the point. Not mincing her words, she launched into the rest of the speech she had been rehearsing for days, most recently just before she fell asleep last night, and, for the final time this morning, out loud with Simon listening in the car as they drove to Gavaza.

"In 1976, around July or August," she began, "Comrade Lightning led a daring attack near here on the farmhouse of a leading Rhodesian Front politician. There was a massive firefight first at the farm house and then in the nearby *kopje*. The politician survived. A number of guerrilla fighters were killed, though some managed to escape. We – my grandmother, myself, our whole family – have never discovered precisely what happened to Comrade Lightning, my grandfather, after that engagement. That incident was the last we ever heard of my grandfather. We do not know whether he was killed in that attack or whether he escaped, and if he did escape whether he was wounded or not."

Not wanting to be interrupted in the flow of what she was saying, she hurried on. "I live in London, Mr Svosve, with my grandmother, Sarah Makoni, the husband of Joshua Makonde, or, as he was known in the war, Comrade Lightning, though I was born here. I left Zimbabwe, the family home near All Souls Mission Mutoko, when I was scarcely more than a baby with my mother Alice. Alice was born in October 1976; she was the baby Sarah was carrying in her womb when the farmhouse attack took place; Comrade Lightning was her father. Tragically, Alice, my mother, died of AIDS soon after we arrived in England and I was then brought up by my grandmother, Sarah. So Sarah has been more like a mother to me than a grandmother; as a result I look upon Joshua – Comrade Lightning – more as my father rather than my grandfather.

"Two weeks ago, I returned to Zimbabwe, my first visit since I left as that young toddler in the early 1990s." Emma's eyes were fixed on Mr Svosve, though she was no longer registering his reaction as she was so emotionally caught up in what she was saying. "I went to stay with my relatives in Mutoko. It was only then – just a day or two ago – I first learned about my grandfather, Comrade Lightning as, back in England, Sarah had deliberately kept everything about him – his time in the war and his disappearance – a secret."

Then, forcing out the words afraid and her voice was going to crumble, she said, "But now knowing as much about my grandfather as I have told you, I need to know what exactly happened at that farmhouse, so close to us here at Gavaza, to the dear and deeply loved husband of the woman I have grown up believing to be my mother. That, Mr Svosve, is why I am here, that is why I have come to Gavaza today."

There was a short pause before Mr Svosve responded.

"That's all very interesting, Ms Makoni, but you haven't explained why you have come to see *me*. What makes you think *I* know anything about this farmhouse attack you speak of, and what happened to your grandfather?"

Then almost repeating the first words he had spoken, Mr Svosve's eyes stopped quivering and he looked at Emma directly and said, "What makes you think *I* can help you?"

Emma was ready with her answer. She told Mr Svosve about Prosper's visit to Mhondoro to try to unearth more information about the farmhouse raid and the fate of Comrade Lightning. She said in relation to the crucial information of what happened to her grandfather during and after that final attack, the main aim of his visit, he sadly had drawn a complete blank: he left St Michael's knowing no more than when he came.

"However," said Emma, "during his conversations the name of a man called Mr Svosve cropped up a few times. A few people told my uncle he really needed to talk to this Mr Svosve who was said to be someone who really knew what had happened on that fateful day, though when he enquired no one seemed to know, or was willing to say precisely why.

"Last week, when my uncle told me about the last firm news we had had about my grandfather, I vowed not to go back to England without discovering what had happened to him. I knew I couldn't face my grandmother, Sarah, without being able to tell her the truth about her beloved Joshua, Comrade Lightning. I owe it to her! She has carried alone the burden of his disappearance for almost 40 years, even keeping it from me, believing if I knew the truth about him, it would have upset me too much as a young child who had already lost her mother. She didn't want me to experience further pain, but it is she who has suffered, Mr Svosve, and she has suffered enough."

Then Emma surprised not only Simon and Mr Svosve, but herself as well: she did something spontaneous, something completely unplanned. Drawing from the depths of her experience as an investigative journalist, she instinctively made a courageous leap in the dark.

Jettisoning Ambrose's advice she should speak sensitively to those who might have been traumatised by the war, Emma sat upright on her chair, looked Mr Svosve directly in the eye and, aware more of listening to herself talk than of speaking, heard herself say in a voice strong and demanding, "The reason I needed to talk to *you*, Mr Svosve is because *you* *…were … there. You* know what happened to my grandfather because you were a witness to the events which took place on that fateful day. You know whether my grandfather died or whether he lived, and if he lived what happened to him. So I am asking you, Mr Svosve, begging you – in honour of my grandfather, for all he stood for and for everything he did – to tell me the truth."

Emma leant over towards Mr Svosve and peered even more closely into his eyes, which were fixed on her face, and said, "The time of silence, the time of concealment, the time of hiding is over. Now is the time for time for you, Shungu Svosve, to tell me – Comrade's Lightning's flesh and blood, his only living offspring – exactly what happened."

Emma had staked everything on her conviction Mr Svosve was their key interlocutor, and her belief that only if she confronted him directly would she discover the truth. Was she right? Simon looked at Emma in astonishment, though neither she nor Mr Svosve noticed as their eyes remained fixed on each other.

For a while no one spoke, and then Mr Svosve broke the silence. His initial reply baffled both Emma and Simon. Still staring at Emma but speaking so quietly they couldn't initially make out what he was saying, Mr Svosve said, "You have his eyes."

As they said nothing, he repeated the same words, still quietly but a little more loudly now. "You have his eyes." This time he seemed to be speaking more to himself than to them as if he had been transported far away in both distance and time ... "You have his eyes."

Then, as suddenly as he had entered into his trance-like stupor, Mr Svosve snapped out of it. He took a deep breath and sat up, his upper body leaning against the back of his chair, as stiff as if he were sitting to attention. As his face changed, his whole body seemed to transform itself from the small, shy and reserved figure of few words of a moment ago to become a self-assured man in control, transformed from someone who spoke hesitantly into a person eager to engage and keen to talk. It was as if what Emma had said pressed a button deep inside Mr Svosve, releasing him from the burden of decades of withdrawal and pent-up tension, loosening him from the prison of his past which had till then bound him to a self-imposed silence. The flood gates had been opened, and over the next few minutes they listened, not quite believing what they were hearing.

Mr Svosve now felt free, free to respond to Emma's challenge, but before he said anything in response to her bold and direct demand for the truth, he turned and spoke to Simon. He first needed to deal with something which was clearly nagging him, a final barrier which had to be lifted before he could speak to Emma with the freedom she had given him and the honesty he believed he owed her.

So, turning to Simon, Mr Svosve said, "Tell me, Mr Robinson who precisely *are* you? How do you fit in? Why have you come here with Ms Makoni? What right do you have to hear what I might have to say about the farmhouse attack and what happened to Comrade Lightning?"

Simon was taken completely aback by Mr Svosve's totally unforeseen interest in him rather than Emma, but he was sharp enough to know he needed to tread with extreme care.

"Mr Svosve, Ms Maconie is my girlfriend," began Simon. "We met in London early this year and have been together ever since. We share everything, we are kindred spirits: what she knows, she tells me; what she needs to confide in me, I will keep secret. As for me, well, I am an Englishman, a Londoner. London is where I grew up and went to school. I am now training to be an accountant and have a job working in London. When Emma said she wanted to come out to Zimbabwe, of course I said I would come with her, and that's why I am here. We are out here together, and Ms Maconie and I are due to fly back to London on Saturday. I don't know whether I will return to Zimbabwe, but I guess some day we will, though as of now I can't say for certain. Certainly from what I have seen so far, this is a beautiful country. That's about all I can say. There is really no more to add."

Although Simon had been careful not to say he'd been born in Zimbabwe, he knew he had been floundering in his response to Mr

Svosve's challenging question, repeating himself and saying things he needn't have said. He felt quite ashamed at his performance. Yet what he had said seemed to have been sufficient to satisfy Mr Svosve, who had decided Simon posed no threat: he was an irrelevance to what he was about to say to Emma. He would have preferred to have talked to her on his own but he didn't see Simon now as either any sort of barrier to his impending revelations.

But before he turned back to Emma, he said, half to himself but loud enough for both Emma and Simon to hear, "I'm glad your name is *Robin*son and not *Roberts*on or else I would need to know far more about you and your family background, Mr Robinson."

Robinson... Robertson... When Mr Svosve mouthed these seemingly harmless words Simon's body tightened as he swiftly went over in his mind what he just said about himself and his past. Then, as he realised he had said nothing incriminating – nothing to link himself to his father or the country's past – he felt the tension leave him, to be replaced by an enormous sense of relief. Concealing all this from Mr Svosve, Simon inwardly thanked Mr Netseka for mistakenly introducing him as Mr Robinson and not Mr Robertson.

Simon made no further comment but sufficient had been said for him to realise not only that Mr Svosve knew a great deal about the farmhouse attack but he had done his research on the enemy. He knew the surname of the commander of the unit which had attacked Comrade Lightning's guerrilla forces was Robertson. Mr Svosve was clearly aware of the pivotal role Simon's father had played on that fateful day. Emma was already on edge, waiting for Mr Svosve to speak, but now it all became terrifyingly real to Simon as well.

Mr Svosve then turned back to Emma and his next four words brought confirmation they would have what they had come for.

He said simply, "Yes, I was there. *Ichokwadi* ("it is the truth")."

It was clear Mr Svosve was now eager to talk. He began by providing a partial summary of what had taken place.

"I not only witnessed the shootout," he said, "but I was involved in the planning undertaken prior to the attack. I did what Comrade Lightning instructed me to do. From that day to this, I have told no one what really happened on that day. I was the first person to come to the aid of Comrade Lightning after he was shot in the corridor of the farmhouse. I was the one who took him away. I hid him. As you said, Ms Makoni, Comrade Lightning was a charismatic leader. To me, as a young impressionable teenager, Comrade Lightning was a remarkable man, to me, he was a real hero – he was then and he always will be. I was not only proud but also honoured to have worked alongside him and for him."

He paused and said, "But there is far more."

Then, casting his eyes down at his hands, which lay open in front of him, resting on his knees, Mr Svosve went on to provide an account of the farmhouse attack, the detailed preparations, how it all went wrong, the chilling aftermath and his reflections on what that day meant for him in the months and years which followed. What he told Emma (and Simon) was the result of decades of soul-searching; it was almost like a deathbed confession, though there was no remorse, no guilt or repentance and no plea for forgiveness.

"We were part of a struggle to create a new society, to build a country which would prosper and with the fruits of progress shared more equitably after decades of minority rule," Mr Svosve began. "But corruption, nepotism, avarice and greed seeped in to eventually take control of our country."

Then, turning to Emma, he smiled and, speaking almost like a priest preaching a sermon, said, "Ms Makoni, I honour you as I have I honoured the blood of your grandfather. Comrade Lightning believed in a different future and fought for it. Sadly, what he fought for has not yet come to pass. But it will! He stands out still as a symbol of a new future. God willing, Ms. Makoni, if it can't be different for me then I live in hope it can be for you, your children and your grandchildren. Comrade Lightning was a torchbearer, a symbol of hope for a better country. You must now be a torchbearer of hope for the next generation as your grandfather was for mine. To most people, Comrade Lightning is now long forgotten, but to me he remains what he always was, a symbol of hope for a better world."

This was not the speech Emma had been expecting, though Mr Svosve's sincerity touched her deeply. She waited for a moment in respect of what he had just said before replying, sounding curter than she had wanted.

"Mr Svosve," she said, "you have clearly so much to say and I deeply appreciate your sharing with us your thoughts about myself and the future of this beautiful country. But please can you tell us about the events we have come here to learn more about, the events which will finally shed light on what befell my grandfather, Comrade Lightning."

"I was never a guerrilla, never a fighter. I didn't go to Mozambique for training," Mr Svosve continued. "But that didn't mean I wasn't involved. Indeed, as I will tell you, I was given a crucial role to play.

"Some months before the farmhouse attack, I had become a *mujiba*. I was still a schoolboy, and although things began in a small way – passing on information about troop movements, providing food, hiding weapons, you know, the usual stuff – they quickly mushroomed into something far bigger. Even in those early days, the guerrillas I worked with were already talking in hushed tones about Comrade Lightning. Then, some months after I had become what was called 'active', I met him and from that very first meeting I was in awe of him. Though, like many other top guerrilla fighters, he was tough, committed and determined, he stood apart and was quite different. But the reason your grandfather stood out, Ms Makoni, was in the way he interacted with those under his command. He not only knew every one of his troops and even us young *mujibas* by name, but you felt he had a special interest in you not only as a soldier or helper but as a human being. Everyone under his command came to trust him absolutely, probably none more than me.

"Well," Mr Svosve was now completely wrapped up in the telling of his story, "after a month or two, he began to take me increasingly into his confidence. He even asked my views about different logistical issues – where to hide larger and heavier weapons, how to move ammunition long distances, where best to place landmines."

He then told Emma how Comrade Lightning had become aware of a farmer who was also a leading Rhodesian Front politician as well as a cabinet minister who lived nearby. He decided he and his farm were to be the target of this new initiative, but this time the target was to be kidnapped not killed. Early on, said Mr Svosve, Comrade Lightning gave the MP the codename "Nelson," chosen for South Africa's most famous political prisoner.

"*He* was," said Mr Svosve, almost certainly, Emma thought, reproducing the exact words Comrade Lightning had used, "to be *our* captured prisoner."

The farm was heavily protected with landmines, booby traps, barbed wire and electric fences and patrolled day and night by armed guards, but Comrade Lightning was convinced the kidnapping would work. The key, he said, lay in the gathering of intelligence.

"As luck would have it," said Mr Svosve, who was beginning to sound like the eager young teenager he had then been, "I knew the son of the MP's – of Nelson's – cook: Mathias and I were in the same class at school.

"I started to visit the farm, supposedly to work on school projects but all the time learning more about the farm's security. I located the farm's saferoom and the building which housed the back-up electrical generator, the electricity and the phone lines. But what proved to be of critical importance was that I managed to pinpoint the precise location of the landmines and booby traps laid between the two barbed-wire fences. I also learned that, as regular as clockwork, two or three times a week in the late afternoon, one of their armoured vehicles would leave the farmhouse to pick up supplies, returning just before dusk. Crucially, the driver always took one or two armed men with him which, I realised, halved the number guarding the farmhouse during that time. I had already noticed, about half a mile from the farmstead to the main road, that the farm road (there was only one) narrowed as it passed between two rocky *kopjes*, and at one point it was only wide enough for one vehicle to squeeze through; now I realised how significant this could be.

"I fed this information back and the plan was developed by Comrade Lightning, the senior members of his unit and, in a small way, by myself."

What Mr Svosve said next began to dovetail with what Emma and Simon already knew about the attack. One group of guerrillas would lay landmines on the farm road at its narrowest point between the *kopjes* after the armoured vehicle left to get supplies, to be detonated on its return, hopefully blocking the road to hinder the arrival of the inevitable back-up vehicles hurrying to reach the farm once the attack had begun and they had radioed for urgent support.

"With one vehicle and half the guards neutralised," continued Mr Svosve, "Comrade Lightning would then lead the attack on the farmhouse, which was to take place as night fell, with a larger group eliminating the remaining guard, cutting the phone and power lines, blowing up the electrical generator, avoiding the booby-trap and carefully defusing the landmines in their path.

"When it was safe to do so, Comrade Lightning would rush into the farmhouse covered by his two closest and most trusted fighters. run down the corridor to the saferoom at the end, blow the lock on the wooden door at the end of the corridor and throw a smoke bomb into the saferoom where he knew 'Nelson' would have run to, giving him the cover necessary to blast open the metal door of the safe room. Under cover of the smoke and in the resulting confusion, he would overcome 'Nelson' and sedate him.

"Some weeks before the attack, Mathias and I had been training a donkey kept at the farm to carry heavy loads long distances, pretending we had merely been playing with the animal. The night before the attack, I was to stay the night, supposedly to work on my school project with Mathias. When the attack began, I was to go to the field to retrieve the donkey, and as Comrade Lightning was sedating 'Nelson,' I was to bring it to the farmhouse door where, with the help of Comrade Lightning and his fellow fighters, the sedated 'Nelson' would be strapped to its back and Mathias and I would make our getaway. We were to head east towards Mozambique under cover of darkness, hiding in villages during the day and travelling only at night until we reached the border. The villagers had been warned of our coming. It had all been scrupulously planned.

"I needn't go into any more details because, in the event, things did not turn out as planned. The kidnapping never took place; everything went disastrously wrong."

"So what *did* happen?" said Emma and Simon together, their voices conveying their growing frustration with Mr Svosve, for it was already becoming clear to both of them that her grandfather had died. What they needed to know was precisely how, and what had happened to his body. Then, as Mr Svosve slowly began to give them the details of the attack as it had unfolded, they listened in silence, bolt upright in their seats, their eyes fixed on the only man who knew. He not only answered the questions they had come for, but he provided them with details about the shootout in the farmhouse, and its aftermath, which not even Simon's father and his Uncle Jim had known.

"For some months before the farmhouse attack," said Mr Svosve, "Comrade Lightning had been aware his unit was being followed by a security force detachment which we later learned had been led by a Corporal Robertson, a man known for his considerable bush and tracking expertise. It was common knowledge that this Robertson had been responsible for the deaths of two other guerrilla commanders and he was determined to kill Comrade Lightning and neutralise the third of these three fighting units.

"Once the plans for the farmhouse attack had been agreed, in order to try to shake off this enemy unit, to pick up the chloroform/sedative needed and to learn how to use it properly, Comrade Lightning's unit went back to Mozambique where they undertook their final training for the assault. A week or so later they returned from Mozambique, initially launching two minor attacks a considerable distance from here – to the north and east of Mutoko – in an attempt to draw the security forces there in the hope they would believe this was where they would operate from for the next few weeks.

"Following the second of these two attacks, Comrade Lightning moved his unit swiftly westwards overnight, intending to have left the Mutoko area well before their departure had been detected by the enemy. We met up as planned early the following morning and the unit picked up the heavy supplies we had helped them to hide a week or so before they went to Mozambique. They then rested for most of the day, ready to launch the farmhouse attack that evening.

"The attack began well. The *Kudu* armoured vehicle left the farm right on schedule and was successfully landmined on its return just before dusk, wedging the crumbled vehicle between the rocks and blocking the road to incoming vehicles. Both the driver and the two guards were killed. Then, covered by machine gun fire from his comrades, Comrade Lightning led the unit of himself and two others to begin the assault on the farm compound, rapidly cutting the phone line and overhead electric cables and blowing up the auxiliary generator. They cut through the outer fencing wire, wove their way safely across the minefield and quickly neutralised the last remaining guard.

"I watched closely, observing every minute detail from where I was hiding up in the rafters of the cow shed nearby." Mr Svosve had clearly relived every detail of the attack many times since. "And Mathias was crouched next to me. We were ready to rush to the front door of the farmhouse with the donkey who was tethered below us, as soon as Comrade Lightning came out and gave us the signal to go!

"Then things began to go disastrously wrong." Mr Svosve paused and started to shift uneasily on his chair; it was clear he was going to find this part of his story difficult to tell. Emma and Simon both sensed the change and Emma felt her heartbeat quicken.

Mr Svosve wrung his hands together as he continued what now turned into a tale of tragedy and failure. "As became clear later, Corporal Robertson's RLI detachment was far closer to Comrade Lightning's unit when they were still in the Mutoko area than Comrade Lightning had realised. Consequently, they were aware the unit had left the area almost as soon as they had abandoned their positions and moved westwards. Robertson followed and was able to track them, though his detachment moved more slowly. Yet they were close enough to the farm when they heard the landmines go off to reach the compound soon after the assault had begun. The RLI enemy unit must either have seen or at least understood what was happening because just as Comrade Lightning ran through the front door of the farmhouse, one of their number reached the compound.

"Things then happened quickly. The enemy fighter followed Comrade Lightning into the farmhouse not ten yards behind. I saw this with my own eyes. As soon as he appeared, a hand grenade went off close to where the two guerrillas covering Comrade Lightning were crouching down. In the ensuing confusion, the enemy fighter was able to pursue Comrade Lightning through the front door of the farmhouse without being fired upon. A moment later, shots rang out from deep inside. By this time Comrade Lightning's two companions had recovered, unharmed but shaken from the grenade attack. On hearing the shots, they immediately ran across the courtyard and into the farmhouse through the front door in pursuit of the sole enemy fighter. As they did so, three more guerrilla fighters from the back-up group who had been waiting a little way off in case of problems ran forward to take up their positions, their AK47s trained on the front door of the farmhouse. We heard more shots ring out from inside the farmhouse, and then – almost immediately afterwards – we saw a figure bent low running out of the front door. It took us a moment to realise this person was neither Comrade Lightning nor either of his two comrades who had been the last to enter the farmhouse. No – it was the enemy soldier!

"By the time the guerrillas covering the front door realised who it was, they opened fire. But it was too late, the enemy fighter had escaped: he had turned sharp left out of the house and run along the farmhouse wall which shielded him from the salvo of bullets which, if they had released them a moment earlier, would have killed him. Shielded by the cover of the house, he was then able to run eastwards – in the direction I was to have taken the donkey and the kidnapped 'Nelson' if things had not gone so disastrously wrong – to join his companions waiting for him crouched behind a low wall five to ten yards away.

"Not knowing what had happened to Comrade Lightning or his two companions who had followed the enemy fighter into the farmhouse but, knowing they would be killed instantly by the enemy if they attempted to enter the farmhouse to try to find them, the remaining guerrillas were forced to switch to the 'disaster plan' they had all hoped they would never have to follow: they retreated to the nearby hill. There they began to fire rockets towards the farmhouse in order to draw the enemy away and towards them.

"At least this part of the plan worked." Mr Svosve sighed. "Once the enemy realised our fighters had regrouped on the hill, all of them – there must have been ten or more – immediately ran from their positions around the farmhouse towards the hill which they started to encircle. As they did so, I heard the deep thudding sound of low-flying helicopters and then saw four or five searchlights which were soon beamed onto the hill where the final battle took place.

"With no enemy troops left at the farmhouse I moved into action, though what I did was totally different from what we had practised. Leaving Mathias and the donkey at the front door, with my torch in my hand I rushed into the farmhouse and ran down the corridor."

Emma felt her body tighten as Mr Svosve moved towards the climax of his narrative.

"The beam of my torch landed on the bodies of the two guerrilla fighters who had followed the enemy fighter in through the front door. They were both dead; one lay on top of and across the other, one rifle was sandwiched between the two bodies, the other lay on the floor beside them. But I spent only a moment taking in the scene immediately in front of me as my attention was drawn to what I then saw at the far end of the corridor. Shining my torch ahead of me, I saw slumped against the still locked wooden door the motionless body of Comrade Lightning. I ran forward and as I covered those last few yards to reach him I heard on the far side of the still-locked door moans and groans from the farmer beyond, still very much alive, though sounding confused and clearly in shock.

"Comrade Lightning's back was propped up against the door, his legs lying apart in front of him," went on Mr Svosve hurriedly, hardly pausing to catch his breath. "As I reached him, I could see he was definitely still alive though only half conscious, if that. His already blood-stained T-shirt was becoming redder still as his blood seemed to be still seeping out of his chest from underneath. His head had fallen and his chin was lying awkwardly on his chest. As I shone my torch onto his face, I could see his eyes were moving, though slowly; he was gazing unfocused into the middle distance. It was clearly a huge effort for him simply to keep his eyes open, but he seemed to be forcing himself to do so. Then I noticed other parts of his body were also moving: his knees, boots and fingers twitched every now and then. Though he didn't seem to want to, he didn't even try to speak. I don't think he was aware of what was going on – he certainly didn't recognise me. I had never seen a dying person at close quarters before but, though he was clearly still alive then, it did not seem to me he was going to live very much longer."

Carried away by what he had been saying, Mr Svosve suddenly remembered where he was and who he was talking to. He turned to Emma and said "I am so sorry, Ms Makoni, to have to recount what I saw, but you did ask me to tell you what I knew. Of all the things I saw that evening, the sight of your wounded grandfather was by far the most disturbing. I shall never forget it."

Emma said nothing. She had heard enough to know Sarah's beloved Joshua had died at the farmhouse; all that was left were the final details which she knew she needed, upsetting though she knew they would be.

"The one thing I knew," continued Mr Svosve, "was I had to get him out of the farmhouse. We – that is, Mathias and I – needed to make our escape and we had to move fast.

"I started to drag Comrade Lightning down the corridor, but I immediately realised I would not be able to get him over the bodies of his dead comrades without help. So I ran back to fetch Mathias and between us – I don't really know how – we succeeded in half-dragging, half-lifting Comrade Lightning to the front door. We managed to raise him up onto the donkey and secure him onto its back, binding him tightly with the ropes and straps which were to have been used to secure the farmer. I instructed Mathias to brush away all traces of footprints and hoof-marks from the ground. There were no donkey droppings to pick up, but I told Mathias to use his shovel to remove the lumps of dirt on which Comrade Lightning's blood had fallen and had begun to congeal, and to brush away the marks on the ground made by his boots as we had dragged his body out from the front door. Mathias then took my torch and with a cloth returned to the farmhouse to wipe away all traces of blood which had fallen on the floor as we had pulled the body to the front door.

"As Mathias was doing this, I left as quickly as I could, leading the donkey by its halter. I turned to wave to Mathias as I left and could see tears were streaming down his cheeks. A few minutes later, I heard footsteps behind me. It was Mathias, who rejoined me when he had finished clearing up. I remember him telling me I had been crying and it was only then that the enormity of what had happened hit me. Up to then, I had clearly been running on adrenaline. Though I was hot and sweating, I started to feel cold and afraid.

"After all," Mr Svosve reflected, "Mathias and I were little more than children – I had just turned 16; Mathias was still only 15.

"Only at that point did I think to check on Comrade Lightning. I put my hand on his forehead and felt a shiver go down my back. It was cold and dry. He was dead. I'd never seen a dead body before, but I knew he was dead; I just knew it. Your grandfather, Ms Makoni, was certainly alive when I came to him in the corridor, but now he was dead – without a doubt. But when exactly had he died? I don't know. I felt no particular or new sadness when I realised he had died as I guess I had been expecting this to happen from the moment I saw him wounded and lying bleeding, almost motionless, but still twitching, inside the farmhouse. However, I did experience a terrible loneliness. Though Mathias was by my side, I suddenly felt as if my life was one big gaping hole."

Emma knew exactly what Mr Svosve meant because this was exactly what she was feeling as Mr Svosve told her the moment he realised Joshua had died.

"I remember only too well what happened next," said Mr Svosve. "There was a brief exchange between Mathias and myself.

"'What shall we do now?' asked Mathias.

"'We must bury him,' I said. 'They mustn't find him.'

"'Where?' he asked.

"'I need to think,' I said."

Then, lifting up his head, Mr Svosve turned to look at Emma and told her he simply didn't know what to do. Everything was so different now.

"I turned and looked at Comrade Lightning and asked myself what he would say; it was as if I was appealing to him for guidance. As I did so I saw in my mind's eye his face looking at me when we were sitting together discussing the farmhouse attack. I saw him turning to me smiling and saying:

> *Always make a plan, young Svosve. Weave it round in your head, chop holes in it, tease out its weakness; revisit it, test it and challenge it again and again until you know, until you are certain it will work.*

"Never did I think I would have to make a plan about how and where to bury *him*," said Mr Svosve. "Then it suddenly came to me, what I should do.

"As a young boy," Mr Svosve's voice was rising excitedly, "I remembered being taken by some older boys to what then seemed to me to be the strangest of places. One day as we were walking in the bush we suddenly came across a succession of deep white-coloured gullies, eerie-looking gashes in the land formed as if by a giant tearing his fingers across the ground in anger to create scars in the earth, five to ten metres in depth. One of the boys said they were called *makaronga*. He told the rest of us that the ground from which the gullies were formed was made from fine grains of sand blown in from the Kalahari Desert which had accumulated over many centuries. In the heavy storms of the rainy season, the power of the gushing rain washes the sandy soil away to create these deep gullies, or dongas, which for most of the year lie dry and bare. During the rainy season, after a big storm, the gullies fill and the rushing water rips the sandy soil off from the steep gully walls. By the end of each rainy season, the shape of each donga will have changed so radically it would be unrecognisable from the previous year.

"What I remembered most about these dongas when I first ran inside them," said Mr Svosve, "was how soft the sandy soil was: press your fingers gently into their sides and they sink in easily.

"It was now late August." He returned to his narrative of what they did with Comrade Lightning's body.

"I knew the dongas would be dusty and very dry. Using our hands and Mathias's shovel, I reckoned we could quickly dig a shallow grave in the sides of a donga and conceal the body. I told Mathias our plan: he had heard about the dongas but had never seen them before. With half a moon now visible in the night sky, we could see our way there in the dark. We turned south and reached the dongas within the hour, both of us sweating from the pace I set.

"Before daybreak, we had buried Comrade Lightning in a shallow grave hollowed out of the side at the bottom of one of the deepest dongas, at a bend in the dry river bed, and filled it in again, smoothing the sides to make it look as though no hole had ever been dug. Ten or 20 yards from the grave, we dug another hole to hide the brush and shovel, as well as the ropes, the straps and the makeshift saddle – indeed, everything which had been on the donkey's back. We then shooed the donkey away and it ran into the bush. I felt sorry for it, but what else could I have done? We then hurriedly brushed over the prints of our shoes and the donkey's hooves with our hands and then said goodbye. I walked back home to Gavaza and reached there as the sun was rising. Mathias walked away in the opposite direction.

"I never saw Mathias again. Wisely, he never returned to his family at the farmhouse. He headed off eastwards, making his way to Mozambique where he had intended to join the guerrillas as a fighter. However, he was told he was too young and would have to wait. I learned later he died the following year when the Rhodesian Airforce bombed and paratroopers stormed through the camps at Chimoio in Mozambique where Mathias and many other young people like him were living. He died as a statistic, one of some 3,000 young people killed in a single weekend in November 1977. The Rhodesians named it Operation Dingo; we called it a massacre."

All this time, Emma sat in silence. At the point when Mr Svosve described Mathias shedding a tear, Emma's eyes welled up and tears flowed down her cheeks. When he came to the moment when he realised Comrade Lightning was dead, Simon took Emma's hands and held them tightly. They had heard what they had come for, it confirmed what they had always feared had happened.

But Mr Svosve had not quite finished.

"I was afraid of going back to the grave for many weeks afterwards, fearful I was being watched, but I knew I had to return before the rains came. So, late one afternoon towards the end of October, an hour before sunset, I walked back to the dongas, careful to look as if I had arrived there by chance in case anyone was catching. Then, when I was sure I was alone, I rushed into the donga, but the body was no longer there. At first I thought it had been removed, taken away by someone or persons unknown. But on closer examination I found traces of clothing, then, some distance away, I saw some bleached bones followed by first one and then another part of the heel of a boot. It seemed pretty clear to me the body had been discovered, dug up and eaten by wild animals, and probably finished off by vultures. In many ways I felt relieved as no one was ever going to find him. I stood in silence and said a short prayer of thanksgiving for Comrade Lightning's life and for my having known him. Oddly, as I walked back home, I wasn't sad. On the contrary, I felt proud I'd been privileged to know not only a quite remarkable soldier but such a kind and gentle human being."

Mr Svosve had now finished and Emma was the first to speak in response.

"Thank you, Mr Svosve," she began. "You have told us what we came to hear, giving us closure on the death of my grandfather. I am grateful to you not only for the full account you have given us but also for the care you took in burying my grandfather and honouring him in the way you did. However, wars do strange things to people."

Emma's instincts were starting to wrestle with what her heart had told her. Taking Simon by surprise, she said, "How do we know – how do *I* know – what you told us is the truth? How do I know you didn't make it all up? You have had 40 years to go over this story, to think it through, to develop and refine it. I don't doubt for one moment you believe what you told us is true as the events of that day clearly live vividly deep inside you. But how can I be sure these events really did happen in the way you said they did?

"Is what you have recounted, Mr Svosve, the truth?" she said, earnestly and with some passion. "I really want to trust you, Mr Svosve, but tell me, how can I? With Mathias dead and a wall of silence from the other guerrilla fighters who might have escaped that day, there are no other witnesses to confirm the veracity of what you have told us. Before I return home and relate what happened to my dear mother, I need to be certain, Mr Svosve. Please convince me; is this too much to ask?"

Unlike Simon, Mr Svosve was neither surprised nor shocked by what Emma had said. Indeed, as she spoke, it struck Mr Svosve forcefully how similar Emma was to her grandfather: it clearly went far deeper than their eyes. Twisting his words ever so slightly, he could hear Comrade Lightning sitting next to him and saying, "tease out the weaknesses of what you are told; test it; challenge it until you know for certain it is true."

"Ms Makoni," he said to Emma in reply, "I respect what you have just said: your grandfather would have been proud of your thoroughness. I can go partway in persuading you of the truth of what I have told you, but I suspect you will not be finally convinced until you see your mother, Sarah, again. She is the only one who will be able to confirm the truth of what I have told you. In a moment you will understand why."

Emma warmed to Mr Svosve once again, noting he had referred to Sarah now as she had done a moment before as her mother, and not as her grandmother.

Mr Svosve then stood up, held out his hand and beckoned to Emma and Simon to accompany him as he walked towards the teachers' house. He looked tired; what he had said seemed to have sapped the energy out of him. He told them he had something he needed to show them and, apologising in advance for what he said was a "mess", turned the key to the triple-locked door of his room and gestured for them to step inside.

* * *

At first, they could see nothing. They were met with a blanket of darkness, due in part to their eyes not having adjusted to the brightness of the African sun and in part to the curtains, thick and doubly-lined, which were tightly drawn across the room's single window. As they peered into the black, Simon recalled what Mr Vambe had told them: no one had ever been invited into Mr Svosve's room or knew what lay behind the door he always kept securely locked.

Mr Svosve apologised for the darkness but instead of opening the curtains to let in the light and knowing his way around, he walked ahead of them, picked up the matchbox lying on the centre table and lit a match which he cupped in his hands to keep it alight as he walked on to the far end of the room. In the flickering light they were just able to make out the shape of a long narrow table touching the end wall. Mr Svosve lit a second match and, as he raised his arm, they could make out the first of what they were soon to discover were brass three-arm candelabra standing at each end of the table. He lit the first of three candles then used the lit candle to light the five remaining candles. As more candles were lit, they saw the wall behind the table was covered almost to the ceiling by a piece of cloth, purple and shiny, almost silk-like. The cloth covering the table, which matched the one on the wall, dropped down a foot or so in the front, giving it the appearance of an altar, the whole edifice creating what looked just like a shrine.

After Mr Svosve had lit the last candle he asked Emma and Simon to be seated. As their eyes grew more accustomed to the light, they independently concluded the table was set up as an altar, though there was no crucifix, tabernacle or any other familiar Christian emblems or artefacts.

Instead, right at the centre of the table was what looked like a small box; it was gold-coloured, rectangular and made of metal, secured with black metal hinges across the top, one set at each end. It wasn't large, about eight inches long and two to three inches high.

Still standing next to the altar, Mr Svosve took off his tie, unbuttoned his shirt at the neck and then removed what they thought at first was a necklace, but which turned out to be a shoe lace to which was tied a small key. He removed the key from round his neck and slowly turned the key to unlock the metal box, which he opened, its hinged top rattling slightly as he did so. Inside the box, resting on the centre of a small raised velvety cushion, as scarlet as a Cardinal's mozzetta, was what appeared to be another shoelace which had been neatly rolled up and was coiled round itself. Mr Svovse held it aloft before letting it unravel in front of them. The cord was black and turned out to be made of leather, fraying at the edges.

Dangling at the bottom they could clearly see a square-shaped cross; it had a hole at the top of the longer of the two cross-pieces through which the leather cord had been threaded. It was made of wood and roughly carved, suggesting strongly it had been made by hand as the surfaces were rough and the sides not quite symmetrical. Mr Svosve then clasped hold of the wooden cross and held it between his fingers as delicately as if it were a newly-born animal. He had clearly done this many times before and they could both see the cross was deeply significant to him; he could have been fingering something as holy as a communion host. After a moment's silence, Mr Svosve handed the cross to Emma and sat down.

He then turned to Emma and said, "You probably don't know this, but some guerrilla fighters wore identity tags around their necks; many did not. However, there was an unwritten rule: no fighter was ever allowed to wear anything personal, nothing which might trace him back to his home, to his life before he joined the guerrilla army, in case he was killed or captured. When I came to bury your grandfather, I discovered this wooden cross around his neck and I knew at once it wasn't an official identity tag: ask any former guerrilla and they will confirm this to you. From all you have said, Ms Makoni, I now believe it was almost certainly given to him by your mother, Sarah; it could even have been carved by her or by someone locally.

"Take the cross, Ms Makoni. I have kept it and have treasured it to honour your grandfather since the day I buried him, but it is yours by right. It is not mine. I was holding it in trust but until today I did not know who I was keeping it for. Now I do. Take it, it's yours. Give it to your mother and watch carefully to see how she responds because her reaction will confirm what you asked me to provide you with just now: the certainty that what I have told you today is indeed the truth or – so help me God – a succession of lies spun and woven to deceive you. If I have told you the truth today, Ms Makoni, she will caress it, hold it next to her heart and tell you how he came to be wearing it. Then you will finally have the answer you asked me to give you."

Mr Svosve then stood up and walked back to the altar. There he lifted the scarlet cushioning from the inside of the still open metal box. Underneath was a small glass vial with a plastic stopper on the top which he picked up and also handed to Emma. He told her it contained sandy soil taken from the exact place in the donga where he had buried her grandfather. A week ago she would not have known what she should do with it but now she did: she placed it carefully in the side pocket of her bag, laying it carefully next to the wooden cross she had just put in.

Very quietly Emma said, "Thank you, thank you, Mr Svosve, for all you have done – for these mementos, but especially for the kindness you have bestowed upon me. I'm sorry if I did not sound as grateful as I should have just then but I am still quite a jumble of different feelings and mixed emotions right now, and it is going to take me a while for all this to sink in."

Simon knew exactly how *he* felt, and it was simply ghastly. At the Reddys' pool on Sunday evening, when Emma had splutteringly said to him, "I think your father killed Sarah's husband", he had felt little emotion, even if he had recognised the pivotal importance of what she was telling him. Now, here and for the very first time, Simon's whole being grasped the enormity of it all – his father had deliberately, knowingly and brutally killed the man whom Emma viewed as her father, bringing death to the family of the one he loved. He felt completely empty and shuddered; his head was spinning and he had to steady himself to stop being physically sick. He wanted to take hold of Emma's hand, but he didn't dare touch her. He was afraid – afraid of Emma, frightened above all else he was going to lose her. For the very first time since they had met, Simon was completely lost for words. He couldn't think of anything he could possibly say to her which would even begin to express how sorry he was for what his father had done: whatever he said he knew would be totally inadequate. It was as if the portcullis at the Tower of London had first rattled then crashed down to separate them and keep them apart, forever. It was a barrier which, Simon strongly sensed, only Emma had the power to remove.

Mr Svosve could feel at least a little of the tension in the room, but he had no idea what had caused it and though he had no wish to pry, he thought he should do something to relieve it. It was now mid-afternoon and they had neither eaten nor drunk anything since arriving at the school early in the morning. He said they must be in need of sustenance and, without waiting for an answer, that he would just pop to the kitchen and bring back some refreshments. In a moment, well before Emma and Simon felt the urge to start talking to each other about what they had learned, Mr Svosve returned with cold drinks, half a dozen large sticky buns and something else they hadn't seen, a cheerful smile. As he placed the tray in front of them, they both realised how much they needed them and in no time had each consumed two bottles of coke and two buns, while Mr Svosve sipped at a Fanta and nibbled at half a bun.

The tension began to lift as their sugar levels rose and they took in the rest of the room where they were seated, which they had begun to take note of in the brief period of Mr Svosve's absence. The altar, shrine or whatever it should be called took up one end of Mr Svosve's room. The rest was filled with countless books and an array of many other of Mr Svosve's clearly treasured possessions. It was an Aladdin's cave of curiosities: ornaments and trinkets; photographs, pictures and drawings; and rocks, withered plants and pieces of shrivelled wood. Some were displayed on tables and bookshelves, some were pinned on walls, and others hung on ropes slung across the room and around the small bed, which lay almost hidden behind the door in one corner.

On either side of the cloth-coloured "altar" stood two huge bookshelves which rose almost to the ceiling. They were bulging with books: thick historical studies and weighty philosophy tomes; some scientific works; a number of biographies and rows of largely classical works of literature. Scanning the titles, they could see books about ancient Greece, China, India and the Middle East, contemporary Europe, the Reformation and the Enlightenment. There were the works of Mao and Marx, Aristotle and Aquinas, books about Darwin and evolution, and novels by Tolstoy, Dostoevsky, Camus, Orwell, Sartre and many others. Dozens of other books were piled up at the end of the bookshelves, their sleeves not visible. A few lay unopened still in their wrappers piled up on the floor.

After Independence, as he explained, Mr Svosve had enrolled for a correspondence degree with UNISA in Pretoria and travelled down to South Africa, sometimes for weeks at a time to attend different summer school courses. This, thought Emma, may have explained why he had not been around when Prosper came looking for him. In Johannesburg he had discovered, he said, some wonderful second-hand bookshops, including his favourite, Collectors' Treasury, where he had been befriended by a kindred "book-a-holic", as he called her. This woman, he said, sent him books he ordered until she died a year or two ago, even posting them off without payment in those periods when Zimbabwe's financial problems meant he wasn't able to pay for them with hard currency. She had clearly meant a lot to him as he was keen to tell them her name: she was Marlene Botha, an Afrikaans woman. He went on to say they had become good friends, adding that most Afrikaans people he had met had been kindly and caring and that he had never personally met an Afrikaner who was a racist, though many clearly were. He said he always instructed the children he taught to respect others, be wary of prejudice and never make sweeping generalisations about different racial or ethnic groups. Emma could hear her grandfather telling a younger Shungu Svosve to prod and test everything and always to be wary of convention in order to get to the truth.

Yet what fascinated Simon and Emma about Mr Svosve's interior, far more than the "altar," the trinkets and the books, were the photographs and pictures displayed prominently across his room. Mounted on picture frames, pinned onto cloth hangings, propped up in front of books, tied to pieces of string strung between book-shelving and taped onto the bare walls with blue tack round Mr Svosve's bed were dozens of photographs, pictures, paintings and drawings with one thing in common. They were all faces. If Mr Svosve's room was a shrine, it was above all else a shrine of people.

As he was eager to explain to Emma and Simon, the pictures and photos displayed were people he most respected and admired – mostly philosophers, theologians and novelists as well as statesmen and politicians past and present. The "chosen ones," as he called them, had been picked over and selected after decades of reading and thinking and, as he explained, he changed the faces he displayed as time went by and circumstances altered his earlier selection. But what he was most keen to tell them was the reason he put them up was not so much so he could look at them, but rather so they could look at him.

"Why?" they enquired.

"To challenge me," he said, as if the reason was so obvious it didn't need to be answered.

"The people you see around you are those I most respect, those whose thoughts and writings have had a profound influence on me. I want them to continue to help shape the way I think about the world because most are beacons of hope for a better and more humane world."

Simon, in particular, was fascinated by Mr Svosve's choice of faces. He was able to pick out many who were familiar as his eyes moved round the room and he called out their names in turn. There was Aristotle and Plato, Martin Luther King and Mahatma Gandhi on the wall to his left. Strung up above them he saw Nelson Mandela, Confucius, Fidel Castro and Che Guevara. Then, as he looked to his right, he was stuck. Emma came to his aid by naming Julius Nyerere and Rosa Parks and the two iconic figures from Zimbabwe's earlier struggle against settler rule, Mbuya Nehanda and Sekuru Kaguvi. After she had correctly named the last two, Mr Svosve told them his grandmother was a direct descendent of Chief Mashayamombe, who came from Mhondoro and was also among those first leaders killed in the initial days of white rule, a connection he said he had mentioned once, with some pride, to Comrade Lightning. Emma immediately remembered this was Jessica's surname, and was sure it must have been the same family. Another eerie coincidence, she thought.

Below the altar, Mr Svosve helped them both with the pictures of Bishop Helder Camara and Ashoka Mauraya. He pointed to the picture of Ivan Illich, an Austrian philosopher, former Catholic priest and radical critic of western society, who, he hastened to add, one must not confuse with Lenin. And he explained why he had placed him next to a picture of Paulo Freire.

Enjoying himself now in a moment of escape from the real world (and in some respects the inside of Mr Svosve's room was created as a sort of escape), Simon noticed Abraham Lincoln and with the film starring Daniel Day Lewis fresh in his mind, he challenged the inclusion of Lincoln in Mr Svosve's "hall of fame." Simon said he hardly deserved to be here given his clearly racist views of black Americans, whom he saw very much as second-class citizens. Mr Svosve explained that while Simon was certainly correct about Lincoln's racist views, he needed to be judged within the historical context in which he lived and not from our vantage point.

"The fundamental point about Lincoln," he said, "was not merely the key role he played in the suppression of slavery, but that he achieved what he did in spite of fierce opposition from his own party and many of his own kith and kin. Lincoln is here for the simple reason he helped to move history along."

This was also, he explained, why the other pictures around his bed included Eleanor Roosevelt as well as Thomas Paine, both key figures in the human rights movement, though not perfect human beings either.

Mr Svosve then pointed to a bespectacled figure whom he told them was the Italian political philosopher and activist Antonio Gramsci. He was here in his hall of fame, Mr Svosve explained, not only because of his opposition to fascism, but because of his belief in spiritual development and the importance he gave to the strengthening of society as a counterweight to the power of politicians.

Finally, he motioned to the small crucifix which was displayed above his pillow and said even Jesus, whom he deeply respected, was a child of his time. "By his silence at least he seemed to be pretty much accepting of society's discrimination of and general oppression of women and, looking back at him today, most would argue he was pretty rubbish in championing the full gamut of human rights of all people.

"But that shouldn't lessen our admiration for him. Jesus was clearly a great human being who provided us, perhaps more than any other person, with enduring insights into what it means to be truly human and in so doing provided us with a unique window into the Divine."

Emma was both impressed and amazed at what Mr Svosve said, and even Simon thought to himself there was much here he would agree with.

Clearly enjoying himself now, Mr Svosve then said he had a collection of faces of people he did not display but which were hidden away in the top drawer of his cupboard. Why? Because, as he explained, although they had

made a significant contribution to humanity they were also guilty of
appalling atrocities. He said he had put Mao in this drawer more than 30
years ago and had kept him there where he was in the company of
Napoleon, whose face he would want to display for the enduring
contribution he made to state-building but which he couldn't because of the
sheer numbers of people slaughtered in the wars he waged.

For Emma, the most interesting of Mr Svosve's comments about "his"
faces were made when they were about to take their leave, and they
concerned other faces which were missing.

"Why," she asked, "do you not have any pictures up of any present-
day Zimbabweans?"

Mr Svosve said he did have one, and he pointed to a small picture of
the former Bishop of Bulawayo, Pius Ncube, which he had placed next to
the one of Helder Camara.

"A very, very brave man," he said. "One of very few of my
compatriots who had the courage to speak out in favour of democracy and
against some of the unlawful killings which have taken place in our country,
even going as far as naming those responsible for them. From the look on
your faces, you don't recognise him but you should because he was a
recipient of the Scottish Robert Burns Humanitarian Award. And you call
yourself British!"

He laughed, adding, "Sadly, the bishop was himself silenced in tragic
circumstances," but didn't elaborate.

"For the rest, it is a depressing tale. When I began to build my hall of
fame soon after Independence, many of the faces looking down on me were
of contemporary Zimbabweans, among them famous politicians, some
household names not only here but abroad. But then, with an increasingly
heavy heart, I was forced to tear them up and burn them one by one as they
didn't even deserve a temporary reprieve in my top drawer. At one time,
my pictures of contemporary Zimbabweans outnumbered the rest. But over
time the majority turned into a minority, then the minority became just a
few, until the few were reduced to two, and now there is just one. It was
more than five years ago," said Mr Svosve with sadness in his voice, "that
I had to remove the face of the last remaining Zimbabwean politician on
display, more than thirty years ago following the mass slaughter of civilians
in Matabeleland that I reluctantly was forced to remove both the first
president of our country and his successor.

"It is with a heavy heart that I have to tell you there are no Zimbabwean
politicians or soldiers alive today whom I would judge in the sweep of
history to be a credit to humanity as a whole. And it is in that context, Ms
Makoni, that I hold your grandfather in such high regard. He fought for a
better world; he laid down his life for the new Zimbabwe to be born and
died still pure, untainted by corruption and self-aggrandisement. As I said
to you earlier today, Comrade Lightning remains for me a symbol of what

might have been as well as a sign of hope for a better future for my, for our country. If I had a picture of him I would gladly add him to my hall of fame, but sadly I do not."

Then, clasping Emma's hands between his and speaking with emotion in his voice, Mr Svosve tried to sum up his time with Emma and what it meant for him, deliberately choosing to speak quite formally.

"As we take our leave of each other, Ms Makoni, I am parting with the only links I had to him, his cross and the sand which surrounded his body. But I do so with pride and honour. Pictures are only pictures and relics only relics. What matters most is what happens in the human heart. That is the test of someone's greatness and the testament of your grandfather, Ms Makoni, is that he is here in my heart and will remain here for ever."

It was now late in the afternoon. Emma was drained, physically and emotionally, and she knew she had had enough for one day. She stood up to signal it was time to go, and Mr Svosve and Simon immediately followed her lead. She said they needed to get back to St Michael's before dark, and Mr Svosve said she was right.

Emma didn't know quite how to thank Mr Svosve, either for what he had given her or, even more importantly, for what he had told her. She knew she couldn't put into words how she felt. Instead, as they rose to leave the room she stepped forward towards Mr Svosve and clasped his elbows firmly with both her hands and leant forward to give him a gentle peck on his cheek. She knew she was forcing Mr Svosve to step outside his social comfort zone but, with all the knowledge he had accumulated in his head of other cultures, she felt he would understand what her actions were meant to convey and she hoped the intended warmth of her parting gesture would bring him solace, even some comfort.

They walked back to the car in silence, but as they stepped into the car, Emma said, "There's one last thing I would like to ask you, Mr Svosve."

"What is that?" he said in surprise as he had caught the jollity in Emma's question.

"You introduced yourself to us as Shungu Svosve," she said. "Why Shungu? It's not a name I've heard of before. As a good Catholic, I would expect you to have been given a saint's name when you were baptised."

"You are right on both counts," he said, chuckling. "I was baptised Simon Peter. But it was a name I discarded a very long time ago. He was, after all, both a threefold liar and the first pope, neither of which I had any wish to emulate. Shungu is a name I gave myself. Why? Well, as you well know (though Mr Robinson will not), it is not merely a Shona word but one which can't easily and simply be put into English. Hannon's dictionary wrongly translates it as 'exhilaration', 'vehement desire' or 'ambition'. For me the appeal of the word Shungu lies in its being a single word which combines the sense of determination and passion to do good with personal integrity and honesty. Why did I choose it? Not because I see myself as a particularly good person, but because I can think of no better word to sum up my own personal philosophy. My name, Shungu Svosve, calls *me* to live a life of passion, honesty and personal integrity with ant-like determination. Why? So I can contribute to making the world a better place and, if I can, especially through my teaching, to help my students to see they should strive to do the same as they grow into adults. That is why I chose to be a teacher."

Simon felt small from what he had heard. When they had first entered Mr Svosve's room, Simon watched as this shadowy, diminutive figure with a slight hunchback shuffled towards the shrine he had built against the backwall of his dark room. As his tiny hands caressed the wooden cross when he lovingly removed it from its box, Simon immediately thought of Tolkien's Gollum fondling his "precious". How wrong he was! He knew now he had been in the presence of a very different person – not a self-centred creature absorbed in hoarding precious things for himself and destroyed by greed. Now he knew the person they had called the elusive Mr Svosve to be an upright and honourable man who, first at war and now through his books and his teaching, had dedicated his life to others.

And with that they parted. As they left the school compound, Emma looked back to see Mr Svosve waving to them as their car, like Mr Vambe's earlier in the day, churned up the dust. It caught the wind and drifted down onto Mr Svosve's clothes. She smiled, waved back and breathed in deeply: it had been a momentous day; one she would never forget.

They travelled back to the mission in almost complete silence as both she and Simon played back in their minds everything Mr Svosve had told them, what they had learned and what it meant for them. There was simply too much to process. Simon knew it would be impossible for him even to start to raise the subject of her grandfather's death with Emma. It was far too early for that. He hadn't yet even got his mind round the question of whether he thought it was murder, still less whether Emma thought it was. Emma's thoughts were far less convoluted. They were focused just then on her own family, on her grandfather, on Sarah and on Alice, and not on either Simon or on any other Robertson. She felt comfortable, as the Quakers would put it, simply to hold them in the light. Anything more would be far too much for now.

They reached St Michael's having only made one wrong turn, a relatively minor one. They provided Father Ambrose and Sister Immaculata with a brief account of what they had discovered and though both of them commiserated with the news of Emma's grandfather's certain death, they found it hard to conceal their delight that Emma's, and Sarah's, uncertainties were now over.

Before retiring for the night, Father Ambrose asked if they would like to delay their departure to Harare the next morning till after the 10:00 am Mass, which he invited them to attend. He said it was a Mass for the whole secondary school and they would enjoy the singing and drumming. They were both far too tired to do anything but accept.

* * *

Once Emma was back was behind the womb-like security of the convent walls and alone, she had the first opportunity to try to take stock of what had happened on this tumultuous day. As she started to try to work out the implications of what Mr Svosve had told her, the doubts and uncertainties she had felt about her relationship with Simon when it first began all of a sudden resurfaced – and then they hit her with the power of a hurricane-force storm.

From the outset, Emma knew she had been worried about the circumstances surrounding her getting together with Simon, especially the succession of coincidences which seemed increasingly to bind them together. There was first the oddity of the chance encounter which had initially brought them together, followed by the feelings Emma had in that dream which drove her to meet Simon properly when she had all but forgotten him, and then his telling her he had been half-expecting her to call. It was as if forces beyond them both had made them meet. Then there was the discovery of their shared African roots followed very soon after, by the weirdness – there was no better word for it – of both their parents switching so dramatically from not wanting them to visit Zimbabwe to their urging them to go. At the time, their becoming a couple seemed even if not simple – because of Robbie – then at least the right thing to do. For Emma, all these coincidences were simply signs her relationship with Simon was something which was always meant to be. What she had struggled with was how to prise herself away from Robbie without – she hoped – losing him. After their day at Hampstead Heath, never for a moment had it ever crossed her mind she would ever leave Simon or be forced to leave him.

But now, sitting on her bed on her own in the pure, almost antiseptic, atmosphere of the convent's most scrupulously-cleaned guest room, everything started to change: what she thought had been firmly set in stone started to crumble; the certainties looked like certainties no more. Then in an instant it came to her and she realised how wrong she had been. She had misinterpreted these coincidences. How could she have done? Now Emma knew Simon's father had killed her grandfather, it all looked so different – as well as so simple.

She and Simon should never have got together: that is what the succession of coincidences had really been telling her. Bright lights had flashed to tell her not to leave Robbie and go to Simon and she hadn't seen them. How and why could she have turned her back on her stable, loving and ever-deepening relationship with Robbie for a set of dangerous coincidences? They were warning signs but she never heeded them. She knew she had found wrenching herself from Robbie difficult, if not impossible, but she had managed to convince herself this was what she really wanted to happen. How could she possibly conceive of living with the son of the man who killed her grandfather, the man who destroyed Sarah's life by killing the only love of her life? And now she knew more about her grandfather, Emma now thought Peter was also indirectly to blame for Alice's death too. After all, if he had not been killed, Joshua would never have allowed Alice to become pregnant as a schoolgirl, become HIV positive and go on to contract AIDS.

She knew none of this was Simon's fault; she only had herself to blame. If only she had listened to her journalistic instincts when early on she had sensed danger in the string of coincidences, but instead she had dismissed them out of hand. Why had she been so ready to do this? She couldn't remember precisely why, but she was now clear she had been so terribly wrong. She had been mistaken, but had she also been misled? Did Simon contribute to her being misled? Would Robbie have her back? Was it too late? What was clearly meant to be, she now knew, was her relationship with Robbie, not with Simon.

Surprisingly, at that moment, Emma didn't feel emotionally distraught at the thought of having to cut herself loose from Simon. She knew it was not only all over between them, but she knew it should never have happened in the first place. She knew she loved Simon but she had also loved Robbie in much the same way, so if she could extract herself from Robbie, she could do the same with Simon, and eventually stop loving him. Time would heal her. At that precise moment, Emma felt her relationship with Simon had all been a dream.

Emma was totally limp, she felt completely drained: she couldn't absorb or give out any more! She was exhausted, physically, mentally and emotionally. She knew she needed to sleep. She pinched herself, but she was numb. She couldn't feel a thing.

Turmoil at the Victoria Falls

A woman is alone in a narrow rowing boat travelling along a wide fast-flowing river. It could be the upper reaches of the Zambezi close to the Victoria Falls, known locally as the-smoke-that-thunders for its ferocity, and it turns out it is. Suddenly she hears a crunching sound and feels a thud underneath her as the boat grinds to an abrupt halt. She is stuck. The boat has become wedged between rocks just below the surface right in the middle of the river.

The woman screams when the boat hit the rocks, and now screams again as, to her horror, she first hears then sees a man struggling in the river behind her to the left, shouting, one arm desperately waving over his head to try to catch her attention, the other fighting the current as he battles to keep afloat. He is too far away for the woman to be able to grab hold of him, but not too far off to recognise him. It is Simon.

No sooner has the woman taken in that the man in mortal danger is Simon than she hears a second cry for help, this time behind her and to the right of the boat. She turns and sees a second man caught in the fast-flowing river, his arms waving frantically, his head repeatedly bobbing up and down as he also struggles to keep afloat, such is the power of the current. This man is not close enough for the woman to be able to grab hold of him either, though she immediately recognises him. It is Robbie.

The men are not aware of each other but both realise they know the woman as, almost at the same time, she hears the word "Emma" ring out from each of them above the noise of the river and the thunder of the Falls beyond. The men are terrified. They repeat her name as they each plead desperately for her to come to their aid. Emma, Emma, Emma ... Emma, they cry out. They know she is the only who can save them. She is their only hope.

Emma's boat carries a red and white lifebelt ring on board. It is right next to where she is seated, securely bound to one end of a long, lightweight rope. The other end is attached to the front of the boat. Emma jumps up and, as quickly as she can, lifts the lifebelt and tosses it out in front of her downriver in the direction of the Falls with all the force she can muster, propelling it into the air to go as far as the rope will carry it before landing on the water beyond her.

As she releases the ring, Emma sees that the two men have now drawn parallel to her boat, Simon to her left and Robbie to her right, though they are still well beyond her reach. Ahead of her, Emma is acutely aware of how near she is to the Falls. The sound of the water cascading to the rocks below is deafening and she can feel the spray from the mighty Zambezi falling onto her from above like rain. She knows the men are being sucked ever closer to the 100-metre drop and certain death.

At that moment, Emma feels an enormous gush of wind all around her: it is so strong, she has difficulty steadying herself. She suspects it's some sort of freak whirlwind. The wind catches the lifebelt ring and for a moment is seems to hover almost motionless above the water. Emma can now see both men ahead of her; they are beyond her boat and they have just noticed each other. Indeed, they seem to be signalling to each other. They then both catch sight of the ring hovering above them and each tries to grab it, but it is too far away – to the left of Robbie and to the right of Simon.

When she had tossed the ring out in front of her, Emma had tried to be scrupulously fair, throwing it equidistant between the two men. But as it now wavers momentarily in the air, Emma becomes agitated, fearing she might have thrown it a little to the right, favouring Robbie, or a little to the left, favouring Simon. As it starts to fall, she looks on in terror as the dying whirlwind seems first to tip the ring closer to Simon then, as if changing its mind, sends it veering closer to Robbie. Emma feels pangs of guilt sweep through her. She shouts out loudly, as if to the wind, "I tried to be fair. I didn't choose who should or would be saved. It wasn't me, it was the wind which made the lifebelt change direction." Her clothes are now so damp with spray they cling to her body as she stands motionless in the boat, helpless and distraught.

Then, as suddenly as the wind had come and added to Emma's frenzy, the men appear to have stopped moving. Although they are still waving their arms about frantically and the water continues to rush past them, they are no longer careering forward to the edge of the Falls. They somehow seem to be stuck in the same spot in the river. Emma screams again; she can't understand what is happening. Her eyes seem to playing tricks on her – or is it her mind?

As she gazes across to the two men in her life, she cups her hands round her mouth and shouts out as loud as she can with desperation in her voice, "For God's sake grab hold of the lifebelt. Hurry! It's tied securely to the boat. Take it and you'll be saved."

The men look back at Emma, perplexed, then shout back to her, their voices clearly audible in spite of the thundering noise of the Falls. They call out, using precisely the same words as if they were actors coached to say their lines.

"Which one of us should take hold of the ring? Which one of us are you trying to save?"

Emma is silent. She's unable to answer their questions. She knows only one man can be saved. However courageous and strong a swimmer he might be, by the time the man who catches the lifebelt ring struggles to reach the second man, the river will have swept him beyond the reach of the lifebelt's rope. Emma's insides are churning, she is tortured by guilt.

Did she throw out the ring fairly, or did she twist it slightly as she let it go, directing it more to one side than the other, and favouring one man over the other? If so, she would be guilty of the death of one of the two men in her life! But which man did she save, and which one did she kill?

Emma sat up. She was sweating profusely and shaking as the cocktail of feelings – terror, panic and guilt – were still buffeting her insides. Then, as she realised she was in bed and had been dreaming, she grew calmer and began to take in her surroundings. She recognised where she was – not in her London flat but still in the convent in Mhondoro. It was pitch dark. She checked the time: it was just after four in the morning.

Just then, Emma heard the shuffling sound of feet slipping down the corridor floor outside her room. She knew at once what it was: a few of the elderly nuns were making their way to the convent chapel to pray in silence before dawn broke. Impulsively, and almost before she knew it, Emma had dressed and found herself sitting in the chapel, alone on a bench at the back. In front of her she could see the shapes of three women sitting motionless and well apart from each other, their bodies dimly lit by the red sanctuary lamp flickering in the distance next to the altar's tabernacle. Emma breathed in the quietness of her surroundings and, without thinking, closed her eyes. She still wasn't fully awake, but she now knew what had made her come to the chapel: it would be the best place to try to make sense of her dream.

As she sat there in the darkness, Emma mouthed silently the words *Oh God, what shall I do?*, uncertain whether she was uttering a prayer for help or letting out a pent-up expletive. It didn't matter. What was important was to try to find answers.

She racked her brain to try to recall how the dream ended. She remembered everything freezing just after she tossed the lifebelt ring out in front of her; she knew Robbie was ahead of her on her right and Simon on her left. She was sure it hadn't ended there and she strained to try to remember. She didn't have to wait long as, slowly at first, the next part of her dream came back to her and with her mind's eye she saw what happened. Her intuition had been right, the chapel had been the right place to come.

Robbie had managed to grab hold of the lifebelt with the tips of his fingers and pull it towards him. Yes, that was right; it was Robbie for sure! But as soon as he had caught it, Robbie immediately threw the ring across to Simon instead of keeping hold of it himself. Emma's eyes travelled with the red and white ring as Robbie threw it, and she saw Simon's startled face as he caught it, uncertain what he should do next. But Emma hadn't waited to look: she remembered turning her head back to see what had happened to Robbie. She was just in time to see his head before it disappeared into the spray of the Falls and the yellowy-white foam on top of the frothy water.

But this hadn't been the end of her dream either. She remembered then suddenly seeing Robbie's head again, but in a different part of the river. He hadn't gone over the edge after all, her eyes had been scouring the wrong part of the river. But if Robbie was alive, what had happened to Simon? Emma relived the panic she had felt in her dream as she remembered turning back to look where she had last seen Simon: he wasn't there and she couldn't understand why. If he had kept hold of the ring after Robbie had thrown it to him, he ought to have been clearly visible right there in the water. But he wasn't. Did Robbie's reappearance mean Simon had immediately thrown the ring back to Robbie as soon as he had caught it? If so, what happened next?

Again and again, Emma attempted to recall her dream's closing moments but, try as she might, everything always seemed to an end in a blurry haze: she couldn't remember who finally held the lifebelt ring, who had reappeared and who had disappeared. It was as if the final frames of an old-fashioned cellulose film had been lost on the cutting room floor.

The harder she tried to remember how her dream ended, the more distressed Emma became, but she never forgot she was in the convent chapel, and she kept repeating the words "Oh God, what shall I do?"

Then, all of a sudden, it occurred to Emma that maybe her dream didn't have an ending. Perhaps it deliberately stopped before revealing to her which of the two men in her life had lived and which had not. But why should it have done this? Emma thought she had the beginnings of an answer to that question as well. Perhaps it was because any death, and loss, would have been too painful for her to bear. Her mind had to close down because there was no pain-free outcome, and if that's what her dream was telling her, what did *that* mean?

Just then, Emma felt an arm touch her shoulder and as she opened her eyes she was surprised to see Sister Immaculata sitting beside her. On finding Emma wasn't in her room when she knocked to wake her just before 6:00 am as they had agreed when they said good night, Immaculata had scoured the convent until she found her in this unlikely spot. They were alone: the first light of the new day had just touched the chapel's windows and the older sisters had all left.

Immaculata could see Emma was extremely upset and had been crying, and she asked her in hushed tones what was troubling her. Already feeling comforted by their physical closeness, Emma found it easy to start opening up to Immaculata, and the more she said, the more secure and reassured she felt. Quite soon, Emma was revealing things about herself she would not have thought possible to share with anyone, not even her mother, still less someone she had only met a day or so ago. With her guard down, Emma spoke with a frankness and an honesty which surprised her as much as it did Immaculata. The whole experience was cathartic. As she talked and Immaculata listened, Emma felt a huge sense of release as she unburdened herself of some of her deepest worries.

She began by quietly recounting every detail of her dream with its emotional troughs and peaks and its uncertain outcome. But as the dream made no sense without knowing more about her relationship with Robbie, Emma then told Immaculata about that. She then gave Immaculata an honest account of what Mr Svosve had revealed. But as the full implications of what he said could not be understood without knowing who Simon's father was, Emma then told Immaculata all about Peter and why and how he had had come to kill her grandfather. This led Emma to tell Immaculata how the previous evening she had convinced herself she had to end her relationship with Simon even though – as she confirmed to Immaculata almost in the same breath – she still loved him. But even before Emma had finished sharing this shocking news with Immaculata, she realised her dream had already challenged her to revise her hasty, and supposedly unequivocal, decision. Indeed, it crossed both Emma's and Immaculata's minds at almost the same time this was probably why she had had that dream in the first place.

As Emma spoke, Immaculata placed her warm hands on Emma's cold ones, every so often squeezing them to help Emma along. By the time Emma had finished, the chapel was bathed in bright sunlight. Then, after waiting a moment to make sure Emma had finished saying everything she had wanted to say, Immaculata smiled and said, "Well, my dear, it's pretty clear to me your dream was telling you that you need to decide which of these two men you will choose to spend the rest of your life with."

Emma felt distraught. After everything she had shared with her, was that all Immaculata could come up with?

"But I *can't* decide," said Emma despairingly. "That's the problem, Immaculata, and *that's* what my dream was telling me."

"No," insisted Immaculata, surprising herself at how strongly she emphasised the word. "What your dream was telling you was that even though it is going to be hugely difficult, not only does a decision need to be made, but it is *you* who have to decide. That's why you woke up, Emma: it was because the *dream* was finished.

"It is not the-you-of-your-dream who will decide, but the real you. It's the you-of-the-cool-light-of-day who needs to decide! What's more, the reason the dream was taking place on the fast-flowing Zambezi right on the edge of the Falls was it was telling you that you need to decide soon. It's urgent, Emma! This whole thing is eating away at you, and hurting you in the process. No more procrastinating, my dear Emma, as my novice mistress would say to us. You have to decide without any further delay.

"And I need to say one more thing, harsh though this may sound as well," said Immaculata, following what her instincts were telling her more than her more prudent self. "You have trusted me a lot in what you have told me about yourself, dear Emma, and I love you for that. But just because you have revealed your problems to me and told me the dilemma you face, please don't think I will somehow help you to make your decision because I won't. Just as your dream hasn't given you your answer, neither will I. It is you who has to decide.

"Emma," Immaculata put her arm around her, "painful though it is and will necessarily be for everyone, now you know what Mr Svosve told you, everything is in place to enable you to make your decision. Have the courage to do so and confront and manage the pain which will follow for possibly all of you."

Emma turned and looked intently at Immaculata. She had been forcibly struck by something Immaculata had just said which Emma realised she hadn't thought sufficiently before about.

"You are right," said Emma. "Now I see it."

"Right about what?" said Immaculata, wondering precisely what she had said which Emma had found so significant.

"Right that it will be painful for everyone, for them as well as for me."

"Of course it will be," said Immaculata, quite surprised by Emma's comment. "If there was one thing which was crystal clear about your dream it was the way it revealed the pain and suffering the two men were going through, terrified they were about to drown, or rather, terrified they might lose you."

"Yes, that's precisely my point," said Emma. "Until you said it just now, it only occurred to me *I* was the one who was hurting. But they are too – of course they are! Now you've said it, it's so obvious, but why didn't I really register this before? What's worse is that I am the cause of their pain. My inability to choose has not only hurt them both already, but the pain will continue at least until I decide and probably well after this for at least two of us. The longer I am unable to decide, the longer everyone's pain will continue.

"You see, Immaculata," Emma clasped Immaculata's hands, "I somehow seemed to have believed, at least deep in my subconscious that I was preventing pain by not making a decision, but in fact I am prolonging pain both for me and for them. You are right. The only way to stop the pain is for me to make the decision I have been shying away from making. Why didn't I see that? How could I not have seen it?"

"Well," said Immaculata, "at least you now know what you have to do to address the pain which clearly exists between the three of you, which is why I said you shouldn't delay any longer.

"Today, dear Emma," she continued, standing up, "today is decision day for you."

Then almost as an afterthought, she added, "Go, Emma, go in the direction your heart is leading you to go."

It took Emma many weeks to grasp the full significance of Immaculata's final remark.

She stood up and Immaculata took hold of her hand and led her out of the chapel. Once outside, they stopped talking in whispers and Immaculata told Emma she needed to eat a really good breakfast. Only then did Emma realise how hungry she was. As they walked together down the corridor in silence, Emma thought Immaculata could be right, today could be decision day. Hard though she knew it would be, Emma felt her time in the convent chapel had injected her with a new dose of confidence to help to decide, to make full use of what Robbie had termed the suspension of their relationship. Emma knew she needed to make a decision she would stick to, and not go back on.

But then she returned to what Immaculata had said about its being painful for everyone, and as she did so, she felt a wave of regret sweep through her, almost as strong as the whirlwind in her dream. She wondered if the man she was about to reject would ever be able to forgive her for the hurt he would suffer on her account. Emma shuddered. And would she be able to tell him to his face how sorry she was for the pain she had caused him? Immaculata was right: she had already stepped out beyond the confines of her dream to face the real world.

BOOK III
RESOLUTIONS

Harmony

Emma and Simon left St Michael's to drive back to Harare later that morning. Father Ambrose and Sister Immaculata walked with them to their car to say their goodbyes, and Simon and Emma thanked them warmly for everything they had done to help them. It was an emotional farewell. After an effusive handshake from Ambrose, Simon slipped an envelope into his hand containing $100 in cash, only telling Emma afterwards. Ambrose was embarrassed but grateful. Immaculata handed Emma a plastic bag which she said was sustenance for the journey. Emma knew what it contained without opening the bag: two bottles of coke and the ubiquitous sticky buns. Immaculata then threw her arms around Emma, her body almost engulfing the younger woman, who by no means slight herself. *My God*, said Simon to himself at such an untraditional display of affection, but Emma knew the reason and Simon was even more surprised as Emma responded in kind.

The school Mass they had earlier attended set the tone for the rest of the day, which proved to be a watershed in their relationship. As Ambrose had predicted, the music captivated them. Lines of secondary school pupils snaked into the church – still green-roofed as Jim had remembered it from all those years before – filling it from side to side with neat rows of obedient teenagers. They sat on the floor, segregated, boys on the left and girls on the right. Emma and Simon were directed to the back and the few benches reserved for important people. As soon as the last students were in their places, the sound of a slow, deep drumbeat from the front, joined almost immediately by the rhythmic shake-shake of rattles, and the melodious voices of first the girls and then the boys announced the Mass had begun.

Throughout the service, the children sang in natural harmony, the deeper voices of the boys whose voices had broken set against those of the girls to create sounds unfamiliar, yet alluringly attractive to Simon's ear. As he sat and listened, Simon recalled the effect a recording of a Congolese Latin Mass, *Missa Luba,* that he had heard as a ten-year-old, had had on him. It also began with a slow, deep drumbeat, then a jingling of rattles followed by high-pitched voices giving a shrill rendition of the *Kyrie Eleison.* He remembered listening spellbound by that music and wondering then what it would be like to be transported to a church in the very heart of Africa to listen to such haunting sounds. And here he was now in Africa: this time it was real. His old vinyl recording played the *Kyrie Eleison,* the *Sanctus* and the *Agnus Dei* in Latin. Here they were being sung in Shona and Emma knew the words: *Mambo tinzwireiwo tsitsi* (Lord Have Mercy); *Musante, Musante, Musante* (Holy, Holy, Holy) and *Hwayana yaMwari* (Lamb of God). At times the students stood up to sing and the girls' bodies swayed as they clapped their hands and swung their hips gently from side to side, just as Emma had witnessed in the secular setting of the family homestead a week ago. At times the beat of the drums quickened and the volume rose to ring round the church, the sounds ricocheting back off the tin roof with such force they could feel the thudding vibrations on their chests.

Simon was captivated by what he heard and what he felt – it was as if his body was locked in harmony with the voices and the drums. His neck tingled and he felt a glowing warmth across his back which spread out along his arms and legs. It all made him think. Did it make any difference, he asked himself, that it was Simon the atheist who was mesmerised by the drums and the singing taking place at a Catholic Mass? Wasn't what he was experiencing just the same as what Emma was feeling right now? The conclusion he came to was it didn't matter. The key thing was that he was uplifted by what he was hearing and experiencing, it engaged his whole person, and, as he turned and looked at Emma, it was evident it was having the same effect on her. How you choose to label such feelings, he decided, was secondary. Simon knew many believers would argue their experience *was* different because they believed in God and he didn't, but he didn't think that was true. Anyway, how would they know?

Towards the end of the Mass, everyone went forward to the altar for communion. Simon didn't join Emma and the others in receiving the host but, having been instructed by Emma beforehand, he crossed his arms on his chest as Ambrose placed his hands on Simon's head for a blessing. Simon didn't think his actions were hypocritical and he did not feel uncomfortable being blessed by Ambrose, though he had feared he would. It was, he said to himself, both a way of conveying a thank you to Ambrose for his kindness to them as well as demonstrating positively how he felt about having engaged intimately with the music – for Simon felt he had not simply been a passive bystander.

However, it was what happened just before Ambrose blessed Simon which had a far deeper effect upon him. As he drew close to the altar, his attention was drawn to one of the drummers, who was preparing to play a solo piece just as Simon walked past him. He was a small boy dressed in a neatly-ironed white shirt and grey trousers and with a serious grown-up look across his shining face. He had moved a little way from the other drummers, so the contrast between the tall powerful drum and the thin and frail-looking figure standing next to it was even more noticeable.

Totally focused, the drummer-boy started to beat his taut animal skin at the centre with the inner palm of his right hand, softly and slowly at first: tap… tap… tap… He then began to beat the drum harder, his right hand moving now from the centre to the edge of the drum's surface and back again. A moment later, the boy's drumming hand quickened as if his brain had instructed it to shift into a higher gear. He then started to pound it even more vigorously and as the volume rose the sound was almost violent. And as he drummed and his hands moved ever faster, tiny beads of perspiration appeared on the boy's forehead and his bright eyes gazed out into the middle distance as if in a trance.

As Simon walked on ahead to feel the comforting pressure of Ambrose's hands on his own forehead, he daydreamed of his younger self at much the same age – 11 or 12, he thought – taking the place of this drummer-boy completely absorbed in his playing, and he reflected upon the very different world this gifted youngster inhabited. What, Simon wondered, would he be doing when he reached Simon's age? Would he have a job or, like most of Zimbabwe's young, would he have joined the ranks of the unemployed? And what would drums and drumming, and the Catholic Mass and Christianity, mean to him then?

The service had raised both Emma's and Simon's spirits and it helped to lighten the mood between them as they set off for Harare. They chatted briefly about how uplifting they had found the Mass and how glad they were to have delayed their departure to experience it. However, their conversation soon dried up as they each retreated into their own thoughts as they tried to make sense of the previous 24 hours. Neither of them was yet ready to discuss what Mr Svosve's revelations meant for them and for their future together.

As they drove on in silence, Simon pondered the state of their relationship, which he obviously wanted to deepen, but which he was even more desperate to become far more physical. It had certainly had its physical dimensions: from the time of their first dinner together in Muswell Hill, they touched and caressed each other whenever they were together. Thereafter they kissed passionately, intimately and often, and Simon had never felt any reluctance on Emma's side to the growing intimacy between them. Indeed, he felt his hunger for her was frequently surpassed by Emma's passion for him. But they had still never slept together and this had continued to pain Simon. For some time now, he had known a little of why that was – it revolved around Robbie. But Emma had only really begun to tell him about Robbie in the final weeks before they left, and he had always been too respectful of her to prod and ask more.

But as he now thought more about what he had begun to call the problem of Robbie – to himself, obviously, he would never say anything to Emma – he wondered whether his reluctance to raise the subject directly with her was due more to something else. He knew Emma needed time because she clearly wasn't finding it easy simply to 'drop' Robbie and give herself totally to him, though he never fully understood why. Now he wasn't so sure. Despite so much evidence to the contrary, could the problem be that Emma was really still in love with Robbie? It then occurred to Simon that perhaps his own reluctance to ask Emma to confirm it was now all over with her and Robbie was due to his fear she wouldn't be able to do this. This thought made him feel not only even more miserable, but extremely vulnerable as well. Simon had hoped, and in many ways convinced himself, that their spending time together alone at the Falls would provide the catalyst for her to come to terms with and confront the reality of what her heart and most of her head had been telling her for months. If Emma were to say yes to Simon completely, and sleeping with him he felt sure was a crucial part of her doing this, she would be able to move on. Then, what he felt for her could be – would be – reciprocated 100%. But things had not turned out as planned. Not only had their trip to the Falls had to be aborted, but what they had learned yesterday from Mr Svosve, confirming the killing of Joshua at the hand of his father, had changed everything. Thinking about it now, Simon feared the issue they faced was no longer when and how their relationship would become more physical and cemented in place forever but whether and how it could be rescued; how it could survive.

When they had driven back from Gavaza the previous day, Simon did tell Emma how dreadfully sorry he was, but she had hardly responded. What he had meant to say was he was sorry it had all happened and there was now so much hurt around. But on reflection he feared she might have interpreted his 'sorry' as meaning he was somehow apologising for what his father, his family, had done to hers, but this wasn't what he had meant at all. He knew – and he felt sure Emma recognised – her grandfather's death had nothing to do with him and therefore there was nothing he, personally, needed to apologise for. But his view now, as he gripped the steering wheel tightly to help manage the sting of rejection he was feeling, was there was nothing more *he* could either say or do to help the situation they were in. It was only Emma who could move things forward. He would have to wait until she was ready to talk. He told himself he was – of course – prepared to wait for as long as it took. Then suddenly Simon's whole world darkened as the terrifying thought came to him that everything was now over between him and Emma. She would soon return to London tomorrow a broken man – incapable of loving another woman as he had loved Emma, his life filled by the routine of work, cheered only by music and the occasional game of cricket, until he sank into old age and died heirless and destined to be quickly forgotten. Simon shuddered and gripped the steering wheel even more tightly.

Emma had spoken lovingly of Sarah's suffering, but he knew she was suffering now. He wanted to show her his love for her had not changed one iota. He wanted to hug her, to hold her close to himself and stroke and smell her hair as he had so often done before. But her body felt taboo to him now as parts of her mind had always been. Simon didn't even feel he could touch Emma. As they sat next to each other, barely a foot apart, he was painfully aware of the barrier between them which yesterday had put so firmly in place.

As Emma stepped into the car and sat next to Simon, she still felt uplifted by the music of the morning's Mass and comforted by the warmth of Immaculata's parting hug, but those feelings soon faded as she began to reflect anew on her problems and to puzzle out how she was ever going to resolve them. Here she was, returning to London tomorrow no nearer to having the answers she had told herself her time in Zimbabwe with Simon would give her: there was scarcely a day left and she had far more problems than she had had when they left. At least in the convent chapel this morning she had convinced herself that the unequivocal decision she had made the previous night to end her relationship with Simon was not merely premature but wrong. But didn't this simply put her back to where her dream had told her she now was, she pondered, still torn between choosing between Simon and Robbie, although now clearer about the urgency of making a decision?

But then, as she thought about it more, it dawned on Emma that her dream – or at least the clear interpretation she had had of it when sitting next to Immaculata – had got it all wrong. Her problem didn't lie in choosing between Simon and Robbie but in working out how to disengage with Robbie so she could be with Simon. The difference was crucial. Her core problem was she was in love with Simon but unable to commit herself to him totally because she felt unable to shake off all the positive feelings she still had for Robbie. This is what her heart had been telling her for months. It was her mind which had frequently been muddling her up and, to the extent that her dream, in asking her to choose between Simon and Robbie, was her subconscious telling her the same thing, it was reinforcing that muddle. Immaculata was correct on three counts. First, she had been right in telling Emma her dream was a clarion call to make a decision and make it soon. Second, she had been right in saying the process would be painful. But third and most importantly of all, Immaculata had been right when, almost as an afterthought, she told Emma to be guided by her heart.

So her dream *had* been wrong in one crucial respect, Emma concluded, for in her heart of hearts, she had known for a long time she had chosen Simon. Her problem – her real problem – lay in working out how to disengage from Robbie. *There*, she said to herself, *I have said it twice now, so I must be right.* Emma knew she was having difficulty thinking straight and how uncharacteristic it was of her to feel she was in such a muddle. As if proof were needed that this was how she really felt, Emma thought back to how, for some time before they set out for Zimbabwe, she had wanted to sleep with Simon, and how she had grown increasingly upset by her inability to convince herself she could. Indeed, this was one of the key issues she had hoped would be resolved before she and Simon stepped back on the plane to return home to England. But the possibility of that happening seemed ever more remote now because there was an even bigger reason why she couldn't: the killing of her grandfather by Simon's father.

This set Emma thinking about precisely how Joshua's death altered her relationship with Simon. As she did so, she was appalled to realise that when she came to her hasty decision last night to end her relationship with Simon that she hadn't even considered why this mattered. But it did, it was hugely important – after all, as she had told herself and even confirmed to Immaculata, she still loved Simon.

It was Simon's father who had killed Joshua and she didn't in any way blame Simon for what had happened. What's more, she didn't think knowing how Joshua had met his death had caused her to love Simon any less: why would it? How could it? It would, however, create enormous problems for her relationship with Peter, both how she felt towards him now and in the future. But as Peter was Simon's father, this must have knock-on effects for her relationship with Simon, she thought.

Then there was Sarah. What she and Simon now knew about Joshua's death *had* to have massive consequences for the relationship between Sarah and Simon's parents. Indeed, it would be bound to shape it because while Sarah had met Simon (and they had got on extremely well), she had still not met Simon's parents. This had been deliberate. Though they had never discussed it, Emma was fully aware Sarah knew she still had strong feelings of affection for Robbie. So, in order not to confuse Sarah – who liked everything to be clear-cut and simple – Emma had decided to postpone the time when Sarah met Simon's parents until she had resolved that dilemma.

Emma knew Sarah, Peter and Cathy *had* to be told Peter had definitely killed Sarah's Joshua. It might have happened in the context of war, but Emma did not think that materially altered the bare facts: dying may just be dying, but killing was killing. Emma knew if their respective parents didn't know the truth of what actually happened, the relationship between herself and Simon would be built upon a lie. Emma knew she couldn't live with such a colossal lie and she also knew she couldn't conceal the truth from her mother. Sarah simply had to know. Likewise, Emma knew Simon couldn't live with himself – or with Emma – if his parents, and especially his father, didn't know who Emma really was.

So, there was a succession of problems thrown up by Joshua's death which affected her relationship with Simon. Most were huge, and as Emma thought about each in turn she didn't know how she – how they – were ever going to solve them. *Oh God*, Emma said to herself, *what a mess we are in! I came out to Zimbabwe hoping I could solve the biggest problem I thought I had – how to break up with Robbie and be more closely united with Simon. I am now about to go back home with a succession of even bigger problems to add to the one I still haven't been able to resolve.* Emma rarely swore but she felt so terrible that only expletives seemed able to give her the release she felt she needed. *What a fucking awful mess I am in – we are in* – she said to herself despairingly.

But then, as she turned everything over in her mind once again, Emma began to wonder whether, perhaps, the problems she was grappling with weren't so insurmountable after all. It suddenly struck her she didn't need to confront and resolve all her problems at once: she should try to tackle them one at a time. And this led her to ask herself where she should start. As she started to mull over this question, Emma suddenly realised she had the answer, and it totally surprised her. Not only were her problems not as big she had just convinced herself they were, but, it turned out, they weren't really problems at all. How could she possibly reach such a conclusion so soon after she had felt at her wits' end? Emma pinched herself as she tried to see the fault in her logic.

This is the way Emma's mind was working; this is what she told herself.

Sarah, Peter and – our families – only have to be told the truth about what happened if my relationship with Simon definitely moves onto a new plane and I am able to resolve the ambiguities and uncertainties I still feel about Robbie. There is no need now to think about the difficulties our families might face and the pain which might be caused in some theoretical, dim and possibly quite distant future. Why do I need to torture myself thinking about hypothetical problems and how they might be hypothetically solved? The answer is simple. Why didn't I think of it before – I don't need to!

As of now, I am free! I am free to sort out my life, to make my own decisions, just as Robbie urged me to do. I am free to focus all my energies on Simon, to be with Simon, to be alone with him, just the two of us. We had hoped for four or five days together at the Victoria Falls and now only have a day and a bit left, but we will have to make do with Harare and less time. But we will be together and I will talk openly, far more openly than I have; we will talk until we resolve all this. Immaculata was right: this has to be done soon, and knowing about Joshua's death has been the catalyst I needed to stir me into action. As of now, Simon is really all that matters. I need to focus everything on him.

And when I know where I really am with Simon, I will be in a position to know where I stand with Robbie. So, I am well on the way to making a decision, as Immaculata told me I must. It's all now fitting into place.

And when the full nature of my relationship with Simon is finally sorted, I will know whether and how Simon and I will tell our families about the events revealed to us by Mr Svosve. Until then I don't need to think about this either. It really is that simple!

As these thoughts whirled around Emma's head, her mood changed. The barrier which she felt had fallen between herself and Simon, creating a no-man's land between them emotionally and intellectually, had suddenly lifted. They could re-engage just as they had before that terrible moment when Simon had recounted to her what Jim had told him when they were at Kariba. The confident and self-assured Emma had returned. She was a free agent once more, in control and starting to feel she was in a good place. She smiled across at Simon but he didn't notice; he was still far away, lost in his own thoughts.

As they drove along, Emma started to feel as close to Simon emotionally as she was to him physically. She saw his thin hands holding firmly onto the steering wheel, his narrow fingers wrapped round the leather. She watched the muscles rise up on his lean, bare forearms, browned by the African sun, as he suddenly tightened his grip on the wheel. As he changed gear, she noticed his thighs tense up then loosen again as his left leg moved to engage the clutch. A fly which had been buzzing inside the windscreen landed on Simon's shirt collar; she flicked it off and as her hand was close, without thinking she brushed the side of his cheek gently with the back of it. He turned to her and saw her smiling at him. Her face had changed; it was no longer drawn but looking relaxed. He knew at once something profound had happened and he smiled back. Only then did Emma realise how much she had missed him these last few days, even though they had scarcely been out of each other's sight. As they drove on, Emma felt a warmth inside her, simply to be sitting next to Simon. They *were* on a journey together and she felt she didn't want this journey ever to end.

Then, all of a sudden, Emma realised how hungry she was, and, smiling, asked Simon if he was ready for their 'gourmet' lunch. It was the first time either of them had spoken for a good half hour, but as soon as Emma spoke she confirmed her mood had changed. The portcullis which had crashed down between them had been raised and, quietly and to himself, Simon sincerely prayed everything would stay that way.

"What is it?" Simon enquired as he tried to peer into the bag now on Emma's lap.

"Nothing but the best, freshly clicked from Tesco this very morning," chuckled Emma. "The finest Coke and the best sticky buns on God's earth, served up with a smile."

"Just what I was dying for," said Simon who was smiling now, and as their eyes momentarily met, they both let out a loud laugh at the same time.

Emma took the first Coke in one hand and the opener in the other, securing the unopened bottle between her legs ready to open it. As she started to prize open the top, it fizzed and she sprayed coke all over her jeans and hands and screamed at her stupidity in forgetting what else bumpy roads do.

"I'm all sticky!" she exclaimed a few moments later, licking her fingers after finishing the last mouthful of her second sickly, sugar-coated bun. "I can't wait for a good shower when we get in; though I dearly love it here, I think I have had my fill of the African bush at least for now."

They had just reached the main, tarred road and from there it was a straight smooth ride back to Harare, no sand to slip on, no more corrugated roads and no decisions to be made at unmarked junctions.

It then suddenly occurred to Emma they didn't know where they were going to stay. They had made no arrangements for the night: there was no plan. Before they left – and it seemed such a long time ago now – Emma had told Simon she simply couldn't return to the Reddys', and he had agreed they would not go back there. But they had been so focused on first arranging their trip to Mhondoro and then so absorbed in it as it unfolded that they hadn't given any further thought to where they would stay when they got back to Harare. Where planning was concerned, Simon always relied on Emma and, preoccupied with everything else she had simply, and uncharacteristically, forgotten. But, back to her old self again, she told Simon she had already thought what to do.

Emma took her phone out of her pocket, switched it on then cursed. Although she saw she had a slight signal she knew it wasn't strong enough to call anyone, never mind to access the internet: scarcely one flickering bar. But then, about 10 miles further on, just after the sign to Beatrice, Emma saw three then four bars suddenly appear on her phone.

"Stop, stop, stop," she shouted, in the hope they wouldn't lose the signal. Simon saw they were about to pass a layby so he braked hard and the car left the main carriageway with a bump. The layby had seen better days: the trunk and branches of its shady msasa tree had been felled long ago for firewood, and its round reinforced concrete table and benches lay broken on the ground, the reinforced metal exposed and rusting and hardly holding together the now crumbling cement surrounds. Emma didn't notice. She had a connection; she was in luck; the signal was strong and she didn't lose it.

Emma googled *Zimbabwe Lonely Planet*. When the website came up and she clicked through to Harare hotels, she saw an advertisement on the right of the display page which she read aloud.

> *Bronte Hotel. Located on the eastern edge of town, the Bronte is sprawled out over peaceful gardens and features colonial-style rooms, which are comfortable but a bit dated.*

She told Simon it said the Bronte was a popular choice with NGOs, which she thought was a good sign. Clicking on to the hotel's own webpage, she was pleased to see it was called 'The Garden Hotel', jotted down the phone number and then called. Reception answered almost immediately and Emma enquired if they had a cheap room for tonight, just the one night. She was told the standard rooms were all taken but they had a superior room which would be $50 more. Without enquiring further what the total price would be, or checking the one-star reviews on TripAdvisor which she always did when searching for a good hotel, Emma said they would take the room. After a brief exchange with Simon, she told the receptionist they should be there within the next hour or so and she gave them Simon's surname, relieved they didn't ask for a credit card number.

Before putting down the phone, she asked directions driving into Harare from the Masvingo road and was told it was easy: 'Turn left on Fourth Street and then ...' But at that point the phone signal died. Rather than being annoyed at having failed to finalise directions, Emma was delighted. She told Simon they had a smarter-than-basic room in what was called a garden hotel which they should be able to find easily enough using Google maps, and if they failed to reconnect they could always fall back on the old-fashioned way of getting directions – rolling down the window and asking someone. Emma chuckled; she was in a buoyant mood.

As she put her phone in her bag, Simon patted her gently on her leg and said, "That's my Emma: I know I can always rely on you to sort out problems which I find insoluble. All I have to do now is drive carefully, watch out for wobbly cyclists and stray pedestrians, keep my eyes peeled for crazy or drunk drivers and avoid the potholes, and we should arrive safely in one piece."

He said he would phone Sheila when they got to the hotel, but he didn't share with Emma what he was intending to tell her. Emma didn't respond and they spent the rest of the journey mostly in silence. But it was quite a different sort of silence than the one which had marked the start of their journey from St Michael's.

* * *

They reached the Bronte a little after four o'clock feeling hot, sticky and weary and in need of a wash and a change of clothes. But they were relieved they had arrived and had only had to ask the way once. Seeing the trees and shrubs as they drove in, they were pleasantly surprised that their chosen spot seemed to live up to its name as a garden hotel.

"Looks like a great place," said Simon. "Well chosen, Em."

They were even more delighted when they saw a swimming pool in the hotel grounds as they walked to reception, with some people swimming and others sitting round tables under the shade of khaki-coloured umbrellas. Emma said she was definitely going to take a dip and, as they walked on to check in, she could already feel her stress levels falling further in anticipation of relaxing as she swam in the pool.

The receptionist was the same man Emma had spoken to earlier on the phone and they recognised each other from their voices. He greeted them, saying "I hope you enjoy your stay at the Bronte. My name is John Gamuchirai. You are most welcome!"

Emma smiled to herself then said, "Thank you. We are exhausted. I am Emma, Emma Maconie, and this is Simon, Simon Robertson."

Though he was cheerful enough, John was clearly puzzled. From her accent he had earlier taken Emma to be foreign but she certainly looked Zimbabwean and the name 'Makoni' seemed to confirm this. Yet her accent, clothes and confident manner signalled somewhere different, probably England. When she wrote her name in the book as 'Maconie' he was even more confused, dismissing his new theory she was English but had Zimbabwean roots. He was used to professional female NGO guests but these were almost all white, unless they were American. He was also used to single professional black Zimbabwean women but they usually stayed on their own or with black partners. Black women staying with white men at the hotel, especially for just one night and without children in tow, were usually neither professional nor foreign. When Emma told him she was a journalist, Simon was an accountant and they had just come from a three-night stay at a Catholic mission in Mhondoro, where they had gone neither for work nor on holiday, he gave up and, having been trained not to pry, simply wished them a pleasant stay.

They baulked at the price of the room, $246, and joked to John how well paid NGO workers must be to afford to stay. They turned more serious when he told them some of their NGO guests almost lived here, working from their rooms for weeks and occasionally months on end. When John asked them if they would like to have dinner at the hotel, Simon took over and said they definitely would. They were given two options – the smarter, more expensive and quieter Emmanuel's or the cheaper Parks restaurant. Having made a quick calculation of how much they had saved by not flying to or staying at the Victoria Falls, where he had already discovered there was no such thing as a cheap hotel room, and with a nod from Emma, Simon the accountant decided on Emmanuel's, after confirming there would be vegetarian options on the menu. Yes, came the reply, there always are.

With only a rucksack each, they declined the offer of having their luggage carried to their rooms but were barred from going on their own by the would-be porter who immediately turned herself into a key-carrier. She informed them her name was Takurai, instructing them to follow her as she led them first up the stairs and then along an outside corridor to their room at the end of the first-floor block.

Takurai welcomed them into their room, opening first the bathroom door then the sliding French doors which gave onto a private veranda just wide enough to squeeze in two metal chairs. She then hovered, hoping for a tip. Simon dug into his pocket and gave her a couple of loose coins without really looking at them. Their key-carrier smiled, curtsied, handed Emma their keys with her two hands outstretched, and was off.

They were happy with their room, which was big, bright, airy and freshly-painted. It was overlooked by nothing but trees and you could see the pool from the veranda, though it was far enough away that the noise didn't seem to carry. It contained two double beds, made separately with sheets rather than duvets, but lying so close to each other they were almost touching. Above and behind the beds on the wall was a picture of a group of elephants drinking at a waterhole, faded and discoloured by the sun. Between the beds and the French doors was a sitting area comprising a small round table and two small padded upright chairs with arms. A small vase of fresh hibiscus flowers had been placed on the table: vivid red petals which changed to deep yellow as the flowers narrowed. Large pistils projected out of the centre of each flower, extending beyond the petals and, with the French doors open, they quivered slightly in the breeze. A handwritten card was propped up next to the vase, inviting them to a free sundowner drink in the bar on production of their room key. Facing the bed was a desk with internet connection and above the desk was a television. The en-suite bathroom was at the back of the room. It was quite small, with a sink and toilet near the door and, beyond, a compact stand-alone shower enclosed by a translucent glass screen with two matching sliding doors which opened outwards, covering the entire back wall. Though simple by European standards, it was by far the grandest room either of them had slept in since arriving in the country.

Emma looked pleased but was less interested in the room's geography than her imminent swim. Announcing this to Simon, she placed her rucksack on the bed nearest the bathroom, landing next to where Simon had thrown his, and began rummaging inside to try to find her swimsuit. She did not succeed before she had scattered a variety of clean and dirty clothes onto the bed around her, as she emptied out almost the entire contents. Then, triumphantly, she waved it in the air, a one-piece black Speedo, before almost running off in delight to the bathroom to change. Though keener to have a shower, Simon's far-stronger desire simply to be with Emma trumped his fear of the pool water being too cold. He said he would follow her down to the pool after first giving Sheila a quick call.

With Emma gone, Simon phoned Sheila as he, in turn, dug deep into his rucksack in search of his own swimsuit. He panicked, thinking he had left it at the Reddys', but then found it right at the bottom, having scattered even more of his clothes across the bed than Emma had. Dreading having to fend off what he knew would be Sheila's prying questions, he was delighted when no one answered. He left as short a message as he thought he could get away with, saying simply they were now back in Harare and staying at a nice hotel, and he would call them in the morning. He felt a little guilty at not naming the hotel but he did not want anyone interrupting the short time he and Emma would have together.

When Simon reached the pool, he could see Emma was the only one in the water and she didn't notice him after he put his towel on a chair and stood and watched her for a while. She was swimming laps and he knew she would be delighted to be doing some serious exercise after nearly two weeks without. Although he could not see her whole body, he was struck by how even more athletic she looked than the few times they had been out running together in London. The muscles of her shoulders glistened in the water as she turned them over when swimming the front crawl, her long shapely legs visible as she flipped over to do back crawl and her long arms stretched out in front of her when she kick-turned at the ends of the pool.

He then bent down to wait for her before she turned again, leaned over and grabbed her hand as she touched the end. Initially surprised, she saw it was Simon, smiled and stood up; then, in a flash and hardly thinking what she was doing, she gripped his hand tightly and pulled him into the water. They both laughed and, though Simon gasped, the water was far warmer than he had feared and in no time, he was swimming alongside her.

Less of a swimmer than Emma, Simon got out of the pool first and, having earlier seen they served tea by the pool, asked Emma if she would like some.

"Yes," she said "as long as I don't have to eat any more of those sticky buns," and they both laughed.

She watched Simon as he exited the pool, one jump up from the side, not by way of the steps, and as he stood chatting to a waiter, drying himself. She had never seen him almost naked before and though she knew he was tall and slim she hadn't really seen just how well-proportioned his body was. Though he didn't have an ounce of extra flesh on him and he was not particularly muscular, he wasn't skinny either. Compared to the flabby flesh all around him, Simon looked fit, his legs firm as he lifted each in turn to rub them with his towel, ruffling his hair and beard as he dried them. She acknowledged to herself how attractive she found him and how pleasing it was simply to gaze at him.

As she saw the tea being brought to Simon's umbrella-covered table, Emma swam to the pool steps and got out. She grabbed the towel she had left hanging over the back of a nearby chair and, rubbing herself as she walked towards him, she sat down next to Simon. They chatted freely about nothing in particular: the pool; the variety and lushness of the surrounding trees, which they both agreed they were hopeless at naming; the other guests having tea, some in swimsuits like them, others dressed and talking so earnestly in groups of five or six, they reckoned they must be NGO workers in the midst of a workshop; the quality of the tea; the friendliness of the staff and how wonderful it was just to be able to sit together and simply 'be' for a change.

After Simon had drained his second cup of tea, he leaned forward and took Emma's hand in his, and said her how happy he was they were together and alone at last. Emma smiled but said nothing. Simon said he was so glad they had made the decision to come out to Zimbabwe, how unexpectedly attractive he found the country and how wonderful it would be if they could have seen more of it together. Emma smiled back but again said nothing. Simon then added how sad it was they had not made it to the Falls and never had a chance to do any game-viewing.

Emma smiled again and nodded, and then said quietly, as if talking to herself, "we are young. The Falls may be old, but they won't disappear in a hurry. They can wait."

Simon didn't know quite what Emma meant and normally when this happened he would have asked her but he sensed she was far away; it was as if she had a 'do not disturb' notice hung across her face. He had no intention of spoiling the sense of wellbeing he was feeling: he was finding just being in her presence so satisfying.

For a while they both said nothing then, noticing the shadows were lengthening and the light was changing, Emma suddenly jumped up and grabbed Simon by the hand, saying "final swim" and "race you" as she ran back to the pool and dived in. Swept up by her enthusiasm, Simon ran after her and dived in too. They swam fast but for only a couple of lengths as Simon was by then exhausted and, smiling, readily acknowledged she had won. The air was noticeably cooler than when they had stepped out of the pool only about half an hour earlier and they were chilled as they stood dripping by the edge.

"Let's go back and warm up under a hot shower," said Emma as she struggled to pull on her T-shirt over her still wet body.

"Yes," said Simon. "It will be dark soon," as he too made heavy weather of putting on his shirt before he had properly dried himself. It was already a little on the small side but now, dampened from the pool water, he was finding it even more difficult pull it across his shoulders and button it up. Emma laughed and stepped in close to help him. He felt the goose bumps rise up to the surface of his body as her fingers touched his skin, her body so close to his he could hear her breathing. He turned towards her and, smiling, said, "and it's getting colder too".

As he spoke, his eyes fell on Emma's wet T-shirt. It clung to her skin, tracking the contours of her upper body. His eyes travelled downwards from her neck and stopped when they reached her rounded breasts and the outline of her nipples below. They put on their flip-flops, picked up their keys and hurried back to their room.

On opening their door, Simon told Emma to shower first, which she did. Fortunately, she was quick so he didn't have to wait long before she opened the bathroom door and, seeing him shivering, his shirt removed, with his towel around his shoulders and the parquet floor wet around his feet, she beckoned him to come in quick. She had left the water running.

Emma was wearing a long floppy T-shirt. As they squeezed past each other, he caught the scent of her perfume.

Emma sat down on one of the two padded chairs by the French doors and, as it was now almost dark, she drew the curtains. She hadn't decided what she would do while Simon showered, though she certainly felt no urge to open her iPad and catch up on the news, her normal default when killing time. So she simply sat and, while she waited, she idly picked up and started fingering the petals of one of the hibiscus flowers in the vase in front of her, cursing mildly as she saw the pollen had spilled onto and stained her fingers.

Simon began to sing and whistle as he showered and she turned her head, wondering why the noise was so loud. She smiled as, rather typically she thought, he had forgotten to shut the bathroom door. As she looked into the steamy bathroom, she could see the outline of his body behind the shower door as he washed, his busy arms bent upwards as his singing became muffled when he washed his head, face and hair. She gazed on as he raised his arms to wash and rinse under his armpits and as he lifted first one leg then the other to swill off the suds. Finally, she could see his arms move from side to side as he soaped the rest of his torso and then held the shower head in his hand to hose himself down, front and back for a final rinse.

As Simon washed and scrubbed, sang and whistled, almost involuntarily Emma found herself rising and walking across the room and on into the bathroom. She stopped right next to the shower door where Simon's shadowy body stood beyond, holding his towel in her hands and waiting for him to pull back the door and step out. She could feel her blood beating in the arteries of her neck.

"Emma," called out Simon loudly from behind the screen. "Can you see my towel?"

"I have it here," came the reply, so close it made him jump. Simon opened the shower door to see Emma standing right there in front of him, smiling. She handed him his towel and he, clearly embarrassed, modestly turned his back to her and started to dry his front. Then, picking up her own towel from the floor where she had left it, Emma began to dry his back with soft and gentle strokes. She then laid down her towel and started to rub and massage his back with her fingers and the palms of her hands, pausing every so often to lean forward so she could caress and kiss his skin. Simon by now had frozen.

Slowly, he turned round and looked searchingly into Emma's face; momentarily, their eyes met. As they drew near each other, Emma's lips touched Simon's, so lightly at first he wondered if she was afraid to go further. Emma was hesitating, but it was because her whole body was trembling in anticipation of what was to come. Then, in an instant, Simon could feel both the pressure and warmth of her lips closing in on his. They kissed deeply and passionately, then kissed again, more deeply and knowingly now, tongue to tongue, as they felt the juices within them rising up and racing through their bodies. Feelings of warmth swept through Emma and began to engulf her and fill her rising breasts. They left the bathroom hand in hand and, with the room now in almost complete darkness, they made their way to the waiting empty bed, Emma dropping her T-shirt to the floor as they walked. She felt her body tingle.

Starting with their faces they touched and caressed each other, hungry for each other's body, hurrying almost as if they were in a race to release the pent-up feelings of months of waiting. Quivering, Emma moved her fingers deliberately but slowly over Simon's lips as his head hovered over her, scarcely visible now as the light had faded so much and so quickly. Then, sooner than Emma would have liked but later than Simon thought he could bear, and with the darkness swallowing them both whole, Emma eased Simon inside her. As she experienced the fullness of him deep within her, she felt her whole body quivering as she dug her fingers into Simon's back and felt his body rise. She held him tighter, pulled him even closer to her as she felt first his back then his thigh muscles tighten, hold taut and then relax. She loved him; she now knew it with absolute certainty. She lay still, feeling calm, at one and completely at peace.

A little while later, Emma cupped Simon's face in her hands and then began to kiss his cheeks, his ears, his eyes and his forehead gently and tenderly with her moist lips. As she did so she became aware of his heavy breathing, as his head dropped down and lay motionless on her breast, his chest rising and falling rhythmically on her stomach as he breathed. She smelt and stroked his hair and twisted it in her hands. He slept on.

In that short period before she gently woke him, Emma's thoughts turned from Simon to Robbie, but for the first time since she and Simon had met, she was gripped by a sense of finality: she was no longer haunted by her twin demons – doubt and uncertainty.

In all the months since she had first met Simon she had thought the answer to her worries about Robbie lay solely within her mind; she believed her rational self would solve the riddle of how she should let go of Robbie. She now realised the answer had not lain in her mind, nor in her body either. Rather, it lay within her whole being, the amalgam of body and soul, her physical and spiritual self, the mix of the everyday, the mundane and the transcendent, the rational and the irrational. Emma felt connected with Simon within the fullness of her whole self, not just a part of her, but the complete and entire person who was Emma Maconie. She knew she had loved Robbie powerful, intently and completely; this was the same, but also entirely different.

True, her body had prompted her to go to Simon and to unite with him in joyous physical intimacy, but in giving her body to him, and he giving his to her in return, they had woven together so much more. They had joined together their total selves; it was as if their whole beings were in harmony. Emma thought back to the music, the singing and the drumming which had so captivated them both that morning, delighting them and transporting them into another world. The uplift and pleasure they had experienced and shared then Emma now saw as adding a new layer to the bond and union she felt between herself and Simon, special as it would remind her – and remind him, too, she hoped – of the day they first made love. She felt she was at one with Simon spiritually as well as physically. Emma felt she had found the liberation she had been searching for but which till then had eluded her. She had been released from the chains of not knowing how to delink herself from Robbie. How good it felt; how good she felt!

But there was more. As she lay with Simon's head resting on her breast, Emma felt she could now engage with Robbie, but in a new and different way – through Simon. With Simon as her bedrock, she would become the woman she wanted to be, hopefully growing into both a better and a more generous woman. Then, as a stronger person, she would be able to re-engage with Robbie, sharing with him far more than she would have been able to give if she had continued to be the 'old' Emma, held back by the doubt and uncertainty of a relationship she hadn't known how to end. What's more, Emma convinced herself Robbie would understand all this because she would also have the courage to tell him the truth. In time, they would be close friends, she felt sure of that. Indeed, at that moment, Emma felt she would still love Robbie, draw from his wisdom, laugh at his jokes and share so much with him as she had done in the past, but it had to be a very different sort of love – she knew that – and it would be. Emma was cocooned in her own thoughts, and reassuring though they were, there was no knowing whether Robbie would see the future in the way she was recasting it. Yet, enclosed in her own world, it never occurred to Emma to doubt that Robbie would.

As these thoughts whirred around inside Emma's head, Simon stirred. His head was still resting on Emma's breast, and she lifted it gently and turned it towards her to help wake him. His deep blue eyes opened and as she gazed deeply into them, she gripped him tightly.

As she did so Emma knew, released from Robbie and feeling totally liberated, that she not only had to make love to Simon again but she had to do so now, at once. It was urgent. Although it had happened only a few moments ago, she saw their first coming together just now in a new light. It had been an act of purification, a cleansing of her old self from Robbie. She was not only totally free to make love to Simon with her full self now, but she needed to make love to him, to give herself to him in what would be her first act of complete self-giving.

So, as Simon turned to Emma, she responded immediately and they made love once again, as passionately and intently as before but far more slowly and deliberately as well. Just like other young couples, they were embarking on a journey of learning about each other's bodies – and Simon had so much to learn – as they renewed and went beyond their earlier desire for each other, entwining and binding their bodies together, hankering after each other, hungry to go on, ravenous for more. When they eventually separated and lay on their backs, bodies still touching, Simon was more wakeful than earlier and it was Emma's turn to be overcome with sleep. Snuggled in close to Simon, Emma rolled on to her side and placed her head on his warm and naked body, her fingers sleepily sliding through the hairs on his chest before she succumbed to sleep. As she slept, Simon stroked her forehead and gently rubbed her cheeks with the back of his hand just as she had done in the car to chase off the fly, and in the next few moments he realised his world had been transformed.

Simon felt complete simply lying close to Emma. The pains he had experienced after falling so deeply in love with her all those weeks ago were now gone: the pain of separation he continued to feel whenever they were apart and, increasingly, the pain of yearning for them to make love. But what replaced Simon's pain was as unexpected as it was different from anything he had ever experienced before. Until now, Simon had never given any thought to how he might feel from knowing – really knowing – Emma loved him as intently as he loved her. But as this totally new dimension of what it was to be 'in love' took hold of Simon, he felt himself being transported to a level of contentment he had never been even remotely aware could be reached. In everything he had read about, in everything he had thought about and in everything he had hoped of being in love, why had he never come across the feeling of pure joy he now felt in the knowledge that a woman could love him with the intensity, completeness and certainty Emma had just demonstrated she had for him? Simon was intoxicated by the nectar of Emma's love, and he willingly lost track of the time as he wallowed in the ecstatic world he had just discovered, hovering between sleep and wakefulness.

It was some time later when, jolted awake by pangs of intense hunger and realising they were lying in complete darkness, Simon gently woke Emma by asking if she knew what time it was. They guessed it was about seven, but it was later, almost eight, and so, with an evening together to look forward to, they hurriedly dressed as smartly as their rucksacks would allow. Emma managed well with her long floral skirt, her neat white blouse, silver necklace, matching earrings and a fresh dose of perfume. Simon said she looked magnificent, as he knew he should, but he really meant it. He managed khaki trousers and a long-sleeved matching shirt which both could have done with a good iron. He redeemed himself by promising Emma he would trim and smarten up his beard, overgrown from a fortnight of inattention, before they returned to bed at the end of the evening.

Emma remembered the free drinks voucher and picked it up as they went downstairs arm in arm, smiles on their faces. After a quick drink at the bar, where Simon had a Castle and Emma a rock shandy and a top-up of salted peanuts to try to fend off their food craving for a little longer, they walked across to Emmanuel's for dinner. Asking their room number, the head waiter welcomed them both warmly by their names and showed them to a quiet table for two in the corner covered with a white tablecloth, a single rose and a burning candle, all neatly laid out under the restaurant's pine-striped ceiling. With sufficiently discreet background music, the ambience was perfect to end such a memorable day, the food delicious and plentiful enough even for Simon, who was ravenous. They ate the freshly baked bread, with Simon cheekily asking for more as they began to drink their celebratory bottle of expensive South African red wine. It was a smooth and silky Pinotage from the Kanonkop wine estate in Stellenbosch which Simon ordered without letting on to Emma what it cost. Like so many other events of the day, their meal remained lodged in their memories long afterwards. For starters, Emma ordered a plate of large prawns from Mozambique, Simon mushroom soup with yet more bread. To follow, Emma had impala and Simon a butternut and leek risotto which they both enjoyed with a medley of fresh vegetables. They ended with a marbled chocolate torte which they shared and which Simon washed down with a glass of 10-year-old KWV brandy. They were back in their room just before midnight and, after Simon had undertaken the care and maintenance job on his beard he had promised, they were soon fast asleep, locked together as one after making love for the final time.

* * *

Emma was roused by the warmth of the dawning sun as it moved across her pillow and caressed her face. She instinctively started to pull the covers up over her eyes, curl up her knees and roll over as she had done for as long as she could remember. But as she did so she suddenly realised she was not home alone in London and, as her body remembered yesterday's love-making, she lay back on her pillow instead and savoured the closeness and scent of Simon's body next to hers as she waited patiently for him to wake. Beams of early morning sunlight danced over her closed eyelids as they shone through the rustling leaves of the tall eucalyptus trees just outside their window. Soon, however, her mood changed as she remembered this was their last day in Africa: by nightfall they would be gone. To fend off her melancholy, Emma snuggled in closer to Simon and tried to force herself back into that state of semi-wakefulness she had always savoured as a child.

Just before seven, they were wakened by a loud knock-knock at their door, followed soon after by another two sharp knocks; it sounded as if someone was desperate to come in. Simon jumped up, grabbed a towel to cover himself and ran across to the door to open it. In walked a white-coated man carrying a tray which Simon indicated he should leave on the table next to the window. The waiter, if that's who he was, departed as speedily as he had come in.

When the door was closed Emma emerged from under the covers where she had rapidly hidden. Still not understanding what had happened, she sat up and said, "Simon, what on earth was all that about?"

He smiled and said his mother had told him whenever they stayed at a smart hotel in Zim to be sure to order morning tea. Why? Because it always came free with the room, because it was a quaint and old-fashioned ritual giving them a glimpse of what the country had been like in the 'bad old days' and because, his mother had assured him, the tea would be exceptionally tasty. Simon then admitted when they were having their drinks at the bar the previous night he had gone to the front desk and arranged for a pot of tea to be brought to their room at seven o'clock the following morning.

"Shall I pour?' he said and Emma laughed as she said yes, admitting she actually loved having a drink in bed before getting up but rarely did so as she was always so time poor.

They drank their tea in bed and his mother had been right; it was delicious. When they had finished they snuggled down again under the bedclothes to renew, reconfirm and relish their love for each other.

A while later, Simon turned to Emma and said to her "Emma, my love…"

"… Yes?"

"I want to sing to you."

"OK," said Emma, hesitantly and curiously surprised, "then sing".

Simon folded his arms behind his head, and, taking a deep breath, he began to sing. Emma had never heard him sing before but as he began, she quickly realised what a melodious voice he had and, as she knew the words of the song he sang she knew so well, she was soon melting. This is what Simon sang:

> How to handle a woman? There's a way," said the
> wise old man…
> "A way known by ev'ry woman since the whole
> rigmarole began."
> "Do I flatter her?" I begged him answer – "Do I
> threaten or cajole or plead?
> Do I brood or play the gay romancer?"…
> Said he, smiling – "No, indeed!"
> "How to handle a woman? Mark me well, I will
> tell you, Sir…

The way to handle a woman... is to love her...
simply love her... merely love her...
Love her... Love her... Just love her!"

"Simon, that's so beautiful," said Emma when he had finished, leaning over to kiss him on his forehead. "I didn't know you were such a romantic! Sing it again for me!" And he did.

When he had finished, Emma said, "How did you know?"

"Well," said Simon "I remember you telling me you had been in a school production of *Camelot* and, knowing you, I figured you probably had the main part."

"I did," said Emma. "I was cast as the Queen, Guinevere, torn between the love of two men, Arthur and Lancelot, and those words were sung to me by Arthur. But he was one of the biggest creeps in the school who just happened to have a good voice and I grimaced, standing in front of him pretending I was enjoying it. This time, Simon, it's so different, so very different. I never knew you had such a lovely voice." Emma leaned over and ruffled his hair.

"Well," said Simon, "I practised the song quite a lot after that day on Hampstead Heath, but then I had to find the right moment to sing it to you. Then, just now, it suddenly came to me that *this* was the right moment. I know it sounds cheesy but I do – simply – love you, and I always will."

"I can't offer you much in return," replied Emma. "I suppose I could give you my rendition of *Shall I compare thee to a summer's day? Thou art more lovely and more temperate: Rough winds do shake the darling buds of May...* which I had to learn at school, but that would be even more cheesy, and, anyway, it's not May so that gets get me off that particular hook.

"But how about this from Yeats? I came across it quite by chance one day in the school library when I was at a loose end. The words got to me at once; in fact, I learned it off by heart there and then, I was probably only 17 at the time, and now I sometimes say it out loud to myself when jogging, so I don't forget it. I was never sure exactly why it got to me in the way it did, it sort of captivated me. But now perhaps I do?"

Had I the heavens' embroidered cloths,
Enwrought with golden and silver light,
The blue and the dim and the dark cloths
Of night and light and the half-light,
I would spread the cloths under your feet:
But I, being poor, have only my dreams;
I have spread my dreams under your feet;
Tread softly because you tread on my dreams.

When she had finished, it was Simon's turn to lean over and kiss Emma on her forehead and, as he did so he said "That's lovely, Em, really, really lovely!" Emma was touched and smiled back at Simon. As she did so she said to herself she was ninety-nine percent certain she had never recited that particular poem to Robbie: it wasn't his sort of thing.

But then Simon's stomach began to speak as it had the previous evening. "Time to get up or we'll miss breakfast," he said, breaking the feelings of warmth and security they were both savouring, cocooned together, lying next to each other, their bodies touching, and Emma sighed in agreement.

She announced she would take a shower first. Simon passed on the shower saying, jokingly, more water had already passed over his body in the short period they had been here than in a normal week at home. They ate a full breakfast. As they were finishing, Emma suggested a walk and Simon readily agreed. They walked out of the hotel not quite knowing where to go but, deciding to head north away from the city, turned left to go up Fifth Avenue. Once on the road they were immediately struck by the rich colours of Harare's spring trees, shrubs and flowers, so near to them as if they were lining their route, so fresh and alive in spite of months without a drop of rain. Yet this was merely the warm-up for what was to come. When they reached the next junction, between Fifth Street and Josiah Chinamano Avenue, and looked to their left, Emma gasped as she grasped Simon's arm. On either side of the street was the most breath-taking display of colour either of them had ever seen.

There, stretching out ahead of them almost as far as the eye could see, were jacaranda trees, their tops overflowing with flowers so dense the branches holding them were completely hidden, their flowers radiant in the morning sunlight. Their countless petals, clustered in panicles, were pressed so closely together they created a jungle of dazzling hues from the indigo end of the rainbow, encompassing all shades from delicate and wistful to dark and bold – deep and strong to more gentle, lighter blues, rubbing shoulders with more modest, lavender-like blossoms and streaks of light purples to create an enormous blanket of riotous colour. The trees were arranged in two neat lines on either side of the road, their old wizened and scaly-barked trunks a witness to their age. In places, the branches from the trees on one side of the street touched those from the other, to create a tunnel-like canopy of flowers stretching out ahead of them and packed together so densely the street below was in semi-permanent shadow. As the flowering season had peaked, petals had started to fall and were already accumulating on the ground below, creating the beginnings of what would soon become a thick carpet of petals, and the air was filled with the buzz of thousands of worker bees drawn to the mild, sweet honey, almost musky fragrance of the pollen, intoxicated by the sheer abundance of it all around them.

Emma said the tree trunks reminded her of David Hockney's paintings of Yorkshire trees. Simon said they looked so like the postcard of Picasso's *Cami Entre Arbres* his parents had sent him from Barcelona a year or so ago and which was still pinned to his bedroom wall. Perhaps, he now thought, that was why they chose it and had sent it to him as they would have known this street. Maybe they, too, had walked down it years ago as young lovers?

As she soaked in her surroundings, Emma linked arms with Simon and they walked along the tarmac between the avenue of trees which seemed to double as both footpath and cycle path. They were greeted by pedestrians and cyclists as they passed by, clearly uplifted like them by the wonderland they were passing through, and they gladly returned their good wishes. After walking five or six blocks, they crossed the road and walked back on the opposite side of the street, arm in arm as the young couple they had become, delighting in their love for each other as they wandered through this magical creation of nature.

Lovely as it all was, Emma and Simon both knew they needed to head back to the hotel as the morning had almost gone and they had so much to do before they flew out that evening. As they reached the hotel, Emma could already feel herself beginning to switch into a very different gear: the clock had struck midnight and the magic was fast disappearing.

She was all too well aware that, having sealed her relationship with Simon, she would now have to start grappling with the array of problems she had convinced herself yesterday morning she didn't need to think about just yet, and which, since early yesterday evening, she had forced herself to keep at bay for a little longer. But she knew she now had to face an even more challenging new reality: with her doubts about her relationship with Simon finally dealt with, the problems she had temporarily parked now needed to be confronted, and a number were going to be even more difficult to resolve. At least, she thought, trying to clutch at straws, I will no longer have to try to solve them on my own: from now on, we can work together as a team.

Within a few minutes, Simon had solved two of the most immediate problems they faced. When they reached the front desk, he asked if they could stay in their rooms till early evening, explaining they were booked on the flight to London that evening. As their rooms weren't needed until the following day, Mr Gamuchirai – who had clearly taken a liking to what he still viewed as an enigmatic couple – kindly waived the day supplement of $50 the hotel normally charged and handed them back their room key. Then, while Emma was busy gathering up their toiletries in their bathroom, Simon phoned Sheila, his main aim being to suggest a way for them to not to have to go back to the Reddys'. Sheila said she and Jessica would pack up all the things they had left at the house and she would bring them over to the Bronte for them; Jim would come to the Bronte with Sheila but instead of their all going out to the airport, he would simply pick up the 4x4, say his goodbyes at the hotel and drive home, leaving Sheila to take them to the airport in her car. When Simon told Emma the arrangements, she was both relieved and impressed, though they both knew these problems were in a different league from the ones they would need to start to work on as soon as they arrived back in England.

As Emma started to gather their things together, they started to talk seriously about how to tell their parents what they now knew, and the more they thought about it, the more they realised how complex it all was. They knew they needed to work out precisely *what* to tell their parents from everything they knew about the death of Joshua, but they soon realised they would also need to decide exactly *how* to tell them and *when* to tell them about these deeply distressing events. This was because they also had to work out how to weave into the narrative of the dreadful news they needed to convey the good news about themselves. Judging how to do this presented them with perhaps their biggest challenge because they realised that if they got either the different bad-news messages or their sequencing wrong, instead of their parents supporting them in their relationship, they could end up trying to wrench Emma and Simon apart.

They chewed this over again as they sat by the hotel pool, where they talked in earnest over lunch. However, they didn't get very far in coming up with the answers they so desperately needed, so agreed that each of them would think everything through individually as they took a swim, setting themselves the task of finding the flaws in what they had discussed while completing lengths of the pool. When they emerged, they shared a large pot of tea under the shade of a pool umbrella and re-engaged, and a more robust plan started to develop. After challenging each other's suggestions and revising them further, by the time they had drained the pot, they seemed – for now at least – to be satisfied their plan was as good as they thought it ever would be. They also knew far more clearly that much of what was going to unfold back in England would be both extremely stressful as well as deeply hurtful.

The first and most fundamental issue Emma and Simon knew they needed to address was whether they *needed* to tell their parents that Sarah's Joshua had been killed by Peter's father: they knew everything would be so much easier for themselves and their parents if they never mentioned this part of the story and simply kept quiet about who had actually killed him. But it didn't take them long to realise they couldn't live with either themselves or their parents if they hid the truth from them. They agreed concealing this crucial fact and keeping it to themselves would not only be dishonest, it would mean their entire future relationship with their parents would be based on a continuing lie, as they had already acknowledged. They both agreed, but now more clearly than ever, that everyone – Peter and Sarah in particular – had to know, had to be told the truth.

However, the more Simon and Emma discussed it, the more they realised their parents didn't need to know the complete story of what had happened straight away. And the more they thought about it, the clearer it became to them not only that they *could* manage the way they imparted the key events to their parents, but they *should* manage it. They would carefully drip-feed to their parents the truth of what had happened (without holding back on any of the crucial facts). Once they had decided this would be their strategy, their plan quickly emerged of exactly when and how they would tell their parents what they knew they had to tell them. This is what they agreed.

As soon as they landed in London tomorrow, Emma would call Sarah – she had already agreed to do this – and tell her she was coming over. Sarah would be nervous, knowing Prosper would have told her all about her mother, Alice – after all, that was one main reason Sarah had been so keen for Emma to go out to see them all in the first place. That conversation would be hard for both of them and they would need time for it to run its course. Emma would then go on to tell Sarah they knew Joshua was dead but wouldn't say anything to her about who killed him – simply that she now knew for certain he had died in battle. She would confirm this by producing the cross Mr Svosve had given her, pretty certain Sarah would immediately recognise it and crumple on seeing it. Precisely how Joshua died – and, crucially, who killed him – would not be broached with Sarah then. At their first encounter, everything Emma would tell Sarah would be true, but she would not tell her the whole truth.

As with Emma's discussion with Sarah, Simon's initial conversation with his parents would have its boundaries and limitations: it would be truthful, but it would be far from complete. He would share with his parents what Jim had told him both about his father's time in the army and his subsequent breakdown. This would also be a painful discussion as his parents would have to acknowledge to Simon that their silence about all this when he was growing up, though understandable then, now looked pretty much like deception. But he would steer well clear of the farmhouse incident and make no mention of Comrade Lightning. Simon realised even covering this ground was going to be hugely difficult but he knew his parents, like Sarah, would be expecting to have this discussion – after all, it was Cathy and Peter who had asked Jim to share with Simon what they felt they had been unable to do. So what Simon would discuss with his parents would be the very issues they had been so keen for him to have revealed in Zim.

Emma and Simon also agreed they should end these initial conversations with their respective parents on as upbeat a note as possible.

When they had recovered sufficiently from the emotional blows which they knew would inevitably come, Emma would tell Sarah and Simon would tell Peter and Cathy they had some really exciting news they wanted to share about their own relationship, but it needed to wait until all five of them – Sarah, Peter and Cathy and the two of them – could be together for them to announce it. The plan was for their initial tête-à-têtes to end with an agreement for them all to gather the following weekend, when they would share their news. They agreed this meeting should take place at Simon's home and, given the difficulties they knew would arise, they decided lunch or dinner would be far too awkward so plumped for an after-lunch start, though they had no idea when they might finish.

When all of them – Sarah, Cathy, Peter, Emma and Simon – were assembled together in the same room, and having just heard their children announcing they had pledged themselves to live their lives together, the news of how Joshua had died would be broken to Sarah, Cathy and Peter. Between them, Emma and Simon would take it in turns – as unemotionally but as accurately as possible, providing enough information as was necessary – to tell them Emma's grandfather had been killed by the father of the person she was in love with, the man she had chosen to live with for the rest of her life. Indeed, they thought they should go one step further and tell them they, Emma and Simon, had pledged themselves to each other not before but after they had learned Peter was the one who had killed Joshua. After all, that was the truth too.

What would happen next? They couldn't predict what the outcome would be and they were deeply worried. They feared for the future of their relationship, for its very survival, knowing that once they had shared the information on Joshua's killing, their future together would be determined by their parents' reactions. They knew if their parents were never able to come to terms with what had happened then there was a real risk their own relationship or their relationship with their parents would be blown apart. They knew both outcomes were possible, and they dreaded thinking of either.

Emma and Simon talked long and hard and they knew there was no other way. Their plan was logical and robust as far as it went, addressing each of their different problems step by step, one at a time. But in the end, they knew the only real solution – if there was one – was completely out of their hands. They could manage the process of telling their parents what they knew, but they couldn't either manage, or foresee, what would happen next.

It was now late in the afternoon and they had about an hour before Sheila was expected. Emma spent the next hour in the company of Simon's iPad. She had lots of emails from work colleagues, most with nods of jealousy wishing her well on her holiday. A few were more specifically work-related.

Rosemary told Emma she had succeeded in negotiating for her to do some key interviews at the upcoming party conferences. Normally she would have been excited and thrilled by the challenge, but instead she shuddered as she knew how out of touch she was. She had hardly trawled the news in the two weeks she had been away, and over the last few days had not given a single thought to what was happening in the world of news and current affairs. For the last 24 hours, her whole world had been Simon. She had so wanted to arrive back fresh, alert, confident and on top of all the day's news stories and raring to go after her African holiday, but now she felt exhausted just thinking about work on top of everything else coming home would entail.

Sheila arrived at the Bronte on time and they were soon repacked and ready to go. Emma was relieved at how sensitive Jim was in saying goodbye. He said how much he had enjoyed her staying with them (and, of course, made no mention of the war years) before wishing them both well, saying how much he was looking forward to seeing Emma again before too long. She felt he had meant it. However, she knew any future relationship she might have with Jim would depend critically on what happened next week in London. Thus, her cheery "hope so, too" to Jim's "hope to see you again soon" was filled, in her mind, with a sense of foreboding. For all the problems she had had in relating to Jim since her return from Mutoko, she never doubted his sincerity. He had been a warm and generous host and she now felt she had been quite wrong to react the way she had done when downing his whiskey to try to escape. Although she didn't know what would happen when she and Simon told Sarah and Peter about Joshua's death, she knew her future with Simon was likely to depend crucially on some sort of act of forgiveness, so, she thought, she ought to start practising forgiveness herself.

Emma asked Sheila if she wouldn't mind stopping on their way to the airport as, she explained, she had not yet bought anything for Sarah. It had completely slipped Emma's mind until she started repacking the cross and vial of sand Mr Svosve had given her and she realised she had nothing herself to give her mother. No sooner had Emma told Sheila what she was looking for than Sheila stopped the car outside a supermarket and Emma popped in. She came out with a bag of mealie meal she knew Sarah would be delighted with, as it was not South African but carried the Zimbabwean brand label and name *Red Seal Superfine*. She also bought a small bottle of Mazoe orange and a small pot of Zimbabwean-made camphor cream. Before they reached the airport, Emma had put the glass bottle in her check-in baggage, crossing her fingers she had surrounded it with sufficient clothing to prevent it from breaking.

Before they knew it, they had checked in, said their good-byes to Sheila and passed through passport control and the x-ray machines. At duty free, Simon bought a bottle of South African KWV brandy for his father and a rather cheap-looking copper plaque of the Victoria Falls for his mother as there was nothing else he could see which she would possibly like. Before they boarded their plane, they both had a final Castle to use up their loose change. As they were finishing their beers, their flight was called and in no time, they were in the seats of their Emirates flight on their way to Dubai, where, as before, they had to change planes. Exhausted and influenced by the alcohol she had drunk, Emma was asleep even before they took off, her head limp on Simon's shoulder. She was too tired even to briefly go through their plans one final time in her head before they took off as she had promised herself she would. Before the aircraft's Rolls Royce engines had started up, both Emma's mind and body had shut down.

- 13 -

Back Home

"Almost there," said Emma excitedly as their aircraft circled above the Sussex countryside before coming in to land at Gatwick. "It looks so lush down below, green as far as the eye can see, such a contrast with the dusty, dry Africa we left behind. You wouldn't think we'd only been gone two weeks, it feels like we've been away ages." Then, breathing in deeply, she added, "it's so good to be back home."

"Yes, it really is," said Simon. "And from up here England looks so quaint: picture postcard fields separated by manicured hedges. Look down there." He pointed out of the window, warming to his theme. "Neat rows of matchbox houses, each with its own miniature back garden, most with what look like toy cars lined up in rows out the front."

"Yes," said Emma, "it's all so small-town and incredibly twee!"

Simon squeezed Emma's hand and they smiled at each other, disguising the nervousness he knew they were both feeling about what lay ahead. Emma had slept well on both legs of their flight back and had eaten well, too. Simon less so. He had lost count of the number of times he had gone to the galley to raid the snack tray; nibbling had always helped him calm his nerves.

Knowing how much time they needed for their discussions with their respective parents, they had been delighted earlier when the pilot announced they were going to be at the gate at least half an hour early. But they spent so much time stacked up over the Thames estuary they missed that slot and ended up landing almost half an hour later than scheduled. Their hearts sank again when they reached the arrivals hall to see it swarming with people moving through passport control at a snail's pace as the eye-recognition e-passport machines weren't working. It was time above all else they needed because they knew their conversations would suffer from being hurried.

First Emma and then Simon called their respective parents once they were settled on the Gatwick Express, and their phones were answered at once. All three of them were at home waiting for news of their arrival, their cheery voices disguising their own nervousness. Cathy and Peter were worried Simon would think they had deceived him about Peter's health and his time in the army. Sarah was more than worried; she was frightened of how Emma would react to knowing she had deceived Emma into believing she was her mother.

Everyone was on edge, though each of them had a different set of reasons for why they were nervous.

* * *

On reaching Sarah's flat, Emma dipped her hand into her bag one last time to reassure herself she had remembered everything. As she rang the doorbell she smiled, telling herself how good it felt to be back. But when the door opened and she saw Sarah standing there in front of her, everything suddenly changed. Quite out of character, Emma burst into tears and her knees started to give way as she felt herself losing control.

As soon as she saw Emma crumple in front of her, Sarah instinctively responded. She stepped forward to stop Emma falling, then drew her close and hugged her tightly, and for a while the two of them stood together motionless on the step. Sarah had herself been nervous before Emma arrived, but now she was the more composed. She had been afraid Emma would rebuff her for her deception but as soon as she caught sight of the younger woman, Sarah could feel her self-confidence return. She knew the reason: as always happened after Emma had been away, when Sarah first looked into her eyes she felt herself reconnected to her beloved Joshua, the strong and self-assured man she might have lost but whom she had never stopped loving.

As Emma started to recover from collapsing in front of Sarah, she told herself her reaction was simply the delayed response she had suppressed from the instant Prosper had started to reveal all those things about her past she had never known as she recalled craving more than anything else during those distressing moments the comfort and security of Sarah, her mother. With her now, Emma had the safety, closeness and warmth she had so sorely missed then and, breathing in the familiar scent of the perfume Sarah always wore at the weekend, she soon recovered. Linking arms, they walked together into the house.

But when Emma thought about this incident sometime later, she recalled the strong feeling of *déjà vu* which she had had as they had hugged each other tightly on her mother's doorstep – it was more powerful than anything she recalled having ever experienced before. For a fleeting moment, it was as if she was a tiny child again, flinging her arms round a far younger Sarah and squeezing her as hard as she could. Was she reliving that moment long ago when Sarah had told Emma her real mother Alice had died? And if she was, what did her tight hugs mean? Was she trying to force Alice back from the dead and be with her again, or perhaps she was telling Sarah – trying to compel Sarah – to take Alice's place and be her mother instead? Was this Emma's very first attempt to try to manipulate the world around her? Whatever it was, it was all so vivid. The one thing she knew for sure was it had all happened before.

Sarah was the first to speak. Avoiding any reference to Emma's emotional collapse, she said cheerily, "Emma my dear, it's so good to have you back and looking so well. You must be tired. Come on into the kitchen and I'll make some tea, the kettle's already boiled. Then we can sit down together and have a really good talk."

By the time they had crossed the hallway and were in the kitchen, Emma's face was dry. As they busied themselves, Sarah continued her monologue. "You must tell me all about the family," she said. "I am dying to have news of Prosper and Emerentiana and all the children, and to know everything that happened."

As the words 'everything that happened' left her lips, Sarah's stomach tightened. She knew full well Prosper had told Emma everything – after all, she had asked him explicitly to do so. But what had Emma's reaction been? How had she taken the news then and what did she feel now? Sarah had been dreading this moment. But what she hadn't considered until now was just how she would react herself. She thought it was fear which was gripping her now, and churning her stomach. But it was more than fear. She was terrified – terrified she might lose Emma for ever.

What if Emma never would never, could never forgive her for what she had done to her? Through her silence, year after year, Sarah knew she had, in effect, lied to Emma about being her mother. The bedrock of any relationship she knew was trust. But their relationship was based on a profound act of dishonesty and then constructed on a succession of subsequent falsehoods. Over the years, deception had seeped out from the spring where trust ought to have flowed. Standing next to Emma in the kitchen as these thoughts raced through her head, Sarah forced herself to retain her smile, but she began to feel weak at the knees and grabbed hold of the countertop to steady herself.

Emma immediately sensed there was a problem and turned to look at Sarah. It was the first time Emma had looked at her properly. Expecting to see the familiar, kind and caring face she knew so well, what she saw shocked her. Sarah's face had aged by years in the two weeks Emma had been away. She looked far worse than she did when she was tired: her cheeks were drawn and her skin had the appearance of a woman far older than Emma knew her mother to be. Or had Sarah's face and features changed more gradually over these past months and Emma simply hadn't noticed, so absorbed had she been with Simon, so focused on making a success of her new job, perpetually worrying about her relationship with Robbie and, in the final few weeks, caught up with the details of their trip?

Normally, even when Sarah's face spoke tiredness, her eyes remained bright and engaging when they met Emma's. Now, though, they had a more distant, faraway look to them, their usual sparkle dulled – but by what? Was it a slight yellowish tinge, or was it just tricks played by the late afternoon sunlight as it was filtered through the kitchen's faded net curtains and fell on her skin? But Emma didn't pursue her worrying thoughts about Sarah's eyes any further because of her shock at realising what Sarah was wearing.

For Emma's arrival back from Zimbabwe, Sarah had chosen a dress Emma knew well: her long dark-grey mixed-wool one with its distinctive deep purple collar and matching cuffs and buttons. Emma knew this was not a dress of welcome; it was a dress of mourning. Sarah's purple dress was the one she always, and only, wore on Sundays in Lent and Advent, in the run-up to Easter and Christmas, periods when the church calls its followers to focus on their wrongdoings and ask God for special forgiveness. And here she was wearing the dress in late September. Emma said nothing.

She led Sarah into the sitting room and told her to sit down, returning shortly afterwards with the tea things. When Emma was seated, Sarah was again the one to speak. Delaying again for a moment or two longer the time before they would really talk, Sarah asked, "How was the journey, my dear, and how's Simon?"

"The journey was good, Ma, though long. We had to change planes in Dubai as we did coming out, and we were late landing, but we slept OK and the food was good," said Emma, who was still distracted, trying to make sense of Sarah's worrying look and her strange choice of clothes. "Simon's really well. He so enjoyed Kariba while I was staying with the family in Mutoko."

"Yes, I do miss home, of course I do," said Sarah. "But it's more the family I miss than the country. I am so used to England now, even to the cold and the darkness. The English weather seems over the years to have dulled my memories of Africa." She sighed as she spoke.

"Oh, Ma," said Emma, "you never told me how beautiful it is: the brightness; the breath-taking rocky outcrops, the dazzling colours of the birds, and most of all, the warmth of the people. So many memories: I will never forget looking up at the Milky Way the first night I was in Mutoko – you never told me how magical the sky is down there!"

As Emma spoke, Sarah felt a sudden twinge of sadness, not only because she lived so far away from home but because she had never been able to share any of this with Emma. She knew it was not the past which she needed to focus on, but what the future held for her relationship with Emma, the most precious thing she had. Sarah had listened closely to every word Emma had spoken since she had arrived. Though she knew they were only chatting, in the space of a few sentences, Emma had used the word 'Ma' three times – Sarah had counted. This, she thought, *had* to be a good omen for what was to come. Perhaps things would turn out better than, in her darker moments, she had been terrified they might?

Emma jumped up and told Sarah to remain seated while she went out to the hallway to fetch her bag. When she returned, she told Sarah to close her eyes as she placed on Sarah's lap in turn the camphor cream, then the Mazoe juice and, finally, the heavy sack of mealie meal. Emma guided

Sarah's hands to each, and Sarah felt then guessed them all correctly first time. As Sarah opened her eyes, they momentarily lit up and Emma caught a glimpse of her old self. Sarah's eyes had moistened, too, with tears of gratitude.

Right on cue, Sarah said, "So much better than the South African stuff we get at Graham's. Thank you so much my dear – my dear, dear Emma."

"My pleasure, Ma," said Emma. "There's not much, but I knew they were what you would have liked more than anything else."

Sarah said she would cook with the new mealie meal later in honour of Emma's safe return. "Washed down with Mazoe, it will be just like home!" she added and they both laughed. It was almost the last time they laughed for the rest of that day.

"Ma," said Emma quietly when they had both finished their tea, "Prosper told me everything. He, Emerentiana and I sat down together on the morning after I arrived and we spoke for a long time. It took the whole morning and a little longer for Prosper to tell me first about you and the war. Emerentiana told me how you adored Alice and how she left the convent to help you bring her up, a feisty child with a determination which would have made her father proud."

Emma then went over the story of how and why they had come to England, of Alice dying of AIDS and how Sarah had stepped in and taken her place. As Emma recounted it all back to Sarah, she spoke with love, not bitterness.

"I know," said Emma, "that after Alice passed away you stood in for Alice and in effect became the mother I had so tragically lost. In the summer of 1994 at the age of 34 – for you too had been a teenage mum when Alice was born – you ceased being my grandmother and took on the role of mother to me, loving me as much as the daughter you had lost, devoting yourself to me and my upbringing."

As Emma came to the end of her prepared speech, she turned to Sarah to gauge her reaction to what she had said. She could see the look of remoteness she had caught when they had been standing side by side in the kitchen had returned to Sarah, who was gazing through the sitting room window into the middle distance. Tears were rolling down her cheeks. Sarah was wrapped up in her own thoughts but Emma had no way of knowing precisely *what* was going through her mind. Was she thinking about Prosper and Emerentiana and the family home where she had grown up, played in as a girl and lived when she had worked as a nurse? Was she thinking of Alice? Was she thinking of Joshua, and if she was, were her thoughts focussed on their happier times together? Or was it their deaths which were now on her mind? Perhaps it was the successive waves of sadness she had had to bear, and bear alone after each of their deaths? Or was she thinking of her life here in England far away and far removed from all that had gone on in the past and which she had concealed from her, from Emma?

As Sarah sat there in silence, Emma lifted up Sarah's hands and held them in hers. They were cold. She brought them towards her and placed them tenderly on her cheeks to warm them. Sarah remained silent, her face still unreadable as she continued to stare fixedly ahead of her, her body uncharacteristically unresponsive to Emma's touch. So Emma then lovingly placed her own hands on either side of Sarah's face and gently turned Sarah's head towards her. Sarah offered no resistance, and as her head moved, Sarah's face began to change as though she was trying to force a smile, although her efforts ended in failure. She was clearly troubled by what was going through her mind. Emma saw and felt Sarah's pain and she was now hurting too.

Emma waited a few more moments, and then said, softly, "why?" Her single-word question carried with it a whole array of other questions. Emma felt she needed many answers: why had Sarah chosen, deliberately and repeatedly, to conceal the truth about herself not only while she was growing up but even after Emma had become an adult? Why were there no photographs of Alice? Why had Sarah decided she had needed to shield Emma from her past, from their past? Why had she never told Emma about her real mother and effectively lied to her by presenting herself to Emma and the rest of the world as her mother? Why had she said so little about Joshua; why had she kept him coiled up within her own heart? Why had she done all this – why, why, why?

Sarah said nothing, so what Emma said next was a far softer extension of her original question. She said, "Ma, I love you so much. Why did you conceal all this from me: why did you feel you needed to do this?"

After what seemed like an age Sarah said simply, "I'm sorry, Emma. I'm so deeply sorry for what has happened. What I did was wrong." Then, after a far shorter pause, as she was now ready to start talking, "Though I don't deserve it, I beg for your forgiveness for what I have done to you. Emma, forgive me. I have wronged you. At the time, I thought what I was doing was right; but as the years went by, I began to have my doubts, but I kept them to myself. Indeed, I kept your true identity to myself for so long I found it impossible to tell you the truth. I shouldn't have done it. That's why I asked Prosper to tell you the truth. Fortunately, he eventually agreed, as I knew he would. I know what I did was wrong. I don't deserve your forgiveness, but I ask for it now."

Emma was puzzled. When she had thought everything through in the cool light of day following the emotional turmoil which tore through her after Prosper had told her about Alice, it had never occurred to her that Sarah had ever believed what she was doing in taking on the role of her mother was a mistake. Indeed, it was obvious to Emma that Sarah had chosen to be her mother because she believed it was the right thing for her to do. What's more, it was Emma's considered view that Sarah had succeeded in creating the well-rounded, self-assured confident young Englishwoman she felt she had turned out to be, comfortable in herself and in who she was striving to become. As the means Sarah deployed were entirely legitimate and the outcome positive, Sarah's actions should be judged not just as commendable but as praiseworthy. Thus, in Emma's view, there were no grounds for Sarah to need to ask for forgiveness.

"What is it, Ma, that makes you think what you have done was so wrong?"

Sarah's reply was swift and simple. "I deceived you, Emma" she said, "and I stand before you now asking you, begging you for forgiveness for what I have done, for what I did to you." This time tears started to trickle down Sarah's checks.

"No," said Emma, sounding slightly more indignant than she had intended. "You didn't deceive me. Everything you did for me was motivated by and based on love, not deception. When Alice died, I had no mother and you jumped right in and filled that role. In doing this, you did no wrong; what you did was right – it was good. When I grew up, you loved me as a daughter: what more could I have asked for than that? My welfare was uppermost in your mind; in fact, you cared for me with such commitment and devotion your entire life revolved around me. As a family we had little and you worked and saved 24/7 for me; you always put me before yourself, just as a mother does. Your life has not been built on deception, it has been driven by love and self-sacrifice. Ma, you suffered the loss, the death, of two great loves in your life: Grandfather Joshua and the fruit of that love, Alice. Your heart died twice over but out of those two deaths a new life has sprung up and that life is me. This new life had to be nurtured. You chose to sacrifice your life, your happiness for me. That wasn't deception, it was an act of self-sacrifice!"

Sarah said nothing, so Emma tried again. She moved in a little closer to Sarah on the couch so their bodies were almost touching and said, "You kept the truth of who I am hidden neither to deceive me nor with the intention of deceiving anyone else. Just think what my life would have been like if I had gone to school believing I had no mother as well as no father. Would I have grown into the strong, self-assured person I have become? I doubt it, and this was not a risk you were prepared to take. Ma. I owe who I am today to your love for me as a mother."

Sarah still said nothing, and during this silence Emma reflected a little more on what Sarah had done for her. She looked at the dress Sarah had chosen to wear today and was disturbed by how Sarah viewed herself and her actions in the eyes of God. *But*, Emma said to herself, *Sarah is not a sinner who needs to be forgiven for serious wrongdoing; she is more a saint. Sarah's actions have been motivated by and driven by love. If, as the Bible says, God is love, what Sarah has done for me is God-like.*

Then, as ever, in her mind Emma started to play the devil's advocate. It could be argued, she thought, that when she had become an adult, Sarah ought to have told her the truth. So that was wrong? But even if she didn't do it then, she's surely done so now, hasn't she?

Terrified Emma might reject her, Sarah clearly had simply not been able herself to tell Emma the truth, which is why she had asked Prosper to do it for her. That was understandable wasn't it? After all, she had lost the two people she had loved, and she could not face losing a third; that would destroy her. Surely that was reasonable? The important thing was she had asked Prosper to tell Emma the truth, and by so doing, Sarah could not stand accused of either lying or deceiving her. Sarah was the one who had been so keen for Emma to go out to Zimbabwe; indeed, she had urged her to 'go soon'. She hadn't done this because she had wanted to hide the truth from her. On the contrary, it was proof she had been keen for Emma to know the truth and know it soon. What terrified Sarah was that on learning who she really was, Emma would simply rebuff her and walk away.

Emma now saw with great clarity only she, Emma, could give Sarah the one thing she so desperately hungered for – the reassurance that she, Emma, still loved her. Although she had listened to everything Emma had said, sitting close to her, Sarah was still afraid Emma was going to reject her. What Emma needed to do was to convey to her not merely that this wasn't ever going to happen but it had never even been a possibility. As all these thoughts whizzed around in Emma's head, she began to feel first a sense of calm then one of elation – the different bits of the puzzle seemed to be sliding into place – and so unexpectedly: what had been happening between the two of them over the past few minutes had not formed any part of what Emma had envisaged would happen today.

What Emma next said to Sarah was this. "Ma, when Prosper told me Alice was my mother and not you, I felt so strongly there and then the need to be with you. I not merely missed you not being there with me to hear the truth, but I missed you as my mother. Then, when Prosper started telling me about Joshua, the husband you loved and my real grandfather, Joshua felt to me more like the father I had lost than the grandfather I had never had. I wanted to know more about Joshua and his life, and, though perhaps I should be ashamed to say this, I felt nothing for my physical father, Kenneth Banda. And this, Ma, is the way I still feel now."

Then, slowly, Emma began to see the strain and tension ebbing from Sarah's face and she felt her mother's body starting to relax a little. A huge weight had been removed from Sarah. As she was later to tell Emma, at that moment she experienced the same sort of release as a penitent does when pouring out her serious sins to a priest in confession when he blesses her and says 'go in peace; your sins are forgiven you'.

What she said as she turned to Emma, smiled and rested the palm of her hand tenderly on Emma's cheek, almost her old self again, was simply, "Thank you, Emma. Thank you."

Then, after a pause, she added, "you are a child of God. I was frightened you would reject me, but now I know my fears were without foundation. My dear, dear Emma."

Emma, however, was by no means finished. Although it was for love that Sarah had hidden the truth about Alice from her for practically her whole life, Prosper and Emerentiana had painted a picture of a boisterous, determined and often headstrong young woman and Emma was hungry for more. She was eager to hear about Alice directly, first-hand, from Sarah.

"Ma, now you are free to do so, tell me about Alice, tell me all about her."

Then, starting slowly and hesitantly but gaining confidence as she spoke, Sarah began to unburden herself of what she had kept secret from Emma and hidden in her heart for so long. For Sarah, speaking about Alice was therapeutic: she was now able to share the closeness of the daughter she had lost, sickly and before time, with the healthy daughter who had replaced her, of both of whom she felt so proud.

Sarah spoke almost uninterrupted for an hour or more. She began when Alice was born and spoke lovingly of the highs and lows of her short life, but focused especially on the happiness she had given to all who had known her. Emma listened in awe. Never had she heard Sarah speak so lovingly of anyone; her love for Alice clearly still ran deep within her veins.

What Sarah said about Alice's final days were brief and poignant. "Her illness spread rapidly after she arrived in London, but she fought it; it was as if she was trying to hold it at bay till she could see your future was assured. I looked after her at first at home but as she became thinner, her cheeks sank into her face and her complexion became powdery. Then, as she became more and more frail, and her skin hung limply over her wasting bones and she was totally bedridden, she was moved to my hospice where, a few days later, totally exhausted, she expired. Before she sank into delirium, Alice made me promise to keep you away from her as she neared her end. I did as she told me, dear Emma, but it was hard, so very hard! I nursed her with a rota of some of my new English friends taking it in turns to look after you.

"Her end was peaceful." Sarah could see Emma was reliving Alice's death as she spoke. "She gradually faded away and was gone. It was a relief. Her body could no longer take the disease. I suffered the agony of her death and the pain of not letting the two of you be together at the end. Emma, my dear, you have no idea how difficult that was for me, no idea at all. Alice hadn't said anything to me about you and the funeral, but her funeral and burial was a quiet and quick affair and I decided not to let you come. Strangely enough, I still think that was the right decision – it was the one thing I never had any regrets about. There was too much sadness around for me to deliberately seek out and create any more. That night, after the funeral, I remember cradling you in my arms and you said, *Ma, don't cry*, and I knew from that time on that I needed to be strong – strong for you.

"She is buried in an unmarked grave in the big cemetery opposite St Mary's. As is our custom, I visited the grave a number of times in the first year after she died and then with a few Zimbabwean friends we had a service round the grave on the first anniversary of her death – you know we call it *kurova guva*, literally 'the beating of the grave'. Since then I have rarely visited the place, but I did so just a couple of weeks ago before you left for Zim to gather up some of the soil from the surrounds for you to take out. Now you know all about Alice, we shall go to the grave together; we will go there soon. Now is the right time. It will then be as she would have wanted it to be."

"Yes, I should like that, Ma," said Emma soberly, "I should like that very much."

It was then that Emma told Sarah she had given the soil to Prosper, and he had scattered it over the family burial ground.

Over the hour or so Sarah had spoken to her so freely about Alice, Emma had listened to every word, and, the more she listened, the more aware she became of her own emotions. As Sarah spoke about the mother she had no memory of, Emma felt little. As the warmth and depth of feelings Sarah had had for Alice came across so vividly, they were almost tangible as she spoke, Emma felt strangely distant from both Alice and from the emotional ties which had clearly bound them together when Emma was a baby and toddler. Emma knew the person Sarah was speaking to her about with such affection was her mother, Emma's flesh and blood, but her heart couldn't engage with what she heard. To Emma, Alice seemed to be a character from a fairy tale or the heroine in a film, coming alive only in the make-believe pages of a book or the images projected onto the silver screen. Sarah was the story-teller, the film-maker without whom Alice could never, would never, be brought to life. Emma felt ashamed at her lack of feeling, and she didn't share any of this with Sarah.

It was beginning to grow dark when Sarah had emptied herself of what she had kept stored away about Alice and they both agreed it was time to eat. They went back to the kitchen and together cooked, using some of Emma's mealie-meal which they added to the stew Sarah had prepared earlier. As they ate, Emma spoke of the warmth she felt around the family fireplace in Mutoko and, as she remembered them, Sarah added to her stories about village life.

When they had finished their supper, Emma cleared away the dishes, telling Sarah to 'just stay put' as there was more she needed to share with her about what she had learned in Zimbabwe. Feeling satisfied after a good supper, relieved her relationship with Emma had survived Prosper's revelations and having cheered herself up further with positive stories about home and Alice, Sarah was relaxed and smiling, almost like her old self, and anticipating good news. But within moments, as Emma began to tell her about Joshua's confirmed death, her demeanour was to change beyond all recognition.

"There is one more thing I learned in Zim, Ma," began Emma, "which I need to share with you. Nothing we have discussed so far, Ma, is new to you – you already knew everything Prosper and Emerentiana told me about myself and Alice. But what I am about to tell you will be as new to you as it was to me when I found out about it just a few days ago.

"What I am now going to tell you about, Ma, concerns my grandfather Joshua Makumbe."

Sarah sat up, immediately attentive but also puzzled. "But how can you know anything about my Joshua? None of us has seen him since he disappeared so long ago, even before Alice was born, and that was some 40 years ago. We know he never came back, but we never knew what happened to him."

Then Emma gently began to tell Sarah about their trip to Mhondoro, who Mr Svosve was, how they had managed to track him down and why he was the key to knowing what happened to Joshua all those years ago. She was scrupulously careful to make no mention of the soldiers who had fought with and killed her grandfather.

She talked at length about Mr Svosve, saying he had been a *mujiba* and had known Joshua for some months before he had died. She explained how Mr Svosve had effectively been a witness at that final attack which took place at a farmhouse near Mhondoro so he could confirm Joshua had been killed, adding that he was known as a charismatic commander and an inspiring leader. Emma said Mr Svosve had told her not only we, his family, but everyone should be deeply proud of him and all he had done.

As she spoke, Emma sensed Sarah wanted to know more about Joshua's death and less about his heroism. Emma was surprised how calmly Sarah took the news he had been killed: she simply sat there quietly listening as Emma told her Joshua was dead, her face registering no new emotion. As Emma was to learn, this was because Sarah had heard so many stories before about Joshua's death, and this seemed to be simply one more tale which could not be substantiated to be added to the list. Why should she place more weight on what Emma was telling her now than on the stories she had heard far closer to the time when Joshua had disappeared? After all, to Emma this was merely a distant war which took place long ago in a far-off land.

So, wearily, Sarah said to her, "Dear Emma, I am glad you found people who were still talking about my dear Joshua; at least it means he is still known for what he did. But unless you can provide me with proof, with the evidence he died where and when you were told he did, then sadly I will have to continue with the 'open mourning' I have now got so used to. I remain as deeply saddened as I always have been from the day I last saw him, but I remain no more convinced about the certainty of his death than I have been since the war ended and he never came home."

"Ma," said Emma, "I've got something to show you." She dug her hand deep into her bag and brought out a folded white cotton handkerchief which she placed unopened on her lap. She then began slowly to unfold the hanky to reveal the small wooden carved cross which Mr Svosve had given her.

Sarah recognised the cross at once. There were no ifs or buts: she knew what it was the instant she saw it. Even before Emma had finished unfolding the hanky, she heard the sudden inward rush of air into Sarah's lungs as she gasped. This was followed by the outflow of a succession of Shona words, first of exclamation and amazement and then of total shock. She began by saying quietly *yowee, yowee, yowee* (my goodness), followed by the word *i-chokwadi* (it is true). Then, in a shrill, high-pitched voice which grew ever louder as she repeated the word, Sarah exclaimed *maiwe, maiwe, maiwe, maiwe* (Oh-my-God, literally, 'mother'). Emma needed no further proof. Mr Svosve had been right. She now knew for certain everything he had told Simon and herself was true.

Then Emma heard a deep groaning, a sort of gurgling or wailing sound emerging from the back of Sarah's throat as if it had travelled up from the depths of her belly. She turned to look at Sarah, and, just as she did so, she saw Sarah bang her back forcefully against the sofa, then twist her arms together as she tossed back her head and raised her legs out in front of her, locking them straight at the knees. She was visibly shaking and Emma thought she was having a fit. Emma tried to calm her down, to stop the shaking and the terrible wailing noises she was now uttering but nothing she did seemed to make any difference.

Emma was scared; she had never seen Sarah so distraught. She was not merely unresponsive but seemingly far away in another world. Before they had eaten, Emma had witnessed Sarah deeply upset, frightened and in panic as she feared Emma was going to reject her for concealing her true identity from her. But this was a different league of emotional meltdown. Sarah's body was being torn apart by waves of misery and despair so intense they seemed too much to bear; it was as if she was possessed.

Eventually Sarah stopped shaking and punishing her body but the gurgling and wailing continued a while longer, accompanied now by an outpouring of tears which streamed down her cheeks, though she didn't seem to notice. She wasn't even aware when Emma picked up the white handkerchief and started to try to dry her face.

A little while later, the groans started to turn into words and Emma could clearly make out Sarah saying again and again, "Joshua, Joshua, Va-

Makumbe, Va-Makumbe, Joshua, Joshua, *madiwa, madiwa, madiwa* ...
(my dearest)."

Slowly, it began to dawn on Emma what was happening. She had been
to a number of Zimbabwean funerals in London where some of the women,
those closest to the deceased, had thrown fits, and moaned and groaned
inconsolably. It seemed to Emma what Sarah was doing now was going
through the process of ritual mourning she had never felt able to undertake
before. Now Sarah had the proof she had never had and a part of her had
always hungered for, she was – finally – able to release the pent-up
emotions inside her which until just then she had not been able to let loose.

As she realised what was happening, Emma no longer felt so
frightened. What she was witnessing was Sarah going through a rite of
passage: her whole being – her body and soul, her conscious and
unconscious self – was being cleansed and purified as at last she could come
to terms with and accept the fact of Joshua's death. Emma's assessment of
Sarah's reaction to what she had told her and shown her were soon
confirmed by Sarah herself. Now lying still, limp and exhausted on the sofa
a good half hour after she first set eyes on the wooden cross, Sarah simply
said "*zvapera*."

And, as if to confirm the finality of what she had said – 'it is finished'
– she leaned over to Emma, picked up the cross and lovingly cupping it in
her hands, caressed it, then brought it up to her lips and kissed it.

She then said quietly, as much to herself as to Emma "I made it for
him; I carved it with my own hands in the months after he went over to
Mozambique. He promised to come back, but he did so only once after he
had joined the guerrilla army. We had one last night together. I will never
forget it. But for that night, neither Alice nor you would have been born.

"He came so unexpectedly. It was dark and I had been asleep but I was
woken by a rustling sound, and as soon as I heard his voice call out 'Sarah',
I knew it was him." She was reliving the last time she had been with Joshua,
more than 40 years ago and six thousand miles away. "As he drew close
and kissed me, the smoke from weeks of sleeping in the kitchens of
villagers who had hidden him hung on his clothes and I can smell him now.
He told me the rest of his unit was three or four miles away and he had to
be with them again before sunrise. He talked and talked, skipping over the
hardships they had to endure, to tell me with pride about the engagements
they had had with the enemy. I remember the way he emphasised the words
'trust' and 'loyalty' as the key ingredients of their successes. Though I had
missed him terribly, my heart filled with pride as he spoke. Then he stopped
talking and asked me if I was ready and I said yes, knowing full well what
he meant. I will never forget the joy I felt as we shared what turned out to
be both the first and last moments of intimacy together.

"Joshua was already awake and alert, lying beside me when I woke: it
was still pitch black. I sensed he had been awake a long time, or perhaps he

had never slept? Though he said nothing, we both knew he was about to go, but I told him to wait. Then I took the cross from the cloth wrapped under my pillow, where I always kept it, and placed it in his hand. He felt it and I lit a candle so he could see it: I will never forget him running his long fingers across one side of the cross before he turned it over to caress the other side of the wood.

"'You carved this for me yourself, isn't it?' he asked me, though he knew the answer. 'It's beautiful,' he told me and I said, 'yes, it is.' I then tied it round his neck and as I did so I felt his chest rising and falling next to mine as I secured it at the back. He kissed the cross then he kissed me, saying, 'With this cross around my neck, you will accompany me, Sarah, wherever fate takes me until I return home to you. Pray for me, my dear one, as I will pray for you; let us pray for the safety of each other. God has been good to give us each other and our love, though new, already runs deep in our veins. You shall bear many children, dear Sarah, and they shall grow up free in the new country I have pledged to fight for and help create. I will wear your cross – our cross – next to my heart until I come home once this dreadful war is over.'

"I then watched Joshua in the flickering candlelight as he put on his boots and quietly picked up his AK47. He then grabbed my two arms firmly, like in a wrist-lock, but also tenderly as a mother would hold a child's arms, and for a moment he held them as I gazed into his eyes one last time. His eyes searched mine as if he was hunting for meaning in the look I gave him as I struggled to keep back my tears and convey a message of hope and optimism. Then he was gone. The last thing I remember was his thrusting a few crusts of bread into his trouser pockets as he went out. He left as silently as he had come and all of a sudden, he was no longer there. I hardly heard his footsteps once he was outside. He had been with me just a few hours, five or six at the most. I sat there motionless til the sun rose, reliving and savouring every moment of our being together. He had said he would return and I solemnly promised to myself I would wait for him until he did, even forever. There and then, I knew if he didn't return, I could love no other man. Joshua was everything I had ever hoped for, everything I had ever wished for. There could be no other."

Then, cupping the cross in her hand, Sarah emerged from her memories, and, turning to Emma, she said, "Now it's my turn to keep Joshua's cross safely round my neck and close to my heart. I will keep it until the time comes for me to join him. And when that time comes, my dear Emma, I shall pass our cross on to you for you to keep, to keep in remembrance of him and me, to keep in memory of us both."

Sarah suddenly sat up and said, her voice strong and her mind focused, "but where is he buried? You didn't tell me where they laid him to rest."

Emma then took hold of Sarah's hand and told her most of what Mr Svosve had recounted to her about the end, explaining how Mr Svosve had taken some of the sandy soil from the spot where they had buried him. However, she didn't share Mr Svosve's theory that Joshua's body had almost certainly been eaten by wild animals and finished off by vultures.

"And the soil, where's the sandy soil he took from the grave, what happened to it?" said Sarah insistently.

"I have it right here, Ma," said Emma as she dug her hand into her bag one last time. "Mr Svosve gave it to me to give to you. He had kept it and the cross safely all these years. Indeed, he had built a sort of shrine to keep them in. He said he had been waiting all this time to return them to the family.

"And Ma, do you know how Mr Svosve knew who I was, and why he gave them to me, why he trusted me?"

"Yes," said Sarah as she looked lovingly across at Emma and gently touched her cheek with the open palm of her hand. "Yes, I know, you don't need to tell me. It is your eyes, dear Emma. You have his eyes. And that's also why I know this Mr Svosve of yours was telling you the truth. Anyone could have stumbled across the cross and gathered up some sandy soil, but only those who knew Joshua and saw you would know. As soon as Mr Svosve saw your eyes he would have seen Joshua again and he would then have known he had found the person he needed to give the cross to, and the soil from his grave.

"Alice didn't, you know," she added, almost casually. "Joshua's eyes were held back for a generation and were then given to you."

Sarah took the vial with the sandy soil in it from Emma and clasped it tightly in her hands with the cross, and then, gazing out into what had now become the early darkness of a September night, she said "We'll go together and pour this sand over Alice's grave."

"Yes, Ma," said Emma. "We shall."

It was well after dark when Emma left her mother's flat and their time together ended with Emma telling Sarah she had exciting news to share about Simon and herself, but it would have to wait until the following weekend. She explained the two of them would meet up with Simon and his parents at his home and what they had to tell everyone would be announced when they were all together. Sarah was delighted and in their last few moments together her excitement grew so that, as Emma had hoped, Sarah was in buoyant mood when they said their goodbyes. As she walked up Moat Crescent and turned to wave to her mother one last time, Emma could see Sarah still had a smile on her face. She felt pleased with this part of her day's work: Sarah had been on two traumatic and troubling journeys but she had now returned with the Makoni-Maconie family bonds still very much intact.

As agreed, she called Simon when walking home and he answered at once. He was sitting in a quiet corner of The Mossy Well on Muswell Hill Broadway, sipping what was by now an almost empty glass of John Smith's and waiting for Emma's call. He thought sitting in the pub opposite *Jenny's* where they first really met would bring him comfort and, in some ways, it had, as he chewed over what had just happened at home and what it all meant for next weekend. As soon as Simon's phone started ringing and he saw who it was, he left the pub and turned to walk down Dukes Lane as it was quieter there and they needed to talk in private.

* * *

Simon's heartbeat quickened as he rang the doorbell at Wellfield Road, Muswell Hill: he had deliberately left his keys at home, fearing he would only lose them if he took them to Zimbabwe. Simon guessed Sheila must have called Cathy to tell her Jim had had the conversation, and as soon as his mother opened the front door, he knew he had been right for both his parents were on edge. His mother was wearing that tortured look she put on to try to conceal embarrassment, while, quite out of character, his father stepped forward to fumble a pre-prepared, but what turned out to be an extremely awkward, hug. Beyond a handshake Peter and Simon were now never physical. They sensed he was edgy too. With confirmation the two sisters had been in touch, Simon's mind quickly adjusted not so much to the substance of what he was going to say to his parents, but the manner in which he had planned to present it.

The underlying unease between them continued to be concealed by their cheerful words of greeting; this Cathy cut short by hurrying them on to the sitting room, announcing she would make tea. As Simon had predicted, she instructed them not to start talking until she was with them. She soon joined them, arriving with a homemade cake, a colossal Victoria sponge which she had baked for the occasion, on the tea-tray and sat down. Cathy and Peter looked across at Simon and, without them saying anything, he knew this was his cue to begin. He started by sharing a few pleasantries about Zimbabwe, saying how grateful he was to them both for encouraging him to go, how he loved the country and how much he had enjoyed getting to know Jim and Sheila. Peter offered a strained smile and said nothing but Cathy, clearly relieved to have her boy back, told him how well he looked. Simon then handed his father the brandy which he was clearly delighted with, the warmth of his smile easing the tension just a little. His mother graciously accepted the copper plaque but immediately Simon could tell, as he had also predicted, she didn't really like it.

Cathy then pressed Simon to share more impressions of the country and he told them how surprised he was Harare looked so modern, how lovely the Reddys' home was and what generous hosts they had been. Then, realising he hadn't yet mentioned Emma, he said how well she had got on with both Jim and Sheila, filtering out the moments when that hadn't been true. He tried to joke about the novelty of living with servants but quickly lost track of the point he was trying to make and hurried on to tell them all about their visit to Nazareth House and how he had vaguely remembered the place. Cathy was delighted, and Simon's confidence rose a little more from the warm smile she gave him. Then, taking a deep breath, he started to talk about his trip to Kariba and felt his heart beating faster again as he told his parents first how beautiful the lake and surroundings were and then how well he and Jim had bonded, knowing this was simply the prelude to his having to move on to very difficult territory. As he and Emma had agreed, Simon tried to make his first substantial remarks come across as comforting and reassuring.

"As you know, Dad, Jim told me about how you two became friends and the time you had been in the army together. He said you had been keen for him to share all this with me."

Peter sat up, forcing a smile, and said, "Yes I did, and I'm glad he did."

Simon then set off talking about his father's commitment and dedication, his bravery and his leadership skills, recounting his successes in tracking down different guerrilla units and listing the awards and medals he had received in recognition of all he had done. He finished by saying simply, "Dad, I am so proud of you for what you did."

When Simon had rehearsed all this, he hadn't given any thought to what he would be feeling in talking so directly to his father – which he rarely – about such sensitive matters. But as he finished, tears started to well up behind his eyes and he realised he really meant what he had just said. However, he knew he had far more to say and hurried on before either Peter or Cathy could butt in. He needn't have been concerned because, for now, all they wanted to do was to hear more.

"As you know, Jim also told me about your illness, Dad. My God, it sounded so terrible, you suffered such a lot. He went on to explain that if you had told us about your illness you might never have got better. But you did: the healing process you went through worked. So, Dad –and it may surprise you to hear this – I see the fact Jane and I knew nothing about the terrible impact the war had on you as something really positive. It is clear evidence, proof if you will, what you did was right. So, this is another thing I feel immensely proud of you about."

There! He had said it! Simon knew bits of what he had said had sounded formulaic and not everything he had said had come across as well as he had hoped it would. To try to relieve the tension a little, Simon then walked across to the tea-tray, poured himself a second cup of tea and helped himself to a second piece of cake but, as he started to eat, he knew this had been a mistake. His parents had hardly moved, so he put his cup down and held back on biting into the cake.

For a while after this happened no one moved. Then, as Simon had expected, his mother was the first to break the silence.

"It was very hard for us," said Cathy as she glanced across at Peter, whose eyes were cast downwards to the floor, his face expressionless and his head stoically still. His mother had only mouthed five words, but Simon already knew they, like him, had rehearsed what they were about to say.

"Your father was very ill," she continued. "You have no idea what he had to endure. Then, for a long time after he had begun to recover, we remained terrified he would have a major relapse, such was the severity and seriousness of his condition." She hadn't used the word 'breakdown' or 'disorder' and Simon wondered whether this had been deliberate.

"If your father was to live the full life he deserved, he simply had to draw a line under the events which had led to his illness and that meant steering clear of any discussion not only of his illness but of the war years themselves," said Cathy, sounding as wooden as Simon had, but with earnestness, if not passion, in her voice.

"We were frightened for you and Jane, Simon. There was a real possibility if either of you two children had ever pressed your father to tell you in detail what he had done in the war, especially when you were younger, it would have risked triggering the return of the illness, and that would have been too ghastly to contemplate. It was bad enough for your father to have suffered. We could not allow you to suffer on top of and because of everything he went through." Simon could almost feel the stresses and strains her father's illness had had on his mother and it made him feel even smaller as he acknowledged to himself he hadn't given any thought to how all this had affected her.

Cathy explained how their move to the UK helped enormously because there were far fewer times when Dad's past was likely to be brought up in conversation. She said most of their English friends knew little about Zimbabwe's pre-independence war and weren't interested in it, and they deliberately avoided seeking out old army friends who had moved to London. Simon reflected on how isolating this must also have been for them: there was so much they had sacrificed when they emigrated he was only now beginning to understand,

She then told Simon how they had come to buy the family home. "By the time we arrived in London with you as a toddler, Simon, and Jane not yet born, Dad's attacks were rare, but we were always afraid they might come back. Fearful of how terrified you would have been even to hear your father's screams, never mind see him when he had a turn, we searched for ages until we found a house whose design we thought would best be able to protect you from the traumas of Dad's possible attacks. You know our bedroom is down the far end of the corridor at the opposite end of the house to Jane's room and yours? Well, that was deliberate. What's more, when we moved in, besides having the house redecorated we had our bedroom and both our offices totally sound-proofed – walls, floor, ceiling and door, the lot, and they put in double-glazing – so you would never hear anything if your father ever had an attack in his sleep or, God forbid, while working at his desk. There was only one occasion when he did. It happened the night we came back from Christmas at your Uncle George's at Catshead and he was prompted, we were pretty sure, by some insanely insensitive remarks George made in front of you two children just as we were leaving.

"You know how he is, Simon," she added, looking across at him. "Well, the noise that night was horrific and lasted for such a long time and I was so involved with looking after your father I quite forgot about you children. So when you and Jane came down to breakfast the next morning, your father and I sat there terrified, waiting for you to ask us what that screaming in the night was about, but fortunately you never did."

"You're right," said Simon quietly, "I never knew."

"It was only later," said Cathy, "that we understood the full cost to the family of keeping everything secret and hidden from you. In deciding not to tell you and Jane about your father's illness we believed we had done the right thing. But then, over the years, gradually at first, it started to look so very different until suddenly your father said to me one day we had been living a lie. And he was right, we had been. The more we continued to say nothing the more dishonest we felt we were being, but what could we do, what should we have done? I was still afraid of what telling the truth would do to your father, Simon. Indeed, I still am."

Simon could see his mother was almost in tears now and he felt wretched. He knew his parents to be honest and truthful people – almost to a fault – so listening to her describing the dilemma they faced pained him deeply.

What his mother said next came as a surprise to Simon even though it was totally consistent with the earlier comment he had made about his father. "I want you to know, Simon," she said, "neither your father nor I have ever been ashamed of what he did during the war. As you have rightly said – and I am so pleased you did – your father *was* a hero, but to me he *still is* a hero, as I hope he still is to you too. You and Jane have every reason to be proud of what your father did. I always have been and I always will be." Although Simon couldn't put his finger on it, this defence of his father sounded odd, almost strange, when it was his mother who was defending him.

Cathy was about to say more, but Peter was stirring. From decades of watching for the signals, she knew he wanted to speak and so she immediately stopped talking. Simon's father began in a rather matter of fact manner, saying he thought the best way to deal with what had by now become a huge problem for the two of them was to urge him to go out to Zim because Jim would not only be willing to help but he would be the only person who really could fill Simon in about his past. What he left unsaid confirmed what his mother had said earlier: his father felt he still didn't have the inner resources to do this himself. As Peter then started to open up in a way Simon had never seen him do before, it was Simon's turn not to move a muscle.

"You have no idea how terrifying it all was," said Peter. "It began with the nightmares, which became more intense and more frequent. They started with the noise of automatic gunfire, the deep thud-thud-thud of helicopter blades, the blasts of landmines going off and above all the shouting which grew ever louder and louder.

"I heard screams right next to me, right here in my ear," he said, pointing. "They were so deafening I felt my eardrums would pierce, so I screamed to try to force them to stop. But instead of stopping, the noise grew even louder. Chaotic sounds of noise and screaming roared around my head; they kept on coming: it was as if they were hunting me down. They taunted and haunted me, and I became perpetually agitated when they stopped as I waited for the explosions in my head to start up all over again. I felt I was becoming mad: I started to have nightmares about the nightmares.

"If that wasn't bad enough, there was the trembling. It began in my feet, which began to quiver. As I tried to control the quivering, my feet started to shake, then my lower legs and as the shaking continued, it felt as if someone was controlling my movements, not me. The shaking sensation then moved up the top and back of my legs and spread to the rest of my body. I tensed my back to try to stop myself shaking all over, but it just continued. I threw my back against the mattress as hard as I could to try it stop it, but I couldn't. Nothing worked. At first these shaking fits happened only at night but then, soon after I began to fear they would occur during the day, they did. When I felt a day-attack coming, I quickly lay down on the floor to try to cope better with what I knew was coming, but I couldn't, and in many ways these day-attacks were worse than the night-time ones. I'll never forget the noise of my head banging against the floorboards. A few weeks after these day-attacks started, they moved me to hospital. They gave me a succession of different drugs which started to play tricks with my memory so at times I didn't know what was happening and whether I was having day-attacks or night-attacks. For days on end, my life became little more than a blur.

"The noise and the shaking weren't half of it. One of the reasons I had to go into hospital was I became disorientated: even before the drugs, my mind had started to muddle present-day events with past events. I started to lose not just my sense but my understanding of reality. This in turn induced feelings of terror. These panic attacks were so much worse than the physical attacks because of their intensity and because when they were happening it seemed they would never end."

As his father was speaking, Simon could see a change come over him. Though he had never seen it before, Simon recognised what it was: the face of fear. The skin on his father's cheeks had tightened and grown paler, losing much of its colour. What was even more disturbing was his eyeballs looked as if they had sunk back into their sockets, not by much but enough to make his whole face appear disfigured. As he noticed what was happening, Simon began to understand why his parents had kept his father's PTSD – for that's what it was – hidden from Jane and himself, and he knew he hadn't seen anything like the worst.

As if to confirm what Simon was thinking, Peter said, "Constant fear is the worst thing that can take hold of a human being. You can deal with even the most intense fear if you can see it has an end-point." Simon was suddenly back at Mr Svosve's, seeing his father in the corridor as Comrade Lightning raised his gun to shoot.

"But if you believe, when you believe, what is terrifying will go on and on for ever and ever," said Peter, "then there is only one word for it: then you know you are in hell."

Simon saw Peter shudder. He looked across at his mother, who was watching his father closely. She suddenly jumped up, rushed across to him and cradled him lovingly in her arms. She had clearly done this many times before and knew instinctively how to calm him down. Eventually she did – her hands gently stroking his head, the tips of her fingers tenderly tracing out lines across the top of his skull before caressing the roots of his whitening hair and massaging his temples.

As his mother was busy with her hands, Simon reflected back to Kariba. He knew he had been shaken by what Jim had told him, but now he realised he had absorbed everything in a very abstract sort of way, as if the description of his father's illness had sanitised him from the reality of it all. But now, as his father had opened up to him and delved a little into how he had been affected by the breakdown, he began to get a real sense of what his father had been through, and his mother too. He not only felt a little unnerved but a little frightened.

His mother's soothing fingers and comforting words worked their magic and soon his father appeared to have recovered. He looked across at Simon as if to say he had finished recounting what he had had to say. Then, almost without thinking, Simon stood up and walked over to his father. As he drew close, Peter stood up and looked at Simon lovingly, his body asking for, craving, contact with his son's. Simon then gave him the longest and tightest of hugs he ever remembered giving him, even as a small boy, and Peter replied in kind, ending with a kiss on Simon's cheek. Even before Peter let out a quiet sob, Simon knew he was in tears.

As they separated, Simon said he saw it as his responsibility to break the news to Jane. It came across almost as an announcement, and both his parents were clearly relieved. "I had hoped you would say that,' said his mother. "Thank you, Simon, you're a strong person and I thought I could rely on you."

When they had all sat down again, the tension rapidly subsided. Cathy topped up their cups, and as they drank, Peter looked across at his son, and, fully himself again, said, "Simon, you remember when you told me you wanted to stop being an accountant, and I came across as negative and unsupportive?" Simon nodded, uncertain where this was leading.

"You know why I said what I did; after all, accountancy has been an intricate part of our identity as male Robertsons for generations. But then, while you were away these past two weeks and I was looking back at my life and the mess I had been in because of my illness, I thought, here is my son, my own flesh and blood, wanting to assist people back onto the path of a meaningful and fulfilling life as others have so ably and professionally helped me to do. And it struck me how wonderful it would be to have a son like that. So, Simon, I want you to know you have my blessing and my full support to move into your new chosen career, mixing medicine with mental health – that is, if you still want to and think it will be for the best. Given all this, Simon, I want to apologise to you for what I said: I am sorry for how I first reacted."

For Simon, what had happened was monumental. Before Peter had said this, even though they had just hugged in a way they had never done before, if Simon was honest he would have to admit to himself he never really *felt* he had had a father. Now he knew – for certain – he did. But all he could say as he fought back his tears was, "Thanks, Dad, thank you so much."

All too soon the magic was broken by Cathy, who had been itching to know more about why Simon and Emma had never made it to the Victoria Falls. No longer sensing she had to pretend she and her sister had not spoken, she said, "Sheila told me you spent the last few days at a mission station – in the Mhondoro area I think she said – rather than going to the Falls. Why the sudden change of plans, Simon?"

Simon knew this seemingly innocuous question had moved them into very dangerous territory. Although he and Emma had made no mention to Jim and Sheila of the link between Joshua's death and Peter and Jim's final farmhouse battle, Simon knew it would only take one slip of the tongue for Peter to make the connection. He didn't think Sheila would have shared everything she knew with Cathy – they had always had an uneasy rather than close, sisterly relationship – so he expected he could tell her things about their visit she didn't know about: that should temper her curiosity, but he knew he had to be careful. There was so much he knew he mustn't share – at least for now. So, treading a fine line between telling the truth and saying as little as he thought he could get away with, Simon replied.

"Well, Ma, it's all pretty simple to explain," he began, trying to sound quite matter-of-fact. "When Emma was staying with her family in Mutoko, she learned things about her grandfather which her mother had never told her. Like so many others, he had been a guerrilla fighter and had never returned home after the war. Emma's uncle Prosper told Emma he may have been killed in the area around St Michael's in Mhondoro, but this had never been confirmed. On learning this, Emma really felt she had to try to find out more; she strongly believed she owed this to Sarah, and when she told me she said she wanted to go there to try to resolve the family mystery. I thought she was right to do so, and I fully supported her. Getting to the bottom of that mystery, so important to Emma's family, was far more important than our going to the Falls simply on a holiday, and I know if we hadn't gone and hadn't tried, Emma would always have blamed herself. When Emma explained the situation on her return from Mutoko, Sheila could not have been more helpful. Actually, we could never have got there without her help."

Then Simon ran through what had happened as quickly as he thought he could get away with. He explained a little of how Sheila had managed to fix up their visit and a little of how the priest at St Michael's, Father Ambrose, had helped them. He told them from the outset Ambrose had cautioned them about resolving the mystery of Emma's grandfather's death both because it had happened so long ago and because levels of political intimidation were still so high that people were afraid to talk, and how surprised they were to discover how right Father Ambrose had been on both counts.

Simon then turned to his father and said, "What's more, Dad, we were told – and you will know this far better than I do – the guerrilla soldiers took on war names which made it even more difficult to get to the truth." Then, to distance himself even further from those events, he added, "in any case it was your war, Dad, and not ours."

Simon had judged things correctly. Pushing the discussion onto his father effectively killed the discussion because Peter was clearly reluctant to ask any further questions. He had no wish either to talk names or to stray anywhere close to reliving past battles.

"Yes, Simon," he said. "So many people died without their relatives knowing where they had fallen. Most were buried in shallow unmarked graves, only to be eaten shortly afterwards by wild animals, making it even more difficult to know precisely not only when and where people died but even who had died. It was all so desperately sad."

Simon and his mother glanced across at Peter but, thankfully, he seemed to be fully in control of himself, and Simon had the opening he had hoped he would be given to round things off by saying, 'Yes, Dad, we found a man who claimed to have been present at the death of Emma's grandfather and after some pretty intense questioning by Emma we were sure he had been telling the truth. But, just like you said, he told us the body had almost certainly been eaten by wild animals, so that was really the end of it. We had found what we had come for. Emma was of course sad but she was pretty sure she had resolved the family mystery."

The exchange had made Cathy uneasy but she couldn't quite put her finger on why. She wanted to ask Simon more questions about their visit to Mhondoro, but knew that for Peter's sake she couldn't, at least for now. So, with some reluctance, she switched to the other matter uppermost in her mind. "And how is Emma, Simon? You have hardly told us anything about her."

Simon knew what she was really asking was the state of their relationship and he was relieved to be able to move onto safer ground and happy to answer the question she hadn't asked.

"I hope you can wait just a little longer, Ma," he said, smiling broadly. "Because next weekend Emma and I would like to invite her mother, Sarah, over here. We want Sarah to be in the same room as the two of you when Emma and I make an announcement, when we share with you something, some things which require us all to be together for both the telling and the hearing."

Simon's eyes were fixed on his mother's face as he spoke. It gave him the reassurance he needed. As he had hoped, Cathy had interpreted his 'something, some things' solely as *good news*. Though he knew he had misled his parents about next weekend's gathering as he had done about the visit to Mhondoro, he felt relief rather than guilt. He was adopting a distinctly Jesuitical view of truth-telling – in essence, never mouthing a lie. Emma had long used this particular moral compass, and Simon realised how comfortable he now felt deploying it to determine right from wrong.

Simon felt satisfied. Today's interaction with his parents had had its traumas, its awkward and difficult moments, as he knew it would, but overall it had gone as well as he had hoped. What he knew for sure was all three of them had travelled a long way.

* * *

"What news?" said Emma earnestly, unable to disguise the nervousness in her voice. But before he could answer, she said, "Things ended OK with Ma, but it was by no means easy, Simon, and we had our fair share of tears. Yes, actually, bits of it were really difficult, actually dreadful – not that that's surprising, we both knew they would be.

"It was terrible to see her when I showed her the cross. I have never seen Ma so distressed. She started shaking and wailing, and for a time she was inconsolable – you know, Simon, I was really quite scared until eventually she quietened down. I know we discussed all this and she now accepts Joshua is dead, and after it all sank in she was almost her old self again, but as she writhed with pain, Simon, I could almost feel the hurt I was inflicting on her and I blamed myself for what I was doing to her. Indeed, if I'm honest, I still do.

"As for telling her I now knew all about Alice, well, I was the one who became an emotional mess then. You know the reason Ma couldn't pluck up the courage to tell me the truth was she felt she had deceived me, had lied to me all her life, and she was terrified I would not merely blame her but I would reject her. How could she possibly think that, Simon? I told her that could never, ever happen. Oh Simon, I found it all so much more difficult as it was happening than when we discussed it back in Zim.

"But tell me," Emma was feeling guilty she had started by asking Simon how his conversation with his parents had gone and then hadn't given him a chance to speak, "what happened at your end? How did it go, and how are things now for the three of you?"

As Simon recounted what had happened, Emma listened. When he started to describe the hurt and the pain, Emma could feel herself hurting again, and as she wanted to pick up every word he was saying, she sat down on a bench she saw just ahead of her on East End Road. By the time he had finished, the autumnal chill in the air added to Emma's distress and she buttoned her light jacket right up to the neck.

She let out a short sharp sob which she knew Simon would have heard and understood, so, as she stood up, she said, "I'll be OK."

"Oh, Em," said Simon. "It's been a hugely difficult day for us all. But, painful though it has been, we seem to have achieved what we set out to do, and our parents have done so too. We are tired as well as emotionally drained, but we should feel pretty pleased with the outcome. Anyway, that's what I thought sitting in the pub waiting for you to call and in spite of all the low points we've shared, I still think that's true."

Then taking in a deep breath, Simon said, "We know it's going to be even more difficult, but at least we'll be together so that should make it a lot easier, shouldn't it?"

He had meant these words to sound positive and supportive, but as soon as he had spoken he knew they had had the opposite effect. Emma stood up to continue walking home, and as she rose she could already feel any optimism she was feeling drain away. A sense of unease and growing anxiety started to take hold of her as she began to feel what they had planned to do next week was all a terrible mistake.

When they had discussed it by the pool at the Bronte Hotel, it had all sounded so robust, so much sounder. With today's objectives achieved, they would simply bring their parents together next weekend and, after informing them they were now well and truly together as a loving couple, they would merrily go on to tell them Peter had killed Joshua, step back and leave it to their parents to respond. But now this all seemed to Emma to be both cruel and heartless. If there was one clear message to emerge from today it was that all three of them – not only Sarah and Peter but Cathy, too

– had already suffered deeply: at different times they had hardly been able to cope with the truth. Now here were Simon and herself about to inflict greater pain on them, possibly more than they could bear. How could they do this? Should they do this? Emma asked herself whether her love for Simon, and his love for her, was so important they were not only willing to risk doing deep damage to their parents, but also to take on the responsibility for the ensuing harm which could well follow. The more she thought about it, the more Emma felt what they were proposing to do was not just cruel and heartless; it was mean, callous and deeply hurtful too.

She felt wretched. After spending so long with Sarah just now, Emma felt herself bound even more closely to her mother than she had been before. Similarly, Simon had just told her that today he felt he had discovered his father for the very first time. Did they really want to risk destroying all the good they had created today? Did they have the right to assume their own love for each other should trump everything else? What presumption!

Perhaps Emma was simply overtired from hours of intense conversation following an overnight long-haul flight? Or perhaps she was simply too dispirited to start revisiting their agreed plan to tweak it or improve it substantially? Whatever it was, Emma felt trapped: she certainly felt she didn't have the energy to start thinking about a workable alternative.

What she said was less definitive. "Simon," she sighed, "we'll talk more on the phone tomorrow, and once we know our work schedules, we'll see each other as often as we can between now and the weekend." But then her fears took over as she added, "I really hope and pray we agree something which will work for everyone because at the moment I'm deeply worried."

Simon said nothing.

As if to provide some relief, Emma's mind switched from her unresolved problems to focus on him. After saying down the phone "Night, night my love. I'm dead tired and need to sleep," she went on, "this is the first night we'll not be together since we've been properly together, and I miss you dreadfully!"

Simon wished Emma a deliberately cheerful-sounding good night down his phone, but he had caught Emma's doubts and was worried. He missed her too and told her so as Emma was turning the key to her front door and he began his lonely walk home on his own.

* * *

When Emma had arrived at her flat earlier to drop off her rucksack, she had been met by a mound of letters, fliers and junk mail which had accumulated on the inner doormat in her absence. As she'd been in such a hurry to get over to Sarah's, she hadn't had time to pick it up, never mind sort it out; all she had done was kick it off the mat and out of the way. But now, when she walked in and switched on the hall light, she noticed a white envelope at her feet in front of her, face down on the mat. She was instantly curious. Had it been there before and she hadn't noticed it, or had it been pushed through her letterbox in the few hours she had been at Sarah's? She bent down to pick it up and as she turned it over and the saw the writing –it was handwritten and had no stamp - her heart stopped.

Emma threw her bag onto the floor and started to tear it open, cursing the tape on the obstructive envelope. As she unfolded the letter, she could see it was long but instead of starting to read it, she flicked the pages over to the signature at the end, even though she already knew who it was from.

Clasping the letter tightly, Emma almost ran into the sitting room, struggling to unbutton and toss her jacket onto the floor before she sat down on the sofa. Feeling exhausted and drained when she had put her key into the front door, she was alert now, having drawn on energy from an unknown source deep inside her. The letter was typed except for the beginning and the end which, like the envelope, were handwritten. In a script she knew so well, it started *My dear Emma*, and ended with the words *With my love – Robbie*. Just below the familiar way he signed his name he had put three xs – X, X, X – which Emma ran the tips of her fingers over as soon as she saw them.

Then, just as she was about to start reading the text of his letter, it suddenly occurred to Emma she hadn't texted Robbie when they landed. Not only did she *always* text Robbie whenever she got back from any trip – like calling Sarah, it had become an ingrained part of her homecoming ritual – she had specifically promised him she would this time. But, completely absorbed in implementing the plan for the day which she and Simon had concocted, sending Robbie his text had completely slipped her mind. She felt dreadful: she couldn't recall ever breaking a promise she had made to Robbie.

My dear Emma

Welcome home!
This has been a difficult letter to write, so I think it's best to get to the point immediately without any further pleasantries.
You have spoken to me about Simon as you knew you would need to, and as I knew you would, and over the summer it became increasingly evident, Emma, that you have fallen deeply in love with him. You know this, all I am doing is simply confirming to you I know it too.
I also know you have found it difficult to talk to me about all this because of our own relationship. You have found it hard to confront the reality that what was happening with Simon would mean our relationship would not merely have to change, it would effectively have to end. Why the reluctance? Because of the deep hurt it would cause. Most immediately,

you knew ending our relationship meant the end of all the great things we had going for us as well as abandoning the plans we had for the future – and, given the deep bond between us, this was bound to be hugely upsetting as well as possibly quite disorienting for you. But I would also like to think the difficulties you had in telling me about you and Simon were because you knew how hurt I would be too. I experienced huge waves of bitterness and anger – yes, Emma, towards you. It was as dreadful as it was destructive.

But, as I said, this letter is not about me and I don't want to dwell any further on myself except to add that I ripped up earlier versions of this letter which went on and on about how awful I felt: though I regret a lot of what I wrote, I have to admit the process was quite therapeutic. Don't be afraid of hurting me anymore, Emma. I have been through the hurt and the pain and am emerging on the other side, stronger, though, if I am honest, at times I still feel quite fragile.

*Anyway, as you know, before you left for Africa we agreed to suspend our relationship, to put it into abeyance – call it what you will – for now, for the time being. Although I was the one who suggested it, almost from the time we parted, I never thought – deep down – this was ever going to work even as a makeshift solution. The problem with my suggesting our relationship could be put on hold is it left **me** with some hope you would come back to me, and it left **you** with a residue of guilt about me and about us. So, Emma, my supposed solution didn't work as I wrongly said it would, and now I know – for certain – it never will.*

*And this brings me to the very heart of what my letter is about. Although it hurts me to say this, what I want to say to you can be summed up in three short words. The purpose of this letter, Emma, is to say **You-Are-Free**. I release you from all the ties which bind us, totally and completely, and not provisionally: **You-Are-Free, Free-of-Me-Forever.***

It is not easy for me to say this but it is the truth. Emma, I recognise I probably still have some sort of hold over you. I know I probably have the power to upset your relationship with Simon if I were to try to exploit any guilt about me you might still have. But while you were away I have been on a journey myself and my better self tells me I mustn't do that. So now let me tell you a little about my own travels.

Almost as soon as you and Simon flew off to Africa, I felt myself rushing headlong into a downward spiral of self-destruction – hurt I spoke about earlier really kicked in then. It became so terrible I knew I needed to talk to someone, and I knew I had to do so quickly. It didn't take me long to realise who could help me. So, late one evening, I called Don Paulo and after I recovered from my incoherent blubbering, we started to talk, and we talked, and we talked, and we talked. Although I certainly felt a little stronger when we hung up, things still seemed pretty unclear and, sensing this, Don Paulo said he would reflect on what had happened to me – and to us, Emma – and what we had spoken about and he would write. True to his word, two days letter I received a long email. At first it upset me a great deal, and even after re-reading what he had written, it still made little sense. Why? Because he had hard, tough things to say. But then, as what he said started to sink in, it began to make more sense and I now know his advice was as wise as it was eloquently put. It was all encapsulated in a few sentences, which he said I should share with you if I thought it would be helpful.

In essence, what Don Paulo said was I needed to support you in your relationship with Simon, not to chip away at it or, worse still, try to manipulate you to end it. He said there was nothing wrong with my feeling bitterness in myself or even towards you, and he told me there was nothing wrong with having feelings of despair. But he told me I had to move on, to put the destructive and self-destructive thoughts and emotions behind me. He said that all the positives which shaped our relationship and bound us together needed to form the basis for what had to be a new and different relationship between us. He told me, Emma – and this was the really tough bit – I needed to stand ready to help and support you, to give you the hope you need for your future. He said even if it took you time to speak to me again, to speak to me properly that is, I needed you to know I would be there for you, encouraging you as you built a new life for yourself. And there was one other thing Don Paulo said which I'm still not entirely sure I really understand. He said if I wasn't prepared to help and support you, then – as he put it – when I came to look back on our own relationship in the years ahead, I would see that it had been based on a lie and not on the truths we believed at the time it had been built on. Yes, Emma, some of what he said was perplexing, but then we both know, don't we, that Don Paulo does have an odd, even mysterious streak to him. In some ways I think it's what attracted us to him.

*As I said, Emma, when I first read his email, with the bitterness of what had happened still fresh within me, I thought it was as unrealistic as it was unhelpful. But then I saw what he said was absolutely right. If I really do want my life to have meaning, if I really do want **everyone** to live fulfilling lives – and for everything that's happened, I know this is what still motivates me and gives meaning to my own life – then I need to be able to say I want to do this for **you**, Emma, and to really mean it. What Don Paulo said was tough and hard to take, but the more I thought about it the more I knew he was ultimately right and the sooner I could rid myself of the festering anger, bitterness and self-pity inside me, the better. He laid before me the ideal: my job is to try to make that ideal become reality.*

There is one other thing I need to tell you which is, in part, related to the change Don Paulo encouraged me to make within myself. You know, Emma, better than anyone else, there have been instances when I have met other women I have felt attracted to, and even women whom I have felt in other circumstances could have been potential partners. You may well remember we talked about it, and – I dread to recall now – we even laughed and made light of it. So, it will come as no surprise when I tell you I have been thinking more about other relationships than I ever did before you met Simon. Indeed, there is a woman who teaches at St Michael's who is quite like you and another I met on my theology course in the summer, both of whom I really like. Now I have written this letter to you, I might begin to look at a potential relationship with one of them in a new light.

But let me return to the main message of my letter. **You are totally free of me, Emma, with no strings attached.** *Act on that freedom: you owe it to yourself and you owe it to Simon. And, ultimately, you owe it to me too.*

There's one final thing I need to say. When you have read, and possibly re-read, my letter, please don't suggest we meet. You need the time and the space to be with Simon free from feeling yourself still bound to me, and I need space and time to build my life anew too. You know, I am far better at talking than writing, but I know our meeting up will only make things more complicated than they are already. So on balance, I think – for now – if you feel the need to respond to my letter, best not to phone, just write.

Oh, and Don Paulo told me to tell you he hoped you would contact him yourself if you felt it could be helpful, though he also said he wouldn't expect to hear from you for quite a while.

With my love
Robbie
X X X

[Posted through your letterbox in the afternoon of the Sunday you arrived back in the UK.]

Emma did re-read the letter, the second time with tears running down her cheeks and with her free hand lying along, and occasionally stroking the arm of, the sofa she was sitting on; it was the exact spot where Robbie had rested his head on that Sunday morning a few weeks earlier, the dying moments of the last time they had been together. As she folded up Robbie's letter and placed it in the top drawer of her desk, the weariness Emma had felt before discovering it returned with a vengeance. She was good for nothing more that evening: she was completely drained and knew she had to sleep.

She didn't have the energy either to unpack properly or take a shower before she slid in between the bedclothes. Then, as she always did – it had almost become part of her DNA – before she fell asleep her mind automatically started to reflect on the major events of the day just ending. As it did so, a sense of quiet contentment came over Emma, first as she relived the joy she had felt when she left Sarah's in the knowledge that the love between them was stronger than ever, and then by recalling the pleasure she had had listening to Simon's account of how his discussions with his parents had ended. Added to that was the new glow she now felt about her relationship with Simon provided by the almost formal blessing Robbie had given them in his letter. In his absence, she could almost sense the closeness of Simon's body next to hers.

But none of that was sufficient. As she fell asleep, Emma was wrapped in an overwhelming feeling of gloom. Immaculata had been right, of course. Robbie had been deeply hurt by what had happened, his letter couldn't have been clearer. So why hadn't he featured in any of the plans she had made either for today or for next weekend, or for any time in the future? How could she have decided merely to send Robbie a text message to say she had landed and then forgotten to send it? How could she have been so callous?

But now things were even worse. How could she even start to make amends if, as Robbie had stipulated in his letter, they couldn't even meet up. Emma went to sleep not merely sad but feeling hurt inside; it was as if a little of Robbie's pain had been transferred to her. If she hadn't been so utterly exhausted, she would have reflected why. Robbie did still have power over her, she couldn't easily shake him off. Why? Because in spite of everything that had happened between her and Simon and even with his blessing, a part of her still loved him.

- 14 -

Alice

Lead Kindly Light amidst th'encircling gloom. Lead Thou me on. The choir had begun to sing the entrance hymn as Emma slid quietly into the bench beside Sarah at the back of the church. They smiled to each other as Emma affectionately patted Sarah's arm.

Though she knew full well what horrors the day could have in store for her, Emma had felt strong and confident as she hurried into St Mary's for Sunday Mass, arriving a little late. Her positive mood was boosted not only by Sarah's welcoming smile but also by the opening hymn. Emma knew it well; the words were by Cardinal Newman, whose writings about faith and doubt Robbie had introduced her to some years ago. As she took in the familiar surroundings, relieved to see Robbie's mother was not in church, she saw the hymn as a good omen for the day ahead. It heralded – she hoped – a day which would be marked by kindliness and light and end in calm, though she knew for certain they would also all be encircled by periods of intense gloom.

It was just a week since Simon and Emma had returned from Zimbabwe. Emma and Sarah had agreed to go and visit Alice's grave after Mass before making their way to the Robertsons' for their after-lunch gathering. Emma rarely went to Mass with Sarah anymore and she was rather dreading it as she knew the negative feelings the service usually induced in her – as it did in most other parishes in England – with its formulaic set-piece liturgy, dreary sermon and dreadfully-sung hymns. But today Emma woke with positive feelings as she recalled the last Mass she had been to – with Simon at St Michael's in Mhondoro – and was hopeful she could recapture the pleasure it had given her and sustain its joyful memory to the end of this one.

There was another reason why Emma had been keen to join Sarah for Mass today: Robbie. It had been a week since she had first read his letter and she must have re-read it half a dozen times since. She had, of course, mentioned the letter to Simon, but she hadn't offered it to him to read and he hadn't asked, which she knew he wouldn't. There were still bits of Robbie's letter which Emma felt she needed to think more about more, especially those sections which referred more obliquely to their shared beliefs, and she had told herself she might discover more if she reflected on Robbie's words – and those of Don Paulo – in the archetypical Catholic setting of the Mass.

When the opening hymn ended and the church became quiet, the priest began the Mass by inviting everyone to make the sign of the cross, and Emma started to daydream. Robbie had written of his anger, bitterness, self-pity and the total despair, and Don Paulo had told him it was OK to feel like this but he had to try – and if needs be, force himself – to pick himself up and move on. Much of Robbie's letter seemed to be telling Emma how difficult this had been for him. Then, all of a sudden, Emma remembered the first time Don Paulo had come over to her flat for supper. They had been discussing what it really meant to be a Christian and he had used those very same words Robbie had: he had said the role of the Christian was to be life-affirming, to sow the seeds of genuine hope where there was despair.

Emma could see Don Paulo now in her mind's eye, smiling across to her and saying, with the strong Latino lilt to his voice, "my dear Emma, the true Christian is someone who tries to make resurrection happen right now, the person who strives to create new life and make a tangible difference." Then, to make sure Emma really understood the radical nature of what he was saying to her, Don Paulo – a Catholic priest – had turned to her (she still vividly remembered the incident) and said, almost casually, that none of the Gospel stories about Jesus physically rising from the dead were true: they were a distraction. Emma had been shocked: what Don Paulo had said seemed so contrary to everything she had been taught. "After all," she recalled saying, "isn't resurrection the centre-piece of Christian belief?"

And Emma had never forgotten Don Paulo's reply. "Yes," he had said, "resurrection is the centre-piece of Christianity, though the true meaning of Christian resurrection has very little to do with dead bodies after they have died – it has everything to do with life here and now, with bringing hope, breathing new life into people and communities when everything appears hopeless. Our job as Christians is to make resurrection happen first within ourselves and then in our broken world. It is this world and not the next, what we do here rather than what happens to us after we die, which really matters."

Emma remembered just how liberating she had found Don Paulo's words. She no longer had to bother about – to struggle to try to believe, against all scientific logic – Jesus being mysteriously raised from the dead after he had died, and to worry about how his disciples half-recognised him as if they were all walking round in a fog. It all started to make sense! And then she recalled the relief on Simon's face during their dinner that night at the Bronte Hotel when she had told him about her interchange with Don Paulo and the profound impact it had made on her knowing she didn't have to believe Jesus had been brought back to life as if by magic. She told him how it had both confirmed and strengthened her commitment to her Christian faith.

"That sounds pretty unorthodox to me, Em," Simon had said.

"Yes, it does, I know," Emma had replied, "but it happens to be what I believe."

"And it's what I believe, too," said Simon. "And I also really like the notion of trying to make resurrection really happen by working to give people genuine hope – I can certainly buy into that too". He had wondered what else was left which separated Emma's Christianity from his atheism.

Emma was jolted back to the Mass as all around people were sitting down for the homily. She listened to the priest's opening remarks and was discouraged when he said *Our quest in this life is simple, to focus our sights on the world to come. Our ultimate aim is to leave this life pure and untainted when we die, for then we will be as ready as we can be to live with Him for ever in heaven.* Emma sighed and switched off. Before she knew it, the time for Communion had arrived and she and Sarah stood up to join the stream of people moving towards the front of the church.

When they had been at St Michael's, all the secondary school children had gone up for Communion enthusiastically. But here, as she walked up the aisle with Sarah, Emma couldn't help noticing how many people remained in their seats. These, she thought, were probably divorced or openly living unmarried with a partner, their status at variance with the church's norms so they felt they had to sit tight. A number of those who did come up to the altar stood in front of the priest with heads bowed and arms crossed and didn't take the host. Some would have been non-Catholic Christians forbidden by England's Catholic bishops to receive communion; some, possibly, were not even Christians. But most would be Catholics, their crossed arms symbolising their acceptance, grudging or otherwise, of their church's view they were not worthy to receive the Eucharist from a church whose founder went out of his way to welcome sinners. Emma couldn't help reflecting on the deep divide between what she now believed and the beliefs of the official church: where, she wondered, was the joy of the resurrection for those marginalised in this multi-tiered system of worship?

As she walked back to her place, it struck Emma how little seemed to have changed since Graham Greene wrote his novels about Catholicism decades earlier. Here was she, a young Catholic unmarried woman going up to the altar to receive Communion though now living openly in a relationship with Simon, following many years of intimacy with Robbie. From the standpoint of Catholic orthodoxy, it would be difficult to think of anything more demonstrably sinful than what she had just done.

No one had written so movingly and powerfully about what would happen to people such as her as James Joyce, whose *A Portrait of the Artist as a Young Man* Emma had read in her last year at school. Here, in Joyce's guilt-ridden world, the sinfulness of every unmarried sexual act is mercilessly laid bare. If unconfessed, it will result in eternal damnation for every one of Catholicism's tortured souls. Joyce's young schoolboy character, Stephen Dedalus, listens to the Jesuit retreat-giver drip-feeding fear of hellfire into him unless he too confesses: he has to, there is no escape. Emma had never experienced either Greene's nor Joyce's guilt-feelings for the choices she had deliberately made: she received the host because she honestly believed doing so was wholly consistent with, and would strengthen, her Christian faith. But she remained angry for those the church still successfully persuaded to feel guilty. As Robbie would often say when they discussed such matters, quoting the words of the Jewish writer Martin Buber, 'nothing so masks the face of God as religion'. How right he was, thought Emma as she returned to her bench at the back of the church and quietly thanked God for the faith which meant so much to her.

The choir began the final hymn, *Praise to the Holiest in the Height*. It was another of Newman's and Emma then realised why he had featured so prominently in today's service: this week was the anniversary of his beatification, the beginnings of the formal process of the church proclaiming him to be a saint. This was not a hymn Emma had ever warmed to and she didn't join in. Instead, her thoughts wandered again, this time to what had happened in the week since she and Simon had arrived back in England.

Emma and Simon had kept closely in touch the whole week. Following their Sunday night apart, he had come over to her flat for two of the next six nights and between times they constantly talked and texted. Besides wanting to be together, both of them were conscious of the need to ensure they were as well prepared as they could be for the coming weekend's gathering. When Simon discovered his parents were taking one of their short city breaks, this time to Paris, and were only returning on the Saturday, he quickly saw the advantage this would give them. It made it far easier for his mother to agree not to host a lunch, as she did when he told her she would have neither the time nor the energy to give to preparing a meal of the standard which Sunday's important event would merit.

With the logistical details taken care of, Simon and Emma could focus on the substance of the event. As they went over their plans again and again, rehearsing every detail, Simon was relieved he had managed to ease, though not entirely remove, the doubts Emma had expressed at the end of their Sunday night phone call about what they had agreed to do. He was now sure there was no longer any risk of her wanting to call the whole thing off, but the incident had made him far more aware of the importance of the chemistry of their being together to maintaining Emma's confidence and carrying it through.

Another plus for Simon with his parents being away for the whole week was he didn't have to worry about the possibility of having to revisit their first-day-back's discussion. When not overnighting at Emma's flat, he busied himself going through the mountain of work which had accumulated in his absence: working until nine at night, he was in the office again just after seven the following morning. The only other major task Simon set himself for the week was to apply to sit his final accountancy exams. Buoyed up by his father's enthusiasm, Simon filled in the forms to write these early in the New Year. Still on his 'to-do' list was finalising the shortlist of medical schools to apply to. Emma was keen to help but they both decided this needed more time than they had this week. What's more, as each of them knew but neither of them dared say it, their world might look very different next week than it did this side of Sunday.

Emma surprised herself with the ease with which she slid back into her work at the BBC, not least because she had felt hugely exposed when she walked into Broadcasting House on the Monday morning and started chatting with colleagues in the lift as she knew the banter always revolved around a current news issue, and she hadn't kept up with the news. Fortunately, work was dominated by the upcoming party conferences news, so no one important noticed. The world of British politics seemed as dead now as it always was in August and she sensed little appetite in the office for 'creating' domestic news stories by proactively hunting for the links between current international news stories and the UK, as they usually did on quiet domestic news-days. Rosemary told Emma things were now moving fast on the Civilisation-type programme ideas they had talked about so enthusiastically in the summer, but she said they would talk more about all that when the party conferences were over.

Emma felt a nudge on her arm. The final hymn had finished and Sarah was motioning to her it was time to leave church. Before she stood up, Emma paused for one final prayer. The time for daydreaming was over and she prayed everything would go well today, whatever well might mean. As she rose and followed Sarah out of the church, she realised she still didn't really know.

The morning had started dull, with heavy clouds in the sky, but when Sarah and Emma stepped out of St Mary's after Mass, the weather had worsened. Not only was it darker, but the wind had picked up, it was raining heavily and it had turned colder – it was now noticeably chilly for a September day. People left the church hurrying. Those with umbrellas raised them and those without tried to keep dry under coats tossed hurriedly over their heads, shoulders hunched. The parish priest stood on the front steps of his church in case anyone wanted to talk, but today few did. He was clearly cold and cut a forlorn figure as he sheltered under a large, bright green umbrella which matched so well that it seemed to be almost colour-coded with his vestments. Emma had always thought church attire looked so out of place when seen outside in the real world and today proved her point once again.

She raised her umbrella and motioned to Sarah to move in close to her to shelter as they turned left to walk down the High Street, both glad they had sensibly decided to wear their boots. It was her new M&S umbrella, bought only this week, as she had forgotten to put hers in her bag when going to work. It was double the price and almost twice the size of the ones sold by the umbrella sellers who magically appear around Oxford Circus to tempt (or was it accost?) sodden commuters and shoppers whenever there is a downpour, and she hoped its claim to be strong, sturdy and 'guaranteed showerproof' would prove to be accurate. She was about to find out.

They reached the cemetery in no time and Emma could see the familiar buildings of The Grange estate just beyond. She had really never registered the first home she had ever known lay opposite the entrance to the cemetery. Indeed, she had never really given the cemetery much thought when young. Her earliest memories of walking along the High Street from their flat to Martin's School and the journey back were focused almost entirely on the distance she had to cover. As Emma thought back to her earliest schooldays, it struck her that it had seemed so much further then than it did now and she shared this thought with her mother. Sarah laughed and told her that, of course, she had had far shorter legs and very tiny feet in those days. Emma was pleased her mother seemed to be in such good spirits; her decision to join Sarah for Mass had clearly been a good one. It was, she thought, a positive omen for the day ahead.

Emma was delighted to see the familiar sight of two or three flower sellers' stalls pitched on the pavement between The Grange and the cemetery. Emma knew both the habits and the friendly faces of her local flower sellers, one always sporting his Lenin look-alike flat cap as he did today, and when she had time she often stopped to chat to them, at least when it was dry. It was all part of the warmth she felt living here in East Finchley. Perhaps her early summer article on the council's plans to limit their number, if not remove them entirely had had some impact? However, there were few potential customers about and the men (they were all men today) seemed more intent on sheltering from the rain than on trying to tempt a cemetery visitor to buy a bloom or two. Through the rain Emma could see the flowers were looking a little sad and she knew why. As ever, they were the leftovers from the Saturday stalls strategically placed at the main exit from the tube station. As they drew near, Emma asked Sarah if she would like her to buy some flowers but she declined so firmly Emma didn't press the point. Sarah told her she would understand why when they reached Alice's grave.

Sarah held on to Emma's arm as they crossed the road to the open wrought-iron gates ahead of them and passed the faded green signs informing them they were entering both the St Pancras and the Islington cemeteries, the bold red signs on the railings telling them once inside they would be digitally recorded on CCTV. The rain was easing now and quite soon Emma was able to put away her umbrella. It had worked up to a point: though waterproof, it hadn't been big enough to shelter them both underneath, so the result of Emma's efforts to juggle the umbrella between the two of them was that they were now both quite wet. For comfort rather than to try to stay dry, they kept their arms locked together.

Emma had never set foot in the cemetery before and was pleased to see flowerbeds immediately ahead of her. Indeed, from the wide tarred road they had started to walk along, it didn't look much like a cemetery at all as she couldn't see any graves. However, it didn't take long for graves to come into view: there were masses of them. A number were imposing, reflecting the wealth of a bygone age, the fading greys and whites of marble or granite slabs with matching upright headstones. The biggest were enclosed by ornate walls or fenced surroundings, and the grandest were topped with statues, angels and even the odd ornamental dog. Most awesome (or was it pretentious, Emma couldn't make up her mind which) were the stand-alone mausoleums, with their Greek or Roman columns, their now-silent occupants competing to outdo each other in death as they probably had done in life. From the dates, the most exotic had been built in Victorian times. One looked like a mini replica of a Greek temple built in austere reddish-brown granite and Portland stone with bronze doors and sombre columns, some now cracked, others covered with green moss at the bottom. But for all their imperfections, these edifices of power still looked impressive as both their sides and columns glistened with the water from the morning's downpour.

Beyond the mausoleums the road dropped down and, as it fell away, smaller roads branched off it to create a hotchpotch of confusing route options as some were not marked. Those that were had odd, seemingly random, names: Viaduct Road, Cross Road, Joint Road and Parkers Road. The road signs were painted green on a yellow background and Emma wondered what this colour combination symbolised. She then saw notices which read 'Police Notice: Thieves Operate in This Area' and wondered what there was here which was so tempting to steal.

They first passed small clusters of older graves hidden among the untrimmed trees and overgrown shrubs, but then they could see stretching out ahead of them rows of newer gravestones and tombstones laid out in lines as straight as soldiers on parade. As Emma took all this in she was beginning to realise just how large the cemetery was – not a town, more like a whole city of the dead.

After passing the last of this long line of graves, the area became more wooded. They walked past sycamores, ashes, cypresses, monkey puzzles and oaks and a scattering of yews, the ubiquitous tree of old English churchyards. In the thickest areas, and with the heavy undergrowth blocking their view, Emma completely lost her sense of direction but Sarah knew where she was heading and strode on purposefully. They next came to an area where a number of the graves were in a serious state of disrepair. Some headstones and crosses had fallen over completely, others were leaning precariously and would soon topple over to join them, eased by the ever-expanding tree roots whose power and energy was drawn from the rich soil below. Nature was creeping in silently and unhurriedly to play havoc with the meticulously constructed, regimental-like lines of cemetery furniture. It was if nature was winning the battle of a slow-motion earthquake. With all the spending cuts, Emma guessed the tending of the graves here had become a remembrance of things past, like so many of the graves' occupants.

Unsurprisingly, the more numerous, older and more humble graves boasted names familiar in those bygone days but which sounded strange to the modern ear – Ida, Bertha, Nellie, Maude, Minnie, Bessie and Florence. The men's names sounded far less out of place, reflecting, thought Emma, the stronghold the (male) monarchy still has on ordinary English folk: lots of Georges, Williams, Charles, Alberts and Henrys, though she did have to smile when she saw the odd Percy, Horace and Otto. Many of these older graves lay hidden or half-hidden among the growing untrimmed bushes of laurel, hawthorn and gorse, their physical concealment only adding to the faded memory of their occupants. Unsurprisingly, many of the newer graves especially bore the names of Turks, Poles, Greeks, Cypriots and those from other immigrant communities. Given their strong sense of community, Emma had imagined on a Sunday these graves especially would be surrounded by relatives visiting their departed loved ones, but there seemed to be few visitors here today, probably, she thought, because of the rain. Emma felt the stillness of the cemetery all around her.

As she had been reading the names on the graves they had been passing, Emma realised she had been lagging behind Sarah, so she quickened her pace, and when she drew alongside her, she tugged at Sarah's arm to reconnect with her. As she turned fleetingly to look at Emma, Sarah's face was as graven-looking as the headstones they were passing and she hurried on. She was still setting a strong pace and Emma sensed they still had quite a way to go. It was now raining again, so she put up her umbrella and linked arms again with Sarah. It felt good to be close again.

A little further on, they passed a single-storey building with a tall chimney on their right as the road they were on started to fall away again. Its name – Islington Crematorium – was boldly displayed on the building, yellow letters on a green background, the reverse colouring to the road signs. Emma wondered how much further they had to go but she didn't ask because Sarah still had that determined look on her face. It was a look Emma knew so well: it had 'do not disturb' written all over it. Whether it was sensing a change in Sarah as they hurried on or because she had seen so much death all around her, Emma's own mood changed. As she had walked ever deeper into the cemetery and read, with growing interest, the wording on the different graves they passed, she had begun to wonder what Alice's would look like. She knew it would be simple, but would it have a flat tombstone or an upright headstone, would it look 'right' by which she meant would it be in state of good repair or would it be one of those which looked unkempt and untidy? But now all she could think about was what she would feel when she read what she assumed would be something like Alice Makoni, Born 24 October 1976, Died 24th August 1994 Aged 18 engraved in stone above her blood-mother's grave.

Just then, Sarah turned to Emma and said, "we're getting close now" but remained preoccupied. Although she had no idea what they were, Emma started to look for signs which might mark the place where Alice was buried, and felt her heartbeat quicken a little. Moments later, after they had passed five fir trees on their right, Sarah pointed to a protruding tap next to the road and announced they were here. Fortunately, it had stopped raining and Emma lowered her umbrella; after shaking it she thrust it under her arm.

They were in a largely open area and the damp air had a fresh smell to it. Immediately in front of them was a group of graves crammed together more tightly than any others Emma had seen. Their ends touched each other as well as their sides and so, if you were heading for the more distant graves, there was no clear route, let alone a made-up footpath. If the grave you were looking for happened to be some way in – and as Emma was about to discover, in their case it was – you simply had to walk over the graves in front of you to reach it.

And this is precisely what Sarah did: she stepped onto the tops of the graves in front of her and by the time she had stopped she had walked over thirteen – Emma had counted them as she followed close behind. Most of the graves had tombstones laid flat on top of them; they were all quite old and on many the writing had faded, weathered by the elements. A number were cracked, and a few were chipped or broken entirely. Their smooth surfaces were slippery as well as uneven, and as she walked over them, Sarah stumbled twice. Emma lunged forward in case she fell, but on both occasions, Sarah steadied herself before Emma's arm touched her. There was a determination in her step. One grave stood out from the rest; it had the statue of an angel on top. As she came to it, Emma read 'Polis Koutroukides born on 20th November 1945, died on 16th July 1963'. Only 17, Emma calculated, losing her concentration as she did so. She slipped herself but didn't fall as she steadied herself with the help of the angel, as Sarah had done before her. She wondered what had happened to this young Polish boy for him to die so young; he had been a year younger than Alice was when she had died.

Emma was surprised Sarah hadn't stopped before they reached the end of the line of gravestones, but then, as Sarah lowered her head and dropped her shoulders to look down at the ground more closely, Emma realised they had come to another group of graves. They were difficult to see as they had no tombstone; they were all unmarked and didn't look much like graves, more like untended rough ground. As she looked more closely, she reckoned there must have been a couple of dozen of them, or maybe more. She could see the distinct mounds of each grave, their tops consisting of hardened, but now wet earth, many with weeds or nettles randomly growing out of them. Some had almost entirely disappeared beneath a web of brambles which had spread out from their roots in the dark trees beyond. Against the shadow of the trees, Emma could see clusters of unpicked rotting blackberries hanging off the thicker brambles under the trees, a further sign, she thought, that no one came here.

Sarah had been back to Alice's grave only a few weeks earlier, but she was having difficulty locating it and for a moment Emma thought she was lost and had come to the wrong spot. But she knew what she was doing. She took one step forward, then, with her foot, started to poke and prod as she pushed away nettles and tried to clear brambles as best she could to find what she was looking for. She stepped to her right and chiselled away with her foot again. From the look on Sarah's face now, Emma could see she knew where she was and what she was doing: Alice's grave was clearly right here, concealed among the other half-hidden unmarked graves its covering abutted.

As Emma watched, she could see the bottom of Sarah's boots were now caked in mud and as she drew in closer, she felt a heaviness to her own boots. What she had anticipated would be a difficult moment had suddenly become even more challenging. Emma had dressed smartly and had wanted to feel presentable as she stood over Alice's grave, and for Emma presentable included being clean. But now here she was, her boots filthy and her clothes hanging uncomfortably on her from the rain. Emma had assumed their arrival at Alice's grave would be a dignified affair, but now it was anything but: she was a mess and felt she was letting Alice down. And Alice's grave – – and Emma now knew it would be unmarked, with no words on it for her to read – would clearly be a mess, too.

* * *

Suddenly, Sarah grabs hold of Emma's arm as she takes what turns out to be her final step sideways, almost falling as she catches her foot on a bramble. Emma can see the distinct elevation Sarah is pointing to, but to her, Alice's grave looks just like those around it: an uneven hump of ground. Its largely clayey soil surface has a green tinge to it, which Emma can see is the result of years of weed growth, not because fresh turf had been lovingly laid on top of the earth to create the familiar grassy mound. As soon as she knows she's reached the right place, Sarah stands upright and motionless at what Emma assumes is the foot of the grave, and she does the same. Sarah looks ahead of her and says nothing and Emma does the same, sensing – again — this is what she's expected to do.

Now they've arrived it's all so different. Emma had been expecting to be overwhelmed by crippling grief as she stood for the first time at the foot of her real mother's grave — *she* and Simon had even discussed how she would cope with her distress. But standing here now, she doesn't feel anything, Then, half-embarrassed and feeling rather ashamed of herself, Emma tries to conjure up feelings of sadness, but she can't because all the signals are wrong: there's no gravestone, no name, birthdate or death-date; there's not even an official cemetery reference number she can see to refer people to the cemetery archives where Alice Makoni's particulars would surely be recorded.

It's as if there is no grave. Alice's had clearly been a cut-price funeral, and all Emma can think of is what sort of marked-down coffin she had been put in, or even if she had had one at all: if there's no tombstone, perhaps there's no coffin either? She knew in Zimbabwe her relatives were buried in sacks – when Prosper had told her that, the thought of this had repulsed Emma even though she had reassured herself that as this was clearly the custom, it must be okay. But you don't bury people in sacks in England, do you, unless you're a fervent Quaker perhaps? Emma knows this isn't the time to ask.

A wave first of bitterness then anger sweeps through Emma. Neither Alice nor her remains matter. A dead newly-arrived immigrant with an unwanted disease, grudgingly allocated a spot in a far-off location, was clearly someone whose memory as well as her remains ought to be hurriedly forgotten. The powers-that-be had her body dispatched like a misaddressed letter to the place where unmarked graves for marginalised people were left, hidden away at the end of the outer edge of London's largest suburb of dead people.

As these feelings start to subside, Emma looks around and examine the grave and its immediate surrounds more closely. She sees a small metal crucifix stuck in the soil at the far end of Alice's grave; it's old and rusty and listing over slightly to the left. Perhaps it has moved over the years as the soil has shifted, or is it standing there lopsided because it had been placed there in a hurry and no one ever thought of pulling it up and putting it back in the ground properly? The grave – or hump – to the right is as bare as Alice's, but the one to its left has a chipped plastic vase half-buried on top of it containing the remnants of what had been a larger bunch of probably once brightly-coloured plastic flowers, as some of the chewed plastic stems lie some distance way away broken and frayed; one is now lying on the edge of Alice's grave, halfway down on the right. Bleached by seasons of summer sun, their colour has almost disappeared. There are no fresh flowers anywhere near Alice's grave, and no vase to put them in if anyone ever brought them here. Emma notices there isn't even a discarded sweet-wrapper anywhere in sight and concludes visitors to these unmarked graves are as rare as picked flowers.

As the two of them stand there in silence, Emma realises how cold she is and she starts to worry about Sarah. As the rain had started to seep into her own boots, and as Sarah suffers from Raynaud's syndrome, Emma knows Sarah's feet are probably numb already. Although it has taken Emma almost 25 years to come to this spot, she knows they shouldn't stay long.

Sarah now stirs. She takes Mr Svosve's vial from her pocket, kisses it, then tries to ease off the top but, seeing she is struggling as her hands are cold, Emma offers to help and Sarah forces a grateful smile. She then takes a step forward, sprinkles half the sandy-soil over Alice's grave, steps back and gives the phial to Emma, gesturing for her to do the same. After emptying the phial, Emma respectfully stands in silence as she waits for Sarah to recite a prayer or say something but, still wholly absorbed in her own thoughts, Sarah says nothing.

Emma thinks she should say a prayer and mouths to herself little more than 'May she rest in peace', uncertain, with no signal from Sarah, what mood her prayer should reflect. Then, as Sarah still says nothing, Emma's thoughts start to wander. Seeing the Zimbabwean soil is far lighter in colour than the earth it has just landed on, she wonders how long it will stand out before it merges and blends in with the old.

Just then Sarah starts to speak, but what she says is quickly over; it sounds more like an announcement than a prayer.

"It is done now," she says. "The soil of Joshua's grave has been united with the soil of Alice's grave. I am now at peace. May God bless them both." Emma waits for more, but it's soon clear that's all there is.

Emma repeats Sarah's words to herself, wondering why she had said what she had; it was odd. Sarah had said *she* was now at peace, but she made no mention of either Alice or Joshua being at peace. Emma knows Sarah is careful with words so assumes she had said precisely what she had meant to say. She also asked God to bless *them both*, not *you both* which suggests, Emma thought, Sarah doesn't believe them to be *here*. But as Emma knows Sarah certainly believes they – or their souls or spirits – *are* alive, she must mean they are somewhere else.

Then, as she thinks about it a little more, Emma starts to understand: Sarah's words are drawn directly from her understanding of how the spirit world works. According to her Shona beliefs, on the first anniversary of their deaths, the spirits of the dead leave the places where they are buried to join their ancestors, and once there, they are at peace. To mark this event, a ceremony takes place at the graveside a year after a person dies which, in many ways, is a more important event than the burial itself. Emma is sure Sarah will have had a ceremony at Alice's graveside a year after she was buried, and that would have been it. With that ritual completed, and with Sarah believing Alice is no longer here, she would feel no further need to visit her daughter's grave. This would also explain why Sarah didn't seem to be particularly troubled by Alice's being buried in an unmarked grave. Emma then remembers how surprised she was when shown the family burial ground by her young cousins in Mutoko as no one had felt the need to place fresh flowers on any of the family's unmarked graves, which also explains Sarah's earlier comment about not needing to buy flowers.

As for Joshua, Emma guessed Mr Svovse had probably returned a year after he buried him in the dry riverbank to say a prayer for him as his soul passed on, but she now realises she had never thought to ask him. Sarah was clearly relieved to have been able to mingle the soil from Joshua's grave with the soil of Alice's, though she didn't believe this would bring him here. The important thing, Emma concludes, is because all the different rituals have been carried out, Sarah is now able to feel at peace, and that is precisely what she had just said. She has done what she had to, and now she can move on. It's all beginning to make sense.

After mulling over Sarah's few words for a little while longer, Emma simply says, "Yes, Ma, you are at peace now." Then, not knowing what else she should either say or do, she turns to Sarah and hugs her, and Sarah gratefully responds.

As Emma feels the pressure of Sarah's body against hers as if to signal everything they had come for had now been done and she can now move away, waves of emotions start to stir within her. They are so different from anything she has ever experienced before that she found them as difficult to describe to Simon afterwards as they are to come to grips with as she feels them now, growing in intensity inside her. She told Simon it started with a sense of oneness and immense peace, which was suddenly eclipsed by a feeling of terror which started as a creeping and growing fear but which took hold with such intensity it seemed to shut down her body, but which, strangely and at the same time, caused her mind to become hyperactive. As she said to Simon, she became disoriented and started to panic as she felt herself swinging violently, like Edgar Allen Poe's pendulum, between intense fear and utter confusion.

What triggers all this in Emma is the stark realisation that the future of her entire family depends solely on her. All of a sudden Emma is palpably aware the very survival of the family rests squarely on her shoulders, and hers alone. Without her, this branch of the Makoni family will simply die out.

As she stands at the foot of her mother's grave, feeling on her cheeks the breath of the woman she had always believed to be her mother, and gazes down at the soil from her grandfather's grave she has just thrown down, Emma becomes acutely conscious of the bond which unites all four of them. She feels it so strongly it's as if they were bound together physically. She knows how deep her bond with Sarah has always been, and the more she has learned about Joshua, the closer she has felt, but this is the first time she has had any feelings towards her blood-mother Alice. Now, though, in the company of Sarah and Joshua, Emma senses a closeness to Alice which is as new as it is difficult to describe – but she feels it, and feels it intensely. She has never felt as tightly bound to all her closest relatives before as she does now. It's as if she has just gone through an initiation ceremony to formally make her a member of the senior family. Emma *is* a Makoni. It couldn't be simpler, and it couldn't be clearer. She feels immensely proud of who she is, totally accepting of the responsibilities she now bears and deeply secure in her new identity. Emma knows it is up to her not merely to choose a partner to enable her to be the mother of the next generation, but that the person she selects has to be worthy of her family. She needs to track down and find a man Joshua, Alice and Sarah will be proud of, someone they will trust, respect and honour as the father of her offspring, the new founding-father of the Makoni clan.

Sarah could have come here alone to pour the soil from Joshua's grave onto the earth which covered Alice's bones, but she chose not to: she brought Emma here because she knew Emma *had* to be here. Sarah needs Emma not just to know but to feel what it's like to be the person upon whom her family is now totally dependent, the only one able to create the new life necessary for their family to live on, and now she does.

But now her mood changes. Emma is hit first by fear and then panic as she sees a huge chasm, an unbridgeable gap, opening up between her and her family as she is brought face to face with the consequences of her love for Simon. She knows exactly what is happening because, though her body freezes, her mind remains clear, but this only adds to her misery. What could be worse than your being fully aware of your body as it sends out ever more powerful signals of acute distress?

Of all the people on earth she could have fallen in love with, of all the men in the world she could have chosen to be the father of her children, why, oh why, did it have to be Simon – Simon Robertson the only son of Peter Robertson, the Rhodesian soldier who had killed her grandfather in cold blood? How could Alice and Sarah possibly accept as the father of Emma's children the son of the man who had not merely murdered Joshua in cold blood, but who had singlehandedly torn their family apart? Joshua could never conceive of, would never accept, her marrying such a person, so how could they? How could Emma possibly have selected this man over any other on God's earth? As Emma stands next to her adopted mother at the foot of her blood-mother's grave, she feels the enormity of what she has done. She seems willing to sacrifice her family, to cause the destruction of the whole Makoni family, for this man. Emma shivers, not from the cold but from a creeping dread of the events which will unfold in the next few hours because of her, because of the man she has fallen so deeply in love with.

As Emma's body remains rigid, her mind continues to race. She tells herself what she has told herself before: she could walk away from Simon and return to the welcoming bosom of her family. But she knows she can't: this is no longer an option. She then recalls that night after their day with Mr Svosve when, behind the security of the convent walls, she did decide she would leave Simon, even though she knew then how much she loved him. But within a matter of hours she had changed her mind and had sealed her decision to become even more tightly bound to Simon that same night at the Bronte Hotel. But then she thought she was choosing between Simon and Robbie: how odd both that choice and her Victoria Falls dream look now. Then she was forcing herself to choose between Robbie and Simon and she could, now she is being forced to choose between her family and Simon and she knows she can't.

Immaculata had told Emma she needed to go where her heart was leading her, but this is precisely what she has done. Almost from the day she first met Simon, certainly from the moment she was captivated by his deep blue eyes, she knew what her heart was telling her. Everything else – from the way their conversations had gone first at *Jenny's* and the twists and turns of their discussions on Hampstead Heath about belief when she had struggled but eventually managed to square that particular circle – had merely confirmed what her instincts had already been telling her. What's more, even if he had said how much *he* was still struggling, hadn't Robbie said in his letter he now had his sights set on helping Emma's and Simon's relationship to flourish? But Emma knows her certainties about Simon now go well beyond all this. She knows she wants him to eventually father her children. There is no other man for her anymore. She has made her choice and there is no going back.

Emma knows the consequences. As she has made her decision about Simon, the Makonis are family no longer. The woman who holds the destiny of the Makonis in her hands is nothing but a treacherous deceiver. They trusted her but she is a traitor and a turncoat. Emma feels the rawness of being alone as the warmth, comfort and security she had just felt are sucked out of her. She is terrified: she can feel fear pulsating through her veins. They are over there and she is over here, totally alone.

Standing in front of Alice's grave, she shudders: this cannot happen! As certain as she is she wants to be with Simon, she is as equally clear she cannot sever her relationship with her family. She knew before coming here she couldn't unravel herself from her love for Simon, now she knows she cannot turn her back on and walk away from her family either. She is acutely aware of the dilemma she faces and almost screams to herself as she tries to force her mind to work even harder to resolve the mess she is in, but she knows she can't bring together two polar opposites. Rarely, if ever, has Emma felt so out of control. She can see no way out, she is stuck, she is trapped, and she feels her helplessness only feeding her fear and confusion.

With no way out, Emma's mind now starts to mimic her body: not knowing what to think, it starts to close down. Then, as her whole being cries out for relief and with her eyes staring in front of her, Emma starts to weep. Tears begin to flow from her in even greater quantities than those which had rolled down Sarah's cheeks the previous Saturday. But Emma's tears are initially shed silently; she doesn't moan, and, other than the blinking of her reddening eyes and a puffing of her cheeks, her body remains rigid, statue-like. Earlier Emma had tried to force tears of sorrow, but she had failed; now her tears are almost gushing from her. They seem to be the release of the pent-up feelings of frustration, fear and confusion that have been building within her, bursting out as tears of distress because she has no idea what she should do. But underlying all this, Emma is also shedding tears of love – love for both Simon and her family – and that's really why she can't stop crying. A moment or two later she lets out a sob as she takes in a quick breath of air, though she isn't aware of it.

Already sensing the change which has come over Emma, on hearing her sob, Sarah moves in closer to her. Placing one arm behind Emma's back, Sarah takes hold of Emma's hand and says to her, "I know how hard it is, my dear, but you can't turn back the clock. You can't undo what's happened, all you can do is move on. I know you have the strength to go forward, for after all, Emma, you are a Makoni like your mother Alice before you and your grandfather Joshua before her. The baton has been handed on to you; you will do it, I know you will. We're all relying on you."

Emma says nothing, but Sarah's words seem to act as a catalyst; they start to stir Emma back into action. It only takes her dextrous mind a moment to apply what Sarah has said to the other side of the dilemma she is facing.

"That's it," Emma says to herself as she realises she has been crying and lets go of Sarah's hand to wipe her eyes with the back of her hand.

"That's exactly it, I have to go forward," she tells herself with even greater conviction now. "Ma's absolutely right, I have no other options; there is no turning back." Then her mind begins to race again and it all starts to make sense. This is the path Emma's mind traces.

> *Although it's not the answer, I have to let the rest of today happen as we had planned it. I know I must stick with Simon, but now I know I can never turn my back on my family: I have to remain tied to both right to the bitter end. I know last Sunday night after talking to Simon I started to feel what we had planned to do was all wrong and just now I started to dread it all again, but now I can see clearly what we had decided to do is **not** wrong. In fact, it's not only not wrong, it's the only thing we can do. Anything else we could do has to be wrong! When Simon and I were struggling to come up with a plan at the Bronte, I had simply **hoped it** would turn out all right. I certainly told myself we needed to tell the truth, but I never really considered then whether what we were planning to do was the right course of action to take. Now I'm not only convinced it is, but I think the **process** is as important as, even more important than, the **outcome**. What we do is*

the key to everything: indeed; I am sure, were I to ask him later, Don Paulo would confirm that pursuing the correct process is the only correct ethical path I can take. What happens is not down to us, we cannot control it and shouldn't try to. It hinges on trust: Simon and I have to trust each other and we each have to trust our families. None of us can turn back the clock on Joshua's killing, but equally Simon and I can't turn back the clock on our love for each other either. There is no going back. As Ma has just said to me, going forward is what we have to do. That is the only answer there is.

Although she is no nearer to knowing what the outcome of this afternoon's events will be, Emma can feel herself growing more confident as she convinces herself of the centrality and the soundness of the process they are about to embark upon. She knows laying before their families the truth is the only honest thing they can do, and she knows everyone to be assembled in the room shortly as honest people. As for the consequences, 'what will be will be', Emma says to herself. Emma is about to venture into the unknown. She is about to push her foot off the bottom of the swimming pool, knowing she will have no control over what happens next. But, in a strange way, she feels if not at peace then at least content with allowing things to pan out without her intervening. On this occasion she feels quietly confident she will be able to withstand whatever the world throws at her. Though normally, Emma is keen to influence outcomes, in some way she feels relief she doesn't have to try to manipulate her world.

As if to confirm the optimism she feels rising within her, the sun comes out. Looking up, Emma can see after the next cloud there is an almost uninterrupted blue sky and they are in for a long spell of continuous sunshine. She feels herself recovering and turns to Sarah and smiles, then notices Sarah has been crying too. For all her traditional beliefs, it is clear Sarah still has a heavy heart and keenly feels the loss of her daughter. Why shouldn't she, thought Emma. Saying you need to move on after something dreadful happens doesn't remove the pain.

"We should get going, Ma," says Emma. "We need to get back home and change into some clean, dry clothes and warm up." Then, in a way she hoped wouldn't come across as an after-thought, she adds, "Thank you for bringing me here, Ma. You were right, I did have to come; it helps it all come together as well as making it a little bit easier to understand everything you had to go through."

"Thank you, Emma," says Sarah. "I know Alice would have been proud of the fine woman you have grown up to be."

Sarah returns Emma's warm and comforting smile and they move slowly away, arm in arm, and Emma wonders if she will ever return. Misty steam starts to rise up from the damp road they step onto, warmed by the return of September's sun as Emma feels a cloud lifting from her heart.

As they started to make their way back up the hill to the cemetery entrance, Emma soon realised Sarah was finding the walk, and especially the climb, increasingly difficult. She sounded breathless and was clearly struggling as first she began to slow down, and then she stopped every hundred yards to rest and try to regain her strength. Emma could see how weary she looked and even started to worry Sarah might pass out. Then, when Sarah had stopped for the second time, Emma saw she had that same look in her eyes which she had first noticed the previous Sunday when she had supposed the odd colouring had been caused by sunlight filtered through the net curtains of her kitchen. Sarah had said she was fine then, but looking at her now, Emma was even less convinced than she had been then. The strange thing was that Sarah had set a cracking pace when they set off for Alice's grave and as far as Emma could recall she hadn't flagged on the way in spite of the cold and the rain, so she'd clearly been fine earlier. It was all very odd, thought Emma.

After passing the Islington Crematorium, the road flattened out for a while and Sarah seemed to recover. But then, when High View Road became Parkers Road, and the road started to climb again and they came to a more wooded area, Sarah became breathless once again, though she only had to stop once before the road flattened out for the final time. When she stopped, Sarah smiled across at Emma as if to say, 'I know you know there's something wrong, but don't ask. The last thing I want is for you to say we should abort today's important gathering at the Robertsons.' I won't let you do this. I'll be just fine'.

Thinking fast, Emma knew she had to change her plans for what the two of them would do before their scheduled arrival at Simon's. Her idea had been to catch the bus outside the cemetery, go straight to Muswell Hill and have a leisurely lunch at *Jenny's*. Showing Sarah where she and Simon had first properly met and eating comfort food, she thought, would help to lift their spirits after the visit to Alice's grave. Emma was keen for Sarah to be in the best possible mood to prepare her for what lay ahead. But the rain, their damp clothes, her own emotional state – so different from the straightforward feelings of sadness she had anticipated having and which she assumed she would get over quickly – and now her concern for Sarah's health meant Emma needed a new plan.

So, as they emerged from the wooded area and turned left onto Cross Road, scarcely five minutes from the entrance gates, Emma took out her phone and logged onto the Uber taxi website. She typed in Sarah's postcode, tapped in a fare estimate and was quoted between £5 and £6. She signed into her account and accepted the quote, praying Sarah would make it to the entrance, which she did. The taxi was there when they reached the gate and their cheerful driver — a former solider with 10 years' service in the Eritrean army who had recently arrived in Britain – was happy to stop off at Emma's so she could pick up a change of clothes for herself before dropping them both at Sarah's at no extra charge.

By the time they had both changed, warmed up and nibbled at a light lunch (neither of them was hungry though for very different reasons), it was already well after one. Sarah said she had totally recovered and, as if to prove it, easily managed the walk up the short hill from Moat Crescent to East End Road to wait for the bus to East Finchley. It came quickly but they then had to wait for what seemed like an age before catching the bus to Muswell Hill and it was after two before they were at Muswell Hill Broadway, considerably later than Emma had planned. As they stepped off the bus, Emma's hands were clammy and her clean, freshly-ironed blouse was damp. She was already a bundle of nerves.

The Planned Encounter

With Sarah at her side and smiling broadly, Emma rang the Robertsons' bell. Simon answered the door while Cathy and Peter remained in the sitting room where he had asked them to wait. He greeted Sarah and Emma as they walked in by embracing them affectionately in turn. When his body met Emma's, her mood changed. Drained by the way their visit to the cemetery had ended, concerned about Sarah's health and having just spent their bus ride worrying how their parents would react to what they were about to tell them, she had arrived downcast. But, touched by the manner in which Sarah greeted Simon, with a warmth far greater than she had seen him express, and overcome by the sense of security which her closeness to him now triggered, Emma's fear and foreboding momentarily left her.

The three of them moved swiftly through the hallway and, as Simon opened the door into the sitting room, Cathy and Peter stood up as one, like actors on a film set drilled to rise on cue. The three adults walked confidently towards each other, their faces beaming, and before Simon could say anything by way of introduction, they had already begun to shake hands. Sensing this was far too formal, and led by Cathy, the three of them then took a step closer and shared a more intimate greeting by grasping each other's elbows in a firm arm-shake. They then all took a pace back at the same time – as if Sarah had joined the acting fraternity – and shared a knowing parental smile.

Cathy then said, "You are so very welcome Sarah. I – or I should say *we* – have heard so much about you and the incredible work you do at the hospice. And you must be so proud of your daughter; Emma has become very special to us too."

"It's so good to be here and to meet you both, too, at last," responded Sarah. Emma knew how formal Sarah was in new social settings but could already detect –or was it merely her hope? – they would genuinely grow to like each other and not merely get along. This seemed to be confirmed almost at once in the cheek-to-cheek embrace Cathy and Emma now shared.

Sarah then turned to Peter, who smiled and said, using his best Shona "You are most welcome!" and they both laughed as he moved forward to give her a traditional Zimbabwean handshake: an upward movement to grip thumbs before and after the normal right-arm handshake. Simon smiled to himself as he saw his father's free arm hover uncertainly behind Sarah's back. Although it didn't quite succeed in making contact, the gesture signalled a rare affection, as Simon knew his father found it difficult even to shake hands with women he didn't know.

He was, of course, far more demonstrative and relaxed with Emma, whom he hugged fondly as he had delighted in doing every time they had met since first being introduced way back in June. He then went on to kiss her lightly on her cheek, something he had never done before. Simon and Cathy both smiled. Neither of them noticed Emma tense up slightly as Peter kissed her. Peter missed this too as he was, as ever, preoccupied with managing his own emotions.

Simon took the lead in motioning everyone to sit down. He and Emma had discussed at length where everyone should be seated for the events which were to follow. Cathy and Peter were seated in the two armchairs close to each other in front of the bay window on the far side of the room. Simon beckoned to Sarah to sit down on the matching sofa opposite, and then he and Emma sat down on the two slat-backed chairs which Simon had brought in from the dining room and had placed equidistant between the armchairs and the sofa. As with the positioning of Cathy and Peter's armchairs, these were close enough for the two of them to touch. Together, the chairs formed as big a circle as the room would allow. Emma sat on Simon's left so she was a yard or so away from Sarah to *her* left, while Simon sat on Emma's right so he was a step away from Peter to *his* right and, to complete the circle, Cathy sat to the right of Peter. The greatest distance was the one which separated Sarah and Peter, who faced each other on opposite sides of the room.

When everyone was seated, Emma glanced knowingly at Simon, surprised how relaxed she felt at that moment. As they had agreed, she spoke first, but merely to welcome them all and announce that Simon would explain why they had asked them to gather here on this Sunday afternoon.

Simon took hold of Emma's hand and squeezed it to give him the confidence he felt he needed to begin, though he knew this, the first part of the afternoon, was the easy bit. He started by telling them how grateful he and Emma were for their encouraging the two of them to go out to Zimbabwe. He said how much they had both really enjoyed being with their relatives, but more than that, their being away had given them the space and time they needed to think more deeply about their own relationship.

Simon gave out a genuine, if nervous, laugh as he said, "I'm sure I fell in love with Emma well before she did with me." She chipped in to insist it was the other way round and he had simply been slower to realise it. Everyone laughed and they both felt things had started well.

Then, becoming more serious, Simon said, "our being together in Zim was crucially important as it removed any lingering doubts either of us might have had about our relationship, and confirmed our being together would be long-lasting; indeed, we have now become what you might call a permanent fixture." These were the words Simon had rehearsed, but as he said them he knew what he had said had come across as wooden.

Emma thought the same. She laughed and said, "what Simon is really trying to tell you is we have in effect become a couple, it's as simple as that, and, of course, we're both delighted!"

Simon's eyes travelled round the room and he could see everyone was pleased, but they clearly wanted to hear more. He continued by saying, "Emma and I are fully aware and respect that you, Mum and Dad, as well as you, Sarah, are more formal and traditional about all these things than Em and I are, having grown up here in modern-day Britain. But what I want to say now is we have reached the stage of our relationship where we have decided to start living together."

Emma felt she needed to rescue Simon once again so quickly added, knowing this was what they really wanted to hear, "Yes, and one day, I'm sure we will get married, but that is very much for the future, not for now, and definitely not why we asked you all to be here with us today."

"But please," she pleaded, "please, don't go around telling everyone we're engaged because this is not the way we, and our friends, think about these things these days and – to be frank – we would be a bit upset if you did. In the way we and our friends see things, we would simply say we are an 'item'. We are now 'together' and this is what we will start to tell our friends and work colleagues. Things are so different now than they were when you were young. We certainly feel it's far too early to start thinking about marriage and children and, to be frank, we don't want to focus on such things for the moment. *This* is about us *now*; the rest is for the future."

Emma felt she had hit the right note. She laughed again, leant over and gave Simon an affectionate kiss, lip to lip, and could feel the happiness rising inside her. Simon could sense the positive atmosphere in the room, and, feeling his earlier tension leaving him, his love for Emma shone out now from his face even if, underneath, it was relief he felt more than anything else because – so far – things were going well. Sarah, Cathy and Peter had heard and could now see what they had come for, and Simon and Emma had successfully communicated to their parents how they wished them to understand their relationship – firm, secure and permanent but modern. As if further proof was needed, Sarah started clapping and Cathy and Peter joined in.

Simon now rose from his seat and he was about to announce they all needed a break – to have some tea – as he and Emma had agreed would happen next, when he felt Emma's hand on his left arm checking him and resumed his seat. Simon could tell she had something pressing she wanted to add and could feel his stomach start to squirm. When they had started to develop their plans for today by the pool at the Bronte, Emma had said at this point she felt she had to make some comment about Robbie: she told Simon it was the final thing needed to clear the air. This was because she knew Cathy had got wind of another important relationship in her life, but, even more importantly, Sarah was aware of how difficult Emma had been finding it over the summer to let go of Robbie, and Emma knew this would be uppermost in her mind when she and Simon declared their enduring love for each other. As they talked all this over – if there was ever a time in their relationship when they had had an argument, this had been – Simon believed he had persuaded Emma not to bring up the subject of Robbie at this juncture, and with great reluctance she had agreed.

Unbeknown to Simon, Emma had spoken to Sarah about Robbie only a little earlier, as they were changing buses in East Finchley. She knew she had to, though she felt bad about it as she knew she could only tell Sarah about Robbie by explaining the new developments in her relationship with Simon, and they had both agreed this should wait until they were all together. It meant Emma breaking her promise. So, after skirting round the subject for a while, Emma had taken the plunge and said, "Ma, you know how much Robbie has meant to me over these past years?"

"Yes," said Sarah and the word lingered on her lips, suggesting the subject had been very much on her mind.

"Well," said Emma, "over the course of these past months, as you are well aware, I have rather agonised over the love I had for Robbie and my new love for Simon. But I am pleased to say all this has now been resolved. As we shall explain further when we're at the Robertsons', following our time together in Zim, I am now totally convinced Simon is and will always be the man with whom I wish to share my life. Robbie knows this, Ma – he has been in touch with me since we came back from Zim – and though of course he has found it hard, as I did until recently, he has given his blessing to us and our future. Robbie, I know, will always be special to me and in time I am confident he will become special to both of us. Needless to say, my relationship with Robbie has already changed, and from now on, of course, it will be totally different from what it used to be."

Sarah had replied with affection, though Emma wasn't able to judge with how much conviction, by saying simply, "I know how hard it's been for you, Emma, but I can see you've made the decision you're happy with, so please don't think I will ever get in the way of what you think is best."

Emma knew it wasn't a ringing endorsement.

Sarah had then added, with almost the same words Immaculata had used, "My dear Emma, go where your heart tells you you need to go," and with that their bus arrived and this difficult exchange came to its natural end.

To Simon's immense relief, it wasn't Robbie Emma wanted to talk about. She felt she needed to say something more to Cathy especially, but also to Sarah, woman to woman, as she could tell what she had said earlier about marriage and children had sounded too vague and vacuous.

"Simon has asked you not to think of us as engaged, still less about our getting married soon," said Emma. "And this is my view too. But I'd like to make a little addition to what he has said. I love Simon as intensely and deeply as if we were 'old-fashioned engaged', as if he was already my husband-eventually-to-be. Ours is no temporary or passing relationship. Simon and I are completely committed to each other; our time in Zimbabwe confirmed this and, so to speak, cemented us together. Being together is not only what we both want but I'm hoping we'll soon be blessed with children." Simon was shocked: they had never talked about having children, so what did Emma mean by bringing this up and by using the word 'soon'? But he pushed these concerns to the back of his mind because he was delighted Emma hadn't broken her promise, as he had feared she was just about to, and talk about Robbie.

As the young – understandably at times tongue-tied – couple had talked, their parents had listened. Except for Sarah's brief clapping, no one had interrupted. Now Simon and Emma had finished what they had wanted to say, the atmosphere in the room was palpably upbeat. Notwithstanding their repeated efforts to prevent it happening, the unanimous interpretation of what the two of them had said conveyed quite the opposite message to the one Emma and Simon had been struggling to articulate. As the three of them understood it, Simon and Emma would be married and were planning, possibly quite soon, to have children, and they were all evidently ecstatic as Cathy, Peter and Sarah were now all wearing broad smiles.

The visible delight on all their faces, however, concealed subtle and unexpressed differences between the three adults in the room. Peter was the most excited. What he had just heard confirmed what he already knew: Simon was deeply in love with Emma, and she adored him, so that box could be ticked. But to Peter what really mattered was what this meant going forward. He knew Emma and Simon were both bright and ambitious go-getters, so their financial future was assured, which meant that box could be confidently ticked as well. But perhaps most importantly, feeling prouder of and closer to Simon than ever before following last week's interaction between the two of them, Peter was aware today heralded the start of the new generation of Robertsons. This is what pleased him the most. After all he had gone through, he could now – at last – take a back seat and watch his family flourish without having to worry any more. He knew how taken he already was with Emma, but now he felt a warm glow inside, sensing her to be already a member of the family.

As ever, Sarah's love for Emma coloured how she felt about their announcement. She knew how happy Emma was with Simon, and Emma's happiness was really all that mattered. However, Sarah had only ever loved one man, Joshua, and if she was honest she would have to admit not really being able to understand how Emma could switch, apparently so seamlessly, from loving Robbie as deeply and completely as she clearly had to loving Simon seemingly just as intensely. This troubled Sarah even though she knew Emma *had* made the switch – that, after all, was what she had told her at the bus stop.

The other thing which worried Sarah was far more practical: she wanted to know how Simon and his family intended to 'settle' matters between them. In many different ways Sarah was still a very traditional person, and none more so than when it came to marriage. She wasn't bothered about Emma and Simon living together before they were officially married. After all, she had done that herself. Living together before marrying in church had always been part of Shona custom long before it reached the shores of Europe and was something the early Christian missionaries, knowing they couldn't alter traditional practice, repeatedly turned a blind eye to. But Sarah's traditions required the family of the husband-to-be to demonstrate their appreciation of the worth of the woman he was marrying before they started to live together. Historically this had usually been done by the exchange of cattle from the groom's to the bride's family, and even in the very different conditions of the war, this is exactly what Joshua's family had done. These days it was predominantly money not cows which were exchanged. Sarah had lived in England long enough not to expect anything for herself from Simon's family, but wasn't he going to give Emma anything, and why hadn't anyone mentioned anything about this? Surely he should at least have given her a ring? But no one had said anything about there being a ring. This bothered Sarah, but she kept her concerns to herself as well.

Cathy was also thrilled by what she had heard: her beloved and only son – and if she was honest, of her two children, the one she had always loved the most – was firmly set on the road to marriage. In time she would become a grandmother and smother her son's children with her love. Before Emma had appeared, Cathy had worried about Simon's ability to relate to women, confirmed by the almost total absence of serious girlfriends in his life. Indeed, at times, she had been concerned he didn't seem to show much interest in women at all. However, Emma was clearly quite a catch: a bright, ambitious, no-nonsense woman who clearly loved her son. All Cathy's instincts told here they were well-matched. Before today, she had worried whether Emma would make a good mother, but even the short time she had had to observe Sarah had convinced her of the strength of the Maconie mothering genes.

But Cathy had other worries. She knew Simon loved Emma and he was lucky to have found her. But she – – 'as any mother would', she said to herself – whether he could have done better. Did Emma's single-mindedness and determination go too far? Was she that little bit too pushy? Would she give Simon the attention he needed; would she help him – push him – to make a success of his new career?

Then there was the delicate subject of race. Cathy was extremely fond of Emma, but she was black and Simon white. She worried about the problems her grandchildren could face first at school and then in adult life as mixed-race children. Cathy had friends, even relatives, whom she knew would raise an eyebrow, or worse, when they knew who her daughter-in-law was. Cathy had already convinced herself this wasn't a problem – for her it simply wasn't an 'issue' – but it did bother her. All these thoughts were in Cathy's mind as she joined everyone else smiling in delight across her sitting room at Emma and Simon's news.

"And now," said Emma, rising up from her seat and beaming broadly, "I think we can all do with a cup of tea."

Simon stood up and was about to go into the kitchen to reboil the kettle and bring out the prepared tea-tray when Sarah jumped up in front of him and began ululating and doing a little dance around them. Emma smiled; it so reminded her of the joy she had felt dancing with her relatives in Mutoko. If there had been any tension in the room while she and Simon had been speaking (and she had sensed none herself), it had now been well and truly broken by Sarah's spontaneous half-dancing and half-jumping, and everyone started to clap. As they did so, Cathy and Peter came across to join the three of them and share in the joy each one of them was feeling. As Emma and Simon breathed in the almost party-like atmosphere which filled the room, they both felt relieved the first part of the afternoon's proceedings had all gone so well.

As soon as he was able, Simon withdrew from the merriment to busy himself in the kitchen, returning as quickly as he could with the tea-tray, and for the next 15 to 20 minutes the room was abuzz with chatter. As time passed, the cups were refilled and the talk was punctuated by the occasional shriek of laughter from Sarah who, more than anyone else, had decided this was the time to properly let her hair down.

Understandably, the conversation initially revolved around Simon and Emma, but it moved on from there, seeming to flow naturally to Zimbabwe as the senior members of the family started to ask each other where they had been born and grown up, and what they missed, having to live in England so far removed from their roots. Simon and Emma were watchful of the conversation straying into the war years, and Emma had warned Sarah to make no mention of Alice 'early on' in the afternoon as it would only be 'confusing'. But they needn't have worried as everyone in the room was clearly aware of the need to prevent the conversation slipping into any potentially difficult areas. After all, all three of them – Sarah, Cathy and Peter – were well skilled in concealing things they believed were best kept hidden.

* * *

With the atmosphere in the room as warm and harmonious as he and Emma had hoped it would be, Simon called everyone 'to order' and asked them to return to where they had been sitting. When they were all settled, the adults looked expectantly across to Simon and Emma. There was a short period of silence before anyone spoke, but long enough for Cathy and Sarah to think at almost the same instant Emma might be pregnant already.

Simon started this part of the proceedings but, like Emma earlier, all he did was say she was the one who was going to speak first. Even before she began, Emma could feel her heartbeat quickening and her hands had already become clammy again. She prayed for the courage to sustain her through to the end of what she had prepared and long dreaded having to say.

"Ma, Peter and Cathy," she began, "what I am about to tell you is without a doubt the most difficult thing I have ever had to say or share with anyone. In the next few moments I am going to lay before you things which will be painful to hear. I will recall events which will be deeply hurtful for *all* of you to listen to because *every one of us* in this room will be affected. It was certainly never Simon's nor my wish to share with you what we are about to tell you and, believe me, we have talked this over so many times, racking our brains thinking of other, gentler, ways of doing so – but we have repeatedly drawn a blank. The only other option, and it is by far the simplest one, would be not to speak about these enormously distressing matters at all, and pretend they never happened. But we know we can't. We are simply unable to keep from you what we now know and remain silent because if we were to do this our entire lives and our future relationship with you would be built on a lie."

Emma paused briefly to take in a large gulp of air. She was already finding this difficult, as she knew she would; but equally she knew she had to go on – she simply had to. The mood had changed and the room was silent. The smiles, the laughter and the merriment had vanished; no one moved a muscle.

"This afternoon," Emma continued, "began with Simon and myself telling you about our love for each other. But, as I am about to explain, our future lives together are dependent on something more than our love for each other and the initial affirmation, support and blessing you have just given us. They require you to know the truth about who exactly we all are, for – and I know this sounds like a riddle – gathered together in this room, we are a different group of people from the ones we think we are. What you do with what I am about to share with you is up to you. All I want now is to present you with the truth as we have learned it, as accurately and honestly as I am able. Once I have told you what we know, you must decide how you feel you should respond. So, let me now lay before you what we discovered while out in Zimbabwe and which we know to be the truth."

Then, with a nod from Simon who looked as worried as she was feeling, Emma launched into the details as bravely as she could.

"Last weekend," she began, "Simon and I deliberately spoke to you individually about what we had learned in Zimbabwe about our pasts and about your pasts. Now is the time to start sharing all this between us."

Then, turning to Sarah, Emma said, "Ma, I first need to tell you when Simon was growing up in north London, he never knew his father – Peter here (she pointed) – had been heavily involved in Zimbabwe's pre-independence war, and, until last week, neither did I. Just as others like him did, Peter went into the army after he left school, but, unlike most others, he was decorated at almost the highest level for his skill, dedication, courage and bravery. Yet, he was so deeply scarred by the experiences he had while in the army that when he left he was deeply troubled in his mind."

Everyone's eyes were now on Peter, but his eyes were cast downwards. His face hadn't changed and he felt fully in control of himself. He had known he would have to share his past with Sarah one day and was grateful for the way Emma had chosen to explain his psychological problems through the prism of the medals he was awarded.

"Peter was so traumatised by his experiences," continued Emma, "he and Cathy chose to shield all this from Simon and his sister Jane when they were growing up." She went on to tell Sarah as sensitively as she could how what they thought had been the right decision at the time turned gradually turned into a nightmare for them as they knew Simon and Jane had to know the truth but couldn't work out how to tell them. Emma then told Sarah what had happened at Kariba when she had been visiting the family in Mutoko. "Simon's uncle opened up and told Simon everything he knew about what had happened during the war years as he had promised Peter he would. You see, Ma, he knew it all because the two of them fought alongside each other in the army; they were best friends."

Before anyone had a chance to speak, Emma then turned to her right to face Peter and Cathy and said to them directly, "And you, Peter and Cathy, don't know what I only learned about myself and my past when I was in Zimbabwe. I discovered Sarah, here, who I grew up deeply loving and always believing was my mother is in fact my grandmother."

Cathy and Peter looked across at Sarah in astonishment.

"For her love of me," Emma continued, raising her arm towards Sarah, and Sarah responded with a motherly smile of affection, "just as you kept Simon in the dark about Peter's past for the best of intentions, so Sarah kept from me that as a teenager she had a daughter named Alice. Then as a teenager, Alice my blood-mother had a daughter and that daughter was me."

Emma then explained how Alice had been born HIV positive, how Sarah had arranged for Alice and herself, a two-year-old, to come to England for Alice to get the drugs she needed and to create a new life for them over here, how Alice died of AIDS soon after arriving and how Sarah stepped in to take Alice's place as her mother. The way Emma described growing up as a confident young girl and how this had been due more than anything else to Sarah's love and devotion to her as she stepped into Alice's shoes to become, in effect, her mother, struck a chord with both Peter and Cathy. It even crossed Cathy's mind she could well have done the same. Emma spoke only briefly about her father, Kenneth Banda, explaining how little she knew and felt about him; it was her way of introducing the subject of her grandfather.

"The most important man in our family," said Emma, "is without any doubt Alice's father, Sarah's husband and my grandfather. Sadly, I never knew him; in fact, he died even before Alice was born. As a teenager, he joined the ZANLA guerrillas but, like so many others, he never returned home when the war ended." For the moment, she left it at that and returned to the way she had discovered Sarah was not her real mother, deliberately avoiding sharing either her grandfather's birth name, Joshua Makonde, or his guerrilla name, Comrade Lightning.

"Then, just as happened with you and Simon," continued Emma, "as I grew up and became an adult, Ma increasingly felt I needed to know the truth about my past and her past. However, again just like with you and Simon, she couldn't bring herself to tell me the truth. So when I was in Mutoko visiting my extended family at the same time Simon was in Kariba with his Uncle Jim, Sarah's elder brother and her younger sister, my Uncle Prosper and Aunt Emerentiana, at Sarah's prompting, told me about Alice and who I really was."

Emma shared a little more of what Prosper and Emerentiana had told her about her family and mentioned the respect they all had for Sarah, then, tracing a path round the room with her eyes and hand, she said, "As I told Ma, here, and as Simon told you, Peter and Cathy, the reason we went to St Michael's Mission was to try to find out more about what exactly had happened to my grandfather, who, as I mentioned just now, never came home after the war ended. Mhondoro was the last place the family had firm news of his whereabouts before everything went silent."

Emma then turned to face Cathy and Pater directly and said, "Simon told you we tracked down a man who claimed to have been a witness to my grandfather's death and that this man – Mr Svosve was his name –said his body had almost certainly been eaten by wild animals so we left as we seemed to have found what we had come for. But there is more to add. As I explained to Ma, this Mr Svosve not only claimed to have been present at my grandfather's death and to have buried him as well but passed on to me a wooden cross my grandfather had worn about his neck. Last Sunday I gave the cross to Ma, who not only confirmed it was indeed my grandfather's but told me she had carved it for him herself. So we now had the proof of his death we needed. As I am sure you can imagine, sharing all this with Ma was simply horrific for her as she relived the pain of the loss of her beloved husband and my dear grandfather as – finally – she had confirmation of his death." Emma cast a quick glance back at Sarah and was relieved to see how strong she looked as she sat listening again to Emma's account of Joshua's death, which last week had caused her such distress.

"And that," said Emma, "pretty much gets us to what all of us now know about our pasts, about your pasts." She paused and rose slightly in her chair, gripping the sides as she did so, as she knew they were now coming to the most crucial and difficult part of the afternoon. The atmosphere in the room grew more tense. All eyes were on Emma. As she breathed in deeply, she heard Simon whisper quietly to her, "You're doing just fine, Em."

"While all this was true", said Emma, "it was not the whole story. Last weekend we deliberately held back key details of my grandfather's death which we learned from Mr Svosve. Now is the time to share them with you, but before we do this, I am going to move over and sit next to Sarah here on the couch, and Simon is going to move his chair a little closer to you, Peter, and Cathy." Then, unable to disguise her nervousness, Emma called on Simon to take over.

"Dad," began Simon earnestly, "I learned from Uncle Jim that in your final few months in the army you had become increasingly focused on trying to track down three key guerrilla commanders who had led a succession of attacks on strategically important targets in the area south and eastwards from Harare, extending up to the Mutoko area. Some weeks after your unit had eliminated two of these three commanders, you picked up the spoor of a group you had been tracking, hoping it was being led by the third commander you had been after. You managed to surprise the group just as they were launching a hugely ambitious attack at the farmhouse of a prominent national politician located in the Beatrice area south of Harare."

From the moment Simon had started talking, Peter had become visibly alert, but when he mentioned the final farmhouse assault Simon could see his father's fingers pressing hard down on the padded sides of his armchair as his leg muscles tightened beneath his trousers. Simon motioned for Emma to take up the story.

"Ma," continued Emma, "this Mr Svosve I have mentioned knew far more than I have so far shared with you. He not only knew about the attack on a farmhouse north of St Michael's but he was there when it happened. He witnessed the whole thing, though he wasn't a guerrilla himself; he was a young *mujiba* who, nonetheless, played a key role in the whole event."

Emma raised her voice slightly as she looked across the room towards Simon and his father and said, "Peter, my grandfather, Ma's husband, whose death Mr Svosve witnessed, was born Joshua Makonde.

"I guess that name means very little to you, probably nothing at all." She willed herself on, praying she had the strength to finish. "But when I tell you my grandfather's war-name – his *Chimurenga* name – was Comrade Lightning, you will know exactly who I am talking about."

Peter froze and Simon could see the tips of his fingers whiten as he pushed them ever deeper into the arms of his chair. Simon looked across at his father's face but couldn't tell what was going on in his mind. Though Cathy had never heard the name Comrade Lightning, she sensed the significance of what was happening and shuffled uncomfortably on her seat. Emma knew she couldn't stop now; she had to hurry on.

"Comrade Lightning was the last of the three guerrilla leaders you had been trying to track down, Peter," said Emma. "What you had always suspected, but had never been able to confirm definitively, was that it was Comrade Lightning who had led the assault on this farmhouse. So you, Peter, and my grandfather were the two commanders who led their troops on opposing sides to what would turn out, though in very different ways, to be your final battle."

"Yes, Dad," said Simon, whose turn it now was to continue their account of what had happened on that fateful day. "And from Mr Svosve we learned far more about the farmhouse attack than even Uncle Jim had been able to tell me only a few days earlier."

"Uncle Jim gave me the details of this attack as you and he remembered them. How you followed the guerrilla fighter who led the assault into the farmhouse. How you shot him in the chest but never knew what happened to him as you immediately had to defend yourself against the two guerrillas who had followed you into the farmhouse and would have killed you if you hadn't managed to surprise them and shoot them first.

"How you then ran out of the farmhouse to lead your men in the final assault on the remaining guerrillas who had regrouped on the nearby *kopje*. And how when you returned to the farmhouse there was no sign of the first guerrilla soldier you had shot in the chest. He seemed to have vanished into thin air.

"Well, Dad, that guerrilla leader you surprised, struggling with the door to the saferoom at the end of the farmhouse corridor, was the same Comrade Lightning you had been hunting. You never knew his identity for sure, but I can tell you the shots you fired on that day's assault were directed at Comrade Lightning. It is difficult for me to say this, Dad, and forgive me for its sounding harsh and cruel but the truth, Dad, is your bullets entered the chest of Sarah's husband, Emma's grandfather, causing him eventually to bleed to death."

Sufficient had been said for everyone in the room to grasp the enormity of what had been said, and, just as Emma and Simon had expected, when Simon reached this point in the story, the reaction from Sarah and Pater was instantaneous. It began with Sarah, who started to whimper on the sofa.

Emma put her arm around Sarah to try to comfort and console her, but she simply sat there sobbing. Then she started to groan before giving off a series of long, low moans which rose to a crescendo and reverberated round the room. Emma recognised the sounds Sarah was making – they were similar to those she had heard her mother make the previous Sunday – but there was a crucial difference. This time Sarah seemed to be far more in control of herself and remained fully aware of her surroundings because Emma noticed that every so often, she shot a glance across the room to Peter, though as she couldn't see directly into Sarah's eyes, Emma wasn't able to read precisely what they were saying.

Just as this was happening, on the other side of the room Peter began first to twitch and then to respond to Sarah's groans and moans with noises of his own. But before these started, Peter's twitching switched to shaking. Simon was ready: he jumped up, leaned over and pressed down on his father's hands to try to control what were now both erratic and frightening movements as his whole body began to shake, far more violently than it had the previous Sunday. Cathy rose to come to Simon's aid. Though the two of them worked together almost as a team, they couldn't control Peter's shaking. Simon couldn't believe how strong his father was – that was terrifying too. It was then, as Peter continued to shake, that a slow croaking sound arose from deep within Peter's throat, half-muffled as if he were choking, or possibly suffocating. It was unlike anything Simon had ever heard coming out of a human being. He knew instinctively his father was in or near to being in a trance and Simon could feel panic starting to take hold of him, fearful of what Peter might do next. To add to his distress, as he glanced across at her, Simon could see from his mother's face how frightened she was: tears were streaming down her cheeks.

What happened next was even more terrifying. Peter wrenched his hands free of Simon's and Cathy's grip and stood up. He pointed with his right arm thrust forward and, with his voice rising, he started to shout, spitting out groups of words staccato-like which boomed out across the room. Simon and Emma could hear clearly and distinctly the clipped sound of a strong Rhodesian accent taking over from the more mellow English accent Peter had increasingly cultivated over his years living in the UK. "Where's-he-gone-hey?   For-God's-sake-what-has-happened-to-him? Where's-the-body? Is-he-dead, or is-he-just-wounded-hey? I-need-answers. I-need-them-now! Find-him, find-him, for-God's-sake-find-him. Quick. Quick. Quick."

As if proof were needed he was back at the farmhouse, reliving his final battle, as Peter spoke, his eyes were looking straight ahead of him, focused in the way they do when you're looking at people right there immediately in front of you. His eyes switched from one imaginary person to the next, his eyebrows rising and his forehead thrust forward as he demanded answers, as he demanded action.

When he had finished firing off all these questions, Peter let out a scream, looked upwards to the sky he saw way above him rather than the ceiling of the sitting room and slumped back into his chair. Peter's side of the room now fell silent, leaving only Sarah's moans to fill the silence which must have continued while all this had been going on, but they were far quieter now than they had been. Soon, Sarah was whimpering again, her voice sounding as if it had been pounded into submission by the violence of Peter's terrifying outburst.

For a while there was silence: no one said anything, and no one moved. Then, gradually, Simon, who had been watching them closely, saw that both Sarah and his father had started to recover. As the tension left them, they looked calmer, and a few moments later Simon judged they were now more or less aware of where they were and Peter had become himself again. As if to announce his trance-like state had left him, Simon's father put his hand on Simon's and patted it as if to say he had recovered and all was now well again, but he still looked drained and didn't smile. Simon knew he had to seize the opportunity: there was more he needed to say.

Though he was hesitant about saying more, fearing he might make things worse again, Simon felt he had to complete what he and Emma had decided they **had** to say concerning the events Mr Svosve imparted to them. Indeed, though he felt simply wretched inside, Simon convinced himself he had an even greater responsibility now to provide the final details of what had happened than he had had before he had started. He drew some comfort from what he had understood from Peter's outburst as he sensed what he was about to say could help to answer some of what Peter had spat out earlier. So, taking a deep breath, Simon completed their story, pausing from time to time to help his father take in what he was saying and to help it all sink in.

Over the course of the next few minutes, Simon recounted how during the shooting inside the farmhouse, Mr Svosve was lying hidden with his friend, the cook's son, waiting close by outside, ready to go into the farmhouse and down the corridor to meet Comrade Lightning. They were to take the sedated and kidnapped farmer whom Comrade Lightning was to have overpowered and tie him onto a donkey to take him to Mozambique.

How the plan had all gone wrong.

How Mr Svosve ran into the farmhouse to discover Comrade Lightning lying bleeding but still alive in the corridor to the safe room.

How Mathias had joined him and together they pulled him outside and strapped him onto the donkey instead, being careful to cover their tracks and remove all signs of the blood and boot marks on the ground before they made their escape.

How they realised Comrade Lightning had died a little while later, still strapped to the back of the donkey.

How they had found a place to bury him that same night in the sandy soil of a donga, a shallow makeshift and temporary grave.

And how, when Mr Svosve returned some weeks later, once he believed it was safe to do so, just before the rains, to remove the body for its final burial, all he found were some remnants of ripped and torn clothing which they recognised to be Comrade Lightning's and evidence of wild animals and vultures having visited the site.

Sarah had, of course, heard some of this from Emma the previous Sunday and she showed little emotion as Simon retold the story she knew – of Joshua's final moments, his temporary burial and the discovery that the body was no longer there. But for Peter it was all new and as the account of what happened fell from Simon's lips it was evident his father was not merely taking it all in but seemed to be drawing some sort of comfort from knowing exactly what had happened because he nodded as he fit together in his mind the final pieces of the jig-saw he had thought would always remain incomplete.

When Simon had finished, the whole room fell silent once again. Everyone was wrapped up in their own thoughts as they tried to make sense of what they had heard and began to try to work out what it meant for them both individually and as the even more closely-grouped people they had become. It was a silence of intense reflection.

For a long time, no one said anything, and no one moved. Emma knew it was not for her to break the silence, and even when she heard herself breathing, she felt she was on land she shouldn't be trespassing on – and Simon felt much the same. To begin with Emma feared the worst. She felt the silence in the room was like the stillness of a dam wall cracking before it burst to send water cascading downstream with such speed and ferocity nothing could prevent the destruction of everything which lay in its path.

Then, as the silence lengthened further, Emma's confidence grew. Sarah hadn't shouted across to Peter, accusing him of killing her beloved Joshua and it didn't look as if she would. Peter had made no triumphant comment about his finally knowing he had succeeded in tracking down and killing the third of the three guerrilla leaders he had pledged to eliminate. More ominously, though, Emma could see no sign of remorse cross Peter's face for what he had done to her grandfather, no evidence of sorrow or regret, no signal indicating guilt for his having done anything wrong. So, at best it seemed what their presentation of the truth had done was to create a stand-off.

Even for Emma, the silence eventually became too long to bear. She began to worry their worst fears were now being acted out: the fact no one was prepared or willing to say anything meant nothing more *was* going to happen; no one *was* going to say anything. The web of words they had so carefully spun, the way they had planned their drip-feed presentation of the truth, was all for nought. Perhaps everyone would leave the room without a further word being uttered, leaving Simon and Emma not knowing where they stood. What then?

Desperately, Emma looked across to Simon but she wasn't able to make eye contact. He was looking down at the floor, and she sensed he was as downcast as she was. Oh God, she said to herself, it's not only all gone horribly wrong but has moved out of reach and is now out of our control. This has turned out to be nothing like we expected: we have created a wretched, irretrievable situation from which we can't escape. Emma's silence began to fill with ominous foreboding.

When Emma was at her lowest, things started to happen. It began with Sarah, who broke the silence by saying quietly, but with determination in her voice, "I would like to speak".

Emma was startled, not so much because it was Sarah who spoke first – though she had not expected her to – but more by the strength of her voice. Sarah sounded again like the strong and confident mother Emma knew of old, not the uncertain, hesitant and teary-eyed woman she had been with for many moments since her return from Zimbabwe.

Sarah then stood up and, looking directly across the room, gathered herself to speak, as if she was about to address a large and formal meeting. She wanted everyone to listen carefully to what she was about to say and they did. No one in the room would ever forget Sarah's speech.

"We are a family deeply troubled by war," she said, and then stopped.

Everyone looked closely at Sarah. They were all puzzled if not confused, and in exactly the same way, by what she had said. Sarah was the only non-native English speaker in the room, and her English was excellent, but surely, she had made a mistake? Why did she say 'we are a family'? Surely, she should have said 'we are two families deeply affected by war' – after all, that was what this whole afternoon was all about. But, as they were about to discover, Sarah had said precisely what she had meant to say.

"We suffered immeasurable pain as Zimbabwe struggled to gain its independence," she continued. "I lost my dear husband, Joshua, and you, Peter, suffered the loss of your health and were deeply scarred.

"My Joshua was such a fine man: *ichokwadi* (it is true)!" Sarah continued, wiping away an unwanted tear from her cheeks. "He fought and died for a better future and I've spent not just years but decades now trying to make sense of it all. I know, because my heart has told me, that my Joshua laid down his life in the hope the country he contributed to creating would be a place where the lives of all Zimbabwe's children would not be determined by privilege or the colour of their skin but by reward for hard work and respect for all. My Joshua gave his life so everyone would have the opportunity to prosper in a land where we could, and would, live united as one.

"But as we now know, the gleaming new Zimbabwe soon tarnished, then rapidly began to rust. And what a rusting it was! For so many of our people, hope has been dashed, to be reborn as despair. Corruption has spread like a cancer, spawning greed which has left so many not only poor, jobless and hungry but as voiceless as they had been before. But this doesn't have to be the end of it; this *must not be* the end of it. *We* have it within *our* power to create a different future."

Although at this point Emma didn't know where all this was leading, she could feel her mother's passion and optimism as she spoke. It reminded her so much of when Prosper had spoken to her that morning under the mango tree with such grace and dignity. As had happened at Alice's grave, so too now: Emma felt proud to be a Makoni.

Then, to everyone's surprise Sarah raised her hand and pointed towards Peter as she addressed him directly, saying "My Joshua died at your hands, Peter, with you both fighting for a better future. My Joshua died and sacrificed his life for a future he hoped to see, but didn't.

"But this doesn't have to be the end. We have the chance few others have been given – we have it within our power to unite our two families who were divided by death to create one family and the new life, God willing, it will bring," Sarah continued.

"Peter and Cathy, I want us to be one family, just as Joshua would have wanted us to be. He died so today's happiness could come about. Here in this room – now – we can create that new Zimbabwe we all hoped for in microcosm. We only have to say yes to these young people. If, after hearing what Simon and Emma have told us, if, now knowing the truth, we are able to bless the coming together of our children, then we will confirm the values you, Peter, and my Joshua fought for and for which he sacrificed his life. What Joshua would want more than anything else would be to know his death sowed the seed for the creation of new life built on the principles he so heroically fought for. *We* can say yes to these young people because *he* would have said yes, too. If we cannot give our blessing to these two young people born out of the struggle, our struggle, then Joshua really would have sacrificed his life for nought, his death would have been in vain. There is nothing better we could do to honour Joshua and everyone who died in our war, our struggle, than to celebrate and rejoice in the love of our two children, Emma and Simon."

Simon was familiar with the speeches and sermons of Martin Luther King; Sarah's words, he felt, would not have looked out of place in the pages of King's writing. Emma was equally dumbfounded. Not unlike Simon, it struck Emma that Sarah sounded rather like a preacher from the American South. Where did she learn to speak like this, Emma wondered, as a feeling of immense pride filled her breast?

But this wasn't the time for reflection. Sarah hadn't quite finished. She turned, looked directly at Peter, whose eyes were already fixed on her, and, as their eyes met, finished with these words. "And so, Peter, though my heart is heavy," she said, quietly but loud enough for everyone to hear, her face speaking gentleness, "I forgive you.

"I forgive you for what happened at that farmhouse near Mhondoro so many years ago but brought alive to us so vividly today. I forgive you for killing my beloved Joshua. I do this to honour Joshua, yes, but also to honour the lives of our children here, Emma and Simon. And if one day they are to have children of their own, I hope – when they are old enough to hear what happened here today – they, in their turn, will honour both Joshua and you too, Peter, as they are told how our two families became one in a moment of shared forgiveness, and that they, in their turn, will remember what they are told."

Sarah sat down and the room fell silent once again. In the moments she had been on her feet, Sarah had changed the atmosphere in the room from fear and foreboding to hope. The silence now was one of renewed expectation; it was a silence which cried out for Peter to break. Simon had read a lot about peace and reconciliation but he never thought he would witness such a scene, live, in his own sitting room. Emma felt very small. The plans she had so carefully woven and spun now appeared so parochial in the face of the towering strength of her mother.

With Sarah's, Simon's and Emma's eyes fixed on Peter's face, to everyone's surprise, it was Cathy who broke the silence. Cathy had become increasingly uncomfortable as Sarah had been speaking. Her first words were far more than a cautious counterweight to Sarah's appeal for forgiveness. Cathy lobbed a powerful explosive into their midst. Challengingly and with a chilling hint of aggression in her voice, her eyes darting between Sarah and Peter, Cathy said demandingly, "What has Peter done for which he needs to be forgiven?"

With almost everyone in the room grappling to understand what she had said and what it implied, Cathy stood up and explained exactly what she had meant. "Forgiveness is certainly a wonderful gift but it can only be bestowed on those who have done wrong," she said.

"Of course, what we have heard this afternoon is really and truly dreadful and, Sarah, I'm truly and genuinely sorry to have heard how your husband Joshua died, and it looks pretty certain it was Peter who shot him. But let's not get carried away or be driven by sentimentality. This was a war and wars are terrible things. Peter may well have killed Joshua, in fact he probably did, but he didn't commit murder. Murder is *wrongful* killing, but Peter was doing what he believed was right. What he did really *was* right, not wrong and no one *ever* needs to be forgiven for doing something right."

Cathy then looked directly across at Sarah and, with one arm outstretched towards her, the other now resting on Peter's shoulder, she shared more of her thinking.

"Peter here joined the army to defend the very values you said your Joshua was fighting for. That Zimbabwe has turned out so different from what we all thought it would be – where so many basic freedoms are denied, where people disappear and where so many are afraid to say what they think – only adds moral weight to the rightness of Peter's actions. He fought to try to stop happening what in so many ways has happened. You are right, Sarah, the hope of the new Zimbabwe did not entirely die, and I am willing to renew the blessing to Simon and Emma I gave them a moment ago as they embark on a new life together. But that's as far as I can go. Peter is a good man, a person of deep integrity, and he was a good man when he took up arms to fight in that war, because the war he chose to fight in was a just war. I am sure he is sorry for what happened to your grandfather, Emma, but please don't ask him to ask you to forgive him for what he did. I'm sorry, Sarah, but you can't, you can never, ask Peter to forgive you for what happened."

Cathy had finished and the room fell silent again. This was a silence of confusion. Simon was deeply troubled by his mother's outburst, though he forced himself not to start to think through the implications of what she had said; now was not the time for that. Sarah was more than troubled; she was shocked and it showed on her face. As Cathy was speaking, Sarah's jaw had dropped and by the time Cathy had finished, the pupils in her eyes had widened as they do when the optician put in drops to dilate them to produce the oddest of stares. Emma's confusion verged on panic. She felt she ought to jump up and defend Sarah but knew this was not the way to go – it would only make things far worse than they now were. Emma's heart was beating fast again but she didn't stir; she didn't want to say or do anything which could push them over the edge of the precipice she felt they had moved perilously close to.

Everyone knew – even Cathy – that Peter now had to speak, and everyone also knew Emma and Simon's future life together lay entirely with him; their future was in his hands, poised precariously as water cupped in his hands. In the silence, Emma and Simon returned to their original seats, equidistant between Sarah on their left and Peter on their right, and clasped each other's hands, knowing they needed to be together for what was to come. They held each other tightly as if the firmness of their grip would ease the pain they felt was about to hit them when Peter spoke. Everyone waited.

Since Sarah had first spoken, Peter had been fully aware of what was happening; he had completely recovered from his earlier trance-like state. He had looked puzzled when Cathy had rounded off her resolute call for non-forgiveness, but he was calm and remained in control of himself. Peter tapped the arms of his padded chair with his fingers as he gathered his thoughts together before he finally spoke. He knew what he wanted to say, he was hesitating only because he was still pondering *how* he would say it. Then, with a voice as confident as Sarah's had been, he launched himself, fully aware of the significance of the words he was about to utter.

"This is not easy for me, both because it all happened so long ago and because I have tried strenuously to forget so much about it," he began, providing the background and context for what was to come. "But you have forced me to recall those terrible events and this has triggered some of the ugly manifestations of my illness as I am sure you knew it might. But I don't blame you for that. In many ways, I knew this day had to come, but as I had vainly hoped it wouldn't, I never really prepared for it, so I can only hope what I say now will sound as heart-felt and honest as it is."

Then, turning to face Simon and Emma, Peter leant forward, clasped his hands together with his fingers interwoven, and said, "Neither last week, Simon, nor so far today have I said much about the root cause of my illness, but I need to now. You see, I didn't become ill because I believed what I did was wrong. I became ill when I realised killing had become a part of me, coming face to face with the horrors of war. My repeated involvement in the killing of many guerrilla fighters in close-combat shootouts ate into me until with the shootout with Comrade Lightning I finally broke. It hit me – deep inside – that death, torture and killing, the sheer brutality of close-quarter fighting, was not just confined to battlefields. Soldiers go out and kill, even torture (though I always thought that deeply wrong) and then return to the warmth of their families, to love their nearest and dearest and live upright lives in Civvy Street, almost as if these terrible things they did never happened. Well, the key to understanding my illness (for illness is what they call it) is that I saw this compartmentalisation of war and 'normal life' as unreal, as an artificial but necessary construct created to try to keep us sane.

"But I realised I couldn't do this." Peter sounded almost triumphant. "In my mind I had torn away the flimsy partition which separated war from everyday life. I found myself no longer able to participate in and witness close-quarter killing and go back to my loved ones, 'parking' these deaths on the doorstep outside and pretending in some way neither these killings nor all the other horrors of war had ever taken place. No longer could I put the killing and hate into one box and put the love, caring and altruism of my family into another box, keeping them apart and seeing my doing this as something perfectly normal. I felt it was all a charade and I couldn't play the game anymore.

But it was worse than this. Human beings killing other human beings not only filled me with deep repugnance, but the revulsion I felt started to spread to the whole of my life until I could only view the rest of the world through the narrow prism of killing. Having first seen war as obscenely abnormal, I now viewed the rest of the world as abnormal as well. This meant I could no longer distinguish between what was normal and what was not; I could no longer judge what was acceptable and what was not; I no longer knew what was right and what was wrong. Everything I saw looked obscene and everything I touched felt unclean. And I recoiled in horror as I realised the central role I was playing in this nightmare: war was violent and society was violent, and the violence in me was keeping this madness alive and perpetuating the violence beyond me."

Peter looked around the room, his face more like a child's than a man's, crying out for sympathy and support, his eyes almost pleading for everyone to understand. "Please don't think I'm trying to make you accept the logic of my thinking," he said. "I am not! But I'm telling you all this now in the hope you can at least begin to see how my way of thinking all made sense — to me that is."

Peter paused for a moment, stretched a little, sat more upright and crossed his legs to signal he was ready to move on. Resuming, he said, "Getting better involved my trying to re-compartmentalise the world, to put back into its box the killing side of humanity with its different layers of darkness and meaninglessness from which it had escaped. We can leave for another day discussion of what constitutes sanity and illness and who judges the extent to which it is society or people who are ill, but I did find reading the Scottish psychiatrist R.D. Laing's writings on the divided self both helpful and restorative: Laing knew the problems of soldiers first-hand and wrote about exactly the sorts of thoughts and feelings I had experienced. It was all hugely therapeutic."

Peter forced a smile. He was clearly relieved to have said a little about the nature of his illness, but both he and everyone else in the room knew this was merely the prelude to the main issue he had yet to address: how he was going to respond to Sarah's challenge to ask her for forgiveness. What no one else knew was that Peter would not have been able to say what he did next unless he had made that detour into explaining the way his illness had shaped and informed his view of the world.

Emma and Simon had certainly warmed to Peter's honesty in talking so candidly about his problems, but they couldn't work out what it implied for what was to come. Likewise, Cathy knew Peter hadn't spoken like this for ten or more years and his outburst had taken her by surprise. She thought what he had just said about his illness had been prompted by what she had said about forgiveness and she was worried because she didn't know how strongly he would support her in what he was about to say. For her part, Sarah was struck by the controlled way Peter had spoken and how carefully he had weighed his words. It reminded her so much of a number of the residents at the hospice she had known who had spoken in the same measured tones and she was fully aware of why they spoke that way: they were all taking strong doses of prescription drugs for acute depression. Sarah sensed Peter was far less in control of himself than he appeared to be and the more he said, the more fearful she grew. If Peter was about to ask her for forgiveness, all this seemed to be moving in the wrong direction.

Peter leant back in his chair as he prepared to address everyone more formally. He was totally in control.

"Sarah," he said, motioning with a raised arm across the room, "has just said she forgives me for killing Comrade Lightning, her husband Joshua." Then, placing his hand momentarily on Cathy's lap, he said, "And Cathy, here, has just said there is nothing to forgive. So, do I ask to be forgiven to enable Sarah to accept my forgiveness, or do I side with my dear wife Cathy and robustly hold out, saying there is nothing I can be forgiven for as I did nothing wrong? Can I solve this dilemma I am faced with? Am I able to bring together what look like polar opposites?" he asked rhetorically as Simon and Emma shifted uneasily and expectantly in their seats.

"Well, yes," he said slowly, "I believe I can." No one moved and Peter hurried on.

"What has happened in this room this afternoon has profoundly influenced, if not actually changed, my view of the morality of what I did when I shot Comrade Lightning in that horrific gun-battle," said Peter. "To understand this, I need to take you on a journey I have just travelled on myself as I sat here thinking over what Sarah had said to me. It is a journey of freedom; a journey of my freedom. I hope you will bear with me as we travel together because you will then understand why I personally need to ask Sarah for forgiveness."

Emma and Simon exchanged glances. Emma's glance spoke of doubt, even worry that Peter had flipped and was returning to the confusion of the trance-like state they had witnessed only a few minutes ago. Simon's glance said, 'be patient, Em, trust him; I'm sure he knows what he's doing'. Sarah's face gave nothing away; she was still listening carefully to every word and eyeing Peter, watching for any movement, any twitch, which might indicate what he was thinking. Cathy looked and felt lost.

"We Rhodesians took up arms to defend ourselves from what we saw not only as an assault on our way of life and our society," said Peter with an even greater confidence in his voice, "but as an attack on the core, bedrock values upon which we believed our society was built. In short, we were convinced we were fighting for the preservation of our freedom, for the way of life we had known, which we believed to be fundamentally good, to be Christian, and which therefore needed – at all costs – to be preserved.

"For their part and from their viewpoint, the guerrillas did much the same. They took up arms because they believed the preservation of *our* way of life and the society *we* had built, was the core barrier preventing *them* from flourishing as human beings. In short, as they saw it, everything we had and we enjoyed blocked their freedoms, denying them the rich and fulfilling life they saw us having and preventing them from living fully human lives.

"Among the most fundamental freedoms the nationalists fought for," he continued, "was the freedom to choose a government which would represent and further the interests of the majority black population. Given the climate of fear and the levels of intimidation which have marked recent elections in Zimbabwe, many would argue even the right to choose the government of their choice is now denied to very many Zimbabwean voters. But the problems are far greater than this. As Cathy has quite correctly pointed out, many of the key freedoms we fought to defend have disappeared just as many of the freedoms the guerrillas fought to have access to have not materialised either: life is as tough today, if not tougher, for the majority than it was before we all took up arms. If, as Cathy has suggested, the moral case for doing something were to be based solely on the actual outcome, then I would have good reason to argue that what I did in killing Comrade Lightning was justified, as was his belief that what he was fighting for would be achieved, but turned out to be wrong in so many ways.

"So, how does all this relate to what has been happening here in this small room 6,000 miles away from Zimbabwe?" he asked. "Well, the first thing we did when we all gathered here today was to listen as Emma and Simon told us about their love for each other. We then all responded warmly to their request for us to give our support and blessing to their new relationship. This we were all delighted to do.

"But why did they then go on to tell us the awful truth about our pasts, most notably that I, Simon's father, had killed Emma's grandfather? Not out of malice, to hurt us and make us relive the horrors of the past, but because they believed *they* were not free to continue their relationship without *our* giving them the green light to do so. As they saw it – as they see it – our history not merely influences their future, but what *we* did *then* has the power to fundamentally shape, even decide *their* lives – *now*. What in essence they were saying is their freedom to be together is not merely dependent upon us but is in effect dictated by whether we choose to give them that freedom, or whether we withhold our assent because of what we all now know about the complex intertwining of our pasts and the horrors which took place all those years ago.

"What this means," he said gravely "is they are asking *us* to make choices. How could I be party to denying Emma and Simon the freedom they are asking us to give them? How could I ever conceive of being in a position to have such control over their lives?"

Peter then rose to his feet and spoke directly to Sarah, addressing her as boldly as she had him.

"When I fought and killed, and when in particular I fought and killed your husband, Sarah, I believed what I was doing was right. Now, however, I see things differently. There is probably nothing more important to me now, nothing I feel more deeply in my bones about, than my children should have the freedom to choose how to live their lives. So, if there was anything I did to help cause the war, anything I did in the war or anything which happened after the war as a consequence of my actions which could cause or create a barrier to their freedom – whether that barrier was put up deliberately or inadvertently – then I would need to be forgiven for my actions."

Then Peter turned to Emma and addressed her directly, saying, "Emma, when I killed your grandfather I did not believe what I did was wrong. However, I do now believe the freedoms he was fighting for were of greater moral weight, or worth, than the freedoms I was fighting to defend because he was fighting for the freedoms of the many, while I was fighting for the freedoms of the few. What he was fighting for were the very freedoms you and Simon will have if we are willing to bless your relationship and this I am more than willing to do. Indeed, this is something I need to do."

What was happening in Peter's mind, though he would only fully understand this many months later, was that he was looking at Emma's life, her past and her future afresh, in a way he had only previously looked at his own life, at his family's life, at Simon's life and Jane's life. Here was a woman born into a poor family in rural Zimbabwe, a representative and symbol of all poor Zimbabwean women. And there he had been, fighting to preserve his freedoms and the freedoms of his family, but at the cost of hers. This, he now knew, was wrong. He knew the freedoms he was defending were certainly real freedoms, core human freedoms which needed to be defended. But he now saw that they were the freedoms of only a minority, not the freedoms of all, because they were dominated by the defence of privilege.

What had led Peter to believe, to know, he had been wrong? One simple thing: he felt it. Emma's freedoms had never before been important, or even relevant, to Peter because he didn't know Emma; but now he did. Her life and her freedoms were now real to him and because they were real he understood their value and knew they had to be respected. One reason Peter felt as he did was his son loved Emma and all his being wanted his son to be happy. But the other reason, though he was not fully conscious of it then, was he had grown to love Emma too. Peter felt increasingly attracted to Emma: the naturalness and warmth of the kiss he gave her when she entered the sitting room this afternoon was evidence of that. It was probably this more than anything else which was pivotal in altering Peter's views on freedom and forgiveness.

Immaculata had told Emma to follow her heart. In many ways it was Peter's heart which had prompted Peter to see things differently. He had found Emma; he couldn't lose her. She was now precious to him. He loved her. And loving her and not wanting to lose her, holding her precious in his sight, meant his wanting to champion her freedoms as well. This not only meant valuing the freedoms of Sarah, Emma's mother, but also those of her grandfather who had died at his hand.

Peter then addressed Sarah directly. "Sarah, here and now I ask for your forgiveness. Forgive me for believing my actions were right then when now I know they were not. I do not ask for your forgiveness for what happened all those years ago when I killed your husband, Sarah, and your grandfather, Emma, because at that time I did not think my actions were morally wrong. But I ask for your forgiveness now because I know if I were not to ask you for forgiveness the freedoms Joshua fought for and which I now believe to have been more important to Simon and Emma than the freedoms I fought for would be denied them. So, Sarah, I am not only sorry for the death of your husband in a war which should never have happened and in which I was an active participant. I am sorry for the narrow and exclusive society we created in Zimbabwe and from which I benefited to the exclusion of so many others. I am sorry for the history of privilege of which I was a part, which stunted the opportunities of so many of our people, the seeds of which led to the war in which I was an active participant. So, in all these different but linked senses, I ask you for your forgiveness. My asking for forgiveness and your granting it is the only way we can give the future our children are seeking and which they deserve."

Peter sat down and stretched out his hand to Cathy, saying, "And to my dearest, most faithful wife Cathy, without whom I would never have had the strength to speak to you all today I need to say this. Don't think ill of me for what I have said here today. As you know more than anyone else, I have always tried as best I can to follow my conscience in all I have done and said. You are absolutely right to say when I killed Comrade Lightning I did not do anything wrong so I did not need forgiveness. Indeed, you might have gone on to say I saw my contribution to Rhodesia's war effort as something virtuous as others clearly did, given the awards they showered on me and which I felt honoured to accept. But the world changes and holding rigidly to views and beliefs which looked morally right in one context can look quite different and wrong in another. Emma here was born a black Zimbabwean, Simon a white Zimbabwean. Today they are both British, living in another country, but their past, or, I should say more accurately, our past, hangs over them. We owe it to them and we owe it to the country where we were born and grew up to give them both the freedom we say we value, the freedom we fought for and moved to this country to give them."

Then, looking over towards Sarah, Peter lifted his right arm and gestured across the room to her. "Sarah here has moved the tectonic plates: in forgiving me she has forgiven us all for the damage we did to her country, to our country, and to her family in the war and earlier. The least I can do is to acknowledge the wrongs I and others committed directly or which we benefited from indirectly and ask for her forgiveness."

Peter was finished. The room fell silent but only for an instant because almost before Peter had sat down, Sarah stood up. Then, repeating what she had said earlier but this time with emotion quivering and lingering on every word, she spoke slowly. "Peter, you are forgiven."

There was one more thing Sarah added. "Peter, you are an honest man and I respect you for your honesty. When Emma marries Simon, I will stand proud having you as part of my family as I hope you will welcome me as part of yours. Because of what has happened today, Emma and Simon and their children, God willing, will become a family which you, Cathy and I will for ever be proud to call ours. In Shona culture, we don't believe things happen by chance. Simon's meeting Emma didn't happen by accident. It was God's wish that they should meet and it is God's wish that today should turn out as it has with our families united. Today provides meaning to Joshua's death."

As Sarah was saying these words, Simon clasped Emma's right hand again. She gripped him as tightly as she could, and he responded in kind. They had just witnessed what they hadn't dared to hope would unfold before them, and they could hardly take it in. Peter had spoken about freedom, and now they were experiencing it, feeling it, relishing it. Between them Sarah and Peter had set them free. Emma was overcome with emotion, and tears of happiness rolled down her cheeks as Simon shed a single tear of relief. It was all over. Their lips came together and they momentarily kissed.

Peter then stood up again and he and Sarah walked towards each other and embraced in the centre of the room, beckoning Emma, Simon and Cathy to come and join them. But as Emma stepped forward, Simon walked over to Cathy and, out of earshot of the others, said "I'm so proud of Dad, but I'm proud of you too, Mum – for everything. Dad hasn't asked to be forgiven for when he killed Emma's grandfather as he did not believe then he had done wrong in killing him, so you were absolutely right when he said he had nothing to be forgiven for then. But he has looked back at those events and has now taken a different view. We should respect him for this. I know, Ma, he couldn't have got through today and said the things he did without you, without your love and support. So, Mum, I am as proud of you as I am of Dad."

Simon held out his arms to hug his mother and, hesitantly at first, she moved towards him and responded to his embrace. As she did so, her thoughts travelled far away from today's events and back to her past.

Cathy loved Simon more than anything in the world and as she felt his body touching hers, with her eyes moist and tightly shut, she saw her boy running barefoot and carefree as a toddler in the hot Zimbabwe summer, wearing his khaki shorts and shirt with his matching sunhat, his sun-screened skin shining as he raced across the irrigated green grass, his hands outstretched, mimicking an aeroplane's wings. She moved further back in time and saw her mother and father laughing when she was a toddler in her bathing costume and sunhat as she splashed in their paddling pool. Next, she felt warm and secure, snuggling in a hot towel in her nanny's arms as she stepped out of the bath on a cold African winter's evening. Then her mind's eye switched and she was standing next to Peter on the day he received his Grand Cross of Valour from the President at State House and the pride she felt then filled her breast once more.

Cathy knew the land of her memories was slipping away when she turned back to gaze one final time across Harare as she climbed the steps of the plane which brought her to live in England, and today she felt the loss of her link with her past even more definitively. But then Cathy said to herself in defiance – *NO! Not only will I never forget, but I will never discard the values which shaped my life and gave it meaning.* Clasping Simon more tightly to her, Cathy knew she could never – ever – bring herself to believe the joy, happiness and freedom of her own childhood, the pleasures of seeing her own children grow up and the pride she felt on witnessing the country's second-highest decoration for bravery pinned on her husband's chest could ever be seen as wrong. Even if the past really was another country, she would never let go of her memories and the moral values which she would always believe underpinned them.

Cathy wrenched herself away from her thoughts. She hoped one day she might love Emma as a daughter, but she knew it would take time. She prayed they would have a son first as she knew it would help. She sighed, wiped away her tears then, taking Simon's hand in hers, the two of them walked over to the others. It was the most difficult three steps Cathy had taken in her life.

It was over. Everyone was exhausted. Drained by the nervous energy they had all played their part in dispensing, they were now relishing the relief they all felt. Underneath, the earlier sense of elation they had shared was struggling to make its reappearance and it soon started to.

The bottom line was that after being confronted by the truth about Peter's killing of Emma's grandfather, Peter and Sarah willingly and Cathy more reluctantly had re-confirmed the blessing they had given earlier to their relationship. Emma wasn't entirely sure she had fully understood how Peter's reasoning, tortuous at times, had enabled him to acknowledge the wrongdoing required to accept Sarah's forgiveness, or, after Simon had gone over and spoken to her, how Cathy was now reconciled with what was happening. Peter's speech had been long and Emma was focused more on the outcome than on how Peter got there. Their coming together now was sufficient; it provided the tangible proof, if it was needed, that reconciliation had triumphed over conflict and alienation. At an intellectual level, Emma knew what this meant: her relationship with Simon had been re-blessed and re-approved, and she could carry the torch of the Makoni family with pride in her breast. But her heart still had to catch up with her head and she knew it would take time before it would.

If she was honest, Emma would have to admit she had always hoped things would turn out for the best but, for all the talking and planning Simon and she had done, she had never worked out precisely how it would. Now she knew why. She hadn't made space for or given much thought to the unexpected, to the twists and turns of human feelings and behaviour. She had certainly not factored forgiveness into her plans, or the unpredictable movements of the heart, and, in the end, it was these factors which had really driven the process and determined the outcome.

When Cathy had spoken up to challenge Peter's need to ask for forgiveness, Emma had had an eerie sense of *déjà vu*, for wasn't that pretty much what she had said to Sarah only a week ago about her not needing to ask for Emma's forgiveness for deceiving her, because she had done nothing wrong? And then there was Robbie. She knew there was unfinished business involving forgiveness with him but she was too focused on today for such thoughts to do more than linger with her for a moment. For now, she knew she would always be grateful that human beings had it within them to forgive, however deep and horrific the hurt done to them.

Their time together stretched out for far longer than any of them had expected as they talked more together, and then in twos and threes. Soon they began to laugh again and eventually they did so from their hearts, aided by Cathy, who served finger food, and Peter, who brought out drinks. It was well after dark before they took leave of each other and said their final goodbyes on the front step.

Simon went to fetch the car to drive Sarah back to her house and then on to Emma's to stay with her for the night. He knew he would have to leave early the next day to be back to Muswell Hill before seven, as his father needed the car to drive to meet a new client in a village north of Cambridge before 10, but he was as desperate to be alone with Emma as she was to be alone with him. They both knew things would eventually adjust to a new normal, but it would take time. For now, everything still felt quite surreal.

* * *

The roads were empty, and they reached Sarah's flat in no time. As they drew up outside, Sarah insisted they simply drop her off and leave, saying she was fine and they were all tired. But then, pulling down the car door handle ready to step out of the car, Sarah hesitated. With the door still shut, she turned back so she could see Simon sitting next to her in the driver's seat as well as Emma, who was leaning forward in the middle of the back seat.

"Good night, my dears," said Sarah. "It has been a long day and I am more than exhausted. I am so happy for you both but I feel we have been through the wringer and I need my bed; I am more than bone-weary. But before you go, there is one last thing which needs to be said and this time it is I who have something important I need to share with you. Sadly, it's quite pressing and can't really wait."

"Yes, Ma," said Emma "tell us," thinking Sarah was going to explain again how she had been able to forgive Peter, or perhaps she was desperate to say something else about their visit to Alice's grave earlier in the day, which felt so long ago now. "What is it you need to say?"

"I will only tell you on one condition, and you have to promise," Sarah replied.

"Yes, Ma," said Emma again, and Simon chimed in cheerily, "we promise".

"You have to promise when I tell you, you will not ask to come in and be with me or say you will call me this evening when you get back to your flat. Everything can wait. We'll have plenty of time to discuss it all later, in the days and weeks ahead."

"Yes, Ma," said Emma for the third time, but now far more alert, sensing Sarah was going to say something different as well as possibly important. She was now more than curious.

"My dears," said Sarah, "what I need to tell you can be briefly said. It is this: I have cancer and it seems to be quite serious."

Emma gasped but, raising her hand, Sarah checked her as there was more she needed to say.

"Even before you went out to Zimbabwe," said Sarah, "I was increasingly feeling far more tired than usual after work, and I seemed to be losing my appetite. While you were away I went to see the doctor, who commented on what seemed to be yellowness around my eyes. He sent me off to Barnet General for a couple of scans and some blood tests, and on the Friday before you came back I was called in to be told it looked pretty likely I have pancreatic cancer. You probably don't know much about it, I didn't at the time, but it's not good."

Then, turning to Emma, Sarah said, "The exhaustion I felt climbing the hill after visiting Alice's grave this morning was almost certainly directly linked to my cancer. They told me I will get similar attacks of exhaustion and these are likely to become more frequent. Unlike many cancers, there doesn't seem to be too much they can do in the way of curing me."

Sarah then opened the door to get out, saying, "I'm fine for now – easily well enough to go to work not only tomorrow but in the weeks ahead. So we'll just have to see how it all goes."

In shock from what she had heard, Emma jumped out of the car, put her arms round Sarah and hugged her tightly. Sarah was in control of her feelings but Emma was not. She didn't know much about pancreatic cancer but from what Sarah had said it was clearly dreadful. Random thoughts whizzed through her mind: was her mother going to die? Yes, probably, but when? *Oh Ma, I need you. Don't die, Ma, please don't die! Why did this have to happen today after all we've been through? I felt alone at Alice's grave, but this is worse: I really am going to be alone, but when? This is terrible: is it really happening?* By the time Sarah wrenched herself away from Emma, saying 'you promised, my dear', Emma was in tears. Somehow, they reached the front door, where they stopped for a far more intense and tender goodbye hug than Emma remembered ever giving her mother. She told her mother she had to come in, but Sarah stood her ground and said 'you promised, my dear, you promised'.

Emma tried again. "Ma," she pleaded, "*please* let me come in. We have to talk more about this now."

Sarah had her key in the door and had opened it when she said one final time, "you promised, Em, and I am going to hold you to your promise."

"Fine," said Emma, knowing she had lost, but she felt anything but fine. "But I *will* come over tomorrow evening after work, and I hope you will be more sensible by then and we'll talk about it all properly. And *that's* a promise!"

"OK," said Sarah, adding, "but I'm working late tomorrow, Em, so don't come before seven."

"OK, Ma," said Emma as she walked back to the waiting car, "I'll let myself in and be waiting here before you get back." Her heart was heavy, her body listless as Sarah's news took hold of her. "And that's a promise too," she shouted as she heard Sarah's front door close behind her. Emma knew she was angry now as well, though unsure whether her anger was with Sarah or whether it came from self-pity.

As she got back in the car, Emma burst into tears. "Why did the day have to end like this," she sobbed. "It's not just unfair, it's cruel; it's unreal. It's my mother, Simon, it's Ma; it's dreadful. Why did she make us promise? I know she's tough, but this was too much. I'll go back, she'll have to open the door. She must!"

"Calm down, Em, calm down," said Simon. "I know how terrible you feel, but this is the way she wanted it to happen. You know her well enough to realise this is how she had planned to tell you and I think we should respect that. I don't know much about pancreatic cancer but from what she says she seems to have bad periods and good ones. I must say the whole of the time she was with us, I didn't at any time sense she was ill. Quite the opposite. She's certainly not at death's door, Em. I think we need to get a proper perspective on what's going on."

Then, sensing he had been too unfeeling in what he had said, Simon added, "we must do everything we can to help her, and we will, Emma. We'll move mountains for her if we have to – you know that! But your Ma's right, we have time. We don't have to start at once; we can leave it until tomorrow."

"OK, Simon," said Emma reluctantly as she tried to pull herself together, "perhaps you're right. I never thought the day was going to end like this. Life always lies in wait to spring its surprises or, in this case, its shocks, on us. If pancreatic cancer is as bad as it sounds, it looks as though our lives are going to have to change radically, and in ways we couldn't possibly have foreseen this morning. Poor, poor Ma. I can't believe this is happening to her. You would have thought she had suffered enough already."

When they reached Emma's flat, they hurried in and sat down next to each other, as Emma googled 'pancreatic cancer'. It made grim reading and, as she discovered more, Emma began to feel once again that sense of aloneness she had experienced at Alice's graveside in the morning creeping through her. Not even her physical closeness to Simon on the day when their future together had been finally sealed brought her any relief.

It had been a bittersweet day, and as it drew to a close, a new gloom had arrived unexpectedly to hang over them. In the coming weeks and months, it would encircle their lives completely.

BOOK IV
RELOCATIONS

Sunday Lunch at Catshead

"Next stop's ours," said Emma, nudging Simon as they drew out of Staplehurst station. He turned and smiled, extracting himself from his thoughts. He loved the English countryside and had been gazing dreamily out across the green fields of Kent. His head was leaning on the carriage window, and Emma could hear it knocking against the glass whenever the train's wheels lurched from side to side as they hit an uneven piece of track. Simon was unconcerned – he was in another world. Emma was keeping a mental note of the stations and reading: she was immersed in Zadie Smith's *Swing Time* and was herself in West Africa. They had already stopped at the two larger stations, Sevenoaks and Tonbridge, followed by the two smaller ones, Paddock Wood and Marden. They were getting out at Headcorn, the next station, so Emma had started to gather her things together as it was also a small station and the stop would be brief.

It was the end of October, five weeks to the day since that momentous afternoon in the Robertsons' sitting room. They were on their way down to Catshead – the ancestral home of the Stander family, currently owned by Simon's uncle, George Stander – for Sunday lunch. Simon's grandfather on his mother's side – Cathy's father, John Stander – and Uncle George's father, also George Stander, were brothers, though both were now long dead. The younger George Stander was therefore technically Simon's first cousin once removed but he had always been known simply as 'Uncle George' and his wife as 'Aunt Margaret'. Cathy and George were close.

Uncle George was the family fixer. If something important needed to be done in the wider world, he was always willing to help and, remarkably, his efforts usually proved successful. Although now semi-retired, Professor George G. B. Stander was still a senior consultant at St Thomas' Hospital, so it wasn't surprising when, soon after Simon told his parents of his decision to change careers and become a doctor – and struggling to decide which medical schools to apply for – they encouraged him to contact Uncle George.

Suggesting Simon talk to his cousin-in-law was not easy for Peter because the two had never got along. They had first met in the old Salisbury when George Stander had come out for their wedding, and it didn't take long for Peter to realise George was the sort of Englishman whom white Rhodesian men loathed – pompous, arrogant, self-opinionated and very full of himself. So when Cathy went over to England to stay with George and Margaret and their young family while they were still living in Rhodesia, as she did regularly, Peter never joined them. The first Christmas after the family moved to England, George and Margaret invited the Robertsons down for the week, and every year after that while the children were growing up, Christmas was always at Catshead. These visits only reconfirmed Peter's initial assessment of George, but Peter learned to conceal his loathing of the other man, and it rarely showed. The problem was that as well as the strong bond George and Cathy had between them, Peter was indebted to him. When Cathy told George they were thinking of moving to England and Peter would be looking for a job, George not only offered to help but effectively got him a job. George had been an exact contemporary at Oxford (Balliol) with John Meadowcraft, who had gone on to become a successful accountant. John had been the prime mover in establishing Falkland, Fairbridge and Hayes in Muswell Hill, which grew in size and reputation to become one of North London's most respected accountancy firms. George knew this and encouraged John first to offer Peter a job and, very soon after he arrived, a partnership in the firm. So, for all the reservations he had about George, and knowing how difficult it was to get into medical school as a mature student, Peter agreed with Cathy's suggestion that George and Simon should get together.

As Simon didn't really know his Uncle George – their paths had rarely crossed since the family had stopped spending their Christmases at Catshead some ten years previously – he told his mother he would be happy to talk to him. Within the day Cathy was on the phone to George, first to give him even firmer news of Simon's planned career move, which she had mentioned rather vaguely to him in the summer, and then to ask if the two of them could meet. She also shared the exciting family news that Simon had a girlfriend who, coincidentally, had also been born in Zimbabwe and, like Simon, had grown up in North London. George expressed his delight with both the news on the career move and the girlfriend and said he would call back to suggest when and where the two of them might meet. He was on the phone to Cathy again within the hour to suggest Simon came down to Catshead for Sunday lunch rather than their having an office meeting in London, and went on to ask Cathy to convey to Simon his insistence he should bring Emma with him so they could make a day of it. If their relationship was as serious as she had hinted it was, George told Cathy both he and Margaret clearly had to meet her.

Over the next 48 hours Cathy had multiple phone calls with George, Margaret, Simon and Emma to fix the date. Simon reminded his mother to let them know he was now a vegetarian and when Cathy confirmed the date to him, she said she had spoken to Margaret about his food requirements, and she had said that would be just fine.

Since Sarah had told Emma about her cancer, Emma had been spending huge amounts of time with her mother and their Sundays together had become even more precious to both of them. So, when Simon asked Emma about joining him at Catshead for lunch and dates started to be discussed, Emma told her mother she didn't need to go and could easily meet the Standers at another time. But Sarah had other plans. Although her condition was worsening, at the end of October she was still working full-time at the hospice and, knowing they were short-staffed, had arranged to work on the proposed day of the Catshead lunch, insisting to Emma she should go with Simon. As Simon knew Emma needed a break, he sided with Sarah, and Emma was persuaded to go.

George was of course delighted to help Simon as best he could, but as Sunday drew closer, he found himself becoming increasingly excited about meeting Emma. These days his weekends were boring: his four children and the grandchildren rarely came to visit and he found almost all the guests Margaret proposed inviting – all their age or older – dull. He could think of nothing better than having a bright young woman – as he was sure she would be – sitting next to him as he made his way through a large Sunday roast and homemade pie, all washed down with a bottle or two of his cellar's best Bordeaux. For her part, Margaret was delighted to host the meal as increasingly George had said no whenever she had suggested a Sunday lunch party with their friends. When the date was fixed, Margaret started working on the guest-list.

As he'd gazed out of the train window, Simon's mind had drifted dreamily back in time. From a very early age, Catshead had made a deep impression on him. Its size, its olde-worlde look and, despite Aunt Margaret's best efforts, its general air of untidiness and neglect and its musty smells had always appealed to him and over the years he had grown to love the house. It was so different from their own home in North London, modern and small and as polished and orderly as a newly-built hospital ward.

In contrast, Catshead was exciting and exotic, and it even had a hint of mystery to it. Large downstairs rooms of wood-panelled walls and bare floorboards covered in fading antique rugs and sofas; highly-polished tables displaying richly-coloured oriental bowls and china ornaments. There were the bathrooms with strangely shaped baths and basins, their old brass taps, their ill-fitting plugs and their leaks; toilets with wobbly wooden seats he dreaded using as he never seemed able to flush them properly; carpeted and almost bare bedrooms with their uneven floors and uncomfortable beds.

It was around the age of eight or nine that the house had really begun to cast its spell on him. He remembered it in winter as dark and eerie with its creaking floors and squeaking doors, its dimly-lit corners and its tall windows which always rattled more at night as the wind seemed to whistle more then. Simon remembered well cosy winter evenings sitting beside giant log-fires in pjs thinking up endless reasons why it was not quite time for bed. In winter, his mother would eventually take him up and he would jump into bed, shivering between the ice-cold sheets as he curled up like a hamster under the thick eiderdown to try to retain his log-fired heat; but by morning his nest had become so snug and cosy it was painful to leave. As the winter sun rose, he would gaze out from under a mound of warm bedclothes at the intricate patterns of ice which had formed overnight on the inside of the frosty windows. He had loved creating clouds in front of his face by breathing in deeply through his nose, drawing up warm air from the depths of his lungs and puffing it out of his mouth in short bursts to hit the room's freezing air.

Outside, in the summer, he recalled playing imaginary games, usually on his own, running in and out of the dark and overgrown bushes, jumping over low-lying branches of ancient yew trees and balancing dangerously as he raced along their exposed roots, his arms outstretched like an aeroplane. His most cherished memory was of the happiness he felt seeing his mother looking more relaxed than she ever did in London. He could see her walking carefree in the rose garden, laughing as she played tennis or drinking tea and nibbling at cream- and jam-filled scones and homemade cakes in the old summer house. She used to raise her hand up in front of her mouth so as not to rudely spit out the crumbs in front of her as she chuckled at Uncle George's jokes. He saw them now in his mind's eye, beckoning him to come over to them. After running to join them, he caught again the reassuring scent of his mother's perfume as he nestled in warm and close to her body, secure amongst the folds of her summer frock...

Emma was already standing up when she felt, then heard, the brakes engage. They walked to the end of the carriage as the train was coming to a stop and jumped out. Headcorn was very much a weekday station, a growing magnet for people working in London but who couldn't afford to live there. At weekends, it was eerily quiet: they were the only ones to leave the train.

Catshead lay some four miles south of the station. Emma had done her homework and found the cheapest way to get there was a bus and a short walk. However, as she discovered, the buses from Headcorn station to Biddenden only ran on a weekday; there was no Sunday service. She had called the local taxi firm, which had an office at the station, but they said it was closed on Sundays. As it wasn't too far, Emma had suggested to Simon they walk. Though it would mean taking the earlier train, she reminded Simon the clocks would be going back an hour that morning so it wouldn't feel they were missing their Sunday lie-in and he readily agreed.

As they stepped onto the deserted platform Emma checked the time on her phone: it was a minute after quarter past; the train was on time and they were on schedule. They linked arms turned right out of the station and were soon out of Headcorn, walking south on the A274, happy to be walking together in the country. Sadly, it began to drizzle so they took out their rain jackets and walked the last half hour in light rain. Fortunately, Emma had remembered her umbrella.

Rounding a bend, Simon recognised the entrance ahead of them before they saw the Catshead sign. They turned to walk up the gravel path, their feet scrunching on the loose cobblestones as they rounded the final bend and the house came into view. The leaves of the Virginia creeper which covered the whole of the front had already turned into their deep autumnal colours, making the house look even more magnificent than Simon remembered it. They half-walked, half-ran up the stone steps to the front door. Simon pressed the doorbell and they heard it ringing deep inside the house. Emma shook the rain from her umbrella, folded it up and returned it to her bag, and they helped each other remove their rain jackets as they stood waiting, sheltered by the porch roof. Next to the door was a well-used cast-iron Victorian boot-scraper and next to that a collection of old walking sticks and golf umbrellas squashed together inside a thin oak barrel whose wooden staves were rotting and metal hoops rusting. They smiled at each other as Emma straightened the front of Simon's coat and wiped a spot of rainwater from the end of his nose. She was about to give him a peck on the cheek when they heard noises so instead they turned to face the door expectantly, waiting for it to be opened.

"Oh," exclaimed the woman who opened the door, the warm and relaxed greeting departing from her face as speedily as it had appeared. It was quickly replaced by a forced smile. "I never realised…" she hurriedly added, but she didn't finish her sentence; her voice trailed off into nothingness in the autumnal air.

"Sorry," said Simon leaping into the void, assuming Aunt Margaret was upset they had not told them they were coming by train, as they would certainly have offered to meet them at the station. He wasn't sure whether she was upset by the distance they had walked or by seeing them standing there in their wet clothes.

"I should really have let you know we decided we would walk," he continued, "as we were keen to take in a little of the wonderful Kent countryside before we arrived, but we hadn't factored in the rain. Never mind, it's only been drizzling; we're not really wet and we'll quickly dry out. Anyway, we are delighted to be here."

Then, turning first to Emma then back to their host, Simon said, "Aunt Margaret, this is Emma, Emma Maconie. I have told her a little about you and Uncle George and about Catshead. Thanks so much for inviting us; we are really looking forward to the day."

Once again Margaret tried a smile, but as before it didn't really work. She held out her arm and shook hands with Emma, but her greeting was brief and far from warm. Aunt Margaret was clearly still distracted. Before Emma could say anything, Aunt Margaret had turned away and was calling out over her shoulder, "George, they are here," in a loud voice. It was apparent she needed support and was appealing for reinforcements.

Emma knew at once what Aunt Margaret's initial 'Oh' had meant, and this was only confirmed by her forced smile, her strained greeting and her need to be rescued. It had nothing to do with Emma and Simon not telling the Standers they were taking the train and not coming by car, and nothing to do with their walking in the rain and their standing on the porch in damp clothes. It had everything to do with Emma being black.

* * *

For as long as she could remember, Emma had encountered this sort of racism: white people who not only viewed black people as different but – often unconsciously and unknowingly – whom their sixth sense told them were, somehow, out of place in their world. For Emma and her young non-white friends, this had been a pretty frequent experience when growing up. It was as if they shouldn't be there; they should be relocated. It didn't matter if their forbears had come from Africa, the Asian sub-continent or from other non-Caribbean countries, they were all lumped together as part of the Windrush generation. Of course, she had also been at the receiving end of vicious and overt racial attacks, as her friends had, though in Emma's case these had fortunately been far rarer.

The incident which had affected her most deeply happened when she was just seven. Soon after starting primary school as a carefree young girl, Emma was skipping along the High Street in East Finchley one day after school, hand-in-hand with one of her two 'Scottish' school friends, Laura McCabe. Laura's mother was looking after them but she was preoccupied with Laura's new-born sister, Amy, who had started to cry as her Mum was pushing her along the pavement in her pram. Suddenly, as they came alongside the Abbey National Building Society with its distinctive red logo, Laura darted out onto the main road squeezing her way past two parked cars. She had been proudly bouncing her rubber ball one-handedly on the pavement – a trick she had recently learned and wanted to show Emma she had perfected – but this time she had failed to catch hold of it and it had bounced into the road. Oblivious of the danger, she had run out onto the road to retrieve it.

From then on, everything seemed to switch to slow motion. There was a loud screeching of brakes, the unmistakeable noise of cars crashing into each other, lots of screaming and people running about in all directions. Emma remembered seeing the heads of the passengers sitting on a red London bus being thrown forward in their seats as their bus came to a screeching halt. She recalled seeing Laura lying still, face down on the road, her head turned away from Emma. She and Laura's mother both started running to her at the same time. But before Emma reached Laura's body, still motionless on the road ahead of her, she was jerked back and picked up by her hair, her right arm and her right shoulder by a tall muscular man.

With a roar in his voice, he threw Emma back onto the pavement like a sack of unwanted, putrid potatoes.

As Emma lay there dazed and shocked, she looked up to see the man leaning over her, his eyes aflame, pointing at her with his outstretched hand and screaming out for everyone to hear, drops of white spittle dripping down onto Emma's face below him as he shouted:

"You black bastard, you fucking black bastard!

"I saw you: you deliberately let go of her hand and let her run out onto the road.

"You killed her. You are responsible. I saw it all. You are *guilty*." He lingered on the word; he had venom in his voice.

"Why did you lot ever come here?" he ranted. "Get the hell out of here. We've had enough of your sort in *our* country. Go back home to fucking Africa and the trees where you belong, and stay there. You…evil… little… baboon." The man spat out these final words slowly and viciously as his anger caused him to tremble.

Even before the man had finished and as he hovered over her, Emma burst into floods of tears; she was in deep shock and was shaking. She tried to scream for help but she was so afraid of the monster above her and what else he might do that she couldn't make her voice work. All she could manage was a low whimper. She knew she was hurting from being thrown to the ground but at that moment she could feel no physical pain. She felt exposed, vulnerable and totally unsafe; what she hungered for more than anything else was the safety and protection of home, her mother and the grown-ups she trusted.

Everything had happened so fast, Emma couldn't grasp what was going on about her. The only thing she clearly did understood was that she was being blamed for what had happened to Laura, and she had no idea why. As people started to gather round her, she became even more confused by the attention being given to her when it was Laura who was hurt. She was also frightened because she didn't understand what she had done wrong.

In the days, weeks and months after it all happened, it was this scene which continually returned to Emma, initially to haunt but then also to trouble her. Emma, of course, knew she was black but she hadn't understood the other words the man had used though she was clear from the tone of his voice they were all words of blame. Until that moment it had never occurred to Emma being black could possibly be the cause of wrongdoing, or worse, could even be something evil, but until she was much older the more Emma thought about it afterwards the more she realised the man had cowed her into believing what he had screamed at her was true. In her child's mind, Emma was telling herself Laura's accident had been caused not merely by what she had done, or not done, but by her being black. It had to be true: this grown-up man had said so.

As Emma lay here on the ground, two passers-by who had seen what had happened from a distance – a man and a woman, both white – ran up to and confronted the man who had abused and assaulted Emma. For a few moments Emma's racist abuser stood his ground as the three of them screamed at each other, but then, sensing the growing crowd was turning against him, the man ran off. The male passer-by gave chase but never managed to catch him. As the two men left the scene, the woman squatted down next to Emma and cradled her, telling her everything was alright and it was the man who had done wrong and not her. Emma was crying now both from relief from the comfort she was receiving following the confusion of the accident and its terrible aftermath, and from the pain she realised she was feeling on the side of her left leg from being thrown onto the ground by her racist assailant. Emma's side was hurting. It turned out no bones had been broken, but her leg remained swollen and bruised for weeks afterwards.

Laura was not seriously injured either though she was badly grazed and bleeding slightly on her right side, on her thigh, her elbow and her cheek. It turned out she had been struck on the left shoulder by a car but its driver had had enough time to brake, and she had managed to slow right down by the time her car hit Laura so she barely knocked her over. However, heavy braking resulted in her car being hit from behind by a white van whose driver had clearly not noticed what was happening, and he hadn't braked. As a result, both vehicles were so damaged they had to be towed away. The road was closed and for a long time the sound of the horns of frustrated drivers rang round the High Street.

Laura was carried from the road and brought to sit next to Emma; they held onto each other's hands again, tightly this time, not knowing what else to do. Laura's mum, though still distraught, was calming down as she realised Laura was not badly hurt and, leaving the pram with a passer-by who offered to help, she came over to Laura and Emma and hugged then kissed them both. Emma remembered this vividly.

What happened next became a blur when she tried to recall it all afterwards. She remembered sitting on the pavement for ages as people walked by, slowed down and stared at them in the way British people do at accidents. Blankets were brought, drinks and biscuits appeared. A policeman arrived and asked the two girls a few questions about what happened and he wrote down the words Emma told him the man had screamed at her, even though she still didn't know what they meant. Moments later she remembered feeling pangs of guilt because she might have told him the wrong words as she didn't know them properly. Eventually Sarah arrived and they were given a lift back home by someone she didn't know, but whom her mother assured her was a friend.

Emma did, however, remember quite clearly what happened next. She sat on the sofa back home, where she began to cry again; it went on for some time though she was never quite sure why, but she did remember shaking as well, and not being able to stop. Then, that same evening before she went to bed and well after she had stopped crying and shaking, Sarah talked to her quietly and reassuringly about what had happened.

"Laura's dropping the ball was an accident, Emma," she said, "it wasn't something you were in any way responsible for, nothing you ever have to feel bad about. Laura knows this and her mum does too."

Sarah then went on to talk about the man who had screamed at her. She talked freely about his racially abusing Emma, his swearing and his physical violence, which she had been told about by the two passers-by as well as the policeman. This is the gist of what Emma remembered her mother telling her then.

"Some white people do say terrible, hurtful and evil things about you because you are black. It's wrong and its's dreadful, but, my dear Emma, it happens. When it happens the first time it's horrid and, just like with you today, you can't really believe it *is* happening. It'll happen again, Emma and the more it does, the more you can see it coming; you'll know the signs. Sometimes you'll see the signs but the person never actually says anything, but it's there, and it hurts all the same. Some white people might tell you you're imagining it; many of those who acknowledge it happens will tell you you'll get used to it. But, Emma, you must never get used to it, and I'm sure you won't. You must never accept what is not right, never, ever."

Looking back on that evening some years later – for that day remained with her for the rest of her life – Emma recalled that what she had really wanted to know then was something quite specific: why her being black could have caused the accident. But she hadn't asked her mother that question, probably because she didn't know how to express in words what she was thinking. What she remembered most clearly was Sarah saying to her, "The fact some people think and believe terrible things about black people doesn't mean they're true."

When she was a little older, Sarah had told Emma she mustn't let these evil actions, evil words and evil thoughts fester inside. She had said, "We will always be proud of our heritage, of who we are as black people and the Africa from which we came. And the best way we can fight racism and its evils is with dignity and pride, not with hate and bitterness." That particular conversation had ended with Sarah saying, "For many years, even decades, to come, we can expect this sort of thing to continue happening to us here in England. It will always happen to us." The way Sarah had said the word 'always' had an air of inevitability and resignation to it.

This was only the second time Emma remembered Sarah ever speaking to her about racism, and she didn't do it very often afterwards except when Emma brought up the subject. This she often did, especially through her teenage years and on to adulthood, as there were plenty of other times when Emma experienced racial abuse, discrimination, prejudice and bigotry, including being aggressively asked where she came from, and she had witnessed friends, male and female, including Robbie, being treated in the same way. But she was never as deeply upset then as she had been that very first time.

What was far more common were incidents like the one she had just experienced with Aunt Margaret. Like all black British people, like all black British women, Emma had been at the receiving end of the look, the quick glance, the muffled remark, the ever-so-slight curl of the lip at the side of the mouth, the raised eyebrow, the condescending smile, the hardly noticeable nod of the head, the surprise at bumping into you, the fleeting pause before a question is answered. She had experienced being treated as if she were simply not there, and had felt that all-encompassing sense of being excluded, of not being part of the 'in' group. She had been at the receiving end of that unmistakable arrogant whiff of disdain. She had been made to feel not so much different as inferior. She had been looked down upon simply and explicitly because she was black.

Meeting and falling in love with Emma had massively increased Simon's awareness of racism. They both agreed it had been fortunate neither of them could recall any time while out together of their being the recipients of explicit racial abuse or prejudice. But when Emma began to point out specific examples of the subtle ways racism impinged on her everyday life, either when it was happening or just afterwards, so it was still fresh in Simon's mind, he began to see for himself how regularly this sort of thing happened and how it must feel. Unconscious racism, Simon could now readily affirm, was not only far more pervasive than even most white people sensitive to racial prejudice would think; it was experienced by the vast majority of black British people almost as a daily occurrence. Simon knew few professional men would admit today to being sexist. However, many claiming they were not prejudiced against women bosses would be willing to acknowledge they would simply prefer their boss to be a man. Similarly, few middle-aged British tennis fans would admit to being racists but deep down many would be happier if they could watch a Wimbledon tennis match on television without both, or even without one, of the Williams sisters playing. The problem, Simon realised, was that racist assumptions and perceptions, as well as fear, colour probably most white people's views of who and what black British are: it was still part of the 'stuff' of large swathes of modern-day Britain. Simon told Emma how this made him seethe with anger, and she said she would be angry if it didn't.

It didn't matter Emma spoke English like any other north Londoner. It didn't matter she felt as English as the next person. It didn't matter she had a sense of pride in being English and cheered as loudly as the next person when the English football, rugby and cricket teams (men and women) won – to the extent she was aware when they were playing. It didn't matter she was as exuberant as a white English person when one of them, black or white, won recognition on the world stage as a singer, film star, actor or writer, when they won an Olympic medal or were honoured with a Nobel prize. It didn't even matter she passionately believed in and tried to champion the values of justice, fairness, compassion, truth-telling, respect, care and tolerance. What mattered was simply that she was black. That trumped everything.

As Emma stood in front of Margaret now, she thought of the conversation she must have had with Simon's mother. Well done, Cathy, she said to herself, for when they had spoken on the phone Cathy had clearly not told Margaret Emma was black.

* * *

As Simon and Emma stepped inside the house, Uncle George was walking towards them, smiling broadly. With arms outstretched he said, "Welcome to Catshead, the both of you. You look a little wet and bedraggled."

"Yes," said Simon, "its's great to be back, Uncle George. I don't think I've crossed the threshold for 10 years or maybe more. I'm sorry we look a little like drowned rats, but, as I explained to Aunt Margaret, we took an early train as we were keen to walk from the station, but Emma's usually impeccable planning failed to factor in the rain."

"Oh, you should have called us, we would gladly have picked you up," said George, failing to pick up Simon's saying they had chosen to walk. "I had assumed you would be driving down. Anyway, there are fires lit in the parlour and in the sitting room. They will be the first this autumn. We always light them to mark the changing of the clocks. I always say it helps to get the body adjusted – so let's go through and you'll soon be dry."

Then, turning to Emma, he said, "So glad to meet you, Emma. I'm sure we'll soon get to know each other today and you'll enjoy yourself enough to come back; and if you do, when you come next time, I hope you'll stay the whole weekend. I must say I hadn't realised you were, er, coloured; it had never crossed my mind. But that's great! I've had plenty of black students at St Thomas' in my time and got to know some pretty well; as you'd expect some are exceptionally bright. I've even had a smattering of black colleagues, though mostly Indian or at least Asian. We all get on so well, just as I do with all my female colleagues on the Faculty. But to be honest, Emma, I've never yet had either an Indian or black person here to Sunday lunch, so you're the first and you're most welcome. Come on, let's move to the parlour and I'll pour you both a drink."

George had barely introduced himself but he had already said enough. Simon shot a glance of despair-cum-resignation across to Emma, who was squirming inside. He felt terrible he hadn't alerted Emma to the sort of person George Stander was, but he hadn't known. Like his father, Simon knew George was pompous but as he had never seen him interacting with people outside his personal comfort zone, he had never realised how racist and sexist he was. Simon then reflected back to the way Aunt Margaret had reacted to Emma when she first set eyes on her and realised what her "Oh" had meant. Simon was now squirming too as he realised he had probably made a big mistake in agreeing for them to come down to Catshead for Sunday lunch. For Emma, though, none of what she had heard surprised her, so she wasn't unusually upset. Although the day was clearly going to be quite different from what she had envisaged, she was determined to enjoy herself. She did wonder, however, whether – or would it be when – either George, or Margaret, or one of their friends would so overstep the mark she would feel she had to challenge them.

George motioned for them to go down the corridor which led to the parlour and, as they walked along, turned to Simon and said, "We've got lots to discuss about your exciting plans of switching to a career in medicine. I thought your father would be dead against it, but I gather from your mother he is quite supportive. That's great! We can start our medical school discussions before our other guests arrive."

George opened the parlour door and politely stepped aside to let his guests go in before him. They were immediately hit by the heat of the log-fire, in front of which lay two black overweight Labradors, fast asleep, and Emma and Simon were now glad they had chosen to wear their light linen jackets. Margaret, who had been bringing up the rear, excused herself at the door, saying she needed to attend to the lunch.

By the time they reached the parlour, Emma had fully recovered from her initial exchange with George and felt herself again. When she stepped inside, she was immediately captivated by the room: it was large, well-proportioned and gave off an air of grandeur. The walls were covered from top to bottom with dark antique oak wood panelling, joined to the ceiling by a wide rim of French-leaf cornicing. From the rose centrepiece an old, dusty chandelier with lop-sided antique candle-light electric lamps hung precariously from the ceiling, looking as dated as if it hadn't been touched since World War II, as George told them it hadn't. The deeply-waxed floorboards, also dark oak, were covered with a massive rust-coloured rug, its colours faded by the sun and its edges unravelling in parts. Above the fireplace on the opposite wall hung an imposing Stubbs-like picture of a large white horse painted against a rural English background. Each of the walls on either side was dominated by large matching oil paintings of the Kent countryside, strikingly similar to the real-life views which Simon had so enjoyed from the window of the train. Taking it all in, and building on what she had already absorbed of the magnificent house and grounds, Emma felt she had stepped right inside the pages of a Brontë novel.

As soon as they were seated, George asked them what they would like to drink as he picked up his own already empty crystal glass from one of the tables for a refill, informing them his pre-lunch drink on a Sunday was always gin and tonic. Thirsty from the walk, Simon would have asked for a beer but as he saw none had been laid out, he said he would join George in a very weak gin and tonic. Emma asked simply for tonic. George added ice and a slice of lemon to their glasses without asking.

As he poured the drinks, George told them two other guests were expected, Leonard Winslow-Smith, or Lennie, and his wife Virginia, known as Ginny, who, like them, were both in their sixties. He explained Lennie was a local psychiatrist who worked at Tunbridge Wells Hospital but also had his own private practice. Ginny, he said, was a ball of energy and after the children had grown up she returned to the world of stained glass and had some sort of link to a studio in Ashford, saying Margaret would fill them in with the details. George said she was also quite heavily involved with a number of local charities including, he said, glancing at Emma, some which helped children in Africa, Malawi he thought, the old Nyasaland.

"Ginny is one of your Aunt Margaret's closest friends," said George to Simon. "I don't actually know Lennie all that well but we thought it would be useful to chat to him, Simon, about your interest in mental health issues – not, I hasten to add, an area I know too much about. We had hoped another couple could come to make up the eight – our closest friends Richard and Jean Winkler. Sadly, though, they are away this weekend. Richard was an estate agent but he is retired now; he puts in two afternoons a week for the National Trust in the summer, down the road at Sissinghurst." He asked Emma if she and Simon were members, and expressed surprise when she said no.

"Like Margaret," continued George, "Jean was originally a nurse but she hasn't practised since the children were born. Now they see a lot of each other, not least on the golf course. They remain stalwarts of the over-60s ladies' group at Charts Hill, you must have heard of it, our local championship course designed by Nick Faldo? We joined when the club started way back in the 1990s but it took on a new lease of life following a devastating fire which burnt the whole place down 10 years ago. The new buildings they put up cost millions and as they needed to recoup the money, we were worried when they embarked on a drive to attract new members. To our great relief, however, the membership committee knew their stuff and devised a pretty foolproof way of ensuring the *nouveau riche* couldn't wriggle their way in."

Unbeknown to George, self-absorbed in information-dumping, Emma raised an eyebrow, which Simon acknowledged with a wry smile.

"But Simon," said George as he handed them their drinks and came to sit down with them by the fire, "I want to hear more about why you decided to change careers and how far you have got in your plans to get into medical school. As I told your mother, I am keen to help as best I can. You do realise, don't you, you'll be the first in the family to become a doctor since I took the plunge almost 50 years ago now? My goodness, how time flies!"

So Simon explained first why he decided to become an accountant and then what had led to his decision to switch to medicine and the reason he had been drawn to mental health, being careful to steer well clear of his father's mental illness even though he was sure his mother had told George a lot about it, at least in the past; he felt sure she hadn't shared last month's sitting-room dramas with him and guessed she never would. Simon explained he wasn't yet clear what area of speciality would best suit him but said he was convinced he should first qualify as a doctor. Then, said Simon, as the course progressed and he met patients and was exposed to the different areas of the mental health profession, he would have a better feel of where his interests and talents lay. George nodded, saying his approach of first concentrating on becoming a doctor before focusing more narrowly on mental health was absolutely the correct one.

"If you were to take the non-medical path of qualifying as a clinical psychologist," said George, "the benefits of finishing sooner if you didn't go on to a PhD would need to be weighed against the severe disadvantage of not being able to prescribe. Having a medical degree gives you the choice of moving into either psychiatry or psychotherapy. What's more, good psychiatrists are pretty well paid as many choose either to move entirely into private practice – a growth industry these days – or to take on some private patients. Most psychiatrists I know have done this," he added, "just like Lennie".

Simon bristled at the way the conversation had slid so easily into the subject of money and he felt compelled to say if it was a good salary he was after, he would have stuck with accountancy. George was a little taken back but didn't show it, though he made a mental note of needing to watch more carefully not only what he said to Simon but how he said it. He also told himself he needed to go easy on the booze as he regularly did at some point on a Sunday, though it never made any difference.

"So," said George cheerily, steering the conversation back onto safer ground, "the first thing you need to do is choose a good medical school. As I am sure you are aware, applying for graduate entry will cut at least a year off the normal undergraduate medical training so, all being well, you'll be able to call yourself Dr Robertson after just four years. The snag is your choice of medical school is more limited as graduate entry is not offered by all UK medical schools and that means it's a lot tougher to be accepted as a graduate entrant than it is for an undergraduate medical degree and that's difficult enough.

"Here," he continued, leaning over and handing Simon a piece of paper he pulled from his jacket pocket. "Here's the current list of medical schools with graduate entry I've dug out for you. As you can see, there are only about 15. Sadly, we don't offer graduate level entry at St Thomas', but if you wanted to opt for London, there's Barts, St George's and Imperial, all of which I would rate highly.

"And this brings me to why I thought it would be good for us to talk because this is where I think I can be of some help to you," said George, smiling as he finished off his second cocktail of the morning. "I happen to know the Dean of Medicine at Barts pretty well, and also a couple of the senior profs there and in the not too distant past I have sat on various committees with two of the people at Imperial who I know are directly involved in student selection, so I would be more than happy to put in a good word for you with them. I am sure this would make a difference, although if it works like St Thomas', as I guess it still does, a quiet word from me will really only work if you were to make Barts your first choice. Outside London I would, of course, recommend Oxford and I'm sure my influence is still strong enough to set you on the path to securing a place at my old *alma mater*, Balliol, once I have told them you are really a Stander, only dressed up as a Robertson."

George guffawed at what he thought was his splendid joke.

"The other schools I am not so familiar with, but knowing you were coming today I asked around at St Thomas' when I was up this week and people I trust said Liverpool, Nottingham and Birmingham were all excellent medical schools. But what's of perhaps even greater importance for you, Simon, is all three seem to have a growing interest in mental health. As I am sure you know, historically mental health was always treated pretty marginally in the core curriculum. When I studied medicine, I am now ashamed to say we spent little more than a month of our five years delving into the world of mental health; the unwritten assumption then was illness pretty much only meant physical illness. Most people who were mentally ill were simply told to pull themselves together, perhaps given a pill to help them on their way and urged to get on with life. It really was as appalling as that!"

George shook his head, and for the first time since they arrived Simon was pleased his uncle had started to say something interesting. He was particularly cheered by what he said next.

"But it's no longer doom and gloom, Simon, I'm glad to say. In fact, my guess is big changes will happen in the next five or so years as the medical profession at last wakes up to what the general public has known for a long time – mental illness is not only real, it is a huge problem. I think, Simon, you're entering the mental health field at just the right time."

Simon caught Emma's eye again. She had also been pleased the professor had managed to scramble out of the hole he had dug himself into when talking about money.

"There is, of course, only so much I can do to help you. Even with my assistance, you'll need to study hard," said George, leaning back in his chair, which creaked under the pressure. Smiling, he said, "But you're still young, you're bright, you're eager to learn and clearly used to hard work and the discipline of exams. So I have every confidence you *will* get a place at a *good* medical school and succeed in your ambition of becoming a first-rate, and possibly even a famous mental health specialist.

"The question is," he said, turning and smiling at Emma, "whether your good lady-friend here can endure those long years of your studying."

"That's not going to be a problem," said Emma, smiling, "providing he continues to support me in my career, though I am banking on him getting into a London medical school because I know I couldn't live with us having to be wrenched apart so soon after we have got together if he had to live in some far-flung city like Birmingham or Manchester."

"And if I may be so bold, my dear, as to ask," said George. "What is your chosen career? You are tall and athletic. Are you a singer or dancer – or a nurse perhaps? We have had lots of wonderful black nurses at St Thomas' over the years, and no bad eggs. In some ways they seem to be more committed to the profession than many of the – I'm not putting this as delicately as I might – so to speak, local girls." When he wasn't able to think fast, George knew the gin was getting to him.

Emma was affronted and knew she couldn't let George's outrageous remark pass. Shifting in her chair she said "I…" taking in a deep breath. But no sooner had she started than George stopped her by raising his hand as the front doorbell was ringing; he stood up, excused himself and left the room.

As soon as George had gone, Simon pleaded with Emma not to get mad, and she smiled and said she wouldn't. In his absence, they had a little exchange about George's fixing methods. The message to Simon was clear: he should be grateful he was so closely related to Uncle George and take advantage of his contacts. In a word, he should choose Barts and Balliol as his first choices, and Uncle George would then move in and bat for him. It all left a pretty nasty taste in Simon's mouth.

"What amazes me," said Emma, "is he doesn't see anything wrong in what he's doing."

"Quite the opposite," said Simon. "Uncle George is happy not only to jump queues, and – if needs be – to avoid having to queue at all, and I'm sure it's not only in the world of medicine where he's happy to deploy such methods. In fact, Emma, it's even worse than this. Uncle George sees using his contacts to help me get into medical school as an obligation to the family. What I'm saying is he would see it as wrong not to pull strings on my behalf. And if you were to challenge him on the morality of doing this, I'm sure he'd tell you this is simply the way things are done, and if you pressed him further, he'd probably say this is the way we do things in Britain. And I suppose in some perverse way he's right because there are plenty of people who really do believe the 'end' pretty much always does justify the 'means'. That's hardly surprising given the number of statues we have erected to British heroes whose lives are held up for us to admire, though many of them were self-proclaimed racists, murderers, slave owners or advocates of slavery, and top-ranking soldiers and sailors happy to order the massacre of civilians for the sake of the Empire or to send tens of thousands of their troops to be slaughtered needlessly."

The more Simon's words and face signalled worries about making use of George's contacts, the more pleased Emma felt. She was ready for what else either George or Margaret, and possibly their other guests, might throw her way. It could be a pretty challenging Sunday lunch and she was comforted by Simon's mood of defiance. He would be her ally.

Emma and Simon rose politely as George and Margaret walked into the parlour with their two new guests. Not only were they all the same age but they were all dressed so similarly they could be mistaken for wearing some sort of uniform. George and Lennie both wore Harris Tweed jackets, though of a different cut; Lennie's was new, George's many decades old, the cuffs already repaired once but again fraying at the edges. Underneath, each had on a classic weekend checked shirt with a floral tie, though of different patterns and colours, George's wide and no longer in fashion, Lennie's newer and thinner. Their trousers were charcoal grey and matched the shape of their bodies: George's looked old and was over-sized and baggy with turn-ups; Lennie's were more modern, thin cut, straight and twin-pleated. They both wore brown shoes, George's well-worn brogues in need of a clean, Lennie's almost brand-new, with highly-polished toe-caps.

For their part, Margaret and Ginny seemed to have bought their similarly-cut bodycon dresses with sleeves, Margaret's navy and Ginny's oatmeal, from the same sections of M&S. Both failed to hide their hips and tummies. They wore similarly-styled sensible shoes with slightly-raised heels, and both had dyed hair and wore redder lipstick than Simon knew Cathy wore these days. Ginny wore a pearl necklace with matching earrings, Margaret the same in gold.

Prompted by Cathy, Simon and Emma had given some thought to what they should wear and they had tried hard to dress as 'Sunday smart' as they could. Simon had bought a new long-sleeved white cotton shirt which had had the merit of starting the day well-ironed. He wore his best dark-blue Levi's, which were dry now and still looked neat in spite of the rain, and leather shoes which, with a quick rub on the back of his jeans as they ran up the steps to the house, were still largely black. Emma had matched Simon with her own white cotton long-sleeved shirt, snug-fitting black trousers, and comfy black slip-on shoes which she knew would be fine for their walk and which had now dried out. She wore her silver choker necklace but no earrings. To crown it all, they both wore – for the very first time – the linen jackets they had bought specially for the trip to Zimbabwe, intending to wear them at their aborted stay at a smart Victoria Falls hotel.

Simon's was a light blue two-buttoned tailored jacket from M&S, Emma's a stone-coloured mixed-stitch long-sleeved blazer which had been on sale at New Look. If out with their friends dressed like this on a Sunday in London, they would have been laughed at for being completely over-dressed, but present company viewed their attempt to dress up as largely a failure.

George introduced Lennie and Ginny to Simon and Emma, and they all greeted each other warmly and sat down, George motioning to Lennie to sit next to Simon. As there had been no looks or worse when they had come into the parlour, Emma knew between the front door and the parlour, either George or Margaret, but most likely George, had told them about her. Then, after confirming they would both have the usual and asking if Simon or Emma wanted a top-up – to which the answer was no – George hurried away to the side-table where the bottles were neatly assembled. In no time, he was back carrying a tray. On it were two small cream sherries, a large gin and tonic for Lennie and his own glass more than half full; it was the second time George had replenished it that morning.

Simon and Lennie discussed psychiatry until they were all called for lunch, by which time they both realised their conversation wasn't going to advance very much further. Lennie came across to Simon as a decent, caring man who was evidently fulfilled by his work; from everything Simon could pick up he seemed to be a committed and successful psychiatrist. However, it was soon apparent Lennie was by nature cautious, reluctant to venture beyond his comfort zones or to proffer views and opinions on matters he knew little about. Perhaps, thought Simon, that's what made him a good psychiatrist?

As the two of them sat and chatted on one side of the fireplace, Ginny, Margaret, George and Emma sat together on the other. To stop George's prying questions, Emma took the initiative and fired off harmless questions to each of them about themselves which they enjoyed answering. When they thought Emma wasn't looking, Ginny and Margaret exchanged knowing glances to say how pleased they were to see how intelligent Emma clearly was.

It didn't take long before George could see Margaret was becoming fidgety. She always liked Sunday lunch to start promptly at one thirty, but Lennie and Ginny had arrived late and it was now well past her self-imposed deadline. So, scarcely ten minutes after he had served them all drinks, George stood up and announced they should eat. He could see the relief on Margaret's face when she hurried off to the kitchen as he led the way into lunch.

As they entered the dining room, George announced with an air of formality out of place for such a small gathering that he would sit at one end of the table and Margaret at the other, the one nearest to the kitchen. He then pulled out the chair to his right and standing behind it gestured for Emma to sit next to him, as she had feared he would, before motioning to Ginny to join their end of the table and take the chair to his left, opposite Emma's. Ginny knew the form and was at her place before George had finished seating Emma. Similarly, Lennie was standing in front of the chair to Emma's right before George was ready to steer him there. That left only the chair opposite Lennie for Simon to occupy, which George pointed to as he moved towards it. With Emma already seated, George asked the others to make themselves comfortable before Margaret joined them, and as he sat down he couldn't resist patting Emma's arm gently as he smiled and told her how lovely she looked. Emma winced, but was already on her guard and was more concerned with how she would react to anything outrageous he might say.

Before everyone had unfolded their crisply-starched napkins and put them on their laps, Margaret swept in, sat down, smiled and then looked back towards the open door of the kitchen she had just come in by. As she did so, a small woman in her early thirties wearing a black dress with a white full Victorian-style lace-trimmed apron pinned to the front of it walked in carrying a tray of steaming-hot soup bowls. Without a word, she placed these in front of each of the guests, serving the women first. Simon and Emma both smiled at the woman as she put their bowls in front of them and voiced a few words of greeting to which she responded with a friendly smile. No one else in the room either looked or spoke to her. When she had returned to the kitchen, Emma asked George who she was.

"Oh, that's Denisa," said George. "Lovely girl. We've had her a couple of years now. She's from Czechia – you know, the former Czech Republic, and – in even older money – Czechoslovakia." He chuckled, proud of how up-to -date he was with the country's successive name changes.

"She speaks such good English, and says she hopes to open an English language school in Prague one day. She's very enterprising. Good for her, I say!"

Emma couldn't resist asking if she had another name, to which George said he could never remember what it was. So he lobbed the question across to Margaret who said she thought it was something like Soroboda then suggested Emma ask her when Denisa came in to collect the dishes. "I'm sure Denisa would love to tell you herself," she added.

Given Denisa's age and the recent publicity about the difficulties foreign workers had in bringing their families to Britain if they didn't have work, Simon asked if she was married, and it was Margaret who again replied.

"Yes," she said. "She has two small girls who are looked after by her mother when she is working over here. Then Anton – that's her husband – comes over to Kent each year for the fruit-picking season, so he's over now.

It's such a good arrangement. He stays close by so they get to see each other on Sundays. That is, unless we have a lunch party. Then we ask her to stay back and help out. She's so willing and always says yes. She's keen to have the extra cash, it all goes towards the money she's saving for her language school, and, of course, we pay her more on a Sunday. Unlike some people we know and some countries I could name, we still believe Sunday should be special here in England."

Margaret then motioned for them to start, announcing it was homemade cream of celery soup. She pointed to the bowl of croutons in front of Simon and asked him to help himself and pass them round.

Wary of the croutons in case they contained bacon, Simon said, "What are they?"

"Croutons of course," replied Margaret brusquely.

"Sorry," said Simon apologetically, "I meant what sort of croutons?"

"Smoky bacon, as you ask. George and I always say they go so well with the celery. I'm sure you'll agree."

Simon didn't want to make a fuss so smiled and passed the bowl across to Ginny without taking any, which led Margaret, who felt affronted as she had specially made them herself, to ask why he wouldn't even try them.

"Sorry," he said again, "but I am vegetarian. I don't eat bacon."

"Oh yes," said Margaret, "Cathy did say something about that."

Sensing a little tension at the other end of the table, George stepped in to announce he had opened a bottle of Chardonnay to have with their soup and poured some into Emma's wine glass after she had given him the nod to say yes, before asking her to pass the wine on to Lennie. When the bottle had gone round the table and Ginny handed it back to George, he was clearly pleased there was enough left not just to fill his glass but to top it up a few moments later.

George then turned to his right and said, "Now, Emma, you'll recall I was asking you just now about your career, your job, but we were interrupted. So perhaps you can tell us all what it is. What *do* you do?"

"Glad to do that," said Emma cheerily. "I am a journalist; I work for the BBC."

"Oh," said George with some surprise. "Do you work for BBC local radio? No," he began a dialogue with himself. "I know, you work for that newish radio station BBC 1 Extra. I was told about it by one of my grandchildren who loves black music. She tells me it's rather good. Is that where you work?"

Before Emma could reply, George stepped in once again – he was clearly enjoying himself – saying, "No, you don't look at all like a pop music sort of person: you don't have the long braided hair or wear those dangly bracelets! Let me try again. I know: you're a TV sports reporter or announcer. Yes, I'm going to plump for that."

"Actually," said Emma who was less annoyed by George's pomposity than by his disdainful attitude towards her, "I do work in television. I am a professional current affairs journalist embracing both domestic and international news, not someone who simply reads a script. I work out of Langham Place with a small team of like-minded colleagues." Then, seeing blank faces across the table, she added, "at the new Broadcasting House building, the BBC's headquarters in central London."

Emma knew she had sounded a bit too venomous but she also knew it was her way of trying to quell the anger rising up inside her as she pinched herself below the table on the tender bits of her inner thighs. This was another way she had learned to keep in control.

Calmer now, she continued, speaking more matter-of-factly. "The BBC set up a new current affairs unit last year and I joined it earlier this year. After my first degree and graduate training, I worked for three or four years in print journalism for a local newspaper in North London but, keen to move into current affairs and television, I jumped at the opportunity this job offered and was delighted when offered the job. As you might imagine, these sorts of posts don't come up very often and the competition was pretty fierce." Emma was well aware she was showing off and had probably gone too far, but she thought George deserved it.

Seeing the absurdity of his flippant remarks, George felt momentarily deflated and fell silent, realising he should cease engaging in banal repartee. Simon smiled to himself. Then Ginny spoke.

"Oh, I had no idea... I am *very* impressed!" she began. "But I'm sorry to say although I see myself as rather a current affairs addict I don't ever remember seeing you on the news. It's funny how there are some people who you remember and others you don't. Actually, I find you can get quite attached to some TV people. I love that Thomas Shafernacker – or whatever he is called – you know, that lovely man who presents the weather."

So it clearly wasn't only George. Emma felt herself under attack and, with the wine starting to go to her head, she wasn't able to hold back any longer. "Thank goodness," she said, "there are a growing number of not only female but also black female professionals working in television now. Most are still presenters, some among the best, like Gillian Joseph and Charlene White, but I am hopeful more like me will go far in current affairs. There was a time when viewers didn't really notice the women on their screens; now it seems it's just black women who don't get seen."

Ginny felt uncomfortable but, as she wasn't quite sure the precise point Emma was making, she said nothing.

As the tension round the table rose, Denisa swept back into the room with an empty tray to collect the soup bowls, to everyone's relief. Margaret followed her back to the kitchen as George stood up to announce he had selected a Châteauneuf du Pape instead of his usual claret to go with the roast lamb as this was, as he put it, such a special occasion. To retain the initiative, he picked up two bottles from the sideboard, clasping one in each hand, and returned to the table to place one at each end, inviting everyone to help themselves and saying no one should hold back as he had plenty more in reserve.

By the time he was back in his seat, Denisa had already put six large dinner plates in front of George and returned carrying a wooden carving plate with an entire leg of lamb on it, its skin crisply burnt, fresh rosemary stalks on top and round the edges, which she ceremoniously laid before George for him to carve. As George began to slice the meat, Denisa and Margaret brought out dishes of roast potatoes, carrots and boiled peas from the kitchen and arranged them neatly in the centre of the table, around which they placed a gravy boat, a bowl of onion sauce and a jar of redcurrant jelly. Like the side plates and the soup bowls, the dinner plates and serving dishes were all Royal Crown Derby, old Imari Japan – as Simon and Emma now knew because George had helpfully told them. As they prepared to eat, the atmosphere in the room was noticeably calmer.

When he had finished carving, George started to pile the meat onto the top dinner plate, which he handed to Emma to pass to Lennie. The women all quietly asked him to give them less and Simon said he would not be having any meat, so would Uncle George kindly pass him an empty plate? He turned to Margaret and, trying hard not to upset her again, repeated the point he had made earlier about his being vegetarian, saying quietly he was sure his mother had notified her well in time.

"Yes, Simon," she retorted, sounding exasperated. "Cathy did tell me you were vegetarian but I didn't think there was any need to make something special as I felt sure when you saw the roast you would change your mind and eat at least a small portion of the delicious lamb. After all, you always ate meat when you came here as a child."

Simon froze but Margaret hadn't finished. "Anyway, I'm sure a little won't do you any harm," she persisted. "It'll do you good and build you up; you always were on the thin side Simon. Our lamb is reared a few fields from here and locally slaughtered. It's quite the best: none of this frozen New Zealand stuff. I've never had a vegetarian to lunch, but as I said, I'm sure you'll soon get over it. After all, if you can change your mind once, you can change it again."

Simon was even more incensed now and felt the anger rise within him. He was itching to respond and would have dearly loved to engage in a discussion of the rights and wrongs of eating meat, but it wouldn't end well so he kept silent. He knew what he wanted to say.

"Aunt Margaret," he would have begun, "I want to assure you I have thought long and hard about vegetarianism. The reason I don't eat meat has very little to do with how it tastes. There are plenty of ways of obtaining the nutrition I need without eating meat and, what's more, well-prepared vegetarian meals are not only nutritious, they are just as tasty as meat dishes – I should know as I make them. I don't eat meat as I believe it is wrong to use animals, sentient creatures like ourselves, as food, and neither you nor anyone else is going to make me change my mind about this in a hurry."

Instead Simon kept quiet and piled vegetables, onion sauce and redcurrant jelly onto his plate, politely declining the gravy when Margaret offered it to him by raising his hand and catching her eye with a knowing glance just before he started to tuck into his food.

Since that dramatic exchange between Sarah and his father, Simon had spent a lot of time thinking about confrontation. He now knew at least a little about the power which forgiveness and saying sorry could have in changing the whole dynamic of human interaction, transforming what would otherwise be an inevitable destructive outcome into something totally different. In the short time he piled the vegetables and sauces onto his plate, Simon managed to force the anger out of himself, and in the glance he gave to Margaret, his eyes spoke of forgiveness. And, as if by magic, it worked. Quietly, so no one else would hear and almost as if she had heard what Simon had said to himself about the power of forgiveness, Margaret said she was sorry; she shouldn't have said what she did. Knowing how difficult it is to say sorry, Simon smiled back at her as if to say it was OK, and from the look she now gave him, he could tell she was grateful.

Emma was surprised Simon had let Margaret's remark slip. She was aware some sort of exchange was taking place, but she hadn't been able pick up what had been going on between the two of them. Meanwhile, unaware of what had just taken place, George, Ginny and Lennie were busy tucking into their lamb.

George had made up his mind a long time ago about most things and meat-eating was among them. As he chewed on his food, George knew the main reason why he ate meat was because he liked it, though he knew if he was challenged he would be able to produce a raft of other reasons to support his belief eating meat was also morally acceptable. To start with, he, his entire family and pretty much everyone across the country ate meat and had always done so. George felt quite strongly there was a very good reason for this: meat eating was one of the things which defined them as English, as British, people. If Simon had challenged him, George would have said eating meat was a manifestation, a fundamental part of the British way of life and culture. He couldn't even start to imagine Christmas without roast turkey, or possibly roast goose, or Sunday lunch without its roast beef, lamb, pork, veal, chicken or duck. For George, eating meat at Christmas and on Sundays goes to the very heart of who the British are.

What's more, he would have been happy to add, millions of people depend on animal farming for their livelihood so it would be inconceivable to ask people to stop rearing animals for food. Of course, George was against cruelty to animals, who wouldn't be? But the sight of sheep on our hillsides, cows in our fields, chickens running loose in the farmyard – these were also the very essence of rural Britain and what it always should and would be. George couldn't see any problem either with loving animals and eating meat; after all, David Attenborough devoted practically the whole of his life to getting us to care about the animal world but was happy to eat meat. Indeed, George remembered him saying on TV once our mouths and teeth are designed for us to be meat eaters. And if that wasn't sufficient, Britain was a Christian country and Jesus ate meat, or at least if he hadn't gnawed at a lamb shank with his Apostles at the Last Supper, the Bible would certainly have mentioned it.

As no one said anything and as, from deep within her British bones, she knew they needed to change the subject, Emma turned to George, smiled and said, "Tell me, George, why is this magnificent house of yours called Catshead? It's such a strange name."

"Ah," said George sighing. He was relieved Emma was steering them away from what might turn out to be a difficult and emotionally charged discussion. For George, the flow of conversation was as necessary a part of Sunday lunch as the roast and the wine but it had to be a particular sort of conversation. Besides light banter, he would never want to disagree with, still less confront, any of his guests, and disagreeing openly with Simon was out of the question; after all, he was family and family relationships are sacrosanct.

"How Catshead got its name is a fascinating story and apologies to Lennie and Ginny who may have heard me before on this. But before I start, Emma, be a dear and pass me the wine. I need a little liquid sustenance to help me clear my throat.

"The land on which this house was built," began George, his glass topped up, "has been with the family for generations; we certainly have land registration and ownership documents stretching back to the 16th century. The present house was built in the middle of the 18th century, which is why it is and looks so typically Georgian. The new house was called Catshead though we don't know exactly when it was so named nor whether the house it replaced was also called Catshead. What also remains a mystery is whether it is coincidence our name – Stander – and the name of our nearest village – Standen – are almost the same. Probably not is my guess, but that's another story.

"But to get back to the name *Catshead*, as far back as the sixteen hundreds, we know the family were in the cider trade. Later they were also involved in the slave trade but that's also a different story." He gave out a belly laugh, forgetting Emma was sitting next to him, and stopped, giving her a look which conveyed the embarrassment he felt.

"What you probably don't know," he continued, "is there is an old English apple called a catshead which was developed in Kent around that time. It grew to become a key ingredient in traditional Kent cider. The catshead apple is pretty rare now in England though it is still grown in the United States, mostly in the southern states, I believe. Anyway, we like to think it is our family which was responsible for creating the catshead variety of apple, hence the house name. The family certainly made plenty of money in the cider business.

"However," he went on, feeling more relaxed and smiling broadly at Emma, "there is another story about the origin of the Catshead name. The family archives tell us soon after the new house was built, in the middle of the 18th century, it was widely believed to be haunted: I have read through dozens of documents which talk of witches, séances, sorcery and all things black magic." George glanced back at Emma, immediately regretting the emphasis he had placed on the word black.

"Well," said George, whose ability to bounce back straight after making offensive remarks continued to astound Emma, "these same archives record a really strange event which happened one morning in late autumn in the year 1745: the severed and bloodstained head of a cat was found impaled on a fence post very near the main house. No one could explain how or why this gruesome-looking head of a cat had got there, even if, as you would expect, the incident led to plenty of discussion, even fear.

"But what was far stranger was a year later, to the very day, exactly the same thing happened: another bloodstained severed cat's head was discovered, impaled on top of exactly the same fence post. More sinister still, the same thing happened again – for a third time – on precisely the same day the following year. This time the archives record fear and panic not only among family members, but right across the countryside for miles around. People were terrified by what was now widely accepted to be witchcraft, or at least an event which could only be explained by resort to the supernatural. In the course of the following year, long-time loyal staff left the family's employment and it became impossible to hire new local people, so they had to advertise as far away as London to get the staff they needed.

"Then, the year after the third incident, when everyone was waiting in fear for another dead cat's head to appear, there was nothing. That was it, both then and forever afterwards. No one ever satisfactorily explained why the head of a dead cat had appeared three years running or why these gruesome cats' head appearances never occurred again. It was all very grizzly! Anyway, it was these macabre goings on which are the other reason why the rebuilt house was named Catshead.

"Which story is true?" asked George rhetorically, beaming broadly round the room. "Well," he said, again answering his own question, "we don't know. When the family assembles we often still debate and discuss it. I like to think the answer could be a bit of both!"

By the time George had finished, Denisa had cleared away the main course and George's uneaten apple pie was now in front of him, and next to it, a jug of cream. He let out his second guffaw of the day as he poured a generous dollop of double cream over his apple pie and tucked in.

With George occupied, Margaret looked across at Emma and, toying with a piece of apple pie at the end of her fork, said, "perhaps Emma can help us by shedding some *new* light on the severed cats' heads? After all, she must know plenty about witches and witchcraft, mustn't she?" Margaret's was neither a flippant nor rhetorical question.

"And why should *I* know about witches and witchcraft?" retorted Emma, not quite believing what she was hearing.

"Well, you are African, aren't you?" said Margaret, sounding almost as shocked in her reply as Emma had been in her response. "And today it's mostly Africans who practise witchcraft, don't they, unless I am very much mistaken?" It was George's turn to feel embarrassed. He knew Margaret was partial to her wine and on occasions, though not too often, she drank a little too much on a Sunday. When she did, she could say things she would afterwards regret. But Margaret wasn't alone. Her close friend Ginny had been thinking much the same.

"Simon, here, is as African as I am," retorted Emma swiftly. "We were both born in Africa – in Zimbabwe – and came over to England when we were still very young. Actually, as I was two when I came to live in England and Simon a little older I have lived more of my life in England than Simon, which surely makes him more 'African' than I am, doesn't it? If, however, you are referring to my ethnicity, I am Shona by birth and, yes, the Shona traditionally believed in witchcraft as have most other people who have inhabited this planet. Even the English did, as George has just been telling us. But I am modern-day English, Margaret, just as Simon is and neither of us has any experience of witchcraft, direct or indirect, I am glad to say."

"Well," said Ginny, "you're not really English, Emma, in the same way as Simon is English." If there was one thing Ginny prided herself on, it was her honesty. "After all," she continued, "you are black, so at least you must be black English rather than simply English."

Like Margaret, Ginny had drunk a little too much and her guard was down. As soon as she had spoken, she knew she should have contrasted 'black English' with 'white English', otherwise she knew she could be accused of racism, and if there was the one thing Ginny was certain of, it was that she wasn't a racist.

As Emma was wondering how she should respond to what Ginny had just said, George threw his two pennies' worth into the bubbling cauldron, saying, "And what's more, Emma, Simon's home is now here whereas your real home – I mean your traditional home – will always be in Africa, in Zimbabwe. Your people must have lived there for dozens of centuries, whereas Simon's family went out to Africa probably less than a hundred years ago."

Rarely had Emma been on the receiving end of so many blatantly racist comments directed at her in such quick succession. This was not racial abuse as she had known it: the short sharp verbal attack knowingly launched and intended to taunt. These people didn't even know what they were saying was racist. This was the first time Emma recalled ever being exposed to such extreme views in a social setting. What her friends had told her about there still being pockets of raw racism alive and well in the home counties of England really was true.

"I really don't know where to begin," said Emma as she gathered herself together. She decided to start with what she knew best, herself.

"Although you clearly find this hard to understand," she said, "not only am I English, but England is my home, my *only* home. My family here in England may be small – there's just my mum and me – but it would never cross my mind to go back to Africa and live with my extended family. I have spent almost my entire life in England and I have no desire to live anywhere else than here. All my close friends are here as is my partner, Simon – my *English* partner. I have not only been to school and work here in England but I am building a career here as I intend to stay – just like pretty much all the other English people I know and who I grew up with.

"But maybe even more difficult for you to grasp is I *feel* English. Not only is England my home, but deep inside me – in my bones – England and Englishness are part of who I am as a person. I am comfortable in my English skin. My family left Zimbabwe to settle here, as the Irish have done for decades and the Romans, Normans, Angles, Saxons and Vikings, and so many other people before them, to create the melting pot which is Britain today. If you go back far enough, I'll bet you'll all find the blood of either an immigrant or a foreign conqueror, or both, flowing through your own veins. Like so many people, I remain grateful to England for welcoming me and allowing me to live here, to live here permanently as my home. There'll be no relocating back to Africa – either for me or for Simon."

Emma could feel her words having an effect on her; she was angry but she kept her cool just as Simon had done moments earlier when Margaret had riled him about his vegetarianism. However, she wasn't finished; there was far more she needed to say.

"What does make me deeply uncomfortable, though, is out and out prejudice." Emma sounded calmer now. "As Ginny so indelicately put it, being black British isn't quite as kosher as being what Ginny called 'British' by which, of course, she meant being white British.

"Maybe you don't know this, but black people have lived in England since Roman times. Today's British black population has been boosted by waves of immigration from both the Caribbean and from Africa and today there are over two million black British people living in the UK. Many families have now been here for generations and pretty much all families, like mine, see Britain, and most see England, as home. In World War II, thousands of black people from the Empire, mostly from the Caribbean but also from Africa, fought and died for this country. What's more, notwithstanding the history of racism in Britain, black people have long been seen in a positive light. Two of Shakespeare's greatest characters – Othello and Aaron – are black.

"But Britishness is so much more than where we come from and how we speak. It is above all about our values. High on the list of British values to be cherished are parliamentary democracy and the rule of law. Successive UK governments, your governments and my governments, have formally and unequivocally rejected racism in all its forms and I am proud of that. Fifty years ago, in the 1960s, our parliament passed the Race Relations Act and it remains a central pillar of our legislation to this day. Sadly, however, although the Act has been successful in helping to stamp out much overt racism in our country, it hasn't made as many inroads into tackling inbuilt racial prejudices, nor in addressing systemic racial inequalities and inequities which still blight our country.

"As I see it," continued Emma, encouraged by the feeling most people round the table were now really listening to what she was saying, "prejudice and perceptions get us to the heart of the matter. In 1978, well before I arrived here, Britain joined other leading countries in formally adopting the UN's Declaration on Race and Racial Prejudice and all British laws are shaped in the context of equal rights for all. This Declaration is also important because it makes a clear distinction between difference and racism.

"We're all different in some way. I don't have a problem with difference. I believe individuals and groups not only have the right to be different, they have the right both to regard themselves as different as well as to be regarded as such."

"Here, here," said George, and Lennie nodded in agreement.

"However," said Emma, "diversity of lifestyles and the right to be different must never serve either as a pretext for racial prejudice or justify, either in law or in practice, any discriminatory practice whatsoever. This is crucial; fundamental, in fact. It is the bedrock upon which all English law is based, and it underpins the very core of what being British means. It's what enables us to both tolerate and smile at eccentricity." Emma cut a glance across at George, who smiled back at her, failing to grasp the implication of Emma's look, as if to prove the point she was making.

"But the freedom and opportunities which come with championing differences come with risks attached," said Emma, warming to her theme. "Just as I'm sure you do, I know some of our politicians have used diversity and difference to whip up and foment racial prejudice, even racial hatred, and the effect has been both swift and terrifying. What's more, they've been enabled by the press to spread their message of hate, and as I work as a professional journalist I think I know what I am talking about here. All our leaders in all walks of life, but especially those in government, need to continually denounce this abuse of press freedom whenever it starts to appear, but they seem more afraid to do this today than they were even a few years ago. And if I'm honest, I have to say how much these developments trouble me – yes, as a black woman, but even more so as someone who passionately believes in British values."

Emma paused and looked round the table. All eyes were on her, and, except for the sound of Emma's voice, the room had fallen silent; even George had put his wine glass down, surprising himself with his keenness to concentrate on what Emma was saying. The silence was almost broken when, a moment earlier, Denisa had walked in to collect the dessert plates but, sensing the mood in the room, she stopped a step beyond the kitchen door and was now standing still, her tray at her side, listening herself to what Emma was saying. Not even Margaret noticed Denisa's statue-like presence.

Everyone could hear the emotion in Emma's voice and in a strange way, as she spoke, her sincerity struck a chord with her fellow diners, prompting them to open up and think honestly about the issues Emma had raised because they mattered to them. It was this which led Lennie to say while he thought it was wrong to make a distinction between black British and British, he also felt people like Simon were not only different from people like Emma because of their different ethnic origins but, as he put it, "because of our history".

"Surely people with Simon's roots – those from white British stock – have more in common with each other than people living in this country whose roots lie elsewhere?" said Lennie. "So, in that sense, Simon could be said to be 'more British' than Emma. I am not sure I have phrased this as delicately as I might, but I hope I have provided you with some sense of what I mean."

"I understand what you're saying," said Emma, who felt far more comfortable now the discussion was no longer so emotionally charged. "But I don't think you have gone quite as far as you might." She knew she had everyone's attention once again.

"Right at the start of the meal," said Emma "Ginny referred to that nice man who reads the weather, Thomas Shafernacker, and I guess her view of niceness carried with it the notion of being British. Tomasz Schafernaker – pronounced 'Toor-marss' – was born in Poland, started school over there before he moved to England, and, to this day, remains a dual Polish-British national. Besides being charming, he sounds English, smiles and jokes like an English person should and uses a range of delightful English expressions and mannerisms, like pretty much everyone who has grown up and gone to school here. Like "Toor-marss" I sound English, smile and joke like an English person and almost certainly have an even greater range of English jokes and mannerisms than he does. And, like "Toor-marss", I was born abroad.

"But there are two ways in which he and I differ. Firstly, I am not a dual national. I am only British. Secondly, his family's roots are Polish, European – yes – foreign, whereas my family's historical roots lie deep within the family of the British Empire. For seven generations, my family imbibed core British values growing up in our corner of the Empire. My grandmother, my mother and I were all born in the British Commonwealth. So ethnically, it would seem Britishness runs deeper through the veins of Emma Maconie than the 'ever so nice' Englishman Toor-marss Schafernaker."

At that point Simon felt it was time to step in to take over the running from Emma. Although George was still listening, Simon could see he was starting to become fidgety and guessed he was itching to move to the sitting room for the brandy and coffee but Simon felt too much would be lost if he didn't intervene now before they adjourned to sink into the comfy chairs where he was sure George, and perhaps others, would nod off. There were things he felt strongly about which needed to be said before this conversation was brought to an end, and he knew they would have far more of an impact if it was he, rather than Emma, who said them.

"I would like to add a few thoughts of my own here on what Emma has said about herself and her Britishness," said Simon.

"Emma has just told you she not only *is* British but how she *feels* British too. Well, a large part of what attracts me to Emma – to add to her being smart and incredibly attractive of course – revolve around the core values which mean so much to her, the principles and beliefs which have helped to mould and shape her into the woman she is today.

"Though she may blush to hear it, Emma is a hugely caring person, a woman of deep integrity, a passionate believer in fair play, justice and freedom. She has a special eye for the underdog and a determination to help those to whom society and the world have dealt a rotten hand. Emma is driven by wanting to make the world, and Britain, a better place. While I would argue these are essentially human values, they are widely believed to be core British values too. To the extent they are, then I can say I am drawn to Emma because of the British values she so clearly has in abundance. I should add she also loves dogs and flowers and the change of the seasons, spring especially. What else? Emma clearly loves the BBC, she works for it. And – oh yes – queue-jumping is as alien to Emma as it is to everyone else round this table. I know, as I have seen her in action when she has challenged queue-jumpers, and to my knowledge she has a 100% success rate!

"But there is one more British value, or attribute, which Emma has and which has very much been on display here today, and that is tolerance. Emma is incredibly tolerant of those who hold racist views. Understandably, racism makes Emma angry; I would be horrified if it didn't! It makes me angry too. Actually, it makes her bitterly sad as well because she has seen first-hand the way racism shatters not only the dreams but the lives of young people, young British people, who are blocked when they apply for jobs for which they are qualified, and hungry to do. She has often used the word 'crumble' to describe the effect persistent racism has on people – on young British people.

"But there is more. Emma is tolerant of the silent unknowing racists – not 'tolerant' as in accepting the wrongness of what they believe and its consequences, but 'tolerant' as in accepting them as persons, as fellow Brits. Why? Well, firstly because she believes in tolerance *per se*. But also because, as she has told me, she believes tolerance can be contagious. Showing respect to someone who has just slighted you, or who knows you disagree with them, can sometimes jolt that person into reflecting on, and asking themselves why, you have chosen to treat them with the dignity due to them as a human being when you have just treated them with such disdain. This in turn can create a new type of self-awareness: juxtaposing one's beliefs with those of someone who doesn't share them can help to tease out and expose these views for what they are – prejudices. And one victory over prejudice and bigotry can lead to another, spreading out to have a wider impact until, hopefully, instead of the victims of racism continuing to crumble, the whole edifice of racism will start to crumble.

"I love Emma in part because we share these values. What I don't share with Emma is her ethnicity. However, our racial and ethnic differences add to who we are, they don't diminish our relationship. On the contrary, they deepen it. And when one day we have children, they will be the richer not the poorer for having parents drawn from different racial groups and British roots, and their lives will add to the richness of modern Britain. They will not merely contribute to the mix and diversity of today's Britain but their existence will make it more difficult for other British people to view the world through the stultifying one-dimensional template of race which hides people as persons and bundles them up into boxes labelled exclusively as only black British or white British, ignoring everything else about them. Racism ought never to have been part of Britain's past, but it has been. Racism should not have any place in present-day Britain, but it still does. Emma and I are keen to play our part in ensuring it will have no place in the Britain of the future."

Everyone was moved by Simon's words, recognising they were spoken from the heart. Even Emma, who knew how well Simon understood the way she felt, was uplifted by his defence of her and the way he had described British values. She had never known him speak so passionately about these things either to others or even to herself.

Simon couldn't resist one final remark, which was received in the half-joking way in which it was said. "You know I'm a vegetarian, and a passionate one at that. If you believe the Sunday roast and meat-eating forms part of what it is to be British, then, Lennie, you would have to conclude Emma here, who still eats meat, is far more British than I am."

He leant back in his chair and smiled across the table to Emma, who smiled back. Denisa saw her opportunity and announced she would take the coffee to the sitting room; it was only then that Margaret realised she had been standing there listening, and for once, she didn't seem upset the clearing up had been put on hold. Margaret stood up and opened the door between the dining room and sitting room, repeating Denisa's invitation to go in for coffee. As everyone rose, George said he would bring up the rear. Once he was alone in the dining room, he hurriedly helped himself to a final glass of red wine.

By the time George was in the sitting room, Lennie, Ginny and Margaret had already sat themselves together on the only three chairs arranged on the one side of the fireplace; it was evident they had had their fill of challenging conversation. Emma and Simon seemed relieved. As the two of them hovered around the small settee and armchair on the other side of the fireplace, George motioned for Simon to take the armchair as he sat down next to him on one end of the settee, patting the other end for Emma to sit next to him.

After serving the coffee, Denisa left but soon returned from the kitchen carrying a tray of different glasses, a large cut-glass decanter filled with vintage port and a large bottle of as yet unopened Rémy Martin. Ginny had a port. The only other person to take a drink was George, who poured himself a large cognac into an oversized brandy glass and gently warmed the bottom with his two podgy hands.

Lennie, Ginny and Margaret distanced themselves further from the risk of having to talk any more to Emma and Simon by starting up a conversation about mutual friends. Having been forewarned by his mother of George's habit of nodding off after a good lunch, Simon thanked him for inviting them down and said how much they had both enjoyed their day. Between sips, George smiled, said he hoped they would come again and told Simon to phone him in the next week or so to let him know which medical schools he had decided to apply to so he could then step in and help.

George's glass was soon empty and moments later he was asleep, his double chin bobbing up and down on his bulging chest as he breathed heavily, occasionally letting out a loud sigh. Emma carefully removed the empty glass from his limp right hand and placed it on the side table next to her, exchanging grateful glances with Margaret, whose look merely confirmed this was how their Sunday lunches always ended.

It was now well past 4.30 and Lennie was keen to leave. Ensuring Margaret was watching, he raised his left arm in front of him, bent it at the elbow, turned his wrist towards him and looked at his watch. Then, in as loud a voice as convention allowed, he said, "Goodness, look at the time. I hadn't realised it was so late. Come on, Ginny, we really must be going; we mustn't outstay our welcome."

During lunch Lennie had gathered Simon and Emma would need a lift back to the station and so he said they would be delighted to drop them off if they were ready to go. Emma had already picked up what was happening and, saying she and Simon needed to get back to London soon, thanked him and said a lift would be great. Leaving George to sleep on, the four of them plus Margaret quietly left the sitting room and made their way via the coat cupboard to the front door where they stood to say their goodbyes.

Simon began by saying how much he and Emma had enjoyed their day and he thanked Margaret for such a lovely lunch. He said he was sorry if the conversation had at times become a little heated, adding neither he nor Emma had meant to sound aggressive but they both felt strongly about a number of things and apologised if they had come over as a little too passionate.

Before Margaret could say anything, Lennie said he had found the discussions on Britishness different and at times enlightening, adding he had been glad to hear first-hand what young Londoners were thinking these days. He said there was much he needed to think more about, and that he was grateful for their honesty.

Relieved it was all over, Margaret was equally gracious in her parting words. Knowing Cathy was certain to call and ask how things had gone, Margaret apologised again to Simon for not taking his vegetarianism sufficiently seriously. Smiling, she said she promised to produce a veggie main course when next they came down which, she added, she hoped would be soon. She then gave a brief hug to all her guests in turn, ending with Emma, whom she said it had been a pleasure to meet and whom she had found most interesting.

"I'll look out for you when I watch the news from now on, and wish you all the very best in your career as a TV journalist," she said graciously, revealing how far she had come since she had opened the front door and first set eyes on Emma.

Emma stepped forward and gave Margaret an affectionate peck on the cheek as if to demonstrate the truth of what Simon had said about her tolerance. She thanked Margaret for having them down and asked her to convey her thanks to George too. She said she had found Catshead fascinating and, responding to Margaret's invitation, told her she too hoped they could come back soon as she was keen to see more of their beautiful house and explore the garden. Emma said the whole meal had been delicious, smiling as she said 'even the meat', and ended by asking Margaret to thank Denisa, especially for sacrificing a precious day off with her husband.

Almost as soon as Lennie drove off, Ginny asked Emma if she played golf. Too weary to engage in a conversation about the irrelevance of golf to penniless young Londoners, Emma merely said she got her exercise through running, which she loved, and though she had tried many different sports, she didn't really have the eye for ball games. "However," she added, "the older I get the more fascinated I am getting about cricket. You know Simon plays, he both bowls and bats and I have been to watch him, he's pretty impressive at both, as he is at catching. He even caught me!"

Then Emma mischievously asked Ginny whether she preferred Tests, ODIs or T20s and what she thought of their having 100-ball games. Ginny looked blank and turned to Lennie for help, who let out a loud laugh, saying, cruelly, she wouldn't even know what the question meant. For the rest of their journey to the station Ginny and Emma remained quiet while Lennie and Simon chatted merrily on about cricket. Lennie was the most relaxed he had been the whole afternoon.

As they got out of the car, Simon thanked Lennie for his earlier advice and his thoughts on psychiatry as a career. Lennie said how pleased he was they had all met, going on to apologise for not being able to help Simon more. He handed Simon his card as they shook hands, telling him to call whenever he wanted. Ginny gave Emma a strained smile as Emma raised her hand to wave goodbye, thanking them both for the lift. In stark contrast, Lennie's smile across to Emma was warm and generous: of all the things Emma had said over lunch to try to persuade Lennie of her Britishness, none was more convincing than the topical question she had just raised about the merits of different forms of the game of cricket. He was clearly impressed.

As the car drove off, Emma took out her phone and saw it was ten past five. Perfect timing: if it wasn't delayed she knew the next London train should arrive in a couple of minutes. The station was empty. With the clocks changing, it was now quite dark and feeling cold: there was already a distinct autumnal nip to the air, though the rain which had been forecast was still holding off. Emma and Simon locked arms as they headed for the near-side platform.

* * *

"Well," said Simon as they stood waiting for their train, "that was different."

"Yes, it certainly was," said Emma. "In every way. It had never occurred to me they would be quite as racist as that. You don't know even how to begin. But Simon, you're such a love: you said some really nice things about me, most pretty undeserved. But thanks most especially for your support. I'm not nearly as tolerant as you gave me credit for but it was sweet of you to say what you did. I fear most of them didn't *really* understand what you were saying, especially Ginny and certainly George. As for Margaret, well, though she doesn't still get it, I feel she's learned a lot, so we should be grateful for that.

"There's something I am growing to love about you, Simon," Emma continued as she snuggled up close to him. "It comes out when you get worked up. You become so articulate – not that you're not articulate anyway – but you suddenly have a new way with words. Your sentences just seem to flow out of you so naturally it's as if you were delivering a carefully prepared speech. I don't quite know what it is, but you take on an aura of authority which is really attractive, quite sexy in fact. I think a couple of times you scared them, you know."

"Well, you certainly silenced them with your eloquence, Em," said Simon as he in turn drew his body close to hers. "I couldn't believe it when they started to ask you about witchcraft, but, as ever, you kept your cool and handled it brilliantly. But none of this would have happened if I had realised how depressingly disappointing Uncle George would turn out to be, and if I had, we would never have agreed to come. I think the reason I was so keen to see him was I had always been rather in awe of him as a boy, but as we now know there is really nothing there much except a love of drink, and he clearly fancied you. It was quite embarrassing, and dreadful for you, and I'm sorry about that of course. Can't he see how pompous and racist he is? I guess not. And none of the others seemed particularly bothered by his supercilious remarks. I guess that's because they're so like that themselves they didn't notice. I liked Lennie, though, even if he was *so* quiet. Of all the people there, he really seemed to listen to what we were saying and I am pretty sure we made him think. He even said as much."

Just then they heard the rails below them rattling and, looking up, they saw the bright front light of the train as it drew into the station. As luck would have it, it stopped with a carriage door right in front of them, and as it slowed to a stop they could see it was practically empty. As they stepped inside they were immediately hit by the warm air; it felt so cosy compared with the chill of the platform they had just left.

When settled, they chatted on, reflecting further on the day, focusing now on some of the conversations which had troubled them the most. Understandably, Simon started by saying how upset he had been by George's advising him to put as his first choice those medical schools where his influence was sufficiently strong for him, effectively, to ensure he would be offered a place. They both knew this was wrong, and Emma agreed when Simon said George's behaviour was a clear-cut case of corruption. "I am not going to be sucked into this way of getting into medical school, however fierce the competition is, and however keen I am to move into medicine," he said. "I've made up my mind. I will definitely not apply to either Balliol or Barts. It would be deeply dishonest. It's a matter of principle, Em." Emma agreed.

From Simon's perspective, what he was doing in agreeing to come down to talk to Uncle George was to tap into his knowledge of the medical profession and to seek his views, even his guidance, on the quality of the teaching in the different medical schools. If he made recommendations, Simon would listen and then make his own mind up. After all, from what his parents had told him, Uncle George had been a fine urological surgeon and teacher in his day, and Simon had googled him and read eloquent testimonials online from his patients and former students to confirm this. He had not come down to Catshead to seek help to get into medical school by the back door.

"What I find so galling," said Simon, "is what George offered to do for me was so clearly at odds with the very British values of truth, honesty and fair play he went on later to assert he so passionately believed in. How could he be so blind not to see the contradiction himself?"

This led the two of them to start chatting more generally about the different ways you can get on in life which are acceptable. "It's not wrong for you to be made aware of a job opportunity by a friend or colleague or to seek advice on how to prepare for an interview," volunteered Emma, "provided you then compete for the job with others on a level playing field, following procedures which are open, transparent and applicable to everyone. After all, Simon, you can't get by in life by sitting on your hands and simply waiting passively for jobs to fall into your lap by magic. You get on by being proactive, searching out opportunities and using your initiative.

"The problem, though, is the playing field can never be entirely level because your life chances are influenced in varying degrees by factors and events which tend to favour you or work against you, many of which are out of your control. In the real world, Simon, we both know it really does matter not only whether you are born black or white but whether you were born male or female, disabled or disadvantaged, a member of the dominant or a minority group. But it's more than this. Even your inborn talents are dependent, for better or worse, on the gene-pool from which you came. So, are your genes based on luck, or, as your Uncle George would put it, aren't they simply the outcome of the way things are?"

"Luck certainly has far more to do with it than we might initially be prepared to acknowledge," said Simon as he thought more about what Emma was saying. "Luck plays a part in which teacher you will have, and in so many of the people you meet in life who one way or another help you along. Being in a certain place at a particular time can play a crucial part in determining what happens in your life. When you come to think of it, Em, luck has been pretty important to both of us in making us the people we are today."

"Yes, it's huge, isn't it," said Emma. "If Mum hadn't managed to get us over to England and if I had stayed in Zimbabwe, I would have gone to school in Mutoko and ended up – if I'd been lucky – as a health worker. Remember that nurse, Farisai, I met on the bus and told you about, Simon? *I* could easily have been the beaten-up third wife of an abusive husband who took most of the little money I earned, forcing me not only to live in poverty, but apart from my only daughter. And we both know I was only able to obtain a British passport with relative ease because of the luck of the date when I arrived in England. Just imagine what would have happened if I had arrived here in the 2010s and not the early 1990s. I received the excellent secondary school education I did because I was lucky to be born a Catholic. I owe my career in journalism and my first job at the *Finchley Times* to David Gould, whom I only met because I was in the same class at school with his son Joe – and we were lucky to get on so well.

"Then there's my job at the BBC. Did I get this, Simon, because I really was the best in the bunch of applicants? I have always thought so, and I still do. But perhaps being black had more to do with it than I have been willing to acknowledge. How much do I owe my job not merely to the Corporation's latest attempt to recruit young black journalists to make its current inclusion strategy work and to help hit its new diversity targets, but also to the consequences of decades of historic racism and black discrimination at the BBC? Think about it, Simon. I was employed on the backs of equally talented black journalists who had applied for similar jobs as me in the past but were rejected because they were black. What this means is their failure to get jobs stacked the cards more and more in my favour; in other words, I got my job because of those the BBC never employed. So the pay I am getting is due in some way to the low salaries they had to live on. When you look at it in this way, I can't help but feel dreadful. In what sense could this be called fair, just and right? You see, Simon, it's all far more complicated than we might think."

Likewise, Simon mused on the tangible benefits his birth and what his family had brought to him already. He was born African but had been able to move to and settle in England because, fortuitously, his mother had an English passport. He was employed as an accountant at Falkland, Fairbridge and Hayes as he was his father's son and because he obtained a good degree at a well-respected university. And he was accepted at Kent to study accountancy because he was able to attend an excellent school as he lived in the catchment area. This he also owed to his father, who could afford to live in Muswell Hill because he had become a partner in a local accountancy firm. This in turn was due directly to George Stander's contacts who had been at Balliol with one of the firm's senior partners and, of course, he knew George because of his wife Cathy, and was it through luck or good fortune they met?

Simon then revisited the medical school/corruption conundrum which a moment ago had seemed far more clear-cut. Seeing how important Uncle George's help had been to his life so far, what would be so wrong in making use of Uncle George's contact just one more time to get into medical school? After all, one of the reasons Simon was in the privileged position he was already in was due to Uncle George. What would be so wrong in making use of Uncle George to ensure his entry into a new career? What's more, his new career choice was being made primarily to help disadvantaged people not to make more money for himself. Wouldn't it be better to take advantage of his uncle's contacts this time round to fund a career to help those who were less fortunate than himself? It would certainly help make amends for the less savoury ways his family had benefited from Uncle George's contacts in the past. Birth, luck, ability, opportunity, talent, skill, race, gender, ethnic group, contacts, family, personality and abilities. They were all part of the mix of life and life chances, of career, of how England worked and ought to work. Neither Simon nor Emma had any clear answers to the different moral questions raised by how they had got to where they were now in life.

Then there was their own relationship. Wasn't the reason they were sitting here together on the train due entirely to luck? But for that chance encounter at Graham's, which would never have happened if Emma had not been rushing and clumsily dropped her mother's groceries all over the shop floor and Simon hadn't – by luck – been there to help her pick them up, they would never have met. But was their bumping into each other due entirely to luck? They met at Graham's because they were buying food from southern Africa, and they were doing this because of their shared southern African roots. This was more than luck, What's more, Emma had consciously and quite deliberately *chosen* to phone Simon after he had left her his number. That wasn't luck either. But what was it? Foresight? Intuition? Was it a biologically driven evolutionary instinct, an unconscious sense he was 'the one' which impulsively and totally out of character drove her to press the keypad on her phone, call him and decide they needed to meet properly?

Some would call Simon and Emma's meeting providential: they met because it was 'meant to happen'. Even if something looks like luck, many people would argue there is always another layer of explanation to what looks at first sight to be coincidences. They say you can always see the hand of God – or the devil – behind every event in our lives. And even if you don't believe in God, most people are often ready to admit their lives are influenced by forces beyond our control. And didn't that mean forces beyond us? So what difference does applying this extra layer of meaning to life's events mean in practice? If the cause of what happens can't be verified, what does it matter if some people call it the hand of God, others, providence, and others chance or luck?

For now, they were happy to put these heady matters to one side. What was most important to both Simon and Emma at this moment of time was simply their having each other. Drained by the emotional overload of the day, hypnotised by the rhythmical movements and sounds of the train, overcome by the warmth of the carriage and musing over the different ways of understanding what luck meant, they soon fell asleep, hands intertwined, Emma's head resting on Simon's shoulder. As they lost consciousness, what they knew for certain concerned their futures not their pasts. It was this which gave meaning to their lives: whether their being brought together had been due to luck, some chance encounter or something else simply didn't matter.

Daffodils

On a bitterly cold Saturday morning in late January, Sarah made the familiar journey to the North London Hospice. It was the first time she hadn't taken the bus. She was going there by ambulance, having just been admitted to the in-patient unit: Sarah was not on her way to the hospice to work but relocating there to die. Over many years, the hospice had provided her with a good living. It was now about to help Sarah in a very different way: she would be drawing on its accumulated wisdom and the skills of its staff to help her complete a good dying.

From the initial diagnosis of pancreatic cancer she was given in mid-September, Sarah's health had continued to deteriorate. The yellowness in her eyes which Emma first noticed in her kitchen the day she returned from Zimbabwe, and the sudden burst of tiredness which overcame her as she struggled up the hill after visiting Alice's grave the following weekend were just the start. In October her eyes grew yellower, her spells of tiredness occurred more often and by the end of that month she experienced other recognisable symptoms of her cancer – lack of appetite and weight loss. The day after the clocks went back Sarah went to work in a uniform which had hung in her cupboard unworn for the last 15 years. Then, just as the doctor had told her would happen, she began to experience discomfort in her abdomen and stomach. At first, she dismissed it as something minor but within a few weeks it had come to dominate her life.

In mid-November, Sarah was invited in for a talk with Dr Fletcher, the hospice's Medical Director, the only person on the staff who had been working there even longer than her. With tact and sadness, he gave her the news she had been dreading: she shouldn't come to work anymore.

"Your contribution to the work of the hospice has been outstanding," he told her, and he knew better than anyone else the truth of what he said. "But Sarah, the time has come to stop worrying about the needs of others and to focus on caring for yourself."

It took Sarah a moment or two to realise he was saying she should stop work at once, so she asked him if that was really what he meant and he said it was, though it was not until she returned home that it all started to sink in. From the first day she didn't go to work, Sarah felt sad and quite lonely and knew things would get worse if she didn't take action. So she created a structure and routine for her days and this helped, as she knew it would from years of giving advice to others. She forced herself outside the flat to take a daily walk and within a few days looked forward to going up to East End Road to see the children pouring out of Christ's College at the end of the school day: they laughed a lot which, strangely perhaps, made her feel good to be alive, and even their bubbling energy seemed to be catching. What gave her a particular buzz was when some of the children started to greet her as they passed, and she was even more thrilled when two or three girls stopped regularly for a chat. Yet, far sooner than she had hoped, she found even that short walk had become too exhausting, and one day she simply stopped going up the hill to the school. Not long after that, she stopped going out altogether.

Her days then became increasingly focused on first trying to fight, then simply to cope with, the advancing cancer. From the start, Sarah had been adamant she would have neither radiotherapy nor chemotherapy and the doctors agreed with her, as they knew neither of these treatments was likely to make any significant difference to her quality of life as the cancer was spreading so fast. What's more, Sarah herself knew what the side effects would be – hair loss, mouth sores and even more vomiting – and, as she told herself, she had enough to cope with without having to 'bother about all that'.

Caring for her body required Sarah to add increasingly strong pain killers to the decreasing amounts of food she felt able to eat. To try to counter her accelerating weight loss, she initially enjoyed eating more of the foods she had loved as a child but later in life had strenuously tried to resist as she knew how fattening they were: steaming mealie-meal porridge eaten with generous amounts of melting butter; mugs of milo mixed with full-cream milk rather than water and laced with a few more spoonfuls of sugar; and peanut butter thickly rather than thinly spread on large chunks of white bread. But, sooner than she had hoped, even these treats grew increasingly unappetising, though Sarah forced herself to continue consuming them as she knew how important it was to try to maintain her weight as long as she possibly could.

She watched more TV and spent longer listening to the radio, but as her world shrank she was happiest when she read her bible and sang old Shona hymns of her childhood or when she prayed quietly to herself. As the long days became weeks, her thoughts turned more inwards and the more she thought, the further back in time she went. However, her mind remained alert to the here and now and she delighted in Emma's and Simon's news, though, inevitably, she was able to engage more with Emma, who came to increasingly cherish the moments when just the two of them sat chatting together. From the day Sarah stopped work, Emma called her once, twice or even three times a day and Sarah was deeply touched by her thoughtfulness. Emma's cheery voice and enthusiasm continued to be Sarah's most powerful medicine. Emma knew this and in late November, as Sarah's growing inability to cope became evident to both Simon and Emma, Emma decided to move in to her mother's flat so she could be with her more or less whenever she wasn't at work. Sarah was delighted, but so too was Emma, who was becoming increasingly aware of the emptiness she knew she would feel when her mother eventually died and was keen to participate in her mother's fight to fend off the day for as long as possible.

Christmas came and went with little celebration. Simon stayed overnight at Sarah's as well for the holidays and he and Emma shared the cooking. It was a sombre few days as both Simon and Emma could see how great an effort Sarah needed to make to try to be cheerful and it took out of her what little energy she had. The day after Boxing Day was also a holiday and Cathy kindly came and sat with Sarah after lunch to give Emma and Simon a break.

They took Cathy's car and drove to Hampstead Heath, had a quick walk and then an early dinner at Dim T in Highgate Village. It was the longest time they had spent alone during the day since their visit to Catshead back in October. However, they were glad to get back to Sarah's flat, both because they were too tired to be able to enjoy themselves and because Emma hadn't been able to shake off the self-reproach which never left her for being away from her mother.

"Ma only has me," she said. "And I already have to spend so much time away from her. It just doesn't feel right not being there with her when I'm not working."

As they began to discuss and then plan their Boxing Day break, Simon had hoped they could recapture at least a little of the euphoria of their first day together but, almost as soon as they stepped onto the Heath, the grass still white from the night's frost, he knew at once the magic would have to wait. They walked, they held hands but they talked little. At one point, Emma said, "It's just not like it was,' but it was the feelings she had had for Simon at the Bronte Hotel she was remembering and had been the keenest to try to recapture. She knew she couldn't; feelings of guilt about her mother trumped everything for Emma.

That evening, when Sarah, Emma and Simon were all together, they had the difficult conversation they had put off for far too long. Sarah herself was well aware of what the next stage of her life would be; the question revolved around not if but when it should commence. It didn't take too long before they had all agreed it should happen very soon, and so – on New Year's Eve – the hospice's Palliative Care Support Service team of nurses and healthcare assistants arrived to start their outreach care programme at Sarah's flat.

Different team members set about their allotted tasks. The nurses came to give Sarah stronger pills to add to the painkillers she was already taking, different doses of Creon to make eating less painful at mealtimes and when she snacked, and antihistamines to try to reduce the increased itchiness of her skin. One morning when Emma was at work Sarah was whisked off to the new endoscopy department at Chase Farm Hospital to have a plastic stent inserted into her bile duct to aid her digestion. It helped for a while but the relief was short-lived.

The health assistants came initially to assist Sarah prepare her midday meal, her day-time drinks and her personal care, but very soon Sarah reluctantly accepted she was too weak to manage herself without their help, and she let them take over completely. She knew losing the ability to attend to her own personal care would mean a loss of dignity and self-esteem but she had prepared herself for it: it was simply one more type of pain she knew she would have to try to manage. During this time, too, a hospital bed arrived to become the centre of Sarah's shrinking world. After two weeks, what had been twice weekly visits of the health assistants became daily visits, and they stayed for longer. When the three-week assessment took place, it was decided a trained nurse should stay with Sarah overnight. She moved into Emma's bed and Emma slept on the sofa. Though she slept poorly, Emma wasn't unduly bothered as she was far closer to her mother and could hear her breathing when she slept, and Emma drew comfort simply from being close.

On a Friday morning before Emma went to work, a week after she began receiving round-the-clock nursing care at home, Sarah took the initiative to announce the time had come to leave home and move into the hospice, saying she was now ready. Feeling wretched, Emma agreed but it was a heart-wrenching moment for her and that night she cried herself to sleep on the sofa. It all happened so quickly: the call was made, a room was free and with the paperwork already completed, Sarah was admitted to the North London Hospice that Saturday morning.

Inevitably, Sarah's cancer threw awry Emma's and Simon's plans for their future together. When September became October, Simon stayed over at Emma's less and less often, and they put on hold the ideas they had begun to discuss about moving into a larger flat together. Emma's work often required her to stay at the BBC for either afternoon meetings or live interviews, and when this happened Simon tried to juggle his schedule to visit Sarah for her, but it was tricky because he was already working long hours as well as studying hard for his final exams, and he didn't always make it. This made him feel even more miserable both because he knew how long and lonely Sarah's days were and because Emma, who was already feeling guilty they were not helping Sarah enough, always blamed herself for letting down her mother. As the weeks rolled by, Simon was not only worried about Sarah's health but became increasingly concerned about Emma's. Sarah was as well, and it was this which in part prompted Sarah to say it was time to have the hospice's Palliative Care Support Service team move in before she felt it was necessary.

When Emma told Rosemary about her mother's cancer, Rosemary at once encouraged her to tell her more. When Emma said Sarah always felt weaker as the day progressed, Rosemary insisted Emma change her work schedule, persuading her to work from home wherever she could, and to come into the office earlier so she could spend more time in the evenings with her mother. Emma was touched by her kindness, not least because Rosemary was known right across the office for expecting every member of her team to work as hard as she did, and no one put in the hours Rosemary did. Those who knew her from old said the reason she had never married was because she was so wedded to the BBC.

It was only after Sarah had died that Rosemary told Emma – in the first of what were to become regular out-of-hours tête-à-têtes – her mother had died from breast cancer when she was only 16.

"I felt terrible when Mum died," Rosemary said to Emma as they sat together in a café off Oxford Street one evening after work. "Even when I knew she was going to die, I spent so little time with her because I was so preoccupied with being a teenager, and the last thing I wanted was for you, my dear Emma, to have to live with the guilt I have carried with me ever since the day she passed away."

Emma was deeply touched, seeing, almost for the first time, a gentleness beneath Rosemary's businesslike and seemingly hard exterior. Before she quite realised what she was saying, Emma had responded, saying, "Do you think my passion for journalism makes me come over as hard and uncaring?"

Rosemary knew at once what she meant. She smiled across at Emma and, hesitating for a moment before allowing her hands to come to rest gently on top of Emma's, she said "No, Emma, you have nothing to fear in that department. I've never heard anyone at work say anything remotely like that about you. On the contrary, you manage to mix your hard work and commitment to journalism with a remarkable sensitivity to others. Your kindness to older colleagues and the time you are happy to spend supporting more junior staff are what people notice about you. And from where I sit, Emma, I have seen you becoming an even warmer and caring person as you have grown into your job. From the day I decided to have you join our unit I could see you were just the person we needed."

Well before this interchange between Rosemary and Emma took place – almost as soon as the interviews Emma conducted at the party conference were over in early October – Emma and Rosemary were thrown together even more closely at work when Rosemary asked Emma to help her develop the initial ideas she had for the series of programmes on what it is to be British today, which Rosemary had told Emma about before she and Simon had gone out to Zimbabwe. However, it took a while before Emma really began to engage on what Rosemary was now calling the *Being British* series as she was so absorbed with her personal life – initially preoccupied with the uncertainty surrounding her relationship with Simon and then coping with the shock of learning of her mother's cancer.

The change occurred quite suddenly and the catalyst was their visit to Catshead. The morning after their Sunday lunch, when Rosemary called

Emma in to share their weekend thoughts on the series, Emma was already fired up with a new enthusiasm for the project, having seen firsthand the importance of first understanding and then trying to agree what British values are, and which matter most. If this wasn't difficult enough, what Emma realised would be even more challenging would be to produce a series of TV programmes which at one and the same time engaged in sufficient depth with the complexity of the issues but were light enough to sustain the interest of what both she and Rosemary hoped would be a huge audience – even bigger and far more diverse than those who first watched Kenneth Clarke's Civilisation series. Emma's ambition went one step further: for the series to make a major contribution to building a national consensus on what it meant to be British today. Or, as Rosemary put it half-flippantly, "to help put the Great back into Britain again". It didn't take Emma long to realise this was exactly the same ambition Rosemary had had for the series from the outset. But what she also learned from Rosemary was the scale of the task ahead in trying to convince the BBC that they not only *should* but *would* be able to produce a series of programmes which bridged the traditional divide between current affairs and politics on the one hand and cultural and reality TV on the other. They watched and re-watched Danny Boyle's opening sequence for the London Olympics and were fully aware what they were hoping to do was even more ambitious. They knew convincing senior management could be done, but it would be a mammoth task.

When not focusing on her mother, Emma's mind went into overdrive as she bubbled with ideas she shared with Rosemary in what by November had grown into twice-weekly meetings in her office. But there was one thought which kept coming back to her. Based on her own experience in growing up black in North London and attending a primary school with pupils whose parents or grandparents came from over 40 countries, her being first with Caribbean-rooted Robbie and now with white-Rhodesian-rooted Simon, and the impact her Catshead lunch had had on her, Emma knew *difference* had to be a central, if not the pivotal theme of the series.

"If Britain is to be great today," said Emma late one Friday afternoon, and Rosemary agreed, "British people who are afraid or contemptuous of other British people need to face their fears. They need to be helped not merely to accept there are different ways of being British, but to go two steps further – to appreciate and then celebrate the differences between us. Possibly even to champion those differences." Emma wondered if Rosemary would want to go that far.

"Possibly," said Rosemary, a note of caution sounding in her voice.

As the nights drew in and they continued brainstorming, some concrete programme ideas began to emerge. One was for the early programmes to focus on people from the UK's different communities – both the older, long-established, as well as the new ones – talking freely about what made them feel good about living in Britain. They would then be prompted to say how their understanding of being British 'adds value' to the country as a whole, to explain which values they see as the most important to them, and to talk about how such values could be more deeply embedded in today's Britain. Emma was delighted when Rosemary said this discussion needed to include people's views about how the more vulnerable and less fortunate members of society ought to be treated. Another of Rosemary's ideas was for well-respected and well-known people to talk about what being British meant to them, and a third would be for groups of young people to do the same.

Emma said, "Here's a novel idea: how about one programme devoted solely to a two-person discussion about British values, those two persons being the monarch and Meghan, Duchess of Sussex."

Rosemary laughed, saying, "I'm sure such a programme would guarantee the success of the whole series, but I very much doubt the palace would agree."

"Well, at least we could try," said Emma, and the more Rosemary thought about it, the more she admired Emma's ability to think out of the box, as well as her brazen audacity.

Then, in the final programmes, the various threads of what different people said would be drawn together not so much to *tell* viewers what *Being British* is today but to stimulate them to reflect for themselves what *they* think *Being British* is, what core British values are and, importantly, how they can be spread, shared, and, possibly, more effectively championed.

Of course, Emma also had many conversations with Simon about the proposed series, and he soon caught her enthusiasm for what she and Rosemary were trying to do. Their most poignant exchange was when they were having supper at Emma's flat the evening she was moving in with her mother, immediately before Simon drove her over to Sarah's. As they sat down with their microwave-cooked meals, Simon turned to Emma and asked a question he had been keen to ask but which he'd held back on asking as there'd never been enough time to chew over the answer: what was it that made Britain great in the past? And by the past, Simon told Emma he didn't mean during the world wars, the Victorian era or the period of history everyone learned about in school, the Tudors and Stuarts. Simon's interest lay further back in history. Unsurprisingly, this was a question Emma had already asked herself, and she was ready with her answer.

Prompted by footage on the centrality of cathedrals from Kenneth Clarke's *Civilisation* series which set her thinking, Emma had been reflecting back in time to the Middle Ages, when Britain's vast cathedrals were built. "Our cathedrals," said Emma, "are not only the most striking as well as the most enduring symbols of Britain, but their being built represents a period when the country felt supremely confident and comfortable with itself."

"Yes, that's true," said Simon, warming to Emma's theme, "but what's even more remarkable is our cathedrals have remained relevant to us right down to today. In spite of the rapid decline in Christianity in Britain in recent decades, with fewer and fewer people feeling the need to go to church on Sundays, the popularity of Britain's cathedrals persists. In fact, as I'm sure you know, Em, the numbers of people visiting our cathedrals continues to rise. And as you certainly know, even though I'm a card-carrying atheist, I really enjoy visiting them myself. I love the great sense of space you have as you step inside. I don't feel I'm being press-ganged to believe in God when I walk round these magnificent buildings and I can happily sit quietly in a corner undisturbed if the mood takes me. Our cathedrals are big enough for all of us with our different beliefs about life and our world to feel welcome."

"Yes, that's just it," said Emma as the remark Don Paulo had made about cathedrals in this very same room came back to her: he had told Robbie and her that it's the people as much as, or more than, the bricks which build our cathedrals.

"What makes Britain great today," she continued, "is the rich diversity of its people drawn from all corners of the globe. A millennium ago, about one and half million Brits built 30 or so cathedrals across our land. That's about 50,000 for every cathedral, fewer than those attending a top premier division football game today. Contemporary Britain is made up of over 60 million people living in thousands of thriving communities and it is these people who together form Britain's living cathedrals. Our new cathedrals are characterised not by uniformity of belief or architecture but by diversity, by the richness of our otherness. If Britain today is a country of cathedrals, it is a country of cathedrals of otherness. Together we form a rich tapestry of people of different beliefs, different ethnicities, different races drawn together to form our united kingdom of four nations, underpinned by the core values we share and the rule of law to ensure they really work for us and don't simply remain in the realm of (lofty) ideals."

Simon smiled across at Emma and said, "You are a wonderful dreamer, Emma. I really think you believe even if it hasn't happened yet, it'll happen soon – isn't it?"

"Yes, I do believe it will," said Emma, "I really, really do. There was so much that happened at our Catshead lunch which at the time made me bitter or angry, or both. But the more I have thought about these series of programmes we hope one day soon will be aired, the more I realise I have a fire now burning within me to continue to make them. Nothing would make me happier, Simon, than to have your Uncle George and Aunt Margaret watch our programmes and end up not only understanding better but feeling proud of what Britain is today and both knowing and appreciating a bit more about the rich diversity of our people."

In mid-January, Emma and Rosemary stopped brainstorming and started to work intensely on putting together the formal Programme Concept Note (PCN) for *the Being British* Series. This was scheduled to be presented by the two of them to the Senior Management Committee at their end of January meeting. As Rosemary had explained, and Emma now knew, PCN approval was the watershed moment as it would trigger the release of an initial tranche of money which would enable them to start commissioning the substantial research required for their ideas for *Being British* to become reality. If their PCN was not approved, they both knew they would be extremely unlikely to be given a second chance, and all their work, hopes and ambitions would have been for nought. After dozens of redrafts, this is how the PCN they presented to the committee began:

> ***Being British*** *will be a series of programmes on modern Britain which is authoritative but which appeals to as wide an audience as possible. The bulk of the programmes will consist of ordinary British people from different communities, old and new, talking about themselves, the values they hold and cherish, how these relate to 'traditional' British values and how such values might be spread more widely across the country. Inspired by what ordinary people say, the programmes will not only inform, entertain and above all educate, in a creative and non-threatening way, but their purpose is to gently ease the audience out of a narrow and partial to a more holistic and all-encompassing view of Being British. By the end of the series, viewers will feel more comfortable not merely living in but helping to champion a modern, diversified Britain underpinned and driven by our shared values.*

That Saturday morning, when the ambulance took her mother to the hospice, Emma went with her. For as long as Emma could remember, Sarah had shared the daily comings and goings of her working life at the hospice, so in her mind's eye Emma had developed strong images of the place. But, as she entered building, Emma was struck by how unfamiliar the place was, even strange, because what she saw bore so little resemblance to what she thought the place looked like. It was only then that she realised she hadn't stepped foot inside since she was a young child.

Growing up, Emma had never thought it unusual Sarah didn't take her to where she worked, and as she grew older she had simply assumed it was normal for people to separate their work from their home life. It was only when she had learned about Alice and after Sarah told her she had died at the hospice that she understood the real reason why Sarah had never brought her here. She clearly didn't want her work friends to know Emma called her Ma or referred to her as her mother, or, worse still, *telling* her outright she was wrong if she referred to Sarah as her mother and not her grandmother.

Now it didn't matter and Emma didn't begrudge Sarah what she had – or rather hadn't – done. Indeed, over the coming days Emma was delighted by the number of people she met whose names she knew and who seemed to know who she was. She was quietly amused how similar so many people were to the image she had formed of them from the many times Sarah and Emma had chatted together in the evenings, giving each other an account of their day, Sarah at the hospice and Emma at school. Emma not only knew their names but realised she was even familiar with the mannerisms of a good number of Sarah's colleagues when they stopped to talk to her.

Though completed way back in 1992, the red-brick building still looked fresh and modern. It had been acquired in the late 1980s from land provided by the Catholic Church which, at the time, seemed surplus to the needs of the then far smaller Finchley Catholic High School next door. As the land given to the hospice was on a steep incline, the rear windows of the upper floors of the building towered above and looked down upon the school buildings below. Emma was delighted Sarah had been given an upper floor room as she would be able to see from her bed the tops of the fir and horse-chestnut trees rising up from their roots in the school grounds.

Emma stayed at the hospice the whole of that first weekend. Sarah's' room was one of the larger ones and had a pull-out bed for family visitors so Emma was able to sleep there over the Saturday night. The following week, at Rosemary's suggestion, Emma worked a 'three-quarter' day: she woke with the alarm at six, was at work by 7.30, left Broadcasting House just after 2.30 and was usually back with Sarah by four. She stayed till around nine, or a little earlier if Sarah had sunk deep into drug-induced sleep. If she was lucky with the buses, she was usually back in her own bed by ten.

On the second weekend, Emma again stayed overnight at the hospice, this time sleeping there on both the Friday and Saturday nights. Sarah slept for most of the time Emma was with her, but when she was awake they were able to chat and only occasionally did Emma think Sarah's mind was wandering. She left the hospice at about five on the Sunday evening – she had been there for almost 48 hours – to enjoy a rare evening alone with Simon, who joined her for the night back at her own flat.

Over a bottle of wine, which Emma felt she needed, drinking two glasses instead of her normal one, they tried to make plans for the week ahead. Emma reminded Simon the PCN Senior Management meeting was taking place on Monday and Rosemary had especially asked Emma if she could attend, saying she expected the all-day meeting to be over by 4 o'clock if not earlier, and Emma, of course, had agreed.

For his part, Simon was beginning a week's work in Finsbury Park early on the Monday. The firm was fielding teams to undertake the annual audit of two establishments located almost next door to each other. One was a relatively new client, the Park Theatre, which, though it had only opened its doors in mid-2013, had already become something of a mecca for North London theatregoers. The other, an older client, was John Jones London, the upmarket bespoke picture framing company which was just round the corner on Morris Place. Simon had been involved with the Park Theatre audit since the company was formed but as he was hoping to have departed for medical school before next year's audit, he needed to bring his colleague, Paul Manners, up to speed on the Theatre's finances and Paul was leading the John Jones audit. So, as Simon told Emma, it was going to be particularly important for him to be there for the whole week. What he was saying, in effect, was if there was an unexpected emergency with Sarah during the coming week, he wouldn't be able to drop everything and come over to help. In other words, it would be Emma's plans which would have to change, not his.

To try to provide at least some respite from Emma's self-imposed gruelling schedule, Simon developed a plan which he prayed Emma would accept. To give her as much of a break as he knew she would agree to, and reminding her she had just spent the entire weekend at the hospice as his ammunition, he proposed that Emma take the tube to Finsbury Park as soon as her BBC Senior Management meeting was over so they could meet up for a quick drink and an early supper. After that he told her she would still have a couple of hours left in the day to spend with Sarah later in the evening. With some reluctance, Emma agreed.

Simon suggested they meet at The Old Dairy on the corner of Stroud Green Road and Hanley Road and asked Emma if she knew it. She keyed the pub's postcode into her Google map and they agreed to meet at five pm at the latest.

The following morning, when they said their goodbyes, Emma had become far keener on the Finsbury Park plan than she had been the night before and was really looking forward to going out with Simon: even half an evening together and away from the current work/hospice treadmill was more than they had managed since Boxing Day.

Her enthusiasm was given an additional boost when Simon left her flat early for work – well before seven. This gave her almost an hour at her computer before she needed to leave home herself. Even though she knew the PCN meeting wasn't about today's news, Emma always felt more on top of things if she had done her daily news trawl before arriving at the office. It was a relief simply to settle down in front of her machine and return to her old familiar routine. However, she hadn't been at her laptop for more than 10 minutes when her phone rang. She assumed it would be Simon calling to wish her luck, but when she saw the number her heart jumped. It was Lynn, one of the senior nurses at the hospice, and one of Ma's closest, oldest and dearest friends.

* * *

"Hello. Is that Emma?" said the voice at the end of the phone line as soon as Emma answered.

"Hi, yes, what is it?" replied Emma nervously. Her voice sounded so different, Lynn wasn't certain she had dialled the right number.

"Is that you, Emma?" said Lynn, with an urgency to her question. It was clear she had something important to say.

"Yes," said Emma, expectantly. "Something's happened, hasn't it?"

"It's Sarah, Emma," said Lynn, speaking deliberately, but as unemotionally as she could. "You need to come, Emma; you need to get here soon. I went in to see her just now, I've just come on duty, and she's not going to be with us much longer. We are nearing the end, Emma. Come as quickly as you can. She definitely won't last the day."

"I'll be right over," said Emma. "I'm coming now." She ended the call abruptly, without enquiring what exactly had happened, without waiting for Lynn to tell her more, without thanking her for calling and even without saying good bye.

Deep down, Emma knew she needed to be by her mother's side as soon as she could. Without really knowing what she was doing, or thinking what she might need, she grabbed her bag and only had her coat half on when she was out of the door, hurrying down the street. It had been snowing and felt raw, and though the snow was starting to settle, it wasn't yet very thick. The main road was still clear but the pavements were already covered with a thin layer of powdery snow. As if by instinct, Emma found herself walking along the edge of the road rather than on the pavement until she reached the busy High Road as her unconscious self must have told her it was less slippery. Her mind was focused on how to get to the hospice as quickly as possible. Her first thought was to call an Uber taxi as it would get her up to North Finchley more quickly, but she dismissed that idea as quickly as it had come to her as she realised it was rush hour: the traffic would be solid and a bus using the bus lane would be faster. She was flustered and knew she wasn't thinking clearly. She quickened her pace and then began to half-run towards the bus stop but slipped, almost fell and changed to a brisk walk. She prayed she wouldn't be too late and cursed herself for agreeing to spend the night at her flat with Simon when she should have stayed to be with her mother.

Walking past her local convenience store on her way to the bus stop, Emma couldn't help noticing bunches of daffodils for sale, temptingly placed outside on a rickety old wooden stand which already had snow on it. The flowers were jammed tightly together in bunches in a large yellow bucket below an old handwritten sign which read 'Frist of the Year'. Emma knew this misspelt sign well as it reappeared regularly during the year to cheer this side of East Finchley, tempting residents to buy pre-season flowers or fruit at outrageously high prices before they became more widely available. The sign usually brought a smile to Emma's face, but it didn't today. It did, however, serve its primary purpose, as Emma impulsively grabbed a bunch and hurried inside to pay, swallowing hard on being told the price. These were the first daffodils of the year Emma had seen, and still not thinking clearly, she thought how nice it would be to give them to her mother, especially after the overnight fall of snow, an early reminder of the spring to come.

Emma's frustration grew as she stood waiting for the bus far longer than she thought was normal and cursed herself for not having taken her warmer coat. Once the bus arrived and she was seated, she looked down and, seeing the daffodils close to she noticed the buds were too small, too thin and too tightly closed to ever open. She was cross for not looking more closely at the flowers before she had bought them and cursed herself again.

Twenty minutes later, as the bus crawled slowly through Tally Ho corner, it ground to a halt and didn't move even when the lights turned green ahead of them. Emma cursed the traffic under her breath as she said to herself *come on, come on, hurry up. Be quick, be quick. I must get there before it's too late*. It was another twenty minutes before they had passed Sainsbury's, only two hundred yards further ahead, and were really moving again. As Emma put on her gloves she realised she had been biting her nails, a habit she had conquered when she was five years old.

As Emma's bus stop came into view, she realised she hadn't called Rosemary to let her know what was happening. It was now close to nine and although she knew Rosemary would be at her desk and could take a phone call before the meeting started at ten, Emma knew she wasn't up to talking, so she texted her instead. Embellishing slightly what she had been told, Emma said she had just taken a call from the hospice to tell her to come over right away as her mother had taken a dramatic turn for the worse in the night and she had to be at her bedside. She added how sorry she was to have to miss today's meeting, but was sure Rosemary would understand. That bit was true, as was the way she ended, signing off by saying she would phone when she had more time and more news.

She sent Simon a text even though she knew he wouldn't see it until lunchtime at the earliest, by which time what she wrote would likely have been superseded by what was about to unfold over the next few hours. But at least texting him made her feel he was close and she knew how much she needed his support, now more than ever.

Emma walked from the bus stop to the hospice as fast as the slippery snow allowed. When she quietly opened the door to Sarah's room she saw Lynn by the bed. Though Lynn managed a smile as Emma walked in, the look on her face reconfirmed what she had half-said on the phone. She gave Emma a hug and motioned to her to sit in the familiar blue armchair which she had already moved to be right next to Sarah's bed. Emma sat down; she was totally focused on her mother and scarcely noticed as Lynn took her coat and the flowers. Similarly, she hardly registered Lynn's health update on Sarah: she had taken in no fluids since Emma had left her the previous afternoon; her breathing had changed dramatically at around four o'clock this morning to the more irregular pattern the team was all too familiar with and Sarah was now moving in and out of consciousness. Lynn said she would leave Emma alone with Sarah and, as she left, quietly closed the door. Emma didn't notice her leaving, nor was she aware Lynn had placed the daffodils in a glass vase on the window-sill and they were beginning to catch the morning sun to add to the warmth from the radiator below.

After Lynn had gone, Emma leaned over to touch Sarah's forehead, first with her lips, followed by her hand; then she stroked Sarah's hair before settling back in the chair and taking hold of Sarah's right hand. Both Sarah's forehead and her hands were noticeably colder than they had been the previous evening. Indeed, her hands were almost chilly. Sarah didn't seem to be aware of Emma's presence: her eyes remained closed and her eyelids didn't flicker when Emma touched her. Even when Emma said "Ma, Ma," close to Sarah's ear and squeezed her hand slightly, Sarah remained motionless.

As Sarah's mouth was open and looked dry, Emma dampened the flannel she always kept on her bedside table, as it had dried overnight, and dabbed it gently on Sarah's lips to remoisten them. She then picked up Sarah's limp right hand again and held on to it. Scarcely had she done this when Emma was sure she had felt Sarah's hand move. She knew a sudden twitch didn't necessarily signal consciousness, but the hand's sudden movement was followed almost immediately by what Emma convinced herself was slight pressure on her own hand. It was sufficient: she was certain Sarah had knowingly squeezed her hand. This brought her the relief she needed – for she now knew she had come in time – and she began to feel some of the tension leave her strained body.

There was a long period of silence and stillness. As Emma sat there she was sure the room was a lot warmer than she remembered from yesterday though she realised she was hot from almost running from the bus stop and the contrast with the cold outside, so it could have been her. She peeled off her sweater, leaving her wearing the white blouse she had chosen for today's meeting she would now never make, and resumed her holding of Sarah's right hand.

Overnight, Sarah's light blanket had been removed and she was now covered with just a single sheet. Emma could see the movement of Sarah's chest beneath the sheet whenever she breathed, which was happening far less frequently than she had ever remembered. Her breathing patterns were irregular and unpredictable. Very occasionally Sarah took in a deep breath and her chest rose sharply, then fell again as she exhaled. It was clearly a huge effort and for some time afterwards her chest lay still; it was as if she had stopped breathing completely. Then, when she started to breathe again, the air travelled in through her nose so quietly, it was hardly noticeable until her distraught face was momentarily calmed. But sometimes she would suddenly gasp for breath as a child does in water if her face has fallen below the surface and she panics. When this happened, her body looked as if it was wrestling with an unseen being, or as if there was only so much air to go round and Sarah was engaged in a struggle to capture it for herself. Emma knew her own imagination was running wild, but her daydreaming helped to keep Emma awake and alert as she sat in waiting in Sarah's warm room.

Sometime later – she had little inclination to check the time; she was engaged in a timeless vigil – Emma raised the sheet to try to make her mother more comfortable. Sarah's chest was openly displayed as either the rear ties on her night-dress had worked themselves loose or they had been deliberately parted to help her breathe. Whatever the cause, it left Sarah's frail breasts exposed. Her ribcage protruded out oddly, and at first glance it looked as if it had become misshapen. Then Emma realised it wasn't her ribcage which had suddenly changed shape but her stomach and belly, which had contracted and hollowed out so deeply as to cause her upper body to appear distorted.

Emma hadn't seen Sarah's naked torso since she had come into the hospice, though she had often given her a sponge bath when she was still at home. Sarah's stomach had progressively shrunk as her food intake dropped, but what she saw now was very different. The cause was her having stopped taking in all fluids; it was as if she was sucking herself dry from the inside. Emma turned to see if her drip needed changing and was ready to quickly call the nurse to replace the bag if it was empty. What she saw shocked her: the whole drip system had been taken away during the night. Emma slumped back in her chair, acknowledging to herself the removal of one more symbol of Sarah's life.

When she had lifted the top sheet, Emma saw Sarah had taken Joshua's cross from round her neck and the leather cord was wound round her left hand. At the cord's end, Sarah was holding the cross between her fingers as her hand rested just below her left breast. Then, suddenly, the muscles in Sarah's hand relaxed and, without the resistance provided by the top sheet, the cord slipped from her grip and the weight of the wooden cross caused it to slide down across the far side of her body and rest on the bottom sheet below. Almost at once, Emma saw her mother's hand twitch as it instinctively searched for the cord and cross but failed in its quest. Sarah let out a quiet moan; it was clear she was distressed. Emma lifted up Sarah's almost skeletal arm and laid it lovingly on top of the sheet, carefully wrapping the leather cord round her hand, more tightly this time, to prevent her losing it again. Sarah's eyes remained closed but, as if re-connecting with the cross had given her a surge of new energy, her chest momentarily rose as she noisily took in one more breath of air and her whole body shuddered as she exhaled, as it had before.

Since Emma had been with her mother the previous afternoon, the nurses had also removed two of Sarah's pillows and she was now almost lying flat on the bed. This gave Emma a different view of Sarah's face from the one she had become used to over these past weeks: from this new angle, it looked frailer than ever. Emma could see the skin hanging as loosely over her cheekbones now as the skin on the back of her hands had hung for the last few weeks. Emma had watched her mother's hands grow ever thinner and more delicate as she had gently stroked them day after day, and as she did again now.

As Emma sat beside Sarah, gently caressing her hand and waiting, time suspended, her ever active mind started to wander. At first, she recalled those moments over these past weeks when her mother had still been well enough for them to chat and interact as mother and daughter, and this consoled her. But then, all of a sudden, she was back in the present sitting next to her dying mother, and this not only made her deeply sad, it also prompted her to remember the things she had wanted to discuss with her mother but they had never got round to speaking about.

There was so much they had both enjoyed of their time together at the hospice, talking about so many different things. Sometimes they had chatted light-heartedly about what was going on in the world and in their worlds – though 'their' worlds now almost entirely meant Emma's world as her mother's world had progressively shrunk and was little more than just this one room. From her bed, simply gazing at the trees outside had initially given Sarah enormous pleasure, and she gave Emma a running commentary on how they changed when the wind rustled their branches, when they dripped with rain or glistened with frost, and when they gradually disappeared as dusk fell. "It was as if," said Sarah, not fully realising what she was saying, "they were walking off the stage." But then even the trees departed from her shrinking world as the drugs took over and she was never wide awake enough to notice them.

There had been moments when Emma had asked Sarah about her past life and their own special relationship, trying to get her to dig, to dig deeper. Though Sarah had appeared happy to answer most of Emma's questions, she had clearly been uncomfortable talking about herself. Emma wasn't surprised. Except in rare unguarded moments – such as when she briefly opened up about the one love of her life when Emma first told her about Robbie – Sarah repeatedly shied away from sharing anything personal, even with Emma. Sarah had always been a practical, 'doing' person. Poor Ma, thought Emma, she had such an incredibly tough life, one shaped by so much death and suffering. Yet for all her troubles, her life had always been built on solid foundations: her love for her beloved Joshua had remained strong for all the time Emma had known her, even though he had been dead for 40 years. In many ways, it was his drive and determination which had inspired her and kept her going.

Sarah had, of course, also tragically lost her own daughter, Alice. What a hardship that must have been for her! Emma tightened her grip on Sarah's limp hand as her thoughts turned to the mother *she* had never known. Emma had tried once again over these past weeks to talk to Ma more about Alice, but Sarah had still resisted. Whether this was because Alice's death had been so painful or because in her mind Emma had 'become' the daughter she'd lost – or whether it was a bit of both – Emma had never able to discover the answer, and now she never would. In a strange way, Sarah had managed to cope with Joshua's death because she never stopped loving him. But did she keep on loving Alice too? She had certainly managed to live with Alice's death by seeing her alive in and through Emma – even to the extent she had let Emma believe she *was* her daughter. And it had certainly 'worked' the other way round: Emma felt the woman whose frail hands she was now holding were her mother's hands, not her grandmother's. But had Sarah developed other ways of coping with Alice's death? This was another unanswered question Sarah would take with her to the grave.

Then Emma's thoughts turned to Alice's death which – it came to her in a flash – she realised had taken place right here, in *this* hospice. Which room did Alice die in, wondered Emma? Sarah would not have forgotten. Was it this one? Dr Fletcher would have known too. Did he choose to bring Sarah to die in the room where Alice had died all those years ago, or did he deliberately keep her away from that room? Did they discuss it? Did Dr Fletcher ask Sarah where she would like to end her days? Emma shifted uncomfortably in her chair, searching her mother's face for answers because she knew she could never ask Dr Fletcher directly herself.

And what had Sarah been thinking all those years ago as she had held Alice's hand when she was dying of AIDS – her skin even thinner than Sarah's, her bones as delicate and fragile as the best china, her whole body at war with itself before it succumbed and she died from the sheer exhaustion of trying to keep herself alive? What did Sarah and Alice talk about when Alice lay here dying? Again, Emma glanced across at Sarah's face, but it kept hold of all its secrets. *They must have spoken about me,* thought Emma, *but what did Alice say? What were her final words to her mother about me? I never asked Sarah that either.*

And there were more questions Emma asked as she picked up the damp flannel and wiped it across Sarah's forehead once again as if it would help her to find the answers. Did Sarah think of Alice whenever she came and worked here at the hospice day after day, week after week and year after year? Did she ever come and visit and sit in the room Alice had died in, or did she try to avoid it? Did she come into the hospice's Room of Quiet and think about Alice? Was it there, perhaps, that she developed her plan about how she would bring me up? What did she do on the successive anniversaries of Alice's death? She must have remembered them. Emma had never dared ask those questions either. To be truthful, though, she had never thought to ask them, even when she had learned about Alice's existence, and now it was too late. There was so much Emma didn't know, so much Sarah had always kept hidden and would now take with her to her grave.

And there was one final hardship of Sarah's life which was being acted out in this very room. Though Sarah proudly carried a British passport and had always been happy to refer to England as her 'new home', Sarah was about to die far from what she continued to consider her real home, thousands of miles away from the land which gave meaning to her life and the village which gave Sarah her own unique identity.

Then Emma's thoughts turned to what she *had* learned about Sarah's life at the hospice over the course of the last few weeks. As Emma had come into contact with and chatted to so many of the staff, she realised more than ever before that the hospice had been a central part of Sarah's world when, naively and selfishly she now thought, she had always thought it was she, Emma, who filled Sarah's entire world.

She knew Sarah was a qualified nurse, she had told her so, and Emma had been to the hospital in Mutoko where she had studied and passed her national nursing exams. This was clearly why she worked at the hospice; but what Emma had never known until a few days earlier as she chatted to the hospice staff was precisely how Sarah had come to be employed there.

Within a week of entering the UK as a refugee and with little idea of where she might find work, Sarah met up with a Zimbabwean man she had been told to get in touch with, a distant relative who had been living in North London for some time. On hearing she was a nurse, he introduced her to his local GP, Dr Chris Hindley, whom he knew had links to southern Africa and the South African ANC and thought might be able to help her. What Sarah's new Zimbabwean friend didn't then know was Dr Hindley had been the leading light in the founding of the North London Hospice and was still actively involved. At their first meeting in his surgery in Highgate, Sarah had told him about her long experience of working with the dying and he was clearly impressed. He asked to meet her again and by the end of their third meeting in a week he intuitively knew that Sarah would not merely 'fit in' but would become a huge asset to the hospice. By the end of Sarah's second week in England, Dr Hindley had arranged for her to be employed here.

There was more Emma learned about those early days as she tried to piece everything together from the odd snippets of conversation she had with the older nurses and doctors. Sarah's nursing qualifications had not been accepted in the UK, so when she had begun to work at the hospice, she was taken on as a health assistant not as a nurse. However, as Lynn and others told Emma, both because Sarah had ingrained deep within her the most important attribute needed in palliative care – the gift of communicating with patients – and because of the long experience of working with the dying she brought with her, Sarah was called upon to do far more at the hospice than the other health assistants. The warmth of her personality, the knowledge she brought with her from Zimbabwe of caring for people dying of AIDS as well as the work she had done with those psychologically damaged by Zimbabwe's war were quickly picked up by the medical team and they realised what an asset she was – just as Dr Hindley had predicted. Time after time, Sarah was asked by patients to sit with them during the final few hours of their life: both they and their families drew comfort and strength from her.

As a result, Sarah occupied a rather 'grey' area in the hospice's pay system and job hierarchy as she gladly took on jobs and ably fulfilled roles more complex and challenging than her official status as a health assistant permitted. As Emma also learned from Lynn, this hadn't led to any serious resentment by other staff. In chatting to everyone she met, Emma became aware of how well-liked Sarah was by all, and how loved she was by many. It was all this which led to management placing Sarah on a unique pay scale in recognition of the contribution she made to the hospice's core mission of 'providing the best care for patients by adding quality and meaning to their life journey'.

But, thought Emma now, if Sarah was so good at working with so many others who were dying, this must have had an effect on her as she fell ill and knew she was soon to die herself. Until now it had never occurred to Emma to consider the different ways people die. Emma had never seen anyone die and she had never thought to discuss with Ma all the different ways a life could end. Though Sarah had certainly not treated death as a matter-of-fact process – it had clearly been difficult and she had suffered terribly – at no time had she seemed the least bit morbid about her death. Emma knew – she could see, she could feel, she could sense – Sarah was dying with dignity. For a moment she thought again of Alice. Did *she* die well, and with dignity? As she had died so young and her death had been so painful, Emma guessed Alice had probably died frightened.

What Sarah had wanted to chat about most over these past days was her early life back home, the period of her life before she came to live in England. Indeed, as Emma prodded, it soon became apparent Sarah had been spending a good deal of time thinking back to those days when sitting alone at home in the long weeks after she had stopped going to work, while she was still well enough to remember. What made her eyes light up and really engaged her was when she and Emma talked about, and Sarah recalled, the events of her childhood: the earlier her memories, the more eager she was to share them. As they spoke, Emma grew to understand why: the younger Sarah was, the happier she had been.

It didn't take Emma long to realise an important reason they were able to talk so freely about those early days was her own recent trip out to Mutoko. She now felt so grateful she had been to the village where Sarah had learned the meaning of home, met so many of her extended family, especially Sarah's brother Prosper and her younger sister, Emerentiana, and had experienced – seen, felt, touched and smelt – the precise spots where Sarah had grown up. Emma's sharing of incidents which took place when she had been in Zim stimulated Sarah to talk about the people, the events and the places which had clearly created such joy for her so long ago.

They took it in turns to tell their own tales of the family homestead, the smell of the animals in their kraals, the dry fields and irrigated vegetables, the birds, the baboons and the insects, the shimmering heat and the night skies with their sounds of croaking frogs, testosterone-charged male baboons and howling hyenas. They both had stories to tell of their visits to the local stores, their walks to All Souls Mission and to nearby villages – Emma just a few, Sarah far more. They laughed as Emma spoke of her embarrassment at being presented with a live chicken on her arrival at the family home and how upset she felt when she had to eat it an hour or two later. They chuckled as Emma recalled the time when she realised a cockroach had been crawling up her legs as she ate in the family kitchen in the evening darkness and said if she had known at the time, she would have screamed.

Sarah told Emma about her earliest memory. Aged about three, she stood on tip-toes in the same family kitchen, watching her mother and elderly aunts cooking porridge as she peered into the steaming black pot early in the morning and felt the heat of the cinders on her bare legs. How excited she was when, a year or so older, she was allowed to add the mealie meal flour to the cooking pot on her own, sprinkling it in, one tiny handful at a time. Yet that was nothing compared with being allowed to mix and stir the porridge with a wooden spoon almost half her height when she had grown six inches taller.

The following year, aged six or seven, Sarah's father announced she was now old enough to join her elder siblings and cousins to work in the maize and groundnut fields for an hour or so after the sun rose on those warm summer's mornings in term time before they all set off for school. Emma vividly recalled Sarah peeling off her socks to point out the scars she still bore at the ends of her toes. These came from cutting herself as she dug the blade of her short-handled *badza* (hoe) deep into the sandy soil to weed the tender young maize plants in her bare feet. This was before she had learned how to avoid the *badza* slicing into her toes as she weeded. Sarah told Emma her older cousins had laughed at her when she cried out in pain the first time she cut herself, just as she did when a year or two later, her younger cousins did the same. Their day's weeding completed, Sarah explained how they were rewarded by each being allowed to pick two – and only two – fresh and juicy mangos from the family trees. These they devoured on their way to school, tossing the gnawed pits away into the bush. They then searched for the tree, whose small branches could be snapped open and, with the thin bark removed, could be used as a tooth pick to remove the strands of mango which caught between their teeth before they arrived at school.

There were many other stories Sarah told Emma, but what came through from all the tales she shared was the warmth and happiness of those days, that time before the war came, the war which changed their lives for ever. As Sarah spoke of those far-off places and faraway times, Emma couldn't help thinking of what Simon had told her of the stories Cathy had recounted to him of her childhood: idyllic memories of happy events which had taken place at the same time and in the same country, but so utterly different.

Their discussions of the family home had reminded Emma of the ride back to Harare with the two young Italians, the Beninis, who had told her about John Bradburne, the Englishman who had run the leper settlement at Mtemwa on the outskirts of the town of Mutoko. She remembered the Beninis telling her he had written poems about the beauty of the land around Mutoko but when she googled his name she discovered he had become quite a cult figure in the Catholic Church with the Vatican now responding positively to the growing numbers of people calling for him to be made a saint.

When Emma mentioned the name John Bradburne to Sarah, she said she had heard of him from Doctor Luisa, who used to visit Mtemwa where she dressed the lepers' wounds and distributed medicines to those who needed them, but she didn't think she had met him. However, Sarah said she did remember being told he was a rather wild character with long hair who wore shorts and walked in a gangly bow-legged sort of way and liked to sing out loud in his low booming voice. Emma found the website of his poetry and was astounded by what she discovered. She learned Bradburne was probably the most prolific of English poets: compared to Wordsworth's 54,000 lines and Shakespeare's 88,000, he had penned a whopping 170,000 lines of poetry and probably more.

Though plenty of the poems she read were not to Emma's taste, a good number were. When she came across poems about the Mutoko area, Emma printed them out and, as Sarah became more ill, began to read them aloud to her. She loved them as they so reminded her of home as Emma had hoped they would. A number helped her to re-enter the land she loved, which delighted Emma almost as much as Sarah. They spoke of the grandeur of the granite hills; the magic of the moonlit nights; the splendour of the baobab trees and walks around All Souls Mission. Sitting now next to her dying mother, Emma started to read some of Bradburne's poems to her for one last time in the hope they could still work their magic. As she read, Emma prayed they would transport Sarah back to her home one last time and bring her the comfort Emma so desperately wanted to try to give her.

Taking the well-worn pages from the inside pocket of her bag where she always kept them now, Emma began, holding the poems in one hand, her free hand resting gently on Sarah's hands and her grandfather's cross:

> *Autumnal tints in Mashonaland*
> *Are less like hints of a Rainbow Strand...*
> *Than those of a realm that tawnier gets*
> *As the sound of Summer goes and the ground unsets.*

> *Rolling off from the edge of time*
> *I'll stroll Mashonaland in rhyme*
> *Confining me to a span that rolls*
> *From here to the Mission of All Souls:*

Emma paused and looked across at Sarah, whose eyes remained closed and who hadn't moved. But, convinced the poems were helping and remembering the way Sarah used to smile across at her and say, "Read me some more; Emma, please read some more," Emma lifted her hand from Sarah's to turn the page, then returned it to its place and continued:

> *Where the baobab trees loom large and oft*
> *Had I worn a hat that hat I'd doffed*
> *As I saw the height and the house divine*
> *O' All Souls Church in the light ashine:*
> *The heat was great in the gate of noon*
> *But my heart was elate and I'd get there soon.*

> *Mashonaland by moonlight is my joy,*
> *When sitting cattle sleep athwart the track*
> *And pangolin goes forth with armoured back*
> *And moths and blithe cicadas make their ploy;*
> *While it is moonlight at the brightest full*
> *And tracks retain some warmth of day where still*
> *Ruminate heifers on their mate the bull;*
> *As I go down from where I spend the days*
> *To where I spend the night in moonlight I*

Discern no manface but Madonna, high,
Holding her Child thereon beyond the haze:
Only in this Mashonaland I've seen
So great a boon upon the Moon, my Queen!

* * *

As she was reading, Emma suddenly put down her poems and sat up straight, sensing a change had come over the room. As she had read the words *'holding her child thereon upon the haze'* her mind had drifted and she saw Mr Svosve sitting across from Simon and herself under the shade of a tree at the school in Gavaza last September. He was telling them when he knew Joshua had died.

> *Only at that point did I think to check on Comrade Lightning. I put my hand onto his forehead. It was cold and dry. He was dead, I knew it...but when exactly he had died I don't know. I felt no particular new emotion when I realised he had died as I guess I had been expecting this to happen from the moment I saw him...almost motionless...inside the farmhouse.*

Emma's free hand was still resting on Sarah's hand and her grandfather's cross, and though it felt the same as it had only moments earlier, she knew it wasn't. Just as young Svosve had suddenly realised Joshua, who he was carrying on the back of his donkey on that awesome night, was dead, so Emma knew her mother, lying beside her, was now dead too. No dramatic change in Sarah had signalled she was about to die or when she had died. She had simply expired. There had been no noise, no rattle in her throat and no discernible movement of her body, except Emma could see Sarah's neck had fallen slightly and was now slumped down on her chest, her mouth drooping sideways at an odd angle. Her whole body lay motionless, creating a stillness which pervaded the whole room. In the corridor outside Sarah's room Emma could hear the chatter of voices, some laughing, but here inside there was silence, and in the quiet of the room, Emma became aware of the noise of her own breathing.

Seemingly nothing had changed, but everything had. The limp hand Emma was holding which had had life in it a few moments before was now lifeless. Moments earlier, Emma had sensed her mother's presence, now she was aware of her mother's absence. The life which had been Sarah was gone as if removed by the hand of a conjuror – it had disappeared, vanished – and Emma felt empty and drained. As it began to dawn on Emma what the finality of death really meant, she experienced a numbness which seemed to be saying a part of her had died with her mother: the orphaned

Emma whom Sarah had rescued when Alice had died had become an orphan once more.

Emma felt alone. She then remembered what Mr Svosve had said when he had realised her grandfather, Joshua, had died:

> *...I experienced a terrible loneliness. Though Mathias was by my side, I suddenly felt totally alone; it was as if my life had lost its meaning.*

This was precisely what Emma was feeling now.

Slowly at first, Emma's body began to catch up with what her mind had begun telling her. Still holding her mother's hand, a few tears started to trickle from the corners of her eyes onto her cheeks, followed by many more which rolled down onto her neck, causing the top of Emma's white blouse to dampen. Then, as if in defiance of the stillness and silence of Sarah's chest, Emma's ribcage rose suddenly as she gasped for air, pausing momentarily before it fell again as the air was forced out of her chest by her pent-up grief. She sobbed as she exhaled, and as her chest repeatedly rose and fell in rapid succession, she started to sob and then began to moan quietly to herself.

Lynn, who had been keeping a look-out through the peephole in the door to Sarah's room, heard Emma sobbing and knew at once what had happened. Pulling the doorknob towards her to prevent it making a noise as she turned it, Lynn came in, quietly walked across the room and put her arm around Emma to console her as she sat down on the arm of Emma's chair. Without turning to look, Emma knew who it was and felt comforted, though Lynn's presence set off a further wave of sobbing, louder this time as Emma released more of the painful hurt from deep inside her. Lynn repeatedly said to Emma, "go with your emotions for as long as you need to", as she cradled Emma's head on her breast until Emma eventually fell silent.

After a pause, Lynn gently and reassuringly said, "Stay with her, Emma. Sit with her for as long as you need. Sarah was one in a million. She had that sixth – or even seventh – sense about human beings. She knew how to comfort those the dead leave behind and she would have known how hard this would be for you. Emma, you loved your grandmother as deeply as a mother, we have all seen that, and you will miss her desperately. You will heal; the hurt and emptiness will go, but it takes time.

"Grieving is a complex process," Lynn continued. "But know this, Emma – and if Sarah were here she would tell you this herself – her time had come. She had been in pain and she needed to go. Don't blame yourself, don't ever blame yourself. What Sarah wanted more than anything else was for you to live. Yes, mourn now; you need to mourn, but do not mourn for longer than you need to, and do not brood. Keep the love you have for Sarah centred within you, and above all be strong and, dear Emma, you have Sarah's example to teach you how to do this. I have rarely seen someone move towards death and pass on with such grace and dignity, and what a feat that was, given the pain the cancer inflicted on her body! She was a great woman. I loved her, too, Emma, as did so many of us here. She'll never be forgotten."

Lynn kissed Emma on her forehead, squeezed her hand and announced she was about to leave. For an instant, Emma felt bereft: she wanted Lynn to stay; she had been touched by her kindness, and the warmth of her breast she had found both comforting and reassuring. Then for some reason Emma's mind switched and she suddenly thought of Rosemary as it struck her there had been one British value they had never discussed but which she now knew had to be included in their series as it was clearly of such fundamental importance – compassion. Surely, compassion for others defines the way society values life itself, Emma said to herself. Why hadn't she thought of it before, and why hadn't Rosemary mentioned it herself? But as Lynn pointed to the red alarm cord hanging from the ceiling above Sarah's bed and told her to call if she needed her, Rosemary disappeared from Emma's consciousness as suddenly as she had appeared, and Lynn left Emma to grieve on alone.

After turning her head to the door to watch Lynn leave the room, Emma didn't look back at Sarah. Instead, she let her eyes rest on the ivory-painted wall above the bed. Unusually for Emma, with Rosemary's brief appearance forgotten, her mind was a complete blank. She couldn't think, she didn't know what to think. She still felt drained and empty though she was no longer sad; nor was she about to cry or sob again. She felt a lot calmer and in control.

Then Emma began to mull something over in her mind. Her mother clearly wasn't here any longer, she knew that! But where was she: where 'was' Sarah now?

Sarah was a practising Catholic and the Catholic priest had been to visit her both at home and here at the hospice. Emma had discussed these visits with the hospice and had herself been at Sarah's bedside for the priest's final visit two days earlier. But what did Sarah actually believe would happen to her after her death? Strangely, they hadn't discussed it. Being Catholic herself, Emma knew what Sarah had been taught to believe: there was an afterlife and Sarah was destined for heaven; her purified soul would live on. As the Creed succinctly put it and as Sarah had repeated week in week out since she learned the words as a schoolgirl, "I believe in the resurrection of the body and life everlasting. Amen." But there was more. Sarah yearned to be with her Joshua again and also with Alice, and with her own mother and father as well; she also believed in the communion if not of all saints then certainly those she had personally known.

Yet, as Emma sat and thought about it, she wasn't at all sure what Sarah *really* believed, or rather – now she was dead – what she really *had* believed. In fact, as Emma began to think more about her understanding of Sarah's views on life and death, what struck her was her mother had been far more focused on this life than on any afterlife, even as death approached. Sarah certainly *wanted* to believe she would be reunited with her loved ones; indeed, she almost certainly *hoped* she would be. Yet, it struck Emma, there is quite a difference between wanting, hoping and even yearning that something will happen and believing – by which she meant *really* believing – it would.

If Sarah *had* really believed in an afterlife, thought Emma, then she would surely have talked about it. Indeed, if she was certain – and that's what belief is – she was going to live a new life beyond the grave, she would surely have been keen to speak about it, if not with enthusiasm then at least with some confidence. But she hadn't and this suggested to Emma Sarah's views lay firmly in the hoping-and-yearning rather than in the really-believing camp.

Emma's thoughts then returned to her own beliefs. Did she believe Sarah was alive somewhere? She knew Simon didn't believe in an afterlife. He believed this life is all there is: when we die, we are dead and that's it. But for Emma things were rather more complex. She knew Christians were meant to believe in an afterlife, but no one has died and come back from the dead to tell us what happens after death so we have no proof of one. Indeed, the lack of any hard evidence stacked the cards strongly in favour of there not being one after all, didn't it?

Clearly *life* is passed on from one generation to the next, so the human race lives on; our own species survives and is sustained. What's more, it is quite possible, providing we care for the planet and don't nuke ourselves into oblivion, that humanity could go on living into perpetuity. So, in a sense, we could almost conceive of humanity as being immortal, of going on 'forever'. What's more, when we die we are remembered – hopefully with affection – by our children who, in their turn, go on to tell their children about us. As a result, most of us are not forgotten when we die.

Of course, that is quite different from individual immortality. We leave tangible evidence of our life in films, photographs and digital recordings; we leave behind words we have written, music, art, paintings and even ideas we have created. In the touch of clothes we have worn or the wearing of jewellery which was once ours, we are remembered. Today, in our digital world, the virtual footprints we have amassed are so extensive they have prompted debate on a new human right: the right to be forgotten. Yet it is not *we* who have survived; all these things are simply manifestations of what has been. What we leave behind is not ourselves but memories and there is a finality to them; they can't be added to. Mozart, Lennon and

Prince certainly continue to live with us through their music, but *they* are no longer with us.

Perhaps, thought Emma, more light could be shed on the question of individual immortality not by hunting for evidence of life when we have died but by looking more closely at life-affirming and especially life-expanding experiences which touch us when we are still alive. We can feel an inner glow within us or a sense of being transported to another level when we are 'touched' by beauty, in music, poetry, sculpture and paintings, in animals and in the human form. The complexity of the natural world can delight us and fill us with 'wonder' and 'awe', as can gazing up at the night sky or trying to take in and reflect on the vastness of our ever-expanding universe. Likewise, we can be 'carried away' with feelings of ecstatic joy and elation when we fall in love, as Emma knew only too well. But for all the richness, the depth, the beauty and the complexity of our world which we passively absorb, and for all the 'stretching' we do to try to tap into the reality of what lies just beyond our grasp – none of any of this proves there is life beyond the grave. Though we may wish, even hope, these deeper and more uplifting experiences will not stop when we die, or at least that our self-awareness will survive in some form when we expire, we have no evidence they will.

As for herself, Emma believed – and this was something she knew she *really* believed – the message of the Christian Gospel was encapsulated in one simple truth, that what ultimately matters is how you relate to your fellow human beings. Provided your life has been shaped and driven by a concern for others, heaven can look after itself – as Don Paulo had told her. Emma remembered how reassuring she had found his words when he had first spoken them to her and she found them reassuring again now.

"Whether there is an afterlife," Don Paulo had told her, "is not something you need to bother too much about."

Emma's eyes fell from the wall and she looked again at her mother's lifeless body. She knew Sarah had been a good person. She had lived to give Emma a life, and she had helped to make the wider world she inhabited a better place, through the work she did, the love she gave and the human being she was. If there is an afterlife, as her mother hoped there was, then Sarah was living in it. Emma could feel at peace knowing what Sarah's life had accomplished. Her mother had made resurrection happen here. She had made her contribution; she had helped to make the world a better place and – ultimately – that was all that mattered.

Emma wrenched herself away from her introspections, stood up, leant over Sarah's body and kissed her on her forehead saying quietly, almost confidentially, "I love you, Ma." She then stretched to force the tenseness out of her body, and looked about her to start the process of rejoining the world of the living. To her amazement, she saw the daffodils she had thought were dead had opened. The whole bunch of what had been tightly-closed buds were now fully in flower, filling the vase with a blaze of yellow. It seemed as if the moment Sarah had moved from life to death, her flowers – which Emma had thought were dead – had burst into life. Emma felt uplifted: she could almost hear Sarah shouting out in the voice Emma knew so well "halleluiah!" It was as if Sarah was saying "My life has ended, but yours lies ahead. Leave this place now: go out and live life, your life to the full."

Emma walked across to the flowers, ran her fingers across the tops of the daffodils before picking one out from the bunch, which she held in front of her as she gazed out of the window. She felt she had been at the hospice for the whole of a very long day and was surprised how bright it was before she realised it was still only early afternoon: the clouds had vanished, the winter sky was blue and patches of white from the early morning snowfall glistened on the branches of the trees. After idly twisting the lone daffodil between her fingers, Emma bent down and kissed it to thank God for Sarah's life.

Then, as she stood there, Emma was jolted back to the extraordinary events which had taken place the first time she had stood at this very same window some two weeks earlier. Just as she had done now, Emma had walked across to the window, though it was far later then and the sun had already set. She had gone over to stretch her legs after Sarah, who had been restless all afternoon, had at last fallen asleep. Because it had been so dark outside and the room was so brightly lit, the window had become a mirror. Looking out, all Emma had been able to see then was her own reflection, and beyond, the reflection of Sarah asleep in her bed behind her. She remembered the scene as clearly as if it was happening again now, standing there at the window and starting to tidy up her hair before feeling self-conscious and stopping as she suddenly realised anyone looking in from outside could see her and observe what she was doing. And two weeks ago, it turned out there had been someone outside eyeing her.

But Emma's biggest shock came when she discovered it was not only a man who was looking up at her, but that man was Robbie.

Emma had been in touch with Robbie since she read the letter he posted through her letterbox that Sunday she returned from Zimbabwe, though, as he had instructed, they still hadn't met or even spoken. When she had woken the next day, Emma continued to feel dreadful for the way she had treated Robbie, especially the hurt she had caused him which his letter so vividly described, and she knew she had to write back to him at once. That evening she did, though it was only a text message, a sort of holding message which started by saying how deeply sorry she was for what had happened, the pain she had caused him, and how upset she was after reading his letter, and which ended by telling him she would write a proper letter as soon as she could.

Emma really did want to write the letter, but whenever she tried, she couldn't because she wasn't able to get beyond saying how sorry she was for the insensitive and muddled way she had ended their relationship. As one day followed the next, though Emma's distress for what she had done to Robbie continued to grow – and she wrote and tore up endless drafts – she still didn't send off her letter. When she finally did, it was three weeks after she and Simon had got back from Zimbabwe and, in part to assuage her feelings of guilt, she texted Robbie at the same time to tell him to expect it. It was only then that she felt she knew sufficient about what she wanted to say, having been helped in part by sharing at least some of her concerns with Simon.

After that momentous Sunday afternoon reconciliation of their families, Emma opened up more to Simon about Robbie than she had ever done before, speaking to him more freely both about many aspects of their six-year relationship and the guilt she felt for the way it had ended – for ended it had, Emma no longer had any doubts about that. They talked most often about Robbie when Simon spent the night at Emma's flat during the working week, which he tried to do whenever he could. Within a week, Simon had sensitively bought a new set of sheets and pillowcases and a new duvet for Emma's bed. She was grateful: it was one more thing which helped her come to terms with the new reality. Emma's relationship with Robbie also lay behind Simon's suggestion they start to discuss buying their own flat.

However, the letter Emma eventually wrote to Robbie didn't add much to what she had said in her brief text message: the more she thought about what she should write, the more she realised she couldn't put down on paper what she had come to believe was the most important thing, which was to speak to Robbie not through the written word but in the flesh, face to face. As time passed, Emma became even more convinced saying sorry to Robbie was the only thing that really mattered, but to do that properly, she was certain she needed to make a formal apology standing in front of him – nothing less would be remotely adequate.

Emma knew Robbie had ended his letter saying, 'our meeting up will only make things more complicated than they are already. So, on balance, I think – for now – if you feel the need to respond to my letter, best not to phone, just write.' But now she not only felt strong enough in herself for them to meet without collapsing emotionally, she was keen to do so for another reason – she wanted to begin to shape the parameters around which a new relationship with Robbie would be built. After all, this was also what in his letter Robbie had told her Don Paulo had said he needed to do, and she knew he couldn't even start to do this without her help. It is true Robbie had also said in his letter that at times he still felt quite fragile, but didn't he also say he was now actively looking at potential new relationships? As her relationship with Simon deepened and became more intimate, Emma felt able to see and talk to Robbie without feeling she would regress, and she convinced herself that, with the time which had elapsed, Robbie had moved well along that path too.

The upshot was that, although the letter Emma posted to Robbie spoke about how sorry she was for her actions, its main purpose was to propose they meet up. Emma left it in Robbie's court to decide when and where this might happen, but she ended her letter by saying she hoped it would be soon. She made no mention of Sarah's cancer. That, too, she thought, would best be shared face to face.

In the days which followed, Emma waited for a text, even prayed for a call, from Robbie and her heart skipped a beat each evening when she came back from work and opened her front door, hoping to see an envelope on the mat with his familiar handwriting on it. But there was nothing. Days turned into weeks and Robbie had still not communicated. One night, in desperation, Emma sent off a second text to ask if he could confirm he had received her letter, but he didn't respond to that either. Then, as Sarah's illness took up more and more of Emma's time and absorbed all her emotional energy, Robbie started to fade from her immediate consciousness. She deliberately sent him a Christmas card very early in December, giving him ample time to send one back, but none came. Emma was at first perplexed, then she grew increasingly worried, but she was so focused on her mother she didn't do anything to resolve the puzzle of Robbie's wall of silence.

* * *

Two weeks to the day before her mother died, Emma is standing at the window ruffling her hair when all of a sudden, her phone starts ringing.

She looks down to see who's calling her. It's Robbie.

She is shocked. Not merely is Robbie the last person she is expecting to hear from, but because he always texts. Robbie has never, ever phoned Emma except in an emergency.

She grips the windowsill with her free hand to steady herself.

Emma hesitates for a moment then impulsively takes the call and lifts the phone up to her ear.

"Hello, Emma," cuts in Robbie before she has time to speak. He sounds earnest, even a little breathless, and immediately goes on to say, "I can see you."

"What?" says Emma, sounding – as she is – a mixture of surprise and confusion, having no idea what Robbie could possibly mean.

"Em, I can see you," repeats Robbie. "You are standing at a window at the hospice. Though you obviously can't see me as it's dark already, the room where you are standing is brightly lit. I can see not only the shape of your body but your whole face as well. It's unmistakably you! When I looked up at the window just now I couldn't believe my eyes, as I instantly knew it was you, and – impulsively – I knew I had to phone you there and then."

Emma peers out of the window but, as Robbie has said, it's pitch dark and she can see nothing. She is feeling now both disoriented and unsettled by what is happening, and doesn't know what to say.

"It's your mother, Em, isn't it?" continues Robbie, who has guessed why Emma is at the hospice on a workday afternoon, and follows this question with a rapid-fire succession of others. "She's there in the room with you at the hospice, isn't she? She's not well, is she? Is it serious? I hope not. Can I help?"

"Yes," says Emma, calming down a little as she subconsciously warms to the reassuring sound of Robbie's voice. "You're right, Robbie. Ma's not only not well, she's terminally ill. She's in the final stages of pancreatic cancer. Oh Robbie, it's been so terrible watching her waste away over the past weeks, and a few days ago it was she who asked to be admitted as a patient as she knew she was nearing the end. It's been dreadful, and I feel so helpless I can't do more for her. She's sleeping now; she does that a lot."

Emma then switches her attention back to Robbie and says, "But what on earth are you doing down there in the dark looking up at a woman standing at a window at the North London Hospice? Why are you here, Robbie? It's totally weird!"

"It's quite simple, actually," says Robbie. "Below your window beyond the fence are the buildings of Finchley Catholic High School. The school's short of a key exam-class teacher, so I've was asked to do some extra teaching here, three evenings a week. That's why I am here. On my way back to the bus stop after my lesson, my eyes are always drawn to the brightly-lit hospice windows as there are always a number of rooms where the curtains haven't yet been closed, but I had never before seen anyone at the window looking out – except for just now. As I steadied my gaze onto the figure I could see standing at the window, I stopped walking and strained my eyes upwards to confirm what I already knew. To my total amazement, I could see – unmistakably, Em-and-Em – it was you."

"It's certainly is an amazing coincidence," says Emma, "not only that you should be working there at the school but what's even more remarkable is I should be standing here at the window just when you were walking past." She knows she is becoming flustered as it dawns on her she is suddenly talking to Robbie after so many months of waiting for him to get in touch she had practically given up believing he would ever make contact. "I had no idea you were doing extra teaching, Robbie. We've sort of lost touch recently, haven't we?" she adds, struggling to make her words sound matter-of fact.

"Yes, Em, we have," Robbie replies noncommittally.

Then, after a split-second pause, he impulsively says, "Would you mind, Emma, if I pop in to see your mum, if that's OK with her – and with you, of course? It won't take a moment to get to you. I'm just around the block."

"Ma's here, she's an in-patient here because she's dying, Robbie," said Emma, who is starting to feel emotionally drawn to Robbie: it happened almost automatically, she'd reacted like this so often in the past. But she checks herself, feeling even more nervous now than when she had seen his number appear on the screen of her phone. "I'm standing at the window because she's sleeping now. They've drugged her up with powerful painkillers, she's on a morphine drip and spends a lot of time sleeping. We're nearing the end, Robbie."

Robbie takes her comments to be his green light but, just to be sure, he presses Emma, saying "So can I come up?"

"I suppose so," she says hesitantly, now fully aware of what's happening, "though I am not sure she will know who you are, even if she wakes up." Emma can feel her heart beating faster.

Within a couple of minutes Robbie is at the hospice. As Emma knows he will have trouble convincing the staff at the door he is a bona fide visitor, she has hurried to the entrance to meet him, and gets there just as they ask him if he is a relative, and Robbie says "no, just a very close friend", and they are pleased Emma is there to confirm what he just said.

As the door opens and Robbie steps inside, Emma gives him a hesitant smile. Then, to avoid any awkwardness she knows their greeting each other with a kiss would trigger, she puts her finger to her lips to tell him to respect the hospice's rules about noise as she leads the way down the corridor. When they reach Sarah's room, Emma holds open the door to let Robbie go in first. Sarah is lying motionless on the bed, clearly in a deep sleep, and as he looks across at her his face speaks of shock. He is visibly shaken as he takes in her wizened and frail body, her drawn and sunken cheeks, and by seeing how much she has aged. He doesn't know what to say. To break what would have become an awkward silence, Emma starts to fill him in, explaining how Sarah had really started to go downhill fast around Christmas and had had three weeks of care at home before she had been brought in by ambulance when the out-patient nurses said they could no longer cope.

"I'm so sorry," says Robbie, his eyes still focused on Sarah face, his hands limp by his side. Then, turning back to Emma, who is still standing a pace or two behind him, he says, "I know she's asleep, but would you mind if I go over to greet her? But if you think it might wake her or disturb her, of course I won't." As Emma is still considering her answer, and taking her silence to denote consent, Robbie walks over to the bed, leans over and kisses Sarah's forehead. Emma is touched and is at once reminded of the way he used to greet Sarah when they came over to her place for Sunday lunch, his tall body bending low over hers as Sarah stood on tip-toes offering her forehead for him to kiss.

Robbie steps away from the bed and then says, "I'll pray for her, and for you too," as he turns to look back at Emma. He then smiles and says, "You look great, Em, in spite of all this…It's good to see you."

"It's good to see you, too, Robbie," says Emma, unsure of what will happen next.

After an awkward few moments when no one speaks, Robbie says, "I'd best be going. Give my best to Simon, and do let me have news about your mother… Perhaps we can see each other and talk properly when this is all over?"

"Yes," says Emma, "I'll do that," uncertain if Robbie had understood her 'yes' had meant she would not only pass his greetings on to Simon but she would get in touch when her mother dies and then arrange for the two of them to meet up as soon as possible afterwards.

Robbie isn't sure either, but feels he shouldn't outstay his welcome and – with a heavy heart – says, "Don't worry, I'll let myself out." He walks past Emma without their eyes meeting, and when he reaches the door he turns, raises his hand and says, "Good bye, Emma, take care," and is gone. Robbie has disappeared from Emma's life as suddenly as he had just re-entered it. They hadn't kissed; they hadn't even touched each other.

As soon as Robbie leaves the room, an intense feeling of emptiness sweeps through Emma and she grips the side of Sarah's bed to stop herself from falling. As she steadies herself, she realises she can't simply let him go. However much she tells herself she needs to be ready for Sarah when she wakes – and she knows this will happen very soon – she also knows she mustn't lose this opportunity for the two of them to talk. So, after a quick glance across at Sarah, Emma runs down the corridor and catches up with Robbie as he reaches the entrance, grabbing him by the elbow just before he presses the button on the wall to release the lock on the entrance door.

"Can we talk now?" Emma asks earnestly, almost pleadingly.

"Yes," says Robbie as the look in Emma's eyes starts to lift the even greater heaviness he had been feeling since their clumsy parting.

"Let's go into the Room of Quiet," Emma says, pointing to the frosted-glass door on the opposite side of the entrance hall. "The lights are off, so I'm pretty sure there'll be no one there, and once we're in, no one will disturb us."

"What about Sarah?" asks Robbie, as they walk towards the door.

"She'll be fine for a little while longer," says Emma as she switches on the lights and picks up a wooden-backed chair and places it next to another, careful not to position them so they are too close together. She arranges the two chairs so they are facing the large stained-glass window which almost fills the wall opposite.

As its name suggests, the hospice's Room of Quiet is the place where people can come if they wish to spend time alone. Although it doesn't say so, it is a non-denominational space deliberately devoid of the symbols of any specific religion, designed so people of any faith or none will feel comfortable there. Around the light-coloured painted walls, a few pictures are displayed: uplifting scenes of rivers and mountains, and cheery, smiling faces of people of different ethnicities, young and old. In one corner, a contemporary-designed candlestick hangs which, with the walls and the pictures, gives the whole room a tranquil as well as modern feel. A corner bookshelf opposite the door houses the holy books of most of North London's main faiths: Judaism, Christianity, Islam and Hinduism, and behind closed cupboard doors, Emma knows – because she had once looked – rolled up prayer mats are kept for those who wish to use them. Though Robbie and Emma are Catholic, as they sit down and take in their surroundings they are pleased to be in a place free of statues and the lingering smell of stale incense; it helps to put them at ease, reducing a little the nervousness they are both feeling.

Having brought Robbie to the Room of Quiet, Emma knows she is the one who has to speak first and, aware how little time they have, she gets straight to the point.

"I've treated you dreadfully, Robbie, I really, really have, and I feel so ashamed," she begins. "And that's the reason I was so desperate to see you, as I tried to explain in my letter. I needed to tell you this myself, in person: I owed it to you, Robbie."

Robbie says nothing, and Emma is glad. She shuffles in her chair as she gathers herself together, struggling to remember what she had rehearsed all those months ago after she had written her letter to Robbie, but which had gradually faded from her consciousness after he had never contacted her.

"I have wronged you in so many ways, Robbie," she continues as her prepared speech starts to come back to her. "It began almost at once when I held back from telling you about Simon, deceiving myself into thinking if it all came to nothing there would be nothing to tell, even as I realised how intense were the feelings I already had for him. That was dishonest of me. Then I wronged you again by not thinking of the pain I was causing you. I was so worried about losing you, Robbie, I could only think of the pain I was experiencing. I was so wrapped up in my own feelings I was blind to yours; I hurt you deeply, and when eventually I started to tell you what was going on, you responded with a generosity I didn't deserve. You told me I was free to choose between you and Simon when deep down you already knew my heart was crying out for him; and even then, I continued to deceive myself into believing I could have Simon while continuing in some way to hold on to you."

As she speaks, Emma stares straight out in front of her as if her eyes are focused on something outside, on the far side of the coloured glass. But, like Robbie's silence, the window reveals nothing as it's pitch black outside. The only thing beyond the stained glass is the darkness and cold of the winter night.

"I said in my text and again in my letter, Robbie, I was sorry for what I had done, but I knew these words were meaningless unless in front of you I could tell you I was sorry," Emma continues, conscious she is almost repeating what she has already said. But she feels she needs to because she is struggling to align her spoken words of contrition with the way she is feeling.

"Only now as I mouth these words to you do I feel they can convey their full meaning," she continues. "So, Robbie, what I want to say to you now, with all the honesty and heartfelt remorse I can muster, is I am truly sorry, so deeply sorry for everything I have done in first deceiving and then going on to hurt you. I know I don't deserve it, but if there is one thing I ask of you now, it is your forgiveness. Why do I need your forgiveness, Robbie? Because I still love you and always will, and because I know the power and potential forgiveness has to wipe the slate clean and enable us to start again. So, if you can find it in your heart to forgive me, Robbie, we might be able to start building our relationship anew, just as Don Paulo hinted we could try doing. I am ashamed of what I have done, Robbie, and I realise my plea for forgiveness can easily be interpreted as yet another selfish act on my behalf, but all I can say is I would not be true to myself if I did not ask for it. I know I don't deserve it and considering the way I have treated you I would fully understand if you walked away without forgiving me. Deep inside, I feel so wretched for what I have done to you, Robbie. Only now, having said all this to you, do I feel able to begin to start trying to make amends for the hurt I have caused you."

Emma starts to cry, silently at first, and Robbie doesn't initially notice. As a young girl, Emma had been schooled by the nuns, who taught her to confess her sins to the priest, and for many years she went through the ritual of regular confession. During that time, she used to think up imaginary misdemeanours she had never committed but which she thought were bad enough for the priest to forgive her; after reciting her shopping list of evils, he blessed her, telling her not to sin again, and she assured him she wouldn't. But there was no remorse from her side and his forgiveness meant nothing to her. It was all words and no content, which is why she stopped going to confession. But now it is quite different. For possibly the very first time in her life, Emma is genuinely sorry for things she did to Robbie. Confessing her wrongdoings to Robbie, Emma can see close up the selfish person she is. She's ashamed not so much of what she has done, but of herself. She has inflicted harm not merely on a fellow human being, which would be bad enough, but on someone she claims to love. What sort of betrayal is that? Emma knows she is crying tears of remorse; she can't stop herself, and she doesn't want to. As her silent cries turn into sobs, Emma's tears expose her to Robbie in all her vulnerability.

When Robbie realises what is happening to Emma, he leans over and stretches out his long arms towards her until his hands reach hers, and says gently, "You are forgiven".

Before uttering these three simple words, Robbie's mind had gone travelling. As Emma was listing the wrongs she had done, Robbie started to relive the bitterness and anger he had felt when he realised he was losing Emma, and he experienced again the deep hurt a man feels knowing he is being rejected by a woman for another man. Then he recalled Don Paulo's advice to move on and not wallow in his destructive thoughts and saw in his mind's eye the remarkable women he had met in Haiti who told him how they had come to forgive the young looters who had robbed them of everything they possessed. Robbie remembered thinking he would never be able either to move on as Don Paulo had counselled him to do or to forgive as the Haitian women had: even if Emma were to acknowledge and express genuine sorrow for the hurt she had caused him, Robbie thought he would always have difficulty genuinely forgiving Emma – going beyond mouthing the words and really forgiving her – for what she had done.

But now the moment has arrived, Robbie surprises himself: forgiving Emma seems to be far easier than he ever thought it would be. The Haitian women had forgiven their looters because one day they knew their sons might become the looters and they would need to be forgiven: their forgiveness was shrewd, though he was sure genuine nonetheless. In contrast, Robbie feels he is able to forgive Emma unconditionally. Why? Because – for all she has done – he still loves her. His is a purifying, almost redemptive type of forgiveness. At the moment he says to Emma 'you are forgiven', Robbie feels strangely uplifted – so much so, he thinks he would have had it in him to forgive Emma even if she hadn't repeatedly said she was sorry and hadn't asked for his forgiveness. Robbie is puzzled; he doesn't understand how he could be feeling this way.

It takes a while before Emma says anything. Through her tears, she says, "Thank you Robbie," but, realising he hasn't heard her, repeats herself. Speaking much louder this time, she says again, "Thank you, Robbie".

Immediately Robbie stands up and is about to lean over and embrace her when Emma, already on her feet, suddenly throws her arms around him and squeezes him as tightly she can. They stand there locked together like limpets. When they eventually separate the right-hand sleeve of Emma's white blouse is sodden with a new wave of tears she has just shed – tears of relief, and tears of joy.

With their bodies joined and motionless, Emma's mind begins to race. She wants to tell Robbie how much she loves him for what he has done, how indebted to him she feels and how grateful she will always be. She wants to tell him that even though she and Simon intend eventually to marry, she will always reserve a special place in her heart for him. She wants to tell him that after Simon, he will always be her mentor, he will be a rock and a pillar for her to lean on. She wants to tell him how much she wants them to build a new and lasting friendship which will endure, as solid and stable as a cathedral. She wants to tell him how she feels with Robbie close to her once again.

But then Emma realises she doesn't need to tell Robbie any of what's racing though her mind because everything she could possibly think of telling him is already being transmitted to him as they are locked together in the tightness of her embrace.

Emma loosens her grip. "I must be getting back to Ma," she says quietly as she starts to disengage from Robbie.

"Yes," says Robbie, "you must," as they walk out of the Room of Quiet and momentarily stand next to each other in the entrance hall. "Do remember me to your mother when she wakes," he adds.

"Yes, I will," says Emma, still wiping the tears from her eyes, and busily trying to tidy herself up. "That's a promise!"

"And I'll be in touch again shortly," says Robbie. "That's a promise too!"

Emma smiles across at Robbie as they both raise their hands to each other. By now they are too far away to touch, though neither of them any longer feels the need.

When he steps outside into the cold winter night, Robbie is ready to acknowledge to himself why he found this evening's events far easier than they would have been if they had taken place any earlier. Tonight's unplanned and surprise encounter with Emma happened the day after his first proper date; the previous evening he had invited Danielle Greenidge out for a meal. She was the fellow teacher at Finchley High School Robbie had mentioned in his letter to Emma, but who only very recently he felt ready to ask out, though he knew she had long been keen. The first thing Robbie did at the restaurant, even before they had ordered their food, was to tell Danielle about Emma, as he knew how important it was to be totally honest with her from day one. In some ways, Robbie felt he should have mentioned Danielle to Emma this evening, but as he promised to be in touch soon, he told himself there would be other opportunities. He also wanted to tell Emma that English-born Danielle's mother was Zimbabwean, like Sarah, and her father Bajan, from the Caribbean like his own father.

As she walks back to Sarah's trying to make sense of what has just happened, Emma thinks back to the exchange which took place between Peter and her mother in the Robertsons' sitting room all those weeks ago. *It's strange*, she says to herself, *how things happened the other way round then: Sarah forgave Peter for killing Joshua not only before Peter had acknowledged the wrong he had done, but even before he had expressed any sorrow for killing him. Perhaps*, she goes on, *what ultimately matters is being able to go through the act of forgiving, not in worrying how you get there, because in forgiving what had been impossible can happen. How amazing it is*, Emma thinks as she quietly turns the knob on Sarah's door, *and how wonderful it is as well that human beings who are deeply wronged have it within themselves to forgive.*

Emma had never read or heard anyone say or even suggest forgiveness was a British value: that having a receptivity for forgiveness, an openness to forgive, were part of what it means to be British. *But it must be*, Emma said to herself, *for what sort of society would we be creating if we didn't forgive? If we're not able to forgive others, how can we expect them to forgive us and if we can't forgive then we will build a society driven and shaped by the shifting sands of selfishness.*

* * *

As she stood at the window, daffodil in her hand, remembering how it had all started with her phone ringing, Emma knew she had to tell Robbie her mother had died but she wouldn't do so just yet. She sighed, walked back to Sarah's bed and laid her open hand across Sarah's brow, saying 'may she rest now in peace.' She then lifted up Sarah's right hand, which still had Joshua's cross wrapped round it; it was colder now. She gently unwrapped the cord and momentarily clasped the cross in her own hand before rewrapping it up and putting it into her bag, wondering what she would do with it. Emma wasn't one for relics or even for keepsakes, but she knew Joshua's cross would always remain precious to her even though knew she couldn't wear it as Sarah had done and wouldn't display and honour it as Mr Svosve had. With that done, Emma felt she had stayed long enough and, just as she was wondering where all her things were and what else of Sarah's things she should take with her today, Lynn popped her head round the corner and said, "Emma, can I come in?"

"Yes, do," said Emma.

"It's well past lunchtime," said Lynn. "I've brought you a sandwich and some tea."

"Oh thanks," said Emma, who, on seeing them, realised how hungry she was.

Lynn handed her a large mug of steaming tea and a triple-layered cheese sandwich and stayed with Emma till she had finished. During this time, she covered Sarah's head and upper body with a sheet and she and Emma chatted quietly together. Lynn told her the hospice would look after all the funeral arrangements, so Emma needn't worry about that, and, she added, Father Maitland had already been told Sarah had died. She had just one question. Sarah had not said whether she wanted to be buried or cremated; indeed, she had explicitly said she had wanted to leave that decision to Emma.

"Well," said Emma before she had really thought about it "I don't really know," but it took her only a moment to realise she already had the answer.

She knew Sarah wouldn't want to be buried in the way Alice was buried and she also knew Sarah would like her remains to somehow be mingled with both Joshua's and Alice's, but also to return to her own home in Zimbabwe. That meant three resting places – the cemetery here in London where Alice was buried, the riverbank in Mhondoro where Mr Svosve had first laid Joshua to rest and the family graveyard in Mutoko – and three different locations had to mean cremation. Over the last few months, Emma had rather warmed to the idea of mingling ashes together and when her time came, she thought she would like Sarah's ashes to be mixed with hers. This meant she should hold onto some of Sarah's ashes to keep for herself, which increased the number of resting places from three to four.

She had just told Lynn she definitely wanted Sarah to be cremated when a new wave of sadness swept through her just as Lynn had told her it would, and she became teary again. It didn't last long this time and as Emma pulled herself together she said she thought it was time for her to go, and Lynn agreed. However, before she left, Lynn suggested Emma might like to give Sarah one last, farewell kiss which she obediently gave her. Lynn pulled back the sheet which now covered Sarah's head, and Emma nestled her cheek near to Sarah's and touched her lips with the fingers of her own right hand. She would be eternally grateful to Lynn for encouraging her to formally and finally say goodbye to her mother.

Lynn took Emma's coat off the hook at the back of the door and gave it to her, remarking how surprised she was the daffodils had come out so quickly. She asked Emma if she would like to take them with her. Emma said she would like them to remain in the room with Sarah's body and, if they were still alive when they moved her, for them to go with her. Lynn assured Emma she would arrange for everything to happen just as Emma had asked.

Lynn then walked Emma to the front door but it took them a while to get there as so many people had been waiting to have a word with Emma and she had to stop almost half a dozen times to speak to them. Clearly everyone now knew Sarah had died and Emma was deeply touched by their clearly heartfelt comments; indeed, she wasn't able to hold back her tears as she moved from one to the next. Dr Fletcher was waiting for her at the front door to give a more formal speech he had prepared and which he gave once almost everyone working at the hospice on that afternoon had arrived.

"As you all know," he began, speaking more nervously than he usually did, "I've asked you all to gather here for a moment to honour our colleague and dear friend Sarah Makoni, who died earlier today. Although we plan to have a more substantial event to remember Sarah, I wanted to say a few words now while Emma is with us. This is a very sad day for all of us here at North London Hospice. In a place which rightly prides itself on the care and attention we give to our residents, Sarah stood out as someone quite exceptional. She was devoted both to her patients and their families, dispensing warmth to them to such a degree it was rare for close relatives not to call on her to be with them when the time came to have to say goodbye to their dying loved ones.

"Sarah was a special friend to me, too," said Dr Fletcher, who suddenly started to well up with emotion, and, uncharacteristically, had to pause for a moment before he was able to continue. "We go back a long way: in fact, we are by far the longest-serving members of staff."

Then, turning to Emma he said, "How fortunate you have been, Emma, to have had such an amazing and wonderful person as a grandmother. I still remember when Sarah first arrived at the hospice all those years ago; she looked so young she could have been mistaken for your mother, and over these past weeks as you have come and gone I can honestly say your love for Sarah has shone out for us all to see. It's as if you had been her daughter, Emma, and not her granddaughter. Sarah has been the mother of our hospice. Godspeed Emma. Our prayers go with you."

What Paul Fletcher did not say when he was suddenly overcome was that he carried within him a deep affection for Emma as well as for Sarah. It began the day Alice died on his watch all those years ago. He never forgot the look in the face of three-year old Emma as she left the hospice that summer evening, clutching Sarah's hand. Her eyes were alert, darting from side to side as if she was searching for something she had lost. No, there was more to it than that. Emma had a determined look in her eye, like a leopard just before pouncing on its prey, its eyes focused with dogged determination on its kill.

Dr Fletcher never remembered seeing Emma after that until only a few weeks earlier, when Sarah was brought in to the hospice as an in-patient and they formally introduced themselves to each other. However, he knew a lot about her. As Emma was growing up, Dr Fletcher would often ask Sarah how she was doing and listened closely if ever Sarah recounted her exploits as she changed from toddler to teenager, and then to student, but he never pried. When Sarah told Dr Paul-uh (as she always called him, having first met him when she still spoke English with a heavy Shona accent and the name had stuck) Emma had got her first proper job as a reporter on the *Hendon and Finchley Times*, he took out a subscription to the paper and read the articles she wrote. This gave him enormous pleasure; he felt proud to have known Emma, though, with typical British reserve, he never said a word to Sarah. Similarly, when she told Dr Paul-uh Emma had applied for and been given a job at the BBC, he started to watch BBC news and current affairs programmes more regularly in the hope of catching one of her interviews. The more he saw of Emma, the young professional TV journalist, the more impressed he was, but he wasn't surprised how good she was because he could see in Emma the adult the determination he had seen in her eyes all those years ago, on the day Alice had died.

As Emma took her leave of the gathering she went up to Dr Fletcher and gave him an affectionate kiss on his cheek. His slightly embarrassed smile hid the glow he felt inside for the attention he had been given by 'his' celebrity. Shy by nature, he hated to be noticed. Indeed, still unmarried, Dr Paul-uh had never really confronted the fact that over the years he had probably sort of fallen in love with Sarah Makoni, the nurse from Zimbabwe.

Then, after receiving many hugs and embraces both from the other people she had got to know and many she couldn't even remember meeting, Emma left the hospice with a lump in her throat. As she walked to the bus, chiding herself once again for not having on her warmest coat, Emma tried to recall what Dr Fletcher and everyone else had said to her, but it was all a blur, just a jumble of warm words. There were two things she did remember. The first was Dr Fletcher telling her the hospice would meet all Sarah's funeral expenses, so Emma wouldn't have to worry about any of that. The second was Lynn and Dr Fletcher both asking her to come back later in the week to tidy up a few admin things, and Emma had said she would.

As she neared the bus stop and began to emerge from what now felt like the unreal bubble of her mother's death and its immediate aftermath, Emma realised she needed to let both Simon and Rosemary know what had happened. She knew neither of them would be free to talk just now but, feeling the need for any sort of human contact, she decided to leave them each a voicemail rather than text them.

To Simon she said, "Simon, my love, Ma died this afternoon. Lynn called me just as I was about to set off for work this morning. Fortunately, I arrived in time and a couple of hours after I had sat with her – I lost track of the time – she died. She passed away so quietly I hardly noticed. I cried a lot, but I think I am fine now. But what I wanted to say is I really do want us to meet up at that pub this evening as planned. You probably won't listen to this voicemail until you've finished work, but I wanted to let you know first. We both knew Ma was about to die, so her death was not unexpected. But I am now feeling a huge hole in me Simon. I'm fine, really I am. But I need you; I need to be with you, Simon, to be close and for us to talk. Love you loads. Bye."

Before she started talking into her phone to Simon Emma felt in control, but by the time she had finished her message she could feel another wave of sadness starting to rise up from inside her and she had tears in her

eyes. It took a while and a series of forced deep breaths to recover enough
to be able to leave her voice message for Rosemary.

To Rosemary she said, in a voice more sombre than she ever
remembered using to talk to her, "Hi Rosemary, Emma here. Mum died
earlier this afternoon and fortunately I was at her side. In many ways it's a
relief but, as I am sure you know, I feel her loss terribly. I trust you got my
text earlier this morning. Please do call when you have a moment. I hope
today's meeting went as well as we had been hoping and, as you will know,
I was bitterly disappointed not to have been there. I don't think I'm up to
coming in tomorrow, Rosemary, but you did keep telling me to take my
time coming back when Ma eventually passed away and I know you meant
it. I feel pretty empty just now, but I'm OK, really, I am; but thank God
I've got Simon. We can talk more when you call. Please do call, Rosemary,
just as a friend."

As Emma waited for the bus and took in her surroundings, she was
struck by the sameness of the world. Everyone was going about their daily
business as if nothing had happened, when for Emma something
extraordinary just had: the world, her world, had changed inexorably: her
mother had just died; Sarah was no more. Everything was anything but
ordinary. Emma felt the urge to shout out and tell those she could see nearby
things were not normal, to run up to people, shake them and look them in
the eye to make them understand this was like no other day; something
momentous had occurred. Just then her bus arrived and as she jumped in,
tapped in her card and felt the warmth of the bus's interior on her cheeks,
she realised how needy she was for Simon.

Stroud Green Road

"Those can't be Alphonso mangoes, can they?" asked Emma in surprise. Her voice was strong and self-assured. "I thought they had been banned and, in any case, it's not the season yet is it?"

"Yes, they are Alphonsos," came the equally confident reply. "Just as it says they are!"

The woman behind the counter hurried on, clearly delighted to answer Emma's question. "The import ban was lifted a while back, but you're right, they are early," she said. The Indian weather was kinder than usual this year, and we've just had our first delivery; the boxes only came in this morning. I've eaten two already: couldn't resist them, they're as good as ever!"

Emma had just stepped off the bus at the back of Finsbury Park station. Leaving the hospice well after 3.30, she had been worried she might be late for her planned rendezvous with Simon at five. However, her ride was quicker than she had feared, and she had a good 20 minutes to walk up to The Old Dairy where they had arranged to meet. Her mood had changed. She knew she needed human company and she had found the boisterous giggles and the sometimes furtive, sometimes raucous chatter of the young adolescents on the bus – going home after the end of the school day – therapeutic. The more she listened to them, the more she felt herself being sucked back into the bubble of her own teenage years. So, with more of a spring in her step than she would have thought possible an hour or so earlier, Emma took a left from the bus stand at Wells Terrace and began her walk up Stroud Green Road.

Behind the stall with the juicy mangoes stood a pretty young woman about Emma's age but far shorter. Under her winter jacket, Emma could see she was smartly dressed, but what caught her attention was the contrast between her fresh complexion and smooth naturally-moisturised face and her dark, alluring eyes. Emma thought her ethnic roots were Greek.

"They're expensive," said Emma, "but I know they always are. My mum first discovered Alphonsos at Good Eats in Finchley Central and was persuaded to try them. Though she had grown up eating mangoes in Africa, Mum knew at once these were different. But as she told me, they were quite delicious and ever since she always used to buy them for me as a special treat."

"So you won't need much persuading to buy some today, will you?" said the woman, laughing. Her bubbliness prevented Emma sinking back into her earlier melancholy, having inadvertently mentioned the person she would, from now on, have to get used to calling her late mother.

In their brief exchange, so much had been communicated which had not been said. They knew how much they had in common: young and self-assured North London women each speaking with a slight though distinct – and in Emma's case slightly put-on – 'norf-Lund'un' twang. They were both clearly happy to remain engaged and continue chatting.

"I don't think I have seen you here before, have I?" continued the woman behind the stall. "Where are you from?"

"*East* Finchley," said Emma emphasising the word 'east'. "Where's your home? Where are you from? Round here?"

"No," said the woman. "My home's further east, sort of between Haringey and Seven Sisters."

"Is your family Greek, or Cypriot?" enquired Emma, the boldness of her direct question reflective of the positive vibes flowing between them.

The young dark-eyed woman laughed again, but this time her whole face lit up. "Ha!" she said, "you're right about Cyprus but we're not *Greek*. Oh my God, what would my parents think! We are *Turkish* Cypriots."

"Oops, sorry!" said Emma, relieved the woman had not taken offence at her *faux pas*, as she immediately explained her mistake. "There were lots of kids in my class at school whose parents were from Cyprus but they were all Greek Cypriots and so I simply assumed you were, too! You're the first Turkish Cypriot I've really ever spoken to. It seems I can't tell the difference. I'm so sorry to have made such a silly mistake."

"No offence taken," said the woman. "But you should be able to tell the difference; after all, you *are* a woman!"

"What's being a woman got to do with it?" asked Emma curiously. "How can *that* enable me to tell the difference between Greek and Turkish Cypriots?"

The woman laughed again as she began to answer Emma's question. "Because Turkish Cypriot and Greek Cypriot women pluck their eyebrows in different ways," she said. "It's just not the sort of thing men ever notice: it seems their DNA prevents them from looking closely at that part of our anatomy." She shrieked with laughter. "Old traditions seem to endure longer here in London than they do back in Cyprus."

"Wow," said Emma. "I must say I'm not sure I could tell the difference either, even though I thought I was an expert on London's ethnicities. But," keen to get on her way, "let's get back to the mangoes as I'm actually in a bit of a hurry. Can you pick out three for me, one unwrapped for me to eat now, and two in a bag for tomorrow, if that's OK?"

As Emma handed over the money in return for the single loose and paper bag of mangoes she said, "Cheers, great talking to you."

"You too. Take care now," came the reply as Emma put the fruit into her bag with some care, worried they might bruise and become squashy, and continued her way up the road. "See you!"

"Hope so," said Emma as she strode off, feeling revived.

No sooner had Emma waved a cheery goodbye than she came to a sign for the Big Yellow Hand Carwash, with its strap line 'take a break, get a wash' only a few paces further on.

She was pleased to see women as well as men busy with their jet-hoses in what looked to be an extremely popular venue: the carwash was full and cars waiting their turn were queuing back along the road. The car-washers themselves were a mix of different faces, though none looked older than 40. Emma thought she recognised white Irish and black and white cockney faces in amongst an assortment of North African, Middle Eastern and Afghan beards – all immigrant car washers working happily side by side. The cars, like the drivers inside them, were a mix of old and new, smart and scruffy, black, white, Arab and in-between. Emma was amused to see a couple of smartly-dressed men driving old, almost clapped-out cars and one man in greasy overalls which matched his face behind the wheel of a car sporting this year's newest number plate.

A few paces further on, she passed a charity shop displaying a huge banner which read 'Shop to End Homelessness'. Though curious to discover what this meant, she didn't stop because beyond she could now see the afro-hair shops she knew coming into view on either side of the road; it was here she was keen to stop and shop.

The hair 'emporia' were dominated by one colour, green, one name and one company: Pak's. Clustered together tightly like houses on adjacent Monopoly board squares just before you turn them into hotels were Pak's Hair World; Pak's Hair Centre, Pak's Hair Boutique, Pak's Cosmetics Centre and two shopfronts bearing the same name: Pak's Wig World. Between them, they sold not only a huge range of wigs but a variety of hair extensions of differing lengths, shapes and sizes, the pricey ones made with natural hair, the cheaper ones with a range of artificial material.

Close to the Pak properties was a cluster of haircut shops, which, if the signs on their windows were to be believed, would wash your hair, perm your hair, or, if you preferred, dye it any colour of the rainbow. There were shops which straightened curly hair and shops which made curly hair straight again. There were also shops which offered the cheaper alternative way of curling and straightening your hair by buying their products for you to do it yourself at home: the DIYs of the hair world. A sign on one shop window read, encouragingly, 'curl restorer: brings curls back instantly'. Immediate psychological relief for the desperate, thought Emma, smiling as she walked past.

Today, Emma was heading for the biggest Pak's store, the one she always went to, Pak's Cosmetics Centre. It was huge, an Aladdin's cave of some 100,000 products if you believed their website. There was row upon row and aisle upon aisle of shampoos, conditioners, hair dyes and all manner of hair accessories. As the store's name indicated, this particular

Pak's also sold thousands of other items linked only loosely with hair: oils, creams, potions and lotions for the skin, as well as nails, eyelashes and so much more. The place was a Mecca for products flown in from all over the world: from Africa, the Caribbean, Latin America, the Middle East and Asia.

Emma chatted briefly to a young woman from Atlanta, Georgia, who was studying in London, both wondering which brand of Jamaican black castor oil they should buy. She then explained to two giggly young teenagers from Tufnell Park the difference between coconut and argan oil as she was choosing some Moroccan argan oil for herself. As Emma left the store with a couple of coins in her hand, almost £20 the poorer, two more items went into her bag.

On leaving Pak's, Emma crossed the road and popped into New Beacon Books, remembering when she saw the sign how good it was. Inside, she was delighted to see they still sold 'black' greetings cards. She bought a couple to add to her dwindling stock. If she had had more time, she would have browsed through the books. As ever, they had a good stock of African American fiction and poetry books, and Emma had previously bought both from here. Still thinking of eyebrows, Emma raised one herself on seeing the end of the section labelled 'Black British Fiction' was just touching the start of the section marked 'Crime'.

Stepping out of the bookshop she turned right and was now on the lookout again for The Old Dairy, but she still couldn't see it. She clearly had still quite a way to go up Stroud Green Road.

Emma knew areas of Finsbury Park had a reputation for muggings, but it felt good to be here. The people she had spoken to and seen today had exuded warmth and friendliness, not hostility, just as they had on all her previous visits to this part of North London. This was the London she knew and loved, the London she felt most at home in, with its mix of ethnicities, religions, races and cultures. What Emma especially liked about places such as this was the pride almost all Londoners she met had in themselves and their neighbourhoods, keen to display the richness of their roots and not too embarrassed to expose at least some of the quirkiness of the different ways they lived. Each person had her own, unique story of how their families came to be here, some arriving generations ago, some recent arrivals, a few from other parts of Britain, most from abroad. But they were all – to a woman – happy to tell you their own story if you asked. Some were uplifting and heroic, many harrowing, some hurtful. Emma's was a mixture of all four.

Stroud Green Road spoke diversity and difference. As Emma hurried on, she made a mental list of all the different restaurants she passed: Chinese, Japanese, Vietnamese and Thai; Nepali, Tibetan, Indian and Bangladeshi; Spanish and Italian, including pizzerias; South African,

Caribbean and, of course, Turkish. She was surprised her list did not include Polish and wondered why.

The food shops mirrored the diversity of the restaurants, though most of the street's ethnic food shops clearly catered for the lower end of the income chain. Emma popped her head inside a butcher's to see displayed shoulders of goat, heads of sheep, feet of chickens sold by the bag and plentiful supplies of different animals' innards. She smiled to herself as she spied out frozen fish from Lake Kariba. She passed vegetable sellers displaying breadfruit, yams, matoke and plantains to fill your insides on a bleak winter's night. On the street in front of one store she saw discerning shoppers pondering whether this night's cooking pot would be filled with sweet potatoes from Ghana, Uganda, Jamaica or South Africa. The shoppers here might be poor but they are spoiled for choice, even if, as Emma knew from popping briefly in, the road's Tesco's and Sainsbury's only gave a rather grudging nod to the neighbourhood's diverse range of shoppers.

Although the more downmarket and basic stores were far more numerous, Stroud Green Road also boasted a number of upmarket delicatessens and bakeries with posher names. There was The Deli at 80, which Emma had just passed, the Boulangerie Bon Matin just round the corner on Tollington Park and the Organic Market higher up the street. The packaged coffees, teas, pastries and condiments these shops sold and the fresh fruit and vegetables on display would satisfy almost anyone at the top of the income chain. The goods sold in this hidden part of North London were as exotic and fresh as any you would find in Harrods or Fortnum's, with the added attraction of being kinder to the pocket.

Unsurprisingly, the diversity of the shops and restaurants was mirrored in the people on the streets. Though the school day had ended before Emma had arrived, there were still plenty of children in school uniform, many of them congregating outside Tesco's or at the nearby bus stop, the younger ones under adult care. She saw Chinese, Thai, Burmese, Japanese, Korean and Vietnamese faces; Caribbean and Western African men and women, young and old, fat and thin. There were fashionably-dressed young mothers in hajibs and short skirts talking earnestly to each other with their hand-held children in tow, walking next to children in the same school uniform firmly holding hands with their khimar-adorned grandmothers in long traditional dress.

She walked past hipsters and would-be hipsters and heard young men who looked like students speaking English in North London accents just like her own. She was smiled at by two old women chattering away in Irish accents and looked at gruffly by a Scottish grandfather upbraiding his North London grandson with an 'I'll tell ya' Ma you-ra a thoughtless bairn' for not buttoning up his coat. Among the most elegantly dressed people she saw was a tall white-haired and proud-with-herself woman who Emma thought was probably of Jamaican origin. She was passed by two fashionable young women, heads down and concentrating, talking earnestly to each other in Russian and, soon after that, witnessed two middle-aged, Eastern European women conversing angrily in a language Emma did not recognise. Could it have been Polish? If so, were they cross they couldn't find a Polski Sklep anywhere along the length of Stroud Green Road?

Unlike the streets of Chelsea or Knightsbridge, Hampstead or Mayfair, here the shops for the poor stood right next to the shops for those with more money to spend, yet Stroud Green Road didn't seem to have that air of exclusivity which hits you when walking down New Bond Street or Knightsbridge. But then the inequalities of Stroud Green Road, though significant, were nothing like as extreme as in some parts of Central London. Emma smiled as she recalled that day in the summer when she and Simon had watched dumfounded as a young man who she thought was Russian, no older than them, walked into a car dealership on Park Lane, handed over the cash and drove out of the showroom in his brand new Brabus.

With her investigative journalist's hat firmly on, Emma thought at least a part of the reason everything appeared so calm and friendly here was that many of the poorer people who frequented Stroud Green Road aspired to live the lives of those who could afford to shop in its more upmarket outlets and eat in its fancier restaurants. Her theory of tangible aspiration and realistic upward mobility seemed to be supported by the names of some of the estate agents she passed: Utopia Properties; Galaxy Estate Agents; Dream Property and Future Homes.

Emma saw a young beggar sitting on the pavement outside Future Homes as she drew near. Feeling guilty none of her £30 of purchases had made a major contribution to 'Shopping to End Homelessness', she dropped a £2 coin in his chipped plastic mug. She often did this as a way of beginning a conversation with her less fortunate fellow human beings, and today was no exception.

Emma chatted to him briefly. He was Tom Pearson, a Geordie and probably a good deal younger than herself, she thought, though he looked older and she was too embarrassed to ask him his age. He had left school with one 'A' level and come down to London eagerly expecting to find a good job. Finding nothing in the centre of town, he was forced to move further out and found a part-time job round the corner on Tollington Park, shifting boxes at night in a warehouse. It had at least paid for a roof over his head and, if he was careful, one good meal a day. But he had lost the job and the roof – he didn't say why, and Emma was in no mood to press him – and for the past few weeks had had to beg to eat. Begging was the only thing he did now when he wasn't sleeping, which, he told Emma, he preferred to do as his most pressing need was simply to keep warm, and he was warmer when he slept than when he begged.

Emma didn't have the heart to ask him whether he had deliberately chosen to sit directly below the sign in the window of Future Homes which read 'houses for sale over £4m'. Nor did she ask him how far his current aspirations stretched, though she was sure at the moment he wasn't thinking of a home at all: he would have been more than satisfied tonight if he could find any place to sleep without fear of being robbed. Feeling even guiltier, Emma bent down and dropped a £5 note into his mug, but before she did, she shook his hand and moved on. She knew he also needed human warmth, probably even more desperately than thermal warmth, and she felt guilty for not having had the courage to give him a hug as she went on her way.

A little further ahead, she walked by four men huddled together smoking thin self-rolled cigarettes outside the local branch of Coral's. Their breath smelt of beer and their eyes spoke of boredom. She guessed they probably looked and smelt much the same whether their horses had won or whether they had lost, and she wondered when, why and how the hope of a better life had been extinguished in each one of them.

Then at last, in front of her, Emma saw at the crossroads ahead a sign over a dark grey building on the corner just beyond the lights displaying the words she had been looking for: The Old Dairy. As she drew near and peered in, she was initially confused as it didn't look like a pub at all: with old furniture, bric-a-brac on the walls and no bar counter or beer pull-handles in sight, it had the air of an antique shop. She was even more confused when she pushed open the door as she was sure she had walked into a café because all she could see were two young mothers with pushchairs sitting in armchairs chatting together over late-afternoon tea and cakes, their sixth senses alert to their sleeping offspring. It was only when she walked through to the back that she saw a far bigger room with its long and bending traditional bar, its bare, wooden restaurant tables, and its familiar display boards drawing your attention to the day's specials. As it was still too early for its post-work clientele, The Old Dairy was still quite empty.

Emma was glad to sit down. The hands on the clock above the bar said it was not quite five. She hoped Simon wouldn't be too late. She knew he wouldn't be early. When he came from work, he was always a bit late: she knew that from their first evening together when he had almost tripped on the step as he opened the door at *Jenny's* in Muswell Hill. She bought herself a J2O orange and some lightly-salted crisps and let out a sigh. She half-expected to feel a new wave of sadness about her mother, who, from the time she got off the bus, had never been far from her mind, but she remained in control of her feelings. Taking her phone out of her bag she checked to see if she had any messages or emails and was relieved there were none, but just as she was putting it away, it rang. Emma glanced down. It was Rosemary.

* * *

"Emma?"

"Yes. Hi, Rosemary. I'm grateful you rang," said Emma. "Thanks."

"I'm so dreadfully sorry, Emma," said Rosemary. "My sincerest condolences."

Rosemary's words triggered the wave of sadness Emma had earlier been expecting and her eyes began to well up with tears. For a moment she wasn't able to speak, and she gulped down a large mouthful of juice to try to steady herself.

Sensing Emma was not herself, Rosemary said, "You must be hurting so inside." She then hurried on, in that emotionally clumsy way Emma had started to notice recently whenever Rosemary strayed from a strictly work-focused conversation. "I told you my Mum died – it's five years ago already – but I didn't tell you then how churned up inside I was when it happened, so I have some idea what you're going through. Tell me you're coping, Emma. You did ask me to call you, and I was glad to, but if this is a bad moment for you just now, I can easily call back later."

"No. Thanks, Rosemary, but I'm OK, really I am," said Emma, feeling she was almost back in control of her own emotions again. "But when Ma actually died, it was truly horrible, and I was really upset. I didn't know I was capable of crying so much. But the hospice staff were so kind and caring, and after a while I found myself coping far better than I thought I would. I'm currently sitting in a pub in Finsbury Park waiting for Simon. He's doing an audit here this week. He should be with me any minute now."

"I'm so glad," said Rosemary, referring both to Emma's present emotional state and to Simon's imminent arrival, "but remember what I said to you on Friday: work can wait. As you know, we're all keen to have you back, but only when you feel up to it."

"Thanks, Rosemary," said Emma once again. "I was thinking I would stay away tomorrow and Wednesday, possibly Thursday too, but I hope to come in on Friday. I think getting back into the thick of things will be good for me. I know I haven't given my best these past weeks, especially since the Christmas break when Mum really started to go downhill fast, and I have felt bad about that. I want to get back into the old rhythm as soon as I can."

"I'm sure you'll bounce right back, Emma. Friday sounds good, but next week will be fine too if, when Friday comes, you still feel you're not quite ready."

There was a silence. Rosemary was hoping Emma was going to ask her about the meeting, and, after a short pause, she did.

"Rosemary, I am dying to hear how it all went today," said Emma. "It'll be a welcome distraction. No, I put that badly. What I meant to say is I'm really keen to hear what happened. Tell me its good news!"

"It went far better than we could have hoped," said Rosemary, "and it also went on far longer than I had expected, which is why I've only now just got out of the meeting."

"Go on," said Emma. "It sounds exciting. What did they say?"

"It *is* exciting, Emma. The headline message is the committee has given us the green light to go ahead. We now have the all-important formal 'agreement in principle' which means funds can be released and the hard slog of undertaking and commissioning all the background research needed can now begin. What's more, it's going to be far, far bigger than we envisaged. But I'm getting ahead of myself; let me start at the beginning.

"It started with the chairman reading out that introductory paragraph to our PCN which, I don't need to remind you, we so agonised over, and in the discussions which followed it was clear the committee was unanimous in wanting the series to go ahead. They were particularly taken with your idea of the programmes deliberately bridging that great BBC divide between politics and current affairs on the one side, and culture and reality TV on the other. As the oldest person in the room wryly said, 'although this is something we have often spoken about, rarely attempted, and never succeeded in doing, this provides us with a great opportunity to try again.'

"Another committee member said launching such a series would be 'a major contribution by the BBC into perhaps the most important debate the country needs to engage in, surpassing even Brexit', and everyone round the table nodded in agreement. The chairman went a step further, saying he believed that, as the national broadcaster, the BBC had an obligation to produce such a series. However, he also warned of the strong opposition likely to come from many quarters including from some higher up in the Corporation than even him. But he said this was a risk worth taking provided the pre-programme planning and research is undertaken with rigour and when every programme broadcast is presented in a fair and balanced way. At that point, Emma – I have to tell you – I started to feel quite nervous as only then did I really begin to understand what an enormous responsibility would be resting on our shoulders. Even for me, Emma, this is really big-time stuff!"

Rosemary's excitement had rubbed off on Emma. Sarah's death was now no longer at the forefront of her mind, nor even gnawing away at her just below the surface.

"Let me now fill you in with a little of the detail," Rosemary continued. "As I hinted earlier, by the end of the afternoon, the committee had agreed something far more ambitious than even we had dared hope for: instead of our producing five or possibly six programmes, they wanted us to plan for around ten. They then started to talk about the programmes going out on the prime-time Sunday evening slot in the autumn and running continuously right up to the start of the Christmas schedule. Inevitably a series on this scale would take far longer lead-in times, far more research and far more people involved than we had thought they would possibly agree to, and that meant a far larger budget, which was also approved without much difficulty. As a result, they would like us to think of a 12-month rather than a six-month preparatory phase, at least a year for research, programme design and development, and a further year for filming and editing. That means at least three years in all – three years, Emma – from now to the date when the first programme is broadcast."

Then, pausing to ensure Emma was ready for what was to come next, Rosemary said, "But the most exciting thing is how keen they were for you, Emma, to take on an even more prominent role than you and I had discussed – and you know how keen I have always been to involve you from start to finish. I took a call at home from the chairman yesterday evening – yes, on a Sunday! He said he had already started talking to a few of his colleagues and they all wanted to know exactly what contribution you had made to the documents we had prepared for the meeting. When I explained how much you had done, he said they had all really been struck by what he called your 'fresh and original' ideas. He then asked me if I could put together a 20-minute compilation of clips of your most recent TV interviews, which I did first thing this morning, and they watched the whole thing while having lunch just before the discussions really got going.

"I'm sure it will take a while to sink in," said Rosemary, unable to conceal in her voice the pride she felt for her young protégée, "but, Emma, they want you to be a co-lead in every stage, from initial design and planning to filming. What's more, after the committee had talked a lot about who would present the series, your name came up as a possibility."

Rosemary heard Emma gasp.

"Don't be surprised, Emma," said Rosemary. "You're smart, professional, hard-working and competent, and fast becoming impressively good in front of the camera, where you command authority while exuding confidence. You come over as appealing on camera, and though still young, you have a pretty clear grasp of what being British today means. You know better than I do, Emma, that some people will say you're totally unsuitable to present the series because you're different – because you're black, because you're an immigrant, even because you're a woman and you're young, on top of your being still relatively unknown. But I would say all these attributes only add to why you should be considered at least as one of the anchors for the series. Nothing was decided today, of course: it's still early days and the issue of whether there should be one or more than one presenter for the series was one of the few areas where the committee failed to agree. In my view it was the more courageous who said the series would carry far more weight if it had just one presenter, as the original *Civilisation* series had with Kenneth Clark, but the more cautious round the table argued for a mix of presenters drawn from different backgrounds for the sake of 'balance'. It will be fascinating to see how that particular conversation runs.

"Finally, for lots of different reasons, not least money and office space issues, the committee was unanimous in requiring all the full-time members of the *Being British* series team to be based in Manchester, and not London. That means, Emma, you will have to relocate there too. You will be on a sort of loose secondment from our unit for all those three years, possibly longer, though I will continue to line manage you from London as I will need to stay here to oversee the rest of the unit's work.

"Anyway," said Rosemary, winding up, "that's more than enough for you to try to absorb for now. *We* have done well, and *you*, especially, Emma, have done exceptionally well. Your enthusiasm, creativity and sheer hard work have been clearly recognised. The committee was really sorry you couldn't make the meeting and talk to them yourself. But when I explained why, they were completely understanding. The chairman wants to have a one-to-one with you as soon as it can be fixed up – ideally early next week if possible."

"In the meantime, Emma, your priorities for now are your far more pressing family matters, so attend to them. All this can wait til you're able to give it the attention it needs. Give my best to Simon. Bye, and take care."

"Bye," said Emma, who realised Rosemary had hung up on her before she had had time to ask her any questions, or share her initial feelings about an imminent move up to Manchester. After laying her phone down on the pub table, Emma looked up and stared into the middle distance as her mind filled with dozens of different thoughts, and a succession of conflicting emotions started to rise from deep within her. She was still looking blankly into the middle distance when Simon rushed breathlessly into the pub and saw where she was sitting. By the time he had sat down next to her, Emma's thoughts were dominated by one thing – having to relocate out of London – and she was filled with gloom and foreboding. The feeling of being totally alone which she had experienced on discovering her mother was dead had suddenly returned.

"Em," said Simon on drawing close to Emma, but his cheerful opening word of greeting tailed away before he had completed it. He had anticipated her being upset, but she looked far worse than he had expected. She recognised his voice and had tried to turn to look at him and to smile but had failed on both counts. As Simon slid into the chair next to hers, he wrapped his arms tightly round her. Pressing his cheeks close to hers, he pulled her head towards him and began gently stroking her hair. He could feel her body tighten, and she began to sob quietly, so he held her a little more tightly, but said nothing.

After a few moments, Emma's body started to relax a little and Simon loosened his grip as he said, "Emma, I am so sorry, so very, very sorry. I read your text when I was grabbing lunch and tried to phone you, but I think you'd turned your phone off. I only picked up your voice mail about 20 minutes ago as I left the theatre offices and I called at once, but you were then engaged. I tried again, three or four times, but gave up as I rushed up the street as fast as I could to get here. My dear, dear Em, I'm so, so sorry."

Emma began to dab at her tears with a fresh tissue she took from under the sleeve of her jacket and then asked Simon to get them both a drink. When he returned and sat down, he searched for Emma's hand under the table and they gripped each other's hands tightly as Emma told him everything. She recounted the events at the hospice in the order they had happened, spending a while describing how distraught she had been after discovering her mother had died and she hadn't realised she was dead. She told him about the daffodils flowering, how kind Lynn had been, the lovely things people had said to her about Sarah and what she had remembered from Dr Fletcher's impromptu speech. When she had finished, she turned to Simon and she looked drained.

"She was a great woman, Em, and such a wonderful, caring and loving mother," said Simon. "I'll miss her, too. She was a person of dignity and great courage and, from what you have said, it seems she died with dignity too. I'm so sorry not to have been there with you, to say goodbye."

Then Simon said, "At least we've got each other, Emma, and that's all that matters now. You're exhausted, Em, it's been a very draining few weeks for you. We should plan a weekend away soon, once the funeral is over. We need time together, just the two of us. We've waited such a long time, Em, for this moment. You will recall as vividly as I do your mother announcing to us she had the cancer the very day of our families' amazing reconciliation. We were wrenched apart by having to devote all our energies to Sarah. But now – at last – we can be together."

"Oh Simon," groaned Emma, "that's just the problem. We can't: we still can't be together. That's really why I feel so utterly wretched." Then, taking in a deep breath, she said "let me explain.

"Just before you got here, I took a call from Rosemary, and, at first, the news seemed to be everything I could have dreamed for. After saying some lovely things about me and Ma she went on to tell me about today's meeting which, of course, I missed. Well, at one level, it's terribly exciting: they have not only approved for the series, but they are now talking about as many as 10 programmes, and, Simon, they have thrown my name into the ring as a possible co-presenter, though that's far from settled. This is even more of a break than my getting the job in Rosemary's unit which was big enough. Simon, this is really big-time stuff!"

"Wow," said Simon, chipping in. "That's totally amazing. All your hard work – under incredibly difficult circumstances – has paid off. I am so proud of you, Em, very, very proud of you. You're going to be even more of a star than either of us could have dreamed would be possible."

"Yes, of course it's great news, and, of course, I am delighted," said Emma, her voice expressing exasperation rather than broadcasting delight.

"But there's the most whopping great sting in the tail. On the very day Ma dies and we both think we're now free to be together at last, Rosemary tells me the series with all the pre-programme planning and research involved is going to be based in Manchester, not London. And that means everyone working full-time on the series will have to relocate up there.

"And you know what that means, Simon." The tears were flowing freely now. "It means my having to live 200 bloody miles away from you, not just for a bit but for five excruciatingly long years! Oh God, Simon, we are being wrenched apart yet again. If there is such a thing as luck, well, we don't seem to have had much of it where our relationship is concerned. We have been continually thwarted in every attempt to do the seemingly simplest of things – to be and to live together."

Then, turning away from Simon and looking down at the table, Emma said, "If you want to know how I feel about my myself, my life and my job now – on the day Ma has died – well, Simon, total crap. Oh my God, what shall I do? I simply don't know. It's all been so sudden; I've had no time to think. You arrived just as I ended my call with Rosemary. Oh Simon, I'm *so* upset. I'm *so* frustrated, all I want to do is scream!"

As Simon listened to Emma, even as he sensed her growing distress, he became more and more elated. No sooner had Emma said 'I want to scream' than he threw his head back and, uncharacteristically, started to laugh out loud. Indeed, he gave out such a loud guffaw he turned most of the heads in their part of the pub. Simon's laugh was a laugh of sheer delight. When he had come into The Old Dairy just now, Simon had been more downcast than Emma could have guessed if she had managed to turn and look at him, and read the worries which were written all over his face. But she had been so wrapped up in her own troubles, she hadn't even glanced across at him as he slid into the seat beside her.

Emma was totally shocked by Simon's outburst and couldn't understand what was happening. Knowing how upset she was, how could he possibly have burst out laughing? What could have taken hold of him? Then, as Simon began to explain why the deep distress *he* had been feeling had been blown away by what she had just told him – why he was not merely no longer deeply saddened by her news, but why he was now ecstatic with happiness – it was her turn to feel a growing sense of elation starting to bubble up from inside her.

"You don't know this, Em, because I never told you," said Simon as he grasped hold of Emma's hand again under the table, "but in the dark and difficult days since Christmas, I began to receive replies in the post from the medical schools I had applied to last autumn. When I was staying over with you, I asked Ma to open my mail and text me to let me know whether I had been accepted or rejected. Well, as the days and weeks went by, I grew ever more depressed as one rejection letter followed another and by last Friday there were just two medical schools left who I hadn't heard from: Kings, London and Liverpool. Why Liverpool, you might well ask, when we agreed I would only apply to London medical schools or those close by? Well, just as I was completing that application form we had spent so much time poring over and deciding which medical school would be my final choice, Dad persuaded me to add Liverpool. He said it would simply be my insurance, my wildcard, if all else failed. Well, I reluctantly agreed and added Liverpool to the list, though I never had the courage to tell you Em. Anyway, when Saturday's post came, Ma knew I was staying at your place so she texted me at once to tell me my rejection letter from King's, and my last hope of studying medicine in London had arrived. Mum, Dad and I all knew that only left me with my wildcard choice, Liverpool.

"And this brings us back to today. After listening to your voicemail on my way here just now, hurrying all the more to be with you knowing your mother had died, a text suddenly came in from Ma. I'll read out what she wrote," said Simon, who took his phone out of his pocket and started to read Cathy's text message out loud. By the time he reached the end and Emma realised what it meant for them, she was leaning over his shoulder reading with him. One of Emma's hands was resting on Simon's shoulder, the back of her other hand was caressing his cheek, and she had begun to cry – this time tears of joy.

> *Simon. Unbelievable news. You've been offered a place by Liverpool. I could hardly believe my eyes when I opened the letter after all the other rejections. Dad is over the moon too. Call me when you can. Hope Emma's ok and Sarah's comfortable. Not sure how you're going to break the news to Emma as it'll mean you'll be apart for another five years. Poor souls. Talk soon. Love Ma xxxx.*

"So my thoughts were precisely the same as yours," said Simon as he switched off his phone, put it down and turned to look directly at her. "How cruel of fate, I thought, to offer me a place in a medical school hundreds of miles away from London and on the very day we should be rejoicing as, at last, we could be together.

"And do you know, Em, what I did next? Well, in the literally few seconds I had between reading Ma's text and stepping into the pub just now, I made up my mind. I decided I would turn down Liverpool's offer and abandon my plans to become a doctor. I knew I had to: after all, I owed it to you, Em, to us. There and then – I didn't need any time to think about it – I could see what matters most to me is our being together, far more than my dream of becoming a doctor, if that meant our being apart. I couldn't hurt you: you have had enough hurt from my family. My father's killing your grandfather almost tore us apart. I knew if I left London it would be me and not my father who would be tearing us apart.

"But now, Em, everything has changed again – and as suddenly as it did just a moment ago. With my place to study medicine in Liverpool and your amazing job in Manchester, I know it *can* work," said Simon triumphantly. "The gods have been looking down on us after all! We can live together, either in Liverpool or Manchester or anywhere in between. The fast trains from Liverpool to Manchester take only three quarters of an hour; I know, I've been on them. That's less time than it takes you now to get from your flat in East Finchley to the BBC in Central London, door to door. Whatever way you look at it, Em, it'll work. It will. You can take this amazing promotion you've been offered and I can take my degree. There is no one, and nothing which can get in our way and stop us now!"

Emma leaned forward and, seeing the joy in his deep blue eyes, gave Simon the warmest of kisses as she cupped her hands round his cheeks and stroked his beard as tenderly as she had on their first night of lovemaking at the Bronte Hotel. "It's like a dream, Simon," she said. "I need to pinch myself."

Simon returned her smile and said, turning round, "let's eat, I am really famished. What's on the menu today, have you looked at the specials, I know they write them up on the blackboard but they seemed to have moved it since I was last here? Do they look any good, what's the veggie option?"

"I don't know what the specials are, I haven't looked," said Emma, "but I'm hungry too, and I'll tell you if they're any good when we've tried them." And they both laughed, found the board, ordered at the bar, ate and when they had finished, agreed how tasty the food had been.

As they step outside into the cold winter's night and link arms to retrace their steps back to Finsbury Park Station to catch the bus to East Finchley, Emma tells Simon about her walk up Stroud Green Road earlier, the different people she had talked to and the thoughts which had passed through her head. When she said the road, the shops and the people she had met had raised her spirits, Simon wanted to know why, because, he said, it all seemed pretty ordinary to him.

"That's precisely my point," says Emma. "To you and me this place feels pretty ordinary because to us it is. Yet to many British people, especially non-Londoners and those who live outside our big cities and beyond the main commuter arteries – especially the Catshead crowd and others like them – it is anything but ordinary. To them, this street, this neighbourhood, even most of London feels not only different; it feels strange, even foreign. For them, this area and this street aren't England because they feel uncomfortable here, out of place as you might say. And that's why I was thinking I could do worse than start the *Being British* series by talking to people here. You know, Simon, the more I think about it, the more excited I am about the whole project."

Just then they pass a couple a little older than themselves talking a language Emma thinks she vaguely recognises but isn't immediately able to name. She stops and, in a way the English have developed into an art form, apologises for even thinking of stopping to talk to strangers, and then apologises again before she asks them if they would mind terribly telling her what language they are speaking.

They answer first by smiling and, as they do so, chunks of gold gleam out at Simon and Emma from between their shiny white teeth.

The woman says "It's Patois, of course. We're Jamaican. Have you never been to Jamaica? Go there, enjoy yourselves, enjoy the country and have fun. You can be yourselves in Jamaica!"

"So you're not English, then?" prods Emma.

"Of course we're English," the woman fires back in shock, accompanied by a rather blank look. "You can be a meat-eater as well as a fish-eater can't you? And you can get enormous pleasure out watching both the Windies and England teams playing cricket even though they're hard-wired to play a totally different sort of cricket. So why can't you be both Jamaican and English at the same time? *Dere's not-a-prob-lem-man!*"

"Exactly," says her companion, who then adds, "Indeed, in my humble opinion, you will be a far better Englishman if you are a Jamaican as well."

Emma smiles and thanks them both as they part, all four cheerily waving goodbye. When they were out of earshot Emma says, "You see, Simon, what insights and gems of wisdom there are to be found right here. We could bring our cameras here and just start filming. I defy anyone not to be moved by these sorts of exchanges, not to want to share the values which underpin them, and not be able to appreciate the sheer power of the messages they convey."

Why, wonders Simon, do we British love speaking in double negatives – is that also linked to the values we hold so dear?

"Of course," adds Emma, "the series must also present the Catshead view of England. After all, it's an important component of the total picture; it's a part of who *we* are. In fact, it is essential beliefs held by the likes of your Uncle George and Aunt Margaret be given airtime not only because they are shared by so many other people but in order that they can explain their Catshead view of what they would like Britain to be to those who find their views distasteful. In some ways, Simon, I see the series as an opportunity for you and me to be challenged too. I need my own views and my prejudices – and, believe me, I have prejudices like every other English woman and man – to be put under scrutiny as well. Why? Because if our divided countries are to become a more united kingdom, *we* have to try to explain to the Catshead world why their view of Britain feels so foreign, so alien to us, and they have to try to understand why we find it so upsetting and we have to understand better the importance of forgiveness. We can't even start to champion our differences until we can appreciate them. And my hope is that our series can make a contribution, however small, to achieving that goal.

"What's more," continues Emma, "for all the faults you and I can see in the way your Uncle George and Aunt Margaret and their friend Ginny see the world, their view of Britain is underpinned by a number of values which I share and which those whose world is Stroud Green Road need to hear. For instance, Simon, your Uncle George and I are both firm believers in the notion of service; we both value loyalty, we both see the critical importance of truth-telling and we both know how fundamental family and tradition are. All these things help to bind us together. What's more, we both believe that people should be helped if, through no fault of their own, they are unable to cope. Though we may differ in the nature and the extent of the help needed, we are both strong believers in the caring state. We also both believe in the virtue, or the value, of tolerance: indeed, in my book, being British and being tolerant seem to be one and the same. The only characteristics of British people I have trouble understanding are self-deprecation and the underlying expectation England will always lose whether it's at football or cricket. But maybe before we start filming, I will have learned a little more about why these things are seemingly seen as virtues."

Emma lets out a loud laugh, and Simon knows the old Emma has returned as he tells her how much he loves her when he hears the intoxicating sound of her laughter.

It's close to eight o'clock; they have reached the far end of Stroud Green Road and pass the bright yellow sign of the fruit stall where Emma had bought her mangoes earlier in the day. The young Turkish Cypriot woman who had served her is long gone and the dark-set man who is now serving his last customers tells them he is about to close so they will need to be quick if they want anything. Emma sees a new sign has appeared, propped up next to the one which said 'Alphonso mangoes'. This one reads 'Sorry all sold out. More in at the weekend'. Simon reads it too.

"That's a pity," he says, "I could just do with one for those for the journey home, they are so delicious."

"You're in luck then," says Emma as she digs deep into her bag, and to Simon's amazement produces the two ripe mangoes she had bought earlier which, fortunately, have survived the evening unbruised.

"You are such an amazingly organised person," says Simon. "Personal trainers may be all the rage these days, but I am quite content having my very own personal planner."

"You're amazing too," says Emma, taking hold of Simon's arm again, as she reflects for a moment on their being together. "Is it luck or providence which brought us together, and is it chance or the hand of God which makes the world go round?" she asks herself. Simon hears her but says nothing, and they walk on in silence as Emma thinks back to what a difference he has made to her life as he tucks into his mango.

Emma knows her views about God, about chance and about coincidences have changed since that day on Hampstead Heath when she had struggled to align Simon's atheism with her Christian faith. Ultimately – she now knows – it doesn't really matter how you choose to label what happens in your life. What matters is to be attuned and alert to the world so you are able to notice events as they unfold before you, so you can respond accordingly. And she recalls her chance encounter with the young beggar, Tom Pearson, earlier in the evening and feels uncomfortable about the tragedy of his wasted life. What does *Being British* mean to him, she wonders? Then she thinks back to her chance encounter and eye-opening conversation with that woman, Farisai, she met on her bus ride to Mutoko. Farisai knew what *Being Zimbabwean* meant to her: enslavement.

In their very different ways, Emma's ever-active mind reflected, the most basic things both Tom and Farisai lacked were freedom and opportunity, the freedom to create their lives as they would wish. And she remembered how amazed she had been at school to learn from her history teacher that a colossal 10 million British soldiers took up arms and fought for political freedom in the two world wars, and over a million died. Yes, Emma said to herself, freedom has to feature prominently in her TV series, not only because it is so central a value, but because its importance seems somehow almost to have been forgotten. It had not been raised by anyone at their Catshead lunch, and in all their conversations about British values, neither she nor Rosemary had given much attention to freedom and the twin pillars upon which it depends: a flourishing parliamentary democracy and the persistent application of the rule of law.

As they turn the corner and Simon is wiping his sticky fingers as best he can on his hanky, Emma sees their bus in front of her. She is quick to hear the sound of the engine change, signalling it is about to leave, and pulls Simon towards her. They run forward and jump in just before the doors close. It is as if the bus had been waiting there just for them, ready – providentially or by chance – to whisk them off to the next phase of their lives. And in a sense it had, Emma reflects, as she snuggles in close to Simon and nestles her still-cold nose under his warm chin. She certainly knows she is departing a wiser and more loving person than she was all those months before when she and Simon bumped into each other at Graham's the butcher…seemingly by chance.

ACKNOWLEDGEMENTS

It has taken the best part of five years for this book to travel from a collection of disparate ideas in my mind to the completed book, and there are many people I need to thank for supporting me on the journey. My family was pivotal in telling me to start writing and invaluable in encouraging me to persevere, and I am exceedingly grateful to them all.

My thanks also go to the loyal group of friends and experts in different fields who provided me with advice on different aspects of the book and who generously gave of their time to comment on all or parts of earlier drafts. They hail from Cyprus, Zambia, Zimbabwe and the UK. Among them I would like to mention Peter Cox, David Harold-Barry, Max Harris, Maria Ioannou, Chris Roberts, Roland Von Nidda, Nick Weeks, Vicky Wilding and Sian Williams. I am particularly grateful to Marina McCarron at Oxford Literary Consultancy for her rigorous review of my first full draft. Her detailed comments, wise words and suggestions (some harsh, most spot-on) were both sobering and provided the impetus for the major re-write I needed to undertake. Thanks also go to my copy-editor at Powerhouse Publications for the considerable work she did on improving the text still further.

I am grateful to Robin Langrishe the Director of Funding at the North London Hospice in Finchley, who welcomed me and facilitated my visit to this impressive institution. When it was founded in 1984, the North London Hospice was the UK's first multi-faith hospice. For more information about the hospice see http://www.northlondonhospice.org/about-north-london-hospice/history/.

A special word of thanks has to go to my wife Abby and daughter Becky, for believing that after spending a lifetime writing academic and technical books and papers, I had it in me to write fiction. It has certainly been a challenge and I am grateful to Abby, especially, both for pushing me to embark on this venture and for her patience as I abandoned her and my family commitments to escape to my garret and converse with my characters.

Finally, this book would not have seen the light of day without the enthusiastic support of Stephanie Hale at *Oxford Literary Consultancy*. Stephanie and her team pride themselves on their reputation for excellence and friendly service, and this, together with their sheer professionalism, has been precisely my experience. So, thank you Stephanie!

558

Tapestries of Difference is a work of fiction and none of the main characters either portray or are intended to represent in any way any person living or dead. However, many readers from Zimbabwe will recognise a number of prominent Zimbabweans mentioned in the book. Almost all are now sadly dead. These are Dr Luisa Guidotti, the poet John Bradburne, Dr. Elizabeth Tarira and Archbishop Chakaipa. A fleeting reference is made of Bishop Pius Ncube. Bishop Ncube is now retired and lives in Bulawayo, Zimbabwe's second city. Mention is also made of Dr Chris Hindley. Chris was co-founder of the North London Hospice in 1984 and for many years a hospice trustee. He died in 2016. I have known each of these people personally, and a number were friends.

I am grateful to Charles Mungoshi and Oxford University Press (East Africa) for permission to reproduce an extract from *Coming of the Dry Season* (1972) and to David Crystal and the John Bradburne Memorial Society (JBMS) for permission to reproduce a number of lines from four unpublished poems of John Bradburne. All John Bradburne's poems can be accessed at http://www.johnbradburnepoems.com/public/home.aspx.

Roger Riddell was born in Birmingham and went to school in England. In 1965, aged 18, he went to what was then Southern Rhodesia as a volunteer secondary school teacher. A year later he went back to the UK and joined the Society of Jesus (the Jesuits), leaving in 1977, before ordination.

In 1970, Roger returned to what had then become Rhodesia where he spent a year learning Shona, the main local language, before starting an undergraduate degree in economics at the University of Rhodesia (now the University of Zimbabwe). After obtaining a Masters' Degree in Development Studies at the University of Sussex, Roger was appointed a lecturer in economics at the University of Rhodesia. However, he was declared a 'prohibited immigrant' by the Smith government, so was not able to take up his appointment. When Zimbabwe became independent in 1980, he was asked to come back as Chair of the first Presidential Commission tasked with recommending how to revive and restructure the country's economy after years of economic sanctions and the country's guerrilla war. Roger spent a number of months criss-crossing the country gathering first-hand, hundreds of accounts from people who recounted the suffering and grievances they endured during the war years. At this time, Roger was granted Zimbabwean citizenship. He went back to live in England in 1984.

For many years, Roger was a Senior Research Fellow at the Overseas Development Institute in London, and from 1999 to 2003 he was the International Director of the UK charity, Christian Aid. He then became a Director of Oxford Policy Management where he remains an Associate. He has published widely on Zimbabwean, African and wider development issues. His most recent academic book is *Does Foreign Aid Really Work?* (Oxford University Press, 2008).

Roger lives with his wife Abby near Oxford and they have three grown-up daughters who, when the family were not living in Zimbabwe, Zambia or the United States, grew up in north London.

31320869R00331

Printed in Poland
by Amazon Fulfillment
Poland Sp. z o.o., Wrocław